Dear Reader,

Thank you for choosing to celebrate more than a decade of award-winning romance with Arabesque. In recognition of its ten-year anniversary, Arabesque launched a special collector's series in 2004 honoring the authors who pioneered African-American romance. With a unique three-in-one format, each anthology features the most beloved works of the Arabesque imprint.

Intriguing, intense and sensuous, this special collector's series was launched with *First Touch,* which included three of Arabesque's first published novels written by Sandra Kitt, Francis Ray and Eboni Snoe. It was followed by *Hideaway Saga,* three novels from award-winning author Rochelle Alers. The third book in the series was *Falcon Saga* by Francis Ray; and Brenda Jackson's *Madaris Saga* concluded the series.

In 2005 we continued the series with Donna Hill's *Courageous Hearts,* Felicia Mason's *Seductive Hearts,* Bette Ford's *Passionate Hearts* and in November, Shirley Hailstock's *Magnetic Hearts.*

Last year the series continued with collections from Arabesque authors Angela Benson, Lynn Emery, Monica Jackson and Gwynne Forster. The book you are holding—*Irresistible Desire*—includes three sizzling romances from Kayla Perrin: *Everlasting Love, Sweet Honesty* and *Flirting with Danger.*

We hope you enjoy these romances and please give us your feedback at our Web site at www.kimanipress.com.

Sincerely,

Evette Porter
Arabesque Editor
Kimani Press

Other books by Kayla Perrin

Midnight Dreams
Holiday of Love
In an Instant
In a Heartbeat
Fool for Love
Getting Even

And coming in August...

Scandalous Affair

Irresistible Desire

KAYLA PERRIN

EVERLASTING LOVE • SWEET HONESTY • FLIRTING WITH DANGER

ARABESQUE®

IRRESISTIBLE DESIRE

An Arabesque novel published by Kimani Press 2007

ISBN-13: 978-0-373-83053-4
ISBN-10:   0-373-83053-X

The publisher acknowledges the copyright holder
of the individual works as follows:

EVERLASTING LOVE
Copyright © 1998 by Kayla Perrin
First published by BET Publications, LLC 1998

SWEET HONESTY
Copyright © 1999 by Kayla Perrin
First published by BET Publications, LLC 1999

FLIRTING WITH DANGER
Copyright © 2001 by Kayla Perrin
First published by BET Publications, LLC 2001

www.kimanipress.com

Printed in U.S.A.

CONTENTS

EVERLASTING LOVE

To Dexter Graham: for all your help regarding
the world of architecture. Thanks so much!

To Pearl, Judy, Henry and Pat at TGH, for letting me
use their computer while I was on deadline!

And to Brenda and Kelsey, a very dear
sister and brother—this one's for you.

Prologue

Rain, heavy and menacing, fell in large droplets on the windshield of her late model, royal blue Chevrolet Cavalier. Her hands clenched on the steering wheel as she maneuvered the car, Whitney Jordan worried her bottom lip. Filling her lungs to their full capacity—to the point where it hurt—did nothing to calm her frantic nerves. If she had known it was going to rain when she had left her mother's, she would have delayed this trip.

It was always worse when it rained—the images, the memories. During those times, she didn't even have to close her eyes in order for the terrifying memories to surge forth. And they were there now, in the forefront of her mind, as strong and as real as the night it had happened.

She could still see the bright lights coming toward her, feel the blood freeze in her veins as icy fear enveloped her body. She could still hear the horrifying crunch of metal and the ominous crack of the windshield.

But the sound she could never forget was little J.J.'s scream. The shrill, terrified sound. And she could never forget the sight of his twisted, bloodied, motionless body on the ground.

The horrifying sight of J.J.'s body zapped into her mind with such velocity that Whitney's jittery hands caused the car to swerve into the oncoming lane.

Gasping, she righted the car, then inhaled a deep, steadying breath. She held back her tears, tears that always accompanied the memories. Everything for her had changed after the accident, and her life would never be the same. She had come out of the crash with her life, but she had lost everything else that mattered.

And now, she was returning to the place where it had all happened. The place where one tragic event had shattered her entire existence. Perhaps that was why the pain and the memories seemed so much stronger now.

Whitney sucked in a sharp breath and let it out slowly, willing herself to calm down. She would get through this. She had to. Once she had accomplished her task, she could leave Chicago and get on with her life.

Without Javar. A wave of nostalgia washed over her as she thought of Javar and of how she would now be closing the door on their life together forever. It wasn't something she wanted to do, but her husband had given her no choice. Some marriages just couldn't survive the challenges thrown at them. Theirs was one of those marriages.

And after an almost two-year separation, it was time to officially end their marriage and get on with their lives.

Glancing in the rearview mirror, Whitney noticed a set of headlights in the distance behind her. Her eyes darted to the road, then back to the rearview mirror. The lights were getting closer as the car gained on her, clearly speeding despite the road conditions. As the car neared her bumper, its driver flicked on the high beams, nearly blinding her. Whitney squinted, trying to lessen the effect of the offending bright lights.

"Okay, okay," she muttered. The car was right on her tail now, doing sixty miles an hour. Mumbling an unladylike oath,

Whitney hit her blinker, signaling her intention to enter the right lane. But as she started changing lanes, she noticed that the car behind her was swerving to the right as well.

"Impatient," she grumbled, directing her car back into the left lane to let the restless driver pass her.

But before she could completely cross over the line, she felt and heard the impact of metal against metal as the car behind her crashed into her car. That was all it took to send Whitney's car sliding on the rain-slicked roads straight into the path of oncoming traffic.

Her heart thundering in her chest, Whitney's mind screamed, *It's happening again!* Panicked, and desperate to avoid a head-on collision, she turned the steering wheel to the right. But it was too sharp a turn, because the car began to spin violently, heading toward the shoulder of the road and the large oak tree that loomed ahead of her.

Shielding her face when she realized there was nothing else she could do, Whitney Jordan screamed as the passenger's side of her car collided with the tree trunk.

The next moment, darkness overcame her.

Chapter 1

Somewhere in the back of her mind, Whitney thought she heard hushed voices and soft sobbing. The sounds were hazy, but were growing clearer each second. She had no idea where she was, only the definite feeling that she shouldn't be here. And despite her mind's haze, she felt sore. The entire left side of her body screamed with pain, and her head felt as though someone had tightened it in a vise.

She had to wake up. Her mind wanted to, even if her limbs felt like lead. Whimpering softly, Whitney shifted in the bed and forced her eyes open as much as she could. A blinding jolt of pain in her head caused her to wince, and she let her eyes flutter shut.

"Whitney? Whitney, honey?"

She felt someone gently squeeze her hand.

"She opened her eyes!" a woman shouted excitedly. "Cherise, go call the nurse!"

It was her mother, Whitney realized, feeling a sense of comfort. Fighting the pain, she opened her eyes once again. Lord, it hurt. And all she could see was a blur of shapes. Why was she here, lying on this foreign bed? What had happened?

A startling mental image hit her—the body of a little boy— and Whitney's heart instantly went berserk. Cold, numbing fear slithered through her veins, and as panic seized her, she fought to suck in small gulps of air.

It felt as though someone was strangling her, forcing the very life out of her.

She tried to speak, to ask the questions she so desperately needed answered. But she couldn't. She could only gasp and cry as she struggled to fill her lungs.

She heard the voices around her grow frantic, and she sensed that people were trying to help her, but she wasn't sure what they were doing. Her eyes, although open, couldn't focus on anything.

And then, everything started fading. The shapes, the voices. The frantic movements around her grew faint. Even the memories eluded her now.

Sleep was beckoning her, and Whitney closed her eyes, welcoming the painless oblivion.

Javar Jordan squeezed his forehead with a thumb and forefinger as he looked down at the sketches before him. Close, but not quite right. He wanted to secure the bid for a new shopping plaza in Phoenix, and these sketches that one of his senior associates had produced were good, but lacked the creative edge necessary to land the job.

And he wanted to land the job. Thus far, after eleven years in business, his architectural firm was one of the most successful in the Midwest. But he had yet to accomplish his big dream: to be among the ten best architectural firms in the entire United States. It was a dream that, with time, he knew he could make a reality. Already, several large clients across the country contacted him directly, offering him substantial jobs. In the Midwest, he was always on the short list for government contracts, and when it came to private projects, he was always one of the first architects to be approached.

So, while his financial security didn't depend on this bid, he wanted it. Michael Li of the Li Development Corporation was one of the most affluent commercial property developers in the country, and if he could land this bid, his dream would be one step closer to becoming a reality. For service and value, his firm, Jordan & Associates, was second to none, and once Michael Li learned what Javar's company was capable of doing for him, he would no doubt offer the firm more lucrative jobs in the future.

If he hadn't been busy working on the Milwaukee hotel project, Javar would have done the sketches for the Phoenix bid himself. Clearly, he thought wryly, he was going to have to.

Javar rubbed his tired eyes, but found that useless in relieving the grit-like feeling that assaulted them. What he needed was some sleep, but he'd have to settle for a short break. Pushing back his black, Italian-leather swivel chair, Javar stood and strolled to the left side of his floor to ceiling windows, and glanced out toward the west. His office was on the thirtieth floor and offered him a magnificent view of downtown Chicago. On Lake Michigan, he could see several boats sailing on the glistening water. Below, he could see West Madison, the street where his firm was located. Crowds of people swarmed the waterfront and Grant Park, enjoying the Taste of Chicago festival. Attracting millions of people each year, the summer event could only be described as a big, street food party. Because of the festival, and the fact that it was Friday, traffic was already jammed in the downtown core. And it wasn't even noon yet. Not that Javar had to worry about rush hour. If he was lucky, he would get out of the office by midnight when the streets would be quieter. The sketches for the Li bid had to be revised right away.

The shrill ring of the telephone on his large, mahogany desk interrupted Javar's troubled thoughts. Expelling an aggravated breath, he turned and reached for the receiver. "Yes?" he barked.

"Mr. Jordan, I know you asked not to be interrupted, but—"

"That's right, Melody," he told his administrative assistant. The strain of another stressful day was evident in his voice. "Tell whoever it is to go away."

In her soft-spoken, delicate voice, Melody explained, "Uh…they said it was important. It's someone from your insurance company."

"My insurance company?" Irritation caused Javar's brow to furrow. If this was about his BMW, he didn't have time for it. "Did he say what this is about?"

"It's a she," Melody corrected. "And no, she didn't say. Only that she needed to talk to you immediately."

Running a hand over his wavy coif, Javar groaned and said, "Put her through."

Three seconds later, a deep female voice asked, "Mr. Jordan?"

"Yes, this is he." Javar's tone was curt. "What's this about?"

"Mr. Jordan, this is Gwynne Creswell. I'm calling about Wednesday's accident. I need to know what garage you had the car towed to, so we can send an adjuster out to examine the damage. I'll also need a copy of the police report, so if you could tell me what district did the investigation…"

Javar rolled his eyes. He was going to have to change insurance companies—soon. This was the second time in the last year they had screwed up his claim.

"Ms. Creswell," he began, his voice calmer than his perturbed feelings. "I haven't had any accident. My car was stolen. As for the district that did the investigation, I've already given all that information to Robert Blacklock, my regular broker."

"Mr. Jordan, I realize that you weren't involved in the accident. I'm talking about your wife," Ms. Creswell explained, her tone indicating that she was sure Javar knew what she was talking about but was just feigning ignorance.

For goodness' sake, Javar thought, groaning inwardly. This woman had no idea what she was talking about. And why was *she* calling him? Was reliable Robert on yet another vacation?

"Ms. Creswell, I have to tell you, I'm not very impressed with Rathburn Insurance at the moment. This is the second time you've screwed up my claims in the past eight months. Not only are my wife and I separated, but she's nowhere near Chicago. She's down South, in Louisiana."

Javar heard Gwynne sigh. "Okay," she stated in a placating tone, "is your wife not Whitney Jordan?"

A silent alarm bell went off in Javar's head, and he lowered himself into his chair. "Yes," he replied, his tone guarded.

"Well," Gwynne continued, "according to the call I got from Avery Rentals, your wife was in a serious accident on Wednesday night, and her rental car was badly damaged."

My wife? Javar's stomach tightened in horror. Impatient, he asked, "What exactly has happened?"

"Surely the police must have contacted you, Mr. Jordan. All I know is that the rental car is supposedly a write-off, and since your wife had your insurance policy transferred to the rental car—"

"My wife has been in an accident?" Icy fear slithered up Javar's spine, causing the short hairs on his nape to stand on end.

"According to Avery Rentals, yes."

"Oh my God. Is she all right?"

Clearly flustered, Gwynne said, "I...I don't know. What's going on here, Mr. Jordan?"

Javar didn't have time to answer her. He didn't have time to hang up the receiver. He only had time to grab his gray Armani blazer and rush out of his office.

Whitney had the strange sensation that someone was watching her and her eyes flew open. Something was wrong, she knew, and immediately, her stomach coiled with dread. Focusing her eyes while she glanced around anxiously, she saw both her mother and her cousin sitting to the right of her bed, worried expressions etched on their faces. This wasn't her mother's place, neither was it her cousin Cherise's. Curious, her eyes took in the orange curtain that was on the left side of her bed, before noting the intravenous stand and bag that were connected to her arm.

She was in a hospital, Whitney realized. Why? What had happened? Her gaze narrowed on her mother's coffee-colored face, taking in the sight of her red, swollen eyes. Whatever had happened must have been something awful, but she couldn't remember what that something was.

"Oh, Whitney!" her mother said as she looked at her, relief evident in her deep voice. "Oh, thank God!"

Whitney didn't like the confused feeling that plagued her. Her mind was a groggy haze, and her body was thrumming with pain. Drawing in a ragged breath, she struggled to sit up.

Electric jolts of pain shot through her head and back, causing her to groan.

Her mother's gentle hand was instantly on her shoulder,

softly easing her back down. "Eh eh eh," Carmen Elliston's mild voice warned. "You just lie back and relax, Whitney. Cherise, go call the doctor."

Whitney saw Cherise's warm smile and bright brown eyes that were swollen from crying before she scampered toward the door. Her mother and her cousin were here, the two people who mattered most to her. But despite the presence of her family, the wary feeling that overwhelmed her just wouldn't go away.

J.J.! her mind screamed, and her pulse quickened. Whitney's throat constricted as haunting images—blood, broken glass, a small lifeless body—flooded her mind. Terrified, she reached out and gripped her mother's hand with all her strength. Her voice was hoarse as she asked, "Where's J.J.?"

Carmen's eyes widened with surprise as she stared at her daughter, but she quickly softened her expression. Bringing her hand to Whitney's face, she stroked her cheek in a gentle soothing motion. "Just lie back and go to sleep, honey. You need your rest."

"Mom, where's J.J.?" Whitney repeated, more frantic this time.

A soft sigh fell from Carmen's lips. "Oh, honey." Worry flashed in her dark, hazel eyes. "J.J., he's…don't you remember, honey? It's been two years…." Brushing at a tear that escaped her eye, Carmen bit down on her bottom lip.

Two years, Whitney thought, fighting hard to remember what was eluding her. And then she did. She remembered it with such force that her body shook. J.J. was gone.

But not recently; two years earlier. So why did it feel so fresh, like it had only just happened?

"W-what happened?" Whitney inquired, swallowing against the grief lodged in her throat.

Whitney's mother returned her eyes to her daughter's. "Oh, honey. I don't want you to worry about that. You're gonna be okay now, that's all that matters."

Whitney tried to shake her head, but couldn't. The discomfort was too intense. Instead, she said, "Tell me."

Carmen unleashed a weary sigh. "Honey, you... You were in an accident, but don't you worry. Everything's gonna be all right now."

An accident? Whitney was shocked, and her mind fought hard to fill in the blanks. Suddenly she remembered the high beams, and driving in the rain.

"It was wet," Whitney said aloud, hoping that the rest of the puzzle would come together.

"Don't even think about that now," Carmen said, patting Whitney's hand. "You need your rest."

The shuffle of footsteps drew Whitney's attention to the left, and she watched as Cherise and a young, attractive woman entered through the curtains.

The young woman, dressed in a white lab coat, strode purposefully to the right side of the bed, and Carmen stood to let the woman get closer to Whitney. Beaming down at Whitney, the woman said, "Welcome back."

Whitney managed a small smile.

"I'm Dr. Farkas," the woman told Whitney, then proceeded to check her pulse. Her olive complexion and striking features indicated a Middle Eastern background. But she was so small and seemed so young, Whitney found it hard to believe this woman was old enough to be a practicing physician.

"Your pulse is normal." The doctor slipped her hand into Whitney's saying, "Can you squeeze my fingers?"

Whitney did.

"Great, Whitney." Dr. Farkas then shone a light in both Whitney's eyes. "Your pupils are fine, indicating no damage to your brain. How does your head feel?"

"It hurts."

"That's understandable." Dr. Farkas smiled and crossed her arms over her chest. "You are a very lucky young woman, Mrs. Jordan."

"I was in an accident?"

Dr. Farkas nodded, her short, dark brown hair gently swaying. "Yes. Do you remember what happened?"

Squeezing her eyes shut, Whitney tried again to remember. Only fragments would come to her—the bright lights, the rain on the windshield. Nothing else. She shook her head, then cringed in pain. "No."

"We're going to keep you another night or two for observation, but the good news is, your injuries are only surface. I hear the tree wasn't so lucky." Again, Dr. Farkas smiled down at Whitney.

Whitney found it hard to get excited about Dr. Farkas's good news. She didn't feel lucky. Not when it hurt to open her eyes or to shift her body even slightly.

Dr. Farkas asked, "Do you need something for the pain?"

Weakly, Whitney nodded. The doctor gave her two small pills and water to wash them down. Whitney prayed they would help ease her discomfort.

"That should help you rest, as well as lessen the pain," Dr. Farkas explained. "I'll be back to see you later today. In the meantime, if you need anything, you can ring for the nurse." Turning to Whitney's mother, Dr. Farkas placed a hand on her shoulder and said, "Mrs. Elliston, don't worry. She's going to be just fine."

"Thank you, Doctor," Carmen replied. Then, closing her eyes for a brief moment, she added, "And thank you, too, God."

Smiling, Cherise moved to the side of the bed the doctor had vacated and took Whitney's hand in hers. "Hey cuz, you okay?"

Whitney forced a smile. "I will be."

"You certainly know how to scare a person. Sleeping for two days straight." She smiled weakly. "The next time you want some attention, just let me take you out on the town."

A chuckled that sounded more like a groan escaped Whitney's throat. It was just like Cherise to try to cheer her up with her playful sarcasm. "I'll remember that."

"Good." Cherise's light brown face grew serious, and she ran her free hand through her long, thin braids. "You get well, Whitney. We can't lose you. Not now."

Whitney gave Cherise's hand an encouraging squeeze, surprised that she had the strength. "I'll…be fine. You…" She paused to swallow. "You don't…have to stay here. You need to work."

"Work can wait," Cherise told her. "You're what's important now."

Whitney tried to turn onto her side, and grunted in agony. Giving in to the pain, she collapsed onto her back. The surge of energy she had recently experienced was now passing. Despite the fact that she wanted to stay awake and spend time with her mother and her cousin, the only two people in Chicago who cared about her welfare, her eyelids were getting heavy, and she longed to close them.

She suddenly realized that Cherise had said, "two days straight." Widening her eyes, she looked at Cherise and asked, "How long have I…been here?"

Sadness marred Cherise's features as tears filled her eyes. Quickly, she brushed them away. "Two days."

"Two?"

"You were unconscious for the first day, then started to wake up, but you never really did. At least not for long. Dr. Farkas said you had a slight concussion."

"Oh, God," Whitney uttered, feeling alert once again. "The car. Where is it?"

"Girl, I tell you that you've been unconscious for two days and you're worried about some dumb car?" Cherise flashed Whitney a sardonic grin. Whitney held her gaze, and Cherise continued. "The car's a write-off. But don't go crazy worrying about that. Your mother has already contacted the rental company."

Relieved, Whitney released a breath she didn't know she was holding. "Thank God...I had insurance."

Cherise's eyes bulging, she said, "Thank God you're okay. Now why don't you close your eyes and get some rest? Your mom and I will both be here when you wake up."

Whitney glanced at her mother and saw her smiling. Her heart warmed. She knew at that moment that she would be okay. She had her family with her.

Drawing in a comforting breath, she closed her eyes, accepting the temporary peace sleep offered.

"Where is she?" Javar demanded at the information desk on the first floor of Cook County Hospital. After calling the local police stations in Chicago to inquire about accidents while sitting in traffic, Javar discovered that his wife had been taken here. The description of the accident scene was hard to comprehend, and as he stared down at the young black receptionist, beads of sweat popped up on his brow. He had to see Whitney. He had to know that she was okay.

"And who would 'she' be?" the receptionist asked, a small smile lifting her full lips.

"Oh. Oh, of course." Javar drew in a deep, calming breath, then continued. "My wife. Her name is Whitney Jordan."

"Thank you." The receptionist checked her computer. Several seconds later, she smiled up at Javar. "She's in room four-nineteen, sir. You can take the elevators at the end of the hall."

Whirling around on his heel, Javar called "Thank you" over his shoulder.

When he stepped off the elevator on the fourth floor, Javar was instantly aware that the hallway was crowded with people. Patients on gurneys in the corridor were groaning and crying from their injuries, and several men and women of varying ages surrounded their sick loved ones or sat on benches or lined the walls. The horrible memory of the last time he had been to this hospital entered his mind, and he stopped, swallowing, fighting the unpleasant emotions the memory stirred. Praying for strength, Javar forged ahead and found room four-nineteen. He hurried inside.

Orange curtains closed off both bed areas. Boldly, he pulled open the first flimsy curtain, but the person he saw there was not Whitney. A young woman with a cast on her arm lay sleeping, and a man and young boy, probably father and son, sat piously beside her bed. The boy was older than J.J. had been, probably ten, but still the sight of him brought back vivid images of J.J. lying on a hospital bed, his small body bruised and damaged. Javar's throat constricted, remembering how it had been too late for his son. Only a few hours after arriving at the hospital, J.J. had died. Javar apologized for the intrusion, then made his way to the other partition.

Carmen Elliston's saddened expression was the first thing he saw as he pulled back the curtain and stepped inside. One look on the middle-aged woman's troubled face and Javar assessed the severity of the situation. It was bad. Alarm gripped him, and as he tried to suck in a breath, he found his lungs wouldn't hold more than a mere gasp of air.

He didn't want to glance down, didn't want to look at Whitney. He didn't want to know that she was injured to the extent that she might die. But even as the thought hit him, Javar knew he had to turn his gaze toward her. He had to see his wife, no matter how badly she was injured. Because if she was nearing the end of her life, then he would spend every minute of it by her side.

Anxiety causing his heart to beat rapidly, Javar's eyes moved to the bed. The sight he saw there made his stomach twist into a tight knot, and he almost cried out in pain. Whitney was lying on the small hospital bed, her head bandaged, her eyes closed. Her normally vibrant honey-brown skin was pale and bruised around her eyes. And her round face was drawn, thin—not full the way it had been the last time he had seen her almost two years ago.

But he could see the soft rise and fall of her chest, the faint, yet steady, breath of life.

Relief washing over him, Javar expelled a hurried breath and stepped further into the curtained area.

Whitney was alive.

Thank God.

Chapter 2

"What are you doing here?" Carmen asked, her hazel eyes shooting daggers in Javar's direction.

"What do you think?" Javar asked, not bothering to try and hide his annoyance. He wasn't about to let Carmen bully him into leaving. Whitney needed him. But as he looked at Carmen and the bitterness in her eyes, he felt regret tug at his heart. Once, she had loved him like her own son. Not anymore.

Outrage sparking in Carmen's eyes, she rose from the black vinyl chair at Whitney's side and approached Javar, determination in her steps. "You have a lot of nerve coming here, Javar. I suggest you leave before Whitney wakes up. You know as well as I do that she doesn't want to have anything to do with you."

Javar stared down at his estranged wife's mother, meeting her cold eyes with an equally hard gaze. "I'm still her husband."

Carmen snorted, then threw Javar a distasteful glance. "Like you know the meaning of the word."

Javar didn't reply because the last thing he wanted to do was argue with his mother-in-law over the events of the last two years. Now was not the time nor the place. He only wanted to visit with Whitney. He needed to determine for himself how well she was doing. Brushing past Carmen, he made his way to Whitney's side.

His breath left him as Javar sank into the chair beside Whitney's bed. She looked so fragile, so vulnerable… His gaze steadfast on Whitney, he said to Carmen, "Tell me what happened."

Tension-filled silence permeated the air. Evidently, Carmen felt she owed him no explanations. After several seconds of waiting for his mother-in-law to answer him, Javar turned and faced her, his eyes imploring her to give him the answer he craved.

She frowned. Then sighed as resignation passed over her features. "There was an accident," she stated monotonously. "Whitney was heading to see you, and…" Carmen's deep voice cracked, and she wrenched her gaze away from Javar's. It took her several seconds to regain her composure, and when she did, she again faced him with anger in her eyes. "Once again, Javar, you're the cause of my daughter's pain."

"How am I responsible for this?" Javar unleashed an irritated breath. "I didn't even know she was back in town. And if anyone should be upset here, it should be me. Whitney's been here for two days and you didn't even call to let me know?"

Carmen was silent, her face contorted with ire. She could quietly fume all she wanted, but she couldn't say anything in response to Javar's statement because she knew he was right. He was still legally Whitney's husband, and he had a right to know what happened to her. Shaking his head, Javar pondered the thought that he might have been too late. And if Whitney had died before he'd gotten a chance to see her, he would never have forgiven his mother-in-law.

Closing his eyes for a long moment, he tried to assuage his stormy emotions. Whitney hadn't died, and what was important now was seeing her get well. Moments later, his voice calm, he said, "Will you just finish the story please?"

Carmen cleared her throat and continued. "The roads, they…it was raining. The police don't know exactly what happened, but somehow Whitney lost control, and she collided with a tree. It was awful, the accident scene."

"I…I remember seeing something on the news a couple nights ago…. Oh, my God." The wreckage he had seen on the news had been horrifying. How could Whitney have come out of that accident alive?

"The police and doctors say it's a miracle she's still breathing."

She could have died. It was as though the realization only now truly hit him, and his stomach lurched painfully. Why? His mind screamed. Why did this happen? Why Whitney? She had suffered so much already. Pushing those thoughts aside, Javar reached forward and delicately stroked the soft, pale, honey-brown skin of her face. In spite of the severe bruising under her left eye, and her swollen, bruised lips, she was still incredibly beautiful. As always.

He swallowed. Until this moment, he had deluded himself by saying that he could go on with his life alone, without his wife. In the almost two years that Whitney had been gone, he had resigned himself to a life without her; his anger had made that resignation easier. But seeing her now, and realizing that he had almost lost her a second time, he knew that he would never truly be fulfilled if he didn't have her in his life again. How could he go on without her, when he knew deep in his heart that he had never stopped loving her? It was time to put aside all the hurt and bitterness and move on.

He brought Whitney's frail hand to his lips and kissed it, then held it against his face.

"Touching, Javar," Carmen muttered sardonically. "But just a little too late."

"What's he doing here?"

Javar didn't have to look up to recognize whose face went with that high-pitched question. It was Cherise Burnett, Whitney's feisty, hot-headed cousin.

Feeling her presence upon him, Javar gazed up at Cherise. Her brown eyes were cold and harsh as they stared down at him, telling him in no uncertain terms that she most definitely did not approve of him being here. Too worried about Whitney to deal with Cherise's wrath, Javar returned his gaze to Whitney's bandaged face. He continued to hold her soft hand against his cheek.

"You actually have the audacity to show up here?" Cherise whispered in a lethal tone. "If you know what's good for you, Javar, you'll get out of here."

Javar ignored her; arguing with Cherise would get him nowhere.

"This is ridiculous," Cherise continued, exasperated. "Aunt Carmen, I'm gonna get the nurse to call security." Pinning Javar with an icy glare, Cherise said, "And Javar, you better be gone when I get back."

That comment was Javar's undoing. "And what do you think the nurse or doctor, or security for that matter, is going to say, Cherise? I'm her husband, in case you've forgotten."

"You're the one who conveniently forgot that, now didn't you?" Cherise retorted, her face distorted with anger. If looks could kill…

A soft moan came from Whitney's lips and Javar returned his attention to his wife. Seemingly restless, Whitney stirred.

"Keep your voice down," Javar said softly, casting a sidelong glance at Cherise. "You're disturbing Whitney, and she obviously needs her rest."

Javar heard Cherise huff, and he could imagine that frown she wore so well pasted on her lips. She got quieter, but the icy quality was still evident when she said, "Well that's another reason you should get lost. For once, think of Whitney, not yourself."

Not bothering to dignify Cherise's comment with an answer, Javar rose from the chair at Whitney's side. This visit wasn't going the way he had expected. He'd hoped for some quiet time to sit with Whitney, but he should have known that her family would be with her, and considering the way things had ended between him and Whitney, he should have known that her family wouldn't be happy to see him. Sighing, Javar brushed past Cherise and Carmen, then strode to the door and opened it.

When he stepped into the hallway, the emotions he'd been holding inside overcame him. Relieved, he expelled a soft moan and leaned forward, bracing his hands against his knees. *Whitney's alive!* His mind screamed. *Whitney's alive!*

And according to Carmen, she had been en route to see him when the accident happened. After all this time and his own stubborn pride preventing him from going to see her, she had finally been the one to make the effort to see him.

And now she was lying in a hospital bed because of it.

It was all so hard to believe. How could the vibrant, lively woman he'd met five years ago now be lying in a hospital bed, fighting for her life? One serious car accident was bad enough to have suffered, but another one?

Maybe it was seeing Whitney in such a dismal state that had Javar remembering a happier time. Whatever the reason, he couldn't help remembering the first time she had entered his life. She'd been a twenty-two-year-old cocktail waitress then, and he was nine years her senior. Still, he'd been fiercely attracted to her. He could remember their meeting like it was yesterday…

Javar followed his brother through the crowd at The Rave, one of Chicago's most popular nightspots. The men were outfitted in dress pants and silk shirts, and the women were all decked out in their sexiest outfits. As Javar made his way through the crowd, he realized that it had been a long time since he'd relaxed. All work and no play, his brother would say about him. At his brother's requests, Javar had finally agreed to an evening of fun.

Khamil, his younger brother by a year, definitely appreciated a beautiful woman, and right now, his eyes were roaming the crowd. Turning, Khamil smiled widely at Javar. "Mmm mmm," he hummed. "The ladies are looking super-fine tonight."

"Down boy," Javar said, then chuckled. "Let's wait until we've had at least one drink before you go on the prowl."

"Why wait?" Khamil retorted. "You know what they say: Wait too long and life passes you by."

Rolling his eyes playfully, Javar patted his brother on the shoulder. "Just remember we're here together. Don't you dare find some honey and take off on me, like you did the last time."

The music was loud, and the walls and floors in the two-level club were vibrating with each beat. The large dance floor, which was to their left, was packed with people energetically moving their bodies to the funky tune. Javar smiled. It had definitely been too long.

"Why don't we go upstairs?" Javar suggested, and he was relieved when Khamil led the way to the winding stairs that would take them to the second level.

It was a wonder they even made it upstairs before the end of the night. Along the way, Khamil met, hugged, and conversed with so many beautiful young women, Javar lost count. It was one thing to be well-liked, which his brother certainly was, but it was quite another to know almost all the single women in a given club.

His brother certainly got around.

As Khamil whispered in the ear of a beautiful, dark-skinned woman, Javar leaned forward and whispered in his ear. "Believe me, Khamil, 'getting around' is overrated."

Khamil threw Javar a dubious glance. "Get real, J. Maybe if you're the Pope, but not when you're young, dark, and handsome, like I am."

Folding his arms over his chest, Javar chortled. His younger brother certainly wasn't lacking in the self-esteem department. In fact, it was obvious he had enough to spare.

When Khamil finally drew himself away from the beautiful woman, he turned to Javar and said, "Javar, this is April. April, this is my brother, Javar."

April looked up at Javar from lowered eyelids, grinning at him seductively. Javar flashed her a quick smile. "Hi, April." Then, turning back to his brother, he said, "Can we go upstairs now? You promised me a drink, and I'm getting pretty thirsty."

Khamil shrugged apologetically at April, and when they were out of her earshot he turned toward Javar, pinning him with a puzzled expression. "Are you crazy?"

"No," Javar replied coolly. "Why do you ask?"

Khamil's mouth fell open in complete surprise. "April— she's a TKO, man! And she likes you! What's up with you?"

Javar smirked and stated simply, "She's not my type." One look at April, and he could tell that she was the type of woman who was out for a good time, not a long time. She was also the type who thought all men should worship the ground she walked on, merely because she was beautiful. She probably wasn't rejected too often. Well, let him be one of the few to reject her. Javar was too old to play dating games. He was thirty-one, and he'd already made one big mistake in his life: Stephanie Lewis. Stephanie was gorgeous, and after she'd pursued him relentlessly, he'd finally given in to her seductive charms. He had found out the hard way that she wasn't interested in settling down, merely in having a good time and spending his money. Now, three years later, he had custody of their two-year-old son J.J.

Khamil slapped Javar on the shoulder. He may have been Javar's younger brother, but Khamil was taller than him by about half an inch. "There's a table over there, man. Let's go sit down and I'll buy you that drink I've been promising you."

"Sounds like a plan," Javar said. Within seconds, he and his brother were seated at a small table near the railing, affording them a view of the dance floor below.

"Holy…" Javar heard Khamil murmur, and Javar lifted his eyes from the view of the people below. Khamil's mouth was hanging open and his eyes were lit up with interest as he looked over Javar's shoulder. A woman, Javar figured, smiling wryly. Turning slowly, he saw the object of Khamil's desire. *Holy was right,* Javar thought, sitting taller in his seat. His own lips parted as he observed the waitress approaching their table. To say she was beautiful was an understatement. She was exquisite, the most attractive woman he had ever seen in his life. A form-fitting red top and black miniskirt allowed Javar a fairly unrestricted view of her body, and he liked what he saw. She was probably five foot six, with a small frame, but curves in all the right places and legs that seemed to go on forever. Her skin was a rich, honey-brown complexion. Her face was round, her eyes were bright and wide, and as she smiled at him, he could see two small dimples peeking at him from her cheeks.

"Good evening, gentlemen," she said, her soft, silky voice gently washing over Javar. "What can I get you to drink?"

Javar couldn't speak. He was completely mesmerized. The gorgeous woman standing before him had affected him the way no other woman ever had. She was exquisitely beautiful, exotic—her round face and almond-shaped eyes indicated an Asian influence—yet there was an innocent quality about her, a genuineness.

Khamil snapped his fingers before Javar's face. "J., she asked you a question."

Embarrassed, Javar lowered his gaze and swallowed—hard. What was wrong with him?

"You'll have to excuse my brother," Khamil said, flashing the waitress a wide smile. "He doesn't get out much."

Javar's lips twisted into a crooked grin, directed at his brother. Turning to the waitress, he said, "Don't listen to him." Her radiant smile nearly blinded him.

She chuckled softly. "Can I get you something to drink?"

Javar's throat was suddenly very dry. "Sure," he managed to say. "I'll take a draft beer. Whatever you have on tap."

She took Khamil's order next, but Javar barely heard a word they said. His eyes were fixated on her full, sensuous lips, and his thoughts were completely focused on how he could get to know her better.

When she walked away, he watched the gentle sway of her hips. As soon as she was out of his sight, he released a breath that sounded suspiciously like a whistle.

Khamil smiled at him. "So that's the kind of woman it takes to wake you up, huh? Too bad she was checking me out, not you, big brother."

"Is that right?" Javar bit his bottom lip and raised an eyebrow in a challenging manner. "Well, I hate to disappoint you, bro, but you're definitely not her type."

Khamil laughed. "Hey, the ladies have a hard time passing up a fine brother like me."

"She's not like all your women, Khamil," Javar stated, knowing deep down that he was right. The waitress was different. Although beautiful, he could tell she wasn't the flaky type of woman Khamil seemed to like.

It wasn't a moment too soon when she returned to their table, carrying a small tray with their drinks. Javar stood to his full six foot one inch frame and reached into the back pocket of his black dress pants. He extended a twenty to her, but as she reached for it, he pulled it away. "Before I give this to you, tell me your name."

Curious eyes met his determined ones. "Excuse me?"

Javar sighed, wondering what had gotten into him. Sure, he was attracted to her, but he wasn't used to losing his cool with women. And he certainly wasn't into cheesy pickup lines or games. And to make matters worse, she looked about twenty— definitely too young for him.

He handed her the twenty. "I'm sorry if I offended you. Keep the change."

"Thanks." The waitress's lips curled into a full, genuine smile, exposing her perfect white teeth. She stuffed the twenty in her apron and spun on her heel. When she had walked away a few steps, she turned back and faced Javar. "And since you're interested, my name's Whitney…"

* * *

"Excuse me, sir. Are you all right?"

The sound of a female voice pulled Javar back to the present and the unpleasant reality. He looked up at the pretty nurse who stood before him. He was still hunched forward with his hands on his knees, and instantly, he stood. No wonder the woman was concerned about him; he must have looked like he was going to be sick.

Javar smiled down at the slim nurse, appreciating her concern. "I'm fine. Thanks."

She looked at him as though she didn't believe him, but after a moment the nurse scampered off.

"Wow," Javar mumbled, thinking of how caught up with the past he had just been. A soft smile touched his lips as he remembered his brother's shock that Whitney had been interested in him. By the end of that first night, Javar and Whitney had exchanged numbers, and two weeks later, they were dating steadily. Despite his mother's protests that she was a gold digging child who wanted to sleep her way into their family's money, Javar married Whitney eleven months after they had met.

He sighed. In recent years, whenever he thought about Whitney, he also remembered J.J., the accident, and how everything had taken a turn for the worse in their relationship.

Now was no time for a trip down memory lane, he told himself. He needed to speak with Whitney's doctor. Running a hand over his short hair, Javar made his way to the information desk.

A middle-aged nurse smiled warmly at him. "May I help you, sir?"

Javar nodded. "Yes. My name is Javar Jordan. My wife is Whitney Jordan. Who is her doctor?"

"Let me just check for you," the nurse said, directing her gaze to a chart. A few seconds later, she looked up at Javar and said, "Dr. Farkas is her supervising physician."

"Is Dr. Farkas available?"

The fair-skinned nurse pursed her lips and shrugged. "I haven't seen her in a little while. She's still working, I know that. I can page her for you."

"Please do." Stepping aside and leaning against the counter, Javar squeezed the bridge of his nose. Whitney. He had to believe that she was going to be okay. He had to do whatever it took to make sure that she would be okay. And that meant getting her out of Cook County Hospital and to a place where the doctors weren't so overloaded with patients that they might ignore his wife's needs.

He couldn't lose her...not now.

"Mr. Jordan?"

Javar turned to face the petite young woman before him.

She extended a small hand. "I'm Dr. Farkas."

Javar's eyes widened, unable to shield his shock. Surely this woman standing in front of him wasn't old enough to be a doctor, especially not Whitney's doctor. All the more reason to get her moved to another hospital immediately.

Apparently reading Javar's concern, Dr. Farkas announced, "I assure you I'm quite qualified."

Embarrassed that she had read his thoughts, Javar cleared his throat, then took Dr. Farkas's small hand in his large one, shaking it firmly. "Sorry. You just look..."

"Young?" Dr. Farkas supplied, then smiled. "I know."

Rubbing the back of his neck with his right hand, Javar nodded absently. "Please, tell me about my wife's condition."

Dr. Farkas folded her arms over her chest. "Mr. Jordan, your wife is a very lucky woman. Since she was admitted two days ago, she's been in and out of consciousness, but she's recently woken up, and I'm happy to tell you that she appears quite lucid. Despite the severity of the accident, her wounds are superficial. She did suffer a mild concussion, but has recovered from that."

Javar met Dr. Farkas's steady gaze with questioning eyes. "What do you mean, 'superficial'? I've seen her, and sure, she's breathing, but she looks like she's in a lot of pain."

"She was in a serious car accident and she's bound to experience a lot of discomfort. Unfortunately, the pain is something she can't escape. But fortunately, she didn't have any internal injuries—"

"What about her head?"

A weary look flashed in Dr. Farkas's eyes. "I understand your concerns, Mr. Jordan, but I assure you the wounds to her head are all superficial. The lacerations will heal nicely."

"How do you know that there's no serious internal damage?"

"Because we've run all the tests possible to detect that, Mr. Jordan," Dr. Farkas replied, her tone authoritative.

"An MRI?"

The doctor's eyes darkened a shade. "Yes, Mr. Jordan. I assure you there's no reason to worry about your wife's recovery."

Frustrated, Javar exhaled. He glanced around the hospital hallway, seeing the numerous patients on gurneys and their concerned family members. Dr. Farkas seemed certain that Whitney was going to be okay, but he couldn't be convinced of that. Not if she remained at this facility. He had already lost one person he loved at this hospital. He wasn't about to lose another.

"Well, Dr. Farkas, I do worry," Javar said, turning to meet her gaze once again. "Cook County clearly has too many patients to care for. I would feel much better if my wife were moved to another facility."

"I have to object, Mr. Jordan. She's had a head injury, and it's inadvisable to move her in her condition."

"I thought she was fine?" He watched as Dr. Farkas's olive complected skin turned a shade of crimson red. He sensed she was angry, that she felt her competence was being questioned. Javar realized he was being demanding without offering any explanations. "Dr. Farkas, I have no doubts that you are a qualified physician. The problem isn't you." He paused. "Two years ago, I lost…my son died here. And whether I'm justified or not, I feel that moving my wife to another hospital will… It will make me feel more comfortable."

Dr. Farkas nodded. "I understand where you're coming from, but I assure you—"

"Please, Dr. Farkas," Javar said.

Looking up at him with concerned eyes, the doctor nodded tightly. "Very well."

"Thank you. I'll make the arrangements now." Turning, Javar strode toward the pay telephones, reaching into his pocket for some change.

Ten minutes later, he had all the arrangements made to have Whitney moved to Rush North Shore Medical Hospital in the Chicago suburb of Skokie. Skokie was much closer to his home in Kenilworth, anyway, and he trusted that hospital's medical care much more than he did Cook County's. Rush would not look like a war zone, which was the way Cook County did. Whitney deserved the best medical attention available. J.J. hadn't been so fortunate.

He returned to Whitney's room with an open mind, but the moment he arrived Cherise threw him a hateful look. Carmen's hazel eyes were swollen and red, and as she looked at him, what he could see behind the anger was sadness…and fear.

He was afraid too. That's why he was having Whitney moved to another hospital.

He cleared his throat before speaking. "I just want you to know that Whitney will have the best care available. I'm having her transferred to Rush North Shore Medical Hospital, where I'm sure she will get the attention she needs."

Carmen's mouth fell open in horror, and she gasped. "She's too weak to be moved to another hospital."

"That's right," Cherise added. "God only know why you're here Javar, but if it's guilt, get over it. She doesn't need you."

"The arrangements have already been made, and an ambulance is on its way. What you can do for Whitney now is get her things ready."

Rising, Cherise said, "You can't do this."

"I happen to be her husband, and she's still on my insurance policy. So, yes, Cherise, I can."

A muffled groan escaped Whitney's throat, and instantly Javar made his way to her side. "Sweetie?" He watched as her face contorted, but her eyes remained shut. "Sweetie, it's Javar. I'm right here."

Whitney's eyelids fluttered open, and her chestnut-colored eyes met Javar's. Confusion flashed in their depths, and her eyes widened. But the next moment, they narrowed, then closed. When she opened them again, her eyes were heavy-lidded, and it seemed like it was a major effort to keep them open, but she did.

Grinning, Javar ran a finger along the silky smoothness of Whitney's cheek. Thank God she was waking up.

"Don't you worry, sweetie," he said, his voice filled with emotion. "I'm here now, and I'm going to take care of you."

Chapter 3

"Javar?" Whitney's voice was faint.

Relieved laughter bubbled from his throat as Javar beamed at Whitney, pressing her soft hand against the stubble on his cheek. "Yeah, sweetie. It's me."

Whitney groaned. "W-what…why…?"

Javar pressed Whitney's delicate fingers to his lips, remembering the way things used to be between them. For a brief moment in time, they had been deliriously happy. Her fingers, now cold and frail, had once lovingly caressed his face, his body. Regret washed over him, and he swallowed the emotions that were lodging in his throat. "All that matters is that I'm here now, Whitney. And I'm going to be here until you get well."

Carmen appeared at the other side of Whitney's bed. "I can make him leave, honey. Just say the word."

Whitney's eyes moved to her mother, then returned to meet Javar's gaze. Suddenly, her eyes grew wide, and her chest heaved as she started to cry.

Javar's stomach churned as he watched Whitney, his heart aching for the pain she was in. He brushed her forehead with his fingers, hoping to soothe her. "What is it, Whitney? What's wrong?"

"J.J.," she sobbed, clenching his hand. "Where's J.J.?" Confusion clouded her face. Then, as though everything became clear, she gasped, then started crying harder. "I—I'm sorry," she cried. "I'm sorry."

Javar leaned forward and nuzzled his nose against Whitney's cheek. "Shh," he cooed. "Whitney, sweetie, it's okay."

"I—it's my fault," she said, her words choked between sobs. "J.J.—he's—Oh God!"

Carmen threw her hand to her mouth, but wasn't able to hold back her tears. Javar looked up at her, perplexed, worried. "What's going on?"

Sniffling, Carmen wiped at her tears. "When she awoke before, she was confused. She seemed to think that she was in the accident that…that killed J.J. But then she remembered. Oh, dear Lord, what's happening to her?"

Javar watched Whitney cry, his own heart breaking. Dr. Farkas obviously didn't know what she was talking about. Whitney's injuries were more than surface. Was she suffering some type of memory loss? Javar bit down hard on his bottom lip, overwhelmed with emotion. Then, turning to Cherise, he said, "Go get the doctor!"

Fighting her own tears, Cherise ran from the room.

"It's okay, it's okay," Javar repeated to Whitney, but his soft words didn't stop her tears. Moments later, Dr. Farkas appeared, followed by Cherise.

"Doctor, something's wrong," Javar explained. "She's almost hysterical."

As Dr. Farkas moved to Whitney's side, Javar stepped aside. "What's wrong with her?"

"She needs a sedative," Dr. Farkas replied. "I'll be right back." Minutes later, she returned with a syringe and inserted it into the tubing hooked up to Whitney's intravenous bag. "This should calm her down."

"She doesn't seem lucid at all, Doctor. She thinks she was in an accident that happened two years ago."

"She's going through a lot of physical and emotional stress. Most likely, her actions now were a response to a dream. I have to tell you, Mr. Jordan, I strongly object to transferring her in this state."

Javar leveled a steady gaze on the doctor. "No offense, but I'm now more convinced than ever that my wife needs to be moved."

Dr. Farkas pulled her lips into a thin, taut line. "As you wish. You'll need to settle your wife's bill at the reception desk."

"I'll be out there in a minute." Javar averted his eyes to Whitney, whose breathing was now calmer, and her tortured expression had relaxed. He walked over to the bed, leaned forward and planted a soft kiss on her forehead.

Whitney was clearly tortured. The accident had injured her physically, but guilt was making her suffer far worse than any physical pain. Gritting his teeth, Javar realized that he had done nothing to help Whitney overcome her guilt when she had needed him most. Instead, he had turned his back on her.

Seeing her like this, in so much agony, pained him. A large lump constricted his throat, making it hard to swallow. He had almost lost her before they'd had a chance to make things right.

Javar moved from the bed and went to the small closet in the corner of the room, where he found Whitney's clothes. "Is this everything?" he asked, turning to face Carmen and Cherise.

Her lips curled downward in a frown, Cherise nodded.

"Good. Please get Whitney's other things ready. I'm going to settle the bill before the ambulance arrives."

* * *

The trip to Rush North Shore Medical Hospital was uneventful, and Whitney was now comfortably resting in a private room. The sedative Whitney received at the other hospital had helped her to relax, and other than the occasional nervous twitch, she didn't seem to be in any pain.

Carmen and Cherise had decided not to make the trip to the new hospital, no doubt because they didn't want to see any more of Javar than was necessary. But they had told Javar they would visit Whitney the next day.

Dr. Adu-Bohene, a longtime friend of Javar's parents, and an excellent physician, was supervising Whitney's care. Javar hated to leave her before he knew the extent of her injuries, but having been told that the doctors wouldn't know anything conclusive until they ran some tests, he decided to head to his office to take care of some business. Now that Whitney needed him, he was going to be there for her. And that meant limiting his time at the office.

It was after four in the afternoon when Javar entered his office building. Murphy's Law dictated that on the one day he just wanted to get to his office to take care of business, the elevator would stop on almost every floor before he reached his destination. When he finally reached the thirtieth floor Javar rushed off the elevator and headed to the office of Duncan Malloy, one of his two senior associates. He spent half an hour going over the specs for the renovations of a waterfront estate in Highland Park, a wealthy suburb of Chicago. The estate was an older home, and some of the remodeling the client wanted just wasn't feasible, at least not without tearing apart part of the foundation, and that kind of work wasn't within the client's budget. However, Javar was certain that Duncan could make alternative suggestions that the client would find satisfactory. As for the bid for the Li project, Javar explained to Duncan that he would be personally handling the project from this point on. He should have realized that Duncan wasn't the right architect for the kind of project Mr. Li wanted; he had a more conservative style, and Mr. Li liked innovative, larger-than-life designs. Javar had just been too busy to take on the project himself. In return, he gave Duncan two of his current sizable projects.

Next, he went to see Harvey Grescoe, his other senior associate. Harvey was clearly surprised when Javar named him acting principal for an unspecified period, but Javar avoided the curious man's questions. While he was good friends with Harvey, he didn't want to get into the complicated story of what was going on in his life right now. He trusted Harvey implicitly, and knew that when he returned, the office would still be running smoothly. When Harvey flashed him a concerned look, Javar smiled faintly and promised to check in with him on a daily basis.

It felt weird, reassigning his duties in order to take a leave of absence. It wouldn't be a true leave; he would still be working on the sketches for the Li bid as well as other business, and he would call the office on a regular basis. Still, it felt strange. Javar had built Jordan and Associates from the ground up. In the beginning, he'd spent long hours at the office, and then long hours at home, determined to prove to his parents that he wouldn't fail. But once he had become established, he still hadn't cut back on his work hours. Even when he had married Whitney, he'd continued to burn the candle at both ends. That was something Whitney had constantly complained about, claiming that he wasn't investing as much time in his marriage as he was in his career. She'd suggested on several occasions that the firm was too large for one man to control, that he should accept either of the senior associates' requests for partnership. Javar hadn't wanted to do that, and as a result, he'd put in the hours necessary to run his business successfully and single-handedly, not thinking of the consequences for his marriage.

And then, after J.J. died, and Whitney had left him, his work had become his life.

Burying the thoughts of J.J. and Whitney in the back of his mind, Javar marched across the plush gray carpet, approaching the double mahogany doors to his office. He'd taken care of most of the urgent matters, but still needed to tie up some loose ends before heading back to the hospital.

Melody had the phone secured between her shoulder and ear when Javar stopped at her desk and looked down at her. When she noticed him, Melody's lips curled into a wide grin, and she promptly ended her call.

"Any messages?" Javar asked.

Melody nodded as she searched the message pad on her desk. "I've got some brief ones here. But check your voice mail." Smiling brightly, she handed Javar the pink message slips.

"Thanks." Javar turned to leave, then halted. "Melody, I'm going to be out of the office for a little while. I'm not sure how long yet. Whatever can't wait until I get back, please give to Harvey Grescoe to handle."

Melody's dark brown brow furrowed with concern, and her eyes narrowed. "Are you sure, Mr. Jordan? What if someone insists on speaking with you, not Mr. Grescoe? Should I contact you at home?"

"That won't be necessary. I will check in with you once a day, as well as Harvey. If there are any emergencies, either you or he can relay them to me then."

Melody stood and rounded the corner of her wide oak desk. She placed a soft hand on Javar's. "Is everything okay? The way you stormed out of here earlier, I was a bit worried."

"Well, don't be," Javar said succinctly, and immediately regretted his abrupt tone. At her startled look, he forced a smile. "I'll be fine."

Javar knew that Melody was interested in him, and physically, he found her an attractive black woman, but after his disastrous relationship with Stephanie Lewis, he'd vowed never to get involved with someone who worked for him again. He'd never returned Melody's obvious affection, yet she still persisted. Never overtly, but subtly, with gestures and heated glances. She had liked him even when he'd been married, and then when Whitney had moved away, Melody had started wearing provocative outfits to work, no doubt trying to get his attention. Although professional, her skirts were definitely tighter and shorter, and her necklines were lower, revealing her ample bosom. Her new style of clothes hadn't been a distraction for him, but it had certainly been a distraction for several other men in the office. Javar was immune to that kind of thing; he had fallen for one too many pretty faces, and he'd learned his lesson.

Besides, after falling in love with Whitney, he knew there would never be another woman who would steal his heart.

Looking at Melody now, her full lips pursed in a concerned pout, he thought for the millionth time that he should have hired an older, frumpy woman to be his administrative assistant. Now more than ever, he didn't need the hassles of unwanted sexual attention. But Melody had been the best candidate after Stephanie, and at the time he had hired her, she'd been married, so Javar hadn't anticipated any complications in their work relationship. But she'd gotten divorced shortly after she had started the job, and ever since the ink was dry on her divorce papers, she'd had her sights on him.

It was ironic, Javar thought, that there were several women vying for his heart, yet he wanted the one who'd had the strength to walk away from him.

"I appreciate your concern, Melody." Javar turned his attention to the message slips in his hand and began to flip through them. With a small grin, he left her standing at the corner of her desk and strolled into his office.

There were three messages from his mother, all of which said Urgent. He would have to return her calls, but only after he had taken care of office business.

He spent the next hour checking his voice mail and returning calls. Satisfied that everything was under control for the next couple of days, Javar stood and inhaled a large gulp of air. Moving to the window, he looked out at the spectacular view of Lake Michigan, which was glittering enticingly under the sun's strong rays. It was another hot late June day in Chicago.

But he had no time to worry about beautiful views, or any frivolous thing like that. Flicking his wrist forward, Javar looked down at his gold Rolex. Five forty-three. He was anxious to get back to the hospital and see Whitney, but he knew his mother would never forgive him if he didn't return her calls. When Angela Jordan said something was urgent, she expected to be contacted promptly. By now, she should have been home from Mercy Hospital, where she worked as a surgeon.

Javar picked up the telephone receiver and punched in the digits to his parents' home. After two rings, Gretta Kurtz, the lovely older German woman who was his parents' housekeeper, answered the phone. "Jordan residence," she said pleasantly.

Even after all the years she had been in the United States, Gretta's voice still held a distinct German accent. "Hello, Gretta. It's Javar. Is my mother home?"

"Oh hello, Javar. Yes, your mother's here. One moment, please."

Several moments later, Angela came to the phone. "Javar?"

"Hello, Mother."

"My goodness, where have you been?" Angela Jordan chastised. "I've been trying to reach you for hours."

It was just like his mother to skip the "Hi hon, how are you?" And give him the third degree.

"It's been a long day," Javar replied, his tone making it clear that he didn't want to answer any questions about his whereabouts. "What's so important that you called me several times at work?"

Angela made a sound somewhere between a huff and a snort, the way she always did when she didn't like the response she got. His mother loved to control—her husband, her children, and anyone else who would let her. She had his father wrapped around her finger, and for years while Javar was growing up, he, too, had done everything possible to please her. Not anymore. Javar was too old for her power games.

"I was just calling to remind you of the dinner party tonight, dear," his mother replied, her tone sugary. When Javar was silent, she added, "The one with Judge Harmon and his family."

And Judge Harmon's daughter, Althea, a successful criminal attorney in Chicago. The perfect woman for him, according to his mother. Javar rolled his eyes heavenward. "I'm sorry, Mother. I can't make it."

Angela gasped. "Why on earth not? We're all expecting you."

"Mother, I never promised that I would be there, only that I'd try. And I can't make it. I've got work to do." The last thing he wanted to do was explain that Whitney was back in town and in the hospital. The mere mention of Whitney's name would make his mother livid.

"In other words, you forgot?" Angela asked, clearly not pleased. "Is that it?"

"Actually," Javar began, "I did forget. I've been very busy working on the Milwaukee hotel project I told you about, and—"

His mother's cold words cut him off. "This is about Whitney, isn't it?"

All the blood drained from Javar's face. "W-Whitney?" he stammered, thrown back by his mother's question. How did she know?

"Yes, Whitney," Angela replied, saying Whitney's name as though it were some horrible disease. "I heard she was back in town."

There was no point denying the truth now. "Yes," Javar responded, his tone deceptively calm. "She is. And she needs me now."

"Because of the accident?"

Javar's brow furrowed. "How did you know about that?"

"Word gets around in medical circles," she replied succinctly. The next moment, her tone softened. "What can you do for her now, Javar? She's in the hospital, they're taking care of her. She doesn't need you."

An agitated sigh escaped Javar's clenched teeth. His mother had never approved of his relationship with Whitney, and she would never understand his need to stand by her now. But that was her problem, not his.

"Mother, please relay my deepest regrets to Judge Harmon and his family. I will not be able to make it this evening. Good-bye."

As he replaced the receiver, he could hear his mother's loud protests. He didn't care. He didn't have time for dinner parties and mindless conversation. And he definitely didn't want to be paired with Althea all evening, thinking of things to say to her, and listening to her ramble on about all her important cases.

All he wanted to do was head back to the hospital and be with Whitney. Grabbing his blazer, Javar headed out of the office.

Whitney awoke with a start. Fear gripped her. Darting her eyes around the spacious room, her stomach coiled in apprehension as she realized that she didn't recognize her surroundings.

Where was she?

She was still in a hospital, that much she could ascertain, but not the same one as before. This one was nicer.

A polished oak table was to the right of her bed, on which sat a crystal pitcher filled with ice and water, and two crystal glasses. In the far corner of the room near the large bay window were two plush sofas and a small oak coffee table. Across from the bed, built into the wall, was what looked to be a twenty-one inch television. A vinyl recliner rested on the left side of her bed.

No, this definitely wasn't Cook County Hospital.

Gathering strength, Whitney reached for the nurse buzzer resting on the oak table. She pressed down on the small, blue button. Less than a minute later, a middle-aged woman dressed in a light pink nurse's outfit entered her room.

"How are you feeling?" The woman asked, an amiable smile gracing her lips.

First Whitney looked at the name tag pinned to the woman's shirt. It read, "Hazel McDonnell, R.N." Then, she lifted her gaze to Hazel's, staring at the pleasant looking woman through narrowed eyes. "Where am I?"

"You're at Rush North Shore Medical Hospital." The nurse proceeded to take her blood pressure, then checked her pulse.

Whitney knew this was going to sound like a dumb question, but still she asked, "Why am I here?"

"Your husband had you transferred from Cook County Hospital earlier."

Javar.... Concentrating, she remembered him being at the hospital, but little else.

"Open, please." Whitney complied, and the nurse stuck a thermometer under her tongue. After about a minute, she removed it. "Are you in any pain?"

Whitney nodded, slightly. "My head."

The nurse clucked her tongue, then gave Whitney's hand a reassuring squeeze. "It's gonna be all right, dear. I'll get you some painkillers, and now that you're awake, the doctor would like to see you."

As the nurse left the room, Whitney laid her head back, willing the pain to go away. She wondered where her family was.

And more specifically, where was Javar?

"How is she, Dr. Adu-Bohene?" Javar asked the dark-skinned African man as he stood outside Whitney's private room.

"Surprisingly, well. The swelling on her head is already going down, and the bruises are starting to heal. All our tests indicate no serious head trauma, or other type of internal injury."

Relieved, Javar exhaled a gush of warm air. "Thank God."

"She'll need to take it easy for a while, of course. I can't say how long it will be before she makes a full recovery."

"I understand." Anxious to see her, Javar averted his eyes to her closed door. "But at least she's out of danger?"

Dr. Adu-Bohene's shoulders rose and fell in a noncommittal shrug. "It looks that way, but we can never be too cautious with a head trauma, as far as I'm concerned. I suggest she stay here at least another couple of days for observation."

Javar nodded, his expression grim. Dr. Adu-Bohene patted his back in an effort to comfort him. "Don't worry, Javar. I'll make sure she's fine…at least physically. As for emotionally, I know this must be hard on her, especially after the earlier tragedy."

"Have you spoken to her?"

Dr. Adu-Bohene nodded.

"How did she seem? As I told you before, I'm concerned she may have a memory loss."

"When I spoke to her, her mind seemed very clear. She didn't mention the previous accident, only her desire to speak with you. Why don't you go in and see her? I'm sure she'll be happy to see you."

His heart warmed at the doctor's words. If Whitney was asking for him, that had to be a good sign. And he couldn't wait to talk to her. Flashing Dr. Adu-Bohene an appreciative smile, Javar said, "Thanks." Then he turned the doorknob and slowly entered the room, careful not to disturb Whitney.

She lay sleeping as he gazed at her. Peaceful, serene, without worry…that's how she looked. *Thank goodness,* Javar thought. She deserved some peace. He was anxious to talk with her, but he wouldn't disturb her now. Her rest was much more important than what he wanted.

Quietly, he made his way across the gray marble floor until he reached the black recliner beside Whitney's bed. Easing himself into it, he took Whitney's hand in his, stroking her soft flesh. As he laced his fingers with hers, he closed his eyes, thinking. So much had gone wrong in their marriage. When they had said their vows in the backyard of his waterfront home that sunny day in May four years ago, he had never in his wildest dreams considered that they might separate, much less after only two years of marriage. But things had gone terribly wrong, and they *had* separated. Was there a chance they could make it right again?

Moaning, Whitney stirred. Javar opened his eyes, throwing his gaze to her face. When he'd seen her last, the day she had moved out, she hadn't been as thin as she was right now. He wondered if she was eating.

Whitney's eyes flew open, and when she saw Javar, she looked startled. After a few minutes, a small grin lifted her lips. A weak smile, yet her cute dimples were clearly evident.

Javar smiled back. "Hi."

"Hi."

A strained silence fell between them, and Javar realized how awkward this situation was. The last time he had seen her, she'd been crying; he'd been angry. Most definitely, they hadn't parted on good terms. Now, here he was at her bedside, playing the doting husband. More than anything, he wanted to right things between them.

"I'm sorry," he murmured, looking down at their joined hands, then into Whitney's dark eyes.

Whitney flashed him a questioning look. "Sorry?"

Javar nodded. "Yes, I'm sorry. For everything." He paused as a wide range of emotions washed over him. "For the pain you're feeling now…for all the pain I caused you to feel before. I know you were coming to see me when you had the accident."

"My mother told you?"

Chuckling mirthlessly, Javar said, "Did she ever."

Whitney closed her eyes pensively, then reopened them. "I'm sorry if she offended you."

"She didn't. She's just worried about you, and I can't blame her."

Whitney nodded.

Javar brought his free hand to his wife's face, and softly ran his fingers along her cheeks. It felt so good to touch her. He wondered how he could have been such a fool to let her walk out of his life. "You came back."

"Mmm hmm."

"I'm glad."

Whitney was uncomfortable, and she shifted in the bed until she found a position she liked. She now lay on her side, facing Javar. "You are?"

Javar nodded, a smile brightening his nutmeg-colored eyes. "Yes, Whitney. Does that surprise you?"

Whitney's eyes roamed the hard, masculine edges of his oval face, the wide, full lips, the thin mustache, the black stubble that lined the sides of his golden-brown face. He was still so handsome, so sexy. But when it came down to it, looks didn't count for anything. Dedication did.

"Kind of," Whitney replied. It did surprise her that he said he was happy to have her back. After the way things had been between them when she left, she hadn't known what to expect when she saw him again. She certainly hadn't expected him to be at her bedside, holding her hand.

"Well, don't be surprised. Things are going to be different between us." His smile faded into a soft frown. "I know I was stubborn before. I was just in pain, and I didn't know how to deal with my anger. But that's all behind me now. I promise you."

A nervous sensation spread through Whitney's blood as she realized the implication of what Javar was saying. He was talking like they had a future to look forward to…together.

Maybe it was the thought of almost losing her that had him thinking of a reconciliation. Or maybe he was just feeling guilty for the way things had ended between them. Whatever the reason for his sudden, bizarre display of emotion, it didn't change the fact that there wasn't a future for them. Their marriage ended nearly two years ago.

After the way he had pushed her out of his life then, she knew that he had never truly loved her. And if he *had* loved her, his love hadn't been strong enough to survive the horrible challenge they'd had to face.

"I'm glad you had the strength to come back, Whitney," Javar was saying when she focused on his words again. "I was wrong to ever let you walk out of my life. But you're back now. And that's all that matters."

How simple, Whitney thought, a wave of coldness sweeping over her. So, Javar was just ready to pick up the pieces? She didn't think so. She was playing by her rules now, not his.

And she had to end this charade before it went too far. The excited gleam in Javar's eyes said he thought she had come back to Chicago for a reconciliation. But after the dreadful pain she had suffered, Whitney knew that she could never turn back the clock to the happier times they had once shared. She didn't want to.

Softly moaning as a jolt of pain hit her, Whitney eased herself higher on the bed. "Javar."

"Yes, sweetie. What is it? Somewhere hurting? You need some water?"

Closing her eyes, Whitney took a deep breath. This wasn't the way she had wanted to tell Javar, but it was clear to her that it was necessary to set him straight now. "About why I was coming to see you…"

"It's okay, sweetie. You don't have to talk now. We've got our whole lives ahead of us." He softly stroked her cheek.

"No." Whitney's word was loud, final.

Javar flashed her a concerned look.

Whitney leveled a steady gaze in his direction. "There…" She paused, gathering strength. "There is no future for us, Javar."

Javar looked at her through narrowed eyes, clearly bewildered. "No…don't think like that Whitney. You survived the accident. You're going to be fine."

"That's not what I mean," Whitney retorted, her tone abrupt. She watched as confusion washed over Javar's face again. It wasn't easy, she realized, asking for a divorce even though their marriage was clearly over. Swallowing, Whitney lowered her eyelids, finding it suddenly hard to meet his questioning eyes.

In a voice barely above a whisper she said, "Javar, I want a divorce."

Chapter 4

Javar stared down at Whitney in stunned silence, his lips parted. Surely, getting a solid right hook to the gut couldn't wind him more than Whitney's last statement just had. Her expression solemn, Whitney had turned her head slightly to the left, avoiding his probing gaze.

Was this why she had come back to Chicago? To get a divorce and get on with her life?

"Whitney, you don't mean that..."

"Yes," she said, then paused. "I do."

Javar shook his head as he looked down at his wife, as though that could make Whitney's words go away. "I know that we've had some rough times, but...I think we can...."

"No," she replied, softly this time. "It's too late, Javar. Are you honestly going to tell me that you want to get back together?" Her eyes narrowed, speculatively. "I don't need your pity, Javar, and I know that's where this attitude must be coming from."

"No—"

"Well, it doesn't matter," Whitney continued, cutting Javar off. "It's been almost two years since we separated. That's why I was going to see you. It's time...we set each other free."

"Whitney..."

"Please, Javar. Don't fight me."

A shiver passed over him. It couldn't be true. She couldn't really want this. Anger, hurt, and sadness flooded through him, and Javar bit his inner cheek to fight the unpleasant emotions.

A divorce? No, he couldn't accept that. "You know, now isn't the time to talk about this. You're in pain…."

"But my thoughts aren't impaired. I know what I want, Javar. And that's to get on with my life."

Without him. Why the sudden hurry? he wondered, but didn't ask. She'd been content with a legal separation for almost two years; while they hadn't divorced, they had both gone on with their lives…apart. Frowning, he supposed he always knew this day would come, but nothing had prepared him for the emptiness he would feel when he actually heard her say the words.

He couldn't help asking, "Is there someone else?"

Whitney sighed, then winced as though in pain. Instinctively wanting to ease her discomfort, Javar brushed his fingers across her forehead. Whitney moved away from his touch, and Javar recoiled his fingers as quickly as if he'd been stung by a deadly snake's poison.

She stared at him for a long moment, as though she couldn't believe he'd asked that question. "No," she finally said. "I don't want a divorce because of some other man."

"Then why?"

"How can you ask me that?" She hesitated, then continued. "I thought you'd be elated that I'm finally asking for a divorce. I hear you're dating some lawyer. Maybe she can draw up the divorce papers."

Stunned, Javar's eyes bulged. She must be talking about Althea Harmon. "Where did you hear that?"

"It doesn't matter."

No, he agreed silently, it didn't matter. There was only one person who would have relayed such a story to Whitney: Cherise. He didn't know how she did it, but Whitney's cousin had a knack for discovering all kinds of sordid gossip. "It's not true," Javar told her, praying she believed him. "I...I haven't dated anyone since we separated."

Whitney shrugged her petite shoulders. "That's really not the point. I...our marriage failed." Her eyes challenged Javar to disagree. "What point is there in continuing to be legally married, when we aren't really married in the true sense of the word?"

Javar clenched his teeth, not liking what he was hearing at all. He wanted to have a real marriage. The vows he had taken he'd meant, and right now, he was willing to do whatever was necessary to earn Whitney's trust, and her love. And if she had meant the vows she'd taken before God four years ago, then she at least owed it to him to make the same effort. Calmly, Javar said, "I don't want a divorce."

Whitney unleashed a ragged sigh. "Please, Javar, I don't want you to contest this. It's over—irrevocably. For goodness' sake, you've never even tried to contact me in the two years we've been separated."

"That's because you wanted to be left alone."

Whitney threw him a dubious glance. "If you'd really wanted our relationship to work, you would have tried harder than that. You knew exactly where I was."

He had known; she'd been living with an aunt in Louisiana. But he'd been too angry to contact her in the beginning, and then, after a while, he'd just pushed all thoughts of her to the back of his mind. He had suffered unbearably after the death of his son, and quite frankly, he had shut down his emotions for months.

"As I said, I was in pain then. I didn't know how to deal with it."

Whitney stared at Javar in disbelief. "And I suppose I wasn't in pain?"

"I never said that. But you hadn't just lost your son—"

"He *was* my son, Javar. I may not have given birth to him, but I loved him as my own. And I had to live with the worst part of it all—I still do. If I had made sure that he was still buckled in...." Unable to go on, Whitney's voice broke.

An intense pang of guilt hit him. God, he was an insensitive fool! Javar took her hand in his and gave it a comforting squeeze. "I'm sorry, Whitney, I didn't mean that the way it sounded. Please, forgive me."

"You see, Javar, this is exactly what I'm talking about. You were never able to recognize *my* pain, let alone forgive me for the accident. Based on what you just said, I don't think you ever will."

"That's not true," Javar replied. "I have forgiven you."

Whitney was shaking her head and grimacing. "You haven't, Javar. If you look deep inside yourself, you'll realize that."

Tears filled Whitney's eyes and Javar felt his insides constrict, but he didn't know what to say or do to make her feel better. It was still painful for him to think about the accident that had caused his son's death.

"Whitney, I..."

"Don't," Whitney said, tears now spilling onto her cheeks. "Don't say anything you don't mean, Javar. I just want you to leave."

The loud sounds of a funky tune on WGCI 107.5 FM filled Javar's car as he sped along John F. Kennedy Expressway. Gripping the steering wheel, Javar pressed down hard on the gas pedal, accelerating at an extremely fast rate. Seventy, eighty, ninety… The wind felt wonderful against his face as he whipped his red, convertible Dodge Viper through traffic at dangerous speeds. One hundred, one-ten…. He hit the brake as he came upon some fool in the left lane who refused to let him pass. He slowed to about seventy before he snuck into the immediate right lane in front of another car, then sped up and cut in front of the slower car in the passing lane.

He was driving like an idiot, but he was mad. Nothing was going right in his life and he needed to do something to alleviate his stress. He was in no frame of mind to work on the Li bid, so he could kiss that good-bye. And Whitney's words still rang loud and clear in his mind: "I want a divorce."

Javar floored the gas pedal, taking his Viper to an even higher speed. He'd been driving since he was fifteen, and knew how to handle a car well. And right now, flying through traffic seemed like the only thing he could control in his life.

A soft, love ballad filled the airwaves and Javar searched the passenger seat for a cassette he could play instead. He picked up an old S.O.S. Band tape, then tossed it aside. He didn't want to hear its unrealistic take on love. Continuing to search, he found a tape of George Clinton. Old-school was his style, and he threw the cassette into the tape deck.

The sounds of "Flashlight" blasted through the speakers, and he tapped his thumb against the steering wheel to the beat. He was so focused on the road before him, he didn't notice the police cruiser until it was right on his tail.

"Damn!" Javar lowered the volume of the music, then began to gradually slow down. He heard the loud blast of the police air horn, and cursing under his breath, he downshifted gears, making his way onto the left shoulder.

He slowed to a complete stop, put his car in park, then opened the car door and stepped out onto the shoulder. He felt the enormous force of other cars zooming by at the legal speed limit, and realized just how much of a madman he had been.

"Get back in the car!" the police officer bellowed as he approached Javar, and Javar immediately did as he was told.

A few seconds later, the officer, a young black man who must have been at least six foot five, reached the driver's side of his car. With the hard top off, Javar felt small compared to the man's height, and suddenly, he didn't feel too in control.

"Do you realize you were doing one hundred and eleven miles an hour?" the officer asked, his look saying Javar had to have known but just didn't expect to be caught.

Javar was used to being stopped by police officers, especially because of the expensive cars he drove. But he was always happy when stopped by a brother; if nothing else, presumptions that he must be involved in something illegal in order to afford such an expensive car didn't exist.

Javar looked up at the police officer and smiled. Being polite was the first step in being able to talk his way out of this ticket. "Officer…" he looked at the name tag, "Williams. I do apologize for my idiotic behavior, but if you'd give me a chance to explain…"

"License, registration, and insurance please."

His hope fizzling, Javar complied, searching the glove compartment for the requested items. He handed them to the officer. "I'm not normally this crazy, but I just found out some bad news. My wife's been in a bad accident—"

"Mr. Jordan, I don't have time for excuses. And there is no excuse for the speed you were driving."

"No, you're right," Javar conceded. This cop wasn't going

to be a pushover. How could he expect him to be when he had been driving like a madman? Time to try plan B.

"If you'll just wait a minute, I'll be right back," the cop said, and started walking back toward the cruiser.

"As you can see, my name is Javar Jordan," Javar called to him. "Nephew of the late Marcel Jordan, who died only a year ago in the line of duty, while serving and protecting the citizens of Chicago."

Officer Williams stopped in his tracks. He turned around and walked back to Javar's car, eyeing him skeptically. "Your uncle was Marcel Jordan?"

Javar nodded. He felt lousy using his deceased uncle to get out of a citation, but at the speed he was going, he wouldn't just get a ticket for speeding, he'd get a notice to appear in court.

"Marcel Jordan trained me when I first started on the job. I rode with him for six months."

"Really?" Javar's eyebrows rose with interest.

A small smile lifted Officer Williams's lips as he nodded. "Yeah. He was a great man. It was too bad, him getting shot like that."

"Yes, it was." A wave of nostalgia washed over Javar as he remembered his uncle. Always laughing, always willing to lend a helping hand. He didn't deserve to die the way he did, gunned down at a routine traffic stop.

"I know," Javar said softly.

"Here." Officer Williams returned Javar's information. He smiled. "I'm not about to give any nephew of Lieutenant Jordan's a ticket. But I have to ask you to please slow down."

"Thanks." Javar nodded solemnly. "I really appreciate this. And yes, I will slow down."

Officer Williams tapped the side of the car. "Have a good evening, sir."

"I will. And thanks again."

As Javar started his car and eased back into traffic, he thought about the donation to the Chicago Police Department he would make in his uncle's name. It was something he had planned to do before, but never got around to it.

He would do it soon.

By the time Javar stepped into his waterfront mansion in Kenilworth, a suburb of Chicago along the coast of Lake Michigan, it was well after nine p.m. He had continued to drive after being stopped by Officer Williams, only at a much slower speed, and instead of the expressway, he'd drive along North and South Lake Shore drives, enjoying the view of the water beside him. Surprisingly, he found the calm, scenic drive even more soothing than his mad rush on the expressway. After having worked out his anger he'd had some time to reflect.

While he was angry with Whitney's request for a divorce, he had to admit that he was also angry with himself. He had hardly been the loving, forgiving husband he should have been. Rather, he'd been cold, spiteful, too blinded by pain to offer forgiveness. She didn't believe he could ever truly forgive her. Was she right, Javar wondered. If he was honest with himself, he'd have to admit that he wasn't really sure.

Javar hopped up the steps on the *Gone with the Wind* staircase in his home two at a time. Turning left when he reached the top, he walked down the large, brightly lit hallway to J.J.'s room. He hadn't changed a thing—not even the bedspread—since J.J. had last been in there alive and well. Inhaling a steadying breath, Javar opened the door, but as the hinges creaked softly, he couldn't bring himself to step inside the room.

Finally, he entered. He took one cautious step, then another, until he was beside the bed. J.J.'s favorite stuffed animal, a large brown teddy bear, lay atop the Mickey Mouse bedspread. Martin was the name J.J. had given his favorite bear. A smile touched Javar's lips as he remembered how Martin went everywhere with J.J. Ironically, he hadn't had it with him the day of the accident.

Javar wasn't sure when it had happened, but sometime during the last year, the intense emotional pain he'd originally felt when he'd lost his only son had lessened. It still hurt to think about his death, but instead of the horrifying images of the accident and his dying son entering his mind when he thought of J.J., Javar remembered the happy times they had shared. Before, he couldn't even enter this bedroom without breaking down. Now, to his own surprise, he at times found it necessary to visit J.J.'s room, to feel closer to his son, to remember the love and happiness J.J. had brought to his life. People had always told him that time would ease the pain, but he hadn't believed them. Two years later, Javar had to admit that those people were right. He would never forget his son, but now, instead of only sadness, J.J.'s room gave him a sense of peace.

But would he ever overcome his guilt? That sudden, unexpected thought disturbed him, and Javar made his way down to his den, where he poured himself a scotch—straight. Sooner or later, the nagging guilt he felt over losing his son always crept into his mind, threatening to drive him insane. He didn't want to think about his guilt, about the fact that he believed losing his son was his ultimate punishment. The drink would help. But as Javar reached for the glass, he couldn't make himself pick it up.

He turned, dragging a palm over his face. Alcohol wasn't going to make him feel better. When he had turned to it after

J.J.'s death, it had only postponed the pain. It was time to find a way to overcome his pain and guilt. Perhaps a little more time.

Feeling a small sense of victory at overcoming the temptation, Javar went back upstairs to his bedroom where he grabbed his keys. Returning downstairs, he made his way to the garage and to his car. The only thing that mattered now was Whitney. He had to make her believe that they had a second chance.

That goal consuming his thoughts, Javar drove from his driveway out onto the tree-lined, dimly lit street. Turning left, he headed toward Skokie, and Rush North Shore Medical Hospital.

Whitney hated hospitals. The bright white walls, the smiling nurses and doctors, the antiseptic smell of medicine and cleansers. No matter how much they tried to make a hospital aesthetically appealing with things like colorful paintings, nothing could mask the aura of sickness and death, not even the maternity ward.

She wanted to go home.

Glancing at the clock on the wall opposite her bed, Whitney saw that it was eleven-eighteen. Now that visiting hours were over for the evening, she felt very alone. Her mother and her cousin had spent a couple of hours with her earlier, and by the time they left, she'd felt much better than she had when she'd asked Javar to leave earlier. He had left in a huff, and Whitney could tell he was fuming. But what did he really expect? That she'd jump at his suggestion of a reconciliation? Had he conveniently forgotten how horribly their short marriage had ended?

Whitney groaned and threw her head back onto the pillow, frustrated. Immediately, a sharp pain exploded in her head. She tried to relax, hoping that would help the agony subside. As much as she hated sitting still, it was necessary that she take it easy.

Ten minutes later, the pain in her head was even worse. Although she didn't like to take medications, Whitney finally gave in and rang for the nurse, who brought her two powerful painkillers.

As Whitney closed her eyes and she felt sleep pulling her into its peaceful darkness, she wondered if Javar was ever going to come back.

Although Whitney had told him to leave, Javar found that he just couldn't stay away. He heard what she had said. He just couldn't bring himself to believe it.

Careful not to make any noise, Javar made his way into Whitney's private room. As her husband, he was allowed to spend the night. And that was exactly what he was going to do.

One look at Whitney sleeping peacefully, and Javar's heart warmed. She lay on her side, her lips slightly parted, the soft sound of her breathing filling the room.

In the closet, Javar found an extra blanket. He took it out and flung it over a shoulder. As he made his way to the small sofa near the window where he intended to sleep, Javar unbuttoned his white silk shirt. He slipped it off and tossed it onto the coffee table, then undid his belt. After dropping his pants to the floor, he bent, scooped them up, and placed them next to his shirt. Now he wore only a pair of white briefs, a white undershirt, and black nylon socks.

Whitney had fallen asleep with the bedside lamp on. Moving across the cold marble floor, Javar went to the small table where the lamp rested and turned it off.

He was about to go back over to the sofa when he heard Whitney's soft moan. His eyes flew to her. Her frail form was bathed in the soft glow of the moonlight.

She looked so beautiful.

Mesmerized, Javar merely stood there, observing Whitney. He'd forgotten how she looked when she slept. Her legs were drawn up in front of her, and she was curled in a fetal position. So childlike and so innocent...

The need to touch her was so great it was like a tangible force, drawing him to her. Unable to stop himself, Javar reached out and touched Whitney's face, trailing a finger along the length of her jaw. But the touch wasn't enough; he needed more. Leaning forward, he planted a soft, lingering kiss on her cheek.

The kiss warmed him all over, made him feel more alive than he had felt since she left him. It had been too long since he'd been loved, he realized. Way too long. He and Whitney had their problems, but they would work them out like married couples should. If it was the last thing he did, he would get her back.

Whitney Jordan, the murdering little witch, was back in town. Like a pesky cockroach, she had refused to die. But that didn't mean she wouldn't. Only that it would take longer than planned.

Caution was the utmost priority. However Whitney died, it had to look like an accident. There could be no questioning, no speculating as to the actual cause of death.

So, there was no time to waste. There were things to consider, like the best way to do the deed. Forget another car accident; she was probably so scared now, she wouldn't get behind the wheel of another car. But what? A drowning? An accidental overdose?

Something that would look like a suicide, that would be perfect. After all, Whitney had at least pretended to feel guilt over J.J.'s death, so who would doubt that she had gone crazy and had decided to end her life after years of living with the guilt?

Hmm. This definitely was going to be fun. Planning the perfect murder was going to be the sweetest revenge.

Chapter 5

Javar was dreaming. About food. Eggs, crispy bacon... He stirred. No, he wasn't dreaming. *Carlos must be making breakfast,* he thought, as he realized the scrumptious smell of eggs and bacon drifting into his nose was very real. As if in response to the tantalizing smell, his stomach growled long and loud. Stretching, Javar yawned and opened his eyes.

Immediately, he bolted upright. He wasn't in his bed. He wasn't at home.

Whitney.

Throwing a glance over his shoulder, Javar saw Whitney sitting up in the hospital bed. A tray of food was in front of her, and she nibbled on a strip of bacon.

When she saw him looking at her, Whitney's lips curled into a timid smile. "Morning."

That smile... Javar's blood grew warmer. His wife's smile had always been her best feature. Warm and sexy at the same time. That smile had wooed him on many an occasion.

"Morning," Javar muttered, then swung his feet to the floor. He was about to throw off the flannel blanket draped over his bare legs, but stopped himself. It had been a long time since he had woken up in the same room with Whitney. A tingling sensation washed over him, one of sexual awareness, but also worry. Would Whitney be uncomfortable with her half-dressed husband in the room?

"Still working like an obsessed man, I see," Whitney said, her chestnut eyes meeting his own. "It's after eleven o'clock, and you're just waking up."

Although he didn't doubt her claim, Javar threw a glance in the direction of the wall clock. He couldn't believe how long he'd slept. Obviously, he had needed the rest.

Today, Whitney looked much better and her bruises had faded significantly. Javar's heart expanded in his chest, overjoyed. For the first time, he felt absolutely positive that Whitney was going to be all right.

"How did you sleep?" he asked.

Whitney washed down the bacon with some orange juice. When she finished swallowing she answered, "Fine. The nurse gave me some painkillers last night, and I was out like a light."

"You look better. How are you feeling?"

"A lot better," Whitney replied, emphasizing each word. "Yesterday, I didn't know how I was going to get through this. Today, I feel like a whole new person." A bright smile lit her eyes for a quick moment before she returned her attention to her food.

"At least you've got an appetite."

Munching on another strip of bacon, Whitney nodded. "The doctor says that's a good sign. I was getting tired of the drip." She glanced at the intravenous bag beside her bed which was connected to her arm.

A slight grin touched Javar's lips. "I'd say so. If you're getting your appetite back, then I'd say you're well on your way to recovery."

Whitney couldn't help chortling. Javar was referring to the

fact that she loved to eat. Besides great sex, food was her next favorite passion. If she wasn't able to eat, that was a sure sign that she was gravely ill.

Javar yawned, and Whitney watched as he stood and gave his tall frame a long, hard stretch. The blanket that had covered his legs fell to the floor, revealing the sexy white briefs he sported. Large muscles grew taut in his corded arms and powerful, long legs as he stood on his toes and extended his body. When he finally relaxed his physique, the appealing shape of his sexy muscles was still evident. Javar's body had always been incredibly gorgeous. His brawny chest was evident beneath his thin white undershirt. His arms bulged in all the right places. But Whitney's weakness had always been Javar's firm, cute butt, which looked ever enticing in his skimpy underwear, even though she only had a side view of it.

As if he read her mind, Javar turned and faced the bay window, allowing Whitney a full view of his behind. Her eyes instantly fell to his lower body, taking in the sight of his sexy butt, and then his golden brown thighs and calves before venturing back up to the part she loved the most. Almost two years had passed since she'd had this kind of view of his behind, and she found herself wishing that the briefs would disappear.

Get a grip! her mind screamed. What was wrong with her, lusting after her husband like some lovesick teenager? Swallowing a sigh, Whitney realized that that was the perfect description for her. Since the breakup of her marriage, she hadn't been physically intimate with any other man.

Now, to her surprise, she realized just how much she had missed. The fact that she was lying in a hospital bed recovering from bodily injuries didn't prevent her body from growing taut with sexual awareness. White-hot desire pooled in her belly, then spread throughout her body.

"Looks like it's going to be another scorcher," Javar said, turning to face her.

Heat engulfed Whitney's cheeks. She looked down at her food, hoping that she had averted her eyes quickly enough; she didn't want Javar to realize that she had been ogling him. If he did, he might just get the impression that she was interested in saving their marriage. Which she wasn't, despite her sexual attraction to him that clearly hadn't died.

"Yes, it looks like it," Whitney replied, pondering the double meaning of their words. She was eyeing the scrambled eggs intently, as if they held the answers to life's questions.

Javar suppressed the grin that wanted to escape. It had only been a quick flash, but he'd seen the desire that had flickered in the depths of his wife's eyes. She was still sexually attracted to him.

They had a chance.

Not that sex alone could repair their marriage, but it could probably work wonders. In the past when they'd argued, they'd always ended up in bed, passionately resolving their differences. Maybe that was what they needed now.

If only it could be that easy. Not only had too much time passed for sex to be an answer, but Whitney was recovering from a major accident. The last thing he should be thinking about was making sweet love to her.

He couldn't stop himself.

But he had to. Moving to the coffee table, he retrieved his slacks and stepped into them. He was tempted to strip and go take a shower, but he didn't want to startle Whitney into a relapse. He had to concentrate on getting her well before he thought of ways to seduce her.

A soft rapping sound at the door drew Javar's attention from his carnal thoughts, and he threw a questioning glance at Whitney. Her eyes meeting his own, Whitney shrugged, letting him know that she had no idea who was at the door. As he continued to button his shirt, Javar sauntered to the door, opening it. What he saw disappointed him.

It was Derrick Lawson, an old friend of Whitney's. A sudden, unpleasant attack of jealousy caused his stomach to lurch. What was Derrick doing here?

"Javar," Derrick said, acknowledging him with a tight nod.

"Derrick." Javar forced a smile. "What are you doing here?"

"I'm here to see Whitney," he replied.

"Well, she's occupied right now," Javar told the tall, fair-skinned man.

Derrick's determined eyes met Javar's. "This is official business," he said, then brushed past Javar.

Derrick strolled into the brightly lit room, and Javar gritted his teeth as he closed the door.

"Derrick!" Whitney exclaimed, a wide grin forming on her lips. A grin Javar didn't like one bit.

"Hey, girl." Derrick strode to the bed and threw his arms around Whitney. She hugged him tightly.

Javar would have mentioned that Whitney had just survived an accident and was suffering physically, if it weren't for the fact that she was giggling like a schoolgirl as Derrick held her. Instead, he folded his arms over his chest and bit his tongue.

Pulling back from Derrick's embrace, Whitney said, "What are you doing here?"

"What do you think?" Derrick flashed a smile that was all charm. "You know whenever you get yourself into any trouble, I'll be here to help you out."

Whitney giggled happily. "Yes, of course. How could I forget?"

It was completely irrational, but Javar wanted to grab Derrick by the collar and drag the man away from his wife. However, he couldn't do that. He would upset Whitney, and Derrick would probably charge him with assaulting a police officer. But he could make sure that Derrick got down to "business," whatever that may be. Clearing his throat, Javar approached the opposite side of the bed from where Derrick had made himself comfortable. "You did say this was official?"

Derrick threw Javar a quick glance, nodding. "Actually, what I need to ask Whitney, I have to do in private."

Javar's body went rigid, and he shot Derrick an I-don't-think-so look. "Whatever you have to say to my wife you can say in front of me."

Derrick's light brown eyes met Javar's head-on. His lips lifted in a wry smile. "No, Javar. I can't. It's about the accident, and I hear you weren't even at the scene. So if you don't mind, I'd like to interview Whitney alone."

Sure you would, Javar thought. His stomach lurched again. He had no right to be jealous, but God help him, he was. What he needed to do was calm down. He couldn't start acting like a possessive fool whenever another man was around Whitney. "Fine," Javar replied, his tone flippant. "I'll just sit over there."

"Javar." Whitney's voice was stern, and he stopped midpivot to face her. A weary look stretched across her face. "Please... just give us a few minutes."

Not wanting to leave Whitney alone with Derrick, a man he knew had always had a thing for his wife, Javar merely stared at Whitney with uncompromising eyes. She met his gaze with a firm, but pleading one.

Finally, Javar sighed. "All right. I'll be outside the door."

"Thank you," Whitney said.

Javar spun around and walked out.

When the door clicked shut, Whitney turned and faced Derrick, beaming at him. "I'm so happy to see you, Derrick. It's been so long."

"I know." Derrick took her hand in his large one and squeezed it. "I have definitely missed that beautiful smile."

"And I've definitely missed your friendship." Derrick had been one of her good friends since grade school. "How's the force?"

"It's good. I'm a detective now."

Whitney smiled. "For real?"

"Yeah, for real."

Whitney was impressed, but she had always known that Derrick would move up the ranks of the police force quickly. "How do you like it?"

"I love it. I'm doing a bit of undercover work here and there, going after drug dealers and other lowlifes. I'm having a lot of fun."

"I'm happy for you." From the time Derrick was a child, he had wanted to be a police officer. His family hadn't supported his decision, especially with the high rate of crime in some areas of Chicago and the danger that police officers naturally face. But Whitney had understood his urge to help his community; she too had been driven into the field of social work for the same reason. Unfortunately because of his job, Derrick found it hard to maintain a long-term relationship; women were usually afraid of losing him in the line of fire.

"Things are going well," he said.

"And how's your family?"

"Good. Mom's great. She's enjoying being a grandmother. And Karen is working for the Chicago Board of Trade."

"Mmm hmm." Whitney threw him a suspicious glance, trying to figure out what he was *not* telling her. Her curiosity got the better of her and she asked, "Any special woman in your life?"

Pursing his lips, Derrick shook his head. "Naw. Too busy."

"That's it? Too busy?"

Derrick chuckled and looked at her through narrowed eyes. "I thought I'm the one who's supposed to ask the questions."

Whitney giggled. Derrick was a master at avoiding her more personal questions. Oh well. One day he would find the perfect woman. "Okay, Derrick. What do you want to know?"

"It's about the accident."

"You're assigned to my case?"

Derrick nodded, then reached into the pocket on his black blazer. He withdrew a small police notebook. "Yep. Like I said, whenever you're in trouble, you know I'm going to be there."

Hugging her elbows, Whitney inhaled deeply. Until this moment, she had avoided thinking about the accident. Derrick's presence on behalf of the Chicago Police Department now made that impossible. And remembering the accident the other night meant remembering the accident two years ago; an accident that she had survived, but her stepson had not.

Whitney inhaled again, hoping the deep breath would calm her. It didn't. From what the doctors had said, it was a miracle that she was alive. A miracle, yet she didn't feel very lucky. She'd finally hoped to put all her painful memories behind her, including the guilt she felt over the first accident. But the second accident had just made the haunting memories fresh.

Derrick's deep, smooth voice brought Whitney's thoughts back to the present. "Do you remember what happened?"

Rain. Oh God, she remembered the rain. A tremor hit her, causing her to shudder. She hugged her elbows tighter.

"It was raining."

Derrick jotted something down in his notebook. "Do you remember what caused you to lose control of the car? Did you swerve to avoid an animal, maybe?"

Whitney shook her head. Felt her nerves go haywire. It had been raining, and… "I was driving in the left lane, along North Lake Shore Drive. There was someone behind me. Another car. Some impatient driver who gave me the high beams, so I indicated to go into the right lane. Only, by the time I was going into the right lane, so was he."

"You say he," Derrick pointed out, interrupting her. "Did you get a look at the driver?"

Whitney clenched her fist, trying to stop the shaking. "I…no. It was dark. I—I just assumed that it was a man. Most women don't drive like that."

"Did you get a look at the car?"

Scrunching her forehead, Whitney thought hard. The action brought discomfort with it. But she had to remember. After several moments, she groaned. Nothing. She couldn't remember seeing a particular kind of car, only bright high beams. "No," she replied, frustrated.

Derrick jotted down some more notes. "So what happened to cause you to lose control?"

Running a hand over her limp hair, Whitney tried again to remember. It had all happened so fast. "I remember that when I was going into the right lane, so was the other driver. As I said, he—or she—was impatient. Probably late for something. I swerved back into the left lane, and that's the last thing I remember. Except trying desperately to gain control of the car, but I couldn't."

"It is possible the car hit you?"

Exasperated, Whitney expelled a pent-up moan. "I—I don't know. I can't remember."

"It's okay. Forensics will check the car for any evidence that the other vehicle may have hit you."

Whitney buried her face in her hands and moaned softly. Moments later, she lifted her head, focusing on Derrick's kind face and the warmth it offered.

He seemed to sense that she needed comfort, and he ran a large hand down her arm, lifting her hand into his. "I know this is hard for you. But I have to ask these questions. I just want to get to the bottom of this."

"I know."

Derrick winked at her. "You're strong, Whitney. You're going to get through this."

Despite her frustration, Whitney was able to smile. "Thanks. That means a lot." The smiled faded, and she bit down on her lower lip, shaking her head. "It was a stupid accident. Probably preventable, but it's too late to turn back the clock."

"Yeah." Derrick looked away for a moment, then returned his concerned gaze to Whitney's face. "How are you doing… emotionally?"

"I'm doing better." Sometimes, she wondered if that was really true. She would take two steps forward, then four steps back. She could never escape the horror of the memories, but she prayed she would be able to live with them.

"Coming back to Chicago is a really big step. I know how

much courage that must have taken." Derrick raised a suggestive eyebrow, and his lips twisted in a frisky grin. "If it means
anything, I'm glad you're back."

"You're too much." Whitney chortled—however weakly—
then playfully punched Derrick's arm. Was he merely being
friendly, or something else? She couldn't be sure. All she knew
was that he was a friend she could trust, count on. "I guess it
won't hurt to tell you," she said softly. "I'm only back because
I'm asking Javar for a divorce."

"It's about time."

Whitney flashed Derrick an amiable, don't-go-there look.
Derrick had never liked Javar. No doubt, because he'd once had
a crush on her. A silly grade-school crush, but ever since then,
Derrick had been protective of her, telling her in no uncertain
terms what he thought of the men she went out with. Thinking
back, Whitney realized that Derrick had never approved of any
of the men she'd dated.

Whitney hesitated, shrugging. "You're right. It is time." She
remembered Javar's plea for a reconciliation, and felt regret wash
over her. So many dreams, so many promises...all of them
broken.

Derrick's eyes softened as he held Whitney's gaze. "I know
this can't be easy. You loved him once."

Her heart pounded at the word *loved.* It sounded so final....
But it was accurate, wasn't it? She cared about Javar, would
always have a special place for him in her heart. But that was
all. Their romantic passion for each other had died two years
ago. Now, she loved him like she loved a friend or family
member. She kept those thoughts to herself though, because
nobody would understand that after all that had happened
between them, she still cared deeply for Javar. Sure, she wanted

a divorce, but not because she was bitter, angry, or even hateful. Their problems were too monumental to work out, and there was no point in delaying the inevitable.

Hopefully, one day, she would find the man with whom she would spend the rest of her days, blissfully happy.

One day, if she could be so lucky twice in a lifetime.

Javar had a plan.

Maybe it was seeing Whitney's reaction to Derrick that had him realizing he had to act soon if he wasn't going to lose her. Hell, who was he kidding. He still felt uneasy—jealous—not knowing what was going on behind the closed doors of his wife's hospital room.

He tapped his fingers against the polished oak table next to the chair he was sitting in, while he waited for Dr. Adu-Bohene. He prayed the doctor would go along with his plan. He thought it was feasible, fair, reasonable. And it might be the only chance he had to win Whitney's love back.

Sensing a presence, Javar looked up. Dr. Adu-Bohene stared down at him.

"You wanted to see me?" the doctor asked.

Javar stood and smiled. "Yes, Dr. Adu-Bohene, I did."

Fifteen minutes later, Javar strolled into Whitney's room, a lively bounce in his step. Dr. Adu-Bohene, the good man that he was, had agreed to go along with his plan. All that was left to do was to break the news to Whitney. If he made it appear like the good doctor's idea, what could she say? Besides, the Whitney he knew had always hated hospitals, and he was sure she would do anything to get released, even if it meant accepting Dr. Adu-Bohene's conditions.

Dr. Adu-Bohene had assured Javar that the most recent tests had confirmed the findings of the first ones. Whitney was going to be fine. She hadn't completely recovered yet from the surface wounds, but Dr. Adu-Bohene had no doubt she would, soon.

Javar was pleased to find Whitney standing at the window, looking outside. When she heard him enter the room, she turned. Her wide eyes quickly narrowed with suspicion as Javar approached her, a foolish grin on his lips. "What?" she asked.

"Where's Derrick?"

"He had to go back to work."

"Good." He hoped that Officer Derrick Lawson was finished questioning his wife.

Whitney's forehead wrinkled as caution flashed over her features. "That's why you're so...happy?"

Javar shook his head. "Actually, I have some good news for you."

Still suspicious, Whitney asked, "You do?"

Javar nodded. "You want to go home, don't you?"

Whitney looked at him with anticipation, a half smile on her lips. "I can go home?"

God, Javar felt wonderful seeing Whitney standing, excited even. He took a step closer, wanting to take her in his arms and brush his lips against the velvety soft ones he remembered. He needed to taste her honeyed sweetness, feel her body respond to his the way it once did....

In time, Javar. In time.

He swallowed, then spoke. "Yes, Whitney. That's the good news. I've spoken with your doctor, and he says you can go home...today."

Whitney squealed, delighted. Turning on her heel, she scampered to the closet, no doubt intending to gather her belongings.

She was so much stronger than yesterday. Life had been cruel to her, yet it hadn't weakened her spirit, her zest.

He watched her for a moment before adding, "On one condition."

The excitement fizzled out of Whitney's eyes as she turned and faced him.

Her tone was wary as she asked, "And what condition is that?"

Chapter 6

"No."

Javar merely smiled, an arrogant, confident smile. Whitney wanted to slap it off his face.

"I mean it, Javar," she added, her hands clenched at her sides. "If that's the condition, then I'm staying right here."

"Oh, come on. The way you hate hospitals…. You can't be serious."

How dare he do this to her! That cocky smile was the telltale sign that he had put Dr. Adu-Bohene up to this. Whitney was certain that the doctor had not suggested Javar take her home to *his* place where she could recuperate. With the help of a hired nurse, of course, to make his proposition seem legitimate. The weasel! Javar knew how much she hated hospitals.

Grunting in frustration, Whitney turned from the closet and marched to the bed. Pain shot through her left hip as she hastily climbed onto the soft mattress. Unable to cover her distress, she cried out softly. Javar was immediately at her side.

Glaring at him, Whitney said, "Don't touch me."

Dark brown eyes held hers. "Whitney," Javar began in a placating tone, "don't you think you're being just a little ridiculous? You know as well as I do that you're going to get well a lot quicker at home, where you can go out to the backyard and relax, soak up some sun...."

"No," she reiterated.

Javar's lips twisted. "I've already hired a nurse. Everything is arranged."

Everything is arranged—like that meant she was obligated to agree! Whitney's eyes were uncompromising. "Well *unar-range* it. I won't agree to that condition."

"Whitney—"

"No."

Javar eased himself onto the bed beside Whitney, his eyes precarious as he regarded her. A frown stretched across her beautiful lips, a sexy pout if he ever saw one. But they weren't playing a lover's game of cat and mouse here. Whitney really wanted nothing to do with him.

Javar wanted to run his thumb along her tempting lips, to kiss the bruises on her face and make all her pain go away. But he knew that was the last thing Whitney wanted. Instead he dug his nails into his fists as he clenched them, hoping that would dull the ache in his groin.

"Whitney, do you really hate me so much that you can't stand to be around me, even to the detriment of your own health?"

She was still pouting, refusing to look at him. Finally, she cast a sidelong glance in his direction. Javar couldn't help thinking how much he loved her eyes. They were the most magnificent eyes he had ever seen, a deep chestnut-brown with a thin layer of royal blue around the outer edge of her irises. Unusual, yet striking. That little touch of royal blue added a peerless spark.

"I...I don't hate you," Whitney finally said, her voice low.

"It's just that…I know what you're trying to do, and I don't like it."

Javar raised a questioning eyebrow. "And what is it that I'm trying to do?"

Whitney's beautiful eyes rolled toward the ceiling, and not in a playful manner. She was deadly serious. A chill snaked down his spine.

"Javar, I want a divorce. Getting me into your house is not going to make me change my mind."

He knew it, saw it in her eyes before she said the words, yet when she repeated her intentions, Javar's insides tightened painfully. Was he making a mistake by forcing her to go home with him? Would his plan backfire? No, he decided, not if he took things slowly. He lowered his eyelids and said, "Well, if you're so certain of that, then what's the problem?"

"I just don't like your deception."

"Whitney, I know you may not believe this, but all I really want is for you to get better." That was the truth. Her health came first. "No, I don't want a divorce, but I can't force you to stay married to me against your wishes. Think about it. This arrangement will be perfect. You can get well in a much more appealing environment, not some depressing hospital. You'll have a nurse at your side twenty-four hours a day for as long as necessary. And if anything, *anything,* seems wrong with your health, we can always have you readmitted to the hospital." Javar shrugged. "I don't know about you, but that certainly seems like a great plan to me."

"I'm sure it does."

"Do you have a better idea?"

Whitney drew in a deep breath and lowered her eyes. Javar made it sound so wonderful, so simple. And boy did she ever hate hospitals! She found them more hazardous to her health in this stage of recovery than helpful.

She looked at Javar. A small grin tugged at the corners of his lips, and his nutmeg-colored eyes regarded her warmly. She didn't want to lead him on. Obviously, he still cared about her. But how would he feel if she went along with his plan, then still pursued the divorce when she got well? Would he hate her? God, she couldn't handle that. There was enough animosity between them.

She was crazy for even considering his proposal. "Javar, if I...go home with you, it won't...change anything."

Whitney suspected his emotions weren't as calm as his voice when he replied, "I understand."

"All right, Javar." She hoped she wouldn't regret her decision. "I'll go along with your plan. But don't think for a moment that I believe this was the doctor's idea. I know you're behind it."

Javar opened his mouth to say something, but Whitney put her hand to his lips, stopping him. A familiar rush of longing spread from her fingers down her arm. How she wished she could erase the events of the past and love Javar the way she had vowed to do.

But she couldn't.

She recoiled her fingers, looked down, then continued. "Javar, please be sure about this. If you're entertaining thoughts of a reconciliation, please don't. I meant what I said. When this is all over, when I'm completely healed, I'm still going ahead with my plans for a divorce."

Half an hour later, Whitney was dressed in jeans and a T-shirt and sitting in a wheelchair waiting to be formally released from the hospital while Javar was settling the bill. Earlier she'd spoken with her mother and had told her about the doctor's condition for her release. Her mother hadn't liked the idea and was very worried about Javar pressuring her into a reconciliation while Whitney was vulnerable. But Whitney had assured her mother that she would be well and out of Javar's house soon.

During a final examination by Dr. Adu-Bohene, he replaced the bandage on her forehead with a fresh one, and confirmed that she was recovering nicely. The large gash beneath the bandage was healing, and the bruises were changing color. A little makeup and she would look as good as new.

She'd nearly had heart failure when the doctor told her and Javar that if she felt up to it, lovemaking would not be a problem. Of course, with caution, he'd added, then smiled knowingly. Whitney hadn't dared to look at Javar's face, since her own embarrassment—and probably longing—would have been evident.

A middle-aged black nurse accompanied Javar as he strolled toward Whitney from the reception desk. The nurse took hold of Whitney's wheelchair, moving her across the sparkling gray floor toward the elevators. Javar followed, silently.

When they reached the first floor, the nurse rolled Whitney's wheelchair to the front door, then said warmly, "Here we go."

Javar helped her out of the chair, then turned to the nurse. "Thanks so much for your help."

The nurse's eyes lit up with unmasked longing. Whitney felt a strange pull in her stomach, remembering the same look of desire on so many other women's faces who had found her husband attractive.

"It was my pleasure." A sheepish grin lifted the woman's lips.

As the nurse sauntered away, Whitney felt an unpleasant surge of jealousy sweep over her. Javar seemed unaware of the nurse's flirtatiousness, as he had with the other women. The countless other women. There were so many, so willing.... After J.J.'s death, Whitney had wondered if Javar was seeing someone. He had refused to make love with her, eventually moving out of their bedroom, and he'd spent more and more time at the office, no doubt with Melody, his lovely secretary, hanging all over him.

Whitney pushed that unpleasant thought to the back of her mind. Her husband was an attractive man, and it would be stupid to get upset whenever a woman gave him a sidelong glance, or a bold one for that matter. Besides, he was still legally her husband, but he had stopped being a real one to her a long time ago. So jealousy was the last thing she should be experiencing.

"You ready?" Javar asked, his words interrupting her troubled thoughts.

He was so handsome when he looked at her like that. She exhaled harshly. She would get through this. "I'm ready," she replied. "Lead the way."

Javar wrapped an arm around her waist, leading her out the main doors of the hospital, then across the street to the hospital parking lot. He carried her small suitcase with his free hand. She had to admit she felt comforted by his touch. She felt strangely warm as she leaned into him for support. Why did he still have to look so good? And why, after all the pain he had caused her, did she still find him attractive? Wryly, she wondered if the bump on her head had anything to do with her body's convenient memory loss; clearly, her body didn't seem to remember Javar's betrayal of his vows.

A few minutes later, Javar stopped beside a gorgeous sports car, a red Dodge Viper. This must have been one of his new "toys." She hadn't seen it before.

"New car?" she asked, realizing that it was a dumb question after the words left her lips.

Javar opened the passenger door for her as he replied, "Yeah. Just got it a few months ago."

In time for the beginning of the spring. How nice.

Javar slipped Whitney's small suitcase into the cramped backseat. This car obviously served only one purpose: to get attention.

"Do you like it?" Javar asked.

Whitney's eyes roamed the gleaming, cherry red surface of the car. What wasn't to like? It was gorgeous. "It's beautiful."

"I'd take the top off, but we're not far from home, so there's no point."

Whitney nodded absently. She slipped onto the soft, gray leather seat, running her hand along the edge as she did. Javar's money had allowed her to drive a sporty BMW while they were together. Unfortunately, that was the car that had been totaled in the accident with J.J. But Javar had also driven a top-of-the-line BMW, and from what Whitney remembered, that was his favorite car.

"What happened to your BMW?" she asked.

"It was stolen."

"Stolen?" Whitney repeated, shocked.

Javar nodded. "Yeah. A few days ago. Right out of my driveway."

The moment Whitney walked into the three-story mansion, a gripping wave of nostalgia washed over her.

She stopped. Stared.

It had been so long.

The black marble floor glittered beneath the sun's bright

rays, which flowed through the high ceiling's skylight. The *Gone with the Wind* staircase with a second level balcony looked grand and majestic as it took center stage in the colossal octagon-shaped foyer. Four of the foyer's eight walls boasted high archways leading to hallways and other rooms on the main level. Hanging above the center of the floor was an elegant silver and crystal chandelier. On the walls to the immediate right and left of the double front doors hung two large paintings depicting Africans in the traditional dress of their native Ghana. Javar had traced his family's roots back to that country. The beautiful paintings had graced the walls when Whitney had left almost two years ago. In fact, looking around, everything appeared the same. Even the small mahogany table to her right had the same white, lace doily on it she remembered. And the large crystal vase atop the doily was filled with fresh orchids. Her favorite flower.

Just like the day she had left.

The exterior of the house looked the same, as well. Pink and white rosebushes lined the long, U-shaped walkway from the sidewalk to the front door of Javar's ultramodern, cream-colored estate. The California-styled roof was an orange-brown. The house had several dozen windows—many bay styled, squared, and circular. Having bought more than two acres of land with a moderate-sized house, Javar had demolished the older one and constructed his dream home. Later, he had shown Whitney the blueprints for the house, explaining that he had designed one with lots of windows because he felt sunlight added life to a home. He'd also told her that his dream house hadn't become his dream home until she had moved in and shared it with him.

"Mrs. Jordan. Welcome back."

Whitney lifted her eyes from the orchids she didn't realize she was staring at until she heard the warm, familiar voice of Carlos Medeiros, Javar's longtime butler. He smiled, excitement dancing in his eyes as he regarded her for the first time in almost two years.

Whitney returned the smile. "Thank you, Carlos."

She hesitated only a moment before moving to him. Wrapping her arms around him, she kissed him on the cheek. Carlos was the one to end the hug, stepping back. Whitney remembered that he wasn't prone to physical affection, at least not with his employer's family. He probably worried that he would offend Javar if he got too close.

Carlos looked down at the small suitcase. "This is all your luggage?"

Whitney saw the surprise in Carlos's eyes and wondered what Javar had told him. "Yes. For now at least." She had more clothes at her mother's, which she would pick up later.

"I'll bring the suitcase upstairs, Carlos," Javar told the man. He turned to Whitney. "Are you hungry?"

Whitney flashed him a knowing look. Was she hungry? When was she not?

Javar chuckled. "Silly question. Carlos, why don't you make some French toast for Whitney. I'm sure she'd like that."

"Absolutely sir," Carlos said, then turned and headed toward the arch at the back of the stairs that led to the kitchen.

Whitney looked at the stairs a few feet away from her. Sunlight spilled onto the winding staircase partly from the skylight and partly from the large, circular window at the top of the stairs. Thick, cream-colored carpeting covered each step. The wood was a polished mahogany, Javar's favorite, that gleamed enticingly under the sun's rays. Throughout the house,

Javar had implemented a style of whites and creams contrasting with black, and the result was quite striking.

"Would you like to lie down?"

Whitney glanced at Javar, at his handsome oval face. Memories were still flooding her, like the time he carried her over the threshold of the patio doors after their garden wedding under the clear, blue sky. Or the first time Javar had carried her up those *Gone with the Wind* stairs to their bedroom, where they had made sweet, passionate love for hours. There also was the time she had made a path of scented rose petals from their bedroom to the pool room, where she had seduced him in the Jacuzzi. The memories were of years ago when they were first married, yet they seemed so fresh, so current.

"Actually," Whitney said, contemplating what she should do as she spoke, "I think I'd like to walk around."

"All right. Your room is the first one on the left, at the top of the stairs. The nurse will be here shortly."

Whitney nodded, then turned to her right, walking down the long corridor. She glanced in a sitting room with floor to ceiling windows facing the backyard. She poked her head in Javar's library, graced with rich wood paneling. Books of all types, including fiction and nonfiction, filled the numerous shelves. Further down the hallway was Javar's home office, and stepping inside she saw his large drafting table near the vast windows. Pictures of houses and commercial properties he had designed and renovated framed the walls, including a poster sized picture of his own waterfront home. An image of the time she had worn a skimpy red number down to Javar's office, seducing him from his work entered Whitney's thoughts. The memory was bittersweet. Her husband had been an obsessed workaholic, even through their newlywed stage. She often had to physically distract him from his work in order to get some love and affection. She didn't mind at first, knowing she could tempt her husband, but later it wasn't as easy to divert his attention. And she had become frustrated.

Whitney stepped out of Javar's office, and continued strolling down the great hallway. She kept walking until she rounded a short corner and reached the double glass doors that led to the indoor pool and Jacuzzi. Opening the door on the right, Whitney stepped inside.

The smell of chlorine hit Whitney as she entered the room. The aqua-blue water in the large, kidney shaped pool glistened beneath yet another skylight. At the opposite end of the pool from where she was standing, thick wooden doors led to a sauna. The Jacuzzi, which was quite large, was beside the pool on the left. Whitney swallowed as a clear image of a very naked Javar in the Jacuzzi, his wet body pressing against hers, invaded her mind.

Whitney shook off the memory, then walked toward the Jacuzzi and the patio doors beside it. She looked out into the backyard, where another inground pool, a hexagon shaped one, lay beyond a large concrete deck at the foot of the steps. Unlocking the patio doors, Whitney stepped out onto the peach-colored patterned concrete and looked over the deck's wrought-iron railing. This was where they'd had pool parties with friends, with chicken and steaks grilling, and loud music pulsating out of the patio speakers.

Whitney walked down the deck steps, past the pool area until she reached the vibrant green grass. The backyard was enormous. A variety of flowers were interspersed throughout the colossal backyard in a brilliant display of colors. On the left was a tennis court as well as a basketball court. To the far left, red rosebushes lined a cobblestone path that led from the back of the house to the beach. Whitney walked along the grass until she reached the opening to the path, the sweet scent of azaleas, petunias, lilacs, and roses filling her nose. She followed the path's curving trail down to the shore of Lake Michigan.

The waters of Lake Michigan splashed against the shore, hitting *Lady Love,* the twin hull catamaran Javar had given to her as a wedding gift. The memories were everywhere.... She couldn't escape them. And she couldn't help smiling as she remembered her excitement when Javar had led her down the softly lit, winding rose path the night of their wedding, to the beach, and to her surprise....

"Come on, Javar. Tell me what my surprise is."

Her husband of several hours flashed her a sexy smile. "It wouldn't be a surprise then, now would it?"

Whitney curled her lips downward in a playful pout. "I know, but... I hate surprises."

"Patience, my dear," Javar said, wrapping his arms around her from behind and kissing her cheek. Desire shot straight through her entire body at Javar's touch. The whole day had been an incredible aphrodisiac—the intimate ceremony, the stolen glances exchanged with her husband, the intoxicating smell of fresh flowers, the orchestra, the exchange of personal vows. Now, the last of the guests from the wedding celebration had finally left, and Whitney hadn't yet made love to her husband. They'd agreed to wait until their wedding night, and Whitney found herself unable to wait any longer.

"Come on." Releasing his hold on her waist, Javar took Whitney's hand and jogging, led her down the path. She couldn't help giggling. When they finally reached the moonlit beach, Whitney's mouth fell open.

"Ta da!" Javar turned and faced Whitney, the love in his eyes making her want to cry. "There you are, sweetie. There's your present."

It was beautiful! Whitney threw her hand to her mouth as she approached the gleaming white boat. The words *Lady Love* were painted on the side in bold, red letters. Whitney didn't know much about boats, but she certainly knew that people didn't tend to name catamarans. "You got me a boat?"

"Yes," Javar said proudly.

Whitney's eyes grew misty as she looked at him. "You named it?"

"What? People can't name catamarans?"

She held the tears at bay, laughing instead. "Not usually. Aren't names reserved for bigger boats?"

"Well, I like to be different," Javar stated with a quick shrug of his shoulders. Then, as he regarded Whitney, his smile faded and his eyes narrowed. "You do like it, don't you?"

Whitney gaped at her new husband. The man she planned to be deliriously happy with for the rest of her life. She threw herself into his arms. "Like it? I love it! Oh, Javar, thank you!"

"Really?"

"Of course, really! This is the best gift I've ever received!"

Javar gazed into her eyes. God, he looked so gorgeous when he smiled at her like that, his eyes crinkling. "Good," he said. "How 'bout a moonlit sail?"

"How about this?" Sliding her hands up Javar's large back, over his corded muscles and wide shoulders, Whitney laced her fingers around his neck. A deep, carnal groan rumbled in her husband's chest. She felt it against her own and her longing intensified. Pulling his head down, Whitney whispered, "You've kept me waiting long enough."

Whitney sighed against Javar's lips as they met hers, smooth and sweet. She kissed him slowly, somehow controlling all the pent-up passion that needed to be released.

Unzipping her simple, knee-length white silk dress, Javar slipped his fingers beneath the material and trailed them up her back. She moaned. This felt good, so good. A tremor of longing rocked her body, and heat engulfed her inner thighs. She stood on her toes and arched against him, feeling the evidence of his desire. Javar groaned and deepened the kiss, delving his tongue deep into her mouth.

Gripping her back, Javar pulled her close. Ever so slowly, he trailed one hand around up her back to her shoulder, nudging the dress off. Then softly, he stroked the fullness of one breast. Whitney's nipple immediately hardened, and when Javar tweaked it with his thumb and forefinger, she thought she would die of the pleasure.

"Oh, Javar!" she moaned against his lips.

Tearing his lips away from hers, Javar brought his hot tongue down onto her throbbing nipple, drawing it into his mouth and suckling. Nothing had ever felt this good. Sensations she'd never before experienced—searing, dizzying sensations—overwhelmed her. The pleasure was so intense that it shocked her, tore the sound from her voice.

Finally, the moan that wanted to be unleashed found the voice to accompany it. The sound was loud and rapturous as it escaped her lips, and sounded foreign to her ears. She felt slightly embarrassed, but she couldn't stop the sounds. The feelings of pleasure were so exquisite....

"Let's move to the boat," Javar murmured.

When Whitney nodded, Javar scooped her up in his arms, carrying her to the catamaran's tramp....

* * *

"You're remembering, aren't you?"

Startled, she whirled around and saw Javar standing a couple of feet away from her, a peculiar expression on his face. Her own face was flushed and she was definitely hot with longing. Her heart beat an erratic tempo.

Lord, what was wrong with her? How had she gotten so caught up in the past? The memory had seemed so real....

Javar took a step toward her, and despite her urge to move away Whitney found she was rooted to the spot. Desire sparked in the depths of Javar's beautiful brown eyes. Holding her gaze, he pulled his bottom lip between his teeth.

Whitney sucked in a sharp breath.

He reached out and ran his thumb across her bottom lip. Why couldn't she respond, why couldn't she stop him? Because the simple touch of his finger on her mouth felt so good.

"You are, aren't you, Whitney?"

Whitney's throat was suddenly so dry and tight it ached. She couldn't say a thing. She wanted to walk away. She wanted to feel Javar's sensuous lips on hers.

"Whatever else went wrong, sex was always wonderful for us, wasn't it, Whitney? We used to love passionately."

She couldn't deny that.

"We can have that again, Whitney. It can be so good."

Whitney's lips trembled under the seductive touch of Javar's thumb. Her breath was so shallow, she wasn't sure she was breathing. Her lips parted, remembering, inviting...

Whitney's pulse quickened as Javar leaned forward, lowering his lips until they were a fraction of an inch away from hers. His lips lingered there, taunting her. Javar's musky, masculine smell flirted with her nose, mesmerizing her.

Nervous, she flicked her tongue out, running it across her bottom lip.

And then his lips were on hers, capturing her mouth in a soft, sweet, mind-numbing kiss.

But he ended it almost as soon as it began, leaving Whitney surprised and frustrated.

Javar backed away from her, his eyes holding her captive. "I'll leave you to your thoughts. I just wanted to let you know the nurse has been delayed but will be here as soon as she can."

Then, ever so calmly, as though he hadn't been affected by the meeting of their lips, Javar turned and walked away, strolling casually up the winding path.

Whitney watched him leave in stunned disbelief.

When he was out of sight, Whitney sank into the sand. She wanted to grab a rock and hurl it at him for toying with her the way he had. What she really wanted to do was get away from this place. She couldn't believe how flustered she felt. One quick kiss, and her entire body was thrumming with wanton sexual desire.

Anger soon replaced her frustrated longing. Javar wasn't going to do this to her. He wasn't going to get her worked up to the point where *she* went after *him*.

No way.

Her days of loving Javar Jordan were long over.

Heaving herself off the sand, Whitney rose and started jogging up the path back to the house. She went in through the back patio doors and scampered through the pool room and back down the corridor she had originally followed. She didn't bother to take her shoes off when she ran up the stairs and straight to her room.

Whitney slammed the bedroom door behind her and locked

it. Her head pounded from overexerting herself. She paused to catch her breath. Then she marched to the phone beside the bed. Picking up the receiver, she held it between her shoulder and ear while punching in the digits to Cherise's home.

The phone rang five times, and just as Whitney was about to hang up, Cherise answered.

"Cherise," Whitney said, breathing a sigh of relief. "I need you to come pick me up… No, I'm at Javar's… I know, I know. It's a long story… Cherise, I really want to get out of here, so if you don't mind, I can tell you the details later… Okay, cuz. Thanks a lot… See ya soon."

As Whitney hung up the phone, she dropped herself onto the edge of the king-sized canopy bed, needing to rest a moment. She lingered there for a few minutes, then made her way to the closet where she grabbed the suitcase and opened it. Her clothes were hanging neatly in the closet.

Without regard for the garments, Whitney grabbed them off their hangers and dropped them into a pile in her suitcase. How could she have agreed to Javar's ridiculous proposition? Coming here was a mistake, and she wouldn't stay here a minute longer.

She had to get out of here before Javar made a further fool of her.

Chapter 7

When she heard the doorbell, Whitney grabbed her suitcase and made her way to the bedroom door. She prayed Javar was busy doing something else, and that Carlos would answer the door. Carlos would be surprised that she was leaving, but she could scurry out before he was able to stop her, or alert Javar. She wanted no hassles.

As she stepped into the hallway, she felt the powerful urge to look to her left. Toward J.J.'s room. She inhaled a deep breath, remembering everything. Little J.J. as he played with her, as he asked her thousands of questions about everything. She had loved that child as if he was her own, yet nobody could understand that.

Swallowing a sigh, Whitney averted her gaze and hurried toward the stairs. The sooner she got out of here the better. The sooner she got away from the pain...

She hurried down the stairs. As she reached the bottom, she saw Carlos and Cherise. The smile on Cherise's face gave her the strength to go on.

Carlos's eyes narrowed as he saw the suitcase in Whitney's hand. She did the only thing she could: lie. "I'm going to get the rest of my stuff. This suitcase is empty. I figure I'll need it."

Carlos nodded. "I see."

"I shouldn't be too long. There's no need to tell Javar that I'm even gone." She turned to Cherise. "Let's go."

Cherise took the suitcase from her, then the two hurried to the door. She was stepping over the threshold when she heard Javar's voice.

"Carlos, is that the nurse?"

Whitney closed the door and started down the concrete steps. Cherise's Toyota was several feet away, but if they hurried....

"Whitney!"

Whitney halted at the sound of Javar's voice, but didn't turn around.

"Whitney, where are you going?"

"Uh...I'm going to get the rest of my stuff."

Cherise looked at her. "Why don't you tell him the truth?"

"Look at me, Whitney," Javar commanded.

She didn't have to look around to know that he was only a few feet behind her. Slowly, she turned. "Javar, I..."

"Give that to me." He indicated the suitcase in Cherise's hand.

Cherise looked at Whitney, as though for approval, and Whitney shrugged. "Go ahead," Whitney instructed her cousin.

Eyeing Whitney skeptically, Javar took the suitcase from Cherise. After a moment his eyes narrowed. "If you're only going to get the rest of your stuff, then why is this suitcase full?"

Whitney felt like a child who had been caught with her hand in the cookie jar. And she shouldn't feel that way. She was an adult who could make her own decisions.

"Well?" Javar prompted.

Cherise walked the several feet to the car, giving Whitney and Javar some privacy. Whitney watched as Cherise rounded the back of the car and went to the driver's side before speaking. "I'm leaving."

"That isn't part of the plan."

"I've changed my mind."

"We had an agreement."

"I'm a big girl, Javar. I'm allowed to change my mind."

"Not in this situation, you're not."

Whitney turned, looked at the old maple trees that lined the borders of his property. Their vibrant green leaves rustled softly as the light breeze flirted with them. The scent of the various roses, some of which she had planted and pruned while she'd lived here filled her nostrils. Once, she had been happy here. Now, she only wanted to leave.

Javar's voice interrupted her thoughts. "You weren't even going to tell me you were leaving? Why? Why are you so anxious to get away from me?"

Whitney opened her mouth to speak, but stopped herself. She couldn't tell Javar that just being around him, being in his home, was unnerving. She didn't want to give him any reason to hope, to read anything into her flustered feelings. "I... just...this makes no sense. We're getting a divorce."

"You may be willing to risk your health to get away from me, but I won't let you." He paused, holding her gaze, making sure she knew he was serious. "For my own peace of mind, I want to make sure you're one hundred percent better—no matter how things end between us."

The fact that he sounded so sincere made Whitney feel somewhat guilty. But why should she feel guilty? She was doing the right thing.

The sound of tires on concrete caused them both to look toward the driveway. A Ford Probe was making its way up the curved path. Moments later, the car pulled up behind Cherise's Toyota and parked. An attractive, fairskinned woman whose hair was a rich amber color, hopped out of the car and hurried toward them. The pale blue outfit she wore made it clear she was the nurse.

"Are you Mr. Jordan?" she asked when she reached them.

"Yes," Javar replied. "You must be—"

"Elizabeth Monroe," she supplied. "Your nurse."

"Nice to meet you," Javar said shaking her hand.

"I'm sorry I'm late," she continued. "When I got the call from the agency…"

"It's okay," Javar said.

Elizabeth Monroe seemed to only now realize that Whitney was standing there. Turning to her, the woman smiled. "Oh, hello."

The wrinkles around her eyes when she smiled were the only indication that she was in her mid-to-late forties. Whitney returned the woman's smile. "Hello."

"This is my wife," Javar explained, moving to Whitney and resting a hand on her shoulder. "She recently came home from the hospital. In fact," he turned to Whitney, looking down at her, "we should all go upstairs so Ms. Monroe can examine you."

"Please call me Elizabeth."

Whitney glanced at the blue car where Cherise sat, waiting. Then she turned back to Javar. "In a moment."

Quickly, she walked to the driver's side of Cherise's car. Cherise saw her and immediately opened the door, stretching her legs out onto the concrete. She seemed confused and perhaps a little annoyed as she asked, "What's going on?"

"I—I'm staying. Sorry."

Cherise's lips twisted. "Okay."

"That's the nurse," Whitney explained. "Javar hired her for me."

"Give the man a medal." She sighed. "They're waiting for you. I'm gonna go."

"No," Whitney said. When Cherise flashed her a perplexed look, she added, "Why don't you stay—visit with me."

She shrugged. "Sure."

Whitney waited until Cherise exited the car before starting back toward the house. If Javar wouldn't let her leave, she'd surround herself with her family. With people who really cared about her.

In the short time Elizabeth had been here, she had set up Whitney's room with the necessities of the modern medical world. Blood pressure equipment stood to the left of the bed as well as a nurse's stand, on which lay a box of latex gloves, a stethoscope and other gadgets Whitney wasn't familiar with. There was even a special pager to summon Elizabeth, if necessary.

"Your blood pressure is high," Ms. Monroe said. She plucked the thermometer from Whitney's mouth and examined the reading. "Your temperature is normal."

"Tell her she needs to rest. She won't listen to me."

Whitney gazed at Javar, frowning. She'd tried to convince him he wasn't needed during this examination, but he had insisted on being here.

Elizabeth spoke to Whitney much the way an adult would speak to a child. "Whitney, you need to rest. Your blood pressure is high, so it's critical you also avoid stressful situations. You may feel better, but you haven't completely healed from the accident. Please, take it easy. That's the only way to ensure your complete recovery."

The nurse ended her visit by giving Whitney two small capsules. "Take these."

"What are they?"

"One's a Tylenol for pain. The other's lorazepam for stress."

Whitney did as instructed. It would do no good to argue. The nurse left immediately afterward, leaving Whitney alone with Javar. She didn't look at him.

"Whitney—"

"The nurse said I have to avoid 'stressful' situations."

"And I'm causing you stress?"

"Yes." She knew her response hurt him, she could feel it, but she wouldn't take it back. Wouldn't offer him any comfort. "I'd like to see Cherise now."

Javar didn't argue. Looking out a window, she only heard the soft sound of his feet on the carpet as he left the room.

Whitney pushed the niggling of guilt aside, or tried to, at least. Maybe she was acting like a spoiled child, but it wasn't easy for her being here. Why should it be for Javar?

Minutes later, Cherise, who had been waiting in the family room down the hall, entered the room. Her gaze was wide-eyed, like a child in a candy store who couldn't decide which of the treasures to sample first. "Wow," Cherise said, running her hand over the delicate carvings in the oak post on the canopy bed. "This room is gorgeous!"

"This isn't the first time you're seeing this house."

"It's just been so long." Cherise's eyes darted around the room, taking in everything with excitement. Whitney followed her gaze to the cream-colored lace canopy, the antique oak dresser, the Queen Anne chaise, and the extravagant entertainment center. "My God, this room is almost as big as my whole apartment."

"This is a big house," Whitney said simply.

Cherise was still exploring. She strolled to the far end of the room near the bay windows and entered the ensuite bathroom. "Holy..." she called from inside. Moments later, she reappeared. "That tub is so big, you can swim in it!"

Shrugging, Whitney changed the subject. "Where are Tamika and Jaleel?"

"With their father," Cherise replied sourly. "For a change."

Whitney knew that Paul, Cherise's ex-husband, was a sore spot with Cherise. They'd been married only four years when Cherise had discovered that her husband was sleeping with other women. Before, she had suspected as much, but hadn't had any proof. When she'd found him in bed with a neighbor, she'd taken her two small children and left him. It hadn't been easy, especially since Paul wasn't regular with his child support payments nor his visitation, but Cherise had survived.

"At least he's spending some time with them. That's positive, right?"

"How positive can it be when he sees them once in a blue moon? He's more of a stranger to Tamika and Jaleel than anything else. And Jaleel is so vulnerable. He needs his father. But Paul is too busy getting his freak on with anything that moves, the K-9."

Silence fell between them. Whitney was suddenly tired and wanted to lie down. But she didn't want to send her cousin home. At least not yet.

When Whitney looked up, Cherise was standing before the entertainment center, fingering the selection of compact discs. "Now Javar," Cherise suddenly said, "he was a good father. Loving, devoted, and wealthy. Man, if the accident never happened, you'd still have all this." She gestured to the room.

Whitney propped her foot on the bed, hugging her knee to her chest. "To tell the truth, things weren't that great in our relationship. In fact, I think that sooner or later we would have broken up, regardless of the accident."

Cherise threw her a look of disbelief. "Are you crazy? Why would you ever leave him? Men like Javar do not come along every day."

"Men like Javar love their work more than their families."

Slipping her hands into the back pockets of her form-fitting jeans, Cherise walked toward her. "He's a hardworking man. Look at all he gave you."

Cherise made it sound like it was only the material things that mattered. Sure, while Whitney had lived here she hadn't wanted for anything that money could buy. She had wanted her husband's love and affection, and that was something she hadn't been able to pay for in dollars—or she would have.

Whitney looked up at Cherise. "All this," she waved a hand around the room, "is overrated."

Cherise rolled her eyes. "Of course. It's always those who have money who say it's overrated."

"I didn't always have money. Or a big house. Or a fancy car. You know that. I grew up on the South side of Chicago, just like you. And I'd choose the South side over this posh neighborhood any day, if I could have the love I wanted."

Cherise shrugged. "I'd choose the money. 'Cause when men decide to wander—as most do—at least you'd have the money to make you feel better. When you're with some fool who can't even hold a job, when he screws around all you have is heart-ache…and hungry mouths to feed. I'd take the money any day."

That is classic Cherise, Whitney thought as she stared at her cousin, chuckling softly. But she had two young children who'd suffered because their father didn't have the decency to support them. But Whitney had lived the fairy tale. She was a student struggling to pay the bills when she'd met Javar, when he'd stolen her heart and swept her up into a dreamworld. A dreamworld that had ended with a bitter nightmare.

"Well, cuz," Whitney finally said. "I'd gladly trade places with you. I would. Because without the rest of the package, money just doesn't mean anything to me."

Whitney felt the strangest sensation, like something was surrounding her, trying to keep her down. Something evil...

Her eyes flew open. She found herself in darkness. The blinds were closed, and only a sliver of light filled the room. She didn't even remember falling asleep.

There...a sound. Shuffling. The bedroom door opened, then closed with a soft click.

She threw her gaze to the door, but saw nothing. She shivered. Someone had been in her room. She held still, paralyzed beneath the bedsheets.

Moments later, she sighed deeply. She was overreacting. It was probably just Elizabeth, or Javar who had been in her room, checking on her.

Still, as Whitney closed her eyes and tried to fall back to sleep, she couldn't shake the cold, eerie feeling that someone was watching her.

Chapter 8

Whitney stirred, opening her eyes, then bolted upright. It was morning now; bright sunlight spilled into the room from behind the blinds. But that wasn't what had awakened her. Something else had.

Voices. She heard voices. Loud, angry voices. Throwing the blanket off her body, Whitney eased herself out of the king-sized canopy bed. The robe she'd worn last night was strewn across the Queen Anne chaise, and she picked it up, slipping into it.

Tying the belt on her white silk robe, she opened the door and stepped into the hallway. The voices were coming from downstairs in the foyer, and they were growing louder. When she reached the mouth of the winding mahogany stairs, she looked down and saw Javar. He was talking with a woman.

Whitney made her way down the thickly carpeted steps. She made no sound as she descended. When she neared the bottom of the stairs, she saw clearly who Javar was talking to—Stephanie Lewis. The street-fine beauty was dressed in a black cat suit and high, thick heeled boots. Dressed to seduce, as always. Whitney paused on the steps, fighting a sudden bout of nervousness. Then, gathering courage, she continued, stepping at last onto the cool marble floor.

"Hello, Stephanie," she said softly.

Stephanie's dark brown eyes flew to Whitney, bulging as she took in the sight of her. Returning her ice-cold gaze to Javar, Stephanie said, "You sonofabitch! So it *is* true. How *dare* you let my son's murderer stay here!"

Whitney cringed. Stephanie's harsh words shouldn't have startled her, but they did. Time had done nothing to heal the woman's pain. She was still angry and bitter, and no doubt still believed that Whitney belonged in jail. Whitney could understand her pain—how could she not—but she had suffered, too, probably more than Stephanie ever would. It was she who relived the accident almost every night, she who questioned her own negligence for not buckling J.J. into his seat. It was she who would take the horrifying images of the accident to the grave with her, as well as her profound guilt.

But for now, she needed to fully heal, then get on with her life. Coming downstairs had been a mistake. "Excuse me," she murmured, pivoting on her heel to leave.

"Bitch, don't you walk away from me!"

Stephanie's crude name-calling caused Whitney's back to stiffen with angry indignation. That was uncalled for. Whipping her head around, she faced Stephanie with a sneer. "No matter what you say to me, Stephanie, your son is never coming back."

"You little...I'll kill you! I swear I'll kill you!" And with her deadly threat, an enraged Stephanie lunged at Whitney. Javar grabbed the angry woman before she could reach her intended victim. Screaming at the top of her lungs, Stephanie flailed her arms and legs, demanding that Javar let her go.

"That's enough, Stephanie," Javar said sternly. "You're making a fool of yourself."

"You should be dead!" Stephanie ranted, staring at Whitney, then succumbed to angry tears.

Whitney watched as Javar dragged Stephanie to the door, a wave of numbing pain sweeping over her. Carlos had arrived and he opened the door.

"Don't come back here again," Javar told her, then deposited her on the front step. Quickly, he closed the door, but Stephanie's crying and ranting was so loud, she could still be heard.

Javar moved to Whitney, a troubled expression etched on his face. "Are you okay?"

She trembled. She was cold, frightened, and she felt so…alone. Stephanie's anger had opened old wounds, causing her to remember all the hatred she had experienced after little J.J.'s death.

"I'm so sorry." Javar wrapped Whitney in the safety of his arms, squeezing her tightly. He was an anchor, a lifeline in a troubled sea. Unable to contain her emotions any longer, Whitney let the tears that longed to fall gush from her eyes and spill onto her cheeks.

"Don't cry," Javar said into her hair, his voice soft and gentle. "Please, don't cry."

Whitney couldn't stop the flow of tears. She let Javar hold her until she had cried all the tears she could possibly cry.

The nightmare was starting again. She'd suffered enough of Stephanie's wrath almost two years ago; she didn't want to relive that now. Nobody, not even Javar had understood the anguish she had suffered, the unbearable guilt she carried in her heart every day. But Lord help her, if she could turn back the clock, she would. She'd bring little J.J. back to life, even if it meant exchanging her life for his.

She should have let Javar come to Louisiana and get the

divorce there. She should have stayed away from Chicago. People hated her here. Hated her for something she hadn't been able to control, or prevent. After the accident she'd received numerous death threats. They had come in the form of letters and telephone calls. The letters had never been sent to her home, but to her job, the All For One community youth center in Chicago's Near West. The phone calls had been at home and at work. It had gotten so bad that she'd been afraid to even leave the house.

When, four months after the accident, Javar was still being cold toward her and the death threats hadn't stopped, the decision to leave Illinois and go live with her aunt Beverly and uncle Theo in Louisiana had been made easily.

Javar pulled Whitney close. "Stephanie...she's an angry, unhappy woman. Don't let what she says bother you."

That Stephanie was angry and unhappy was an understatement. Whitney pulled back and looked up into Javar's dark eyes. "Stephanie is a lot more evil than you give her credit for."

Javar shrugged. "She's suffering. Pain can make people do crazy things."

"Like threaten to kill someone else?"

Javar ran his hands down Whitney's arms, taking her hands in his. "She didn't mean that."

Whitney shrugged out of Javar's embrace, a wave of anger washing over her. "Why are you so sure, Javar? You heard what she said." Whitney huffed. "She's probably behind all those death threats nearly two years ago."

Javar's eyes bulged as shock sparked in their depths. "Death threats? What are you talking about? I don't remember any death threats."

The sudden memories caused a chill to pass over her, and

Whitney wrapped her arms around her body. "I…after the first accident, I received numerous death threats…after J.J.…."

"What?" Disbelief sounded in his voice.

"It's one of the reasons I left."

Troubled lines etched Javar's golden brown forehead. "Let me get this straight. You were receiving death threats while you were living here and you didn't tell me?"

Whitney didn't like the anger in his eyes. Unable to face him, she turned her back to him. Javar immediately grasped her arm and spun her around. He looked down at her with eyes that said he couldn't believe what she'd done. "Answer me, Whitney. Why wouldn't you tell me something like that?"

"Because."

"Because? That's your answer?"

Tears poured from Whitney's chestnut eyes and spilled onto her bruised cheeks. Javar's gut clenched. He wanted to comfort her, but how could he when he felt so…angry? Yes, he was angry. He was her husband, and she hadn't trusted him.

"Whitney, you owe me an explanation."

Outrage sparked in her eyes. "Think about it, Javar. Why wouldn't I tell you something like that? Because you were barely saying two words to me then, that's why. I had already burdened you enough. I didn't want to add to the stress in your life."

That hurt. Knocked the wind out of him. And the worst part was, Javar knew Whitney hadn't said that to make him feel like a lousy husband. She'd said that because it had been the truth. Angry with her for the death of his son, he had closed himself off emotionally. Like a fool, he had left her to suffer all her pain and guilt alone. He still felt angry, but now only with himself.

An apology would never make up for all the agony he had caused her. He could only hope it was a start. "Whitney—"

"Save it," she retorted, angrily brushing away her tears. "Nothing you say can change the past."

She spun around, ready to climb the stairs. She halted, turning back to face him. "Why are you doing this to me?" Her eyes implored him to end her suffering. "Please, Javar, just give me a divorce. Please, just let me get on with my life."

Please, just let me get on with my life. The words haunted Javar as he thought about them for the millionth time as he sat hunched over the drafting table in his home office. He should be concentrating on his work, on the Li bid, but he couldn't.

Let her get on with her life… Lord help him, he couldn't. Not yet. Not until they'd had a chance to work through their differences, resolve them.

Javar stood, stretched. Placing his hands on his hips, he walked to the large bay window and looked outside. The sudden movements of a robin frightened him, flying from the flowerpot on the window's edge. He watched the bird as it flew over the flower gardens, past the tennis and basketball courts to the left, finally stopping when it reached the pine trees that bordered the north side of his property. The landscape was beautiful—the gardener had seen to that. When Whitney was here years earlier, she had done a lot of the gardening herself, except the property was too vast to do it all.

He slowly let out a deep breath. He had all this property, yet he hardly used it. *When was the last time I used the pool,* he wondered, *or even took a walk in the backyard?* He'd done those things when Whitney was here, when J.J. was still alive.

His eyes settled on the basketball court. His mind wandered as he stared. Like it was yesterday, he remembered J.J. out on the basketball court, dribbling a ball as best he could. The image was so clear he imagined J.J. was actually out there, wearing his Chicago Bulls jersey. J.J. had loved the fact that his favorite player on the team shared his last name. When he told others that fact, his little eyes had widened with pride.

Javar shook his head, tossing the image aside. J.J. wasn't out there now; he never would be again. Javar's chest tightened painfully the way it always did when he thought of his son. Gone too soon.... He'd never have the chance to be a real father to J.J., the kind of father he had failed to be.

But he could be a real husband. If Whitney let him.

Javar strolled back to the drafting table. Looking down at the sketches, he shook his head. How could he come up with something appropriate for the Li proposal in less than two weeks? If he had the time to concentrate only on that, maybe, but he had Whitney to consider now. Whitney, who had always told him to take on a partner at his firm. If he did win the Li bid, he would be extremely busy with designs, budgeting, traveling to Arizona—even more busy than he presently was. As his firm's only principal, everything ultimately rested on his shoulders— meeting with clients, hiring interior designers. How could he prove to Whitney that their marriage mattered most if he continued to burn the candle at both ends? Maybe he should just forget the Li bid.

Oh, but he wanted to win so badly.... He frowned. Maybe later, when he had more time to weigh the pros and cons, he would make a final decision about what he should do.

Right now, all he could think about was Whitney, and his startling revelation. She had received death threats after J.J. had died. Someone who held her responsible for his son's death.

Could it have been Stephanie? Cunning, faceless threats didn't seem to be her style. Then who? He scrunched his forehead as he thought, realizing there were probably several of his and Stephanie's family members who might have resorted to something that immature.

But there was one person whom he could easily exclude from that list, he realized, a smile touching his lips. The one person in his family who had accepted Whitney with open arms.

An idea hitting him, Javar grabbed his car keys and headed out of the house. There was something he needed to do.

Whitney didn't realize she'd dozed off until the knocking on the bedroom door awoke her. She sat up, feeling somewhat groggy, and called, "Who is it?"

"Feel up for some company?" Javar asked.

Maybe it was the hurt look in his eyes this morning when she'd asked him to let her get on with her life, or maybe it was the nagging feeling that she was being unfair. But Whitney found she wanted to see Javar, to work out some sort of truce.

As she unlocked the door and turned the knob, she said, "Javar—", then halted when she saw he was not alone. The next instant, her eyes grew wide and excitement caused her heart to beat rapidly. She stood only mere seconds before stepping forward and throwing her arms around her surprise visitor. "Grandma Beryl!"

"Whitney!" Grandma Beryl held her in a tight embrace.

Javar said, "I'll be in my office."

Looking over Grandma Beryl's shoulder at Javar, Whitney slipped out of the older woman's arms. "Javar...thanks."

"No problem." His lips curled slightly in a grin. Then he was gone.

Whitney turned to Grandma Beryl, her grandmother-in-law.

Dressed in a bright floral cotton dress that flowed around her ankles, Grandma Beryl was slim and gorgeous. She had a sense of style that many women lost as they grew older. Once a week Grandma Beryl made a trip to the hair salon, treating herself to a hot oil treatment and sometimes a touch-up of the raven color she dyed her hair. As a result, her shoulder-length tresses were thick and vibrant. Without a gray hair on her head, and with her smooth, almost wrinkle free milk chocolate complexion, Grandma Beryl didn't look a day over sixty-five.

Whitney took Grandma Beryl's hands in hers. "I am so glad to see you, Grandma Beryl."

"Oh, Whitney. It has been much too long."

"I know." Whitney turned, leading Grandma Beryl to the cream-colored leather sofa. Grandma Beryl favored her left leg, due to troubles with arthritis. They both sat.

"What were you thinking, scaring us to death like that? Nearly getting yourself killed…" Grandma Berry snorted. "And nobody even told me about it until you'd come home."

"Javar probably didn't want to worry you."

"I should have been there for you," Grandma Beryl said, emphasizing each word. "Hospitals are about as uplifting as the thought of being in a coffin. That must be why they didn't tell me. They must have thought the sight of you in that hospital bed would send me to my grave."

Whitney squeezed Grandma Beryl's hand. "Grandma Beryl, you're too strong to die."

Grandma Beryl chuckled. "And too bad. You know what they say. Only the good die young."

Whitney smiled fondly as she looked at the mischievous gleam in Javar's grandmother's eye. She loved her so much. Despite the fact that blood didn't tie them, she and Grandma Beryl were as close as any blood relatives, even more so. "I see you haven't changed," Whitney said good-naturedly. "Still refusing to move into this house?"

"I do not need my grandson to take care of me. I am still absolutely able to take care of myself."

"We all know that. But this place is so big. There are so many rooms...."

"It's not downtown."

For as long as Whitney had known Grandma Beryl, she had lived in a gorgeous condominium close to the Magnificent Mile. She preferred her privacy more than anything else, as she was a widow who liked to date.

It was then that Whitney noticed the huge ruby ring on Grandma Beryl's left hand. Whitney lifted her thin hand, examining the ring closely. The large ruby was oval-shaped, surrounded by a thin layer of diamonds. "Grandma Beryl, this is some ring! Planning on settling down soon?"

Grandma Beryl flashed Whitney a wry grin. "I am having too much fun to settle down, dear."

Whitney didn't doubt that. But she knew that after Vincent, Beryl's husband, had died of a heart attack at the age of sixty-five—right after he had retired—Beryl was devastated. She had gone on, but she'd closed off her heart to the possibility of deep romantic love. Having married at seventeen, Vincent had been the true love of her life.

Grandma Beryl shifted on the couch, crossing one leg over the other as she faced Whitney. She pinned her with a level stare. "You, on the other hand, do not look like you've been having any fun."

"I...well, I'm recuperating."

The stare grew more intense. "Recuperating has nothing to

do with what I'm talking about. Life is hardly fun when you're not sharing your life with the man you love. When you've asked him for a divorce."

At Whitney's shocked expression, her grandmother added, "Yes, he told me. After I gave him the third degree. Told him that there's no reason for you to be apart."

"Grandma Beryl..."

"Don't Grandma Beryl me. I've been in love, you know. Was married forty-five years. And I can still remember what it's like to look at someone with love in your eyes. That's the way you looked at Javar five years ago. You still look at him that way now."

Whitney hadn't even had an opportunity to look at Javar during the brief time he'd been in the room. She told his grandmother that.

"I saw your reaction. It was immediate. And it was undeniable."

"What you saw was surprise," Whitney replied quickly. "Then gratitude. I was happy to see you."

"Mmm hmm." But Grandma Beryl was eyeing her skeptically.

What else could Whitney say? Grandma Beryl wouldn't understand. She was a romantic, and when she believed two people belonged together, her opinion couldn't be swayed. "When I'm all better, Javar and I will be getting a divorce."

Grandma Beryl pursed her lips, her expression saying she didn't believe a word Whitney said.

They sat together and talked for a long while, remembering old times, until the nurse came to examine Whitney. When Whitney had left Chicago almost two years ago, she'd tried to forget everything about her time with Javar. She'd called

Grandma Beryl on occasion, but in her quest to shut out the bad in her life, she had ultimately shut out the good. Grandma Beryl was part of the good. From now on, they would stay in touch.

She was only divorcing Javar, after all.

Stephanie Lewis pushed the dining room chair back with such force it fell over and clattered against the hardwood floor. Food was the last thing on her mind.

Kevin, her older brother by a year, stood and placed a hand on her shoulder. "Steph, you've got to calm down."

"How would you feel if your dead son's father had the nerve to let your son's murderer live in his house?"

"Javar's a fool."

Stephanie grunted. She and her older brother hadn't always been close, but they'd formed a bond after J.J.'s death. They both hated Whitney and wanted her to pay for her crime. "Why didn't she just die in that car accident? I swear, that woman has nine lives."

Kevin turned Stephanie to face him, planting both hands on her shoulders. "Think of the bright side. At least we know where she is, right?"

"Right."

"And you know what they say. Don't get mad; get even."

Stephanie was silent for a moment. Then she frowned. "That place is like Fort Knox. I can't even get in there to spit in her face."

Kevin's eyebrows rose and he cocked his head to the side. "Don't be so sure, Stephanie. Where there's a will, there's a way."

Chapter 9

"Hello?" Whitney held the receiver to her ear, waiting for a response. She only heard the sound of soft breathing. "Hello?"

Click. In the silence of the room, the dial tone filled her eardrum.

Irritated, she glanced at the clock radio. Three-eleven a.m. Who on earth would be calling her at this hour? Only a select few knew any of Javar's three home numbers, and even less knew which line she was using.

She turned on the lamp and looked at the caller I.D. Private name, unknown number.

It was only a crank call. Or more likely, a wrong number. Nothing to worry about she decided as she lay back on the pillows and pulled the comforter around her neck. She closed her eyes, but sleep wouldn't come. Her nerves felt like they were trying to pop out of her skin.

Although Whitney hated relying on any type of drug, even aspirin, maybe taking a stress pill now wasn't such a bad idea. Maybe that would help her sleep. Not that it had done much good yet. She seemed to waver from groggy to wired, but never truly stress-free. At least her headache had lessened.

She sat up and hugged her knees to her chest. No amount of pills would help her get over the past. Only one thing now could possibly help her mental healing. And she couldn't avoid it any longer.

Whitney slipped out of the warm bed, her feet sinking into the plush carpet as they touched the ground. The house was silent, and she made no sound on the carpet, yet she tiptoed, not wanting to wake anyone.

Slowly Whitney opened the door to her bedroom, being careful not to make any sound. She paused only a moment before turning left and heading down the wide hallway.

Seconds seemed like hours, but Whitney was finally there. She stopped in front of the door, not sure if she had the strength to go on. Only once since the accident had she been in J.J.'s room, and then she had broken down and cried uncontrollably, overwhelmed by the guilt. How could she go in there now and face all the memories that she had tried to forget? But how could she not? The past would always haunt her if she didn't try to come to terms with it.

Her stomach fluttered with anxiety. It had been so long…

Slowly, Whitney reached out and grasped the brass door handle. She felt the onset of tears, but fought them. She had to do this. She had to go on….

The first thing she noticed when she stepped inside the room was that everything was the same. J.J.'s posters, his stuffed animals, his model train set by the window. Whitney couldn't suppress a gasp. Her little J.J. Her darling, precious son.

Dead. Because of her.

No! her mind screamed. It was an accident. J.J.'s mother Stephanie and even members of Javar's family hated her because they thought she was guilty of a crime. The only crime she'd been guilty of was loving J.J. like her own son. Yet Stephanie and her family, her mother and father-in-law, her sister-in-law, they all thought she should be in jail for killing J.J. Why didn't they realize that living with the memories of the accident, living with her own pain and guilt was worse than any jail could ever be? Although J.J.'s death was a senseless accident, she would always blame herself.

And so would Javar, Whitney thought, her stomach clenching as a sharp pain shot through her. How could he even think he wanted a reconciliation? Despite what he said now, he couldn't. Not after the way he had looked at her with such anger, such disgust, when J.J. had died. Not after he had insinuated that she had not taken the best care of J.J. simply because he hadn't been her flesh-and-blood son. The look of betrayal in Javar's cold eyes would always stay with Whitney, haunting her almost as much as the sight of J.J.'s immobile body on the side of the road.

Haunting her almost as much as her own privately suffered, profound guilt.

Wrapping her arms around her body, Whitney tried to fight off the chill that came with the memories. But it was a chill that started in her heart and worked its way outward, and she doubted she'd ever get over it. But she had to try.

Slowly, placing one foot in front of the other, Whitney moved into the room, toward J.J.'s car-shaped bed. The blinds were open, and the soft glow of the moonlight as well as the exterior houselights illuminated the room well enough that she didn't need to switch on a lamp. She lowered herself onto the bed, lifting J.J.'s favorite stuffed animal, his teddy bear Martin, into her arms. The animal he believed would protect him in the dark of the night.

If only he'd had Martin with him that day… Whitney sighed wistfully, knowing that no stuffed animal could have saved

Javar Junior. If only it hadn't been raining. If only she'd been able to control the car before it flipped over.

If onlys weren't going to bring J.J. back. Nothing was.

She didn't know she was crying until the salty taste of tears met her tongue. Holding Martin to her body tightly, she cried and cried until there were no more tears. Then she said a prayer, asking for the strength to go on with her life. But most of all, she prayed for the strength to forgive herself for being the one who had survived.

She shook her head, dismissing that thought. No, she didn't wish she were dead. In fact, she suddenly realized, what she probably felt most guilty for was being glad that she had survived. How could she so selfishly be happy for life when a five-year-old boy was dead? Yes, she decided, her stomach twisting with a newer, sicker, more poignant feeling of guilt. She was glad that she had survived. She was glad she wasn't cheated of her life the way J.J. had been. But God help her, if she had to live through that accident again, she would gladly exchange her life for J.J.'s. J.J. hadn't been driving the car. J.J. wasn't responsible for making sure he was buckled in.

The onus was on her. Only her.

As Whitney sat there on J.J.'s bed, with Martin in her arms, her eyelids grew heavy. The pain of the memories was more than emotional, it was physical, causing her head to pound and her chest to ache. Her body's need to heal, its need for peace, finally won out and lured her into a restless sleep. She dreamed....

One hand on the steering wheel, she looked down at the boy beside her and smiled. He smiled back, his small dimples winking at her, and her heart expanded in her chest. How she loved him! He was so handsome, just like his father, except his young face was rounder. She loved him so much, as if he was her own flesh and blood. Since her marriage to his father, he'd been asking for a brother or a sister. Maybe they would give him one soon.

"How about some ice cream?" she asked. The sky was a clear blue and the day was perfect for such a treat.

"Yeah." He nodded enthusiastically. The next moment, he directed his gaze to the shore of Lake Michigan, pulling his T-shirt up over his chin.

She ran a hand over his hair, then looked out at the road before her. Suddenly, the sky turned black. Pitch-black. She couldn't see a thing in front of her. And then there was rain. Everywhere.

A scream.

Whitney's blood pumped wildly in her veins as she looked to the right. J.J. was gone.

She glanced at the road, saw a small body. Slammed on the brakes…

The scream tore into his consciousness, forcing him awake. *Whitney!*

Javar threw off the covers and bolted out of bed. Through the door. Down the hall.

He burst through the door of Whitney's bedroom and in the darkness ran to her bed. It took him only a moment to realize that she wasn't there.

Where was she?

Again, she screamed, her voice a shrill and desperate sound, and Javar knew. Charging out of the room, he ran down the hall to J.J.'s room, the only other place Whitney could be. As he threw open the door to J.J.'s bedroom, panicked sobs filled the air. Immediately, Javar was at her side, drawing her into his arms.

"No!" she screamed, sounding hysterical. She squirmed, trying to free herself from his strong embrace. "I'm sorry. So sorry. Oh please, you have to believe me!"

"Whitney." He held her tightly, and when she didn't calm down, Javar framed her face with his hands. Despite his direct contact and the fact that he was staring into her eyes, she continued to fight to be free. "Whitney," he repeated, forcefully.

In the soft moonlight, he saw her face contort with grief, then confusion, and finally understanding. He had gotten through to her, drawn her back from the depths of pain. The sobs stopped but she froze, almost as if she didn't know what was happening.

Javar reached for the bedside lamp and turned it on. When he looked down at Whitney, she sat silently staring at him, seemingly dazed.

"W-what happened?" She asked.

"I was hoping you could tell me." Javar slipped an arm around her and rested his chin on her head. His body reacted to the intimacy, coming alive with heat. It had been so long since he had been beside Whitney like this, in a bed, even if it was his son's. He forced the wayward thought from his mind. "You were screaming."

"I...what am I doing here?"

Javar flashed her a puzzled look. "You...don't know?"

Glancing around, she seemed even more confused. She opened her mouth to speak, but then stopped.

"Whitney, you're in J.J.'s room."

After a long moment, she nodded. "I was...I was thinking... about him."

"What's going on?"

Both Javar and Whitney turned at the sound of Elizabeth's voice. She stood in the doorway, wrapped in a pink terry-cloth robe. Moving away from Whitney and sliding to the edge of the bed, Javar said, "Everything's okay."

Elizabeth averted her eyes, as though embarrassed that she had intruded on something. "I—I heard the scream...."

Whitney merely stared at the nurse, clearly not sure what to say.

"What are you doing out of bed?"

"She doesn't seem to know how she got here," Javar explained.

"Do you have a history of sleepwalking?" Elizabeth asked as she strode toward Whitney with determined steps.

Shaking her head, Whitney replied, "No."

"Hmm." Elizabeth's brow wrinkled. Taking Whitney's wrist in her hand, she checked her pulse. "Your pulse is rather high. Did you take your pills earlier?"

Whitney stared up at the nurse, thinking that she reminded her of a drill sergeant. She suddenly felt like a young child who'd fed her broccoli to the dog under the table. "I...I didn't swallow them."

Elizabeth sighed. "Whitney, you must take those pills as prescribed. They'll help you relax, help you sleep, help you heal. Clearly, you're suffering from anxiety, so much so that you got up in the middle of the night and came into this room." She placed a hand on Whitney's back. "Come on. Let's go back to your room."

Javar was on his feet in an instant, wrapping an arm around Whitney's waist. The smell of her delicate floral shampoo flirted with his senses. Being close to her like this, even though she was healing, he wanted to run his fingers through the silky strands of her raven hair, lose himself in the smell and feel of her.

"Help her into the bed," the nurse instructed, pulling Javar from his fantasy. He did as the nurse said, leading Whitney to the bed and helping her under the covers. Elizabeth appeared with two pills in a cup and handed them to Whitney along with some water. "Here. Take these."

Whitney took the two small capsules from Elizabeth and popped them into her mouth, then downed them with a swig of water. There was no point arguing. Tonight's episode had left her frazzled, and she'd give anything for a decent night's sleep. She handed the glass back to the nurse and said, "Thanks."

"That should help you get through the rest of the night." Elizabeth looked at her with a stern expression, then sighed. "I'll check on you later."

After the nurse disappeared, Javar turned to face Whitney. She saw concern in his dark brown eyes as he took her hands in his. "Whitney, you've got to take your medicine. You know that."

"I...you know I don't like taking pills."

"This isn't about liking or not liking prescribed drugs. You need them now, whether you like it or not."

Whitney shrugged, then pulled her hands from Javar's. She shifted away from him on the bed. It wasn't what he said or the firm way in which he said it that bothered her. It was being so close to him like this. His musky smell, his sexiness, unnerved her. Made her remember the dreams and hopes she'd had as a young bride. "I...I was feeling better."

Javar frowned. "Whitney, you were almost killed in a car accident. And the only reason Dr. Adu-Bohene let you come home with me was because he trusted me to help you get well. That's why I hired Elizabeth, to help you get well. Whitney, you cannot skip your medication at this stage in your recovery."

"I know."

Javar looked down at Whitney, saw the sadness in her eyes. He was acting like a parent, not a husband. She needed his comfort, not a lecture.

He reached out and stroked her arm. "Do you remember your dream?"

Whitney shook her head. She did remember that she was dreaming about J.J., but she didn't want to tell Javar that. She wanted him to leave and let her rest. "I'm okay, Javar. You can go back to bed."

"Not until I know you're okay." He trailed his hand up her arm, over her shoulder, to her jaw.

The action was foreign yet painfully familiar. Javar was wearing only cotton pajama bottoms, exposing his brawny, sexy chest. He had only a sprinkling of dark, curly hair on his golden-brown chest that thickened at his belly button and went lower. It was a beautiful chest, a chest on which she could vividly remember raining kisses. A chest that had held her in a lover's embrace on numerous occasions.

She wanted to reach out and touch it now, felt the urge like a moth drawn to a flame. Dressed only in a silk nightie, things could easily escalate. All Javar would have to do was reach out and slip the material off her shoulders, over her breasts....

The unexpected image caused Whitney to shudder. It also caused her to come to her senses. What she needed was for Javar to leave. Now.

"Javar, thanks for checking on me. I'm okay now."

"I found you in J.J.'s room, Whitney. And you have no idea how you got there."

His eyes held hers, told her he didn't believe her, wouldn't leave her until he knew that she was okay. "I," she began, then paused. "Look, I was thinking about J.J., and I just wanted to be close to him."

"Do you always have nightmares...about the accident?"

"Sometimes," Whitney admitted, her voice only a whisper. "But it's getting better. The dreams come less now."

"Is there anything I can do?" Javar asked, wishing there was, knowing there wasn't.

"No." Lying back on the pillows, Whitney half sighed, half yawned.

He wanted to say something else, but thought better of it. Now was not the time. Not only was she tired, there was the chance she might not believe his words were sincere. Folding his arms over his chest, he watched his wife a moment longer.

"I'll be fine," she assured him.

Taking that as his cue to leave, Javar rose from the bed. He shouldn't be leaving her bed. She shouldn't be in a guest room. They were husband and wife and she belonged with him in his bedroom, in the bed they had shared as a married couple.

"Good night, Javar."

Javar sat back down, planting both hands on either side of her body. He began to lean forward. Whitney sucked in a sharp breath, unsure what he was doing. Unsure she would be able to resist him if he advanced toward her.

To her surprise, he planted a soft, lingering kiss on her forehead. His warm lips on her cool skin caused a jolt of electricity to heat her blood. Goodness, he was still so sexy.

"Good night, Whitney," he whispered, his warm breath fanning her forehead. "I'll see you in the morning." Then he stood and sauntered to the door, his strong muscles moving beneath his sleek, golden brown back.

When he was gone, Whitney released her breath. Then, trying

to put Javar out of her mind, she reached for the bedside lamp and turned it off.

Her brain said she was happy Javar was gone. Her heart said she was a liar.

Despite the fact that he'd worked a sixteen-hour day and had to be up early for another hectic day of investigative work, Derrick Lawson couldn't sleep. Whitney was on his mind. Had been for most of the day.

He was worried about her. How could he not be? She was staying with Javar, a man who had turned stone cold when she'd needed him the most. Javar might be a well-respected businessman in the community, but Derrick didn't trust him as far as he could throw him.

Javar would hurt her again, Derrick was sure.

Grumbling because there were only three hours left to sleep before his alarm went off, Derrick rolled out of his queen-sized bed since he couldn't sleep. It didn't matter that it was summer, the hardwood floor was cold on his bare feet. Slipping into the slippers his mother had given him for his last birthday, Derrick walked the short distance to the light switch and flicked it on.

Turning, he saw the framed five-by-seven picture of Whitney on his dresser. It was taken years ago, when she'd been a freshman at Northwestern University. That was a simpler time, before she had met Javar and fallen head-over-heels in love with him.

Derrick chuckled mirthlessly. He'd always hoped that Whitney would fall in love with *him,* but one look in her eyes after she'd met Javar and Derrick had known that he didn't stand a chance. Whitney's eyes had never lit up with that special spark when she'd looked at him. However, with Javar, that spark was there like a constant flame. She had loved him, and he'd hurt her. Abandoned her.

But a trip down memory lane reminiscing about the one girl he'd always loved was not why Derrick had gotten out of his bed this early in the morning. It was the unsettling feeling in his gut. The one that had him thinking constantly about Whitney's accident. Wondering…

Had it really been an accident? Or had someone deliberately run her off the road—tried to kill her? *Kill.* The word was so strong, yet he was very familiar with death—with murder. With the passions that could lead to deplorable crimes.

And that was exactly what was bothering him, as he began to give consideration to a theory he prayed was wrong. If Whitney's accident wasn't really an accident—if it had been a deliberate attempt to harm her—then Derrick could think of only one person who would go to such lengths. One person who had the motive to want to hurt her, and who now had the means.

Derrick prayed he was wrong. For if he was right, that meant that Whitney was in danger at Javar's house. Because Javar held her responsible for his son's death. And he may just want to see her dead in return.

Chapter 10

As she did every morning since the accident, Eleanor Scherer sat at her small breakfast table with the morning newspaper before her. Her glasses perched on the bridge of her nose, she searched for any report of the accident she had witnessed. The morning after the car crash, she'd found a story that stated there had been a serious accident on North Lake Shore Drive late the previous evening, and that a young woman had been taken to the hospital with critical injuries. Then, Eleanor had felt terrible. She didn't know her, but that poor woman didn't deserve to be run off the road the way she had been. Eleanor had wanted to call the police and tell them what she knew, but something had stopped her.

She was afraid.

A chill swept over her as she remembered the fear she'd experienced that night. After the driver had run the woman off the road, he had slowed down. Now, she knew he'd been waiting for her to catch up to him. She had, and she'd been brave enough to look over at the car, attempting to see its driver. Fool she was, she had forgotten the one rule of the streets: Mind your business and nobody else's.

The car's windows had been tinted, and in the dark, Eleanor hadn't been able to see the driver. But she was sure he had seen her. She'd just been so shocked at what he had done that she'd stared, and she knew he had seen her. Every detail of her aging face. And no doubt, her license plate too.

Eleanor rose and made her way to the cupboard where she kept her pills. She would only take one. If Harry was still alive, he could help her make the right decision, but she was alone, and she was so very confused.

She could almost feel the effects of the Prozac immediately after she swallowed the pill that she knew would calm her nerves.

One more day, she decided. She'd wait one more day. If there wasn't a follow-up report stating that that poor woman had died, then she would forget about it. There was no need to go to the police if the woman was alive and well. No need at all.

"Carlos," Javar called as he walked quickly into the kitchen. When he didn't immediately see his butler, he called him again.

The door to the walk-in pantry opened and Carlos appeared, a bag of flour in his hands. His eyebrows rose as concern flashed on his face. "Yes, Mr. Jordan?"

"Carlos, are you aware that the alarm system was turned off? It appears to have been off the entire night."

Shrugging, Carlos said, "No, sir. When I retired to bed, the alarm system was activated."

"Well, how is it that I found the alarm deactivated this morning?"

Carlos ventured toward the kitchen's island, depositing the bag of flour on the granite counter. "Miss Templeton came early. Perhaps she forgot to reactivate it after she arrived."

Miss Templeton was Javar's housekeeper, who came in three times a week. Biting his inner cheek, Javar silently acknowledged that she could have forgotten to reactivate the alarm. It wouldn't be the first time either of them had forgotten to do so, so why did he feel uneasy about it this morning? His sixth sense was telling him something, but what?

"I suppose you're right," Javar finally conceded. When he'd discovered that the alarm had been deactivated, he'd done a check of all the rooms in the house, looking for anything of value that might be missing. Nothing of obvious value, like his art collection, had been taken. "I'm guilty of forgetting to activate the alarm myself sometimes, but while Whitney is recovering, I'd feel a lot better if the alarm were always on. Can you please check it consistently, Carlos?"

"Of course, sir. I'll speak with Miss Templeton as well, if you'd like."

"Please," Javar replied.

Carlos nodded. "Certainly." He paused. "What would you like for breakfast?"

"Actually, Carlos, I'm not very hungry. I'll just grab a cup of coffee."

As Javar was walking toward the coffeemaker, he noticed a black, silk scarf on the seat of one of the breakfast chairs. Forgetting the coffee, he walked to the chair and retrieved the scarf. With the initials A.J. embroidered in shiny red thread, the scarf was unmistakably his mother's.

Javar turned to Carlos. "Carlos, was my mother here?"

Pounding his open palm lightly on his forehead, Carlos said, "Yes, Mr. Jordan. I forgot to tell you. She dropped by while you were out yesterday, she and your sister, Michelle. She said she would call you later. She didn't?"

Javar fingered the delicate silk, wondering. His mother and his sister. "No. She didn't call me last night. Did she say why they dropped by?"

"I believe they wanted to visit your wife, but she was sleeping. And since you weren't here, they left."

Innocent enough, Javar thought, knowing that with his mother and Michelle nothing was really innocent. Michelle had taken after their mother, knowing just how to control a situation to get what she wanted. Neither his mother nor Michelle had approved of Whitney as his wife, although Michelle had at first tried to give her a chance. Having discovered that Whitney's personality was so different from her own, Michelle later decided she didn't like her.

Sighing, Javar wondered how siblings, or even a parent and child, could be so completely different.

One restless night and Whitney felt like lead flowed through her veins. Her limbs were so heavy she could barely lift her body, and her head ached. Even worse, her stomach felt like it contained some vile concoction that needed to be regurgitated.

"You don't look well," Elizabeth was saying as she checked Whitney's pulse. "How do you feel?"

"Awful," Whitney moaned. "I feel nauseous."

"Taking your pills on an empty stomach can cause nausea. You should have some breakfast."

"Yes, that sounds great." Even bread and water sounded wonderful right about now.

"Open." Elizabeth stuck a high-tech digital thermometer in Whitney's mouth. "You look like you could use some more rest. Would you like me to have Carlos bring you some breakfast?"

Whitney shook her head. She'd spent too much time in this room as it was. Surely it would be more beneficial to her recovery if she went outside, enjoyed the fresh air and nature.

The thermometer beeped, signaling that the temperature had

been computed. The nurse pulled it from beneath Whitney's tongue and checked the digital display. "Hmmm. Your temperature is a little higher than yesterday. You have a low-grade fever, indicating your body is fighting an infection. I'm just going to check your wound."

The nurse lifted the gauze that covered the gash on Whitney's forehead. "Oooh," she said, pursing her lips. "Well, now I know what's causing your fever. This cut is infected." She turned, moved to the nurse's stand, searching its contents. Moments later she produced a bottle of medication. "Are you allergic to penicillin?"

"No."

"Good." She opened the bottle and dropped a pill into her hand. "Take this."

Whitney groaned. "More drugs."

"I know this isn't fun, but soon enough you'll be completely healthy again."

"That day can't come too soon."

"I'm sure." Elizabeth cleaned Whitney's wound and rebandaged it, then handed Whitney a glass of water to drink with the pill. "Here you go."

Whitney mumbled her thanks, then swallowed the antibiotic. The day when she was healthy again wouldn't come too soon, indeed.

"Something smells *wonderful*," Whitney almost sang as she walked into the kitchen. Bright sunlight spilled into the room, filling it with warmth. Already, Whitney felt revived.

Hearing her voice, Carlos looked up from the tray of biscuits he had just removed from the oven. The corners of his dark eyes crinkled as he smiled tenderly at her.

"Good morning, Mrs. Jordan."

Walking toward him, Whitney said, "Carlos, please call me Whitney. You know I prefer that."

"I'm sorry, Mrs—Whitney. The biscuits are fresh. Would you like some?"

"Please. Three." Whitney strolled to the fridge and opened it. After scanning its contents, she found the carton of eggs and took it out. She placed it on the gray granite counter, then opened a cupboard and took out a frying pan.

"Mrs. Jordan, what are you doing?"

Whitney couldn't hide her amusement at Carlos's shocked tone. She knew Javar paid him well, but she found it unnecessary to have him prepare something as simple as scrambled eggs for her when she was perfectly capable of doing that for herself.

Whitney turned to Carlos. "I'm making scrambled eggs."

"Oh no, Mrs. Jordan."

"Whitney."

"Whitney," Carlos repeated. "Please, sit down and relax. You are still sick."

"I'm fine," Whitney told him. At his concerned look, she reached out and squeezed his hand. "Honestly, Carlos. I'm quite capable of preparing eggs for myself. I appreciate your concern, though."

Whitney turned and walked to the ceramic-top stove, bringing the frying pan with her. She sensed Carlos's eyes on her, but she didn't turn around. He took his job seriously—too seriously sometimes. But she knew he only meant well.

Opening the cupboard above the stove, Whitney looked for some cooking oil. She found none. "Carlos," she began, "where's the oil?"

"You should be resting, Mrs. Jordan." When Whitney turned

and flashed him a look that said she was not an invalid, he said, "In the pantry. But please, let me get it for you."

Carlos scampered off, and Whitney concentrated on the stove, turning on the element. She'd never get used to these new flat-surfaced stoves that lacked the coils. Sure, they were easy to clean, but without the old-fashioned elements she always feared she'd place her hand right on top of the darn thing and burn herself!

Her breath snagged then, and she froze for a moment. Once while helping her in the kitchen, J.J. had reached for the top of the stove, almost placing his hand atop the invisible element. She'd grabbed it just in time, saving him from burning himself horribly.

J.J. Would it ever get any easier?

A hand was on her back, helping her. "Mrs. Jordan, please. Let me prepare the eggs."

Inhaling a deep breath, Whitney waved him off. "I'm okay." She took the bottle of canola oil from him. "Thanks."

Whitney set about making her breakfast. The eggs sizzled as she cracked them and dropped them into the skillet. Originally, she had set out to make scrambled eggs, but now she opted for fried instead. It was faster, and right now, she needed to get something in her stomach as quickly as possible. Without any food in her stomach, she was queasy and light-headed.

When the eggs were done, she turned to see Carlos beside her with a plate and a glass of orange juice. She smiled at him. Bless him. He was a wonderful person who truly loved his job. On the plate were three biscuits, just as she'd requested.

Plate in one hand and the juice in the other, Whitney walked to the breakfast counter and slipped onto a stool, allowing herself a view of the spectacular rose gardens. After breakfast, she would go for a walk. Maybe even venture into the pool. She did love this house, and it saddened her that she would have to give up both Javar and this spectacular place. But as Luther Vandross had so eloquently said in one of his love ballads, "a house is not a home." Without the unconditional love Whitney had only dreamed of, this house would never be a home for her. It had never really been.

"Mind if I join you?"

At the sound of Javar's deep, sexy voice, Whitney shuddered. Why did he have to sneak up on her like that! Swallowing a piece of the buttery biscuit, Whitney turned and looked up at her estranged husband. He was wearing a simple white T-shirt with khaki shorts, but the shirt made him look so enticing you would think it was cut from the world's finest silk.

She lifted her eyes to his. "Good morning, Javar."

Easing himself down onto the stool beside her, Javar asked, "How are you feeling this morning?"

"Better…now that I've got some food in my stomach."

"No doubt." He smiled softly, and Whitney felt her stomach tighten. If things were different between her and Javar, this might be a time where she was compelled to reach out and stroke his face. He was smiling at her so lovingly now, as though they had never had the problems they'd had. But she held her hand where it was, letting the moment pass.

Javar said, "Why don't you join me on the patio?"

"Umm…" Whitney's mind scrambled for a suitable reason to turn him down. She could find none. He was only offering companionship, and she couldn't very well avoid him all the time while she was staying in his house. "Okay."

"Let me get that for you," he said, lifting her plate. Whitney took juice and followed Javar as he walked to the right, then out the patio doors. The moment they stepped outside, the heat enveloped her like a blanket of warmth. She paused, turning her face upward to enable the sun's rays to reach the entire surface of her face. Closing her eyes, she allowed herself to enjoy the moment.

"Whitney?"

Hearing the concern in Javar's voice, Whitney opened her eyes and faced him. "There's nothing like the sun to make one feel one hundred times better," she said, walking toward the wrought-iron patio table. A large cream-colored umbrella rested in the middle of the table, open and providing shade. She reached for a chair.

Javar placed his hand on hers, stopping her. Instantly, Whitney felt his warmth. She looked down at his large hand where it covered her smaller one, remembering the time she had looked forward to his touch. A time when things weren't strained between them. A time so different from now.

"Let me," Javar stated simply.

Nodding, Whitney slowly pulled her hand from beneath Javar's, telling herself that she didn't really like the way his hand had felt on hers. Her body didn't believe her, evidenced by the fact that her hand now tingled where Javar's had been. Slowly, that tingling sensation spread throughout her arm and to the rest of her body.

It was lust, she assured herself. That's all it was. It had been years since she had been touched by a man, especially one as attractive as Javar, and her body couldn't help responding to his warm touch.

"Sit," Javar said.

Whitney did, wondering why she hadn't noticed him pulling out the chair. The cool iron on her heated skin was exactly what she needed.

Javar pulled out a chair and sat next to her. "I didn't realize the rest of your body was bruised."

"Hmm?"

"Your legs," Javar explained. "I saw the bruises."

"Oh." Whitney glanced down at her white shorts, then back up at him. "I try not to think about it."

Nodding, Javar said, "Do they hurt? Your legs, I mean?" When he'd seen the purplish-blue bruising on her beautiful, slim legs, he almost gasped. Instead, he bit his inner cheek. He needed to be strong for his wife. Besides, he didn't want to make her uncomfortable by gawking at injuries she'd no doubt much rather forget.

"Everything still hurts, a little."

Javar supposed it would for a while. The emotional scars would take much longer to heal, if last night was any indication. Clearly, Whitney harbored guilt over J.J.'s death, and it was much more intense than he ever would have thought.

Whitney turned her attention to her food, and Javar watched her eat for several minutes. At least some things never changed. Whitney still had a voracious appetite, which was good. Eating was necessary to keep up her strength.

His eyes roamed the delicate features of her round face, the exotic-looking eyes, the high cheekbones, the full lips, the ever-so-slightly upturned nose. Her honey-colored complexion wasn't as pale as before, and the bruises were fading. Except for the cut on the left side of her forehead that was still bandaged, one wouldn't know that she'd been in a horrific car accident.

Emotions got caught in his throat, and he swallowed. Clearing his throat, he said, "So tell me what you've been up to in Louisiana."

Whitney finished chewing before turning her gaze to him. "The same thing I was doing here. Working at a youth center."

"Hmm." Javar's reply was curt.

When Whitney had lived in Chicago, Javar had never liked the fact that she worked at an inner-city youth center. He felt her job was dangerous, and among other concerns worried that someone might follow her home and try to attack her. Ironically, his wife's only threat of danger had come from a human invention, and later from someone close to him. He still could not believe that someone had been crazy enough to threaten her.

Whitney fiddled with the remaining eggs on her plate. "I love what I do. Especially working with the younger ones. Some of them have nobody in their lives to turn to, and they turn to me. I feel like I'm making a difference. Like I'm important to someone."

Javar doubted that Whitney's last comment was meant for him, but still his jaw flinched. She didn't have to say it. He knew. He hadn't made her feel important, even when things were good between them. Sure, the times they were together were amazing, but when it came down to it, he put his work first. And Whitney had never been able to accept his explanation that he was working hard to provide for her. On numerous occasions, she told him that she didn't care about money or a big house. She just wanted him.

He said softly, "I'm glad you're having a good time in Shreveport."

Her eyes flew to his. "That's not what I said. The last two years have hardly been a picnic, Javar. I've been trying to get on with my life, which isn't easy. But I do enjoy my work. In fact, it's what helped me get through the...the past two years."

"I didn't mean to imply—"

She paused, staring at him, as if trying to determine whether he was sincere. Finally, he saw her chest heave as she inhaled deeply. "I know."

"Tell me more."

As a smile touched her lips, cute dimples winked at him. "Some people don't like working in that kind of environment. They find it depressing. So many of the young people come from troubled families. They have brothers who've been murdered, sisters who are crack addicts. I see it as a challenge. An opportunity to help influence lives in a positive way.

"Take Terrence, for example. He's only fourteen, but most people would be willing to give up on him. He's got a fiery temper, a bad attitude, but that's all just a facade. Deep down, he's a hurt child who needs some guidance. He saw his father gunned down before his eyes, and his mother ended up turning tricks to support a drug habit. She died. Now, he lives with his grandmother. I've connected with him. When I first met him, he was cold, distant, running with a bad crowd. Now, he's not as cold, not as angry. With my help, he's discovered that his aspirations to be an artist aren't unrealistic. He's still fighting the temptation of gangs, but Javar, I swear, it makes me feel so good to see him find some self-confidence. Realize that he's a worthy human being with something to contribute to the world."

As Whitney spoke, she was animated. Her eyes were bright, alive, and she exuded such a sense of commitment as she spoke about a young man whom others would rather forget. Just seeing her talk about what she loved made Javar realize that she truly was dedicated to helping troubled youths, to making a difference. That job was as important to her as his architecture was to him. And much more noble.

"I think what you do is truly wonderful, Whitney. It's great that there are people like you out there who are willing to dedicate their lives to helping people. Sometimes we take for granted that everyone has had the same start in life, and therefore can achieve the same things."

"It's such a great feeling when I can help them learn the meaning of self-worth."

Placing her chin on her hand, Whitney sighed happily. "What about you, Javar. How's your work going?"

"Busy. Really busy. I'm trying to land a bid for a shopping complex in Arizona."

Whitney sensed a "but" in his tone. She said it for him.

"But…I've been too busy. And now with your accident…my mind's preoccupied. I've got so many other things on my plate."

Shaking her head, Whitney gazed at Javar. "Have you taken on another associate, or made one of your present ones a partner?"

"No."

"Javar. My goodness, do you want to work yourself to death? You're only one person, after all. How much do you think you can do? How creative can you be when you're burned out?"

She was right, he knew. That was why he hadn't been able to come up with something dynamic for the Li bid. He already had too much to do, too much responsibility on his shoulders. But he always met his goals. "I guess I threw myself into my work to take my mind off everything."

"That's not the way to do it."

"And running away was?"

"I didn't run away. You forced me to leave."

"I never told you to go…."

"Not in so many words. But you gave me no choice."

Javar said, "If our marriage was important to you, you would have stayed and tried to work things out."

"Really?" Whitney asked, pushing her chair back on the concrete and rising. "If our marriage was important to *me?* I was the only one trying to keep our marriage together!"

Javar rose, met her gaze with hard eyes. "Why don't you just admit that you were unhappy and looking for a way out? You said yourself that I was married to my job, not you. And then when J.J. died, you found that way out...."

Angry, Whitney slammed both palms on the table. "How dare you!"

"I needed time to grieve, Whitney. You didn't want to accept that."

"And what about me? For God's sake, Javar, I was grieving too. Why couldn't you accept that?"

Unable to deny that accusation, Javar stood, silent.

"Why don't you admit that you still blame me for the accident. An accident where *I* could have been killed!"

He hesitated only a second before saying, "No, I—"

"Puh-lease!" In that fraction of a second when he had hesitated, Whitney had her answer. God, she was incredibly stupid to have believed otherwise. To let herself hope. The only reason he had her here and was "taking care" of her was out of pity. Or maybe just to make her life miserable. She pivoted on her heel and was about to stalk off, then stopped. Slowly, she turned back to Javar. "If you wanted to make me suffer for killing your son..." Her voice broke, and she wasn't sure she could go on. Swallowing her rage, she did. "You're doing a very good job, Javar. I'm more miserable than I've ever been!"

As she turned and started to run, he hastened after her, grabbing her arm. He pinned her with a pained gaze. "Maybe you're right, Whitney. Maybe there is no point in trying to work things out when we're obviously making each other miserable." Though he said it as a statement, it came out as a question.

Her bottom lip quivered as she looked up at him, into the eyes that she had once regarded with fondness. If he wanted her to reassure him that they had a chance, he would wait forever. A reconciliation was not in their future.

Pulling her arm from him, Whitney turned and hurried down the steps. He called her name, once, twice, but she didn't turn around. Propelling her legs as fast as they could carry her, she didn't stop moving until she reached the beach.

Chapter 11

"Whitney!" Javar called again. She didn't turn. Instead, she hobbled toward the beach, even though she seemed to be in pain.

Javar watched as Whitney ran down the path toward the beach, wanting to follow her but knowing that he shouldn't. How had a lovely breakfast together turned into such a disaster?

He ran a hand over his head. Man, she was stubborn. Almost two years away from her and he'd forgotten how determined she could be. Why couldn't she just listen? Beneath her vulnerability was fiery anger. Anger directed at him that prevented her from even listening to anything he had to say.

But what had he said? All the wrong things. He hadn't meant to sound selfish in his grief; he understood that Whitney had suffered too. But, at least he was making an effort.

Javar sighed. He hated to admit it, but he had to accept the fact that Whitney was right. How would they ever work things out if they couldn't even speak civilly to one another?

The not-too-distant ring of the telephone interrupted his thoughts. He would let it ring. Speaking with anyone now was the last thing he wanted to do. Hopefully Carlos would think he and Whitney were still together and not disturb them.

The phone stopped, then immediately started ringing again.

Where was Carlos? Maybe it was someone from work trying to reach him. Grumbling, Javar ran toward the patio doors and the kitchen.

Once inside, he grabbed the receiver from its cradle on the wall. "Yes?" he couldn't help barking.

"Whoa. That's no way to greet your sister."

Running a hand over his hair, Javar said, "Oh. Oh hi, Michelle."

"I don't think I like that any better. You certainly are in a funky mood."

"Yeah, I guess. I've got a lot on my mind."

"I missed you in church yesterday. We all did." Her voice was smooth and sweet. "Javar, I'm worried about you."

Nosy was more like it, but Javar bit his tongue. "Well, sis, I'm fine."

"If you're okay, then why are you at home today? Javar, in all the years you've had your business, I don't think you've ever missed going to the office, even when you should have stayed home."

Clearly, his dear sister was fishing for information. Or confirmation of what she already knew. He said, "I'll be working at home for a while."

"Working at home?" She made it sound like a prison sentence. "Why?"

Michelle was good. Smooth. To someone who didn't know her, she might actually seem concerned as opposed to manipulative. "Michelle, you must know that Whitney is here. That's why I've been home. I want to be here as she recovers."

"Oh, that's right," Michelle said, sounding as though she truly had forgotten. Javar knew better. "I heard about the accident. How awful."

"Yeah, it was. Thank God she's alive, and she'll make a full recovery."

"Oh, that's good to hear." She paused. "So, what exactly is happening with you and Whitney? I mean, are you getting back together?"

"We're talking." Javar's tone was guarded. "That's all."

"Hmm. I hear she wants a divorce."

Stunned, Javar asked, "Where did you hear that?"

"That doesn't matter. Is it true?"

Javar replied, "Like I said, we're talking."

"Well, if it's true, then I think you should take it and run. That girl was nothing but a gold digger."

Michelle had never really liked Whitney, Javar knew. Now, he wondered. Wondered about the death threats Whitney said she had received. Wondered if Michelle was capable of such cowardly acts.

No. He couldn't see it.

But... Michelle had been particularly vicious once in high school, but she was also younger then and more immature. Still, she had known what she was doing when she sought to sabotage the reputation of a classmate, all because she had wanted the girl's man. After spreading rumors to the effect that the girl had slept with a married man and aborted his baby, that girl lost her boyfriend and numerous friends. People hadn't cared whether or not the rumors were true. They were only interested in having something to talk about, something to divert attention from their own boring lives.

"...ruined your life," Michelle was saying when Javar tuned in again. "You deserved much better."

Rolling his eyes to the ceiling, Javar said, "Michelle, I've got to go."

"Wait!" she cried. "Uh, I need to talk to you about something."

"Talk then," Javar replied curtly.

"Not on the phone. I need to see you in person. Tonight."

Javar's lips twisted, skeptical. "Can't this wait?"

"No," Michelle replied quickly. Her voice softened. "It can't. It's about, um…the renovations. Uh, you remember. The addition to the house that we're thinking of. Curtis and I would really like to get started as soon as possible, before the summer's over. Unless you'd like us to find another architect." She chuckled.

"You know you won't have to do that." He suspected there was more to this sudden visit, but didn't say so. "All right. I'll be by at seven."

"Make it six."

Whitney wasn't sure how long after she had arrived at the beach that her heart stopped racing. Over and over, the ugly scene with Javar had played out in her mind until she'd finally made a conscious effort to forget it. The only thing thinking about it had accomplished was worsening her headache.

Now, Whitney sat on the back end of *Lady Love's* tramp, trying to relax. The rhythmic swooshing sound of the waves as they lapped at the shore had a calming, almost hypnotic effect. There was a slight breeze off the water, cooling her body from the heat of the day. It also cooled her anger.

Javar… A mirthless chuckle fell from her lips as his name floated around in her mind. Sure he loved her. Sure he forgave her for the accident. And yesterday a cow jumped over the moon!

But why did it matter if he didn't love or forgive her? She

didn't want a reconciliation. However, she had loved him once, and being here, being near him, reminded her of all she had lost.

Whitney shifted on the tramp, stretching a big toe so that it touched the water. Instantly, she recoiled her foot, the frigid water a shock to her system. Instead, she lay back, letting her feet dangle, and closed her eyes.

Just because she wanted a divorce didn't mean she and Javar couldn't be friends. She had her own demons to deal with, so did he, but maybe—hopefully—they could learn to put their ill feelings aside. After all, they had loved each other once. Maybe in time they could have a great relationship as friends.

The shrill cries then sudden departure of a flock of seagulls drew Whitney's attention to the left and the thick cluster of tall pine trees that bordered Javar's property. Concentrating on listening, she heard rustling movements, but that was probably the breeze.

Wasn't it?

Like the birds had done, Whitney suddenly wanted to flee. Despite the sun's heat, she felt her skin prickle with the onset of goose bumps.

She scrambled off the tramp, almost tripping as her feet hit the sand. Footsteps. Oh God, she heard footsteps! Yet she couldn't see anyone as she frantically looked around.

Stop acting crazy. You can't hear footsteps on the sand!

That thought scared her even more. Anywhere in the thick of trees someone could be waiting… Watching…

She tripped. Gasped. Dug her fingers into the sand and pushed herself to her feet. Then started running. Somehow, she knew her life depended on it. The path to the house was only steps away, and if she could reach…

A scream tore from her throat, her heart pounding in her chest like a frantic boxer. The next moment she felt like a complete fool. It was only a squirrel that had darted out in front of her. A harmless squirrel, for goodness sake! Not some big, bad person who was out to harm her.

Still, Whitney felt like eyes were watching her, shooting daggers at her back.

As she hurried up the bush-lined path to the house, she glanced backward several times. Nothing. Only the sense that she should be afraid.

And she was.

Michelle and her husband lived in the mature, well-established Chicago suburb of Evanston. Slowing his Dodge Viper to a crawl, Javar hit his indicator and turned left into the circular driveway. The landscape was a vibrant green, complemented by an array of colorful flowers. Set amid mature maple and pine trees, the Country French home was quiet and serene on the outside, but Javar mentally prepared himself for a battle inside.

Javar parked his car and killed the engine. Moments later, he was at his sister's front door. Just as he raised his hand to ring the doorbell, the door swung open.

"Hey, Javar," Michelle said, a wide smile on her narrow, cinnamon-complected face. Stepping forward, she hugged him. "Come in, come in."

"Hey, sis." Looking down at her, she seemed genuinely happy to see him. Maybe he was wrong to assume her motive to get him over here was anything other than what she'd said. "You're looking great."

Dressed in a simple pink, form-fitting summer dress, Michelle looked top-notch. After having two children, she'd gained unwanted pounds. Immediately after giving birth to her daughter a year ago, Michelle had started a strict diet and exercise plan—complete with a physical trainer—that had helped her regain her trim figure. She hadn't breast-fed as she found it primitive, and not having to nurse a baby had allowed her to concentrate on working out.

"Thanks," Michelle said, running her perfectly manicured hands over her hips.

"Uncle Javar!" came a young cry, and as Javar looked up, he saw his nephew, Michael, running down the curved staircase at full steam.

Bending to meet him as his little feet hit the white porcelain floor, Javar scooped him up into his arms. "Hey, Michael! You're getting big, man."

"I know," he said succinctly.

"You know…? Well I hope you never get too big to be my favorite nephew."

"I'm your only nephew."

Tilting his head, Javar stared at Michael with narrowed eyes. Michael was four now, a year younger than J.J. had been when he died. At the time, Michael had only been two, and too young to have known J.J. Every time he saw Michael, held him, Javar thought of his son and wondered. Wondered what he'd look like today, how he and his younger cousin would get along.

"Uncle Javar, did you hear me?" Michael asked, cupping Javar's face firmly.

"Hmm?"

"I said I'm your only nephew."

"You are so smart, you know that, Michael?"

"I know."

Chuckling, Javar set Michael down, patting him affectionately on the back. He rose and faced Michelle. "Where's Sarah?"

"Sleeping," Michelle replied. "Finally." Turning to Michael, she said, "Why don't you go to your room and play for a while?"

"Uncle Javar, will you come with me? I want to show you my new police car."

"No," Michelle said sternly. "Your uncle and I need to talk." She placed a hand on his little shoulder, gently nudging him. "Go on."

A pout pulling his lips downward, Michael slowly began to walk away.

"I'll come see your car in a few minutes," Javar called to him.

Michael turned and flashed him a bright smile, then ran off.

Michelle watched her son run away, then smiling, shook her head. "Some days, I swear."

"He's a good kid," Javar said, remembering J.J.'s own enthusiasm and energy at that age.

Linking arms with him, Michelle said, "Let's go to the living room. We can talk there."

She led him to the right, out of the two-story foyer, down the short hallway, and into the large, brightly lit living room. Shaped in a semicircle, the part that was circular was one great window. The view was beautiful, facing a wooded ravine.

Javar sank into the teal-green leather sofa, releasing a sigh. "Where's Curtis?"

"Hello, Javar."

At the familiar voice his stomach knotted, and Javar whipped his head around. In the entranceway of the living room stood his mother. She was elegantly dressed in a beige flowing pantsuit. If she was here, instead of Curtis, then that meant Michelle and his mother were up to something. Something he was sure he wouldn't like.

Javar stood and greeted his mother, although what he felt like doing was reaching out and strangling Michelle. Why had she lied to him, lured him here under false pretenses? He turned to Michelle. "You don't want to discuss any renovations, do you?"

Michelle's expression was serious as she said, "No."

"So why lie? If you wanted me here to talk about something else, why didn't you say so?"

His sister merely folded her arms over her chest and shrugged.

"I asked her to set this up, Javar," his mother said, her voice deep, authoritative. "We need to talk."

Suddenly feeling ambushed, Javar moved to the window, away from his mother and sister. He gazed outside, into the shadows of the trees. "I don't appreciate being manipulated." He heard soft footfalls on the hardwood floor. His mother. He didn't turn around.

Angela Jordan said, "Would you have come here if she told you we wanted to discuss Whitney?"

Not a chance, Javar thought. Neither his mother nor his sister had anything good to say about his wife. Why stay here and listen to their opinions? Turning, he said, "I'm leaving."

Angela reached out and gripped his arm with the speed of a bullet. "Javar—"

"Why should I stay?"

"Because." It was Michelle who had spoken. "This is family business."

"It's *my* business." Javar couldn't help raising his voice. "Not yours, nor yours," he added, looking at his mother and his sister in turn.

"You'll want to hear what we have to say." Angela's brown eyes held his in a steady, uncompromising gaze.

Javar didn't like her tone. He didn't like the fact that she didn't respect his choices. But if she wanted to get in his face, he'd make sure she regretted it.

Michelle placed a palm on his back. It felt cold, even through his cotton shirt. "Sit, please." When Javar glared at her, she added, "My God, Javar. We are not the enemy!"

Against his better judgment, Javar dragged his feet across the floor, depositing himself on the love seat. He wasn't about to sit beside either of them.

Angela and Michelle took a seat on the sofa. Clearing her throat, Angela spoke first. "Stephanie called me. She told me what happened."

Javar rolled his eyes. He could only imagine what Stephanie had to say.

"Goodness, Javar," Angela said, her tone letting him know that she was disgusted. "What were you thinking? Manhandling her?"

"She threatened my wife. I threw her out."

"You've changed, Javar," Michelle said. "Ever since you met Whitney…"

He grasped the love seat's arms, ready to heave himself off the chair. "I think I've heard enough."

"Wait," Angela said sternly. "There's something you should know."

Javar released his grip on the chair's arms, silently agreeing to stay. For the moment. "And what is that?"

Angela and Michelle shared a concerned glance, then slowly, Angela reached into her purse. She withdrew a medium-sized manila envelope.

"You think you love her, Javar," his mother began, "but you don't even know her." Angela rose and approached him, placing the envelope on his lap. "We had her investigated."

"You what?" Incredulous, Javar sprang to his feet, letting the envelope fall to the floor.

"She's a gold digger, Javar. You should thank us for getting the proof now before you got further involved with her," his mother said as she bent to retrieve the envelope.

Glancing down, Javar saw several scattered photos. Color and black-and-white photos of Whitney with some man.

Michelle appeared beside Angela, helping her scoop up the last of the pictures. Picking up the last one, Michelle forced it into Javar's hands. "You think she loved you? You think you were so special to her? Well, get over it. She never loved you. After she killed your son, she went on to the next man. *Men,* probably. See this guy here?" Michelle indicated the picture in his hands.

Although Javar didn't want to, he looked down at the glossy photo. In it, Whitney sat beside a thin black man, attractive nonetheless, his arm intimately draped around her shoulder. They were both smiling at him. They seemed happy.

Javar tore his gaze away, meeting Michelle's chocolate colored eyes. "It's only a picture."

"Is it? Javar, this guy was a millionaire. Coincidence? I don't think so."

His heart pounding, Javar glanced down at the picture in his hand. Whitney and that man had been lovers? No, he didn't believe that. Is that why she wanted a divorce? But she'd told him there was no one else in her life.

"Like Michelle said, Javar, we're not the enemy." Angela gave him the rest of the pictures, as well as a folded piece of paper. "That's the investigator's report. Read it."

His throat was so dry, Javar didn't think he could speak. But after a moment he found his voice. "It's not what you think."

"Oh really?" Angela scoffed, her face contorted with skepticism. "If she wasn't sleeping with him, then why did he leave her money in his will?"

"He's dead?"

"Yes, and he left her two hundred and fifty thousand dollars."

His gut clenched. Ached. Why hadn't Whitney mentioned this to him?

Michelle touched his arm softly. "Don't you see? This is a pattern for her. Rich men...milking them for their money. That's all you were to her, Javar. A rich man who could give her the kind of life she wanted."

"And now that you know, you don't have to feel guilty about divorcing her," his mother added.

Javar inhaled a steadying breath. "That's my decision to make."

"What?" Angela stared up at him in stunned disbelief.

"You heard me."

"My God," Michelle uttered, her expression as confused as her mother's. "What is wrong with you? Haven't you heard—"

"I will not be bullied into making any decision." Javar spoke slowly and clearly so they would not mistake his words.

"So...she's still going to be living at your house?"

"She's recovering from an accident. I can't kick her out on the street."

Angela replied, "She has her mother. She has two hundred and fifty thousand in the bank, for goodness' sake!"

Javar had heard enough. It was all a lie. He didn't know how his mother had done it, how she had gotten the pictures, who'd done the phony report. But if he was making a mistake with Whitney, then it was his mistake to make.

He brushed past his mother, stalked to the entryway of the living room. He heard his mother's and sister's hushed, angry voices, but that didn't deter him.

Michelle spoke when he reached the hallway. "Javar, if you let that murderer stay at your house, then you're no longer welcome here. I won't let you see Michael or Sarah."

Javar hesitated. He was about to turn and respond. But he couldn't make himself do it. He couldn't, wouldn't, allow himself to be manipulated. "Please explain to Michael that I had to leave," he called over his shoulder.

Javar proceeded, hurrying down the hallway to the front door, the pictures and letter scrunched in his fist.

Javar still wasn't home. Since their argument, Whitney hadn't seen nor spoken to him, but through her bedroom window she had seen his red Viper pulling out of the driveway. Now, it was almost midnight, and he wasn't home yet.

Without Javar at home, the house was extremely quiet. Almost eerily so. At least when they'd been newlyweds, even when Javar had spent long hours at the office, J.J.'s little voice had filled the house with laughter. Now, there was an emptiness, almost as if the house lacked a soul.

Whitney flipped through the television channels, stopping when she found a rerun of a comedy show. After watching for several minutes, she turned off the television and placed the remote control on the glass coffee table.

Television wasn't going to distract her from the fight they'd had earlier and the fact that she was worried.

Not worried, she decided. Javar was a grown man who could take care of himself. But she was concerned. Earlier in their marriage, when they argued Javar would leave, either going for a long drive or going to the office. And after J.J.'s death, he had turned not only to long hours at the office, but also to alcohol. As far as she could tell, the alcohol had only been a temporary crutch, but she hoped that while he was angry with her now he didn't do anything crazy.

The phone was ringing, Whitney realized. The main line. Jumping off the sofa in her bedroom, Whitney ran to the door and threw it open. The closest phone was in Javar's room, so she turned right, heading to the south wing and the master suite. She opened Javar's bedroom door and hurried inside.

The machine picked up before she could answer. Stopping, she stood and listened. What if Javar had gotten himself into some trouble and someone was calling?

A woman's voice filled the air. "Javar, hi. It's Melody." Pause, then, "We need to talk. Call me, tonight if you want. I'll be up till about three."

A mix of emotions overcame Whitney: confusion, anger, jealousy. Melody, Javar's administrative assistant who had a definite thing for him. She doubted this was a business-related call. Javar had told her that he had not been involved with anyone since their separation. If that was the truth, then why was Melody calling him at almost midnight?

Strangely rattled, Whitney crossed her arms over her chest. As she walked back to her bedroom, she told herself she didn't want to know. It didn't matter. Was none of her business.

Man, her head was hurting her! When she reached her room she headed straight for the pills she had to take, this time longing for them. She dropped one for pain and two for stress into her mouth. Swallowed them.

Prayed they would dull the ache in her heart.

It was amazing what you could accomplish when you re-directed your energy. Blocked creatively for days, Javar now knew exactly what to do for the Li proposal, and was doing it. Creative genius was flowing from his brain right to his fingers, and from there right onto paper. The sketches were rough, of course, but could be re-done. Right now, all he wanted to do was get his ideas down on paper and perfect them later.

After working for hours at his office, Javar was finally satisfied. He knew he could land this bid. And the sketch he'd just completed was no doubt one of his best. Innovative, modern, with a touch of old classic designs.

All this energy, passion that needed to be released, just from the argument with his mother and sister.

Not just that argument, a voice said. The voice was his own internal one, he realized, although it had seemed to come from somewhere else.

His eyes moved to the chair in his office where he'd placed his jacket…and the pictures. The pictures of Whitney and another man. Another rich man.

His heart began beating furiously again. The two hundred and fifty thousand, the story that his wife had seduced some rich man…that he could discount. Could if it weren't for the photos. Despite his resolve, he had flipped through the various shots the private investigator had taken.

The pictures were clearly taken on different occasions, as both Whitney and the man wore at least three different outfits. The photos spoke a truth he couldn't deny. But how much of the story was true?

Would Whitney have married this man if he hadn't died?

Moving to the floor-to-ceiling windows, Javar tried to push the thoughts of Whitney and her friend out of his mind. What Whitney had done in Louisiana was none of his business.

Then why did he feel like jumping in his car and driving home, where he could finally get to the truth?

Grabbing the pictures, his jacket, and his car keys, that's exactly what he did.

She was dreaming. Dreaming that someone was in her room, wrapping thick hands around her neck. Pressing...

Gasping, Whitney's eyes flew open, and to her horror she realized she wasn't dreaming. Someone was over her, hands on her neck. A balaclava covered her attacker's head, preventing her from seeing his face.

A surge of adrenaline shooting through her body, Whitney grabbed at the attacker's hands. She tugged, scratched.

Managed to scream.

Her attacker paused, as though startled and not sure what to do. As he glanced over his shoulder toward the bedroom door, Whitney took the opportunity to grab at his face.

He was too quick for her, knocking her hand away. The next instant he rushed out of the room.

Knowing she shouldn't but unable to stop herself, Whitney jumped from the bed and hurried into the hallway, following the perpetrator. She screamed again, a loud, desperate scream that could wake the dead.

As she followed the intruder down the staircase, she silently wondered, *Where is Javar?*

Chapter 12

Javar heard Whitney's scream as he entered the house from the garage. Weariness seized him and his feet moved faster, propelling him to the front of the house. As he ran through an archway into the foyer, he heard heavy footfalls as someone raced down the stairs. A figure in black whizzed by, heading for the front door.

"Javar!"

He heard the fear in his wife's voice without having to turn around. Good God, some creep had attacked Whitney!

Anger burned in his veins, refueling him. That man would live to regret he had ever attacked his wife! He charged after the intruder, down the front steps and out onto the concrete sidewalk. With each step, he gained on the man. Finally, he extended his body, reaching for the intruder's arm. His fingers closed around the cottony fabric of the man's long-sleeved shirt.

The man kept going across the concrete driveway to the lawn, pulling his arm free from Javar's grasp. Javar couldn't let him get away. Pumping his arms to accelerate his speed, Javar quickly gained on the intruder. Closer…closer…

Javar lunged forward, tackling the man from behind. They both fell onto the ground with a loud thud. Javar held the man as he squirmed, but the man dragged himself forward, kicking the legs that Javar held.

The man got the better of Javar as his thick boot landed squarely on Javar's chin.

Recoiling in pain, Javar eased his hold on the man a little, but it was enough to give the man an avenue for escape. The intruder rose to his feet, once again taking off into the darkness.

Javar got up, ready to take off once again when he heard Whitney yell, "No, Javar! It's not worth it!"

His chest heaving from ragged breaths, Javar glanced at Whitney, saw her running toward him, then back at the silhouette of the intruder. He wanted to go after the jerk, but he didn't want to leave Whitney alone. And the man had too much of a head start now.

"Oh, my God, Javar!" Whitney had stopped her mad dash and was now standing before him, her face contorted with fear and concern. Reaching up, she touched his face with her long, delicate fingers. She probed, softly massaged. "Honey, are you okay?"

Javar knew it was a slip of the tongue, a word tossed out carelessly considering the situation, but he couldn't prevent the immediate reaction he felt. His loins suddenly burned, ached for his wife. And the way she was touching him was not helping matters. Her fingers softly caressed his skin, awoke a longing in him he had once thought dead. Man, it had been so long since a woman had touched him.

Not just any woman. This woman.

But there was so much between them, so many problems, so many bitter feelings. Drawing in a ragged breath, Javar captured Whitney's hand in his, pulled it away from his face. "I'm okay."

"Javar, there's moisture on your face. I think you're bleeding."

"I'm okay," he repeated forcefully, immediately regretting his tone. Sadness flashed in Whitney's brown eyes, and in the pale moonlight, he could see the shiny moisture brimming beneath her lids. He thought of only one thing he could say to mask his attitude. "I'm sorry, I'm just mad. Did he hurt you?"

Whitney shook her head, but it looked more like a nervous twitch. God, her whole body was shaking. She didn't look ready to answer any questions.

Still, she spoke. "He…was…in my room…."

Javar swept her into his arms, pressed her soft body against his. Releasing a moan, she sagged against him, wrapped her arms around his waist and held him tight.

"Oh, Javar."

An electric current shot through his body, but this time it wasn't a sexual response. It was the response of someone whose heart felt warm because he was needed. The response of someone who realized that despite a lot of pain in his relationship, he was able to offer comfort, and that comfort was being accepted.

"I was sleeping…" Whitney murmured.

"Shh." Javar kissed her forehead, let his lips linger. "Let's go inside."

Whitney nodded, continuing to hold Javar's strong body as he moved slowly, walking across the lawn toward the house. Strength radiated from him, went from his body directly into her pores. Filled her with warmth. He was offering comfort, and she readily accepted.

Thank God he came home when he did. If he hadn't…

She didn't want to think about what might have happened if Javar hadn't shown up when he did. Right now, all she could think about was being in Javar's arms and how good it felt to be both offering comfort and receiving comfort. How good it felt just to hold each other after all this time.

"How did this happen?" Javar demanded, staring at Carlos. "Tell me how someone got in here without tripping the alarm."

The middle-aged man shrugged his shoulders, the dark circles under his eyes evidence of his fatigue. Somehow, he had slept through all the commotion. "I don't know, sir."

"Was the alarm set?"

"Yes. I checked it before I retired for the evening."

Javar slammed his palm against the wall in the foyer where the security box was. "Well, it's clearly not set now. Damn. Does this mean someone forgot to activate it, or that the creep who broke in here knew the code?"

Again, Carlos shrugged, considering the options. "Perhaps Miss Monroe forgot to activate it."

"Did she say where she was going?"

"No," Carlos replied. "She said nothing to me."

"Hmm," Javar hummed absently. The nurse was another of his concerns. She wasn't in her room. In fact, she was nowhere to be found. Why would she have gone out without letting anyone know she was leaving? He had hired her as a twenty-four-hour nurse. What if Whitney had had a relapse in the middle of the night and rang for her?

Walking back and forth, Javar paced the black marble floor. Something wasn't right. If the nurse had accidentally forgotten to activate the alarm tonight when she went out, it was still too much of a coincidence that this would be the night an intruder just *happened* to break in and find he didn't have to disable an alarm.

Javar paced to the alarm system, stopping to examine it again. That only told him what he already knew. The box was intact, so the intruder clearly had figured out the code.

Or had someone told him the code?

Javar cast a sidelong glance at Carlos, his brain working overtime. Carlos's eyebrows rose and he shifted uncomfortably beneath Javar's probing gaze, as if sensing the direction of his thoughts.

Carlos said, "Surely you don't think this was deliberate?"

"I don't know what to think, Carlos. All I know is that someone attacked my wife—in her bed—and that that person gained access to this house without activating the alarm. Now, that was either a lucky break for this guy, or he knew the code."

"I don't know, sir."

Javar's expression softened as he stared at his butler. For the past seven years he had known Carlos, trusted him. Whatever had happened here tonight, he knew that Carlos was not involved.

"Of course you don't know, Carlos," Javar said, then heaved a long sigh. "Thanks for helping me look around. Please, go back to bed."

"Do you want me to call the police now?" Carlos asked.

Javar shook his head. "No. Not tonight. Whitney's not up to any questioning."

Nodding, Carlos walked away, toward his room on the main level.

Wild, crazy ideas whirling in his mind, Javar headed to the kitchen. He found Whitney sitting at the breakfast table, her hands wrapped around a mug of hot tea. Her eyes lowered, she looked like she was praying.

Maybe she was.

Her eyes rose to meet his as she heard his footsteps. "Did you find out anything?"

Shaking his head, Javar replied, "Nothing." He didn't want to worry her with his concerns. Not yet. "Do you know where Elizabeth went?" he asked. He found it highly suspicious that tonight of all nights, she was nowhere to be found.

"No. I saw her around ten-thirty, and that was the last time. She gave me my medication. She didn't mention anything to me about going out." Whitney raised an eyebrow curiously. "Why?"

Javar shrugged, then leaned a hip against the kitchen's island. Changing the subject he said, "You haven't had much of your tea."

"I…I don't feel like it."

Javar took a few steps toward Whitney. "Drink it. It'll help settle your nerves."

A timid smile left Whitney's lips. "You sound like Elizabeth."

Just one smile, but it made so much of a difference to her whole demeanor. Every part of her exuded such warmth when she smiled. Even when he knew that under the circumstances, she didn't want to be smiling.

As though she heard his inner thoughts, Whitney's smile faded. She said, "You don't think this was a random attack, do you?"

She knew him so well, Javar thought. Knew that he was keeping his true thoughts from her. Still, he wasn't ready to admit his suspicions. Instead he asked, "What do you think?"

"I…" Whitney's voice trailed off, and she gripped her mug harder. "I don't think it was random."

It was what he was thinking, but hadn't wanted to voice. It

would be so much easier if the attack *had* been random. "Why do you think that? Because of the threats you told me about?"

"Partly." Whitney released her grip on the mug, and with a forefinger traced the outline of the rim. "But there's more. Earlier today, when I was at the beach, I thought...felt like someone was watching me."

"Right here?" Fear snaked down Javar's spine. "On this property?"

Whitney nodded. "I thought I was overreacting. You know, with all the medicine I've been taking. That maybe I wasn't thinking straight."

A hand on his jaw, Javar walked toward the counter by the stove. He stood a moment silently, then banged a fist on the gray granite counter. Turning to face Whitney, he asked, "Whitney, do you have any idea who might be doing this?"

Bringing her mug to her lips, Whitney took a long sip of the hot herbal tea. As far as she was concerned, the list of suspects was lengthy. She started with the most obvious. "Stephanie." She paused a moment, then added, "Unless you've made some enemies at work. Gotten a bid that someone else wanted and now they're trying to get to you through me."

"That's a possibility," Javar admitted. "Although I really doubt it."

Whitney doubted it too. She glanced down at her tea, then returned her eyes to Javar's dark gaze. "I don't know what to think, Javar."

Gnawing on his lower lip, Javar walked toward Whitney. He stood behind her chair and placed two strong hands on her shoulders.

Whitney shuddered. And not because she was cold, or scared. Because as Javar touched her, she had to admit to herself that she wanted him. Wanted his warmth, his strength, his affection.

"Let's go to bed," he said softly, his deep voice washing over her like a gentle breeze.

He didn't mean it *that* way she tried to convince herself when her body reacted to Javar's words, her heart beating erratically at the erotic thought. He couldn't. He must mean their respective beds. But God help her, Whitney found herself hoping he had meant they'd share one bed. His bed.

"C'mon." He patted her shoulder, then helped ease her chair back.

Whitney stood, instinctively reaching for him, placing an arm around his waist. She felt the stirrings of desire deep in her belly, and it spread lower.

They walked silently up the spiral staircase. When they reached her bedroom, Javar stopped. So did Whitney's heart. As Javar pulled out of her embrace, she looked up at him. "Javar…" Her voice trailed off, unable to express the words in her heart.

"Whitney?"

"I…"

She was shaking again. Earlier, she had seemed strong, but Javar now realized that she had been putting on a brave face. She was scared. Glancing down at her hands he saw that they were trembling. Until now, the thought that someone actually meant to hurt Whitney had seemed unreal somehow, incomprehensible. Now, however, the severity of the situation was all too real.

Someone had broken into his house. Someone had invaded Whitney's room. Someone had tried to kill her.

"Javar…" She was clenching and unclenching her robe. "I…don't want to be…alone."

She didn't need to say another word. Pulling her close, Javar nuzzled his nose in her raven hair, inhaling her flowery scent. Again, he felt his loins ignite with a desire too long denied, but he fought to keep the reaction under control. Whitney didn't want sex, he told himself. She wanted his comfort.

Moments later, they were at his bedroom. Casting a quick glance at Whitney, he opened the double doors. She seemed suddenly cautious, tense, staring into the room from wide eyes.

"It's okay, I won't bite," Javar said, attempting humor.

Whitney's eyes flew to his, as though shocked to think she looked unnerved. She flashed him a shy smile, then slowly ventured into the room, staring around with interest.

Javar was still wearing the T-shirt and shorts he had worn all day. "I'm going to change. Make yourself comfortable."

Whitney watched as Javar walked across the plush rose-colored carpet to his dresser. He opened a drawer and withdrew pajamas, then disappeared into the large ensuite bathroom. A memory hit her, a memory of another time, and she shivered. She recalled the gigantic Jacuzzi, how on occasion they would fill it with bubbles and frolic in there together. How frolicking would lead to passionate lovemaking.

Whitney tried to shake off the image. She turned, directing her gaze to the large gas fireplace and then the sitting area. A black leather sofa and matching love seat sat atop the plush carpet. A black entertainment center rested against the wall, complete with a giant screen television and a CD player with numerous selections beneath.

Whitney shifted her gaze toward the king-sized bed. The iron posts at the head and foot of the bed were black, matching the color scheme in the room. The furniture was the same as when she'd lived here, but he had changed the accessories in the room. In fact, any proof that she had once shared this room with him was gone. There were no pictures of the two of them, none of the dainty statuettes she had bought. Nothing. Her touch was evident in the rest of the house, but not here, where she had spent every night with Javar.

There was a lump in Whitney's throat, and she swallowed it. Tried to. It wouldn't go away.

At that moment, Javar exited the bathroom. Their eyes met and held. Maybe it was the stress of the accident, or even tonight, or maybe it was the realization that she wanted things to work out for them but feared they never would, but Whitney suddenly felt winded. Overwhelmingly sad. Her desire for Javar fizzled, giving way to doubt. One night with him would not erase the gap between them that was as wide as the Grand Canyon.

"I'll take the sofa," Javar said.

No, Whitney wanted to say, but only stood there.

"Whitney?"

"Whatever you want," she finally said, her heart pounding in her chest. She was a coward, afraid to ask for what she wanted.

Her head lowered, she walked toward the bed. As Javar's hand wrapped around her upper arm, she halted, gasping.

He looked down at her from heavy lids. "Don't you want me to sleep on the sofa?"

Whitney swallowed. All she had to do was tell him what she wanted. All she had to do was say no. It was that easy....

"Hmm?" he prodded, his hand tightening.

She looked up at him, into his dark eyes. Something sparked in their depths, something powerful, something electrifying.

Suddenly, the doubts were gone again, and there was only need. The need to be held, to be touched, to be loved.

Turning to him, Whitney pressed her body against Javar's. She answered him now the only way she could, by showing him what she wanted, all the while praying he would not reject her.

She slipped her hands beneath the open pajama top, ran her fingers up over his chest. Her fingertips stopped over his heart, and she could feel its frantic beat. It matched her own.

Whitney's hands ventured upward, finally resting at his nape. She heard the sharp intake of breath, felt it as she pressed her breasts against his chest, but wasn't sure if it came from Javar or from her.

"Whitney..." His voice was deep, captivating.

His eyes drew hers to his like a magnet, pulling, energizing. Tilting her head back, she merely stared at him, wanting his strength, wondering if he would offer it.

He did. Wrapping his hands around her small waist, Javar pulled her closer. As he held her tightly, he lowered his head, his lips ever so slowly approaching hers.

Whitney's lips parted, waiting. The pull between them was so strong, she wouldn't be able to stop herself if she tried.

Javar's lips met hers, tentative at first, teasing. Softly he kissed her mouth, the top lip, the bottom lip, the corners. Whitney's eyelids fluttered shut and she moaned, digging her fingers into the curly hair at his nape.

"Whitney," Javar murmured, before claiming her lips urgently. His tongue played over the flesh of her mouth, slipping inside, forcing its way past her teeth, connecting with her own. Hot was the only thought in Whitney's head. His tongue was hot. His body was hot. She was hot.

She arched against him, pressing her curves into his solid

muscles. Heat pooled in her center, spreading to the rest of her body, making her delirious with longing. It had been so long. Too long.

Javar's hands were suddenly inside her silk robe, delicately running over her back, her buttocks. Back up to her shoulders. Gently nudging the robe off her body. Letting it fall to the floor. The material fell in a heap around her feet.

Pressing his fingertips into the soft flesh of her back, a groan rumbled in Javar's chest. Everything about Whitney was sweet temptation. Her soft lips, her smooth flesh, the way she had her arms wrapped around his neck as if she would never let him go.

He tore his lips from hers, looking into her eyes. They were dark, glistening pools of desire. In no uncertain terms, the passion in her eyes told him not to stop.

He didn't. Moving his lips over Whitney's face, Javar kissed her forehead, the bandage that hid her cut, each eyelid, the tip of her nose, her cheeks, her lips. With every part of his being, he drank in her sweetness. The desire he felt for her now was only equaled by their wedding night, the first time they had ever made love.

When he flicked his tongue over her earlobe, Whitney shuddered, digging her nails into his shoulder blades. Javar's body went up in flames. He scooped Whitney into his arms, carrying her to the massive bed.

It was time he reclaimed his wife. There were no questions now, no concerns. There was only him and his wife and the all-consuming need for her that had to be released.

As he laid her body atop the comforter, he gazed into her eyes. He had to be sure she was sure. "Whitney…"

She cupped his face with her hands, drew his lips to hers.

Again, a moan escaped her lips as she kissed him, told him in no uncertain terms what he needed to know.

He eased his body down beside her then captured her lips in a soft, sensual kiss. God, he had been so lonely without his wife. God, how he needed her now.

Reaching out, he slipped a fingertip beneath the spaghetti strap of her silky white nightie. Gently, he fiddled with the material, dragging it down, then back up, then down again. Whitney dropped her head back, moaned, invited. Javar accepted her invitation, pulling the nightgown off her shoulder and exposing one breast. He drew in a sharp breath as he looked at her, drank in the sight of her beauty. His hand slipped lower and he cupped her fullness, relishing the feel of the hardened tip against the palm of his hand. As Whitney arched against his hand, her head hanging backward, her teeth sinking into her bottom lip, Javar lost all control. He replaced his hand with his mouth. Nearly died from the pleasure.

"Oh, Javar…"

Whitney pulled at his clothes, dragging his pajama top urgently from his body. She wanted to feel his chest against her breasts. She wanted to be skin to skin. Heart to heart.

How she had gone so long without loving Javar, she didn't know. She only knew that she wanted this special moment to last forever. In her heart, there was no yesterday, no tomorrow, only now.

When their bodies finally joined, their coupling was slow, gentle, beautiful. Like two lost souls finding each other and savoring every inch of each other reverently. They clung to each other, giving, receiving. Together they reached that special place of spellbinding passion and earth-shattering pleasure.

Afterward, Javar pulled Whitney's body against his, wrapped

his arms around her possessively, like he used to do on the other occasions when they had made love. She covered his hands with hers. Together, they lay silently.

The moment was so familiar, it was haunting. It was as if no time had passed since they'd last been together. Yet it had.

As Whitney drifted off to sleep in the comfort of Javar's arms, she couldn't help wishing tomorrow wouldn't come. But it would. And with it would also come reality.

Chapter 13

It was too soon to be pregnant, Whitney told herself as she sat on the floor beside the toilet in her ensuite bathroom. But man, did she ever feel sick. One minute her stomach would lurch and she would run from the bed to the bathroom, only for her stomach to settle as soon as she got there. If she could only get whatever it was out of her system, she knew she would feel better. It was the back and forth, teeter-tottering that she couldn't handle.

Finally, it was once again apparent that she was not going to throw up. Groaning, Whitney rose to her feet and walked to the white marble sink with brass fixtures, where she splashed her face with cold water, then cupped her hands and captured some of the liquid. She drank several handfuls, but that did nothing to ease the nasty feeling in the pit of her stomach.

She turned from the sink and dried her hands and face on a towel. The only thing to do now was to go back to bed.

Her bed. Shortly after six a.m., she had snuck out of Javar's bed and returned to her own room. Having awoken from a pleasurable sleep to find herself in his arms, she realized the major mistake she had made.

How had she let things get so out of hand last night?

Because she'd wanted comfort, closeness. Because Javar

offered her those things when she had needed them. That was all, she told herself. As she walked back to her bed and crawled under the covers, she told herself that what had happened last night between her and Javar would never happen again.

In his sleep-induced state, Javar reached for his wife. Reached, and felt air where her body should have been. His hand stretched over the cotton sheets as he continued to search for her warm body.

His eyes popped open as soon as the realization hit him.

Whitney wasn't in his bed.

Looking around the room, he quickly surmised that she wasn't there either. And there were no sounds coming from the ensuite, which meant that Whitney wasn't in the bathroom.

Sometime during the night she'd gotten up and left him.

Rolling over onto his back, Javar groaned. Last night had been…incredible. And he was a fool. He'd allowed himself to believe that when Whitney had come to his room last night— to his bed—that that had been the beginning of a reconciliation. Yes, there were things that had to be worked out, and to be honest, they weren't going to be easy. Still, he hadn't expected to awake to an empty bed.

Javar groaned. He shouldn't have gone against his better judgment last night. He shouldn't have fallen into bed with Whitney. But his yearning for her had been too strong.

Slipping a hand behind his head, Javar wondered if making love had brought them closer, or only added to the distance between them.

When Whitney heard the soft rapping on her door, she froze. God knew, she wasn't ready to face Javar. Wasn't ready to deal with the grave mistake she'd made last night.

The door began to open. Whitney grabbed her pillow and dragged it over her face. If she had to, she'd play dead. She had nothing to say to him.

"Whitney?" a voice called softly. Elizabeth.

Slowly, Whitney moved in the bed, feigning someone awaking from sleep. She pulled the pillow away from her face and looked up at Elizabeth from narrowed lids.

"Good morning, Whitney." The nurse's smile was pure saccharine. "It's time for your medicine."

Whitney sat up for the nurse and they went through their morning routine. When she plucked the thermometer from beneath her tongue, Elizabeth said, "Good news. Your temperature is back to normal. That means your infection is healing."

The nurse lifted the bandage from her forehead, then said, "Oh yes. That's healing nicely now." Moments later, she rebandaged Whitney's forehead with fresh gauze and tape. "Shouldn't be too much longer before you're good as new."

Whitney asked. "Are you sure about that? I feel awful. Really, really nauseous."

"Hmm." Elizabeth's face contorted with concern. "I can only suggest that you make sure you eat. Taking these medications can be harsh on your—"

"Elizabeth." The voice was unmistakably hard, barely containing its anger. Whitney's eyes darted to the bedroom door. There Javar stood, his hands planted firmly on his hips, a scowl distorting his handsome features.

Clearly startled, the nurse's eyes bulged as though frightened. Turning to face him, she replied, "Yes, Mr. Jordan?"

"I need to speak with you," Javar said sharply. He was going to get to the bottom of last night's incident, and Elizabeth's part in it, if any. "Out here, please."

Wiping her palms on her pale green pant outfit, Elizabeth walked briskly toward him, her expression wary. Behind her, Whitney watched him curiously.

When the nurse stepped into the hallway, Javar reached for the brass handle of the bedroom door and closed it. Then, folding his arms over his chest, he turned to face Elizabeth. He got right to the point. "Where were you last night?"

Her eyebrows rose and fell. "Last night?" she repeated, as though she couldn't believe the question.

"Yes, last night," Javar replied, irritation evident in his voice. "Last night, when you should have been here, taking care of my wife."

She withered under his hard gaze. "I was...out. At my... boyfriend's."

"Why didn't you mention that you were going to be gone for the night?"

"I...Mr. Jordan, I apologize. I made sure that Whitney had her medication last night, and then..." She shrugged, as if the rest was self-explanatory.

"I'm paying you to be here, Elizabeth. Twenty-four hours a day unless it is arranged otherwise."

"Did something happen last night? Did Whitney need my—"

"Yes, something happened last night, Elizabeth," Javar answered, his voice rising an octave. "While you were out, Whitney was attacked by some creep who broke into the house, right in her bedroom."

"My God," Elizabeth exclaimed, bringing a hand to her heart.

Javar continued. "The alarm didn't even go off. Probably because you forgot to reactivate it when you rushed out."

Elizabeth's mouth fell open at the allegation, but she closed it promptly. Her eyes narrowed pensively, as though in thought, and after a few moments, she shook her head. "I reactivated the alarm when I left. I'm sure of it."

Javar was about to ask her if she knew anything about the break-in, but thought better of it. All of a sudden, the idea seemed ridiculous. He was grasping at straws if he believed the nurse he'd hired from an agency, whose credentials were top-notch, was somehow involved in the attack on his wife.

Frustrated, he blew out a ragged breath, letting his shoulders sag. "I'm sorry if I came down hard on you, Elizabeth but I'm sure you can understand my concern. My wife was attacked last night, *in this house,* and the alarm didn't go off. There was no forced entry from what we can tell. I know criminals are more sophisticated these days, but…" He let the statement dangle in the air.

"Top-of-the-line security systems can't even guarantee one's safety," Elizabeth said, shaking her head. "Gosh, I'm so sorry. What did the police say?"

"Nothing. Yet. It was so late when everything happened last night, and Whitney was so shaken up…. I decided to let her rest and call the police today."

Rest…yeah, right, a voice teased from somewhere in his subconscious.

Javar bristled at the intrusive voice. The direction of his thoughts quickly went to last night, to the image of Whitney's closed eyes as she cried out his name. His hands dropped to the front of his groin as he felt the first stirrings of desire. The last thing he needed right now was to embarrass himself in front of Elizabeth.

He said, "Actually, I'll call them now." Turning on his heel, Javar made a hasty retreat to his bedroom.

* * *

"Sorry," Whitney mumbled when her elbow hit Javar's arm as she brushed past him on her way to the dishwasher. The large kitchen suddenly seemed too small for the both of them. She hadn't come downstairs until ten, thinking that for sure Javar would have already had his morning coffee and read *The Chicago Tribune.* Instead, he was only now making an appearance in the kitchen. She took that as her cue to leave.

"Whitney."

"Hmm?" She didn't even look up as she opened the dishwasher and placed her plate in the rack.

Javar sighed audibly. "Is this how it's going to be now?" he asked. "You rushing out of a room as soon as I enter?"

Rising, she found his nutmeg gaze scrutinizing her. "What are you talking about?" she asked, pretending she didn't know. "I've finished my breakfast. No point—"

Javar was grinning wryly. "Sure." He walked toward her. "Look, about last night—"

"Gosh, I'm feeling pretty tired," Whitney said, cutting him off. She was not ready for this conversation. Probably never would be.

"So you're not up to talking to the police yet?" Javar asked.

"The police?" Whitney asked, before realizing what Javar had obviously been referring to when he'd said "last night." Heat spread across her face, and she was thankful her darker complexion prevented Javar from seeing her blush. "Oh, yes. The police. Uh, sure. Yeah, we should call them now."

"You're not tired?"

Whitney shook her head. "Uh, yeah. But they should be notified now. After all, the break-in happened last night."

Pressing his lips together tightly, Javar tried not to chuckle.

Whitney was trying to avoid him, all right. If she didn't look so cute when flustered, he might just want to press her for some answers. But he'd let her sweat. At least until after the police were contacted.

Turning, he walked to the kitchen phone. He lifted the receiver from its cradle and placed it to his ear.

"Wait," Whitney said. When he turned to face her, he saw her walking toward him. "Call Derrick. Detective Lawson."

"Why?" Javar asked, a sudden surge of jealousy causing his stomach to twist into a knot. "We're in Kenilworth. Derrick works for the Chicago P.D."

"I know. But, well, I trust Derrick. I'd just feel better calling him first, at least."

The mention of Derrick, her insistence that he call him, had Javar remembering his visit with his mother and his sister last night. Had him remembering the pictures of Whitney and that man in Louisiana.

He swallowed. Tried to suppress the memory. Tried to ignore the tightening in his chest.

One night of great sex. That's all he and his wife had shared.

"Javar?" She was looking at him with a puzzled expression. "Are you going to call Derrick?"

Javar nodded tightly. "Sure. What's the number?"

Long after Derrick had arrived at the Jordan home, he finally took a seat across from Whitney in the living room. With Javar, he had searched the seven-thousand-square-foot house from top to bottom. Now, he sat on the antique-styled sofa, a frustrated frown playing on his lips.

"You didn't find anything, did you?" Whitney asked, already knowing what his answer would be.

Derrick shook his head. "No sign of forced entry in the least. With a house this large, there are often places that an intruder can gain access, but he or she would usually leave some sign of that. Or at least trip the alarm. In this case, it looks as if this guy was invited in through the front door and even took off his shoes."

"He had shoes on. At least I think he did," Whitney said.

"I'm sure he did," Derrick said. "He just left no trace of them. Not even a smudge of dirt on the stairs. Nothing for us to go on."

Javar, who was leaning an elbow against the fireplace mantel, pinched the bridge of his nose with a thumb and forefinger, clearly frustrated. "In other words, this looks like a professional job."

"The guy knew what he was doing," Derrick conceded.

Javar asked, "So what now?"

"Well, I'm here as a friend," Derrick explained. "Kenilworth is way out of my jurisdiction."

"So we should call the Kenilworth P.D.?" Whitney asked.

Derrick's shrug was noncommittal. "If you do call them now, they're going to wonder why you've waited as long as you have. Technically, since you were attacked, Whitney, what happened last night wasn't a break and enter. It was a home invasion. Cops get a bit testy when people wait hours to call them, for no apparent reason."

Crossing to the sofa where Whitney sat, Javar took a seat beside her. "Whitney was too shaken up to talk to the police."

But not too shaken up to make love, Whitney thought, suddenly wondering about her warped priorities.

"They could have come in, started dusting for prints and so forth. Now, they'll say the evidence has been tampered with."

"But there wasn't any," Whitney protested. "You said so yourself."

Derrick shrugged. "I can't advise you not to report this crime. I'm only giving you my opinion."

Javar said, "So basically you're saying that not only will it be a waste of time, but the police won't be too impressed with us for having waited so long to call them."

Pursing his lips, Derrick nodded.

Although she wasn't looking directly at him, Whitney could tell Javar was angry. Angry at his helplessness. Inhaling a deep breath, Whitney turned to face him. "Let's just forget it. There's nothing we can do about it now."

Derrick asked, "Did either of you get a look at this guy? Maybe there have been similar crimes in the area—"

"I doubt it," Javar said sourly. "And no, we didn't get a look at him because his face was covered."

Whitney rose from the sofa, slapping her hands against her thighs. "I just want to forget this ever happened. There's nothing that can be done now, and the more we talk about it…"

Javar rose to meet Whitney, placing his hands on her shoulders. She stiffened at his touch, at this simple gesture that many a married couple shared. But they weren't really married. Only in name, and that was soon to be resolved.

He must have sensed her unease, because he pulled his hands away from her and walked to the bay window. A pang of guilt tugged at her heart as she watched him, thinking once again how her need for comfort last night had caused a greater rift between the two of them.

The phone rang, jarring her from her thoughts. Javar quickly turned from the window, saying, "I'll take it in the kitchen."

When Javar was clearly out of earshot, Derrick stood and approached Whitney. Concern marred his handsome features, as no doubt, it did hers.

"Whitney," Derrick began softly. "I've got to tell you, I have a bad feeling about this."

The curious slant of his eyes, the firm set of his mouth and the skeptical tone in his voice all told Whitney that Derrick was talking about more than the misfortune of last night's occurrence. Arching a brow, she met his eyes with curiosity in her own. "I don't follow you...."

Derrick glanced over his shoulder, then back at her. "Whitney, I think it's time you faced some things."

Alarm caused her stomach to lurch. In response, she wrapped her arms around her belly. "What kind of things are you talking about?"

"How have things been here with Javar?"

Her face grew warm as she remembered last night. Until then, things had been pretty straightforward. She was staying here only until she was completely healed, and then she would get a divorce and move on with her life. Last night complicated the situation, but her plan was still the same. She finally answered, "Tense."

Derrick nodded, as though he expected that answer. "I have to tell you, Whitney. I wonder about Javar's true motives."

Intrigued, she asked, "What do you mean?"

"I mean," Derrick continued, pausing for effect, "I wonder if he's saying one thing but means another."

"You've lost me."

Derrick placed a hand on his hip, glancing around again. He stepped toward Whitney, closing almost all the distance between them. "The accident... I haven't had a chance to tell you, Whitney, but it's looking less and less like an accident. More and more like a hit-and-run."

Gasping, Whitney threw a hand to her mouth. "What are you saying? That someone deliberately hit me, then took off?"

"I can't say whether or not it was deliberate, but Forensics has found traces of black paint on your car. That indicates contact with another car. But now, in light of the attack on you last night, I have to wonder if the hit-and-run wasn't random."

"You mean, like someone's stalking me?" The very thought terrified her, chilled her to the bone. But if she were to be completely honest with herself, she had to admit that she knew coming back to Chicago might be dangerous for her. She was a hated woman here. All because of another accident on another Chicago road two years ago. Clearly, someone wanted her out of the way permanently.

"Not just someone," Derrick replied. "Someone who has a personal vendetta against you."

"Like Stephanie Lewis," Whitney said softly, wondering if Javar's ex-girlfriend would have gone as far as she had threatened.

"Actually, I was thinking maybe Javar."

"Javar!" Whitney exclaimed.

Derrick threw a nervous glance around the room, then placed a hand on Whitney's arm. He lowered his voice as he said, "Yes, Javar. Think about it. He has a motive for wanting you dead."

"That's crazy!"

"Is it?" Derrick challenged with the raising of an eyebrow. "You were behind the wheel in the accident that took his son's life. After that, he wanted nothing to do with you. Now, you return to Chicago and all of a sudden he wants to play husband? I don't buy it."

"Javar wouldn't want me dead," Whitney replied, confident of that fact. He may never forgive her, but he wasn't a killer.

"How can you be so sure? If you ask me, you being here in his house is just a convenient way of keeping an eye on you. You're vulnerable here, and he knows that."

Shaking her head, Whitney said, "No." She turned from Derrick and moved to the window, her thoughts whirling around like a tornado in her brain. Stephanie, yes. Other members of Javar's family, she could see that. Javar, never.

She heard the shuffling of Derrick's clothes as he moved up behind her. "Whitney, I'm sure this is hard to believe, but think of these facts. Who encouraged you not to call the police last night?"

Whitney spun around, tilting her chin upward to meet Derrick's gaze head-on. "Javar was worried about me. He didn't want to put me through the stress of answering questions in the middle of the night."

"How convenient," Derrick said, not bothering to hide his cynicism. "A little too convenient, if you ask me."

"Javar wasn't even here when the guy broke in. He came just as he was taking off. Javar chased him, tried to tackle him…."

"But he let him get away. Again, convenient."

"Why are you doing this?" Whitney asked, incredulous.

"Because I care about you, Whitney. Trust me, my cop instincts are telling me that something is wrong with this whole picture, and his name is Javar."

Her chest was so tight, it was hard to breathe. She felt like she was suffocating. She felt like she was going to be ill. Suddenly, her legs were as weak as jelly and her knees buckled.

Derrick reached for her and caught her before she fell. "Whitney?"

The moment of weakness passed, and she inhaled a deep, steadying breath. She pulled away from Derrick and walked to the armchair, where she took a seat. She asked, "Are you finished?"

Derrick seemed determined to make her believe his accusation. Squatting on the floor before her, he took both of her hands in his, staring at her with a worried expression. "I know this is upsetting, Whitney. But think about it. It makes sense."

"What makes sense?"

At the sound of Javar's voice, Whitney threw her gaze to the living room entrance. Derrick quickly rose to his six foot plus height. Gleaming onyx peeked out at Whitney and Derrick from narrowed eyelids, the intensity of the glare causing a chill to pass over Whitney.

"What makes sense?" Javar asked again.

"That the intruder probably won't strike twice at the same place," Derrick said, his own eyes uncompromising as he walked toward Javar. "Don't you agree?"

Whitney watched, waited. Suddenly, Javar's response to Derrick's question was extremely important to her. Her gut wrenched with guilt for even considering that Derrick might be right in his accusation.

"You're probably right," Javar said, but his voice lacked conviction.

Whitney commented weakly, "Derrick doesn't want me to worry."

Derrick turned then, flashed her a look that said he was worried about her. Whitney rose from the armchair and approached the two men. "Derrick, thanks so much for coming over here. I know you must be busy."

Derrick hesitated, seeming almost reluctant to leave. But after a few seconds, his lips curled into a smile. "Any time you need me, Whitney, you know where I am."

"Thank you. I'll see you out."

Placing a hand on his upper arm, Whitney led Derrick out of the living room and down the hallway to the foyer. A quick glance over her shoulder told her Javar was there, watching them intently.

Derrick noticed as well. He planted a chaste kiss on Whitney's forehead, said a quick good-bye, then exited, taking the front steps two at a time to his white Honda.

"He really cares about you," Javar said as Whitney closed the door.

"Yes," Whitney said, nodding. "He's one of my oldest friends."

Javar held his retort in check, not wanting to let his jealousy get the best of him. Man, when had he started feeling so insecure? *Since Whitney told me that she wanted a divorce,* he answered himself silently.

"I'm feeling tired," Whitney said, turning on her heel and heading for the stairs.

"Wait." Javar reached out and placed a hand on her arm. Her eyes widened as she looked up at him. She was either startled, or scared. He couldn't tell which.

"Javar…please."

Javar pinned her with a level stare. "Whitney, you can't avoid me forever. We need to talk."

"There's nothing to talk about."

"Not even last night?"

"Last night was—" she hesitated "—a reaction to the stress of the situation."

Sarcasm flashed in Javar's eyes as he stared down at her. "A reaction?"

"Yes," Whitney said quickly, thinking desperately to come up with more words. "I was afraid. I needed someone."

"Just someone?" Disbelief resonated in his voice.

Squaring her jaw, Whitney said, "I needed someone. You were there."

"Why do I find that so hard to believe?"

Whitney pulled her arm free, then started up the stairs. Javar followed her, darting in front of her path, blocking her avenue of escape. She could always retreat, but he would be there again, preventing her from getting away.

"Why are you doing this, Javar?" Whitney asked, heaving a frustrated sigh. "Last night doesn't change anything." But as she said the words, her heart was pounding wildly in her chest. Being so near to him, she felt the powerful pull to reach out and touch him. Biting her inner cheek, she fought the urge. Fought to keep her thoughts focused. Last night had been a distraction. Albeit an unforgettable one.

The muscle flinched in Javar's jaw. "Damn it, Whitney. Why are you being so cold? You made promises to me when we got married—"

"And you broke them, Javar. Every one of them. Like 'for better or worse.' Remember that vow?" She felt her eyes mist, and she paused, forcing the tears back. "I made myself clear in the beginning. I want a divorce. Stop this pressure. I'm not going to cave in."

"Fine."

"Thank you."

Javar moved out of her way, and Whitney started up the stairs. Nervous energy caused his hands to jitter as he watched her ascend quickly, desperate to get away from him. All reason fled his brain and he blurted out, "Guess Derrick will be there to help pick up the pieces."

Anger sparked in her eyes as Whitney turned to face him. Retracing her steps, she marched toward him, a hand outstretched. "This has nothing to do with Derrick. I already told you that."

"It's pretty obvious he has a thing for you. The fact that he doesn't like me makes things less complicated. For him at least."

"I'm sure Melody feels the same way," Whitney retorted, regretting the words as soon as they left her mouth. It was just that Javar was making her so angry with his holier-than-thou attitude, she couldn't help stooping to pettiness.

"Melody—"

"Called here last night," Whitney completed. "Oh, around midnight. A little too late for a business call, I'd say."

"Melody is my employee."

"I'm sure."

"Okay. That's it." Wrapping his fingers around her wrist, Javar led Whitney down the hall. If they were ever going to have a chance at a future, they had to clear the air on all the issues. But they would do it in private, not in the foyer where his butler, his housekeeper, or the nurse could walk by at any moment.

"Javar!" Whitney cried, trying to wring her arm free from his strong grip. "Stop this stupid Tarzan act, will you!"

Despite her protests, Javar led Whitney to his first-floor office. He didn't let her go until she was safely in the room. Turning, he locked the door behind them.

Whitney marched toward him, both hands firmly placed on the curve of her hips. "Let me out of here."

Javar looked down at his wife with uncompromising eyes. "Not until we've had it out, Whitney. And I mean everything."

Chapter 14

Whitney growled. Spun around and paced to the desk. Then she turned toward him again, her chest heaving with each angry breath. She spat out, "This is ridiculous."

"I meant what I said. We're going to clear the air once and for all. So go ahead. Ask me what you want to ask me. Whatever you want to know. I'll answer you honestly. Then let's put it behind us forever."

"This isn't going to save our relationship."

"Maybe not. But at least we can make some sort of truce and try to be friends."

Whitney walked to the mahogany desk and propped a hip against it. "I have nothing to say."

"Fine. I do." From the back pocket of his slacks, Javar produced the picture of Whitney and that man, his stomach clenching as he did. For some reason, he'd slipped the picture into his pocket this morning. Silently, he reminded himself that he really had no claim to Whitney, not if he didn't have her heart. Still, he wanted an answer. Flashing the picture before her face he asked, "Who is this?"

"Where did you get that?"

"That's not important. But I want to hear from you who he was, what he meant to you."

She flashed him a distasteful look. "I owe you no explanations."

"Were you involved with him?"

Through narrowed eyes, Whitney asked, "Did you have me investigated? Is that it?"

Javar sighed, suddenly overwhelmed with shame. He hadn't personally had her investigated, but by throwing this in her face, it was as if he had hired the detective himself.

"You did," Whitney stated, disbelief clouding her beautiful face. "God, Javar. Why?"

"I didn't," Javar told her, his tone softening. "But my mother, and my sister—"

Whitney huffed. "I'll bet. What did they tell you? That I was sleeping with him?"

Javar didn't deny the truth. He nodded. "Were you?"

"Javar! God, I've already told you the truth. I won't repeat myself."

"Whitney, they told me that this guy left you two hundred and fifty thousand dollars in his will."

Her chin held high, Whitney held his gaze. Her eyes said she wasn't about to dignify him with a response. But then her eyes lowered to the ground and she took a deep breath. When she lifted her eyes to his again, they portrayed such sadness that guilt gnawed at his conscience. Her shoulders sagged, and her eyes glistened with unshed tears. She said softly, "He was a friend. A very dear one."

"I gathered that much." Somehow he prevented his feelings of guilt from infiltrating his voice. "Did he leave you all that money?"

Whitney brushed at a tear that spilled onto her cheek. "His name was Leroy. He had AIDS. His entire family disowned him when they found out. We connected, but not in the way you think. We both worked at that youth center. We both had lost a lot. He wasn't about to leave his money to a family that disowned him because they didn't like the lifestyle he led." She chuckled mirthlessly. "Maybe they would have reacted differently if they had known that he'd received a chunk of money from his deceased lover."

"So he left the money to you because he had nobody else to leave it to?" Javar guessed.

"He didn't leave it to me. He made me executor of his will, but he left his money to the center. To the inner-city children he loved so much."

If it was possible to shrink away and disappear, Javar would have. As it was, he felt about two inches tall. Deep in his heart, he knew that this story was twisted—to make Whitney look like a scheming, conniving gold digger. Now he had the proof. God, he felt like an idiot for ever listening to his family's lies.

"I'm sorry," Javar said, knowing he sounded lame. But he *was* sorry. Sorry for being such a fool.

"And you wonder why I want a divorce," she whispered before moving from the desk and walking to the window.

Javar said nothing. What could he say to that? What he wanted to do was reach out and touch her, make her believe that they had a chance if they could get past all the obstacles keeping them apart.

"You don't even trust me." Turning, she looked at him pointedly. "Why would you want to stay married to me?"

Running a hand over his head, Javar groaned. "I do trust you. It's just that—"

"That you don't believe a word I say. Great basis for a marriage." Last night he had made love to her. Today, he was acting like she had betrayed him and was unworthy of his trust. For his family, everything boiled down to the fact that she had come from the Chicago projects and not from money. In Angela Jordan's eyes, that made Whitney a gold digger in the first degree. Forget love. To the Angela Jordans of the world, the Whitney Jordans of the world didn't understand the meaning of the word.

Whitney's head began to swirl again, making her weak. Last night's attack, Derrick's suspicions, Javar's lack of trust were all too much to deal with right now. Moving from the window, she strode purposefully to the door. But she didn't make it. On the way she suddenly felt too dizzy and she stopped mid-stride, falling to the floor as darkness overcame her.

"You stupid fool," the voice hissed. "What on earth is wrong with you?"

"She woke up," the second voice replied. "She screamed. I couldn't take any chances, so I got out of there. Then he came in…."

"I want no excuses. You've been paid to do a job. *Very* well, in fact. You *will* do it."

"I plan on it, but it's not as easy as I thought it would be. Do you still want it to look like an accident?"

"At this point, I just want her dead." Pause, then, "Any way you can do it."

Javar took a break from pacing the carpet when he heard the door to Whitney's room open. As the nurse stepped into the hallway, he reached her in two long strides. He asked, "Is she going to be okay?"

Elizabeth looked up at him, flashing a sheepish grin. "Yes. Her body is reacting to the fact that she's overexerted herself, and that she's stressed. I injected her with a sedative, something stronger than the stress pills, but it will help her get the sleep she needs."

"Thank you." From the moment she'd fallen into a heap on his office floor, Javar was worried. What had he been thinking, pressuring her to answer his questions? She had enough stress to deal with and he had only succeeded in making matters worse for her.

He took a step toward the door, but Elizabeth darted in front of him, stopping him from going any further. "Mr. Jordan, the best thing you can do for your wife is to let her rest. Believe me, she'll be out for hours. This is the perfect time to take care of some business, if you need to. You can see Whitney later, when she wakes up."

Elizabeth was right, he knew it. He couldn't help Whitney now. If she even woke up and found him in her room, she might get more stressed out. That thought caused a knot to form in his chest, restricting his lung capacity. He was her husband, yet he had caused her more stress than probably anybody else who had claimed to love her.

"Trust me," the nurse added.

Javar nodded. The nurse was right. This was the time to take care of some business.

Marching to his bedroom to grab his car keys, Javar knew exactly what he was going to do first.

Stepping into Island Breeze was like stepping out of the United States and onto a quaint Caribbean island. Located in downtown Chicago, Island Breeze was one of the few authentic Jamaican restaurants in the city.

The upbeat sound of reggae music played over the speaker system. Fake palm trees, complete with sand at their bases, were placed sporadically around the restaurant, giving the place a definite island feel. The spicy smell of jerk chicken and curried goat filled Javar's nose as waitresses clad in floral sarongs and bright tube tops hurried by with various Jamaican dishes loaded on trays.

He would bring Whitney here if it wasn't for the fact that Stephanie Lewis was one of the restaurant's managers.

Presently he stood, hands in the pockets of his khaki slacks, his eyes scanning the crowd. The assistant manager had promised to call Stephanie for him, and he now stood waiting for her to make an appearance.

When he saw her round a corner, he turned his back. The last thing he wanted her to do now was run from him. And he didn't want to cause a scene by going in there and dragging her out. But he would, if necessary. If she refused to talk to him.

Seconds later, he turned. She was steps away from him. When she recognized him, her eyes grew wide, startled, but she didn't turn and run. Instead, she continued toward him. "Javar. What are you doing here?"

His voice was deceptively calm as he said, "Stephanie, do you think I could see you outside for a moment?"

"I've got a restaurant to run...."

"This won't take long."

Stealing a glance over her shoulder, she said, "Okay."

As she took Javar's arm, leading him to the glass-enclosed foyer, Javar couldn't help thinking that he was surprised at Stephanie's cooperation.

She leaned against the wood paneling. "Okay, what's so important that you came to my workplace to talk to me?"

"Like I said, I'm going to make this quick. Did you have anything to do with the attack on my wife last night?"

Her mouth fell open, incredulous. "What?"

"You heard me. Not too long ago, you threatened Whitney, right in my home. Now, she's been attacked by someone who clearly meant to do her serious harm. I want to know if you had anything to do with that."

"Get a life, Javar. My world does not revolve around your precious Whitney."

He didn't really expect her to answer. But he wanted to show her that he meant business. If she had anything to do with the attack on Whitney's life, she would pay.

"Listen to me, Stephanie. And listen good. I don't want to see you anywhere near my house. I don't want to see your brothers anywhere near my house. I don't want to hear from my mother how I 'manhandled' you today. I want you to stay the hell out of my life and stay away from Whitney. Because if you don't, you'll have to answer to me. So if you had anything to do with what happened last night, forget about trying again. Got it?"

Stephanie's eyes glared pure hatred. But beneath the anger he could tell she was afraid. Which was exactly what he wanted.

"Got it?" he asked again, his voice rising.

"Go to hell," she snapped.

It was about as good as he was going to get, he knew, but at least he had the answer he wanted in her eyes. She wasn't stupid enough to mess with him when she knew he meant business.

Her lips twisted in a sour pout, she said, "I heard you."

"Good." He glowered at her, making sure his message was clear.

Then, without another word, he turned and walked away, all the while feeling the heat of Stephanie's indignant gaze burning a hole in the back of his head.

Somewhere, there was a phone ringing. Somewhere far off, out of her reach. She wished someone would answer it.

Whitney bolted upright, fighting with the cotton sheets that seemed to entrap her. Finally, she struggled out of their grip and reached for the phone beside her bed.

"Hello," she said, her voice sounding as groggy as her mind.

"Whitney?" That was her mother's voice.

"Mom," Whitney said in reply. Sitting up, she placed the phone in her lap.

"My God, you sound horrible. What's happening over there? I thought you were supposed to be getting better…."

"Hi, Mom. I was just sleeping. Gosh, what did that nurse give me?"

"I don't know. But you don't sound well at all."

The grogginess was starting to fade, but it still hovered in her mind, making her less alert. "I'm okay," she lied, remembering last night and the fact that she hadn't told her mother what happened. Telling her mother would only worry her beyond belief, and Whitney wasn't about to do that to her. "What's up with you? I called you a couple of times but you were nowhere to be found."

Her mother chuckled softly. "I'm taking the advice you've been giving me for years. I've been spending some time with Robert."

Whitney squealed, delighted. "And…?"

"And, it's been…nice. He's a sweet, sweet man. He knows the meaning of the word *gentleman,* that's for sure."

Whitney smiled into the receiver, matching the one she knew was on her mother's face. "Good. I'm glad to hear it."

Her mother's tone grew somber. "I'm sorry I haven't been to see you, but you know how I feel about Javar."

"I know. And don't worry. I'll be out of here soon, and back with you."

"Are things okay over there? Really?"

Whitney lied, "Mmm hmm. As good as they can be, considering everything."

"I don't like the way Javar is making you stay there. Like some kind of prisoner."

Think about it, Whitney. Javar has the motive…. The words seeped into her thoughts, making her shudder. Derrick couldn't be right, could he?

"I just hope Javar isn't trying to pressure you into getting back together with him," Whitney's mother was saying. "After the way he treated you, really."

The phone line beeped. "Mom, hold on a sec, okay? That's the other line." Whitney clicked over. "Hello?"

The sound of slow, heavy breathing filled her ear.

"Hello," Whitney repeated.

More breathing, along with unidentifiable muffled sounds in the background. Maybe street sounds. Perhaps a club.

"Who is this?" Whitney said, her voice rising with anger. She hated cowardly, spineless people who had to hide behind faceless threats and other immature mind games.

Click. The dial tone resonated in her ear. Because her mother was on the line, the caller I.D. did not display the second caller's number. As she clicked back over to her mother, Whitney's mind worked overtime. Was that a crank call, or something more sinister? Something like a warning that whoever wanted to hurt her wasn't finished yet?

"Who was it?" her mother asked, interrupting her thoughts.

"Wrong number," Whitney replied absently, hoping that was the truth.

"Well, honey, I won't keep you. You sound like you could use some more rest, and I want to make sure you recover quickly, so you can finally get on with your life."

"No, you don't have to go."

"Yes, honey, I do," her mother replied, a hint of playfulness in her tone. "Robert is taking me out tonight. And I want to make sure that I look my best. You know how it is."

"You'll look beautiful, as usual," Whitney told her, meaning every word. At forty-eight, her mother was gorgeous, and looked about ten years younger. She'd been without a man for too long, since her father had left her eight years ago for a younger woman. It had been a devastating event in her mother's life, but she had gone on. Her strength was remarkable, and Whitney only hoped that she could be half as strong as her mother in the coming years without Javar.

If she was doing the right thing, why did that thought hurt so much? There was a nasty lump in her throat, just thinking about the prospect of finally ending her marriage. It wasn't going to be easy, she suddenly realized. Maybe it would be the hardest thing in her life. But it was something she had to do. She couldn't live a lie anymore.

"…okay, honey?" her mother was saying.

"Hmm? Oh, well have fun."

Her mother hesitated a moment before she asked, "Whitney, are you sure you're okay?" Concern was evident in her voice.

"Yeah. I'm okay. Go on. Go get ready. Have a great time."

"Okay, honey," Carmen said. "Look, if you need anything…"

"I know, Mom. Love you."

"I love you too."

Whitney replaced the receiver and sat quietly for several minutes. The crank call had unnerved her, more than she wanted to admit. Or was it the fact that Derrick's suspicions still floated around in her mind, confusing her?

"Stop this," she said aloud. Just earlier today, she'd gotten angry with Javar for his lack of trust. She could not, would not, distrust him now.

Javar sat in his parked car, his cell phone at his ear. He listened to the rings of his mother's mobile phone, and after the fourth one, a recorded message came on. Angela Jordan's voice was smooth and cheerful as she instructed the caller to leave a message.

Javar did. He said, "Mother, Javar here. This is just a quick message. I know the truth about the pictures and the money. But then, you probably do too. Anyway, I want you to stop this plan of yours to sabotage Whitney. You're not going to influence me one way or another. I know you care about me, but you've got to let this go."

He flipped his phone closed, praying his mother would not only hear his message, but that she would really listen.

"What's wrong, Stephanie?" a pretty, dark-skinned waitress asked.

"Nothing," Stephanie snapped. "Don't you have work to do?"

The waitress recoiled as if physically stung, taking a few steps backward before she turned and hurried out of the kitchen.

Stephanie watched her go. Watched others come. All the while, she was seething. She needed an outlet for her anger. Javar couldn't come to her place of business and treat her like a bag of dirt. She couldn't let him get away with that.

Forget the restaurant. Turning, she marched to her office, her thick heels clicking on the orange tile floor. She slammed the office door shut, locked it, then dropped into the swivel chair. She grabbed the sleek black receiver of the phone and placed it at her ear, then began punching in the digits to her home.

The phone rang...and rang. *Why wasn't anybody around when she needed them?*

With her finger, she broke the connection, resting the receiver against her forehead. Maybe she could reach Kevin on his cell phone. Hopefully, he wasn't in the middle of a delivery.

She punched in the digits to Kevin's phone. After four rings, his answering service picked up. Angry, she dropped the receiver in its cradle and stood. What now? She was going to go crazy if she couldn't vent. And her brothers were the only ones who understood her feelings and agreed with everything she said. She could count on them.

She would try Keith's pager. He worked as a custodian at Northwestern and couldn't be reached by phone. But if he had his pager on him, he could go to the nearest phone and return her call.

Stephanie paged him, leaving the number to the restaurant instead of a voice message. That way, her brother would know immediately that it was her who had called.

Less than two minutes later, the office phone rang. Stephanie grabbed the receiver. Anxiously, she said, "Keith?"

"Steph, it's me. What's going on?"

"Javar, that punk, was here today. Getting in my face and

threatening me. I swear at one point I thought he was going to hit me, right here where I work!"

"Okay, Steph. Calm down. Where is he now?"

"He's gone now, probably back to Whitney. That's why he was here. To tell me to make sure we stay away from his precious Whitney. The woman who murdered my son. Hell, what if he comes back?"

"Don't worry, Steph. Javar won't hurt you. Kevin and I will make sure of that." He paused, then said, "We waited too long to deal with him, but we will now. And when we're done, he'll know never to mess with you again."

As Stephanie replaced the receiver, a smile tugged at the corners of her mouth. For the first time since Javar had made his surprise appearance, she released a long, satisfied breath.

No way, Javar couldn't treat her like a bag of dirt. He would see who had the last laugh.

Chapter 15

His heart racing, Javar ran from Whitney's bedroom down the spiral staircase to the first floor. Where was she?

A quick run through the first-floor rooms and he discovered that she wasn't in any of them. He didn't like this. The nurse had said that Whitney would sleep for several hours. God, had that sedative rendered her helpless against a second attack?

Retracing his footsteps, he ran back to the foyer and through the archway that led to the kitchen. Rays of sunlight brightened the kitchen, but Javar hardly noticed. His nape prickled with fear as he realized nobody was around.

He scurried to the floor-to-ceiling windows and looked out at the vast backyard. He caught movement out of the corner of his eye, and he looked to the south. Carlos was walking alongside the rosebushes toward the house.

Javar ran outside, down the concrete steps and onto the grass. He called, "Carlos!"

Seeing him, Carlos quickened his pace. "Mr. Jordan, is something wrong?"

"Yes," Javar answered, slightly out of breath from both worry and from having run through the entire house. "Whitney...I can't find her. She was supposed to be sleeping..."

Relief softened Carlos's features. He replied, "She's at the beach, sir."

"The beach?"

"Yes. She was heading there only a few moments ago."

"Thanks." Javar turned, heading to the concrete path that led to the beach. After what Whitney had told him yesterday, why would she even consider going to the beach alone?

He saw her sitting on *Lady Love,* with her back facing him and her feet dangling over the side. She wore black jeans that were rolled up to her knees and a pink tank top. Supporting her body with outstretched hands behind her, Whitney seemed not to have a care in the world.

Relief flooded him, allowing his heartbeat to return to normal. Whitney had always been strong-willed, and it didn't surprise him that despite her fears yesterday, she was out here at the beach again. Still, he wished she would keep a low profile until this whole mess with the attacker was resolved. Like Whitney, he suspected Stephanie, but until there was concrete proof, he couldn't be sure that she was the one who was actually behind the attack.

While he made no sound on the sand, Whitney must have sensed his presence for she suddenly whipped her head around, a startled expression stretched across her features. When she saw him, she visibly relaxed but said nothing, instead turning back and staring out at Lake Michigan.

A jolt of electricity attacked his stomach, spiraling through the rest of Javar's body. Whitney was a vision of loveliness. Even in jeans and a tank top, she was irresistible. Her smooth, honey-brown back flirted with him from beneath the material of her top, inviting him to taste of its sweetness again. And he wanted to. Like a moth drawn to a flame, Javar was drawn to Whitney, knowing he might get burned but not caring if he did.

She'd said sex for them last night had been a reaction to her distress. Well, reaction or no reaction, he wanted more of what she had to offer. She was like a drug, intoxicating, tempting.

The lake was calm today, gently lapping at the shore. No wonder Whitney was drawn here. It was peaceful, serene, calming. This was his property, yet he hardly made it out here. But then, he hadn't wanted to. *Lady Love* sat on his private beach, and just coming down here reminded him that Whitney wasn't in his life.

But she was here now. On *Lady Love.*

Javar slipped out of his shoes and socks, leaving them in the sand as he continued toward Whitney. When he stepped into the water, it was cold, and he quickly jumped backward onto the sand.

Whitney giggled. Looking up at him, she said, "Weren't expecting that, were you?"

A warm sensation washing over him at the sight of her smile, Javar smiled back. "No, I guess I wasn't."

An awkward silence fell between them, and Javar looked out at the water, watching as the gentle waves rolled toward the shore. He wished his life could be as rhythmic, normal, predictable even. Chaos and excitement were overrated.

He ventured into the water again, rounding the back of the boat to get at the tramp where Whitney sat. He slipped onto the boat beside her.

She didn't turn, but said, "It's so peaceful out here. That's what I love about it. So beautiful."

"It is," Javar agreed, staring out at the waves. With the sun shining brilliantly on the lake, it looked like it was sprinkled with gold.

"How often do you get out here?" Whitney asked. She turned

and faced him then. "Hmm? How often do you come down to this piece of heaven and just relax? Enjoy the beauty of nature that God has blessed us with?"

I would, if you were here, Javar said to himself. But he said, "Not very often."

"That's what I thought." She stretched a toe into the water, swirling it around. "When are you going to stop working so hard?"

"I have to work hard."

"You don't have to work as hard as you do. You can take on a partner. Maybe two. Your company is thriving. You've already proven to your mother that you're a success."

"This isn't about my mother."

Whitney flashed him a wry grin, saying she knew better. She knew that Angela Jordan hadn't approved of her son's desire to be an architect, as opposed to a doctor like his parents. But he had stood his ground and shown them that he could make a life for himself on his own, even paying back all of the start-up capital they had given him. Whitney admired Javar's fierce independence. But she wondered if that same independence hadn't left him incapable of giving and receiving love. Certainly, in their relationship, that had been the case.

Whitney said, "At the rate you're going, you're going to be dead of a heart attack before forty."

Javar shook his head, a smile playing on the corner of his lips. "I don't plan on dying anytime soon. You should be happy, I've actually taken a few days off. Since…your accident."

"I know. I also know that it must be hard for you. Staying away from work when it's so important to you."

"You're important to me too."

His piercing gaze penetrated her through to the core of her

being, and despite the heat, Whitney shivered. He wanted her, his eyes said, as clearly as if he had voiced the words. The crazy thing was, she wanted him too. There were residual feelings in her heart for this man, and she needed to get them out of her system before she went on. Maybe more nights like last night would give her enough physical satisfaction that she could walk away and keep her heart intact....

Goodness, she was crazy. She should be mad at Javar right now, but for some reason she felt strangely euphoric and couldn't be angry if she tried.

Looking at Javar, she sighed inwardly. She felt the pull to stay and give their marriage another chance just as strongly as she felt the pull to go and get on with her life. She wondered if it was this hard for other couples who broke up. What tomorrow would hold, she couldn't be sure. The only thing she did know for sure was that Javar had had nothing to do with the attack on her life. In his gaze she saw a hint of sadness mixed with warmth, but not hatred. And he would have to hate her to want her dead.

"About before," Javar said, interrupting her thoughts. "I'm sorry."

"I'm sorry too." And she was. For the events that had transpired to keep them apart. For the rift that was probably too wide to close between them. But Javar was right. They should at least try to be friends.

"Feel like going for a sail?" Javar asked.

The other times they had sailed on this catamaran, they had ended up in each other's arms, teasing each other with words of love. A couple of times, they had even made love on the boat's tramp under the moonlight. If she went out there with Javar now, she would lose all perspective. Lose all control, was more like it, she thought wryly.

"I really shouldn't," she finally replied, noticing the disappointment that flashed in Javar's eyes. "I need to…go in and…take my medication."

It seemed to pain him to do so, but Javar said, "Okay."

Javar stepped down into the water and stood before Whitney. "Let me help you."

He didn't wait for a response as he reached for her waist and scooped her up. His strong hands pressed into her back as she wrapped her own hands around his neck. The energy that passed between them was tangible and undeniable. She was still attracted to her husband.

God help her.

Carrying her past the water, Javar deposited her on the sand. But even as her feet touched the ground, she still kept her hands around his neck, her eyes locked with his. Her heartbeat accelerated as his warm breath fanned her forehead. She was weak now, too weak to resist him if he wanted to take her.

Looking down at her, Javar dragged his bottom lip into his mouth. Conflicting emotions warred on his face and Whitney held her breath, waiting, wanting.

Javar's Adam's apple rose and fell as he swallowed. Taking her hands from around his neck he said, "You better go."

It was like getting doused with a cold glass of water. Her desire fizzled as quickly as someone flicking off a light switch, and reason took over. "Yes," she replied softly. "Are you coming?"

"Actually, I'd like to stay here a while longer. Think."

"Okay." Turning toward the house, Whitney started off.

"Whitney?"

She turned, the familiar heat of longing starting to burn in the pit of her belly. "Yes?"

"How about dinner tonight? Here, at the house." He smiled weakly. "I'll cook."

It was at moments like this that she was most vulnerable. When Javar's full lips curled in a sincere, sexy smile. When she saw that he was being thoughtful of her feelings. During these times, it was so easy to remember why she had first fallen in love with him.

A sheepish smile playing on her lips, Whitney said, "Sure." But even as she said the words, she knew that she was walking into dangerous territory.

"Great," Javar replied, his lips growing into a wide smile. "Let's make it eight o'clock. In the dining room."

Nothing. Derrick slammed the file against his cluttered oak desk, then fell into the chair behind it. Absolutely nothing.

Bringing a palm to his face, he squeezed his forehead, as if that could force all the answers he needed into his brain. "Think," he said aloud. "Damn it, think!"

Derrick spun the chair around to face the desk and flipped the file open. Running his finger over the text of the pages, he scanned the contents for what must have been the hundredth time. The strongest evidence right now was the finding of black paint on Whitney's rental car. But without any idea *which* black car that came from, it was like looking for a needle in a haystack.

Then, there was Whitney's account of the accident, of the bright lights in her rearview mirror. But she couldn't identify even the type of car, so again, that information was useless.

Oh, there'd been witnesses. All of whom had been interviewed, but their accounts of the accident scene didn't hold water. Most had come to the scene after the fact and hadn't actually witnessed the accident, despite their helpful suggestions as to what must have happened.

He needed to get the proof soon. It existed, and he would find it.

He had to. Whitney's life depended on it.

Whitney shouldn't feel nervous about dinner with her husband, but she did. Standing before the mirror in her bathroom, her stomach fluttered as if it had a thousand trapped butterflies inside desperate to be freed.

Bracing her hands against the white marble counter, Whitney let her head fall forward. Why did the thought of spending an evening with Javar have her so stressed? She raised her head, staring at her reflection in the mirror. She knew the answer to her question. At least her heart did. Despite everything, she was falling for Javar again. Against her better judgment, she was tempted to give their relationship another chance.

Javar was trying, she knew. He was making more of an effort than she was. But did he really and truly forgive her for the accident? Could she ever forgive him for the way he had treated her after J.J. had died?

Whitney sighed. They had meant so much to each other once. And after last night…

"Last night was only sex," Whitney muttered to her reflection, but the peculiar gleam in her eyes told her she was lying.

Okay, so she was attracted to Javar. So the sex between them was fabulous. That wasn't enough to base a future on.

But it's a great start, the voice in her head told her. The voice that loved playing devil's advocate.

Till death do us part... That was part of the vow she had taken. If Javar wanted to make a genuine effort at repairing their marriage, could she really say no?

Eleanor Scherer drew in a deep, steadying breath as she climbed the steps of the police station. A bout of nervousness caused her stomach to tighten. Even now, she wasn't sure she was doing the right thing. When a surreptitious glance over her shoulder proved nobody was watching her, she continued.

Last night had been the worst. After the newspaper had failed to give her the answers she so craved, she'd been wracked with guilt. Finally, when she had fallen asleep, she dreamed of Harry, her dear, sweet, deceased husband.

He always knew the right thing to do. Harry, who was so courageous. Much more so than she. In a dream, he had come to her and told her to do the right thing.

And that's what she was doing now.

She hesitated when she saw all the hustle and bustle within the police station. Whispering a silent prayer, she forged ahead to the reception desk.

"I have some information," she blurted out to the receptionist behind the desk. "About that accident last week. It wasn't really an accident. Someone tried to kill that poor lady."

Chapter 16

Whitney stepped through the French doors into the mammoth dining room, immediately noting the dimmed lights and the two red candles burning at either end of the large mahogany dining table.

Flashing her a wickedly sexy, charming smile, Javar rose from the chair where he was seated and moved to the sideboard where a portable CD player lay. Moments later, the soft, seductive sounds of Johnny Gill filled the air.

Whitney's heart went wild. Her mind said she should turn and flee. Yet her feet remained firmly planted where they were, on the sparkling cherry wood floor.

Dressed in all black, with the first few buttons of his loose fitting silk shirt undone, Javar looked so sexy. Whitney couldn't help remembering other romantic evenings they had shared. More specifically, she remembered the time shortly after they'd been married when they were in this same dining room, and Javar had seduced her with his eyes. Instead of dinner, they'd feasted on each other, making love on the large dining table, and eventually in the bedroom. She couldn't look at the mahogany table without remembering the wonderful passion they had shared there.

She tore her gaze from the dining table and looked at Javar.

His nutmeg eyes had darkened to onyx, heated desire evident in their depths. Slowly, determination in his steps, Javar approached her.

Whitney's eyes took in the length of him. His long, lean body; the sprinkling of black curls at the opening of his silk shirt. He was still so incredibly handsome, so incredibly sexy. So irresistible.

When he was mere inches away from her, a shiver of desire snaked down her spine. With the bittersweet feeling, sanity crept back into Whitney's brain. Sexy or not, she couldn't do this. She couldn't stay here and get caught up in the past. She turned on her heel, determined to leave.

Javar grabbed her arm, and Whitney stopped. The feel of his long, strong fingers wrapped around her slender forearm caused her skin to tingle, and she remembered too easily the way he used to hold her when loving her. Remembered how wonderful last night had been. Knew she wanted to experience that again.

She felt his head nearing hers, felt the heat of his breath on the side of her face. Her knees almost buckled on the spot.

His face stopped moving when his mouth reached her ear. With a deep, sexy voice he murmured, "Don't go."

It figured, the moment he was about to leave the office and go home that his private line would ring. Grumbling, Derrick doubled back and searched for the phone among the files on his desk. When he found it, he lifted the receiver and brought it to his ear. "District Two, Detective Lawson speaking."

As he listened to the police officer on the other end of the line, Derrick's eyes grew wide with excitement. "You're sure? Wednesday, June twenty-sixth?"

"That's what she says," the officer from District Four replied.

"And you believe her? She doesn't seem like a flake?"

"It's hard to tell. But I'd say she knows something."

Derrick allowed himself to smile. This could be the break he was waiting for. "Where is she now?"

"She's sitting in an interview room. Seems real scared. I don't know how long she'll wait."

"I'm on my way." Hanging up the phone, Derrick grabbed his blazer.

Then, he ran.

A tremor of desire rocked Whitney's body as the sweet sound of Javar's voice vibrated in her ear. Memories of last night invaded her mind, exciting her. Sex had always been wonderful for them and she could easily fall into his arms again, if only for the comfort she knew loving him would bring. And the excitement. And the passion. God, she was tired of being so lonely.

She swallowed. Part of her wanted to run. She had left Javar, after all, and she'd had a good reason. She was afraid. So afraid of being hurt again. Because she had to admit that he had the power to do that, to break her heart, and she didn't know if she could deal with that kind of pain again. Last night could be explained away, but if she fell into her husband's arms right now, that could mean disaster.

But still her feet did not move.

"Dinner's in the oven."

He may as well have been speaking Chinese, her brain wasn't processing his words. She couldn't think, only feel. Looking up at him from what must have been dreamy eyes, Whitney stammered. "D-d-dinner?"

"Mmm hmm. I made barbecue chicken." But his eyes said, "Let's skip dinner. You're all I want."

"Oh, ch-chicken. That's what that, uh, smell is." God, she sounded pathetic! You'd think she and Javar had never been lovers the way her longing for him was now consuming her entire being.

"Take a seat," Javar told her. "I'll get the plates."

He backed away slowly, pinning her with a heated gaze and a beguiling smile. Her heart fluttered; her breath snagged in her throat. God, her mouth even watered, and she doubted it had anything to do with the spicy aroma of barbecue chicken!

When he finally disappeared, Whitney released the breath she'd been holding. She whimpered. How dare Javar—Johnny Gill! He knew how much she loved his smooth love melodies.

If she didn't know better, she'd say that Javar was setting her up to be seduced. Worse still, she hoped he was.

"Okay, dinner is served."

Whitney's head spun around at the sound of her husband's voice. As he carried the two plates of food into the dining room, she ventured toward the table, not wanting him to know just how frazzled she was. If he could seem unaffected by the sexual energy fizzling in the air, then she could at least pretend not to be affected by it either.

Javar placed one plate at the head of the table, and the other to its immediate right. The table could easily seat fourteen, but even Whitney conceded that the opposite end of the table would be too far away for an intimate dinner. Because that's exactly what this was.

"Let me get your chair," Javar said, gently brushing a hand over her shoulder as he moved behind her.

The gentle touch made her shudder. She drew in a slow, deep breath in an effort to quell her desire, but it was no use.

Javar pulled out her chair, and she sat. Her senses were extra-sensitive, for even as he pushed her chair beneath the table and his shirt lightly touched her skin, she found that utterly erotic.

It was Johnny Gill, singing about losing self-control, that had her losing all hers.

She concentrated on the food, trying to put Javar's alluring musky smell out of her mind. The chicken…looked like chicken, she mused. She concentrated harder. It looked like barbecue chicken, accompanied by rice pilaf and steamed broccoli.

Javar reached across the table and took her hand in his. She knew what was next. Whenever they dined together like this, he liked to hold her hand while saying grace. Closing her eyes, she bowed her head.

"Lord, we thank you for this food and pray that you bless it and make it good to our bodies. We also thank you for the gift of life…and love. Amen."

"Amen," Whitney whispered. Slowly she opened her eyes, noting that Javar still held her hand.

But it was only for a moment. He slipped his hand away, and immediately, Whitney's felt cold where it had only a second ago been warm.

Again, Javar seemed unaffected. Lifting the bottle of wine from the chilled carafe, he filled her wineglass with the rose colored liquid first, then his own. Zinfandel. Her favorite.

Javar lifted his crystal glass and twirled the stem between his fingers. Following his lead, Whitney lifted hers. His eyes held hers as he said, "To finding peace, and happiness."

He touched his glass to hers, clinking crystal against crystal. A soft *ping* sounded in the air. Even when he brought the delicate crystal to his lips and took a sip, his eyes never left hers.

Finally, he picked up the silver fork beside his plate and scooped up some rice.

Whitney couldn't seem to get her brain to let her do the same. It was working hard enough to keep her nerves under control.

Javar seemed to notice her reluctance, and his eyebrows drew together in a questioning look. "You're not hungry?"

"Hmm? Oh, yes. It just…looks so wonderful." *Okay, enough of being this pathetic,* she told herself. Picking up her fork, she spiked a piece of broccoli. She brought it to her mouth, popped it inside, then began chewing.

See? It's not that hard, her inner voice said.

The meal was actually very good. Excellent, in fact. The combination of spices Javar had used on the chicken had resulted in a tangy, spicy flavor that was simply delicious.

"You sure you didn't have Carlos help you with this meal?" she asked, playfully.

"No way. Hey, you know that I can cook. Or have you forgotten?"

She shook her head. "No, I haven't forgotten. Your culinary skills are still excellent, I see. This is a terrific meal."

"Thanks." His eyes crinkled as he smiled. "Wait until you see what I have for dessert."

"Oh, you have to tell me!" Whitney exclaimed. She loved dessert. She loved food, period. And Javar knew that.

Humor danced in Javar's eyes at Whitney's response. "You'll find out soon," was all he said.

They fell into silence as they ate the rest of the meal, Johnny Gill followed by Barry White provided the mood music. Everything was so romantic, so like the way Javar had been when they were first dating. Maybe that's why she had felt so nervous about tonight. If things didn't go well, there probably wouldn't be any other nights like this. There probably wouldn't be any more chances to make a go of their relationship.

And suddenly, she wanted that chance.

Javar told Whitney to stay seated when she offered to help him get dessert. Maybe the few glasses of wine she drank were clouding her sanity, but she found herself looking forward to what would come after dessert.

A little while later, he returned with a bowl of vanilla ice cream topped with cherries jubilee. "I admit I didn't make this," Javar said.

"It looks delicious," Whitney said.

"Here." Javar dipped a spoon into the bowl and captured some of the dessert. He held it in front of Whitney, but when she opened her mouth and moved her head forward, he pulled the spoon away.

He chuckled as Whitney's eyes grew wide. Then, slowly, he brought it to her mouth and pulled it away again.

"Javar! Stop teasing me!"

She was smiling as she said the words, and Javar felt a blanket of warmth wrap around his heart. He loved this woman. Had always loved her, even though he'd lost sight of that. But if he had learned anything, it was that love wasn't always enough.

Javar pushed the irksome thought from his mind, concentrating instead on feeding Whitney. This time, he allowed her tongue to flick out and taste the dessert before he slipped the spoon into her mouth.

"Mmm." Whitney both moaned and giggled, closing her eyes as she savored the flavor of the ice cream. Some of the melted dessert trickled down the side of her chin, and she brushed it away with a finger.

Javar couldn't help reaching out and touching the smooth skin of her chin, helping to wipe off the ice cream. Their fingers collided. The giggling stopped. So did Whitney's fingers, beneath Javar's.

She looked so beautiful, he wanted to lean forward, press his lips against her, taste the dessert on her mouth. He held his desire in check and spoon-fed her again.

"How is it?" Javar asked, though he didn't need to, given her earlier response.

"Absolutely heavenly," she replied, her voice husky. She took the spoon from him, dipped it into the dessert, then lifted it to his mouth. Like he had with her, she pulled the spoon back just before it could enter his mouth, teasing him. Bringing the spoon closer, she rotated it around his mouth, slowly, seductively. Javar couldn't help laughing, and Whitney did too when he surprised her by seizing the spoon in his mouth.

They continued the playful routine until the last spoonful. But instead of putting the dessert into her mouth, Javar trailed the spoon around the outline of her lips, leaving a path of melted ice cream as he did.

Whitney knew what was coming next. Wanted it. Leaning forward, she brought her lips to meet Javar's. When their mouths were a mere fraction of an inch from each other, he hesitated. Pulled back.

"Whitney," he said, his voice barely above a whisper. "I— I've missed you so much. You have no idea."

Whitney placed a palm on his cheek, relishing its warmth. "I do, Javar."

"This...tonight...it's not about sex. And it's not about old feelings. It's about..."

"Finding peace and happiness and love," Whitney said, completing his thought.

Javar nodded. "Whitney, I promise I'll change. Work less, whatever it takes. Just say you want me as much as I want you right now. That you're willing to try."

Whitney's heart stopped. Oh, she wanted to say yes. Wanted to so badly. But the thought scared her.

But she was also tired of being lonely. And without Javar, she certainly was lonely. Without Javar, she didn't know if she'd ever find the happiness she so craved.

She moved her fingers down the side of his jaw, over his chin, and finally to his lips. "I'm willing to try, Javar. But...I can't make any promises."

"No promises," he agreed. With a hand, he held her own against his mouth, kissed her fingers. His mouth felt cool against her fingers, and they tingled from his touch. The sensation spread down her arm and to the rest of her body.

Her eyelids heavy, Whitney looked up at Javar from lowered lids. Javar's eyes were clouded with desire. Slipping a hand behind her neck, he swept her hair aside, then braced the back of her head with his hand. Slowly, he drew her closer to him, closer, until their lips finally met in a sweet, sensual, glorious kiss.

His lips were cool and he tasted of vanilla, but he also tasted of something else. On his lips, she tasted passion and temptation, and as if she had waited for this moment all her life, she moaned into his mouth.

Passion ignited. Temptation consumed them like a burning inferno. Scraping his chair back, Javar rose, his lips still connected with hers. He wrapped muscular arms around her back, pressed her against him as if he couldn't get enough of her.

Javar's tongue urged her lips apart and slipped into her mouth, dancing with her own. Here, now, she wanted him, with Barry White crooning in the background. But what if Carlos or Elizabeth walked in and found them?

Javar must have read her thoughts because he broke the kiss and said, "Let's go to the bedroom."

The walk upstairs hand-in-hand seemed like it would never end. The hunger for her husband was overwhelming in its intensity, and it shook her to the core of her being. Never had she wanted anything as much as she wanted her husband right now.

He stopped outside the master suite, enveloped her in an embrace. Kissed her neck, her lips. Javar's muscular chest pressed against her soft breasts, and Whitney's nipples hardened in response. He fiddled with the door handle behind him, and the moment it opened, he swept her inside.

Javar's tongue delved into Whitney's mouth with urgency as his hands found the zipper at the back of her black dress and drew it all the way down. She pressed her buttocks into his hands, and he cupped them, squeezed them. Slipped his hand beneath her dress and felt the lacy trim of her panties.

Whitney wanted to feel him, too, and after undoing a few buttons she slid her hands beneath his silk shirt, running them over his chest, through the sprinkling of curls on his brawny flesh. She found a small, taut nipple and squeezed, then leaned forward and flicked a tongue over it.

Javar moaned, a deep rumbling in his chest. Gripping her by the shoulders, Javar pulled Whitney up to meet his lips. He nipped, sucked, trailed his tongue to her earlobe.

When his tongue found one of her most sensitive spots, Whitney whimpered. After their lengthy separation, they still knew how to please each other, how to turn each other on. In his arms, she felt right. Felt like she belonged. Felt like she had come home.

They came together like desperate lovers, lovers who had been denied too long. Their passion was like a thirst that couldn't be quenched. They clung to each other as they loved wildly, not wanting to let go of the new bond they had found. Together, they moved in a sensuous rhythm all their own, one that brought them to a height as great as the stars.

And when they had loved until they could physically love no more, they lay breathless in each other's arms. Words weren't necessary to make what they had shared any more special. So there were none.

Javar's slick body snuggled against hers, Whitney fell asleep, a feeling of contentment wrapped around her heart like a blanket of warmth.

Chapter 17

Javar awoke with a start. Glancing beside him, the rumpled but flat sheets told him that his worst fear had come true.

Whitney was gone.

Javar rolled onto his back, heaving a long-suffering sigh. He wouldn't go after her. Not this time. If, after last night, she didn't want to be with him this morning, if she wasn't ready to attempt a reconciliation, then he didn't know what else he could do. He had given her everything last night, heart and soul.

A soft, lingering moan interrupted his thoughts. Lifting his head, Javar strained to identify its source. Silence rewarded his efforts, and he wondered if he had imagined the sound. But seconds later, he heard it again.

It was coming from the ensuite bathroom.

Whitney.

He threw off the covers and sprang from the bed, charging into the bathroom. There he found Whitney huddled on the floor beside the toilet. In one quick stride he was at her side on the floor. One touch on her clammy skin and it was obvious she was trembling.

His heart ached for the pain she was clearly suffering. "Whitney…sweetie."

She looked up at him, her eyes round and gleaming with

tears. "Javar, I feel awful." She coughed, then quickly poised herself over the toilet. The coughing ceased. She slapped the toilet seat and slid back onto the white marble floor. "I wish I could just puke and get it over with!" Soft sobs fell from her lips. "It hurts. Oh God, it hurts."

Javar rose and darted to the sink. He turned on the brass cold-water faucet, then grabbed a hand towel and slipped it beneath the cool water. In moments he was back at Whitney's side again, pressing the damp towel against her forehead, over her face.

It happened then. Whitney's chest heaved as she succumbed to a coughing fit. Bracing her hands on the toilet, she leaned over the bowl and vomited. And vomited again.

With one hand, Javar rubbed her back and with the other kept the wet towel against her face.

"Why is this happening?" Whitney asked. "I'm supposed to be getting better."

Javar jumped to his feet. "Let me call the nurse."

"No," Whitney said, a hint of panic in her voice. "Don't leave me."

"Okay," Javar conceded, lowering himself once again. "What do you want me to do?"

"Help me…help me back to bed."

Wrapping an arm around her, Javar lifted Whitney from the floor. He helped her to the bedroom, where he laid her on the bed.

He said, "Stay here. I'm getting Elizabeth."

Whitney clutched her stomach and moaned in response.

Minutes later, Elizabeth was there, handing Whitney a glass of water. "Drink this," she said.

Whitney moaned, as if it was too painful to sit up. Javar

lowered himself onto the bed beside her and helped her up. "C'mon, Whitney. Drink this. It'll make you feel better." To the nurse, he said, "Why is she in so much pain?"

"It has nothing to do with the accident," the nurse replied, her tone confident. "This kind of violent reaction indicates to me that her body is reacting to something she ingested. She could have a case of food poisoning. What did she eat last night?"

"I ate the same thing she did, and I'm fine," Javar replied, his tone dismissive.

"Indulge me," Elizabeth said.

Javar cast a sidelong glance at Whitney, who was lying back on a pillow, moaning softly. His stomach churned at the sight of her, and the air gushed out of his lungs. Turning back to the nurse, he said, "We had barbecue chicken, rice, uh, some broccoli. A little wine…"

"Wine. There we go."

Javar's brow wrinkled as he stared at Elizabeth quizzically. "What? I don't get it."

Elizabeth strolled toward Whitney, stopping when she reached the bed. Looking down at her, Elizabeth asked, "Whitney, did you take your medication last night?"

Whitney's eyes fluttered open. "Yes," she replied, her voice almost a whisper. "Sometime…in the night."

Elizabeth sighed and faced Javar. "Mixing medications with alcohol can cause this kind of reaction."

A wave of guilt washed over Javar. This was his fault. "Well, what now?"

"Has she vomited?" Elizabeth asked.

"Yes," Javar replied.

"Well, that's the best start. She has to get the toxic mix out of her system. Other than that, lots of water. Maybe some hot tea will help her feel better."

"Okay. I'll make her some. Stay with her, please."

Javar felt like kicking himself when he went downstairs. How could he have been so stupid? His only concern had been of creating the perfect romantic evening. It was just that Whitney had seemed so much stronger, he'd forgotten about the fact that she was still taking medication.

He was so flustered from seeing her in such anguish that he could hardly find the teapot, let alone boil hot water. But finally he did. He prepared a pot of mint tea. When he was a child, that's what his mother used to give him for an upset stomach.

Minutes later, he was back upstairs, the tea and a mug on a tray. But as he entered his bedroom, Elizabeth shushed him.

"She's sleeping," she said. "Thankfully."

"Okay." He blew out a relieved breath. "Good. That's good." Javar walked to the sitting area in his room and placed the tray on the coffee table. He continued to the large window, cocking a hip against the ledge. Outside, the sun was shining brilliantly in a cloudless sky, but Javar couldn't appreciate the moment.

He dragged a hand over his face, stretching the skin as he did. "I was going to go in to work, but now…" He fell silent.

Elizabeth sauntered over to him and placed a delicate hand on his arm. "Go," she urged. "This isn't serious. Whitney will be fine. You go to work."

"But Whitney's in pain…."

"She's sleeping, and trust me, she'll feel a lot better when she wakes up. I'll be here with her, like you're paying me to be."

Her closemouthed smile was sincere, and looking at her upturned lips, Javar felt a modicum of relief. "I feel so helpless. Like there's nothing I can do for her."

"You're doing plenty. But if you want to do something else, why don't you help me transfer the equipment from her room to this one. I don't want to disturb her sleep."

Javar nodded absently, still deep in thought. Finally, he met the nurse's gaze. "Okay. Okay."

After he had helped transport the blood pressure machine and medicine tray, Javar eased himself onto the bed beside Whitney. Lifting her hand to his mouth, he pressed his lips against her soft, warm flesh.

The nurse had assured him that Whitney would be fine, but he couldn't shake the feeling of foreboding. Like a premonition that told him he might lose her.

Maybe that was because every time he saw his wife in pain, he remembered his guilt. And that guilt made him fear losing her, the way he had lost his son. Initially, he hadn't wanted J.J.—hadn't welcomed the news that Stephanie was pregnant. Involved with his work, he hadn't been excited about the prospect of becoming a father. And he hadn't wanted to be tied to Stephanie for the next eighteen years, minimum. If anyone was a gold digger, it was Stephanie. She hadn't wanted J.J., only the money Javar could give her. Stephanie had made that clear when Javar had refused to marry her, and to spite him, she'd dropped J.J. on his doorstep, giving him custody.

He had loved his son, while resenting Stephanie. And now, J.J. was gone. Whitney didn't understand that the reason he had been so angry after the accident was because he couldn't come to terms with *his* guilt, not hers. Sure, he'd initially blamed her, but when he'd had time to cool down, the residual blame had been for himself. That's why it was hard talking about the accident, even now, because the burden of guilt was still there, like a lump lodged in his heart.

Now…he couldn't lose Whitney. But he'd turned his back on her after the accident, almost the way he'd turned his back on J.J. before he was born. Would he lose her, too, as further punishment for his faults? He silently prayed that that would not happen.

The nurse was there then. "Javar, you should go. Let her rest."

Solemn, Javar rose. A worried expression marring his features, he turned and faced Elizabeth. "Are you sure she'll be okay?"

"Javar…"

He turned and faced Whitney the moment he heard his name fall from her lips. Her eyes still closed, she shifted on the bed, seemingly getting comfortable.

"Javar…" she repeated, and this time her lips twitched with a smile.

Thank you, God. He realized now that he hadn't wanted to leave her until he'd had a sign, something to give him some hope. Now, he had the sign he needed.

"Mr. Jordan," Elizabeth said, a bright smile gracing her lips. "Whitney will be just fine."

What was the point in coming to the police station to make a statement if you weren't going to make yourself available for questioning? Derrick wondered as he held the receiver to his ear. Ever since he had arrived at District Four last night and found that the witness had left, Derrick had been trying to reach her. After unsuccessful attempts last night, he decided that he would call her first thing in the morning. Yet Eleanor Scherer, a possible witness to Whitney's hit-and-run, wasn't home.

Still holding the receiver to his ear, Derrick grabbed his mug of lukewarm coffee, downed it in three gulps. As he replaced the mug on his desk, his patience paid off. The phone on the other end of the receiver stopped ringing, and an elderly woman's breathless voice said, "Hello."

Derrick sat forward, placing his elbows on the edge of his desk. "Hello. I'm trying to reach Eleanor Scherer."

"This is Eleanor Scherer."

Derrick silently mouthed, *Yes!* To her, he said, "This is Detective Lawson of the Chicago Police Department. I understand you came by the station yesterday."

"Oh yes. Yes, I did."

"You witnessed a car accident on the evening of Wednesday, June twenty-sixth. Is that correct?"

"Mmm hmm. Yes. It was awful, what happened to that poor woman. Is she all right?"

Derrick nodded, although it was only for the receiver's benefit. "Yes, Ms. Scherer. Thankfully, she's going to be fine."

Eleanor exhaled a gush of air into the receiver, sounding relieved. "I was so worried. After what happened that night…" Her voice trailed off.

"I know." Derrick paused, then continued. "Ms. Scherer, I would really like to get together with you to speak about what you saw."

"Well, okay. I don't know if I'll be of much help, but I felt I should come forward. Tell you what I saw."

"Believe me, I'm glad you did." Soon enough, he would figure out if she was one of the flakes or if she was actually a credible witness. But for now, she was his only hope. "Can you come to District Two this morning? You can give me your statement…."

"Certainly, Detective. What time?"

"How about eleven o'clock?"

"Okay. I'll be there."

"And you know the directions to the station?"

Eleanor chuckled. "Oh yes. Chicago's my hometown. I was born and raised here."

As Derrick ended the call, he allowed himself to hope. Eleanor Scherer *would* be the witness he had longed to find. Whitney's life depended on it.

Javar's Italian dress shoes sank into the soft gray carpet as he stepped off the elevator on the thirtieth floor. A large brass sign that read "Jordan & Associates" hung on the cream-colored wall, beneath which an arrow pointed to the right. Javar turned in that direction, toward the several feet of smoked glass that led to his company's offices. The double doors were propped open, and Hilary Robbins, the company's receptionist, sat at a large oak desk. Dressed in a simple but elegant pale blue dress, the mocha-complected woman looked impeccable.

She smiled up at Javar as he approached her desk. "Hello, Mr. Jordan. Great to see you."

"Morning, Hilary," he said, returning her smile. He didn't slow his stride as he rounded the corner, and walked down a long hallway that led to his office at the opposite end of the floor. There was an extra pep in his step, that was certain. And it all had to do with Whitney. Now that he knew she was going to be okay, he allowed himself to remember the incredible night they had shared. The night was much more than great lovemaking. Last night symbolized a new beginning for them.

A few of the draftspersons seemed surprised to see him, but pleasantly so. He nodded and said hello to everyone he passed, feeling somewhat foreign in his own company. He'd been away from work less than a week, yet it seemed like years.

He quickened his pace, anxious to get to his office and sort through his notes before heading to the boardroom for the ten o'clock meeting with his associates and project architects. As he neared the mahogany doors of his office, he saw Melody standing at the corner of her desk, a black man in baggy jeans and a loose fleece shirt partially obstructing his view of her face. Intrigued, Javar's forehead furrowed. Casually dressed, the man didn't look like the type who usually frequented his office. He and Melody were huddled so closely together, as though sharing some secret, that Javar became curious. Was this man a friend of Melody's?

Melody's eyes were lowered, fixed on some spot on the ground, so she didn't notice Javar approaching. But the moment she lifted her gaze and saw him, her eyes grew wide, clearly startled. Then her hand was on her visitor's chest, pushing him away as she said something to him in a hushed tone.

The young man retreated, turning his head as he did. Cold, hard eyes met Javar's, but only for a moment. The man quickly averted his gaze then shuffled past Javar. Javar's neck swiveled with the man's movements, watching him as he walked away. Narrowing his eyes, a peculiar feeling snaked down his spine.

"Good morning—"

"Who was that?" Javar asked, spinning around to face Melody.

His administrative assistant looked like a deer caught in a car's headlights with that bug-eyed, somewhat dazed look.

Javar was even more curious at the reaction. His forehead furrowed as he looked her. "Melody?"

"I'm sorry. Uh, he's a…a friend. Um, he dropped by to say hi."

Something wasn't right about the way Melody was acting.

Javar eyed her with curiosity for a few moments longer, but when she turned and started shuffling papers on her desk, a voice told him not to press her. Not yet, at least. Maybe the man was a new boyfriend and she was flustered only because she didn't expect to be caught taking a few minutes from her work to talk to him.

Javar cleared his throat. "Did everyone receive the message about the meeting?"

"Yes." Melody moved around to her black leather chair, standing before it. "I sent memos to everyone and I was told they would all be there. Except of course Andrew Feldman, who is in Minneapolis."

"Great."

"Oh," Melody said, waving a hand in front of her as if to magically stop him from walking away. "Your brother called."

Javar arched a brow. "Khamil?"

Melody cracked her first smile of the morning. "He's your only brother, isn't he?"

"What did he say?"

Melody sat. "He asked when you were going to be in New York, so I told him the dates. Then he said for you to call him."

"Yeah, I'll give him a call," Javar said, more to himself than to Melody. "Any other messages?"

Melody passed him a stack of pink message slips a couple of inches thick. "Only these. Oh, and Althea Harmon called. A few times." She raised an inquisitive eyebrow, her eyes imploring Javar to offer her an explanation.

He didn't, because he owed her none. "Thanks, Melody."

As he started off, Melody asked, "How's Whitney?"

For an instant, Javar was startled. Then he remembered that the last time he had called the office he'd told Melody about

Whitney's accident—including the fact that she was staying with him—because she'd asked several questions....

"My wife is recovering nicely," Javar replied, tossing in a smile for good measure.

Melody's smile was clearly forced.

If he didn't have a successful business here, Javar might consider packing it in and moving with Whitney to another state. Start fresh. Maybe that would give them the advantage they needed.

No, he decided as he stepped into his office. What he and Whitney needed was time. Time to sort through their problems and build a strong marriage that would withstand any external pressure. Somewhere along the line, they had lost sight of that. But last night, they had recaptured some of the love they'd once shared.

"Enough about last night," he said aloud, lowering himself into his soft leather chair. He was here to work, and work he would.

Javar spent time going through his phone messages, returning the urgent calls and leaving the others for later. Along with the agenda for this morning's meeting, he went over his schedule. The trip to New York next week was something he couldn't put off. He needed to present the interior design team he had hired to the Domning Corporation, the client for whom he was designing a ten-story hotel just outside of Manhattan. He anticipated no problems, but still, this trip could not be avoided. It would only be a day. *Maybe Whitney could come with me,* he thought, a smile lifting the corners of his mouth.

After he finished with his urgent business, including having Melody confirm his travel reservations, Javar headed to the boardroom for the meeting. As he neared the opened double doors, he heard voices.

"...hear she's had a breakdown. That this second accident sent her over the edge...." That was Kathleen Morrison's voice, one of his project architects.

"Poor thing." That voice belonged to Peter West, Javar's chief draftsperson.

"Apparently, that's why he's got her there. Who knows how long she'll be *recovering,* if she ever completely does."

"Wonder why he's calling this sudden meeting?"

These were people Javar worked with, people he had known to be utmost professionals. Yet they were stooping to rumors and gossip. Whitney's name hadn't been mentioned, but he wasn't stupid. That's who they were talking about. Javar wondered where this spiteful gossip had originated. Melody?

"I can only hope—"

Clearing his throat, Javar stepped into the large boardroom and made his presence known. Kathleen stopped mid-sentence, her face flushed with embarrassment when she saw that Javar was standing in the doorway. Peter flashed a smile at Javar, but the guilty look in his eyes could not be camouflaged.

"Morning, everyone," Javar said, his tone exuberant. He moved to the mahogany boardroom table, taking his place at its head.

Curious eyes from other staff members, and even his associates bored into him as he opened his leather folder and slipped a pen from his tan Armani blazer. Though he felt like throttling Kathleen and Peter for gossiping, he smiled instead. He wanted to get this meeting over with as soon as possible so he could get back to what was really important: Whitney.

At least Richard Sanders, the newest project architect he had hired, had been sitting at the table going over a file instead of participating in gossip. Clearly, Richard had his priorities straight—like being loyal to the boss.

Javar looked around the table. All his project architects were present: Robert Dick, Alex Carlisle, Diane Williams, Kathleen Morrison, Richard Sanders. Peter West sat quietly at the far end of the table. Jerry Price, his junior associate, occupied the second seat down from Javar on the right. The only two missing from this meeting were Harvey Grescoe and Duncan Malloy, his senior associates.

Flicking his wrist forward, Javar eyed the time on his Rolex. Two minutes after ten. He pushed his chair back and was about to rise when the two senior associates came hurrying into the room.

"Sorry," Harvey mumbled as he closed the doors.

Javar tapped his Mont Blanc pen on the table as the two men sat down on either side of him. When they were seated, he opened the meeting. "Good morning, everyone. I know a lot of you have questions about my absence, and I'd like to end the speculation by taking a moment to answer those." Lowering her head, Kathleen averted her eyes. Peter was concentrating on the folder before him. Javar continued, "By now, you all must know that my wife was in a car accident a week ago. Well, I'm happy to report that her injuries were not serious and she is now recovering nicely. I've been home with her, supervising her care, but should be back to work full-time next week. To those of you who sent cards and flowers, my wife and I thank you.

"Now, on to company business." Javar looked down at his notes. First, he wanted to know how the final inspection of Simmons's House, a quaint bed-and-breakfast that had been completed a year earlier, had gone. "Alex, how was your trip to Springfield?"

Alex replied, "Simmons's House is doing very well. Everything is up and running smoothly. The property is in topnotch shape from the shingles on the roof to the plumbing. And the Simmonses are very happy. So far, the bed-and-breakfast is doing extremely well."

"Great," Javar said. It pleased him when his clients were happy, and when the loose ends of a deal were finally tied into a nice bow. He turned his attention to Kathleen. "What's happening with the proposal for the industrial mall in Oak Park?"

"I've narrowed the contenders down to five construction companies," Kathleen explained. "Maybe later, you can look over the list and their packages...."

"Yes, I'll do that." As sole principal, it was Javar who made the final decisions as to which companies they hired.

"I have some news," Harvey announced, and Javar's eyes went to him. "In your absence, I hired an interior designer for the motel in Gary, Indiana. Janine Kelley and her firm."

Javar nodded. "I know her work. It's impressive."

They spoke a while longer about more company business. Peter West and his technicians had successfully completed the blueprints for the Manning Group, a company that had hired Jordan & Associates to design a low-level apartment complex in St. Louis. Jerry Price had finished the miniature model of a strip mall for another client, and both the model and the budget were ready to be presented to the client, who would be flying into Chicago in a week.

Javar closed the meeting, scheduling a second one for that afternoon with his associates so that they could go over more intricate business matters. Everyone filed out of the room, heading back to their respective jobs. Everyone except Richard Sanders.

"Mr. Jordan..."

Javar turned and looked into Richard's face. "Yes, Richard?"

"I've come up with a proposal budget for the Li bid. Do you have time to go over it?"

The Li bid. Running a hand over his hair, Javar groaned inwardly. He was still debating forgetting the whole thing, given the time commitments he already had. If he submitted his proposal, if he landed the bid... Would that leave any time for Whitney?

There was a solution, Javar realized. There had always been a solution. However, he hadn't wanted to consider it before. But if he was going to make an honest effort at saving their relationship, now was the time.

"Give me the proposed budget," Javar told Richard. "I'll go over it and let you know what I think."

In his mind, he was thinking of the stunned faces of his associates when he made his surprise announcement this afternoon.

When Whitney awoke, she was momentarily startled to find herself in Javar's bed. But only briefly as memories of last night quickly flooded her, making her lips curl. Javar...last night...everything had been incredible.

"Whitney."

The nurse's voice shocked her, and Whitney whipped her head to the right. Elizabeth dropped a novel and rose from the sofa in the sitting area, a bright smile on her face as she walked toward her.

Whitney's mind scrambled to find a reason for the nurse's presence. After a moment, it did. She remembered being as sick as a dog this morning.

"How are you feeling, Whitney?"

She sat up, gathering part of the down comforter in a bundle on her lap. "I'm a lot better, thank you."

"That's good."

"Where's Javar?"

"He's at work," Elizabeth replied. "I'm not sure when he'll be back."

"Hmm." She felt a strange pull in her stomach. She had been awake only a few minutes, and already she wondered when Javar would be home.

"Can I get you anything? Some soup?"

Whitney looked up at Elizabeth and smiled. "Soup sounds great." Glancing at the digital clock beside the bed, Whitney exclaimed, "Holy!" It was after two in the afternoon. "I slept that long?"

Crossing her arms over her chest, Elizabeth chuckled. "Clearly your body needed the rest. I'll go get some soup. Is chicken-noodle okay?"

Whitney nodded, and Elizabeth scurried off.

When the nurse was gone, Whitney threw the comforter off her body and got out of the bed. Thank God she felt better; this morning she didn't know if she would survive. All right, she conceded, that was an exaggeration, but still, she'd felt so sick that she was surprised she now was out of bed and walking around.

She moved to the window and looked outside at the front lawn. It was a gorgeous summer day. A light breeze flirted with the leaves of the maple trees and, even though the windows were closed, she could hear the joyful songs of the sparrows among the trees' branches. She wished Javar were here, that they could do something together on this beautiful day. Maybe even take *Lady Love* for a sail.

Whitney stretched, and her stomach fluttered from a residual bout of nausea. A thought invaded her brain for the second time in two days, the thought that maybe she was pregnant. Whitney quickly dismissed that thought. It was absurd…wasn't it?

The nurse returned with the food and a smile. On the tray was a large bowl of chicken-noodle soup, beside which was a spoon and a package of crackers. The nurse brought the tray to the sitting area where Whitney was, and Whitney quickly took a seat on the black leather sofa, sinking into its softness, accepting the tray from Elizabeth.

"Thanks," Whitney said, reaching for the spoon.

"Do you need anything else?"

Dipping the spoon into the delicious smelling broth, Whitney replied, "No, I'm fine. Thanks a lot."

"Okay. I'll be downstairs if you need me." Elizabeth walked a few steps, then stopped suddenly and turned around. "Oh, let me get your antibiotic. The infection may be gone, but you have to finish the prescription as a precaution."

"Of course."

It was when Elizabeth handed her the pill cup that the thought hit her. Whitney bristled at the implication, fear crawling down her spine. No, it couldn't be.

"Whitney…your water."

Whitney's head flew up. She saw Elizabeth holding a glass of water. "Uh…no. I mean, I'll take it with the soup. I don't want to mix hot and cold."

Elizabeth stood above her, waiting.

"The soup's a bit too hot," Whitney explained. "I'll take the pill in a few minutes." At Elizabeth's skeptical look, Whitney added, "I promise."

When Elizabeth left the room, Whitney dropped the yellow-and-white capsule into her hand, staring down at it as her brain worked overtime. Then, she went to the nurse's stand and opened the other two bottles that contained the painkiller and the capsule for stress. She thought hard.

Last night, after she had taken the stress medication and painkiller, she had awoken feeling wretched. She had also awoken feeling nauseous the morning before—after having taken these pills.

Since the accident, she hadn't felt one hundred percent. The pills were to aid her in her recovery, but now that she thought about it, she couldn't be sure whether the pills had helped her at all.

A weird, numbing sensation swept over Whitney, causing her legs to wobble. She stepped backward until her legs hit the mattress, and it was then that her knees buckled. She fell onto the king-sized bed. Suddenly, she was horrified.

Was somebody trying to *kill* her?

"No," she said aloud, rising. The antibiotic in hand, she marched back to the sitting area and her soup. She was expecting too much too soon. Despite the fact that the accident hadn't been life threatening, she was hardly as healthy as she had been before. She had to expect bouts of nausea, headaches, and any other type of temporary discomfort until she recovered completely.

Deciding that it was the stress of the accident that had her conjuring such crazy ideas, Whitney tilted her head back, opened her mouth, and dropped the pill inside.

She couldn't believe that Derrick was right. There was no way that Javar wanted her dead.

Chapter 18

"What?" Duncan Malloy asked, his eyes wide with shock.

"You're kidding." Harvey Grescoe added, seconding Duncan's surprise.

Harvey and Duncan both sat on the opposite side of Javar's desk. Javar crossed one leg over the other as he sat in the swivel chair in his office, then eyed each one in turn squarely. "I couldn't be more serious."

"But…" Duncan began. "Why now?"

A smile played at the corners of Javar's mouth. "Everything's okay on the home front, if that's what you're asking. I've just…had a sudden change of heart."

Harvey swallowed, apparently speechless.

"Well?" Javar said. "Does your reaction mean neither of you is interested in a partnership?"

"Of course I'm interested," Harvey replied. "I've been interested in a partnership for a long time. You know that. It's just that I'm…surprised. This seems sudden."

"It's something I've been considering for a long time. And since I couldn't narrow my choice down to one of you, I decided to offer you both a chance at a partnership, and see who'd be interested." He shifted his gaze to Duncan. "Duncan?"

"I'm definitely interested, but I'd like to think about it."

Javar nodded. "That's fine. I don't expect an answer today." He inhaled deeply. This hadn't been as hard as he had anticipated. And instead of dreading the thought of taking on a partner or two, Javar now felt a sense of relief. He had worked with both Harvey and Duncan for years. He valued their talent as well as their friendship. And it was time he rewarded them with the offer of a partnership in Jordan & Associates.

Minutes later, Javar rose and saw both men to the door.

"Thanks again, Javar," Duncan said. "I'll let you know."

"I look forward to your decision," Javar said.

As Duncan stepped into the hallway, Harvey lingered. When Duncan was out of earshot, Harvey turned to Javar and said, "Better get ready to change the company signs. I don't need any more time. I accept your offer of a partnership. Whenever you want to go over the details, I'm ready."

Javar and Harvey shook hands, then agreed to wait for Duncan's decision before discussing the actual business of the partnership.

When Harvey was gone, Javar walked back to his desk, a wry smile lifting his lips. He hadn't thought about the company name, and thus the signs. No longer would the signs and stationery read Jordan & Associates. They would read Jordan, Grescoe & Associates, or Jordan, Grescoe, Malloy & Associates. Yikes. His baby would no longer be only his.

But despite the thought, Javar smiled. Whitney would definitely approve.

"C'mon, Whitney," Derrick said into the receiver. "Pick up."

"Hello?" It was the butler, Carlos, who answered the phone.

"Carlos," Derrick said. "This is Derrick Lawson calling again. Is Whitney awake yet?"

"Yes, she's awake, Mr. Lawson. But she's not here."

"Not there?" Derrick's stomach fluttered. "Where is she?"

"She stepped out. She may be down by the beach."

Derrick blew out an irritated breath. "All right," he said, his mind contemplating what to do. "Look, can you tell her that I called? That she should call me as soon as she gets in?"

"Certainly, Mr. Lawson," Carlos said.

Derrick broke the connection, then sat silently for a moment. In his moment of repose, the door to his office burst open.

"Lawson," a male voice said in an urgent tone.

Derrick spun around and faced Detective Kurt Mulvany. His face was contorted with both anxiety and excitement. Instantly, Derrick was on his feet, knowing that something was wrong.

"Lawson, remember Whitfield?"

Derrick nodded. How could he forget Whitfield? He was one of the biggest drug dealers in the Chicago area, but he somehow always evaded the law. "What about Evan Whitfield?"

"Just got a call from an informant. Says he knows where Whitfield hides his stash and can lead us to him. The captain is sending us both out on this one. C'mon. We've got to move now."

Adrenaline surged through Derrick's veins as he grabbed his light blazer and followed Kurt out of the office. Both men— every cop in the city of Chicago, in fact—had wanted to nail Whitfield for a very long time.

Duty called now, which meant that Derrick wouldn't be able to talk to Whitney until much, much later.

Curtis Nichols paced the beige tile floor in the garden room of his home, listening to the hollow sounds of his wife Michelle and his mother-in-law Angela's laughter. He, Michelle, their son, Michael and his parents-in-law had just finished dinner. The dinner had been a reunion of sorts, as Marcus had just returned from a week's conference in Miami for plastic surgeons.

It should have been a cheerful event, and yes, there was laughter. However, not even the laughter and smiles could cover the sour atmosphere.

As if he sensed Curtis's thoughts, Michael came running into the room. He wrapped an arm around his father's leg.

"Where's Uncle Javar?" Michael asked, surprising the adults in the room. "Why isn't he here too?"

Michelle's laughter stopped cold. Her eyes grew wide. As she held her daughter on her lap, Sarah's small hand grabbed at Michelle's lips but Michelle didn't seem to notice. "Michael," Michelle began, "I already told you Uncle Javar couldn't make it tonight. He's busy."

"But why?" Michael demanded. "He always comes over." When Michelle said nothing, Michael looked up at Curtis.

Curtis shrugged. Before bending to lift his son, he cast a perturbed glance at Michelle. She had gone too far when she gave Javar that stupid ultimatum. The fact that Javar wasn't here now, when he usually would have been, wasn't lost on his young son. And the circumstances under which Javar was not here was what made this evening seem so fake.

Curtis could not, however, tell Michael that his mother had ordered his uncle to stay away unless he did what she wanted. Instead, he said to Michael, "You know your uncle can be very busy sometimes. I'm sure he would be here if he could be."

"But I never got to show him my new police car last time. I want him to see it."

"I know," Curtis said, hugging his son close. Over Michael's shoulder, he glowered at Michelle, who was watching him intently. "But why don't we call him a little later, see if he can come by sometime soon?"

"Okay," Michael agreed. Curtis returned his son to the floor and watched as he ran out of the room.

Walking toward Michelle, Curtis said, "Do you see what you're doing? It's not right, you keeping Javar away from our son. Michael's the one who's suffering."

"What's going on?" Marcus asked, his forehead wrinkled as he looked from his wife to his daughter to his son-in-law.

Curtis arched a brow, challenging Michelle to tell her father the story.

Michelle rolled her eyes to the ceiling and frowned. "I…" she began. "I told Javar that as long as Whitney is staying at his place, not to bother coming over here."

"Aw, for goodness' sake!" Marcus uttered, rising from the wicker chair. "He's your brother, Michelle. Why would you do that?"

"Because he's letting a murderer stay in his house!" Michelle retorted.

"We tried to talk to him," Angela added, rising to meet her husband. "He won't listen to reason."

"I'm gone a week and this is what happens?" Marcus asked, disapproval showing on his face.

"What was I supposed to do? Tell him that I approved of Whitney coming back into his life?"

"You were supposed to keep your nose in your own business," Marcus replied, pinning her with a level stare.

Sarah started to fuss, and sighing, Michelle rocked her, trying to calm her down. She said, "Dad, you don't understand."

Angela placed a hand on her husband's arm. "Of course we love Javar. But after we showed him the pictures and he chose to ignore our concerns, we felt—"

"Those stupid pictures," Marcus said scathingly. "When are you going to get over this?"

"Our son is going to ruin his life if he reconciles with Whitney!" Angela's tone rose an octave.

Sarah burst into tears. Groaning, Michelle stood and walked out of the room.

Curtis followed her, leaving Angela and Marcus arguing in the garden room. When he caught up with Michelle, he said, "Sooner or later, Michelle, you're going to have to grow up. Accept responsibility for your life, not Javar's. He's a grown man. As much as you may not like his choices, you cannot meddle in his life."

Shaking her head, Michelle rolled her eyes again. "He's my brother," was all she said before she stalked off.

Curtis grunted when she was out of sight. Her obsession with Whitney Jordan was taking its toll on their relationship. He guessed it was also taking a toll on Angela and Marcus's relationship, as well.

Javar was at the door of his office when the phone rang. He stopped mid-stride, contemplating whether or not he should answer it. It was already early evening, although he had only planned on spending half a day in the office. Taking care of business had taken more time than he had hoped.

Turning around, Javar decided to answer it. Another message on top of the ones he already had was not what he needed. He grabbed the receiver. "Javar Jordan."

"Ja-va-r!" his brother almost sang. "What's up, guy?"

Javar's face broke into a smile. "Hey, Khamil. I'm fine, man. Fine."

"You still coming to New York?"

"Oh yeah," Javar replied, his tone saying that the possibility of doubt didn't exist. "I'm leaving Sunday night."

"I was beginning to wonder. I hadn't heard from you...."

"I know. I've been busy. Real busy."

"So I hear. What's this about Whitney being back in town? Mom told me she's staying at your place."

Javar groaned. "Don't start. I've heard enough from Mom and Michelle, man."

"Start what?" Khamil asked. "I'm not going to give you a hard time. You know me better than that."

Nodding, Javar said, "Yeah, I do." His brother had let him live his own life, and if he had any opinions of what Javar did or didn't do, he kept them to himself. "It's just that Mom's driving me crazy here. I can just imagine what she told you about Whitney...."

"Hey," Khamil said, cutting him off. "I'm a lawyer, remember? I'm good at sifting through fact and fiction. Don't sweat it."

"Sorry," Javar said.

"So, how is Whitney? She had an accident?"

"Mmm hmm." Javar explained to his brother the events of the past week, and how Whitney was now recovering.

"That's great to hear." Khamil paused. "So, does this mean that you two are getting back together?"

"Is that what Mom told you?"

"Forget what Mom said. I'm asking you."

Javar exhaled deeply. Despite last night, it was too soon to say what would happen for him and Whitney. He said, "We're seeing if we can work things out."

"All right, J." The enthusiasm in Khamil's voice indicated his sincerity. "I always did like Whitney."

"You mean you've gotten over the fact that she chose me over you?"

"Hey…" Khamil protested, but there was laughter in his voice. "I *let* her choose you. I had too many other women, remember?"

Javar chuckled. "Sure. Speaking of women, anyone you're serious about yet?"

"I'm serious about my work."

"All right," Javar said, agreeing not to press his brother. One of these days he would find the right woman. "Sooner or later you're going to have to give up that playboy lifestyle."

"Just let me know if things don't work out with you and Whitney," Khamil said, mirth in his voice. "She still as fine as she used to be?"

"What do you think?" Javar asked, a vision of Whitney's long smooth legs invading his mind. His wife was fine all right.

"You better hold onto her, J. You may not luck out and find a woman as hot as her a second time."

"Really?" Javar said, lowering himself into his swivel chair. He had a feeling this conversation would not end soon.

"Hey, you can't help it if you weren't born with my good looks." Khamil was laughing.

"Remind me not to invite you to our second wedding," Javar said. But he was laughing too.

Whitney sensed Javar's presence before she actually heard him. Sitting up on the lawn chair, she turned around.

Javar's lips curled into a smile as he looked at her. "Hi."

Relief washed over Whitney. Seeing Javar now, smiling at her with such warmth, she knew that he cared deeply for her. He was not responsible for any attack on her life. "Hi," she said softly.

Javar walked toward her. He held his blazer over a shoulder, and the top buttons of his cotton shirt were undone. As usual, he looked incredibly sexy. As usual, she felt drawn to him.

When Javar reached the lawn chair, he reached out and stroked Whitney's face. "I take it you're feeling better."

"Yes," Whitney replied, holding Javar's hand against her face. Bringing his hand to her lips, she kissed his warm flesh. A hint of his musky cologne flirted with her nose, and Whitney took a deep breath, trying to ignore the feeling stirring in the pit of her belly.

Javar squatted, then leaned forward and planted a soft kiss on her lips. "I missed you today."

"I missed you too." Whitney smiled. "How was work?"

"I did something that I think you'll be proud of."

"What?" Whitney asked, her eyes narrowing as she flashed Javar a quizzical look.

"Today, I offered my senior associates a partnership in the company."

"What?" Whitney's mouth fell open.

"I said, I offered my senior associates a partnership in the company."

"You're not kidding?" Whitney asked, stunned. Jordan & Associates meant everything to him, and before, Javar hadn't even wanted to consider giving up his majority share.

"No," Javar said, "I'm not kidding. I meant it when I said that I wanted us to save our marriage. Having a partner or two will mean less work for me, and more time to spend with you."

Touched was how Whitney felt. Genuinely touched. And dare she think it, loved. She framed Javar's face with both hands. "Javar...I know how much your firm means to you."

"But you mean more." Rising, Javar changed the subject. "There's still some time before the sun sets. How about going down to Grant Park? The Taste of Chicago is still going on."

Grabbing Javar's extended hand, Whitney stood. "Oooh, you sure know how to tempt me." The Taste of Chicago was an annual affair, where culinary delights were served by more than seventy of Chicago's finest restaurants. Whitney and Javar had gone together for the two years that they were married, feasting on the extraordinary food as well as enjoying the various entertainment. Looking down at her white sundress, Whitney asked, "I don't have to get changed, do I?"

"No," Javar replied, wrapping his arms around Whitney and pulling her close. "But I do."

"You look fine. Great, actually."

"But a little too formal for where we're going." He kissed her forehead. "Want to come with me upstairs while I change?"

Whitney chuckled. "Oh, I don't think so. We could get... delayed."

"Some delays are good," Javar said, cocking his head to the side.

Whitney pulled out of his embrace. She was tempted.... But no. They should go out. Sex was only one part of their relationship, and they had proven that they were still compatible that way. They needed to prove that they could spend an evening together, doing something as a couple and still enjoy each other's company. "Go get changed. I'll meet you in the foyer."

Biting on his lower lip, Javar flashed Whitney a mock-dejected look. Whitney smiled wryly, then shook her head. Javar turned, jogging into the house.

It took him only minutes to change and meet her downstairs. "Want to take the BMW?" Javar asked.

"Your car was found?" Whitney asked.

"Mmm hmm," Javar replied. "I've got it back and it's as good as new. I'm itching to take it for a spin."

"Sure," Whitney said.

Javar slipped his hand into hers, holding it tightly. "It's in the garage."

They shared a look then, a look that said they'd both like to forget the festival and go back upstairs. Whitney swallowed, trying to shake the feeling.

"Let's go," Whitney said to Javar. She giggled as he groaned.

Seconds later, they were at the garage door. Javar closed the door, then entered the security code into the box on the wall. While he fiddled with that, Whitney walked ahead of him into the garage.

Her eyes roamed the four-car garage, but she didn't see the black BMW. The red Viper was there, the gold Jeep Cherokee, the black convertible Mercedes, and...

Whitney froze. Her eyes focused on the car that looked familiar, the one that looked like the BMW Javar loved. But the car she saw was not black.

It was the same 700 series BMW, she suddenly realized, but it was now a deep maroon as opposed to its original black.

Oh, God, Whitney thought, her stomach fluttering as the implication of the realization hit her.

God help her.

Chapter 19

Whitney's eyes darted to Javar's. "You...you painted your car?"

Javar nodded. "Yeah. You don't like it?"

Whitney walked down the garage steps, moving to the BMW. With a fresh paint job, the car looked brand-new. She didn't know why, but an icy numbness spread through her body, enveloping her in fear.

Yes, she did know why. Because Derrick had said that the car that had run her off the road was black. Because Javar's car was conveniently reported stolen around the time of her accident. And now, it had a new paint job, erasing any possible evidence.

"Whitney? Is something wrong?"

When Whitney looked up, Javar was already at the driver's side door, while she stood at the base of the steps, immobile. "Why?"

"Why what? Why'd I paint the car?"

Whitney nodded.

"Because there was some damage to the car when the police found it. I figured I may as well paint the whole thing a new color. I was getting tired of black, anyway."

"Oh."

"Well, are you coming, or are you waiting for me to come and get you?" Javar raised a suggestive eyebrow.

Okay, Whitney. Don't drive yourself crazy. This doesn't mean anything. And it didn't. This was just a coincidence. The new paint job had nothing to do with her accident. Deep down, she would know, feel it in her gut if Javar was lying to her. She wouldn't be falling for him…again.

Javar was walking toward her. "You *do* want me to come get you?"

Whitney shook off the unpleasant thoughts and forced a smile just before Javar wrapped an arm around her waist and drew her close. He planted a soft, lingering kiss on her lips, and despite Whitney's thoughts of only a few minutes ago, her body warmed.

Javar broke the kiss and locked eyes with hers. "We can always go back upstairs…."

Shaking her head, Whitney said, "No. I'm looking forward to the festival." Slipping out of his embrace she moved to the car. "Let's go."

Their bellies full—his anyway—Javar and Whitney now lay side by side on a blanket in Grant Park. Each propped up on an elbow, they looked out at the water and the various boats sailing in the distance.

There was a light breeze that played with Whitney's raven hair, tossing it every which way. Whitney had long given up trying to keep it down. Whether a perfectly styled coif or a wind-messed one, his wife still looked gorgeous. With her facial bruises covered by makeup, she looked healthy. The only sign that she'd been in an accident was the bandage on her forehead.

Javar reached out, stroking her face. Whitney's eyes turned to him, and she smiled.

"I want to ask you something," Javar said.

"Go ahead."

"Next week, I have to go to New York on business. I was wondering if you'd come with me."

Whitney's eyes narrowed. "Really? You never used to—"

"I know, but that was before." He trailed a thumb over her lips, tempted to replace his finger with his mouth. "I have to leave Sunday night, and I was thinking that if you went with me, we could check out a Broadway play, or something. Oh, and Khamil says he'd like to see you."

"Khamil... How is he? I haven't seen him in ages."

"He's fine. Busy."

"Does he have a girlfriend yet?"

Javar rolled his eyes playfully. "You know Khamil. He's like Teflon when it comes to women. Nonstick."

Whitney chuckled. "Yeah, I remember. New York…"

"It would only be for a day. I'd really like you to come with me."

"And while you're doing your business?"

"You'll be getting pampered. How does a day at the spa sound?"

Whitney moaned. "Mmm. That sounds wonderful."

"So you'll come?"

"Do I look like I'm crazy? Of course I'll come!" She laughed.

Whitney's enthusiasm was addictive. Javar laughed along with her, leaning close and pressing his nose against hers. God, it felt so good just sitting around like this and laughing. How had he ever lost sight of the important things in life? What good was working hard, earning a ton of money, if you couldn't share it with someone you loved? If you couldn't laugh or love?

As Javar pulled back and stared into the eyes of his wife, he knew without a doubt that their days ahead would be filled with plenty of laughter. And love.

* * *

"Grandma Beryl!" Whitney exclaimed, jumping up from the quilt on which she sat. "What are you doing here?"

Grandma Beryl cocked a slim hip as she flashed Whitney a mock-indignant look. "I have to eat, too, now don't I?"

Chuckling, Whitney drew Grandma Beryl into her arms for a big, warm hug. "It's so good to see you, Grandma."

Grandma Beryl squeezed Whitney tightly. "Whitney, dear. Oh, I'm so happy to see you up and around." Slipping out of Whitney's arms, Grandma Beryl moved to Javar and wrapped her arms around her grandson.

"Hey, Gram," Javar said, stooping to kiss her on the cheek.

"Javar, I can't believe you're here watching a sunset, instead of at the office."

Javar chuckled, then flashed Whitney a look that said his new outlook on life was because of her. Turning back to his grandmother, Javar said, "Well? Aren't you going to introduce us to your...friend?"

Grandma Beryl turned back to the elderly gentleman who was with her, placing a hand on his upper arm. The man was probably just shy of six feet, and slim. His skin was the shade of a shelled almond, and his eyes were a distinct green. "Henry," Grandma Beryl began, a hint of pride in her voice, "meet my grandson, Javar. The one I've told you so much about."

"Good things, I hope," Javar said.

Henry chortled. "Of course." He extended a hand and Javar shook it. "Pleased to meet you, Javar."

"Likewise," Javar said.

Grandma Beryl smiled as she waved a hand in Whitney's direction. "And this is Javar's beautiful wife, Whitney."

"Hi," Henry said, shaking Whitney's hand firmly.

"Hello, Henry," Whitney said, a bright smile on her lips. To Grandma Beryl, she raised a curious eyebrow. Grandma Beryl averted her gaze, seeming to blush. Whitney would have to ask her about Henry later. He seemed nice enough, still extremely attractive despite a few wrinkles, and judging from the way Grandma Beryl was holding onto his arm, he was someone special.

"It makes me so happy to see you two out, *together,*" Grandma Beryl said. "I take it things are going well?"

Whitney glanced up at Javar and found him looking at her too. His eyes seemed to ask her if she was going to answer the question or if he should.

Javar took the lead, nodding as he returned his gaze to his grandmother. "I'd say…things are going very well. Wouldn't you, Whitney?"

Forced to answer his question on the spot, unwanted questions and doubts suddenly invaded Whitney's mind. She wanted things to work out, and they seemed to be…. Smiling shyly, she replied, "Yes. Things are definitely looking up."

Grandma Beryl squealed with delight. "Oh, I knew it. I'm so happy for you. A love like yours doesn't come along twice in a lifetime…" She paused, then cast a sidelong glance at Henry. "Unless you're extremely lucky."

So Henry was a *very* special man in Grandma Beryl's life. As Javar pulled Whitney closer, she smiled at the thought that her grandmother had found happiness again. Grandma Beryl definitely seemed to be in love. If anyone deserved to be happy, it was Grandma Beryl.

Would she find that kind of happiness again, Whitney wondered fleetingly. With Javar? They were getting closer, but…

"What were you two doing?" Javar asked, interrupting Whitney's thoughts.

"We were going to walk along the beach," Grandma Beryl replied. "Burn off some of the calories we just ate!"

"Feel like company?" Javar asked.

Grandma Beryl's thin lips lifted in a wide smile. "You bet."

"What a day, what a day," Derrick said, plopping himself on the plush sofa in his small living room. Evan Whitfield, Chicago's biggest cocaine dealer, was now behind bars.

His heart still beat rapidly from the excitement of the hunt, then the catch. Having found Whitfield's "warehouse," Derrick and five other detectives were able to catch Whitfield red-handed. Twelve kilos of cocaine had been seized, with a street value of more than three hundred thousand dollars.

Derrick threw his head back. His sense of victory was minimal. Yes, he was thrilled that Evan Whitfield was behind bars, but there was another pressing concern. Whitney. He needed to tell her about the latest development in her case.

Raising his head, Derrick glanced at the wall clock. It was eleven thirty-three. It was late, but he still had to chance calling her. In the long run, despite her doubts now, she would thank him. Javar was a dangerous man.

Derrick reached for the phone on the end table. Cradling the receiver between his ear and shoulder, he punched in the digits to Javar's home.

The phone began to ring.

When Whitney and Javar stepped into the house through the garage, the phone was ringing.

Javar's forehead wrinkled with speculation. "Who's calling here this time of night?"

Whitney shrugged. "Hmm. I wonder. Aren't you going to answer it?"

Javar looked down at her, his eyes getting a shade darker as his desire pooled in their depths. "Nah."

"But it could be important."

"If it's important, whoever it is will call back," Javar said simply. "Preferably tomorrow." As he pulled Whitney into his arms, he made it clear that he had other things on his mind. Things much more important than answering the telephone.

Whitney swallowed as the flame of passion stroked her body. After a wonderful evening, she now wanted to be with Javar. No intrusions.

"Okay," she whispered, slipping her hands around his neck. "Let it ring."

Chapter 20

Soft, whimpering sounds lured Javar out of sleep. Bolting upright, he realized that Whitney wasn't beside him.

The bathroom light was on. Jumping out of bed, Javar ran into the ensuite bathroom, the sense of déjà vu hitting him as he saw Whitney naked on the floor, crouched over the toilet…again. The stench of vomit filled the air. What was happening to her, Javar wondered as he ran to her side. The distressed moans coming from her lips pained him as though someone had stuck a knife in his gut.

"Whitney." He felt so helpless as he looked at her and the vomit that covered the floor. "Oh, God."

She wrapped an arm around his neck and sagged against his chest. "Javar. I feel…"

"Shh. I'm here now. It's going to be okay." A reaction to alcohol, his foot. Last night, Whitney hadn't had a drop of alcohol. If she was in this kind of pain, then there was something else wrong besides mixing alcohol with her medications. He was taking her to the hospital. God, what if she had internal injuries from the accident?

"Hang on, honey," Javar said, bringing her to the bed so that he could put some clothes on her. "I'm going to get you some help."

* * *

An hour after Javar had brought Whitney to Rush North Shore Medical Hospital, he paced the floor in the waiting room, anxious to see the doctor. Dr. Adu-Bohene, whom he would have preferred to deal with, was not working this early in the morning, so Javar had no idea who was supervising Whitney's care.

Hearing footsteps, Javar turned around. A tall, lanky gray-haired man approached him. Dressed in a white lab coat with a picture ID on his lapel, the man was clearly a doctor.

"Mr. Jordan?" the physician asked.

"Yes." Javar nodded. "Yes, that's me. How is my wife?"

"Your wife," the doctor announced, a grim expression etched on his pale face, "is suffering from an opiate overdose."

"Wh- Overdose? What are you talking about?" Javar asked.

"Morphine," the doctor said, explaining the type of overdose in layman's terms. "Urine tests determined that your wife is suffering from a morphine overdose. That's what's causing the nausea."

"My God."

"We've got her in a room, and we're administering the antidote, naloxone, through an intravenous tube to counter the effects of the morphine. She can't go home yet."

Javar was too stunned to speak. An overdose? How, why? What on earth was going on?

The doctor spoke. "Do you know anything about this?"

Javar flashed the older man an incredulous look. "Of course not. My wife…she was recently in a car accident, and she's been under the care of a nurse." He paused, ran a hand over his face. "None of this makes sense. The nurse was regulating her medications. As far as I know, she wasn't even taking morphine."

"Not even for pain?"

"No," Javar said, resolutely. "She was taking Tylenol for pain. Penicillin for an infection. And a stress tablet, lora—"

"Lorazepam," the doctor completed. "You say she had a nurse supervising her care."

Nodding, Javar said, "Yes." His breaths were shallow as he faced the fact that this wasn't a nightmare. Somehow, Whitney had suffered a morphine overdose. "Is she going to be okay? I have to know."

"Yes. She'll be fine. A morphine overdose usually causes nausea, grogginess, a sense of euphoria sometimes, but it can also lead to death. Your wife is very lucky."

Javar grunted, squeezing his forehead with a palm. "Damn it! Why is this happening?"

"I'd like to speak to the nurse, verify the medications she gave Whitney."

Javar swallowed. Tried to relax. "Okay. Sure. You can call her. She should be home." He gave the doctor the number. "If she doesn't answer the phone, let me know. I can...go wake her."

"Thanks."

The doctor turned to leave, but Javar darted toward him, placing a hand on his arm. "I...can I see her?"

"Not yet, Mr. Jordan. But the moment we've stopped the antidote, someone will come out and get you."

After being assured that Whitney would be asleep for hours, Javar decided to return home and question Elizabeth himself. It didn't matter that it wasn't quite six a.m. He stormed down the hallway to her room, pounding on the door when he got there.

Elizabeth opened the bedroom door moments later, holding the two open ends of her pink robe closed. "What's going on?"

"Why don't you tell me?" Javar asked, stalking into the bedroom.

The nurse flashed him a perplexed look. "What are you talking about?"

"Whitney is in the hospital," Javar announced, glowering at her. "She's apparently overdosed on morphine. Care to explain that?"

"Morphine? I have no idea—"

"Don't you? You're her nurse."

"Yes," the nurse said, taking a step backward. "But I didn't give her any morphine. She was taking Tylenol for her pain."

"That's what I thought," Javar hissed. "Until I found out otherwise."

The nurse seemed flustered, speechless.

Someone was trying to poison Whitney. Trying to kill her. The realization knocked the air from Javar's lungs. God, how had this happened? Had the nurse been paid off by somebody to switch Whitney's medication? She had to have been, because she didn't know Whitney personally. But who? Stephanie?

"Who paid you?" Javar asked, anger causing his voice to rise.

"I...I work for you, Mr. Jordan."

Javar took a threatening step toward the nurse whom he had trusted. The nurse who had betrayed him. "Stop lying to me! Who paid you to poison my wife?"

Tears glistened in Elizabeth's eyes. "I...I don't know what..."

Unable to look into the woman's face, Javar turned around and walked to the bedroom door. "I want you out of here Ms. Monroe. I'll give you an hour."

Then he was out of her room and making his way to his bedroom. There, he collected the bottles of medication that Whitney had taken on a daily basis since the nurse's arrival. Javar pocketed the three bottles, then headed back downstairs. He was going to get to the bottom of this, if it was the last thing he did.

Whitney awoke slowly. Her eyelids were heavy and hardly wanted to open, but sensing unfamiliar surroundings, she opened them wide and looked around.

She was in a hospital. Again. Why?

Glancing to the right, she saw Javar's form by the window, where the early morning sunlight was beginning to light the sky. She called to him. "Javar."

Javar whipped his head around, moving to Whitney's bed in three quick strides. "Hey," he said, smiling. "You're finally awake."

Whitney looked at Javar through narrowed eyes, knowing that with his cheeriness he was trying to avoid the reason that she was here. Well, she would get the answers she needed. "Javar, why am I here?"

Pain crossed over his features, and Javar released a hurried breath.

"What is it?" Whitney asked, her heart racing. "What?"

Javar lifted her hand into his, staring into her eyes. "Whitney, the reason you've been feeling so sick, vomiting...is because you've suffered a...a morphine overdose."

"*Morphine?* I haven't been taking morphine."

"You thought you weren't, but apparently, you were. I brought in your medications, and the doctor has confirmed it. The stress tablet and the painkiller had both been tampered with, consisting of morphine instead of what you thought you were taking. The penicillin was the only pill not tampered with."

She heard his words, but her brain didn't want to accept what he was actually saying. "Wh-what do you mean, tampered with?"

"I fired the nurse," Javar said in response. "I figure someone, maybe Stephanie, paid her to switch your medications." Javar sighed. "Gosh, I don't know."

No. Whitney shook her head, unable to believe Javar. Oh, God. Someone really wanted her dead. Someone really was going to stop at no lengths to make sure she was out of the way.

Derrick believed that person was Javar. Pinning him with a suspicious gaze, Whitney stared into his eyes, hoping to find the truth there. Could it be true? Could Javar want her dead?

Motive, means, opportunity. Javar had them all.

Javar's eyes narrowed as he analyzed her gaze, then widened in disbelief. "Tell me you don't think I had anything to do with this...."

Whitney tore her eyes from Javar's, her heart aching. "I..." Her voice faltered, but somehow she found the strength to continue. "I don't know what to believe."

Javar rose, indignation flashing in his eyes. "C'mon, Whitney. You know I had nothing to do with this."

Did she? Her heart didn't want to believe the horrible possibility, but her brain... God help her, she didn't know what to believe. She didn't trust Javar. "I don't..." Whitney's voice broke. "Too much has happened, Javar. Too many crazy things since I moved into your house."

"Our house," Javar retorted, stressing the words. "And I'm as baffled by all this as you are, believe me."

"I need time." Whitney couldn't look at him. It was too painful.

"Time? For what?"

"To think, Javar!" Whitney replied, frustration evident in her voice. "Please, just go."

"No, I'm not going to leave you. Not now."

Whitney whimpered. Her heart was breaking and she couldn't do anything to stop it. "Javar...please."

"Why are you doing this?" he asked, sounding sincerely perplexed. "I love you, Whitney."

Those were words she had longed to hear, yet Whitney cringed, her stomach aching. They had been trying to work things out, and Javar's proclamation of love should have warmed her heart. Instead, she was so confused that all she could feel was pain. If Javar had been behind the attacks on her life, then everything he had said about wanting to reconcile was a lie, and that hurt more than she thought she could bear. This was what she had feared most; trusting Javar again, giving him the power to crush her heart.

"If you really care about me, you'll leave."

Javar shook his head. "No. I'm not going to leave you. Not until you tell me that you don't think I would ever hurt you."

Whitney met his eyes then. She thought she saw genuine distress there, as well as confusion. God, this was so hard. She wrenched her gaze away, settling back on the bed.

"Whitney?"

She said nothing, unable to give Javar what he wanted. How could she, when she didn't know the truth?

Javar groaned, and Whitney sensed resignation in his tone. Finally, she heard his soft footfalls as he walked away.

When he left the room, the tears came. Didn't stop. Couldn't stop.

Letting Javar back into her heart had been a mistake. They didn't have a future.

Let that be Whitney, Derrick thought as he rushed out of his apartment bathroom and hurried to the living room phone. *Please.*

Grabbing the receiver, he brought it to his ear. "Hello?"

"Derrick."

She sounded breathless, like she had been crying. Derrick propped himself against the arm of his sofa. "Whitney, is that you?"

"Yes."

She *had* been crying, Derrick realized. Instinctively, he knew that Javar had caused her tears. "What happened Whitney? What did Javar do?"

"I'm in the hospital," Whitney explained. "I've overdosed... on morphine."

"What?" Whitney overdosed on a painkiller? He found that extremely hard to believe.

"I didn't take it. Well, I didn't know I was taking it. I thought I was taking my prescribed medications, but instead..."

"Someone tampered with your medication?"

"Yeah," Whitney replied softly.

"And you think it was Javar?"

"I don't know," Whitney admitted. "I don't know what to think. I keep thinking about what you said."

Derrick paused, preparing for the next blow he would deliver. "There's something else you should know. About the accident."

"What?" Whitney asked, the pitch of her voice rising.

"Well," Derrick began, somberness lacing his voice. "I've got a definite lead in your case."

"You do?" She almost sounded like she didn't want to know.

"Yeah. I spoke with a witness to your accident yesterday. She says she definitely saw a car tailing you that night. Her impression of the event was that someone tried to run you off the road."

"Oh, don't say that, Derrick. Don't tell me that."

"Whitney, I know this isn't easy, but from what you've told me, it's pretty obvious now that someone has been out to get you since you came back to Chicago. And the witness's version of events makes that fact even harder to dismiss. I don't know. Maybe the accident wasn't deliberate. Maybe it was some teenager out for a joyride who got a bit stupid."

"The accident happened more than a week ago. Why didn't this witness come forward sooner?"

"She was frightened. She thought maybe the driver of the other car got a look at her, and would come after her if she went to the police."

"And now?"

"Now, her conscience was getting the better of her."

There was a pause, then Whitney asked, "Well, did she get a look at the driver?"

Derrick shook his head. "No. But she did get a look at the car."

Whitney blew out a hurried breath into the receiver. She asked, "What kind of car was it?"

"A late model, top-of-the-line BMW. Definitely black."

Whitney felt a sharp pain in her chest, and she brought a hand to her heart. "Oh, no. No."

"What is it?" Derrick asked. "What's the matter?"

"Javar…he…" This was too hard. So many coincidences! Or were they? Was Javar as guilty as he now looked?

"What? Javar what?"

"His BMW…it was black. Now, it's maroon. He just had it painted."

"What hospital are you at?" Derrick asked, the words coming out in a rush.

Whitney told him the hospital, and the room number.

"Have you called the police yet?"

"No," Whitney replied, hardly able to breathe.

"Okay. Hang tight. I'm on my way."

Whitney replaced the receiver, then lay back on the hospital bed. Her lungs hurt as they strained to take in air, as the oxygen strained to flow through her blood. Her mind pounded as it searched for answers, searched to make sense of this whole sordid situation.

Javar… What hurt the most was that she had allowed herself to hope, to dream. And now, that dream had come crashing down. Maybe Derrick could take her to Javar's to collect her things. She couldn't stay at his house any longer; that was certain. Not when she knew the truth.

No, she conceded with a frown. She didn't know the truth. She knew what Derrick suspected. She knew what Javar said. And man, was she ever confused.

She heaved a wistful sigh. Just a couple of nights ago, she and Javar had gotten over a hurdle and come close to recapturing what they had lost. How could she believe that the Javar who had courted her so lovingly in recent days could possibly want to kill her? Remembering those days, her mind couldn't even contemplate that reality.

But then there was the Javar who had lost his son, the Javar who blamed her for J.J.'s death. Could his sweet words and whispered promises really be some sick plan to get her to trust him again, only so that he could get close enough to kill her?

Her heart fluttered in her chest, as if telling her that it couldn't believe that. But her brain… There were facts she couldn't deny. Regardless, this test of her faith had proven to her one crucial thing: she didn't have a future with Javar. How could she, when she couldn't truly trust him? There were too many complications in their relationship, and with Javar in her life—along with his interfering family—she would never truly be able to get over her demons.

But if the answer was so simple, then why did Whitney's heart ache at the very thought of walking away from Javar and never looking back?

Why did she feel as if her whole world was coming to an end?

When the phone rang, Javar nicked his chin with the razor, muttered a curse, then ran into his bedroom to answer the phone. He said anxiously into the receiver, "Hello."

"Javar. Hi."

The sound of his father's voice, not Whitney's, caused Javar to groan. Not that he wasn't happy to hear from his father, but he was concerned about Whitney, and was hoping desperately that she would call.

Javar said tightly, "Hi, Dad."

"I sense that I've caught you at a bad time," Marcus Jordan said.

Javar blew out the air in his cheeks. "Kind of. I was expecting a call."

"I won't keep you. I wanted to call and say hi since I'm back in town, and I also wanted to say bye, since I'm heading out again tonight."

"Wow. You've been pretty busy. Another conference?"

"Yeah. This one's in Hawaii, so I'm looking forward to it."

"I bet."

An awkward silence fell between them, and Javar didn't know what to say. His father had never been a big supporter of Whitney, and he had no doubt heard his mother's version of what Whitney had and had not done. He loved his family dearly and wanted them to accept the woman he loved.

Marcus cleared his throat. "I heard about the fight you had with Michelle and your mother."

Javar was immediately defensive. "Dad, if you're going to tell me to apologize—"

"No," Marcus said quickly. "I'm not going to tell you to apologize." He sighed. "In fact, I'm calling to apologize…on your mother's behalf."

Surprised, Javar's eyebrows rose.

Marcus continued. "Look, I admit that I was worried when you started dating Whitney. She came from the projects…"

"Neither you nor Mom was born with silver spoons in your mouths," Javar said, thinking that that was the worst part of all. While his parents hadn't come from poor backgrounds, they had certainly worked to acquire their status among the upper-middle class.

"I know. And I wasn't finished. What I was going to say was that even though I originally had my reservations, I respected your decision to marry her. And I respect your decision now. If you want Whitney in your life, then I will accept her in mine…with open arms."

The revelation was so unexpected that Javar was speechless. Sure, his mother had been the more vocal opponent of his relationship with Whitney, but he hadn't expected his father to embrace her with open arms. Closing his eyes for a second,

Javar opened them, truly feeling touched. "Thanks, Dad. That...that means a lot."

"I'm tired of the quarrels, all the resentment. Whitney has suffered enough. So have you. We all have."

Javar shook his head at the irony. Now, of all the times for his father to make this call, it was when Whitney might finally want him out of her life. Javar silently groaned.

"Something's bothering you, isn't it?" Marcus asked. "More than this problem with your mother and Michelle."

"Yeah," Javar admitted, clenching a fist. "A lot has happened. Too much to get into over the phone. But Whitney and I may be going our separate ways after all."

"I'm sorry," Marcus said. "I mean that."

"Thanks." Javar moved to his bed and sat on it. "That's who I was hoping would call...."

"I won't keep you then. I'll see you when I get back."

"Okay. Enjoy your trip. How long is it?"

Marcus replied, "Five days." He paused. "By the way, I've spoken with your mother about this whole...mess. She should be calling you, to apologize personally."

Javar rolled his eyes and wanted to say, "When pigs fly," but instead said, "Thanks again, Dad. I really appreciate having you in my corner."

Javar ended the call, feeling a modicum of satisfaction. The conversation with his father meant a lot.

Rising from the bed, Javar returned to the bathroom and picked up the razor he had thrown in the sink. His eyes met their reflection in the mirror, and for a long moment he stood there, staring.

Yesterday, his brown eyes had had a spark, life. Today, that spark had been replaced by sadness. After everything, getting close again, making love, the dream was still out of his reach. It loomed before him, teasing him, taunting him.

He had lived without his wife for almost two years. Two long, painful years. He had been too stubborn, too hurt to seek her out and try to save their marriage. Now that he had put his heart on the line once again, and now that they had almost seized the dream, fate had dealt their relationship an almost deadly blow.

Not fate. Someone. The person who was trying to harm Whitney—*kill* her, for God's sake. Javar was paying for that person's actions.

His stomach churned when the next thought hit him. Someone didn't want him and Whitney to be together, and would stop at nothing to fulfill that goal.

"Damn!" Javar slapped a palm against the sink's marble counter. Whoever was doing this was very clever. Whoever was doing this was setting him up to take the fall!

Chapter 21

"I don't want to call the police," Whitney announced, running a hand through her hair.

Derrick, who sat on the edge of her hospital bed, looked at her as if she had completely lost her mind. "Whitney, you can't let him get away with this."

"He said he would never hurt me." She sounded like a woman in denial, she knew, but she just couldn't convince herself of Javar's guilt.

"What did you expect him to say?"

Whitney drew in a deep breath and shrugged. "Look, I've made my decision."

Derrick stood, paced the floor for a few seconds, then sat again. "You know that someone tampered with your medication. You know that someone attacked you while you were sleeping. You know that someone ran you off the road." He paused, reached for Whitney's chin and tilted it, forcing her to look at him. "Javar had access to your medication. He had access to you in your bedroom. That we know for sure. We also know that he drove a black BMW, which he reported missing around the time of your accident. He could have hired a thug to attack you, then let him get away. Whitney, he has the motive, the means—"

Whitney dug her fingers into his arm. "Derrick, please. I can't. I just can't." She paused, grimaced. "The doctor probably thinks I'm a druggie. Let's leave it at that, okay? I just want to…get on with my life. That means leaving Javar…leaving this whole affair behind me." She sighed, frustrated. "I don't want to have to see him every day for months in a courtroom. Don't you understand that?"

Derrick flashed her a look that said he didn't understand. "I'm a cop. I like to see the bad guys put behind bars. But," he shrugged, "I guess I can understand your position."

Whitney placed a hand over his. "Thanks, Derrick. You're a dear friend."

"I know." He smiled.

Whitney returned his smile with a weak one. "Hey, I'm waiting on the doctor to come back and give me the okay to leave. The morphine is out of my system, but he… Well, I should be out of here soon. And I'm going to need a ride to Javar's." She hesitated. Swallowed. Tried not to cry. "To get my things."

"Hey," Derrick said, stroking her arm. "Don't worry about it. I'll take you to Javar's and help you pack. Whitney, don't cry…."

But she couldn't help it. A hot tear escaped her eye and spilled onto her cheek. With the palm of her hand she brushed it away. But then there was another one in its place. Angrily, she brushed that one away too.

"Come here," Derrick said, offering Whitney his arms.

She went to him, pressing her face into his jacket. "It's just so hard, you know."

"It's going to be okay. You'll get over this," Derrick told her. "Everything's going to be fine."

Whitney accepted the comfort he offered, but she doubted there was any truth in his words. With Javar out of her life, how could anything ever be right again?

Javar's heart leapt to his throat when he heard the phone ring. Moving from the window in his office, he ran to the black cordless phone at the corner of his mahogany desk.

"Whitney?" he said into the receiver.

"Uh, no. This is your sister."

"Oh." Javar's already foul mood plummeted even further. "Michelle. Hi."

"Let me guess, you're not happy to hear from me."

"Weren't you the one who told me you didn't want me in your life if Whitney was still in mine?"

Javar heard his sister's sharp intake of breath. "That…that's why I'm calling," she said. "I want to apologize. For being so…unreasonable."

Javar heard a voice in the background, Curtis's voice. He chuckled inwardly. So, this was why Michelle was calling. She certainly didn't seem to be doing it of her own free will.

"You do?" Javar asked.

"Yes," Michelle said. "I shouldn't have given you that ultimatum. It was childish."

"That it was."

"Anyway, I just want to say that you're welcome to come over anytime you want. Michael misses you."

The mention of his nephew's name made Javar smile. "I miss him too."

"And… Whitney…she's welcome too."

Twice in one day. The gods of cruelty were certainly laughing at him. "Thanks, Michelle. I hope you mean that."

"Why would I call if I didn't?"

"Okay," Javar conceded, giving her the benefit of the doubt. "Well, since you'll probably hear this from someone else, I may as well tell you that things between Whitney and me…well, I don't think they're going to work out."

"Oh." Michelle sounded surprised. "Why not?"

Because someone has screwed up my life royally, he wanted to say. But he said, "It's a long story. Another time."

"Well," Michelle sounded infinitely more cheery than when she had first called. "Like I said, you're welcome to come over. I'm sorry for being so pigheaded."

"Apology accepted. Listen, tell Curtis I said hi. I've got to run."

"Sure."

Javar ended the call, holding the receiver against his chin. Could his sister have been responsible for the attempts on his wife's life? She certainly hated Whitney enough to do it. Or was it Stephanie, as he had originally thought?

What did it matter? Whoever was responsible for the attempts on Whitney's life had succeeded in ending his relationship. That was all that mattered now.

"Are you sure?" Cherise asked, hugging Whitney tightly.

Pulling from her cousin's embrace, Whitney nodded. "It's definitely over."

Whitney took a seat on the rose-colored sofa, and Cherise sat down beside her. Then she told her cousin everything. About the accident that wasn't really an accident, about the attack in her bedroom, about the morphine overdose and her hospital stay, about Derrick's suspicions that Javar was behind everything.

"You don't believe that, do you?" Cherise asked, her forehead creased with disbelief.

Whitney shrugged, then brought a leg up onto the sofa with her. "What Derrick says sounds plausible, but…"

"But you don't believe it."

Admitting what her heart knew to be true, Whitney shook her head. "I think Stephanie Lewis is behind all of this. She hates me for 'killing' her son. And when I first went to Javar's after the accident, she threatened me. Javar was there."

Cherise reached out and patted Whitney's leg. "Then why? Why are you giving up on your relationship?"

"Because," Whitney said quickly, inhaling a steadying breath. "Because ever since the accident, there's been nothing but pain. And we can't seem to get past it, Cherise. We tried, but it didn't work. And I can't do it anymore. I just can't."

"I hear you," Cherise said. "It's kinda like me and Paul, you know. There was love there, but we lacked something else. And the relationship died."

Now that Whitney had retrieved her belongings from Javar's, she wanted to forget about him. She wanted to forget about the attempts on her life. She asked, "Where are the kids?"

Cherise chuckled mirthlessly. "With Paul. They'll be home later tonight."

"Good," Whitney said. "I can't wait to see them."

Maybe surrounding herself with her family would help her forget the man she was leaving behind.

Hours later, Whitney woke up to a quiet apartment. Never in her entire life had she slept as much as she had in these last several days.

Yawning, Whitney rolled over in the bed. She should call her mother and let her know what had happened, that she was no longer at Javar's.

She knew what her mother would say. That as much as it was hard to fathom, Whitney couldn't ignore the evidence. The pills. The new paint job on the BMW. The accident… It would be too easy to call it all coincidence, her mother would say. Which was true. And, God help her, Derrick made a pretty convincing argument for Javar's guilt.

"But why?" Whitney asked aloud, knowing that the four walls would not whisper the answer to her question. Why pretend he wanted a reconciliation? Why take her into his home to heal? Why hire a nurse?

To get close enough to kill me. That thought caused a shiver to snake down her spine. As much as she wanted to deny it, it *could* be true. The Javar she had known years earlier would never have been capable of anything so heinous, but maybe the loss of his son had been too great. Maybe that loss had changed him, made his heart so cold that only the thought of vengeance would ever warm it.

If only she could make up her mind as to what she believed, instead of teeter-tottering between arguing for Javar's innocence, then arguing for his guilt.

The only thing she knew for sure was that she had made the right decision leaving Javar's home.

Sitting up on the twin bed, Whitney fought the overwhelming sadness and reached for the phone. She placed the receiver to her ear and was about to punch in the digits to her mother's number when she heard a voice.

"…treating me like this? Why're you acting so holy now, like you never wanted me? Because of her? She doesn't even want you, for God's sake."

Whitney knew she should have hung up the phone, but for some strange reason, she was compelled to listen. If Cherise was talking to Paul, her ex-husband, then it was obvious that despite the tough attitude and tough face she showed the world, she wasn't really over him.

"Answer me," Cherise demanded. "Why are you dissing me for someone who doesn't even appreciate you? If it's because she was hurt…"

The strangest, eeriest feeling passed over Whitney. Her hand tightened around the receiver as she waited to hear the man's response, needed to hear it.

Finally, he spoke. "Cherise, I already told you how I feel. I'm trying not to hurt you, but you're giving me no choice. I want to be with Whitney. Only her."

Whitney opened her mouth to gasp, but no sound would come out. The voice was unmistakable from the first moment he'd spoken. And when Whitney heard it, she froze, and a numb feeling enveloped her body. The strength came now, propelling her to act. Hastily, she replaced the receiver and sprang from the bed. Grabbing her purse, she ran to the bedroom door.

She halted. Clutched her stomach. God, was there nobody she could trust? First Javar, now Cherise… Who next? Derrick? Her mother?

Shaking her head, Whitney swallowed against the lump in her throat. Never her mother. That much she knew. And that was the only safe place she could go before she could make arrangements to go back to Louisiana.

She threw the door open, then stopped mid-stride. Dark brown eyes pinned her to the spot.

"Whitney, wait," Cherise said, her voice softer than the look in her eyes. "Let me explain."

Chapter 22

"Get out of my way," Whitney said, moving forward.

Cherise blocked her path. "No, Whitney. Not until you let me explain."

"Explain? I may have hit my head in that car accident, but my hearing is perfectly fine!"

"I...you weren't supposed to hear that."

"No doubt!" Whitney took a step forward, but Cherise was in her face, stopping her.

"Listen to me. Whitney, I'm sorry..."

"Like hell you are!"

Cherise glanced down the narrow hallway. "My kids are sleeping."

"I don't—"

Forcefully, Cherise took Whitney's arm and dragged her into the bedroom. Then she closed the door behind them.

Whitney crossed her arms over her chest. "Save it, Cherise. I already feel like a fool!"

Approaching her slowly, Cherise's lips pulled into a taut line. When she was about a foot away from Whitney, Cherise spoke. "Whitney, it's not what you think. Javar..."

Stepping backward, Whitney said, "Don't. Oh God, I've been a fool!" She squeezed her head with both hands. Cherise and Javar... Suddenly, she needed to know. She deserved to know. "How long, Cherise? How long has...*this*...been going on?"

As Cherise stood, her arms wrapped around her torso, her bottom lip quivered. Finally, she spoke. "You have to believe that I'm sorry, Whitney. I don't know what I was thinking."

"Neither do I," Whitney retorted. "How could you? How? You're my cousin. You're my family. How could you do this to me, lie to my face..."

"Because!" Cherise's eyes were now misty. "Whitney, you don't even want him..."

"And you acted like you couldn't stand him! Like you were angry with him for how he'd turned his back on me! Now you want him?"

"Well if it's any consolation, he doesn't want me," Cherise spat out.

Turning, Whitney marched to the bed. Dropped down on it. "Why? Why Javar?"

Cherise brushed her tears away. She no longer seemed apologetic, only angry. "Why not?" she challenged. "You don't want him. Or do you?"

Her heartbeat accelerating at the thought, Whitney avoided the question. "Javar is not a commodity. Even if I don't want him, I can't just give him to you." Glancing up, Whitney saw the defiance in Cherise's eyes. Her cousin had always been pig-headed, feisty. "Besides, given our history, why couldn't you have gone for someone else? There are other fish in the sea."

"Not like Javar."

Whitney cringed. This all had to be some horrible nightmare. "I guess if you gon' do wrong, do wrong right, huh?"

Cherise continued, "That's not what I mean." She sighed.

"What I mean is that I have two children to think about. Look at where I'm living. A man like Javar could give me the kind of life I deserve. Why are you the only one who should have that kind of man?"

"I don't have him. And I'd never want a man who didn't want me."

Cherise's face contorted with sarcasm. "Oh, that's right. I forgot you live in a friggin' fantasy world. Well I live in the real world, and in the real world I have two kids to look out for."

Whitney whispered, "Sounds like you're the one living in a fantasy world."

"Look, I apologized—"

"Did you?"

Cherise groaned. "There's no pleasing you."

Whitney was about to respond, but bit back her retort. This was getting nowhere. She was the fool. She should have seen the signs. Ever since she and Cherise were young, Cherise had always coveted the nice things she had, even the simple things. Now, she wanted her husband, and in her own crazy way, she was justifying her lies.

Rising, Whitney stared at Cherise long and hard. "Just how badly did you want Javar?" At Cherise's perplexed look, she asked, "Badly enough to try to kill me?"

"You're crazy!"

"Am I? You were there, in my room at his house. You could have tampered with the pills. You knew the moment I arrived in Chicago. How do I know you didn't try to run me off the road?"

"Whitney, I would never do that!"

Oh, God. It could be true. Cherise could have wanted Javar badly enough to want her out of the way—permanently.

Whitney headed for the door in long, quick strides, knowing she couldn't spend another moment here with Cherise.

When she opened the bedroom door, Cherise was at her heels. "Whitney—"

Whitney kept going. Hustling as quickly as her legs could take her, she ran to the apartment door, grabbing her suitcase that still sat in the vestibule. She didn't look back as she jetted through the door and down the apartment hallway. It was only when she reached the main street that she stopped to catch her breath.

Where was her mother? Whitney stood on the porch of her mother's town house, straining to hear a sound inside the house. The interior hall light was on, as always, to keep unwelcome visitors away, but the house was quiet.

Whitney knocked again. Waited. Still, no response.

She fished into her purse for her key. Opening the door, Whitney went inside.

At a moment like this when her heart was racing and her nerves were frazzled, Whitney didn't welcome the eerie quiet of the house. She wanted noise, happy voices, loud voices, to distract her from her thoughts. Even a crying baby would be welcome at this moment.

Placing her suitcase on the floor beside the stairs, Whitney sighed. Her mind worked a mile a minute, trying to make sense of tonight's events. Trying to dismiss the new, devastating possibility. Could Cherise be behind the attempts on her life?

Biting her bottom lip, Whitney sauntered into the living room and sank into the worn, comfy sofa. She reached for the television remote and hit the "power" button.

A late news broadcast was in progress. "…dead tonight in

more gang violence. The young boy was apparently hit by a bullet meant for someone else...."

Whitney shivered. She changed the channel. Normally, she watched the news, depressing as it was. But tonight, the last thing she needed was to be reminded that there were bad people in the world, some of whom might actually want to kill her. Pulling a leg up onto the couch, Whitney flipped through the channels. News. More news. A late-night trashy talk show. Groaning, she switched off the television.

As she walked through the small dining room and into the adjoining kitchen, Whitney thought she heard a sound. She paused. It was faint, but someone was knocking on the front door. Slowly, she walked through the kitchen to the main hallway and went to the door.

She glanced through the peephole. Javar!

"Whitney," he called softly.

Should she say something? On one hand, she wanted to tell Javar to get out of her life, but on the other, she didn't know whether she could trust him. If she let him know she was in here, would he bust down the door and try to harm her?

"I know you're in there. I saw you through the window."

Her body grew rigid. This wasn't right, being afraid of her own husband. But although her mind told her she should be cautious, her heart told her she had nothing to fear. There was no way Javar could hurt her, at least she didn't want to believe he could. Even if he did, would he be foolish enough to try and kill her, right here at her mother's home? She doubted it.

"Please, Whitney. I just want to know that you're okay."

With that, Whitney threw caution to the wind and opened the door. There stood Javar, one arm above his head resting against the door's frame. His eyes showed concern as he looked down at her.

She met his eyes with a hard gaze. "What did you think, Javar? That I would be in here crying my eyes out?"

"Cherise called me. She said you were…distraught. That you left and didn't have a ride. She was worried."

"Yeah right."

Javar stepped into the foyer then, closing the distance between them. "She told me that you heard…our conversation."

"Oh, yeah. I certainly did."

"It's not what you think." Javar's eyes implored her to believe him.

"So Cherise said." Whitney turned, walked a few steps, then faced Javar again. "How long has…has she *wanted* you?"

"I don't know," Javar said. "I don't care. All I know is that I never encouraged her advances. Ever."

"Then why didn't you tell me? God, you could have at least saved me from making a fool of myself with her."

Javar shrugged. "I figured since there was nothing going on, there was no reason to tell you. Besides, we were trying to work out *our* problems. Cherise has nothing to do with us."

Her face hurt from frowning. Her head hurt from pounding. She heaved a long-suffering sigh. "Fine. You've made your point. Now leave."

"I meant what I said before. I love you, Whitney. God knows, I'm telling you the truth."

"It's over." But she couldn't meet his eyes as she lied and said. "I've…called a lawyer. I'm filing for divorce."

Javar closed his eyes pensively, and Whitney watched his Adam's apple rise and fall as he swallowed. Slowly, he opened them. "If this is about Cherise—"

"It's about us," Whitney replied quickly, her throat constricting. "It's not gonna work. It's not."

"How can you say that? We were getting so close...."

This hurt; there was no denying it. Pushing her husband away when her heart ached to embrace him... Her nerves were frazzled from the anguish of this moment, and she didn't know how much longer she could handle being in the same room with him, staring at the man whom she could no longer deny she still loved.

"Please, Javar. Don't make this any harder than it already is. Just go."

Javar's eyes held hers for a long moment, and when she saw the sheen of tears her breath snagged in her throat. God, she wanted to go to him, tell him that nothing else mattered but how they felt for each other. But she couldn't. Because the cards were stacked against them and they were just too high to leap over.

"Just tell me...tell me you don't believe that I tried to hurt you...."

Whitney's body shook as emotions overwhelmed her. Her throat was so tight she didn't even know if she would be able to speak. Her voice a mere whisper, she finally replied, "No. I—I don't believe that."

Javar nodded tightly, then quickly turned on his heel, heading for the door. The gasp that wanted to escape got lodged in Whitney's throat as she pressed her lips together. She covered her mouth with one hand and held onto her torso with the other, the physical pain wrenching her insides into a tight knot.

Javar never turned around, not even when he grabbed the doorknob and closed the front door.

And finally, Whitney couldn't hold back the gasp. It escaped her lips as a flood of tears escaped her eyes.

Javar was gone from her life. Forever.

Summoning all her courage, Stephanie walked up the stairs to Javar's monstrous home. The home that could have been hers if she'd had the chance to regain Javar's love. But he had fallen in love with Whitney. And because of Whitney, her son was dead.

She pushed that thought from her mind. She had a job to do. Soon enough, she would have her revenge. Javar would know that he couldn't get away with dissing her for their son's murderer.

Stephanie looked back at the car where both her brothers sat. Kevin nodded, silently encouraging her. Part one of her plan was about to be executed. Her brothers would execute part two. This was Javar's own fault. He had driven her to this.

Stephanie raised her hand, rang the doorbell. Moments later, Carlos swung the front door open.

Stephanie pushed past him, stepping inside. "Where's Javar?"

"You are not welcome here," Carlos told her.

"Yeah, yeah, whatever. Get Javar for me."

"If you do not leave—"

"Get Javar," Stephanie repeated, louder this time. "I won't leave until you do."

Carlos glanced around worriedly, as if unsure what to do. *Let him glance all he wants,* Stephanie thought. *I'm not leaving until I accomplish what I came to do.* She had to get Javar into the foyer.

Javar must have heard her, because he was in the hallway

now, walking hurriedly toward her from somewhere on the first floor. "I told you not to come back here."

"Yeah, well, too bad. I want to talk to you."

"I have nothing to say to you. Get out."

"No." Firmly, she stood her ground.

Javar turned to Carlos. "Carlos, will you please excuse us?" There was no mistaking his anger.

"What do you want?"

"My son's things. Everything. You're disrespecting his memory by having his killer right here in this house."

As Stephanie had hoped he would, Javar grabbed her forearm and led her out the front door. At that moment, Keith lunged at Javar, snaring him in a headlock. Although she was expecting the action, even Stephanie was surprised when it happened. With his hand securely around Javar's neck, Keith, who was almost as tall as Javar, ushered him down the front steps. Before Javar could react, Kevin was there, planting a sucker punch in his solar plexus.

Javar groaned, but fought back then, squirming in an effort to free himself of Keith's powerful grip. Kevin leapt at him, tackling him to the concrete. When Javar landed on the hard surface, Keith kicked him in the rib cage causing Javar to writhe in pain.

Stephanie stood to the side and watched.

Keith said, "Next time you think about attacking my sister, you better think twice."

His breath coming in ragged gasps, Javar looked from Stephanie to Keith to a now-standing Kevin, his eyes narrow slits. The anger in his gaze was so strong it seared Stephanie's skin.

"That's right," Kevin added. "You want to get to Stephanie, you have to go through us. Remember that."

Grunting loudly, Javar lunged for Kevin's legs. He surprised Kevin, knocking him to the ground. Stephanie screamed. Moving quickly, Keith nailed Javar with a boot in the back. Javar yelled out in pain, releasing his hold on Kevin as he did, falling to his side.

"Okay," Stephanie said, grabbing Keith's arm. "That's enough."

Blinding pain was all Javar could feel spreading through his entire body with the force of an electrical charge. He clutched his side, willing the agony to subside. "Cowards," he spat out, eyeing Stephanie, whose face was contorted in a grimace.

"Stay away from Stephanie," Kevin said, meeting Javar's eyes with hatred in his own. "This is the only warning you'll get."

Javar wanted to lurch forward and rip that devilish smirk off Kevin's face. But he was no fool; he was outnumbered. Besides, his side hurt. He wondered if a rib was broken.

He watched as Stephanie and her brothers ran to the Ford Tempo parked in his driveway. Inhaling deeply to keep his mind off his body's physical suffering, Javar got to his knees, watching helplessly as the trio sped away, tires squealing.

Javar was in the midst of standing when Carlos ran through the front door and down the concrete steps, a harried expression etched on his features. "Sir! Sir, are you all right?"

"Call the police," Javar said, wincing as he stood to his full height.

"I called them from my room when I heard the commotion," Carlos replied, moving to stand beside Javar and offering him an arm for support.

"Good," Javar said, before groaning.

Stephanie and her brothers would see who had the last laugh.

Chapter 23

Long after the word came that Stephanie and her brothers had been arrested, and long after Javar had given the police a formal statement, the pain lingered. And not the pain from the actual assault—nothing was broken, only bruised—but the pain in his heart. Pensively, he sat in the leather recliner by the floor-to-ceiling fireplace in his den, trying to come to terms with the foul events of recent days. Trying to come to terms with his loss.

Javar had tried to reach Whitney after the attack, but each time he had called her mother's, the answering machine had come on. At this hour, he was sure she was there, but she was most likely deliberately avoiding his calls. Like almost everybody in America, her mother probably had a call-display feature on her phone that allowed her to see who was calling.

He needed to reach her, needed to let her know that Stephanie and her brothers had been arrested. He needed to let her know that the people who had tried to harm her were behind bars.

He needed to tell her that he loved her, always would. That without her, his life wasn't complete and never would be. But she wouldn't even talk to him.

With a moan, Javar wondered if there was even any point in trying. Whitney had made herself very clear. She didn't want him in her life.

So, since he hadn't been able to reach her, he did the only thing he could: he left a detailed message on her mother's answering machine, letting her know about the turn of events and ultimate arrest. At least that should stop her worrying, if she was indeed worried about someone trying to "finish her off." Stephanie's arrest should give her some much needed peace of mind.

Javar reached for the glass of straight Scotch on the table at his side, but his hand stopped in the air. He recoiled it, brought it back to his side.

Forget the Scotch, he decided. It might help ease his physical discomfort, but it would never numb the ache in his heart.

Whitney heard the soft protest of the door's hinges as it swung open, but she didn't turn around. Quietly, she sat on a wicker rocking chair, her legs curled under her as she stared out the window at the activity of the morning. Staring, but not seeing.

"Whitney," her mother said softly. "You need to eat something."

"I'm not hungry, Mom."

Carmen's clothes rustled as she walked toward her daughter. She placed a hand on her shoulder. "Honey, you can't sit here like this all day. You've got to get out, get on with your life."

Whitney didn't reply.

Carmen sighed. "Cherise called for you."

"I don't care."

There was silence for a moment, then Carmen said, "Well, I think you need to hear this. Javar called—"

"Mom—" Whitney protested, casting a sidelong glance at her mother.

"Hear me out," her mother stated firmly. "Javar called with

some news. He said that Stephanie Lewis and her two brothers were arrested last night. Apparently, they went to his home, beat him up pretty bad."

Whitney turned and faced her mother then, her heart leaping into her throat. "Oh, my God. Is he okay?"

"In his message, he said he was." Carmen paused, raised a speculative eyebrow. "He also said that the police believe they were the ones who tried to kill you."

"I knew it," Whitney muttered, rising. Her heart was beating wildly in her chest, concern for Javar taking precedence in her mind. "I...should c-call him." She moved to the phone on the night table, reached for it, but didn't lift it.

She couldn't call Javar. How could she, after last night? Her body ached to lift the receiver and see for herself how he was doing, but after last night, she realized that it was best to let things be. Not only did she not want to give Javar false hope with her concern, but it would be too difficult to talk to him. To hear the deep, sexy voice of the man who was no longer hers.

As she recoiled her fingers, Whitney silently wondered if time would ever numb the pain in her heart.

Three days later, Javar still hadn't been able to reach Whitney. On a couple of occasions, he had spoken with her mother, who surprisingly, did not seem as bitter when she spoke with him as she had been right after the accident. In fact, Carmen seemed apologetic when she told him that Whitney didn't want to talk to him.

Today, Javar was missing Whitney even more intensely than the last few days. Today, she was supposed to accompany him to New York for his business trip. Instead, he was going alone.

It was poignant, tangible, the desolation he felt now that she was gone from his home, his life. After Stephanie's arrest, he had hoped that Whitney would take his calls, that she would be willing to give him another chance.

Instead, she was going ahead with her plans to become his ex-wife.

Javar almost didn't want to go to New York; it wouldn't be the same without Whitney. But he had to. Just because Whitney didn't want him anymore didn't mean that he had to let his business suffer. Without Whitney, his business would become his first love again. Because without Whitney, there would never be another woman in his life. As final as it might sound to others, Javar knew he would never love again.

The phone rang, and for a split second, Javar allowed himself to hope. But as he reached for the receiver in his home office, Javar braced himself for the reality that Whitney probably was not the person on the other end of the line.

She wasn't. "Hello, Javar," said his mother.

"Mom."

"I heard about Stephanie. I'm sorry."

"Yeah, so am I." More than his mother would ever know.

"To say the least, I was very surprised. I never thought she would resort to physical violence. How is Whitney?"

Javar rolled his eyes to the ceiling. "Mom, I'm sure Dad told you that Whitney and I are…that things aren't working out."

"Well," Angela began sheepishly, "he did mention something about that. But I thought that after the arrest, you would have spoken to her."

"No," Javar said quickly. "I haven't. She won't take my calls."

"She's at her mother's, I guess."

"Yup." Out of his house, out of his life.

"Hmm," was all Angela said. Then, "Stephanie... What a story. Has she admitted to running Whitney off the road and causing that horrible accident?"

"To be honest, Mom, I don't know. She didn't even want to admit that she had her brothers attack me. But the police believe the case against her is pretty strong."

Angela sighed. "Well, at least that's over now."

"Yeah."

"Look, there's another reason for my call. I...I'm calling to apologize," she said cautiously. "I'm sorry we fought last week. I'm sorry I was intruding in your life. I just love you so much that I get carried away sometimes."

Javar hesitated before answering, debating whether or not to let his mother off the hook so easily. Sighing, he decided there was no point in continuing the feud. He had enough stress to deal with. "Apology accepted."

"Oh, good. Look, maybe we can get together later tonight, have some dinner. Your father has gone off again, so I'm here alone."

"Actually, I can't," Javar replied. "I have an evening flight. I'm heading to New York on business. But maybe later this week."

"Sure," Angela said. "That would be fine."

"Great. I'll be in touch when I get back. Take care, Mom."

"Take care, dear."

Javar ended the call and headed upstairs. He may as well double-check that he had everything he needed for his trip.

Anything to keep his mind off Whitney.

Whitney didn't know how she got through these last few days since leaving Javar's home. Looking for a lawyer had drained her, left her feeling empty, and she still hadn't found one that she was happy with. Most wanted to go after Javar for half of this and half of that, but all Whitney wanted to do was go on with her life. She didn't care about maintaining the kind of lifestyle she had been accustomed to while she was with Javar.

Some lawyers had smiled at her and told her not to think of her life as coming to an end, but as a new beginning. Somehow, Whitney found that extremely hard to do.

So, after a couple of days, she had given up on the search for a lawyer—for now—and instead had done the one thing she thought would take her mind off Javar. She had gone to the All For One community youth center in Chicago's Near West where she had volunteered years earlier.

Meeting with her old friends and making some new ones, Whitney had smiled for the first time in a long time. Being with the children energized her, but still, when she came home in the evening, Javar invaded her mind. Javar kissing her. Javar making sweet love to her. Javar telling her that he loved her.

It would never be easy if she stayed in Chicago, Whitney realized. There were too many memories here, too many ghosts. What she needed to do was head back to Shreveport and resume the life she had been living there. Getting back to work at the youth center there would help her concentrate on other things. Help her forget Javar.

Restless, Whitney lay on the couch, her thoughts of Javar more poignant today for some reason.

Maybe it was because her mother had just left with Robert for an evening of dinner and dancing, leaving her feeling alone because she didn't have a man in her life.

Maybe it was because it was Sunday, the day she should have been going to New York with Javar.

Her stomach fluttering, Whitney realized that that was what was really bothering her. All thoughts led back to Javar. Would she ever forget the way his eyes crinkled when he smiled, the way his gentle touch ignited her skin, the way she felt when wrapped in his powerful arms? God, would she ever get over him?

"I have to," she said, standing. "I have to."

When the phone rang, she was so thankful for the welcome distraction from her thoughts that she just grabbed the receiver. "Hello?"

"Whitney. Hello."

Whitney's back stiffened when she heard that voice. Angela Jordan. Why was she calling her?

"Whitney? Are you there?"

"Yes," Whitney replied, her tone guarded.

"This is Angela Jordan."

"I know who this is."

"Good." Pause. "I guess you're wondering why I'm calling you."

"Mrs. Jordan, I don't have time for games."

"I understand." Her tone was syrupy, and Whitney wondered all the more why her soon-to-be-ex mother-in-law was calling her. "I'm calling because… I want to apologize."

"Apologize?" Whitney asked, a bit incredulous.

"Yes. Please, hear me out. Over the years, I haven't exactly been nice to you."

"That's an understatement," Whitney threw in.

Angela cleared her throat. "Well, you know the situation. I don't have to regurgitate the facts. I only wanted to say that I heard about the whole mess with Stephanie, and that I'm sorry about it."

"Why are *you* sorry?"

"Because I don't think I made things any easier. Perhaps even added fuel to Stephanie's fire."

Whitney drew in a deep breath and let it out slowly. "Mrs. Jordan, I just want to forget everything. Okay?"

"I understand, dear. This isn't working. I should do this face-to-face."

"Do *what?*" Whitney asked. Javar's mother had never liked her and probably never would, and she didn't see the point in having a conversation with her.

"Whitney, I would really appreciate it if you gave me the opportunity to apologize in person. That way, you'll know I'm sincere."

"It really doesn't matter," Whitney said.

"But it does, Whitney. I'd really like to get over the bitterness of the past and let bygones be bygones. Please, say you'll come over tonight. If not for dinner, then for tea."

Whitney found the whole idea of having tea with Angela Jordan a little daunting. "I…" Her mind scrambled for a logical excuse. "I don't have a car."

"Oh, I can have a driver come and get you." Pause. "Whitney, I think this is very important, for both of us. Please don't say no."

The words "No, thanks" were on the tip of Whitney's tongue, but she held them back. Angela Jordan was one of her "demons." One of the demons she had to face sooner or later. Maybe spending time with her would help Whitney face one demon and move on.

She was crazy for even considering this, Whitney knew. Still, she said, "All right, Mrs. Jordan. I'll come."

Chapter 24

Something wasn't right. Javar felt it in his gut, in his soul. Something... But he couldn't put his finger on what.

It was just after six-thirty in the evening, and his flight was in a couple of hours. Driving along I-90, Javar looked out at the steady flow of traffic, trying to shake the wary feeling in his gut.

The feeling wouldn't go away. "What is it?" he asked aloud, speaking only to the windshield of his BMW.

It hit him then, the cause of his anxiety. His mother. Or rather, their phone conversation. His mind worked frantically like a computer virus program to isolate the one piece of information that nagged him.

They had spoken about Stephanie and Whitney. She'd apologized for interfering in his personal life.

Stephanie. That was part of it, Javar realized. But what about her?

Has she admitted to running Whitney off the road and causing that horrible accident?

The words came into his brain clearly, almost as if his mother spoke them from within the car. Icy fear slithered down Javar's spine, as he considered the implication of that question.

How did his mother know that Whitney had been run off the

road? Even Javar hadn't been sure about that, and he certainly hadn't mentioned that possibility to anyone.

Definitely not to his mother. Or his father. Or his sister or brother. So how did his mother know?

Maybe someone else had told her. Derrick maybe. Stephanie? But those options didn't seem likely.

Javar signaled and veered his car to the right, exiting the I-90 before he reached Chicago O'Hare International Airport. He had to turn around and head east to his mother's.

He had to find out the truth, once and for all.

When the driver pulled into the driveway of the Tudor-styled home in Highland Park, one of the wealthiest suburbs of Chicago, Whitney looked out at the grand house she hadn't seen in more than two years. Surrounded by lush forests, the home was ultimately private. She remembered that this house had every luxury known to man, from gold fixtures in the bathrooms to a private bar in the master bedroom. Her in-laws also had a fifty-foot yacht in the boathouse, a boat she recalled they hardly used.

The driver pulled the Mercedes to a stop in the winding driveway, then exited and opened the back door closest to where Whitney sat. The driver was a young black man, probably no more than thirty, and definitely not the man she remembered as being the Jordans' driver.

Whitney stepped onto the pastel-colored interlocking stone cautiously, her hands shaking from a bout of nervousness. *I can do this,* she told herself, annoyed with her fear. Angela Jordan was a woman just like she was, albeit a very controlling one. *Just get this over with, let her say what she has to, and then get out.*

The driver escorted Whitney to the front door, which swung open as she arrived. Angela Jordan flashed a smile as wide as the part in the Red Sea, and to a stranger, it might look as if the woman was genuinely happy to see her. But Whitney doubted that.

"Whitney, come in," Angela said, waving her arms in invitation.

As usual, Angela looked dazzling in a flowing red pantsuit, her preferred style of clothing. Her ebony hair was styled in an elegant chignon, and simple pearl earrings dangled from each ear.

Whitney looked around the massive foyer. A gigantic brass-and-crystal chandelier hung from the top level of the house to just below the railing of the double staircase. The beige-colored marble floor, highlighted by a rose-colored marble trim, glistened beneath the artificial light from the chandelier. Everything was spotless, from the floor to the exquisite paintings on the walls.

Angela placed a hand on the back of Whitney's arm, gently leading her down the great hall. "Why don't we go to the sunroom? The sun is setting, but the view of the lake is breathtaking this time of evening."

It was. The sky was a dazzling array of oranges and reds, just above the peaceful-looking water. The backyard was pretty impressive, too, Whitney thought, looking out at the large oval-shaped pool illuminated by night-lights. There was also a pond in the distance, and an array of colorful flower gardens.

"What can I get you to drink?" Angela asked. "Tea? Gretta made some fresh lemonade before she left for the night."

"Uh, lemonade sounds great."

Smiling, Angela scurried off, leaving Whitney to explore the sunroom. The room was made totally out of windows, except for the ceiling, but that even boasted a skylight. French doors trimmed in polished oak led to the backyard and the pool. The room boasted high ceilings, over which looked part of the upstairs hallway by way of a balcony. It was absolutely gorgeous.

"Here you go," Angela almost sang.

Whitney turned to face her, immediately reaching for the extended tall glass of lemonade. Until now, she didn't realize how dry her throat was and how in need it was of quenching. "Thanks."

"Please, take a seat." Angela motioned to the cream-colored sectional.

Flashing a timid smile, Whitney moved to the comfortable-looking sofa and sat. Angela took a seat next to her.

"I'm glad to see you're looking wonderful," Angela said.

Whitney took a sip of the lemonade, wetting her throat before speaking. "Thank you, Mrs. Jordan. You look great. Red really suits you."

Angela nodded her thanks for the compliment. "Well, I won't bore you with mindless chatter. I'll get right to the point." She adjusted herself on the sofa so that she could face Whitney head on. "Whitney, I am truly sorry for the way I've treated you in the past, even very recently. I know I hurt you, and I can only hope that you can find it in your heart to forgive me."

At Angela's words, Whitney exhaled a gush of air. Never had she expected to hear her mother-in-law say anything like what she just had, especially not face-to-face.

The effort must have taken a lot of courage, Whitney realized, and to her surprise, Angela seemed sincere. Whitney had always wanted a mother-daughter type relationship with her mother-in-law, but while married to Javar they had never achieved that type of closeness. There had been much bitterness, anger, regret. Now more than ever, Whitney wanted to put the negative feelings behind them.

"Thank you for that," Whitney said softly. "I appreciate your effort."

"After what happened with Stephanie, I realized that life is just too short to waste being angry for foolish reasons."

Whitney put the glass to her mouth and took a large gulp of the lemonade. "I have to admit, I was a bit wary of coming over here...."

Angela chuckled. "You were? Well, you needn't have been." She rose, saying, "I've got some spring rolls warming in the oven. Nothing much. Just something Gretta made to nibble on. Care for any?"

"Sure," Whitney replied.

Twirling around, Angela glided out of the room.

Whitney drank some more lemonade. Then widened her eyes as her lids suddenly felt very heavy. *Whoa.* She felt strange all of a sudden.

Rising, Whitney stretched, then stumbled backward onto the sofa. Her head was spinning.

What was wrong with her?

Oh, God! Whitney's mind screamed, fighting off the impending darkness. She'd been set up!

And as the darkness crawled into her brain, numbing her mind as well as her body, Whitney's last conscious thought was of Javar. Of what a fool she'd been to push him away.

Javar.

Javar heard Whitney's voice in his mind, almost like she was calling out to him, asking him for help.

His heart pounding, Javar floored the accelerator. Quickly gaining speed, he drove toward Highland Park like a madman. A madman on a mission.

This time, if he got stopped for speeding, he would gladly accept a ticket.

Because he knew in his gut that Whitney needed him. And he sensed that time was running out.

"Is she out?" Angela asked Steve, the young man she had hired to help her do this deed. It was amazing how far people were willing to go for a few thousand dollars.

Steve lifted Whitney's eyelids, then let them close. "Yep. She's out cold."

Angela blew out a relieved breath. "Good. She'll be out for a while. Let's get her out to the car."

She watched as Steve lifted Whitney's limp body and threw it over his shoulder. He seemed to thrive on this kind of activity, but then for what she was paying him, he should.

"Let's go," he said.

Angela hurried ahead of him, leading him to the door that led to the garage. A sense of satisfaction flowed through her blood, but she wouldn't allow herself to celebrate yet. The deed wasn't quite done. But this time it would be. She would make sure Whitney died if it was the last thing she did.

And Whitney deserved to die. She was a gold digger who wasn't fit to be her son's wife. And as far as most people were concerned, she was also a murderer.

That was the only part Angela regretted. Even now, it made her incredibly sad when she thought about it. Javar Junior should not have been in the car that day; when Whitney had left her house that day almost two years ago, J.J. hadn't been with her. How was Angela to know that Whitney would stop and pick him up on the way home?

Angela popped the trunk on her black Mercedes, watching as Steve dropped Whitney's body inside. J.J.'s death was still Whitney's fault, regardless of the fact that the brakes had been cut. If Whitney had had him buckled in, J.J. would still be alive today, as was Whitney.

Steve closed the trunk with a thud, then hurried around to the driver's side door. Pushing the painful memories of her loss aside, Angela followed him.

Tonight it would all be over. Tonight, vengeance would be hers.

Chapter 25

Almost all traces of the sun were gone from the sky when Javar turned onto the street where his parents lived and headed toward their grand home. Because he was in a residential area, he was forced to slow down, but he was still anxious to get to his mother's home and question her about their earlier phone conversation.

As his hands clenched the steering wheel, the wary feeling in his gut intensified. Whitney was in trouble. He knew it, sensed it. But he prayed his worst fear wasn't true. He prayed his mother wasn't involved.

He was almost there. The large oak tree he had climbed as a child loomed in the distance, and he increased his speed a little. As he was almost at the winding driveway, he saw his mother's black Mercedes Benz pull onto the street and turn right, heading north. Heading away from him.

Javar's stomach tensed. Watching the car gradually pick up speed, he aborted his original plan. He was sure his mother was in that car. Stepping on the gas, he followed her.

After about a ten-minute drive, the car ahead of him slowed, turning into a dark, secluded area along the coast of Lake Michigan.

Javar slowed his car, not wanting his mother or whoever was in the Mercedes to realize that their car had been followed. Pulling to a stop, Javar killed the engine and parked. Then he hopped out of the car, following the trail the Mercedes had taken by foot.

The foliage at this part of the beach was thick and dense. Fear prickled Javar's nape, as he knew instinctively that whatever was going on here was not good. Crouching as he jogged, Javar advanced to some bushes so that he could watch without being seen.

Parked amidst high bushes, the Mercedes's lights were off now, but Javar could hear the steady hum of the car's engine. Then, the driver's side door opened slowly and a well-dressed man exited and looked around cautiously.

Javar ducked, straining to see through the bushes. The man walked toward the back of the car. Moments later, he popped the trunk.

That was when Javar saw his mother exit the car from the passenger's side door. Also eyeing the area with caution, Angela crept to the trunk of the car.

His mind knew then what his heart wanted to deny, and when he saw the man extract a body from the trunk, his whole being shook.

It was Whitney. Limp and seemingly lifeless.

Javar held back the well of emotions that wanted to overflow. Instead, he acted, charging through the bushes and shouting an angry cry.

Angela whirled around, clearly stunned, and as he neared the two, absolute horror passed over her face as she realized who the intruder was.

The man, who'd been holding Whitney's body against his,

let her drop to the ground when he saw Javar charging toward him. As Whitney landed on the hard earth with a thud, the man was already sprinting through the bushes.

Javar didn't care about the man, whoever he was. Running to Whitney, he dropped to the ground beside her, scooping her up as quickly as he could.

"God, oh God," he muttered as he took in her features. Her lips slightly parted, her eyes closed, she looked... "No. Oh, God."

Anxiously, he pressed his ear to her face, desperate to find a sign of life. He was trembling, fear spiraling through him from the inside out. If Whitney was dead...

"Sweet Jesus," he murmured, "please don't let her be dead. Oh, please!"

Drawing in a deep breath, Javar held it, realizing that he needed to be still. And then he felt it. It was soft and faint, like a whisper, but it was there all the same. She was breathing.

Looking heavenward he said, "Thank you. Thank you." But he knew the battle wasn't over. He had to get Whitney out of here, get her to a doctor.

He was lifting her from the ground when his mother said, "Javar."

He looked at her then, saw the anguish in her eyes. But beneath the anguish, he saw the hatred. The hatred that had led her to try to commit murder.

"What did you do to her?" Javar asked.

"It's just a...a strong sedative..."

"What were you going to do? Throw her in the lake while she was helpless?"

"I'm sorry," was all his mother said.

Anger consumed him then, like flames blazing out of control.

"*Sorry?* My God, you tried to *kill* her, and you're sorry? Sorry for what? That you got caught?"

Angela whimpered, then threw a hand to her mouth.

Javar started off, Whitney in his arms. If Whitney had only been given a sedative, then he could bring her home—where she belonged. As long as the paramedics said she was okay.

Angela ran in front of him, blocking his path.

"You don't understand," she said, sounding hysterical. "I was doing this for you, don't you see? Sh-she was using you. Sh-she killed your son!"

"Get out of my way," Javar said slowly, unable to look at his mother. This was a nightmare, so incredibly hard to fathom that he wanted to put as much distance between him and his mother as possible until he'd had a chance to think.

Javar moved forward, and Angela matched his movements, stepping backward ahead of him. "God, Javar! Don't look at me like that! I did this because I love you. I wanted to protect you!"

Her line of reasoning was so pathetic, Javar didn't even bother to respond. Brushing past her, he ran with Whitney to his car.

She may be his mother, but she had tried to kill his wife. After securing Whitney in the backseat, he reached for the car phone on the front seat.

While he dialed 911, his mother sat on the ground, bawling like a spoiled child.

Wet. Something wet was dripping on her face. Whitney stirred, moaned softly. She wanted to open her eyes, but her lids felt so heavy....

Man, was she ever groggy! When was she ever going to be herself, feel one hundred percent again?

She bolted upright as a memory hit her. A memory of Angela Jordan, of being at her place. But it was Javar who was with her, pressing a wet cloth to her face.

Where was she? Narrowing her eyes, Whitney glanced around. Her breathing calmed as a sense of relief washed over her. She was at Javar's place. Javar was with her, comforting her.

He took her in his arms, hugged her, holding her so tight that she didn't think he wanted to let go. He held her even tighter, relief evident in his grasp.

Whitney held onto him, drew from his strength for a long moment. It felt so good to be in her husband's arms.

When Javar pulled back and looked at her, Whitney's body immediately yearned for his. God, she was a fool. And a liar. There was no way she could live without Javar. How had she tried to believe that she could?

"How do you feel?" he asked.

"I'm okay," Whitney replied, resting a head on his strong shoulder.

"I was so scared…."

Lifting her head, Whitney looked at him. Something horrible had happened, she knew that much, but she couldn't remember a thing. "What happened? I remember being at your mother's, but…"

A frown tugged at Javar's lips, and melancholy flashed in his brown eyes. "You—you're not going to like it."

He explained to Whitney the events of the evening, ending with the horror he felt when his mother admitted being behind all the attacks on Whitney's life; his mother and some hired thug. He was only glad that he wasn't too late. As he spoke, his voice broke, and Whitney's heart ached. Though her own life had been jeopardized, she felt the need to comfort him. Reaching out, she gently stroked Javar's face, bringing a finger to his mouth.

"You saved my life," she said softly.

Javar nodded, the grim expression still etched on his face. "The story gets worse."

Whitney cocked an eyebrow. She wondered what could be worse than learning that his mother had wanted his wife dead. "Worse? Worse how?"

Javar drew in a deep breath, then covered her hand with his, holding it against his lips. Suddenly, his face contorted as an internal struggle played out on his features.

Whitney's brow furrowed in concern. "What? Javar, you're scaring me…"

He closed his eyes then, sniffling as he opened them. A tear escaped, slowly trickling down his cheek. Whitney watched him, baffled, feeling as though someone was squeezing her heart, cutting her life source.

"J.J.," he finally said. "She…she killed…" His voice trailed off.

But he had said enough. Enough to cause the eeriest sensation to sweep over Whitney, making her body tremble. "What do you mean?" Whitney asked, the words barely leaving her throat.

Javar sighed and said, "She admitted everything. All this time, I was angry with you…but she did it. She cut the brakes…"

This was too unreal, too unbelievably horrible. As Whitney looked into her husband's eyes, saw the torment in their depths, she almost couldn't breathe.

Somehow she found her voice. "You mean…?" Her head was shaking, and her body felt so incredibly cold.

"Yes!" Javar exclaimed. "Damn it, she did it. She killed him. She killed my son!"

It all seemed too bizarre to be true. For so long, Whitney had blamed herself for J.J.'s death. If she had only buckled him in, if she had only been able to stop the car from spinning out of control…. She remembered hitting the brakes, but that they had not wanted to cooperate with her efforts to control the car. But she had blamed herself even for that.

And now… It wasn't her fault. That first accident had been sabotage.

Oh, God.

"She wanted to kill you," Javar was saying. "But she—she killed my son."

It was like reliving the whole horrible nightmare over again, watching Javar grieve as he had two years ago. Fighting her own tears that threatened to fall, Whitney framed Javar's face with both hands, forcing him to look at her.

"Everything was a lie. It was all a lie," he said.

"Oh, Javar. I'm sorry."

"No," he said sharply, taking her hands in his. "I'm sorry. I'm sorry for being so blind. Why didn't I see this? Why?"

"It's not your fault." Whitney's reserve of strength began to crumble. "Oh, God." Slipping her arms around his neck, she pulled him close. "Oh, God."

And there they stayed, in each other's arms, grieving anew for what they had lost. Grieving for little J.J., the innocent victim who had died because they had loved. Grieving for the years of misplaced guilt. Grieving so they could start to heal.

That night, two hearts reunited. Two lost souls found their way home.

Epilogue

Whitney glanced up at the jib and watched the wind play on the small orange ribbons that she and Javar had used to trim the sail. There was a light breeze, but it was enough to move the sleek white boat through the water. Beside her, Javar controlled the sail, much like he controlled her heart.

Her husband…this time forever.

Javar cast a sidelong glance in her direction, smiling as he caught her staring at him. They had come a long way; her round belly was a testament to that fact.

It was almost a year to the day when Javar's mother had made a final attempt on her life. The Jordan family was stunned and hurt by the news, and shortly after Angela's arrest, Marcus filed for divorce. Even Michelle, who had never liked Whitney, disowned her mother when she learned what her mother had done. Michelle had explained to Whitney and Javar that although she and her mother had hired a detective to investigate Whitney, she hadn't been part of her mother's warped murder plan. Both Whitney and Javar believed her.

Initially Angela had pled temporary insanity in court, but later changed her plea to guilty. She was convicted of murder and attempted murder, and was now in prison for at least the next fifteen years.

Despite everything that happened, Whitney and Javar had triumphed, beating all the odds against them. Because instead of concentrating on the obstacles, they had remembered their love for each other, the very love that had brought them together in the beginning.

"My ears are burning," Javar said.

"At least your ankles aren't swollen," Whitney retorted playfully.

"You're beautiful," Javar said, and the spark in his eye told her his words were one hundred percent true.

"Come here," Whitney said, patting the tramp beside her.

Javar fiddled with the sail, then joined his wife, placing a hand on her belly as he sat beside her.

"I know we said we'd never keep anything from each other," Whitney began, "but there's something I have to tell you."

Javar arched a thick eyebrow, his lips pulling into a tight line. His tone guarded, he asked, "What do you mean?"

"I mean," Whitney replied, her lips curling into a smile, "that I haven't been completely honest with you."

Javar sensed she was being playful, but was still confused by her riddle. "Okay. What haven't you told me?"

"Oh…that we're having two babies." She wrinkled her nose, then said coyly, "Please don't be mad."

Javar's mouth fell open and his eyes grew wide. "Twins? We're having *twins?*"

Whitney nodded, then squealed. "Yeah. I just found out."

"Sweetheart!" Javar wrapped her in an embrace—as much of an embrace as he could, considering her belly. "Oh, that's fabulous news!"

"Yeah, I thought so."

Javar planted a kiss on her lips, then pulled away to look at her. The smile was gone, replaced by a more serious expression. Whitney knew he was remembering J.J. They would never forget him; he had a permanent place in their hearts. But they were moving on, together.

"I have news of my own," Javar said.

"You do?"

"Yes." He took Whitney's hand. "Remember when my firm didn't get the Li bid, I told you I wasn't upset because I was working on something else? Something much more important?"

"Yes."

"Well, that 'something else' is finally coming together. I've found the perfect place."

Whitney eyed Javar quizzically. "What are you talking about?"

"It isn't finalized yet, but there's an old house close to Burnham Park that I want to buy. It's big. I want to fix it up, and—" he paused, then continued "—turn it into a youth center."

"Javar?" Whitney asked, surprised.

"I'm going to name it the J. Jordan Jr. Community Center…as a tribute to J.J. What do you think?"

Whitney reached out, ran her fingers over the planes and grooves of Javar's face. "I think that's an absolutely wonderful idea. J.J. would be so proud."

Javar smiled weakly. "I know."

"I love you, Javar Jordan," Whitney said, trailing a finger along the outline of his full mouth. "So much."

"I love you too."

And then their lips met in a soft, lingering, breathtaking kiss. A kiss that spoke of their promise, of their profound commitment to each other.

A kiss that spoke of everlasting love.

SWEET HONESTY

To my Jamaican "posse," the Perrins and McKenzies:
Much love to you all!
And to Dane: Gone too soon, but always in my heart.

Prologue

It's April Fool's Day, Samona Gray told herself as she glanced nervously around the store. *This must be a joke.* Her brain could think of no other reason why Roger Benson, her boyfriend of only two months, had led her into Milano Jewelers, a quaint jewelry store in Chicago's Near North.

The hand that held hers was damp with sweat, but Samona preferred to blame that on the heat of the beautiful spring day. Anything else—like the fact that he was actually considering engagement-ring shopping—was just too unsettling to think about.

"Roger, what are we doing here?" Samona asked, glancing around the store. Gold, diamonds and other expensive jewelry glistened beneath the ceiling's pod lights. The floor was a sparkling polished oak. Everything was beautiful, and maybe if this had been a time in the not-so-distant past, with a very different man, she would have been excited. Now, it felt like her insides had been churned in a blender.

On more than one occasion Roger had talked about how beautiful a person she was and how he cared for her, even though she'd told him she wasn't ready for a serious relationship. She didn't know when she would be ready again. Roger had seemed slightly disappointed, but had agreed to an open, casual relationship—no commitments. However, in the last few days he had started talking about the "future." He'd mentioned some investments and how he hoped they'd pay off soon. If they did, he could "settle down" and buy a house. From all he'd said, Samona had sensed he'd wanted her in that future, but this?

"You'll see," Roger said in response to her question. His hand still possessively holding hers, he led her to a display case. This particular one boasted a variety of gold chains. Samona released a cautious breath. Maybe she was wrong. Maybe Roger hadn't lost his mind.

There was only one clerk in the store, an attractive, slightly plump lady who appeared to be in her mid-fifties. She looked like Audrey Hepburn. Presently, she was talking to the only other customer in the store, a middle-aged man.

"Do you like that one?" Roger asked, pointing to a thin gold chain with an emerald heart pendant.

"Uh, that's nice," Samona replied, deliberately not sounding enthused. She wouldn't add that it was too expensive a gift unless he actually offered to buy it for her.

The door chimes sang, and when Samona looked up, the clerk was beside them. Now she and Roger were the only customers in the store.

"Hello," the clerk said. A spark of recognition flashed in her eyes and a smile spread across her face as she looked at Roger. "You've been here before."

Roger's hand tightened around Samona's then, almost as though he was nervous and Samona wondered why. Again, her stomach dropped.

His smile was charming and confident as he faced the clerk. "Yes," he replied. "Mrs. Milano, right?"

She nodded. "That's right. Not only good-looking, but smart too." She looked at Samona as she said the last words.

Samona forced a grin.

"What brings you by today?" Mrs. Milano asked. "Ring shopping for this beautiful young woman?"

Samona stole a glance at Roger, anxiously awaiting his response. *Please let him say no,* she thought. *I can't deal with this....*

"I'm looking for a little somethin' for my lady," he said, not giving Samona the answer she craved. One hand was comfortably nestled in the pocket of his long, leather coat; the other still clung to hers like a lifeline. "When I was here before, Mr. Milano said he was designing some new pieces. Is he here? I'd like to see his new creations."

"Right now, he's out doing some banking," Mrs. Milano said. "Before the banks close. But I think I know what you're talking about. Those new rings are over here." With a nod of her head, she signaled for Roger and Samona to follow her.

Oh no, Samona thought.

"They are quite magnificent, if I do say so myself," Mrs. Milano said as she strolled toward the display in question, her shoulder-length auburn hair swaying gently. "Any particular carat size?"

"Beautiful," Roger almost sang as he peered into the glass display. Releasing Samona's hand, he pointed to a huge pear-shaped diamond. "Can I see that one right there?"

Samona swallowed her shock.

Mrs. Milano smiled. "Excellent choice."

The next part happened fast. As Mrs. Milano began to unlock the display case, Roger grabbed Samona in a headlock. Then instantly, seemingly out of thin air, something cold and hard was rammed against her temple.

A gun. Samona knew it without having to see that that's what the icy cold metal was.

Fear spread through her blood, rendering her ice-cold. And numb. And stiff. If Roger's arm wasn't around her neck she would surely collapse.

This was just so bizarre, so real and unreal at the same time that her mind didn't know how to process what was happening.

Roger had a gun to her head! The image was so jarring it was like she only just realized it. Her chest felt heavy, like something was crushing her, forcing the air from her lungs. She tried hard to suck in oxygen, but couldn't. Her head whirled. Good God, what was happening?

"Give me everything you've got!" Roger screamed. The soft-spoken man Samona had known now sounded loud and hateful.

Mrs. Milano's eyes bulged as she saw the gun, but she didn't scream. Instead, she stood rooted to the spot, seemingly paralyzed with fear.

"Move it!" Roger demanded. "Or I'll kill you both!"

Mrs. Milano whimpered then, a soft cry of protest. Yet her hands flew into the display case, grabbing as much as she could. She dropped the precious jewels onto the counter.

Roger yelled, "Put them in a bag!"

"Y-yes," she stammered. "Th-they're j-just over th-here." Hurrying to the cash register, she cast a quick worried glance at the front door.

"Don't worry about it. Nobody's getting in here, and nobody's getting out. The place has been secured."

Mrs. Milano paled at Roger's words, and it was obvious she was holding back tears. No doubt, she had hoped that someone would walk in and interrupt this robbery, that someone would save her.

Samona had hoped the same thing. But as Roger's arm

pressed against her windpipe, as he jerkily moved around taking her with him, she saw her hopes and dreams dying. She saw the faces of her second-grade students and wondered how they would react to the news of her death.

Of her murder…

"Hurry up!" Roger screamed. "I don't have all day."

"Please. Please don't do this. Th-this is all we have…."

"Shut up and keep filling that bag!"

The pressure against Samona's throat was so great and the effort to fill her lungs so hard, she began to gag. Awful wheezing sounds were coming from her mouth. Each time she tried to inhale, she forced oxygen from her lungs instead. She needed air in her body, needed it desperately.

"Stop that, Samona," Roger whispered in her ear, his voice deadly. "Stop that, or I swear I'll kill you right now."

But she couldn't stop herself. As she gagged, her chest heaved, and as a natural reflex, she grabbed the arm that threatened to snuff out her life.

She felt the sharp, blinding blow then, but only for an instant. Because the next instant, the floor rushed up to meet her.

Chapter 1

"Lawson," Captain Boyle bellowed from across the hallway. He stood in the doorway of his office like a giant, his large, pale hands planted on his thick waist. His voice easily carried across the room from his office to the office of Derrick Lawson, detective with the Chicago Police Department. "I need to see you in here pronto."

Immediately dropping the file he'd been leafing through on his desk, Derrick rose. The captain had retreated into his office. Quickly, Derrick crossed the open area filled with filing cabinets, desks, computers and billboards of wanted suspects to the captain's office. When Captain Boyle made a request—or a demand, as many of the officers at this district liked to call it—you responded as quickly as humanly possible.

"What is it?" Derrick asked as he stepped into the office.

"Close the door and take a seat."

Derrick did as told, sitting opposite the captain's large, cluttered desk. It was always cluttered with various folders, but today there were photos scattered across the older man's desk. Photos of a beautiful black woman Derrick immediately recognized. Samona Gray, the girlfriend of notorious Chicago criminal, Roger Benson.

"She didn't show yesterday," Captain Boyle said, assuming

Derrick knew about whom he was talking. "Her own boyfriend's memorial service, and she didn't even make an appearance. Talk about taking the meaning of keeping a low profile to an extreme." He frowned, then continued. "She hasn't messed up once since the robbery, Lawson. Not once." He picked up a candid shot of Samona that had been taken while she was under surveillance, then tossed it back with a snort. Placing his elbows squarely on the desk, he said, "It's time for Plan B."

Naturally, Derrick was sitting in Captain Boyle's office because Plan B involved him. He leaned back in the worn chair. "What exactly do you have in mind?"

"I don't need to tell you that this is a high-profile case. It's not the kind we can easily let die a natural death. Nor should it be. A woman was murdered."

"I agree."

Captain Boyle ran a hand over the bald spot on his head. "The commander and I have been talking, and we finally think we have a way to nail this woman. We've got a special assignment for you."

Derrick was afraid that that was the reason for his being there. "Sir, I don't think I can do a special assignment right now," he began. "As you know, I'm still very involved in that huge heroin bust. I'll have to go to court, and I don't know when I'll be free."

"I'm not asking you." Captain Boyle's stern, abrupt voice made it clear that Derrick had no choice. "As I said, the commander and I have discussed this, the mayor has been involved in this conversation, and we want to find that jewelry. Not to mention solve the murder. We're not going to continue to be made a fool of by some pretty young woman who thinks she can beat the system."

Especially since Captain Boyle's ex-wife, a young, beautiful woman, had made a fool of him by leaving him for an older, wealthier man. Ever since his divorce, the captain had been especially bitter where beautiful women were concerned.

"So what you're really saying," Derrick began, "is that I'm going to do some sort of undercover assignment? Is that it?"

"Yes," Captain Boyle said. Loudly, he cleared his throat, something he tended to do often. "I want you to know that I personally recommended you for this, Lawson. You're the best man I have for the job." When Derrick opened his mouth to speak, the captain continued. "You're a damn fine detective, Lawson. You've proven yourself over and over in this district." He paused. "I know you really enjoy working in Drug Enforcement, but you're the only one I think can handle this job."

Derrick interjected at that point. "I appreciate your faith in me, but I'm sure there are other people in this office, in the city of Chicago, who can do this." It meant a lot that the captain respected him; he didn't easily give compliments. Derrick hoped that would score him some points now. If the captain knew he didn't want to do this assignment, maybe he would assign someone else to the job. "I don't see why it has to be me."

"Are you saying you're refusing to do this?" Captain Boyle's stern eyes met Derrick's head-on.

"No," Derrick said slowly, his hopes fading. "I'm not refusing. But I am hoping you'll reconsider your decision because of my other commitments, mainly the work I need to do on that heroin case."

"I understand your concern," the captain said, his tone abnormally soft. Derrick's eyes must have reflected his shock, for Captain Boyle cleared his throat and continued in his normal boisterous tone. "Look, the mayor approached the commander about this, and the commander approached the captains of all the districts. We chose you. The mayor is counting on you to bring this case to an end, and I've already given him my word that you'll be cooperative. We've taken the steps necessary to cover the work you've been doing in drug enforcement. So that's not a concern. What is our concern is that you're single, you're attractive and you're good at what you do. We need you on this, Lawson. This isn't a question. I've only brought you in here to tell you what your new assignment is."

Derrick didn't know whether to feel proud or angry. He did not appreciate the way Captain Boyle was forcing this on him at the last minute, without even having told him that he might be considered for a special assignment. He was not enthused when he asked, "What exactly is this special assignment?"

"You're going undercover. We need you to get close to Samona Gray." He looked down at her picture and scowled. "We need you to get her to trust you. And when she trusts you, we believe she'll finally break down and tell you where the stash of hidden jewelry is. Only a few pieces were recovered from the explosion that killed her boyfriend, which leads me to believe there's a stash somewhere else. Maybe she'll even admit to her part in the murder. Nothing will bring that poor woman back, but at least we can get justice for her husband."

Derrick nodded. He remembered seeing Angelo Milano, the victim's husband, on the news. He had been so distraught that at the funeral he had thrown himself onto his wife's coffin as it was being lowered into the ground. "How long do you anticipate this assignment will last?"

"We're hoping it won't last more than a month, but we're being realistic. We don't want you to rush the issue. Take as long as you need to get Samona to open up to you. There's no point scaring her off before she's given you the information that we need." Captain Boyle shifted in his chair, something else he tended to do often. "I know you know all of this already, because as I've said, you're an excellent detective. You've done great undercover work in the past, although nothing this...personal. But I trust you. In fact, we're all counting on you."

Great, Derrick thought. *No pressure at all.* But he said, "When do I start?"

At that moment, Captain Boyle produced a thick manila folder from the clutter on his desk. How he knew where anything was was a wonder to Derrick. "First thing Monday morning."

"Monday? It's Friday evening right now. That's not enough time for me to tie up any loose ends—"

"I know what day it is. Have you heard anything I've said? This is urgent. Forget the loose ends. I'll get in touch with you about your present cases when absolutely necessary. But for now, think Derrick Cunningham. Sci-fi writer."

"Sci-fi?" Derrick didn't even like science fiction.

"Yes. It was the best thing I could think of given the time."

Derrick groaned. Then shrugged. What else could he do?

"We've rented you an apartment in the same building where Ms. Gray lives to make it easier. She lives on the second floor of an old Victorian-styled home. You get the third level." Captain Boyle shifted until he was comfortable. "This is the file on her."

Derrick's eyes bulged at the file's thickness. Reaching for it, he took it from the captain. "All this?"

"Yes. I know, it's thick. I'm sorry you didn't get more notice, but that's the way things go sometimes. Mrs. Milano certainly didn't get any notice before her brains were blown out."

Derrick made a face at the captain's crass words. Opening the file, he said, "This is everything?"

The captain cleared his throat and continued. "Yes. Everything is there from our surveillance of her, as well as all the information on the crime. You'll need to read that file on the weekend to get an idea of what Ms. Gray is like, what she does, where she goes—that sort of thing. Then, as soon as you can, make contact. I cannot impress upon you how urgent this case is. And you'll report to me personally on this case, not Lieutenant Grigson."

"What about the Oak Park Police Department?"

"What about them? You think the mayor of Chicago is going to trust that small, Mickey Mouse force to handle this case? The suspect may live in Oak Park now, but the robbery happened in Chicago's north end. This is our baby."

Derrick was sorry he'd asked. He wondered why the northern district officers weren't continuing with this case. Probably because they were too close to it already, and Samona might recognize one of those officers. It was very unlikely she would recognize anyone from District Four where Derrick worked, as it was located in Chicago's south side.

"Any other questions?"

"No," Derrick replied. But he really wanted to say, "Why me?" He didn't want to do this. He was knee-deep in a drug investigation that was more important than this case as far as he was concerned. Why didn't the captain give this assignment to someone else? Anyone else?

Frowning, Derrick silently admitted that he knew why. While he wasn't enthusiastic about this new assignment, he did accept the fact that he was probably the best choice. As a single male he was a better candidate to do undercover work than married or committed men.

Captain Boyle continued to speak, going over various specifics of the case, but Derrick tuned him out for several seconds. He flipped through the numerous pictures of Samona Gray. In most of the pictures she wore braids, but in a few she had straight hair. Picking up a black-and-white photo where her hair was straight, Derrick studied it.

She was indeed beautiful. He didn't know where the shot was taken, probably as she walked down a Chicago street unaware that a camera was even on her. Her ebony hair was windblown, and she had a peculiar expression on her face. It wasn't so much peculiar as it was wary, Derrick realized. Almost as though she knew she was being watched, followed, not free to live her life without scrutiny. And in her eyes he saw sadness, or was it guilt?

What had led her to commit the crime of robbery and murder? The answers were not written on her attractive face.

Derrick cocked an eyebrow. Suddenly, he was intrigued. Intrigued about this new case. Intrigued about Samona Gray.

He hated her.

The man who stood above her was large, angry, cold and menacing. His face was red and covered with perspiration. He stared at her intently, his large arms folded over his wide chest, his legs parted and stiff. Every other second, the vein in his neck jumped. That scared her. And the way his dark eyes bored into her made it clear that he would tear her limb from limb if it weren't for the two other men standing in the small, musty room.

He leaned forward, slamming his heavy palms on the table. She flinched. "Stop lying, Samona. We know you did it. Where is it? Where's the money?"

Samona shivered despite the warmth of the muggy room. "I—I don't know. I've already told you…"

"A woman is dead because of you. Did you get your thrills when you blew her head to bits? Huh? Did it turn you on?"

"N-no. Y-you're wrong. I—I didn't d-do that."

"Didn't you?" He looked at her like she was nothing more than dirt.

Samona met his eyes. "No. I could never—"

The man cut her off. "Do you want to spend the rest of your life in jail, Samona? Do you? It's not a pretty place. You'd be fresh meat but not for long, not after the women there get a hold of you." His low chuckle was pure evil. "Is that what you want, Samona?" When she merely whimpered, the detective edged his face closer, until his lips were only a mere inch away from hers. "How long does a pretty girl like you think she can last in prison?"

Samona squirmed in her chair, gripping the edges until her fingers hurt. Why was this happening to her? Why wouldn't they believe her? She didn't have the answers they needed. She had told them that over and over, but they told her she was a liar. She was afraid in here, afraid of these big men with their loud voices, with their accusatory stares. Why couldn't they see that she was telling the truth?

"Fine." The man stood to his full, intimidating height. Briefly he faced the two other large men in the room. When they nodded in obvious response to some secret code, he slipped the gun from his holster and immediately brought the cold barrel to Samona's head. "You blew it, lady. Now you're going to die!"

"No! No, please!"

The two big men were holding her arms now. They were going to kill her. She tried to struggle, tried to free her arms…

Samona's desperate cries pierced the air. Panting, she awoke and found herself tangled in the sheets. Fighting the sheets off, she bolted upright in the bed. Her body was damp with sweat, and her heart raced as though she'd just run a marathon.

Her eyes focused in the dark room. Recognizing her familiar surroundings, Samona released a long sigh and buried her face in her hands. She'd been dreaming. Thank God. She could relax.

Relax... The word brought with it mixed emotions. While she could relax for the moment, she could never truly relax. Not while she knew that her worst nightmare could still become a reality.

She took a few moments to herself, forcing air in and out of her lungs in an even rhythm, willing herself to calm down. She could not have another panic attack like she'd had the day of the murder.

Glancing at the bedside digital clock, she saw that it was only 3:08 a.m. That didn't surprise her. Ever since the robbery and murder, she hadn't slept one restful night. She wondered if she ever would again.

She'd been accused of being involved in that robbery. The police believed she helped commit the murder.

She was going to go nuts. Throwing off the thick down comforter, Samona stretched her feet onto the floor. The polished hardwood floor was cold despite the warm temperature in her room. Sliding her feet into the pair of slippers she kept by her bed, she rose. Slowly she made her way to the bedroom door.

Exiting the bedroom, she walked into the living room, almost mechanically. No longer did she have pep in her steps. Not since that horrible day at the jewelry store. Samona did what had become routine every night when she awoke. She moved to the small window and slowly eased the lace curtain aside, peering into the dark night.

Nothing. Only the soft rustling movements of the various mature trees. A few cars were parked on the street, but not the white van she had become accustomed to seeing in the last two months. Her racing pulse calmed.

Turning, Samona walked to the plush sofa, the floor mildly protesting under her weight. She collapsed onto the soft material and stretched out, staring at the ceiling in the night-darkened room.

Two weeks, she thought. It had been two weeks since she'd last seen the van. Two weeks since she had moved into this new apartment in Oak Park, a suburb of Chicago.

Maybe they hadn't found her. Not yet, anyway. But she had no doubt that they would. When the police wanted something accomplished, they pulled out all the stops.

And the Chicago police did want her.

It wasn't that she was hiding. She had nothing to hide, even though they didn't believe that. She had only moved because she wanted some peace for a change. The last two months had been so difficult, so stressful, she needed some time to think or she would lose her sanity.

And she hadn't moved far. Just from River Forest to Oak Park, still in Chicago's Near West. While it hadn't been a conscious effort to confuse the police, she couldn't deny that there was a part of her that hoped they would assume she'd moved far away. Especially the media. It had only been in the last few weeks that they'd slowed down their relentless pursuit of her.

She hadn't even gone to Roger's memorial service yesterday because she hadn't wanted to be the object of the media's scrutiny, and they would no doubt have been there. Unflattering pictures of her would have made the headlines, and that was something she could not deal with. People would have seen her with her new hairstyle and she would be more easily recognized on the street. She couldn't stand that. Not now, when she had found a measure of peace, no matter how fleeting it was. Despite her proclamation of innocence, the people in this town still thought she was guilty.

She *was* guilty, she thought, squeezing her forehead. Guilty of being a fool. She should never have gotten involved with Roger. If she hadn't, she would still have her life. She would have her job, her freedom and everything else that mattered. Now, she had nothing.

A lump formed in her throat at the memories of what she had lost. She would always berate herself for going against her better judgment and dating Roger. He had just seemed so nice when she'd met him at her school. He'd been the uncle of one of her students, picking up the child because her mother could not. Never had she imagined he would turn out to be a jerk.

More than a jerk. He was a lying criminal, and she wasn't sorry that he was dead.

The violence of her thought caused her to shudder. Rising from the sofa, she told herself that she didn't really wish him dead. She wished he hadn't fled town and gotten himself killed. That way, she could at least give him a piece of her mind.

It was still hard to believe that he was actually dead. By chance she had been watching the six o'clock news a few days ago and had learned that Roger had been killed in a boat explosion in Detroit.

Her mind whirling with thoughts, Samona stood and walked slowly to the bedroom, her arms wrapped around her torso in an attempt to ward off the chill that always accompanied the memories. It would do no good to think about Roger, his death and the suspicion that still surrounded her. She couldn't tell him off even if she wanted to, so she had to find a way to purge herself. Somehow, she needed to find a way to get her life back.

Climbing into bed, she pulled the thick comforter around her neck. The bed was big and as she curled into a ball, she felt so small in it.

Alone, that's how she felt. So incredibly alone.

Pulling the comforter tightly around her, Samona willed herself to sleep. But she knew that she would not find any peace anytime soon.

Whack! The racquet hit the squash ball with such force that it struck the wall and blasted back in less than a second. Nick Burns, a fellow Chicago PD detective and one of Derrick's close friends, extended his arm in an effort to make contact with the ball, but he missed and ended up on his knee.

"Holy, Lawson," he exclaimed, grimacing as he rose. "What are you trying to do? Murder the ball? Murder me?"

Derrick leaned forward and rested his palms on his knees, watching the black ball bounce. "Just playing some competitive squash, man. Can't you keep up?"

"Squash, my foot. Is Boyle's picture painted on that thing, or what?"

Derrick snorted, remembering yesterday's events at the office. As the ball dribbled near him, he reached out and snatched it.

"Guess that means you're pissed."

Derrick tossed the ball in the air and batted it with the racquet. Like a bullet it sped toward the wall then back toward them.

This time, Nick was able to hit it. But Derrick paid no mind as the ball hit the wall and volleyed back. "What I don't like is that I was the last to know. Sheesh, you think Boyle could have at least clued me in?"

"I think it was all last minute," Nick said. "You know the mayor has been breathing down the commander's neck. Partly because Mr. Milano has been breathing down his."

"Mr. Milano is getting on my nerves."

"Hey, he lost his wife. I'd want some answers too."

Derrick nodded, conceding that fact. If he'd been married and his wife was murdered, he'd probably be a royal pain in the department's butt too. "The point is Mr. Milano has to realize we're doing all we can."

"He thinks that Gray woman should be arrested."

"Who doesn't?" The little Derrick had read of the file convinced him of that. "She's in this mess up to her ears but we can't prove it. There was no murder weapon at the scene, so there's no proof she fired the gun that killed Mrs. Milano." Derrick had also learned from the file that the Milanos did not have security cameras installed in their store. A tearful Angelo Milano had told the investigating officers that he was going to do it soon. Now, with his wife brutally murdered, he had decided to close the store. "And Ms. Gray was found unconscious at the scene, with a nasty gash on her head."

"You think she's innocent?"

"I just said I think she's guilty. But there are other cops who can prove that. Why does it have to be me?"

"Yeah right." Nick's breathing had slowed. "Like me? I'm sure my wife would love that."

Derrick wanted to protest, but he knew nothing to say. Nick had been married for only three years, and had a young daughter. He wasn't going to get any long-term undercover assignments. Besides, he was white—definitely not the man for this particular job. Derrick, on the other hand, was single, attractive, black—and even bore a slight resemblance to Roger.

The fact that he looked a little like Roger could work either way, but the captain was hoping that fact would work in their favor.

Nick patted Derrick on the back. "Don't worry about it. I'll take all the glory on the drug bust when we go to court."

"Don't even say that, Burns."

"Then just make sure you put this case to bed real soon."

"You're right." Derrick slapped Nick's shoulder.

"Ow!"

"Man, you're such a wimp nowadays. Must be married life."

"Oh really?" Nick retrieved the ball and held it up, ready to serve. "Let's see who's a wimp now."

"C'mon, Jen. Pick up."

Samona's nervous hands played with the phone's spiral cord while she listened to the phone ring. Four… Five…

Jennifer Barry, the only person she considered a friend, wasn't home. With a groan, she returned the phone to its cradle, then sank into the sofa.

She needed to talk to somebody. Jen was the only one she kept in touch with from William Hatch Elementary School. Jen was the only one who believed her without a doubt. Four years earlier when Samona had first started working at the school, she and Jen had become fast friends. They were very close and could talk about anything. Men, the lack of good men and everything else in between. Jen was more of a sister to her than Samona's own had ever been.

In recent months, Jen had started dating. Her friendship with a local accountant was becoming more serious. That's probably where she was this Saturday night. With Ken. Samona was happy for her because Jen hadn't had a decent relationship in years. Still, she wished Jen was available for her now.

Samona closed her eyes, thinking about her friend. She could see her dark, round face right now, her big, brown eyes. If she were sitting here with her, Samona knew she would be cross-legged on the sofa with one eyebrow raised saying, "Girl, you're a lot stronger than you think. Just keep telling yourself you'll get over this and you will. Believe that; hold on to that and have faith. Things will work out."

That's the kind of person Jen was—always optimistic when there didn't seem to be anything worth being cheerful about. Always able to make her friends see the positive in any situation. Always there to ground her. Always there, period.

Jen was the one good thing Samona had in her life. If nothing else, she could hold on to that.

Oddly enough, just thinking of Jen as if she were there with her gave Samona a sudden surge of strength.

Gave her hope that in the fall she'd be back at William Hatch Elementary School with a new second-grade class.

Chapter 2

Samona Gray didn't look like a criminal. But having been a cop for seven years, Derrick knew that looks were deceiving. He had arrested many criminals that did not fit any stereotypical description.

Since Captain Boyle had given Derrick the file on Samona Gray two days ago, today was the first day he had truly studied it. "Interesting" was the only way he could describe what he had learned. If there was a type more noncriminal than Samona Gray, he didn't know of one.

Samona was a thirty-year-old teacher—a second-grade teacher no less. She was petite, five-foot-four. And she looked like a second-grade teacher—clean-cut, innocent. Hardly rough around the edges, the way the girlfriends of many low-life criminals were.

Derrick stretched his pajama-clad legs beneath his kitchen table and crossed one ankle over the other. Who would've thought that a second-grade teacher would be involved in a jewelry store robbery? A murder? She taught babies, for goodness' sake. Sweet little children who probably thought the world of her. Goodness, couldn't teachers be trusted anymore? Derrick shook his head ruefully. This case just proved that there was no way to really know who was a criminal and who wasn't.

Flipping through the folder, Derrick found and studied the picture of Samona he liked best, the one where she had been caught smiling. What had made her smile? he wondered. Maybe she had been with a friend in this picture, but only Samona had been photographed.

What made her turn to crime? Frustrated, Derrick sighed. Not only was she involved in this jewelry store robbery and murder, but there was a definite possibility that she was involved in two other unsolved jewelry store robberies in Chicago in the past six months. Derrick flicked his finger against the edge of the picture. Two other robberies... Was this sweet-looking teacher involved in those as well?

Sweet. Not for the first time, Derrick acknowledged his impressions of Samona. Sweet, gentle-looking. Under normal circumstances, she was the type of woman he might try to get to know better on those rare occasions he gave dating a second thought.

Derrick dropped the picture into the manila folder and rose from the small, round table. He stretched, then yawned. This case had kept him up most of the night.

He may as well get dressed and take his belongings to the car. Luckily, the apartment he would be using for the duration of this assignment was furnished. All he had to do was bring himself, his laptop, the pertinent police files and some other necessities.

An undercover assignment with a beautiful woman. Derrick chortled at the irony of it all. Some men would love such an assignment. Not him. At this point in his life, he hardly thought of women. After his heart had been broken by the one and only woman he had ever loved, Derrick didn't think he'd pursue a relationship for a very long time. As the saying went, his heart wasn't in it.

Derrick walked through his small apartment toward the bedroom, hoping this assignment would not last long. He wanted to get back to drug enforcement, his true love. Not that getting the people responsible for the jewelry store heists and murder wasn't important, but to him, getting drugs off the street was a much more important matter. He saw what drugs did to people, how many lives had been ruined because of them. Working in Chicago's inner city, he especially saw the devastating effect drugs had on that community. It was a community he loved because he had grown up in it. Anybody he could save from the powerful allure of drugs and street life was a small victory won.

After a quick shower and change into a decent suit for church, Derrick retrieved the large duffel bag from his bedroom and brought it to the car. He couldn't help thinking about his new persona. No longer was he Derrick Lawson the detective. He was now Derrick Cunningham the writer. An artist, just like Samona.

As had happened before he started any undercover operation in the past, Derrick's stomach fluttered from a bout of nervousness. The captain was convinced that the best way to get close to Samona was to be similar to her in terms of likes and dislikes. Not only would Derrick be posing as an artist like her, but he'd be posing as a loner with a troubled past. Derrick didn't like deceiving people, but in this case he could justify his actions. One, he was paid to do a job, and he did as was told. Two, lying to Samona in an effort to get her to trust him would help get one more dangerous criminal off the street. Hopefully she would feel a kinship with him. Hopefully soon.

Derrick knew her schedule. Samona Gray, despite the fact that she was a criminal, or perhaps because of it, kept a low profile. She didn't venture far from home, but did go to Grant Park daily to work on her art. Sometimes she went a little farther north along the Lake Michigan shoreline to Oak Street Beach. Samona could be found in either the park or on the beach when working, depending on the number of people in either place.

Grant Park was where Derrick would make his move. Soon he would be there with a notebook in hand, a lonely writer looking for a friend.

"That was a good service today," Derrick's mother said as she spooned white rice onto her plate. "Pastor Rawlins spoke the truth, didn't he? People in a position to help, pattin' others on the back and tellin' them to pray. Why can't they realize that *they* may be the help?"

Derrick, his mother, Sharon Lawson; his sister, Karen Montgomery; and his brother-in-law Russell Montgomery, were gathered around the large mahogany table for dinner at his mother's house, the way they did most Sundays after church. It was the one time in the week they all tried to get together.

"You're so right, Mom," Karen said, chewing a bit of food. "That's what I love about Pastor Rawlins. He speaks the truth, and he speaks it straight." Karen's fourteen-month-old daughter, Emily, sat in a high-chair beside her. Emily was a happy baby who normally loved to eat, but right now she was more interested in playing with the mashed potatoes on her plate.

Glancing at his family members in turn as each spoke, Derrick picked at his food. His mind was occupied. He would miss his family in the upcoming weeks. For the duration of this assignment he would have minimal contact with his family and friends, if any contact at all. The assignment was too risky to jeopardize.

He couldn't even risk an overheard phone call from his new apartment.

"Derrick, you seem awfully quiet," his mother said. "You've hardly eaten a thing. Please tell me it's not my cooking." A smile touched her lips. When Derrick didn't reply—merely grinned faintly—she continued, "My baby's not coming down with somethin', are you?"

He spiked a baby carrot with his fork. "Just thinking."

"If you're not sick, then it must be work. Must be a case botherin' you."

Even as a child, Derrick could never keep the fact that something was bothering him from his mother. While he had been close to his father, he had been closer to her. Softly, he replied, "Yeah, it's work."

His mother twisted her lips and gave him one of her sidelong glances, the one that said she was worried about him.

"What is it, D?" his brother-in-law asked.

Derrick faced Russell. "I'm starting a special assignment tomorrow. I'll be working on a pretty high-profile case."

"Really?" Karen asked, her brown eyes growing wide. "Drug related?"

"No. I'm off the Drug Enforcement Unit until this case is solved, and I'm not sure how long that will be. I can't say much more than that, except that I won't be available for a while. So, if you don't hear from me, if you don't see me, don't worry."

"What do you have to do?" his mother asked solemnly. She dropped her fork and knife on her plate. Suddenly she wasn't interested in her food either.

Derrick gave her a you-know-I-can't-tell-you-that look. When concern clouded his mother's eyes, he added, "All I can say is it's nothing dangerous. But I will be doing undercover work."

"Undercover?" his mother asked. "I don't know if I like the sound of that. I've never heard of any undercover assignment that wasn't dangerous."

"You must be watching too much TV," Derrick said playfully, but his mother didn't laugh.

Derrick then said, "I give you my word."

His mother didn't seem convinced. "I know you hate when I say this, but I just wish you weren't a cop. I worry so much."

"Mom," Derrick said, reaching across the table and taking her hand. "I can take care of myself. I've been a cop for a long time."

"But you can't stop a bullet," she quickly said, then averted her eyes. "I'm sorry, honey. I shouldn't—"

"It's okay. But I do promise you, Mom, I will be fine." Still his mother did not seem reassured, and though it hurt him that his mother didn't accept his job, he understood her fear. It was the same fear that many of his friends and family had, because they knew that being a police officer was a dangerous job. Since the death of his father seven years ago, his mother had become more protective. She was afraid of losing either of her two children.

Derrick knew she was lonely. She never openly admitted that she was, but with no husband and her two children grown and out of the house, she must be. That's why he tried to make it to Sunday dinner with her every week.

Karen must have sensed her mother's fear as well, for she took her mother's free hand in hers and gently squeezed it. "You know Derrick always takes care of himself."

"Hey, at least no one can accuse you of having a boring life," Russell joked.

Derrick chuckled. "Maybe when I'm not knee-deep in paperwork."

Russell shrugged. "At least that's more exciting than quality control."

"Stop complaining," Karen said, her eyes teasing as she looked at her husband. "You can't always have the best of both worlds—money *and* excitement."

"Ain't that the truth," Mrs. Lawson said.

"Mmm hmm," Derrick agreed. Not that he cared about money over his career. He loved his job and was happy as long as he could pay the bills and have a pretty secure existence.

For a while longer they spoke and laughed as they ate, and Derrick was relieved the topic of conversation didn't venture to his undercover assignment. He was glad that while his family worried about him and the work he did, they respected the privacy that surrounded his cases.

When he was ready to leave, his mother hugged him long and hard, as though she didn't want to let him go. "I'll miss you, son. I hope you're okay."

"I will be," Derrick assured her. He took her hands in his. "And I'll keep in touch as often as I can."

"Please do."

He said goodbye to Karen, Russell and little Emily, then skipped down the front steps to his car.

As he drove away, his mother stood on the front porch waving, a sad look in her eyes.

Samona ripped the sheet of paper from the easel in one smooth movement and crumpled it into a ball. Tossing it onto the floor, it landed atop the other crumpled pieces. She moaned and closed her eyes.

"This isn't working," she said after a long moment, slapping her charcoal-covered hands against her thighs. The black charcoal stained her jeans. Groaning, she heaved herself off the wooden stool and tried to brush her soiled jeans as best she could. She only made it worse.

She scowled at her easel, tempted to throw it, the charcoal and smudge stick out the window.

Who was she trying to fool, she thought, walking to the living-room window. Ever since Roger's memorial service, she hadn't been able to concentrate on anything.

"Ms. Gray, what is your part in this robbery?"

"Ms. Gray, are you faking your injuries?"

Samona squeezed her eyes shut, trying to block out the memories. She had to forget about the past two months. But how could she, when it was always there? Always there like the scar in her hairline. It wasn't very visible unless one looked closely, but she could still feel it. Thanks to Roger, she'd needed six stitches and therefore would always have a physical reminder of the worst day of her life.

Samona peered through the window at nothing. The street was quiet except for the occasional car driving through. This area of Oak Park was home to many seniors, and she was happy for that. The police would be less likely to look here for her.

More than once Samona had considered fleeing the state and starting over, despite the police orders that she not leave town. If she left town, maybe even the country, she could start again with a clean slate. She had a sizable amount of cash from her parents' estate and generous life insurance policy. Moving somewhere where people didn't know her was definitely an option. If two months had passed and the police still had no concrete proof to arrest her, then surely she was home free....

No, she couldn't do that...wouldn't do that. Running away like a coward was not the answer. Besides, if she ran, the cloud of suspicion would always follow her. Any day the bubble could burst on her new existence and she could be dragged into jail. She would be humiliated before her new friends, and maybe by that time even her children. No, running wasn't an option.

She wanted her life back. And that meant staying in Chicago and clearing her name.

Samona turned and walked back to her easel. Maybe she could clear her name by the end of the summer. Maybe she could return to her teaching job in the fall.

Maybe she should stop thinking about all she could not control right now. Thinking about maybes and what-ifs only made her remember how dismal her life was. Right now, she should go to Grant Park with her sketch pad, the one place she felt at peace. The sunlight, the cool breeze off the lake and other people made her feel a part of something. Made her feel like she wasn't alone.

"He's not dead. I know it."

At Alex's words, Marie abruptly stopped kissing his neck. In the darkened room, she stared at him in disbelief but he stared only at the ceiling. Pouting, she slid her lingerie-clad body off his naked one. She may as well have been kissing a dead dog.

All he ever talked about was Roger. Roger this, Roger that. She was angry too; he had ripped them both off. But there was a time and place for everything. Now was definitely not the time.

"I swear, I'll get that money."

Since the news of Roger's death, Alex was so angry he scared her sometimes. "He's dead, Red."

"He damn well better be. 'Cause if he ain't, I'll kill him."

"His body was burnt to a crisp, remember?"

"Yeah." Alex didn't sound convinced.

"C'mon, Red. Don't do this."

He dug his fingers into her shoulder and faced her. In the softly illuminated room, Marie thought his eyes looked like the devil's. "Don't do this? Do you think I can let him get away with what he did?"

Marie deliberately took his hand off her shoulder. "If the police are certain that he's dead, why aren't you?"

"Because I know him." Alex lay back on the pillow. "They don't call him The Worm for nothing. That man, I tell you, can worm his way out of anything."

He seemed calmer. Marie placed a hand on Alex's chest, twirling a few strands of the curly, dark hair. Maybe if she could divert his attention, this night would not be a total waste. When she spoke, her voice was low and sexy. "Why stress yourself over Roger? It's not like we're broke or hard up. We take care of ourselves. We have been for a long time. So if he skipped town, who cares? At least he's the one the police want—not us. This couldn't have worked out better if we'd planned it."

Alex grabbed her hand and stopped it, squeezed it. "He ripped me off. That's the point. I don't care who the police are looking for. I care about the money that he stole from me. Nobody rips off Red and gets away with it."

Marie yanked her hand from Alex's firm grip. This was useless. Exasperated, she rolled over and turned her back to him.

This was not her idea of an exciting night. There hadn't been very many exciting nights lately. All because of Roger. A dead guy who had gotten what he'd deserved.

The whole Roger thing was getting stale. As far as she was concerned they had enough stolen goods to cash in big and be on easy street for the rest of their lives. What was the point worrying about Roger? Sometimes Alex's ego never failed to amaze her.

Alex shuffled then, and the next moment he had his arms wrapped around her thin waist. Gently he stroked his fingers across her belly. In no time Marie was hot. She turned to face him, snuggling her body against his chest.

Alex said, "I want you to find out where she is."

A cold wave swept over Marie and she froze. "Who are you talking about?" But she knew.

"Don't play dumb. His girlfriend—that's who I'm talking about. The way Roger talked about her, I'm sure she knows where he is."

"How am I supposed to find out where she is?" Marie could not hide her anger.

"You're very resourceful," Alex said, running a hand down her arm. "I'm sure you'll find a way."

With that, he rolled over, away from her. Marie knew what that meant.

She had no choice. She had better find out where Samona Gray was, and soon.

Chapter 3

The moment Derrick saw her, he froze. While the pictures he'd seen had enabled him to recognize her, they did her no justice.

It was hard to describe her, but beautiful was not accurate. She was more than beautiful; she was extraordinary, captivating, even in a simple T-shirt and faded jeans. Her straight hair was pulled back and covered with a baseball cap.

Straight, not thin braids like in most of the pictures. Jet-black hair. Shoulder-length hair. Hair that he knew would be very flattering if it was left hanging around her oval-shaped face as opposed to tied back. Like in the picture of her where she was smiling.

Her skin was smooth and looked like caramel. Her eyes were big and bright, and though they looked sad now, he could easily picture warmth there, laughter and happiness. She had full, sensuous lips, lips he found himself wishing he could see with a smile instead of a frown.

Nothing about her seemed evil and conniving. Nothing about her seemed cold and ruthless. Instead, she seemed innocent and vulnerable, not at all like the accomplice to a major crime.

With her hair straight, she especially looked like a grade-school teacher. A sweet, caring grade-school teacher who loved her students and thought the world revolved around them.

As she shuffled past him in the hallway of the old house, she glanced up at him for only the briefest of moments to acknowledge that she'd seen him. Then she was gone, the delicate floral scent in the air the only lingering proof that she even existed.

So that was Samona Gray, murderess.

Moments later, remembering why he was here, Derrick stepped toward the door marked One and knocked. After a few seconds it swung open and a middle-aged woman with bleached blond hair appeared before him.

"Mrs. Jefferson?" Derrick asked.

"Oh, hello. You must be Derrick." She sounded much more pleasant than she looked. The blue eye shadow she wore matched her eyes, but her makeup could not hide the dark circles beneath them. Her round, pale face seemed wrinkled beyond her years. If the cigarette in her hand was any indication, she was a chain-smoker and that habit had contributed to her harsh features.

Derrick nodded. "Yes."

"Come on in." She held the door open wide so that he could pass, and closed it when he had stepped inside. "So you're the gent who needs this place so badly." Mrs. Jefferson cast him a sidelong glance. "When your agent called, I told him that I don't usually rent the top level. I keep it for family and such, since my daughter usually comes to visit with her husband for an extended period of time and I like to have it available. But then when he told me what you were working on, and that you'd only need the place for a little while, well I figured, what's the harm?" She chuckled. "It didn't hurt that he offered to pay me triple the price. You must be working on some masterpiece."

Derrick smiled tightly as he followed the older woman into the living room of her home. There were cheap ornaments everywhere and hundreds—if not thousands—of magazines and tabloid newspapers. Cluttered did not adequately describe the place. He wondered if she was related to Captain Boyle.

"Sorry about the mess," she apologized. Bending over the sofa, she pushed some magazines to one side. "Please, have a seat."

"That's okay, Mrs. Jefferson," Derrick said politely. "I'd actually like to get the key and get settled in."

"You don't have a lot of stuff, do you?" Before Derrick could reply, Mrs. Jefferson continued. "It is furnished. I told your agent that."

"I've got myself, the clothes on my back and a few other things."

"Hmm." Mrs. Jefferson gave him a slow once-over then, and the gleam in her eye said she liked what she saw. "Very nice." Smirking, she added, "Clothes, that is." She rubbed her palms against her pink sweatpants. "Oh, don't mind me. It's not too often I see a man as cute as you in here. 'Cept when my son-in-law comes over. He's a looker, he is."

"Do you have any other tenants here?" Derrick asked, changing the direction of the conversation. "I'm sure my agent told you how important it is for me to have a certain amount of quiet for my work."

"Oh, just one. She's lovely, she is. Doesn't cause any trouble. She's quiet—maybe too quiet."

"So she doesn't throw wild parties and entertain people all hours of the night?" Derrick smiled, disguising his question as a joke.

"Heavens no. Samantha's as quiet as a ghost. I never see anyone coming to visit her. Hmm. If you ask me, I think she's running from something, but then who doesn't at some time in their life?"

"True," Derrick said simply. So Samona had given her an alias. It made sense, though Mrs. Jefferson didn't seem like the type who kept up with the current news and he doubted Samona had to worry about being recognized here. "Well, this other person sounds like a model tenant."

"She sure is. She's been here a coupla weeks and if I hadn't seen her a coupla times, I'd a thought the house was empty. 'Cept for me, of course."

"I'm glad to hear that." He had learned probably all he would about Samona from Mrs. Jefferson. "Now, the key…"

"Oh, of course. You've got writing to do. Writing a big best-seller, are you?"

"Trying. We'll see."

"Well that New York agent of yours seemed pretty impressed with your work. Science fiction, is it?"

"Yes."

Mrs. Jefferson shrugged. "I don't much care for fiction, myself."

"Really?" Looking around the room, Derrick was genuinely surprised.

"Books, that is," Mrs. Jefferson added as she followed Derrick's gaze. "But I do love my magazines."

"It's a free country. I've always believed that it doesn't matter what you're reading, as long as you're reading."

"'Course I'll buy your book when it comes out," she said with a big smile.

Derrick shifted his weight from one foot to the other. "I appreciate that. Now, I'd really like to get settled in…."

"Oh that's right. You don't need to hear me rambling. Just give me a minute."

She scurried off into the kitchen, stepping over piles of junk.

Magazines, mostly. A few minutes later, she was back. "Here you go. It's just one key but I do have an extra one, in case you get locked out. I keep all the extra ones here."

"Thanks," Derrick said, accepting the silver key.

"Would you like me to show you the room? It's just up the top of the stairs, when you can't go no higher."

"I'm sure I'll find it." Derrick tossed the key into the air, then caught it.

"Okay. Maybe it's best if you settle in first, then I can show you around."

Derrick agreed, thankful that he was able to finally leave Mrs. Jefferson's apartment. He met with several chatty people on the job and was used to dealing with them, but he certainly hoped Mrs. Jefferson would give him the space he needed.

After all, he wasn't really here to write the next science-fiction bestseller. He was here to investigate Samona Gray.

As Samona shut the car door and started the engine, she wondered about the man she had seen entering her home on Maple Avenue. She'd only caught a quick glimpse of him, but it was enough to arouse her curiousity. He was tall, at least six feet, with an athletic build, and very attractive. There was something about him that reminded her of Roger—the Roger she had liked. Not in a dead-ringer kind of way, but in a more general way—like his almond-colored skin and his square-shaped face.

What had he wanted? He didn't look like the door-to-door salesman type—definitely not the type she had met in the past. Whatever he wanted, he would certainly get an earful from Mrs. Jefferson.

Oh well, Samona mused as she backed her Jeep Cherokee out of the three-lane driveway. She would never know. It was just as well.

When a shadow fell across her sketch pad and lingered there, Samona's head whirled around. What she saw caused her breath to snag in her throat. Certainly she had been thinking about him since their brief encounter, but so much so that her brain had conjured up an image of him?

It was no illusion, Samona realized. He was real. It was the man she had seen at her Oak Park home, his thin lips curled in the cutest smile she had seen in a long time. A smile that was directed at her. She couldn't help the frisson of energy that passed through her.

But she didn't like it. She wasn't here at the beach to meet anybody, especially not another man, even if it was the man from her apartment. That smile, that curious spark in his eyes, could only be construed as suggestive. She didn't need a man in her life—especially not another pretty boy like Roger. Not now. Maybe not ever.

That didn't stop him from speaking to her. "Hello. You're the woman I saw earlier, aren't you? From—"

"Are you following me?" The words came from her mouth before she could stop them.

He smiled, a slow, easy smile. "Hardly. But it's obvious to me that great minds think alike. Who would think that within a couple of hours of our first meeting we'd both be at the same spot on the beach?"

"Yes, who?" Samona mumbled, more to herself than to him.

"Mind if I join you?"

She should say no. It was as easy as that. But for some reason, she felt compelled to say yes.

She compromised. Shrugging, she said, "It's a free country."

The man chuckled, a low throaty sound. As he did, even his eyes seem to smile. He lowered himself beside her on the sand. Extending a hand, he said, "I'm Derrick."

Samona looked at his hand for a moment, not wanting to seem too eager to get to know him. For she didn't want to know him. The last thing she needed was a man before she had straightened her mess-of-a-life out.

Derrick pulled his hand back, casually placing it on his knee. His long, lean legs were covered with black jeans, and he wore a long-sleeved denim shirt. She wondered if he wasn't warm in that outfit. As if he read her thoughts, he began undoing the buttons of his shirt. For a moment, Samona stared, speechless, wondering what he was doing. Certainly he wasn't going to strip his shirt….

Beneath the denim shirt was a white T-shirt. Samona was relieved. Men—she'd never understand why they wore so many layers even in warm weather.

He slipped the denim shirt off, draped it across his lap, then looked ahead to the water. His eyes squinted in the glare of the sunlight. Looking back at her, he said, "It's a beautiful day, isn't it?"

Samona managed a tight nod. She quickly realized that he was getting comfortable next to her. She didn't want that. Picking up her charcoal, she looked down at the sheet of paper before her, hoping he would take her subtle hint that she wanted to get back to work.

"You can get to know me now, or you can get to know me later. But you will get to know me."

Her head whipped around. "*Excuse* me?"

Derrick faced her with a charming grin. He looked even more handsome now than when she had first seen him, because his smile touched his eyes. Thinking about it now, she wasn't sure Roger's smile ever touched his eyes.

"I'm your new neighbor," he said. "I'm renting the apartment above yours."

"Oh." She felt like sticking her head in the sand. "Well, I'm sorry for seeming so…cold. It's just that I don't usually talk to strangers."

"That's a good rule to live by."

He seemed nice enough, but the last thing she needed was a new, sexy neighbor who wanted to get to know her. She said, "I guess if we'll be neighbors I can't very well call you a stranger."

"Not for long, anyway."

Samona forced a smile, though she didn't like his response. She wanted her space, her peace.

Derrick looked at her and said, "What are you working on?"

"Just a sketch," Samona replied less than enthusiastically.

"An artist? Wow, I'm impressed. Do you do that for a living?"

Samona turned to him then, a questioning look in her eyes. She had hoped that by now he would have gotten the hint and taken off. Why wouldn't he just leave her alone?

He must have read her mind, for he said, "I'm bothering you, aren't I?"

It was then that Samona realized just how rude she was being. Dropping her sketch pad, she hugged her elbows. Just because things had gone badly in her life did not mean she had the right to treat a stranger badly. This man, whoever he was, was only trying to be nice. She at least owed him the decency of replying to him in a friendly manner. She tried to give him a genuine smile, but under the circumstances knew she failed. "I'm Samona."

The moment her name spilled from her lips she realized her mistake. She should have lied. What if he recognized her name? What if he asked her questions about the robbery?

But she was relieved when he merely said, "Samona. Different. I like that."

This time her smile was sincere. He didn't recognize her. He had no idea who she was. Her shoulders sagged with relief.

"So what's a beautiful lady like yourself doing here at the beach in the middle of the day, all alone?"

"I'm not alone. Look how many people are around me." Samona gestured to the various people playing beach volleyball and lazing around on the sand.

"Okay," Derrick began. "Dumb question. But you know what I mean. None of these people seem to be *with* you."

"I came here to work," Samona explained. "You were right. I'm an artist."

"I figured that. We artists can usually spot one another."

"You're...an artist?"

"Not a visual one. I'm an artist of the written word."

For the first time, Samona registered that he had a notebook in hand. How she hadn't noticed it before, she didn't know. Now, she was curious about this man who was going to be sharing her home. Shifting so that she faced Derrick head-on, she said, "Oh. You're a writer?"

"That's what I said."

Samona flashed him a wry grin. "Okay, dumb question. I guess what I really wanted to ask is what do you write?"

"Fiction. A bit of this, a bit of that."

Samona raised an eyebrow. "That doesn't tell me much. What kind of fiction?"

Derrick watched a mother happily chase her little boy on the sand, buying some time. He had hoped she wouldn't ask that question. He still found it hard to see himself as a writer—a science-fiction writer especially—and he wanted to sound believable when he answered her question.

He paused too long for she said, "You don't like to talk about your writing?"

Derrick nodded, glad that in his moment of thought, he had perhaps seemed not so extroverted. Perhaps like a man with something to hide. He had to remember that he was supposed to be a loner. Facing her, he said, "You know, I should let you get back to your work. That's why I came here as well. To write. I shouldn't have interrupted you."

He started to stand, but Samona grabbed his arm. It was a strong arm, corded with taut muscles. "Wait a minute. You can't leave like that. Not now that you have me all curious."

Derrick settled back onto the sand and wrapped his arms around his knees. His eyes followed a couple walking by.

"Hey, I'm an artist like you and I know how hard it is to share your work sometimes. So if you don't want to tell me what you write, fine. It's okay to say so."

"It's not that," Derrick said.

"Then what?" Samona prodded.

"It's just…" His voice trailed off.

To say she was curious was an understatement. The man who had seemed quite comfortable with conversation had now clammed up at the mention of his writing. "I'm sorry. I shouldn't pry."

"I write science-fiction novels," Derrick said. He didn't face her.

"That sounds interesting." Certainly nothing too bizarre to talk about. She wondered why he wouldn't look at her.

"I used to write grittier true-to-life novels. About dysfunctional families, that sort of thing. But my agent didn't think it would sell."

Samona nodded. She knew what it was like for an artist trying to do something different and daring in a commercial world. It was a much harder sell than the safe, the tried and true. "And you feel like a sell-out?"

Shaking his head, Derrick finally faced her. "I love science-fiction too. If I didn't, I couldn't write it."

Talk about sending some serious mixed messages. Samona wasn't sure what to think. Only that he was somewhat private about his writing. That she could understand. She felt that way about her artwork. Some of her paintings—especially the ones after the whole criminal mess—she had never shown anyone. They bared too much of her soul.

Her eyes roamed Derrick's light-brown face. He had the faintest of mustaches and a small black mole on his chin. She didn't know of any black science-fiction writers—not that she knew of many science-fiction writers at all. Finally she said, "If you're a famous writer, then maybe I should hear it from you—not the landlady."

Derrick chuckled, then Samona chuckled too. She was certainly curious and persistent. The important thing was she was warming up to him. "No, I'm still a nobody. I'm not published yet. Trying though."

"That doesn't make you a nobody."

He sifted sand between his fingers. "I know. But I hope to be published one of these days. Soon."

"I'm sure you will be. As long as you're persistent, it will happen."

"You didn't tell me about your artwork," Derrick said.

"There's not much to tell. I don't do it professionally. I t—" She stopped before she gave up too much information on herself. This man was a stranger, and even though he seemed nice, she had best remember that.

"What were you going to say?"

"Nothing important."

Derrick realized two things at that moment. One, Samona wasn't stupid. He sensed that she was the type of person who would only give up intimate details about herself with someone she really trusted. Two, he was definitely wrong about her. She wasn't a snob. At least not in the way she dealt with people. If she felt that her money made her a better person than others, she didn't show it.

"I'm new in town," Derrick said.

"Really? Where are you from?"

"Toronto."

"Toronto?" Her expression said she was surprised. "You grew up there?"

Derrick nodded. "Born and raised."

"Funny, you sound like a Yankee."

Derrick smiled. "I'm good at adapting to different environments."

She rested her face on her palm. "What's a Canadian doing in Chicago, writing science-fiction, no less?"

Derrick faced the water. "Another time." Returning his gaze to her, he said, "Maybe over dinner sometime?" At Samona's wide-eyed response, Derrick added, "Just as a friend. Friendly dinner, maybe a movie..." He let his statement hang in the air.

Samona's eyes fell to the sheet of paper before her, and Derrick knew that she was uncomfortable. She wasn't ready to go too far in this new relationship. But at least she had warmed to him. That was a good sign.

There was no need to push her. He had plenty of time to get to know her, to gain her trust. Plenty of time to get the goods that would put her away for a long, long time.

"One...more." Derrick grunted as he used his upper-body strength to pull himself for one last chin-up. His muscles burned as he achieved his goal, and he let himself drop to the thickly carpeted floor. He loved working out, pushing himself to the limit, going on to another level. He felt invigorated by this workout, even if it was shortened because of his new assignment.

Because of Samona Gray.

Stretching his arms to soothe his muscles, he thought about her. She wasn't at all what he had expected. After studying the files, he knew she had inherited a fair bit of money. But she didn't look like she had money. Judging by her physical appearance—plain jeans, plain T-shirt, plain shoes, plain hair, plain nails—she didn't seem like the type who cared for a fancy lifestyle. Comfortable was her style, not glamorous. So robbing a jewelry store for a couple of hundred-thousand in jewels, when she already had that kind of cash from her parents' life insurance policy, didn't make sense.

Maybe this look was new, part of her attempt to stay low-key. Maybe she really did fancy the finer things in life. Maybe she had spent all the money she'd inherited and now needed more. So many questions. No answers.

Derrick leaned over and touched his toes, stretching his back. He stayed there a moment, pondering. Something didn't sit right with him about this whole robbery Samona was involved in. Though people who had enough money to live comfortably didn't tend to be involved in unsophisticated jewelry store robberies, Derrick could stretch his imagination and see her doing that. But the murder bothered him. To take such a risk for more money meant she needed it. Needed it why? Was it possible she'd borrowed money from a loan shark, made a few bad investments?

As Derrick made his way to the gym's indoor track, he dismissed those ideas. Samona didn't seem the type to get involved with a loan shark, but one never knew. There had to be another reason. Maybe she'd somehow ended up running with the wrong crowd and had been influenced by them. A thirty-year-old woman being influenced at this stage in her life? Derrick frowned, thinking that didn't make much sense either.

He began to jog, hoping that would erase the questions from his mind. It would do no good to think of her reasons; all that mattered was that she was guilty. No matter how innocent she seemed, she was involved in a capital crime. One woman was dead. Samona had been left at the store alive. If she hadn't been an accessory, wouldn't Roger have killed her too? Why leave a loose end? It was more likely that her injury had been staged, and that she was lying low until she could leave town and freely spend her illegally acquired money.

As Derrick made his way around the track, he gritted his teeth. There was a time when he trusted his gut feeling, when he knew a premonition was dead-on. But after what happened a year and a half ago, he didn't know if he could totally trust his instincts anymore. As a cop, that wasn't a good thing.

Eighteen months ago, he had broken a rule of policing: he'd let his personal feelings get involved. When Whitney Jordan's life had been threatened, he'd thought with his heart, not his head. He had been in love with her ever since grade school and that had clouded his objectivity. A year and a half ago, someone had been trying to kill her. Derrick had been convinced that her estranged husband, Javar Jordan, was behind the attacks because he hadn't forgiven her for the accident that had killed his young son. Despite the other possible suspects—and there had been a few—he had zeroed in on Javar.

Though he didn't like to admit this to himself, part of him had been hoping that Javar was behind the attacks. Part of him had been hoping that Whitney would realize what a jerk Javar was. Part of him had been hoping that Whitney would finally, after all the years of loving her, return his affections.

It was later proven that Javar's mother had been the one trying to kill Whitney. Javar, who had claimed he'd wanted a reconciliation with his wife, had been sincere. Derrick, who had been hoping to start a relationship with Whitney, had been out of luck. When it came to Javar, as always, he hadn't stood a chance.

Now, Javar and Whitney were happily married and the proud parents of twins—a daughter and a son. Whitney had the family she'd always wanted, and was happier than Derrick had ever seen her. Married life agreed with her. Javar agreed with her.

Derrick stopped jogging and leaned forward, catching his breath. He wanted to forget about the one time in his career when he'd had a serious lapse in judgment. Able to accept that

that wasn't just any case because Whitney had been involved, he had tried to put the whole thing behind him.

He had been successful. Until now.

Now, the pressure that had been put on him by the department to solve the Milano case had him questioning his judgment again.

Slowly, Derrick walked to the change room. He made a silent vow that this case would be different from Whitney's case. This time, he would stick to the facts only. He wouldn't let his personal feelings get involved.

Which shouldn't be hard, he figured. Unlike Whitney, he didn't know nor have a bond with Samona. This time, nothing would prevent him from doing his job to the best of his ability, without any biases.

Chapter 4

More nightmares haunted Samona during the night. She had tossed and turned and screamed and awoken in sweat-drenched sheets, afraid. It wasn't quite six this Tuesday morning, but Samona was too afraid and restless to sleep any longer.

She sat with her legs curled under her on the sofa, a hot mug of tea in her hands. Even after two months of not having to go to school, part of her missed her routine. Getting up at six-thirty, having her morning Earl Grey tea, getting to the school by seven-thirty, welcoming her students by eight. Though teaching had its down sides, there was nothing that could replace the joy she felt when she saw the look of understanding in a child's eyes, when he or she finally "got it." It gave her such a sense of satisfaction, a sense of importance that she could make a difference.

Samona blew on her tea to cool it, then took a cautious sip. It scorched her tongue. Grumbling, she placed the mug on the oak coffee table before her but spilled some liquid onto her hand as she did. God, could she do nothing right?

She closed her eyes, tempted to cry. The tea wasn't the problem. Her life was. How many more days would she feel like this—so utterly empty? Until the official end of the school year next week? Would she then finally forget her morning routine, forget the various lesson plans in her mind, forget her students? Or would it take longer to get over this emptiness because of the cloud of doubt that still lingered over her and her future?

Samona knew the answer to that. She would always feel uneasy until she was free. Free to do what she loved most: teach.

School normally ended this week, the first week of June, but because of two major snowstorms in March the children missed several days of school. Therefore, the allotment for "snow days" meant school would end the following week instead. With the end of the school year so close, Samona couldn't help but think of her students.

She sighed. While she missed her job, she wasn't so much concerned about herself as she was about the children. She wondered how they were doing without her. They loved her, and she them. To lose her so far into the school year could be devastating for them. There was so much they didn't understand and naturally wouldn't as far as her situation was concerned. She hoped their parents and her fellow teachers had come up with a thoughtful explanation of her absence.

Samona reached for her tea. This time when she sipped the liquid, it was cool enough to drink. She wondered about little Eric, the one child in her class who needed extra attention. Was he getting the attention that he needed? After a slow start to the school year, he had finally started making great strides after Christmas. At first, he'd been abnormally shy, not saying much more than two words for the day. He didn't have any friends, and the other children could not understand why he was different. Samona had tried all she could but most of all had been patient and encouraging, showing him that she had confidence in him. Her patience had paid off. Eric had finally begun to trust her, talking to her with much more confidence. He had even taken great pride in bringing in and showing her his favorite books from home: mostly about reptiles. When she had read his books to the class, he had been ecstatic. The year-end art unit dealt with reptiles, and Samona had been very much looking forward to seeing Eric blossom even further.

But would he wither without her? Samona took a long sip of the warm tea, trying to calm her nerves. That was what worried her the most. After all the progress Eric had made, with a new teacher she wondered if he would feel his trust had been broken, if he would withdraw into his shell.

She closed her eyes. It was so unfair, the way she had been taken from her class. Not only for her, but for the students. She wasn't like some teachers who only taught for the money. If allowed, she would teach for free. She loved the children, and getting paid to spend time with them all day was like getting paid to breathe. She wanted to inspire her students the way her teachers had inspired her. To touch their lives in a positive way and fuel their dreams. Without dreams they believed were attainable, children could become frustrated and even turn to crime. Maybe that's what had happened to Roger.

Roger. He was also on her mind. Roger Benson, dead at thirty-three.

It was still so hard to believe he was dead, that his memorial service had been on Saturday. After she'd learned of Roger's death, she'd picked up the *Chicago Tribune* yesterday, knowing there would be a story in there somewhere about it—possibly about her. She'd been relieved when she saw the front-page headlines had been occupied with something else: the horrible story of a house fire in the projects that had killed four young children.

She hadn't been able to bring herself to look through the paper for news of the story, mostly because she was afraid she would see a picture of herself. Right now, Mrs. Jefferson didn't know who she was, but if her face was plastered in the papers again it wouldn't be too long before she figured it out. The only papers Samona saw in Mrs. Jefferson's apartment or the recycling box were tabloid papers, so she had felt reasonably safe that the older woman would not discover who she was. But if the media began reporting about her and her suspected involvement in the Milano case, Mrs. Jefferson would surely learn the truth.

All this thinking was driving Samona crazy. She needed to know if there was anything in the paper about her. She couldn't really rest until she did.

Placing her tea on the coffee table, Samona rose and went to the small kitchen table. That's where she had put the newspaper. Even as her hand reached for the paper, she wasn't sure she could bring herself to actually pick it up. Finally, she did.

Carefully flipping through the pages, she found the headline she sought. The heading read: MAN SOUGHT IN JEWELRY STORE MURDER DEAD AT SEA. She blew out a steady breath, then read the article.

DETROIT (AP)—Roger Benson, the Chicago man whose name has been linked to inner-city crime, was killed yesterday when his cabin cruiser exploded and sank while moored at a local marina in Detroit, Michigan. He was 33.

Police had identified Benson as a prime suspect in the robbery of Milano Jewelers and the brutal slaying of Sophia Milano on April 1 of this year in Chicago's Near North. He was also suspected to be involved in two pre-

viously unsolved jewelry store heists in the Chicago suburbs of Skokie and Glencoe.

U.S. Coast Guard and Detroit City police have not ruled
out sabotage as the cause of the explosion. At this time, however, they concede that the explosion could have been accidental, perhaps caused by the non-venting of gasoline
fumes.

A Coast Guard spokesperson noted that boats with in-
board motors have to be vented by a fan before starting,
to avoid the danger of a spark touching off an explosion.

Samona paused. Swallowed. Nothing had been mentioned
about her in the first few paragraphs. Thankfully. She scanned
the rest of the article.

According to the Coast Guard, Roger's body had been burned
beyond recognition, but amazingly his ID had been salvaged.
Some of the stolen jewelry had also been recovered aboard the
charred remains of the boat. The ID, jewelry, and the fact that
several people placed Roger at the scene, had confirmed his
identification.

That was no way to go, Samona thought. Although any
feelings she had had for Roger died the moment he stuck a
gun to her head, she did feel some sympathy for him. He'd
never had a chance to change his life, to try to make amends.
And to be burned beyond recognition—nobody should die that
way.

She wondered what went wrong. The article had given a few
possible reasons, including sabotage. Was sabotage really
possible?

Roger was dead. Really and truly dead.

Her name was finally mentioned at the bottom of the article.

Chicago-area resident Samona Gray is still under investigation in relation to the Milano Jewelry theft and murder. Thus far, however, police have not been able to positively link her to the offense.

This was a small victory, Samona conceded, a half-smile playing on her lips. If she wasn't mistaken, the reporter's lack of interest in her was proof that at least some people were starting to have doubts about her guilt. She wanted to jump and squeal with delight, but she stayed seated. It was too soon for any victory parties yet.

Even though the ringer on her phone had been turned down, when it rang Samona was rudely startled from her sleep. Throwing her hand around wildly, she reached for the phone but it wasn't there.

She bolted awake, realizing she wasn't in her bed; she was on the sofa. The phone was across the room. It must have rung at least six times, and it wouldn't stop ringing. Maybe that was someone from her school…

She hurried to the phone and grabbed the receiver. Before she could say hello, a male voice said, "Samona, hi."

She was momentarily startled because she didn't recognize the voice. "Y—who is this?"

Click.

She frowned into the receiver. Who on earth…?

That didn't make sense. Who would call for her and hang up when she answered? She didn't have Caller ID so she could not see who had called. She dialed "*69," but that only told her that the number of the last person who had called her was unknown.

Dragging her feet across the floor to her bedroom, an uneasy feeling spread through Samona's body. She couldn't shake the feeling even as she slipped into bed.

"Good God, who is it now?" Samona said aloud when the phone awoke her again. She had finally drifted off into a dreamless, comfortable sleep. Groaning, she dragged the second pillow over her head and let the phone ring. When it wouldn't stop, she reached for it, annoyed. If this was the person who had called before… "Who is this?"

"Hello, Samona."

Her stomach lurched painfully at the sound of the familiar voice. It was a voice she hadn't expected to hear. A voice she didn't want to hear.

"Samona, are you there?"

Samona found her voice then, although barely. "Yes. Yes, I'm here."

"It's Evelyn."

"I know."

Silence. "It's after eleven o'clock. You're not still in bed, are you?"

"I don't have a job, remember?" Samona quipped.

There was a pause, then, "You certainly are hard to find."

"That's the way I wanted it."

"Even with your family?"

Family. Even now, the word brought a heaviness in her chest and a pain in her heart. She had no family. None that mattered, at least.

"Samona…?"

"How did you find me?"

"What's important is that I did find you."

That was Evelyn—never answering a question she didn't want to. "This is an unlisted number. If the operator gave it out to you—"

"I didn't get it from the operator."

That didn't make Samona feel any better. She'd had her number unlisted for a reason—to avoid everybody, especially Evelyn and Mark.

"Samona—"

"Evelyn, what do you want?" Just talking to her sister brought all the painful memories of her breakup with Mark surging forth. A breakup her sister had caused. Her sister had never liked her, and the first opportunity she'd had she'd stolen the one man Samona had cared about. She didn't want to talk to Evelyn now. Maybe she never would.

"I heard about Roger. About his death."

"Spying on me?"

"Don't do that, Samona."

"Why not? Isn't it true? That's how you got my number, isn't it? I certainly didn't drop you a note with my change of address."

"I didn't call to upset you."

"Yeah right."

Evelyn sighed. "Why do you have to do that, Samona?"

"Do what?" Samona's stomach was twisted into a painful knot.

"Get so defensive."

Samona stood. "Why do you suddenly feel the urge to be a sister? Out of some sort of guilt?"

"I'm worried about you. Why else do you think that I'm calling?"

"Oh, I don't know," Samona said, sarcasm dripping from her voice. "Maybe to rub in my face what a screwup I am."

"Samona, don't do this."

"Why not? You certainly didn't make any secret of how you felt about my choice of boyfriends. First you said you couldn't stand Mark, then you slept with him. And then Roger—when you'd first called me after what happened, I actually thought you were concerned. Until you made it sound like I was responsible for what happened."

"I've apologized for that, Samona. That came out wrong."

Samona kept going, for if she didn't she might break down and cry. "Even now, I'm not sure you believe me. But then why would you? Just because you're my sister? That's never meant anything to you."

Samona heard her sister groan, and for a moment she wished things were different. Wished her sister had really been her sister in the true sense of the word. But she hadn't been. She'd been her rival, and then her enemy.

"Samona, I just want to know how you're doing. I haven't heard from you in a long time, and I'm worried. I know you find that hard to believe, but it's true."

Samona could not help her outburst of laughter. Her sister cared? That was a joke. Her sister had not cared about her for a very long time. But now, probably because their parents were dead, her older sister felt some obligation to her.

"Evelyn, you don't have to do this. I don't know if you think that this is going to gain you some points somewhere, but I'm okay. Just go on with your life as you usually do. And of course, say hi to Mark." She was surprised her voice didn't crack.

"Samona…"

"I'm serious, Evelyn. I'm a big girl, and I can take care of myself. So, don't lose any sleep over me." Before she lost her courage, Samona hung the phone up.

The room spun and Samona sank into the softness of the bed. It didn't make her happy to do this, to shut her sister out of her life. But what else could she do? There was no point pretending that she and Evelyn got along. Maybe for a short time during her life they had actually been true sisters, but that was a long time ago.

Her nerves were frayed and her brain felt like it would explode. Samona immediately punched in the digits to Jennifer's home. It rang a few times before Samona realized that Jennifer was at work. It was only eleven-eighteen in the morning.

Work. Jennifer was probably in the staff room right now with the other primary teachers. Talking, laughing. That's where she should be right now. Should be, but wasn't.

Samona disconnected the line and began dialing another number. A second later, her hand froze above the phone.

A chill swept over her. She had been about to call her parents' home in Dallas. But her parents were dead.

There was no one else to call. She swallowed a sob.

"No," Samona said aloud. She squeezed her forehead hard. She wasn't going to do this. There was no point sitting around thinking about what could have been, what should have been, but what wasn't.

She thought of Derrick, her new neighbor upstairs. He would be the perfect distraction from her troubling thoughts. Maybe she should take him up on his dinner offer.

It was too early for dinner right now. Maybe tonight.

Chapter 5

Derrick turned when he heard the back door creak open. There stood Samona on the back porch, staring at him as though she hadn't expected to find him here. In fact, she looked startled, as though *he* had intruded on *her.*

After a few moments, she ventured down the few steps and onto the grass, toward the picnic table. Toward him.

Quickly, he shut the notebook before him and placed his elbow on it.

"Hi," she said.

"Are you following me?"

He caught her off guard, and after a moment of wide-eyed shock, her lips curled into a weak grin. "Uh, no. I live here, remember?"

"Ah, that's right." Derrick snapped his fingers.

His attempt at humor didn't impress her. Something was bothering her. She seemed very uncomfortable.

Silence fell between them. Samona fiddled with her fingers, wringing them so hard he was sure it must have hurt. He was about to say something when she dropped onto the seat next to him.

She said, "Are you writing?"

Derrick nodded. "I'm getting some thoughts down."

"That's good. It's really peaceful here. You can get a lot done."

"Or drive yourself crazy."

Samona flashed him a faint smile. "Yeah. I know that feeling."

"Anything you want to talk about?"

She shook her head. There was silence, then she said, "Beautiful day, isn't it?"

"This conversation is beginning to feel like déjà vu."

She looked at him with a puzzled expression. After a moment she seemed to get the gist of his words. "Oh, you mean yesterday? Yes, you're right." She stood. "Well, I don't want to bother you. I know you want to work. I'm going to…pick some flowers."

"Flowers?" Derrick threw his gaze to the flowers lining the backyard fence. They were dazzling in their varying colors and sizes, but Derrick couldn't tell a petunia from a hole in the ground. The only ones Derrick could identify were the pink and white roses. Horticulture was not his forte.

"Mrs. Jefferson doesn't mind. And my apartment needs some life."

She walked off then, to the edge of the vast backyard and the bushes. The white sundress she wore flowed around her ankles, flirting with them. She truly was beautiful.

Derrick made a show of opening his notebook and picking up his pen. But Samona didn't notice. She wasn't looking. She was stooping, sifting through the bushes and picking various wildflowers.

Several minutes later, she stood and walked toward the house. Derrick rested his cheek against his palm and stared down at his notebook. When he heard Samona near him, he looked up, but she merely smiled at him and continued to the back door.

Seconds later, she was gone.

Samona sat staring at the vase of fresh flowers on her coffee table. She liked the selection. The blues and pinks and violets with vibrant green leaves helped add a spark of life to the room.

You need a spark in your own life, a voice told her. She stood and crossed the hardwood floor to the large square window, but the voice followed her. Ever since she'd seen Derrick earlier, she debated going to see him for dinner tonight. One minute she thought she would, the next she figured she wouldn't. Right now, she didn't think seeing him was a good idea.

She wiped her sweaty palms on her sundress. She wondered about him, about what brought him to this particular house in Oak Park. Of all the places he could have gone, he'd ended up here. Jen would laugh and say that this was a sign—a sign for her to get a life. Certainly, he was attractive and he seemed like a nice guy…

So what? Roger, too, had seemed like a nice guy. So had Mark.

But Derrick was her new neighbor. He was new in town and didn't know anybody. It wouldn't hurt to get to know him, spend some time together.

Samona had been staring off into space, so mesmerized by the rhythmic swaying of the maple and spruce trees, that she hadn't noticed Derrick outside. She only noticed when he tooted his horn and waved.

Immediately, she moved away from the window. Had he been waving to her? Why had she moved away from the window like a frightened cat? God, he was going to think she was a nutcase.

Well, she had her answer. Forget dinner tonight.

* * *

Derrick couldn't sleep. He lay awake, a hand propped behind his head, staring at the ceiling for a long time. Maybe he should count all the little mounds. Maybe that would finally put him to sleep.

He nixed that idea with a sarcastic chuckle. He'd already tried counting the number of stripes in the orange and white wallpaper, but that hadn't helped him sleep. He'd even tried counting sheep, but that hadn't worked either. Nothing could take his mind off Samona and this case.

She had picked wildflowers to brighten her place. That was just another piece in this confusing puzzle. A woman with high tastes would not get on her knees in the dirt and pick flowers to brighten a room. She could call a florist.

"Don't try to find a reason for what she did." Derrick spoke the words out loud, hoping he could remember to focus on the facts of this case. They were important—not her motives.

This case wasn't going to be easy, he thought, rolling over. Samona was too hard to figure out. On the beach and today in the backyard, he thought he'd made some headway with her. But he was learning that she was fickle and unpredictable. Samona Gray teeter-tottered between hot and cold, friendly and introverted. When he'd waved to her and she'd stepped away from the window, it was like he'd taken two steps forward and three back.

Derrick snuggled against his pillow, willing himself to sleep. Tomorrow was another day. Maybe she would come to him then.

Alex was getting sick of this town.

There was too much heat here with the whole Milano case, and it was time he moved on. Maybe somewhere warm, like

Jamaica or even Trinidad. With the money he was expecting, he could live like a king there. No more paint peeling from the walls. No more cockroaches. No more bad plumbing.

Marie didn't have to go with him. From the way she talked, he figured she didn't want to leave Chicago. All her friends were here, and her family. So, if she didn't want to leave all that, that was cool with him. It was time he got himself some fresh meat anyway. Marie was getting stale.

She no longer thought the way he did. She couldn't understand him. She complained all the time. Mostly she complained about Roger, telling him he should forget him. But Alex couldn't do that. Roger owed him a huge chunk of money. That money would allow him to leave town and never look back.

Yawning, Alex sat up in Marie's small bed. What was taking her so long? Nobody needed to use the bathroom that long, not even a woman. She was avoiding him. Ever since a couple of nights ago.

Marie's problem was that she was too jealous. She didn't want to find Roger's ex-girlfriend because she thought he had a thing for her. Alex lay back down. Samona wasn't the kind of woman who interested him. She was cute, but Roger said she'd never given him any play.

"Hey, Marie!" Alex finally yelled. "Don't use up all the hot water!"

Minutes later, she appeared at the bedroom door, her face plastered with goop. "What did you say?"

Alex threw the covers off and rose. "Have you found her yet?"

Marie made a face, then said, "I'm working on it."

"Working? Everything is riding on this, Marie. My future. Our future."

"I know."

He approached her slowly. "Then what are you waiting for?"

She moved to the small dresser made of particleboard and acted like she was looking for something, but Alex knew otherwise. She was stalling.

He walked up behind her, slipping his hands around her waist. She flinched. "Marie, I'm counting on you."

"I know."

He cupped her breasts. Hearing her moan, he smiled. He loved teasing her; it was so easy to do. "I want results, Marie."

Leaning against him, she stroked his thigh. "I'll get them."

"You'd better." He released her, left her standing, then returned to bed. Whirling around, she looked at him with surprise. And maybe a bit of anger. He wanted to chuckle, but didn't. Marie didn't like to be rejected.

But he had to make a point: this business with Roger came first. She came second. There was no other way. Once she helped him get what he wanted, he would be all hers.

Chapter 6

Samona parked her Jeep but stayed seated for a moment, waiting until a group of people passed. Looking in the rearview mirror, she adjusted her baseball cap. Never had she worn so many hats in her life, but she couldn't risk being recognized.

Finally, when a man strolled by with a shopping cart full of bags and disappeared, she stepped out onto the asphalt. Instinctively, she dropped her gaze, concentrating on the ground. It was a practice she'd become accustomed to, even when she went to Grant Park to sketch. With straight hair and a hat she looked different than when her picture had been splattered all over the papers and on the news. She blended with the crowd.

This particular grocery store was a small one, half an hour from her home. Although two months had passed since she was a daily news item, people knew her in Chicago's near west. It wasn't only the fear of being recognized that bothered her, but it was dealing with the questions when she was. At the neighborhood corner stores she had been asked so often, "What's happening with the case?" or just plain looked at with doubt and disgust that she couldn't stand it anymore. This drive was out of the way, but worth it for the little extra peace it gave her.

There was a stiff breeze, one strong enough to shift her hat.

Before it flew off, she caught it. She kept a hand on her head until she reached the store's doors.

Inside, she searched for the items she needed most. Bread, eggs, cereal, chicken breasts, juice and rice. The store wasn't too crowded and she shopped with relative ease.

She felt like making cookies today. As a teacher, she often liked to bake cookies for her students and surprise them. Shortbread cookies with sprinkled sugar on top, chocolate chip—any sort of treat. Maybe she could bake some for her new neighbor.

Derrick. Why couldn't she get him off her mind? She shouldn't be seeing him, much less baking any cookies for him. Yet she found herself walking toward the baking aisle.

She rolled the cart slowly, searching the shelves. She didn't know what Derrick liked. Sometimes he reminded her of a little boy in a big man's body—his cute smile, those charming dimples, his silliness. Chocolate chip, she decided. He should like that.

She stopped in front of the shelf with a variety of "just add water" cookie mixes. She reached for a chocolate chip package but didn't quite hang on. Slipping from her fingers, it dropped to the floor.

As she bent to retrieve it, so did somebody else. He reached it before she did. The person, an attractive black man who looked fortyish, stood to his full height, smiling as he handed her the package. "Here you go."

Running a nervous hand over her throat, Samona smiled her thanks and accepted the package. She was about to turn back to her shopping cart when she caught the quizzical expression on the man's face. "Thanks," she said, in case he was offended.

His smile immediately faded. Samona's skin prickled and she quickly turned to her cart.

"I know you…." the man said behind her back. It was a statement that sounded like a question.

"I don't think so." Samona fiddled with her baseball cap, still not facing him.

"Yes," he said. He came around to the front of her cart. "I do know you. You're that woman—the one involved in that murder case."

She felt trapped. She couldn't get away. Moving backward, she pulled her cart with her. "No…"

The man's voice grew louder as he became confident in his recognition of her. "It is you. I can't believe they let people like you walk the streets. After what you did…"

His voice got the attention of the few other shoppers in the aisle. Her pulse pounded in her head so hard she could hear it, like a haunting echo. She had to get out of here. Abandoning her shopping cart, she turned and scurried to the door.

"You can run," the man said in a boisterous voice. "But you can't hide. They'll catch you one of these days."

Samona ran until she reached the front door. Brushing past people in her rush to get out. A bag fell from a woman's hand as she bumped into her, and startled, the woman yelled, then called Samona an obscene name. Samona ran, afraid to look back.

Outside, the warm air enveloped her and she gulped it in frantically. She clawed at her purse, searching for her keys so she would waste no time getting away.

Away… Nowadays, she was always running. She wished she was stronger, strong enough to face her accusers, but she wasn't. She was a coward.

As she ran to her car, afraid to look back, tears of frustration fell. They clouded her vision as she scrambled inside her car and drove off.

* * *

Much better, Derrick thought as he climbed down from the old chair, clapping his hands together in satisfaction. The piece of wallpaper that had gotten his attention last night was finally back where it should be: glued in place. After searching the cupboards and closets, he'd found some glue and had gone to work.

He had too much time on his hands, he acknowledged, but what else was he to do? Having gone to the beach and Grant Park in search of Samona and not finding her there, he had returned home. He'd even left an afternoon blues concert in the park, and he loved blues. All because he'd hoped to find her home and make contact with her once again.

He hadn't. Her Jeep had been gone for hours, and he wondered where she was.

He cocked an eyebrow. Was she perhaps meeting with someone regarding the jewelry? Where was it? Only a fraction of the stolen pieces had been recovered after Roger's death, and Derrick wondered if Samona knew where the rest was. She had to, unless she'd been ripped off by her boyfriend.

Maybe she had been ripped off. Maybe that's why she was still in Chicago, as opposed to somewhere exotic and tropical.

Derrick strolled to the window and peered through the lace curtain. From here, he had a view of the wide driveway at the side of the house. Samona's Jeep was not there.

The flowerpots hanging outside the window caught his attention. The flowers within were withering from too much sun. His own plants at home were probably withering too. Maybe he should go water them.

Derrick shook his head and smiled ruefully. If he was considering going home to water his plants, that was a sure sign he was bored.

* * *

Samona wasn't sure why she was there, but she now sat in her Jeep beneath a tree outside William Hatch Elementary School. She could only stare at the large, old building where she had once been welcome. Now, she was a foreigner here. A criminal.

The incident at the grocery store had only proven to her once again what a mess her life was, how much she had lost. That she would always be running until she was proven innocent. She had driven around for a while, not wanting to go home, not wanting to go anywhere. She had ended up here.

Remembering… She couldn't think about anything that had happened in the last two months without getting that nasty lump in her throat and pain in her chest. Her parents' death had devastated her and she'd never thought she could suffer a worse pain. But she had. Because of this case.

Looking out at the large school she loved so much, Samona wiped at a stray tear. Though no children were there now, she could easily picture plenty on the grass, laughing and running happily. In the spring, the primary grade students especially spent a lot of time out on the sprawling lawns working on nature projects or just having fun. She remembered the Easter egg hunt more than a year ago. Her class had gotten so much pleasure out of first painting the boiled eggs, then hiding them for the kindergarten classes. She smiled at the memory.

The happy memory was quickly replaced by a disturbing one. The one person she'd thought would understand her and stand by her was Matthew Hendrix, her principal. Matthew, whom she'd known to be so kind and gentle and fair. But she had been wrong.

She would never forget the way he'd looked at her that day he called her into his office. With suspicion, with doubt. With disapproval.

"Samona," he'd begun. "I'm not going to beat around the bush. With everything that's happened, I think it's best that you take a leave of absence—until everything blows over."

"A leave of—" Disbelief washing over her, she couldn't bring herself to say the words. "You don't really mean that?"

"Yes, Samona. I do. Parents have called the school, expressing their concern. I have an obligation to them."

"But I'm not guilty," Samona protested.

It was only a slight twitch of his lip, but it said so much. So did his gray eyes. He didn't believe her. "Well, until this is all resolved."

"No. Please, Mr. Hendrix. Don't..." She hated begging, but he couldn't really ask her to leave the job she loved most in the world.

"We have a teacher to replace you starting tomorrow."

"Tomorrow?" Samona had gasped. Then she had watched, helplessly, as Mr. Hendrix stood and gestured for her to leave. Just like that. Without asking for her side of the story. Slowly Samona had risen and walked out of the room, hoping to maintain the shred of dignity she had left.

Her life was ruined because of Roger. Roger, who had died and left her to deal with the aftermath of his crimes.

She understood now why people turned to alcohol. And right now, she wished she was a drinker. Wished that some hard liquor could wash away her problems. Make her numb. Make her forget.

But she hated alcohol, so she didn't even have that.

She had nothing.

* * *

When Derrick opened the door, he was certain he would find Mrs. Jefferson. To his surprise—his pleasant surprise—he saw Samona standing before him.

"Hi," he said.

"Hi," Samona replied softly.

Her voice was merely a hoarse whisper and he realized instantly that she had been crying. Darn, he thought, not a crying woman. He was no good with them, never had been. Samona may be a criminal, but with her red eyes and soft voice, he couldn't help feeling some sympathy for her.

"Something's wrong," he said.

She nodded, and although she smiled, her eyes misted.

"Come in." Derrick held the door wide and she slowly sauntered inside.

"I'm sorry," Samona said, wrapping her arms around her torso. "I didn't come here to…cry. I was hoping…maybe we could do that dinner thing you were talking about. You know, that friendly dinner you suggested."

Derrick should have been happy that Samona was here of her own free will. The sooner she trusted him, the sooner he would get the goods on her, the sooner he would get back to the drug enforcement unit. But he wasn't happy, not while she seemed to be in so much pain.

"Sure, I'm still game for dinner. When do you want to do it? Tomorrow? Later in the week?"

"What about now?"

"Now? Oh…"

"This is a bad time," Samona said.

"No. No it isn't. I was just about to eat, actually. But if you'd like to go out somewhere—"

"Here is fine. I would actually prefer that."

She glanced around his apartment, and Derrick realized then that he was being a bad host. "Why don't you take a seat." He gestured to the living room.

Samona stepped into the large room cautiously, slowly looking around. Like hers, it was furnished with old antique-styled furniture and beige lace curtains. It seemed perhaps a bit too feminine for a man, but if Derrick was only here to write, she was sure he didn't mind. Like her, he wasn't making this his permanent home.

"I'm still getting organized but take a seat where you can. Just give me a minute." He walked off toward the bedroom.

As Samona strolled into the living room, she wiped her eyes once more, hoping to erase all evidence that she had been crying. She hadn't meant to start crying when he had opened the door, but her emotions had overwhelmed her. Now, she wanted to take charge. Take charge of her life and be strong. She'd been so out of control, so emotionally unpredictable in the last two months. That had to change.

She took a seat on the rose-colored armchair. Her new neighbor didn't have many things. There was a pile of magazines and some novels on the wooden coffee table. Leaning forward, Samona took a closer look. They were all women-issue related, and she realized that the books and magazines were probably Mrs. Jefferson's. As she continued to glance around the room, she figured the only thing here that was Derrick's was the laptop computer in the corner of the living room on a small desk. That, and the stack of loose-leafed papers and notebooks surrounding the laptop. His work in progress. His fictional masterpiece.

Like her, he must have come to this place with only the

clothes on his back and a few belongings. She remembered him on the beach a couple of days ago, how he had clammed up when she had asked about his writing and how he had seemed somewhat disillusioned when he'd talked about family. Samona wondered for a moment if he was running too.

She heard his voice from the bedroom, but was unable to make out what he actually said. Moments later he joined her in the living room again and said, "I hope you don't mind pizza. I tried to cancel it, but it's apparently already on its way."

"Oh…you ordered out."

"Since I'm new to the neighborhood I haven't had a chance to shop. So my fridge is empty. Not much to make a meal with."

"Of course. That makes sense. Yes, I like pizza."

"Maybe later you can tell me where a grocery store is. Since I know where nothing is in this area."

She inhaled a sharp breath. "Uh, yeah. Uh, of course."

Derrick took a seat opposite her on the matching sofa. As he leaned forward resting his elbows on his knees, he smiled at her again, a smile that was totally charming and disarming. For a fleeting moment she imagined those sexy lips on hers, gently teasing, warming, making her feel alive. She hadn't felt alive in two months.

She shuddered, surprised at the thought. That she was having this fantasy about a man she barely knew reminded her once again just how alone she really was.

"Do you like vegetarian pizza?" he asked.

She stood. "I'm sorry. I don't really want to intrude on your dinner."

"You're not intruding. Please stay."

She fiddled with her hands, twisting her fingers, then finally sat. "You're probably wondering who this crazy woman in your apartment is."

"No."

"I'm not usually like this. But right now… I don't know. I'm going through a…bit of a rough time."

Derrick nodded absently, wondering what she meant by "rough time." Did she mean that it was hard being a criminal? Or did she mean that she regretted her actions? The criminal life didn't seem to suit her, judging by the amount of stress she was going through, which confirmed his earlier thoughts. Somehow she must have been coerced into criminal activity.

"I insist that you join me for dinner. It's never fun to eat pizza alone. But if you're a big eater, I have to warn you that it's a small pizza—only six slices." He had hoped for a smile out of her, but didn't get one. He added softly, "I'm a good listener. If you want to talk."

Samona ran both hands through her hair. "I appreciate that. But I can assure you, you don't want to hear about my life. Now your life," she paused, resting her chin on her palms, "that sounds like something interesting. Something I'd love to hear about."

"I don't know about that."

"You're a writer. That's exciting."

"And you're curious."

Samona nodded.

Derrick clapped his hands together. "Okay. Ask whatever you'd like to know about my writing. I'll answer as honestly as I can."

Samona crossed one leg over the other, leaning back into the chair. "Hmm… That's a tough one—not!" Finally, she smiled. "What are you currently working on?"

"That's easy. I am working on the next great science-fiction blockbuster."

"Really?"

"Not quite. But my agent has a lot of faith in me."

"That's great. I'm really proud of you…even though I don't know you."

"But you can, if you'd like to."

Samona looked down, picked at a piece of lint on her black shorts, then looked at him again. "What's your book about?"

"Are you a science-fiction fan?" When Samona shook her head, Derrick was relieved. That would save him a lot of explanation, prevent him from having to lie more than was necessary. "If you don't like science fiction then what I write would probably bore you to tears." He hoped that would satisfy her.

It seemed to because Samona nodded. "You're probably right. But one of these days if you don't mind showing me what you're writing, I'd love to read it. Although maybe you're like me. Maybe you don't like showing anyone your work before it's ready."

Derrick was glad she said that because it gave him an out. "As an artist I guess you would understand. I really don't like to let anyone read my work—except my agent."

"Then tell me this. How does someone like yourself who is unpublished get an agent? I've got a few friends who want to be writers, and they find the process really hard."

"It is very hard and I'm very lucky. A friend of a friend knew somebody who knew an agent and they hooked me up. I was as stunned as anyone when I learned that the agent loved my work. It was only partially completed, so my agent suggested that I take some time to go away and finish the book because she thinks it can really sell well."

"So you might just be the next Stephen King, huh?"

Derrick chuckled. "I don't know about that."

Samona laughed, a soft laugh, a sexy laugh. A laugh that for some reason warmed Derrick's heart. At least she wasn't crying anymore.

She seemed so vulnerable, it was hard to see her in the role of criminal, but that's what she was. Derrick best not forget that.

"I just realized this," Samona said, standing. "You probably don't have any plates to eat on."

"I saw some in the cupboard."

"But did you REALLY *see* them? If you haven't washed them, I can guarantee they're dusty. Do you have anything to wash them with?"

Derrick responded with a crooked grin, and Samona laughed again. That was certainly a laugh he could get used to.

"Then I'll be right back," she said, rising. "I've got some clean plates and some clean cups." She walked across the hardwood floor in the living room to the door. As her hand touched the brass knob she turned and asked, "Do you have anything to drink?"

"No," Derrick admitted, shaking his head. "Well, I have some Gatorade in the fridge, but that's not exactly appropriate with dinner."

"That's okay," Samona said. "I'll bring something up."

By the time Samona returned, the pizza had arrived. She brought two full shopping bags with her. Placing the bags on the kitchen counter, she took out plastic plates, plastic cups, forks, knives and paper towels. From the second bag she withdrew a bottle of ginger ale, a Tupperware container and Ranch and Italian salad dressing.

The plastic plates made Derrick think of an insecure exis-, tence, of someone always on the move. Would she be moving again? This time out of town?

"I hope you don't mind ginger ale," Samona said cheerfully as she walked toward the table in his kitchen. "It's all I had."

"It's better than what I had."

Samona busied herself with setting the plates and forks on the table as well as the cups and pop. She opened the pizza box and took a good whiff, closing her eyes as she inhaled the aroma. Derrick couldn't help thinking that she suddenly seemed more alive than she had in any of the pictures he had seen. With something to do, she suddenly seemed happy. Or was it the company?

Derrick didn't want to admit it to himself, but it mattered. It mattered if she liked him or not. He didn't know why it mattered, but it did.

"Well I'm ready to eat if you are."

Derrick joined her at the table and helped himself to three slices of pizza and salad from the Tupperware container. He chose the Italian dressing.

"This is great, Samona. I really appreciate this."

"No problem. I figured you'd like the salad. You seem health conscious."

So she was beautiful *and* perceptive. "It's great. Everything."

"I wish I had something to spice up the salad—some cucumbers or mushrooms or something. But I didn't get to…shop… today."

He watched her carefully as pain flashed in her eyes. Something must have happened today while she was out. He wondered what.

"Samona, I meant what I said. If you want to talk…"

"Let's just say I had a really crappy day and leave it at that."

"Are you sure?"

"Derrick, your pizza is getting cold." She sunk her teeth into a slice.

Derrick followed her example, knowing he couldn't push her.

They ate in silence except for the occasional, "This is really good," "Would you like another drink," "Go on, have the last slice." Little by little, Samona had retreated into her impenetrable shell. Clearly, the happiness had been an act. Either that or forced. She was still polite, still smiling at him every now and then, but it wasn't a true smile. Not while sadness was always there in her eyes.

This case got harder by the minute. He couldn't just arrest Samona and throw her in jail; he had to get to know her, and getting to know her meant he would care for her in some way. How could he not, when she always looked at him like a helpless puppy?

How had he ever let himself get suckered into this undercover assignment? It wasn't going to be easy at all.

Chapter 7

Samona Gray was an enigma, a puzzle Derrick couldn't put together. Long after awaking the next morning, he still lay in bed, staring at the ceiling, wondering. She was so unlike any criminal he had ever known. A criminal he now sympathized with, which was definitely a problem.

"Okay, the facts," he said aloud. He recited the facts of the case, noting the points on each finger. She had the means, the opportunity, but the motive stumped him every time. "Maybe there is no motive because she didn't do it."

Immediately, Derrick threw off the covers and climbed out of bed. Where had that thought come from? Why on earth would he question her guilt? Sure, he didn't know the "why" behind her action, but she *was* guilty—it was up to him to get the proof.

A few tears and he was getting soft. Sheesh.

His instinct was way out of whack. He couldn't trust it anymore.

He slipped on a pair of socks then walked out to the living-room phone and called Nick at the office.

"Detective Burns here," Nick said when the receptionist connected the call.

"Burns, it's Lawson."

"Lawson, just the man I wanted to talk to."

Derrick's brow furrowed. "Why? What's up?"

"I've got some interesting news. A P.I. has been searching for Samona."

"A private investigator? Are you sure?"

"Yep. No one we know of. This guy isn't licensed or bonded. But he's been doing some heavy digging at the PD, calling around for all kinds of information. More importantly, the guy wanted to know where she lives right now."

"Did you talk to him?"

"Nope. I didn't get any of the calls. I just heard about it."

"Hmm." Derrick wondered who wanted to find Samona and why.

"So what did you want?"

"To talk." Derrick ran a hand over his hair. "I've gotta tell you, Samona doesn't seem like a criminal."

"And what exactly does a criminal seem like?" Nick asked.

"I know," Derrick said. "But this is different. From what I've seen, she doesn't have a mean streak, a cunning side… I don't know. I just know this is tougher than I thought it would be."

"What—can't see past her beauty?"

"It's not that—"

"Then what is it?"

"All right. There are a couple of things bothering me about this case. One, if this case is tied to the other jewelry store robberies in the last six months, why was there a lot less jewelry taken? The last two heists netted more than four million total; this time the thief only got about two hundred thousand in jewels, according to Mr. Milano. Two, nobody was murdered in the other robberies. Why this one?"

"I hear you," Nick said. "There are definitely some inconsistencies. But that doesn't mean anything. All it means is that this robbery got sloppy. You never know with street thugs. Often, the violence escalates as the crimes increase. That could explain the murder. Or maybe Mrs. Milano resisted. Some people are too stubborn. They're so interested in saving everything they've worked for that they forget about saving their lives. It's sad, but true."

"You're right."

"You know all this. You didn't need me to tell you this. So what's the real reason for the call?"

"I don't know. I guess I was just hoping this would be over by now."

"In four days? Come on—what's this really about?"

"Nothing." Suddenly he felt foolish. Nick was right. Maybe Derrick couldn't see past Samona's beauty and her charm, and was being fooled the way she had fooled many others. "The truth is I'm starting to feel out of the loop. I just wanted to touch base."

"Well, thanks to you, we're all busting our butts on the heroin case to pick up your slack."

Derrick chuckled. "Okay. I won't keep you. I'll be in touch."

"Lawson," Nick said just before Derrick hung up.

"Yeah?"

"There's a rumor floating around that Mr. Milano isn't impressed with how the police are handling the case."

"Meaning...?"

"Who knows? This is America."

"Don't I know it."

"You want to feel sorry for someone, Lawson, you remember Mrs. Milano. You think about what she went through while Samona and her boyfriend spilled her brains."

Derrick nodded into the receiver. "Thanks for that beautiful visual image. I needed that just before breakfast." But Derrick did need it. He'd been beginning to lose objectivity.

"No problem, man. Any time."

When Derrick replaced the receiver, he had one thought on his mind. He wanted to resolve this case as soon as possible. He wasn't going to be conned by Samona as Mrs. Milano had been.

Moments later, in an effort to speed this case along, he knocked on Samona's door. She wasn't home.

There was a cool breeze in the air, making the heat of this June day bearable. Samona sat on a wooden park bench opposite a water fountain. Oak Park was a small community, and here, surrounded by trees and the lulling chirping of the birds, she felt a modicum of relief, of peace. Maybe she would come here more often.

Downtown Oak Park was both historic and peaceful. The stately old buildings, the intimate antique shops, the beautiful flower gardens—they were all compelling reasons for her to come here and sketch.

The maple trees rustled in the wind, and Samona watched their fluttering shadows on the ground. Their movements were mesmerizing, and much more interesting than the blank sheet of paper before her.

Maybe she could capture their movements on paper. Maybe, if her mind was on work—not on Derrick Cunningham.

She thought of Derrick's eyes, the way they crinkled when he smiled. They were like windows to his soul, and what she saw was both compelling and sincere.

During their pizza dinner last night, he was nothing but a gentleman. She knew he wanted her to open up about what was bothering her, but he didn't pressure her. He let her know he was there for her, and that was it.

Samona smiled. Thinking of him, remembering his thoughtfulness last night, made her smile. He was just so...nice. She liked nice.

She liked Derrick.

"Mrs. Barry, there's a call for you on line three." Jennifer Barry dropped the other half of her sandwich into the Tupperware container and rose. Walking to the staff room phone, she wondered who was calling her in the middle of the day.

"Hello."

"Hello, is that Jennifer?"

"Yes it is."

"Hi... You're a good friend of Samona's, aren't you?"

"Who is this?"

"I'm sorry. This is Samona's sister."

Evelyn, Jennifer thought. Samona's estranged sister. "Hi. Evelyn, right?"

"Uh...yes."

"Samona's mentioned you." Not often, but she had.

"Oh, of course."

"Any particular reason you're calling me?"

"Yes." The woman sighed. "I'm worried about Samona. I heard what happened to Roger."

"You did? All the way in Dallas?"

There was the slightest of pauses. "Yes. I'm following the case. I'm sure you can understand that. Look, the point is I'm worried about her, and since I'm in Dallas, I can't very well check on her. And when I called her, she seemed very distressed."

Evelyn had Samona's new phone number? "Well," Jennifer said. "That's understandable. She's going through a lot."

"I know. That's kind of why I'm calling. I was hoping you could go see her today, after school. I'd feel so much better, knowing someone was there for her."

So Evelyn was feeling guilty. Jennifer said, "Actually, I haven't seen her in a while. I'd like to make sure she's okay too."

"Then you'll go? Today?"

"Yes, Evelyn. Right after school."

As Marie hung up, she couldn't help but chuckle. Man, she was good. Alex would be proud of her.

That was a lot easier than she thought it would be. She'd only been guessing that Samona had a sister; if she'd been wrong and Jennifer had gotten suspicious she simply would have hung up.

But she'd been right. And she had not only learned Samona's sister's name, she'd also learned that she lived in Dallas.

Marie threw herself backwards on the bed, kicking up her high-heeled feet as she laughed. Yes, she was good.

Hours later, when Jennifer drove out of the school parking lot and down the tree-lined River Forest street, she had no idea that the black Mazda parked at the curb was waiting for her. She had no idea she would be followed.

Jennifer hurried up the steps to the front door of the house and hit buzzer number two. Since Samona's sister had called her earlier, she had been worried.

Samona answered the door a couple of minutes later. When she saw her, her eyes widened in surprise.

Jennifer grinned. "Hey, Sammi."

"What are you doing here?" Samona asked. She opened the door wide, inviting her friend inside.

Jennifer was about to tell her that Evelyn had called, but thought better of it. Samona might not like to hear that her sister was checking up on her. "I was just thinking about you. Wanted to see if you're okay."

Samona closed the door then wrapped her friend in a tight embrace. "Thanks. I really needed to see you. You're the best, you know that?"

Jennifer pulled away from her and smiled. "So they tell me."

"Well, come upstairs." Holding her friend's hand, Samona led the way.

"The place looks nice," Jennifer said, looking around as she moved to the living-room sofa. Beige was the dominant color in the room, with splashes of rose. Beige wallpaper, beige lace curtains, rose-colored sofa and matching armchair and a rose-colored rug on the beige hardwood floor.

"It's okay, but it's not home." Looking around, Samona regretted the fact that she hadn't been able to decorate the place the way she would have liked. She didn't mind the color scheme, but the place didn't have her touch. Didn't, because it wasn't hers. She missed the small two-bedroom house she had rented since landing her teaching job, with a studio for her artwork. But the media had made that place a nightmare, stalking her, never giving her any peace. When she'd finally approached the landlord about breaking the lease immediately, he had happily obliged.

"How are you? Really?" Jennifer asked.

Samona ran a hand through her hair, for a moment expecting to feel her braids. But her braids were gone, gone because she had changed her look. "It's still hard. I just keep waiting for the nightmare to end."

"I called you when I heard about Roger. But you weren't home."

"I unplugged the phone. I didn't want any calls from the media. This was an unlisted number, but those vultures have their ways of tracking you down."

"Hmm. I hear you." Jennifer took a seat on the sofa and patted the spot next to her.

Moving slowly, Samona sat beside her. "I still can't believe it. That Roger is really dead."

"I was totally shocked when I heard the news. I thought about you immediately…wondered how you were feeling."

Samona leaned forward, resting her elbows on her knees. "I'm not sure what I felt when I first heard the news. I was so stunned I was literally numb. Then after a while, I got angry. Angry because he had the nerve to get himself killed and leave me here to deal with the aftermath."

"Angry because he can't clear your name."

"Yes. If he ever cared about me, and he said he did, then couldn't he have come forward from somewhere—wherever he was—to tell the police I had nothing to do with the murder? He could have sent a letter, made a phone call. But he did diddly. And you know why? Because this was all part of his sick plan. To make me pay for a crime I didn't commit so he could go to the Caribbean and spend the rest of his life like a king."

Jen's shoulders rose and fell. "Well, he's dead now. He didn't get his wish."

"And as much as I think he deserves it, I really can't wish him dead. With him dead, my life is screwed for God knows how long. Maybe forever. Maybe I'll always be viewed as a murderer, even if the police can't prove I am one."

Jennifer rubbed her arm. "Sammi, you can't think like that."

Samona pulled a leg onto the sofa with her and hugged it to her chest. "How can I not? Suspicion alone caused me to lose my job, to have to leave may home… Why I'm even in Chicago anymore I don't understand."

"Because you have integrity. You don't believe in running from a problem. And you want the world to know you're innocent. Running will only make people more suspicious."

Samona looked at her friend and smiled weakly. "You know me so well. Why can't everyone else know me the way you do?"

"Because they're idiots," Jennifer said succinctly. "They're too easily swayed by public opinion."

"Yeah, well, it would be nice if my colleagues supported me. I still can't believe Mr. Hendrix turned against me."

"Politics, my dear. You know it and I know it."

Facing Jennifer, Samona rested her cheek on her knee. Her friend was right. All along, Samona had tried to blame Mr. Hendrix for his actions, but he wasn't free to make the choices he made. Not without the scrutiny of the board and parents. Given the circumstances, he'd really had no other choice to make. Still, privately he could have told her he was behind her. The fact that he hadn't meant that he wasn't.

"Don't do it," Jennifer warned. "Don't…"

But Samona couldn't help it. The hopelessness of the situation hit her, and tears fell from her eyes. Lifting her head, she brushed them away.

"Listen to me, Sammi. Life is full of challenges, of ups and downs. You accept and appreciate the good times, but you can't run from the bad. You deal with them and go on."

"How can I go on when this cloud of doom is hanging over my head?"

Jennifer gently squeezed Samona's shoulder. "You can't think like that. You have to think that no matter how dark and frightening the night is, the sun always rises in the morning."

Samona grinned through her tears. "What would I do without you?"

"Oh…" Jennifer paused, searching for words. She finally flashed a weak smile and said, "You'd be fine. I'm sure of it."

Samona nodded, feeling stronger now. Jennifer was right. Somehow, this horrible night would finally end.

"Now," Jennifer began, pushing herself off the sofa. "Sit tight. I'll make us dinner."

"Okay." Samona ran the back of her hand across her face, making herself presentable.

Several seconds later, Jennifer called from the kitchen, "I guess we have to order in. You've got nothing but milk and margarine in here."

"Oh, that's right," Samona called back. "I forgot to do some shopping."

Jennifer was at the living-room entrance then, her hands on her hips in a motherly scold. The next second, she giggled. "How does Chinese sound?"

"Perfect."

Hours later, Samona and Jennifer stood in the house's doorway, saying their goodbyes.

Jennifer reached for the door, but it opened before she could turn the knob. Gasping a little, she stepped backwards, before the door hit her.

"Oh, hi," she said when Derrick stepped into the foyer, raising a curious eyebrow.

"Hi," Derrick replied, smiling politely. "Samona."

Samona grinned. Derrick didn't stop to chat, but rather made his way to the steps and then up the stairs.

"Whew!" Jennifer said when he was out of earshot, fanning herself with her hand. "Who was that?"

"Derrick. My new neighbor. He's renting the top floor."

Jennifer's eyes lit up. "Then what I said about your days getting brighter, I think that's going to happen a lot sooner than I thought." She giggled.

"Get out of here," Samona said, giggling too.

"Good night."

There was a faint knock on the door, and when Samona heard it, her heart rate sped up. It was either Derrick or Mrs. Jefferson. She hoped it was Derrick.

It was. "Hi," Samona said softly.

"Hey, Samona. Is your friend still here?"

Samona shook her head. If Mark had asked her that question, she would have wondered if he were interested in Jennifer. With Derrick, it was different. She knew he was asking only because he was curious. "No. She left about an hour ago."

"In that case, I was wondering if you had any plans for the evening. And if not, maybe you'd like to spend some time with me. I was thinking of maybe a walk on the beach or maybe even a movie. I think the blues festival is going on in Grant Park…."

He really did have nice eyes. Striking, hazel eyes. Just the way he looked at her made her skin warm. Samona wondered if maybe she was coming down with something.

"Samona?"

"Tonight isn't a good night," she finally replied. Derrick was dangerous. She should stay away from him.

"Oh." Derrick tried to mask his disappointment, but she saw it in his eyes. "Okay. I'll see you later."

He turned and started to walk away when Samona said, "Wait."

Derrick spun around. "Yes?"

God, she was crazy. Crazy for even considering spending more time with Derrick. But she liked him. She couldn't deny that.

"Tonight isn't really a great night, but I was thinking about tomorrow. Maybe we could check out Ernest Hemingway's birthplace. You know, since you're a writer and he was a writer. After all, you are in Oak Park—the place where he grew up."

"Tomorrow?"

"If you're busy..."

"I'm not."

"So, what do you say?" Samona hoped he would say yes.

"I can't wait."

A smile touched her lips. Doing something with Derrick—anything—was better than sitting at home feeling sorry for herself.

"I found her."

Alex's face lit up with a genuine smile and he pulled Marie into his arms. "Come here."

He kissed her long and hard, his hands traveling over her body. "I knew you could do it."

Marie shrugged out of his embrace and walked toward the living-room window. Alex had been so up and down lately, one minute hot, the next cold, Marie didn't know what to think. Maybe she was overreacting, but she felt like she was being used.

"What's your problem?" Alex's voice was no longer sweet, but harsh.

"Why do you want to find her so badly, anyway? You have a thing for her?"

"Don't play jealous. It doesn't suit you."

"What am I supposed to think?"

Alex moved toward her then, and once again took her in his arms. "You're supposed to think that I'm looking out for you. That's why all this is so important to me. Samona means nothing to me. It's the jewelry I care about."

Marie pouted then looked into his dark eyes. Lifting a hand to his face, she stroked his dark skin. She really did love her man and didn't want to share him with anybody. "You sure?"

"Of course I'm sure. This jewelry is our ticket to a very secure future. Once we get the money we deserve, all our dreams will come true."

Surrendering to his kiss, Marie prayed that was true.

Chapter 8

Ernest Hemingway's birthplace was a beautiful Victorian Queen Anne–styled home on Oak Park Avenue in Oak Park. The house had been refurbished to look as close to the original as possible, a project that was ongoing. Everything looked fabulous, from the fireplace with a carved oak mantle in the parlor to the rose-patterned cornice moldings on the main level.

Samona loved old houses. In this one, the mix and match of designs in the living room—the green-and-white striped wallpaper with a floral border, the Nottingham lace curtains, the flowered carpeting—strangely matched. Definitely, the odd combination added character. Old houses had so much more mystery than modern ones.

Samona especially liked Grace Hemingway's bedroom, which was one of the rooms that had been completely renovated. It looked just as it had in the late 1800s—there was even an original picture of the room as it had been then, to which visitors could compare the new version. Everything was accurate. The room was very feminine, with a dressing table draped in white organdy and a beautiful iron bed. Lace even hung over the dressing table mirror, pulled back like curtains. Adjoining the room was the nursery where Hemingway had spent his first few years.

Derrick seemed genuinely intrigued. He, Samona and a few tourists spent a good part of the afternoon touring the various rooms of the house and watching videos about the Hemingway family life. It had been like taking a step back in time.

The director of the house was a pleasant older woman who was sincere in her excitement for the house and Hemingway's work. She extended an invitation for them to return whenever they desired. As Derrick and Samona left, she stood on the porch waving.

Samona slipped into the passenger's seat in Derrick's white Honda, glad that he had parked under a sprawling maple tree that provided ample shade. She rolled down her window. "To think I've lived here how long and have never checked out Hemingway's birthplace."

"I don't know what it was like before, but the renovated version looked great. Really authentic. Though I don't think I could have lived back then."

"Why not?" Samona challenged.

Derrick raised an eyebrow. "I kinda like modern plumbing."

"Oh. Me too."

Derrick slipped the key into the ignition. "How about some lunch?"

"Sure."

"What do you feel like?"

Samona pursed her lips. "Hmm. Anything. I'm easy."

Derrick turned to her and said, "I hope not."

Her face grew hot. But strangely, Derrick's comment stirred a desire within her she'd long thought dead. "I didn't mean it that way."

"I know. Bad joke." Derrick started the car and the engine of his late-model Honda purred. "Since I haven't seen much of downtown Oak Park, I wouldn't mind checking it out now." That was true. He didn't live in this part of Chicago and didn't get here much.

"There are a lot of neat little shops down there, and a few great places to eat."

"Sounds good. Let's go."

Within minutes, they were parked and out of the car in downtown Oak Park. Samona swallowed hard. Though she'd found nothing but peace here before, she suddenly worried about being recognized. She couldn't handle a repeat of the grocery-store incident with Derrick around.

"Are you okay?" Derrick asked.

His voice brought her out of her thoughts. No, she wasn't okay. But how could she tell him that she just wanted to go home now? She couldn't. Inhaling a deep breath of the warm summer air, Samona stepped away from the car. "I'm fine. I was just…lost in my thoughts for a moment."

"You sure?"

"Mmm hmm."

She was trying to be strong, Derrick knew. For a moment he felt guilty about doing this to her. Obviously, she was uncomfortable in public. At Hemingway's house, she hadn't taken off her floppy hat; she'd even angled it over her forehead to obscure her face. She didn't want to be recognized. Who would, if they had done what she had done?

They found a small, quaint deli with a patio and an awning that provided shade. They both ordered turkey on a Kaiser roll and juice. At their table, Samona took a seat with her back facing the street.

"So," she said, lifting her sandwich. "How does Chicago compare to Toronto?"

Derrick washed down his food with his orange juice. "Chicago's cool. I like it."

"Yeah, me too."

"Have you ever been to Toronto?"

Samona shook her head. "Never. But I've heard lots of great things about it."

"It's a great place." That much Derrick could say with confidence. He had been to Toronto before with his family, even if it was several years ago.

"When do you plan on returning?"

Derrick didn't answer right away. Partly because he had bitten off a piece of his sandwich. Partly because he wanted to make Samona wonder. "I don't know."

"You must know how long you plan on renting the place in Chicago…"

"As long as is necessary."

Just like before, Derrick had shut down when Samona asked about himself. More and more she knew he had something to hide. What was he running from? Something as horrible as she was?

She wanted to find out. Wanted to, because maybe she and Derrick had more in common than he knew. If she could get him to trust her with his story, maybe she could trust him with hers. Maybe she could ease her burden.

"Remember what you told me the other night? About you being willing to listen to me if I had anything to say? The same goes for me. I'm a good listener as well."

"There's nothing to say."

He couldn't even look at her as he said the words. But Samona understood. Some things just weren't easy to talk about. As he had with her, she gave him his space.

"I guess I'm not the only one who's had a rough time."

"No, you're not."

Samona didn't know what else to say. She couldn't very well expect him to open up when she hadn't. As a result, they both ate in comfortable silence. Although they were more like strangers because they didn't really know much about each other, it seemed to Samona that they were becoming friends.

When Derrick returned home, his answering machine was flashing. It had to be work. Nobody else had his phone number here. Hitting the play button, the machine whirred softly as it rewound.

"Boyle here." The captain's loud voice filled the small bedroom. "We need to talk ASAP. We may have a big problem with this case. Milano's lawyer contacted the commander today. He gave the department a stupid ultimatum, saying that if we don't solve this case in a week, he's going to sue us. The commander isn't happy, and neither am I. The heat is on, Lawson, and I can only hope you're making progress. Call me and let me know what's happening."

The message ended with a series of loud beeps. Derrick groaned. The captain's message was the last thing he needed to hear. He had tried his best, but was no closer to solving this case than when he had started.

Already anticipating Captain Boyle's reaction to his news, Derrick reluctantly picked up the phone and dialed.

It seemed the nightmare was just beginning.

Long after Samona had returned home, she sat huddled on one corner of her sofa, trembling. She was so cold, no heat could warm her. She was so confused, she didn't know what to do. And she was so afraid.

The cause of her fear lay at the bottom of the garbage can in her kitchen, ripped into several tiny pieces.

One minute she had been happy, the next terrified. That was how quickly things could change, she knew. In an instant.

It had taken only an instant for her to return home and see the note slipped under her door. It had been written on a letter-size piece of paper, folded twice. At first, she'd thought it was a note from Mrs. Jefferson. As she read it, she'd learned otherwise.

For a moment, she had only been able to stand and stare. Stare as her body quivered. The unsigned note told her in big, bold letters that she had been found. She was being watched. The person who wrote the note wanted the jewelry Roger had stolen.

Samona closed her eyes, placed her chin on her knees. If this was all a bad dream, why wouldn't it end? She knew nothing about the jewelry, knew nothing about the murder. Why did nobody—except Jennifer—believe her?

Until now, it hadn't occurred to her that Roger had been working with somebody else, but it made sense. He couldn't have pulled off such a crime alone. That's what the police believed; it was why they suspected her. Now, Samona knew Roger had worked with a partner. Maybe more than one.

She should have known. Maybe she had heard something, seen something, but she'd drawn a blank where the robbery was concerned. Having a gun put to her head had incapacitated all her senses. All she could think about then was dying.

And now somebody thought she was involved. What would he or she or they do to her? If they thought she knew where the jewelry was, how far would they go to get it?

It scared her. Scared her into wishing she could snap her

fingers and disappear. Somehow the culprit had found her apartment, and had made it up here to slip a note under her door. Unnoticed.

She wasn't safe. In an instant, the security she had found in the last couple of weeks died.

Just as easily as they had found her, they could, in an instant, kill her.

Derrick's fingers paused over the laptop's keyboard, an uneasy feeling washing over him. Samona... For some reason, his mind was on her. His stomach churned as he thought of her and the hairs on his nape stood on end. Had something happened in the short time since they returned home from their date? Was she okay?

Maybe he just felt bad for lying to her, for making her suffer in public today when he knew she was afraid of being spotted. All this pretending and trying to get close to her was wearing him thin. He was a cop with integrity, and he didn't like being lied to. He didn't like lying, either. He wished there was another way to get at Samona. He wished he could just tell her who he was and force her to confess. But he couldn't do that. Not only would it not work, but it would send Samona running again. This time she would probably leave the state, if not the country.

Derrick's fingers hit the keyboard and a clicking sound filled the silent room. He wrote notes about what happened today, how he felt he was finally making some good progress after a week on assignment. He had called the captain, but Boyle had merely reiterated what he said in his earlier message. Samona needed to be arrested, and soon.

The problem was she had not yet opened up to him. He didn't doubt that she might because she did seem weighted down with her problems. Even tortured. Many people had a breaking point and felt the need to confess their crimes eventually.

Derrick ended his report and closed the laptop. This new development with Milano had him stressed. People like Milano just didn't understand the reality of police investigations; they took time. Suing the department would get him nowhere.

Derrick rose and paced. It was the start of the weekend and he would normally enjoy a competitive squash game with Nick this evening. Yet he was stuck here.

The sooner he wrapped up this case, the sooner he could get back to his life. The only way to do that was to spend more time with Samona. Crossing the living room, Derrick headed to the door.

A blood-curdling scream filled the silence of the old house.

Instantly, Derrick charged down the stairs.

Samona!

Chapter 9

His adrenaline pumping, Derrick charged through her door. A quick glance around the living room told him she was not there. Hearing her soft moans, he rushed into the kitchen. There she stood, shaking a hand over the sink. It took him only a second to realize she was bleeding.

He rushed to her. "Samona. My God, what happened?"

She turned on the faucet and held her injured hand under the flow of water. She winced.

Immediately Derrick took her hand in his and checked the cut. Thankfully, it didn't look very deep. Maybe all the blood scared her. "It's not that bad, Samona. There's just a lot of blood. What happened?"

"I was cutting potatoes..."

Derrick glanced at the counter then, noting the cutting board and about three peeled potatoes. The one that was cut in half was sprinkled with blood.

She seemed on the verge of tears. "I'm such a fool."

"Don't say that," Derrick said. "Accidents happen. And as I said, it's not serious."

"But if I'd just been paying attention..."

She seemed more upset than she should have been over a simple mishap in the kitchen. Derrick had seen his mother nick herself, burn herself and even cut herself several times. She never got this upset.

Derrick tore off a paper towel from the roll above the sink. He wrapped it around Samona's finger, applying pressure to it. "Do you have any Band-Aids?" he asked.

Samona nodded. "In the bathroom."

"Okay. I'll get one."

Samona watched him rush off, thoughts swirling around in her mind like a tornado. To him, she must seem like a nutcase. First the other night with their dinner, now this. She cut her finger and had totally overreacted and now that he'd come to her rescue, he must think she was so fragile. Maybe she should just tell him about the note, explain to him what had her so on edge.

She was about to do just that as Derrick returned. But as she saw him stroll around the corner, she stopped herself.

No… Her eyes flew to his as a thought hit her. It was a disturbing thought, but one that made sense. Who else but Derrick could have placed that note under her door? He had access to her apartment; he knew when she'd been out today…

She was such a fool. Here she was spending time with a man she knew nothing about. She only knew his name and where he said he was from. Silently she berated herself for her lack of judgment. Derrick could very easily be behind this. It made sense.

"Give me your hand," Derrick said.

Derrick saw the nervous rise and fall of her chest, the fear in her eyes. In an instant he realized she was afraid of *him*. Why? What had happened in the moments that he'd gone to the bathroom?

"Samona…"

"Uh, I want you to leave. I've…got this under control. Uh, thanks for coming."

It didn't make sense for her to be afraid of him, certainly not when the gash in her finger was her own fault. Or was it? Derrick stared at her intently, wondering what was wrong, hoping she would confide in him. But she didn't. And he couldn't pressure her, not without blowing his cover.

The look of fear was still in her eyes as he turned and quietly walked away.

In bed that night, sleep eluded him. Samona's eyes haunted him. Something had happened downstairs, something she was afraid to share. He wondered what.

Derrick pondered his reaction to her scream. The moment he'd heard her desperate cry, he had forgotten that she was a criminal he was supposed to investigate. All he had thought of was getting to her, helping her. And then when he'd seen the blood, his heart had pounded wildly in his chest. He'd had the strongest urge to protect her.

Maybe he was just a sucker for a woman in distress. He had wanted to protect Whitney Jordan too. But at least he had been in love with Whitney. He'd had a stake in her safety. She had been his longtime friend and he would not have stood around and let anything happen to her if he could prevent it.

But he hadn't grown up with Samona. He knew her only in one light—as the criminal he was investigating. So why should he care if she seemed in pain? Any pain, stress or other problems she was suffering now were a direct result of her own actions. She had chosen her path and was now dealing with the aftermath of that choice. It was a cruel reality that many didn't learn until they'd gotten involved in criminal activities and been caught. Derrick saw it every day. Young men and women, some-times even children, learning the devastating results of their actions the hard way. It wasn't uncommon to see a grown man weep.

But none of that affected Derrick the way the look in Samona's eyes had. Her beautiful brown eyes had been filled with fear. That wasn't faked. Something had happened. Some-thing since their date earlier. Something that really scared her.

Maybe he had lost his objectivity. Frustrated, Derrick stood and stretched. He was glad the gym he went to was open twenty-four hours. Nights like these, he needed to relieve his stress.

Samona couldn't sleep. Remembering the night's events, she alternated between being scared and feeling like a fool. Surely, Derrick would think she was crazy. Either that or an emotional basket case. She wasn't sure which was worse.

Partly because of his confused look when he'd come from the washroom, Samona had forced herself to calm down and think. From the time she'd met him earlier this week, Derrick had always been there for her, helping her, trying to make her feel better. She knew now that there was no way Derrick would have put that note under her door. They had spent the day together and had come home at the same time. When would he have had the chance to slip a note under her door? Not only that, but why would he do it? Derrick didn't know her. He was new in town and had no idea who she was.

Every time she had told herself this evening that she didn't know Derrick, that she couldn't trust him, her heart had told her something else. It told her to look at his eyes, the windows to his soul. She saw nothing devious there. Only kindness. Other than that, she got a glimpse of his own pain. He was a good person like she was, trying to work out whatever problems he had in his life.

Rolling over, Samona hugged the pillow, relieved. Derrick could not have been responsible for the note. It didn't make sense.

It was the middle of the day, yet the knocking at the door made her shudder. The note had been delivered in the afternoon. What if the person who'd written the note was at her door now? Sitting on the edge of her bed, Samona's hands literally shook. God, she was so afraid. Afraid because she didn't know whom to fear.

As the knocking persisted, she could hear a faint female voice. Mrs. Jefferson. Of course. Who else would it be? Samona's heart relaxed. If it had been the person who was stalking her, would he have knocked? Samona sensed he'd break the door down in an effort to get at her.

Samona quickly rose, knotting the belt on her terrycloth robe. It was after noon, but she hadn't dressed. She'd only recently awoken after another sleepless night. Moments later, she opened the door.

"Samantha," Mrs. Jefferson said, clearly relieved. "When you didn't come to the door right away, I was about to call the police. After what Derrick said, I was so worried about you. Thought maybe you were dead inside."

"Derrick…said something?"

"He said I should check on you, make sure you were all right. That you didn't seem okay. Guess I overreacted. Looks like you were just sleeping."

"He did?"

"Yes. On his way out just a little while ago. I came up here as soon as I could."

Samona's brain was still registering the fact that Derrick had been concerned enough about her to speak to Mrs. Jefferson. A wave of guilt washed over her. If Derrick had gone to Mrs. Jefferson, he must have realized that for a moment she was afraid of him. She wondered if he'd ever stop surprising her.

"Thanks for coming, Mrs. Jefferson. I'm okay. I just cut myself last night and was a bit upset. Nothing to worry about."

"You sure? Derrick seemed very worried."

Samona nodded, a smile lifting her lips. Derrick took the meaning of nice guy to an extreme. She had never known a man to be that concerned about her—not even Mark.

"Yes. I'm sure." Suddenly she was more sure than she had been for a while.

"Okay. Go on back and catch up on your beauty sleep."

"Wait," Samona said. She drew in a deep breath. "Did someone come here yesterday looking for me?"

Mrs. Jefferson shook her head. "Not that I can recall. Hmm. Nope."

Samona frowned. "Nobody? Not even a courier? Somebody who told you to leave something for me?"

Her hands on her hips, Mrs. Jefferson was clearly thinking. Again she shook her head. "Nope. Nobody came here yesterday."

Goose bumps broke out on Samona's arms and the back of her neck. She had hoped Mrs. Jefferson could give her some answers. In fact, she had counted on it. For if Mrs. Jefferson hadn't let anybody in to drop a note off for her, then that meant the culprit had somehow gained access to the house without anybody knowing.

"I'll be sure to let you know if somebody drops by today."

"Thanks," Samona said absently. Somehow she knew if that person returned, they wouldn't be knocking on Mrs. Jefferson's door. And this time, they may be breaking down hers.

Chapter 10

The trip to his apartment was uneventful. Partly because he wanted to get Samona off his mind, and partly because he was going crazy with boredom, Derrick had decided to take a trip home this Sunday morning. He'd needed to do something. Being at the apartment in Oak Park, he was tempted to go see Samona, but after the way she had looked at him a couple of nights ago, he knew he had to give her space. The investigation would backfire if she truly became afraid of him.

At his apartment, Derrick had watered his plants—a poinsettia he'd had since Christmas and a big, green and red wide-leafed plant his mother had given him, which he didn't know the name of. Other than that, he'd checked around to make sure that everything was okay. It had been. Even his plants hadn't suffered without him.

He checked his answering machine. There had been one call from his mother. She had wanted to know if he was okay. He had returned her call, but she wasn't at home. Strange, he thought, since this was a Sunday and she always served Sunday dinner at her home. Perhaps there was a luncheon at church, or perhaps Karen and Russell were hosting dinner this afternoon. He didn't know.

When he returned to Oak Park, Derrick took his time climbing the stairs. He was being very quiet, subconsciously listening for any sound in Samona's apartment. He heard none. But that didn't stop him from going to her door.

He should stay away, especially after Friday night and the look of fear she had given him. But how could he stay away, when as a detective with the Chicago PD, it was his duty to investigate her? Whether he liked it or not, he had to spend time with her. He'd spent two days away from her and it was now time to re-establish contact.

He knocked. In less than a minute she opened the door. When she saw him, her face lit up with a big, bright smile. That smile... His skin grew warm beneath it and he relaxed. Relaxed, because he suddenly realized that he cared. Cared that she didn't fear him. Even though she should.

"Hi," she said happily.

"What's up?" Derrick asked. She was certainly a different person than she had been two nights ago. Derrick wondered why.

"I want to apologize for the other night," she said. "You always seem to find me at my worst. Believe me, I'm not usually such a downer."

"I didn't think you were."

Samona flashed him a wry smile. "You're too nice of a guy to tell me otherwise."

"Hey, we all have our bad days. I certainly know that."

"Yes, I think you do."

Derrick leaned a shoulder against the door frame. "You seem much better."

"Thanks. I am."

"Good. Because I hate to see a pretty woman cry." His lips curled ever so slightly in a grin. "If you're up to it, I'd like to invite you to spend the day with me."

Pretty woman. Samona was surprised at her reaction to his

words. Until now, she hadn't really known what he thought of her. Now, she couldn't deny the fluttering in her stomach. She suddenly realized that it mattered to her that Derrick thought she was attractive.

"Working," Derrick stressed when she didn't reply. "Since you love working at the beach, why don't we go there?"

Samona was about to say "Okay" when it registered what Derrick had said. She flashed him a puzzled look. "How do you know that?"

"Know what?"

"Know that I love working at the beach?"

Darn. How had he let that slip out? "Uh… I just assumed… since I found you there the other day with a sketch pad. If you don't want to go to the beach that's fine. I just want to see you keep smiling. So if there's somewhere else you would prefer to work, I'm game as long as it makes you happy."

It was too good to be true. Someone putting her needs first. "No. The beach is fine. Or maybe Grant Park. Give me a few minutes to get my stuff."

Grant Park was absolutely beautiful. The sun shone brilliantly in a cloudless blue sky and birds filled the air with song. As it was Sunday, dozens of people were there, walking, in-line skating, playing various sports in the fields or enjoying the free concerts. With the water calm and tempting, many people had taken their boats for a sail.

Derrick, dressed in khaki shorts and a T-shirt, sat on a park bench while Samona sat on the colorful quilt blanket she had brought. Derrick was busy writing in a notebook and Samona was busy sketching. The two had been working in companionable silence for more than ninety minutes.

Derrick stood and stretched, the muscles in his almond-colored legs growing taut. Samona couldn't help looking at him. He was a beautiful creature. Strong. Sexy. Nice. She'd always been a sucker for nice guys.

Sitting down, Derrick threw his head back, covering his face with his notebook.

"Don't," Samona said. "I was almost finished."

"Don't what?"

"Don't cover your face. I need to see you to sketch you."

Derrick lifted his head and raised an eyebrow curiously. "You're sketching me?"

Samona shifted on the blanket, repositioning the sketch pad in her lap. "Yes, Derrick. I said don't move."

Because she told him not to move, Derrick chuckled and ran a hand over his face.

"Hey," Samona chastised. "I warned you. If you want to end up looking like Frankenstein…"

"Okay." Derrick tried to sit still. No one had ever sketched him before, and he felt self-conscious. He wondered if Samona liked what she saw.

"I should never have told you that I was sketching you. Now you've gotten all stiff. Just relax."

Derrick made a conscious effort to relax. "Give me a second." He lolled his head back and rolled his shoulders. After several seconds, he sat up straight. "All right. I'm relaxed."

Samona giggled watching Derrick. She didn't know what it was about him, but he always made her smile. Maybe he had been a class clown growing up. Whatever his special ability was, she loved it.

"You can still write if you like. You know, pretend I'm not really sketching you. I'm almost finished."

"Naw. I'm enjoying the view. Not every day is as perfect as this one."

Samona wasn't sure if he was talking about the view of the water, of the activity in Grant Park or of her. But his eyes were on her as he said the words, and her pulse pounded in her ears with anticipation.

After a moment, Derrick looked away. It took Samona several seconds to catch her breath. Whoa, that had been an intense moment. Was Derrick trying to send her a message?

Silence fell between them and Samona continued to sketch and smudge to accurately re-create the grooves and angles of Derrick's face. And his dimples. She couldn't forget those incredibly sexy dimples.

Finally, after several minutes she was finished. "Ta da." She presented him the pad in a grand style. "Here you go."

Derrick reached for the pad, his lips pursed in thought. As he scrutinized the picture, his eyes narrowed.

Samona shifted on her feet, then swallowed. She fiddled with her floppy hat, wanting to take it off but didn't dare. It was only a casual sketch, an impromptu thing she'd decided to do just because, but she was suddenly nervous. Nervous that Derrick wouldn't like it. Holding her breath, she waited.

"This is good."

Samona released a long, slow breath. "Really? You really like it?"

"Yeah," Derrick said, nodding. "It's excellent."

Samona smiled. That meant a lot. Maybe more than it should. "I'm glad you like it."

His eyes seemed to dance as he looked at her. Again, Samona felt the tension of his heated gaze. "You are one talented lady."

"Thank you." She folded then unfolded her hands in a nervous gesture. "You can have it—if you like."

"I like." She seemed to beam because of his comment, and strangely, it made Derrick happy to see her happy. His eyes moved from her to the picture. He hadn't lied. He was genuinely impressed. Samona had captured him accurately, right down to the small mole in the center of his chin.

Samona returned to her blanket, sat down, then crossed her legs. It was a simple movement, hardly seductive, but Derrick noticed. Noticed in the way that a man notices a beautiful woman. Noticed her beautiful, slim, nicely shaped legs, her cute butt beneath the pair of tan shorts. Her smooth caramel skin. Her small waist, her small breasts. He liked looking at her.

Seemingly fidgety, Samona uncrossed her legs and stretched them out on the blanket. She cast a sly look at him over her shoulder, and Derrick wondered if she was silently inviting him to join her. Regardless, he felt compelled to do just that. Closing his notebook, he dropped it onto the grass then slid onto the blanket beside her.

"I think it's time for a break," Derrick announced.

"I agree." When Derrick stretched out beside her, Samona couldn't help giving him the once-over. Her eyes roamed the length of his body, his wide chest, his strong arms beneath his cotton shirt, his thighs. Her gaze fell to his legs, similar to hers in complexion, then rested on the scar that began at his knee and stretched to his mid-calf. She didn't have to ask to know that the scar had been obtained painfully. But she asked anyway, "How did that happen?"

"My scar, you mean?"

Samona nodded.

Derrick had seen her eyes linger on his legs and wasn't surprised when she asked him about the scar. This was his chance, his opportunity to "open up" to her in hopes that she would trust him, then open up to him as well. He now felt uneasy at the thought of lying to her and said, "I'm not sure you want to know."

"I do."

Derrick drew in a long, slow, steady breath and released it in a rush. His voice was a mere whisper when he said, "Families can be cruel."

Samona felt the overwhelming urge to reach out and stroke Derrick's face. His eyes were a mixture of many emotions, and she knew he was in pain. She wanted to say something to him, but couldn't. She sensed what he had gone through was horrible and her words would be meaningless. The only thing she could do for him was listen. "If you want to talk…"

Reaching for a blade of grass, Derrick snatched it and shredded it. Then he sighed, a long, sad sound. "My father."

Samona's heart ached for him. She had been right. They did have something in common—pain in their families. She waited, giving him the time he needed.

After several seconds, he spoke again. She wished he would look at her but his eyes remained firmly on a spot on the blanket. "My father used to beat my mother. When I tried to stop him, he would beat me. I got the scar one of those times. He was beating my mother really bad, and I ran at him, pounding my small fists on his body as hard as I could. He grabbed me and threw me. I flew in the air and landed on the glass coffee table. It broke and sliced my leg."

"Oh my God." Samona threw a hand to her mouth.

"I was…maybe seven. I can't remember." Derrick's voice was void of emotion, but Samona knew his heart ached. Ached the way hers did every time she talked to Evelyn or thought of her sister's betrayal.

Sitting, silently watching him, Samona didn't know what to say. What could she say? After a long moment, Derrick continued.

"The beatings went on for years. It was always the same—my father drunk, angry or just plain hateful. Any little thing set him off. My mother and I—we were so afraid of him." Derrick paused, bit his lip. "I'd made a vow to protect my mother, but I failed."

Samona's stomach lurched painfully. "Did—your mother—" How did you ask somebody about something so painful?

"She lost an eye. It could have been worse—she could have lost her life. But I should have protected her."

Samona didn't think. She acted. Her hand reached out and gently rubbed Derrick's arm. "Derrick, don't blame yourself. You were only a child."

"I should have called the police. That was the least I could do. But I was too afraid—afraid that he would get so angry he would kill my mother."

Samona's fingers trailed upwards on Derrick's arm and found his face. She framed it. "You did the best you could."

Derrick moved away from her touch. Her hand lingered in the air, then after a moment, feeling somewhat awkward, Samona pulled her hand back and placed it on her chest.

"I should have done better."

"No," Samona said softly. "Don't say that, Derrick. There are so many things in life that we just can't control. I know that. I learned that the hard way." Just remembering her own pain caused her voice to break. "I...lost my parents. I know it's not the same as what you went through, but the pain was just as intense. And the guilt."

Derrick looked at her then, gazing intently into her eyes. "Guilt? Why?"

"Because," Samona said quickly, then stopped. She seemed to be searching for the right words to say. "Because I should have been there for them. I didn't spend enough time with them. If I hadn't been running from my sister and my problems like a spoiled child, I would've been there for my parents."

He captured an ebony wisp of her hair and twirled it around a finger. "Why were your running?"

"Because I had my share of problems with my sister. But I should never have let that take me away from my parents. Even if I couldn't deal with what my sister had done, I didn't have to leave town. I didn't even go to see them that last Christmas because I'd wanted to avoid my sister. And then they died...." Samona's voice trailed off.

She seemed so overwhelmed by her guilt and pain that Derrick felt for her. And he felt like a jerk. His story had been fiction; hers was the truth. "Don't," he said. "From what you just said I'm sure you had your reasons for leaving. I'm sure your parents understood that as well. It won't do any good to beat yourself up now. I know it's a cliché, but you can't turn back the clock. And you have to ask yourself, would your parents want you to be sitting here grieving like this, blaming yourself for something you couldn't control?"

Samona wiped her tears. Derrick was right. Her parents knew she loved them, always would. Wherever they were now, she was sure they knew that. But still, every time she thought about how they had died without her seeing them one last time, the guilt overwhelmed her.

"I guess you're right," she said softly.

"But there's more, isn't there?" Derrick asked. "Something

that's going on now—more than what happened with your parents?" He was pushing, and he wondered if Samona would take the bait and tell him what he wanted to know. Wondered if he really wanted her to. For if she did, he would have to arrest her. Derrick swallowed, but the lump in his throat wouldn't go away. He felt like a heel, conning her.

"Yeah, there's more."

He didn't breathe.

"I guess I just feel very alone sometimes. I have nobody to turn to, to share my problems with. My parents are gone, and my sister and I don't talk...."

"Why not?" Derrick asked gently.

"That's a very long story."

"What about boyfriends? Or a former boyfriend you're still close to?"

Samona shook her head. "No. Any man I have been close to has betrayed me."

Derrick ignored the shame overwhelming him and continued. "Really? I find that hard to believe."

"It's true. I don't know why." Her petite shoulders rose and fell. "Maybe I'm not special enough."

She couldn't be a criminal, Derrick decided. It was impossible. As much as his brain told him she was involved in the jewelry store robbery and murder, his heart told him it wasn't true. There was just something about her, something inherently good. Something too vulnerable, too sweet. He could pry, ask her more about this boyfriend who had betrayed her. He should. But part of him didn't want to know.

"You're very special." Much to his surprise, he edged closer to her and slipped an arm around her waist. He felt her stiffen at his touch and that should have stopped him, but it didn't. He couldn't help himself. Pulling her close, he brought his face near hers. Her eyes held his for several moments, startled, questioning eyes. He could get lost in those eyes. For a moment, he was.

As he brought his lips slowly down onto hers, he told himself that this was just part of the plan to get to know her, to get her to trust him. But his heart told him that was a lie.

Her mouth was soft and sweet. Like an exotic flower. He ran his lips over hers ever so gently, simply enjoying. The action seemed almost foreign to him in its arousing effect and he realized just how long it had been since he had last kissed a woman. Pressing his hand against her back, pulling her closer, he parted his lips and began to kiss her. Softly.

Samona sighed and her eyes fluttered shut. Derrick's lips were like a feather, softly touching hers, teasing her. A tingling sensation spiraled from her stomach outward to her skin, down her arms and legs to her fingertips and to her toes. The wonderful feeling took over her entire body. She couldn't remember ever feeling this reaction to Mark when he'd kissed her, and she had been in love with him. Or so she had thought.

She felt safe in Derrick's arms. Like maybe her world wasn't falling apart. As he pulled her closer, she arched into his embrace. She slipped an arm around his back as he deepened the kiss. His tongue was warm, persistent, thrilling. If this was a dream, she didn't want to wake up.

Slowly his tongue mated with hers, dancing together as though they always had. He should stop. Pull away. Right now. End the kiss. But he didn't want to. Couldn't. Not when it felt so good.

Finally, Samona placed a hand on his chest and gently eased him away, breaking the kiss. She was so beautiful, her lips glistening, her eyelids closed. Derrick's mouth immediately felt cold. He looked down at her as she slowly opened her eyes. In a breathless whisper, she asked, "Why'd you do that?"

The attraction he was feeling for her made no sense. Sitting up, Derrick rested his elbows on his knees. "I don't know."

Samona's stomach fluttered. She had hoped for a different answer, but sensed that Derrick was as confused and shocked by the kiss as she was. Bringing a hand to her lips, Samona trailed a finger along the outline of her mouth.

It was a wonderful kiss. Though startled when Derrick had drawn her close, Samona had to admit that she had been hoping he would kiss her all day. Hoping, despite the fact that she didn't want to get close to another man. Her life was too screwed up for any relationship.

But God help her, if Derrick were to take her in his arms again, she would let him. Let him kiss her. Let him take her to a place where there were no worries.

Derrick spoke then, ending the fantasy. "It's been a long day. I think we should go."

Chapter 11

Later that evening, Samona still remembered Derrick's kiss as she sat on her living room sofa, staring. Staring, but seeing nothing.

His kiss. *Him.* Derrick had made her feel so alive, so incredibly desirable for the first time in a very long time. That was something she'd needed, had wanted, but hadn't known Derrick could give that to her until he'd actually placed his sensuous lips on hers. Now, her lips still tingled with electricity....

The shrill ring of the telephone drew Samona from her musing. She welcomed the distraction because Derrick had monopolized her thoughts. Hopping off the sofa, she hurried across the warm hardwood floor to the telephone stand. She answered it on the third ring. "Hello."

"Samona...hi."

Samona froze, her hand gripping the receiver. "Evelyn."

"How are you, Samona?"

"Didn't we go through this a couple of days ago? I think we said all we needed to say then."

"Please don't hang up."

"Fine. Make it quick."

"Okay. I'm going to be in Chicago tomorrow. I'll be there

for a three-day business trip. I was hoping…maybe we could get together."

Samona's stomach clenched. "Why?"

"Because we haven't seen each other for more than two years."

"So why start now?" She sounded harsh, like she didn't care. But it was the only way. It was the only way to try to avoid the painful memories of her sister's betrayal.

There was a short, tension-filled pause before Evelyn said, "We have a lot of things to work out, Samona, but…I think we can. We need to. You're the only family I have left."

"Aren't things going well with Mark?" Samona was not able to hide the sarcasm in her voice.

"Mark is fine. I'm fine."

"See…" Samona's throat was suddenly tight, aching with suppressed emotion. "You have your family right there in Dallas. You don't need me. You never did."

Evelyn must have heard the pain in her voice for she said, "Samona, I didn't call to hurt you."

Samona muttered, "You could have fooled me."

"I'm trying to make an effort. Maybe it is a little too late, but I'm hoping that you'll give me a chance. We've let this go on way too long."

"We? You're the one who wasn't happy unless you were hurting me. Don't you put this on me—"

"You're right. I'm sorry. *I've* let this go on too long. Samona, I want to try to make amends…."

Samona didn't know what to believe. Her sister actually sounded sincere. But she was still hurting. Maybe always would when she thought of what her sister had done.

Samona frowned into the receiver, fighting to keep the tears at bay. Maybe her sister was right. Maybe enough time had passed and it was time to try and save their relationship. Giving in, Samona asked, "What time are you getting in tomorrow?"

Evelyn gave Samona all the details of her stay in Chicago, and Samona scribbled the information onto the notepad beside the phone. "Okay. I'll see if I can spare some time."

"I hope you can. I'd really like to see you."

"We'll see." Samona wiped a sweaty hand on her shorts. "I'm not making any promises."

"I understand."

Samona was about to hang up when she heard her sister call her name. Her heart pounded painfully in her chest. "Yes, Evelyn?"

Evelyn said softly, "Thanks."

Samona held the small notepad to her chest long after she had hung up the phone. Inhaling deep breaths did not ease the ache in her heart. Twice in a week Evelyn had called her when they hadn't spoken more than twice in two years.

If only it were easy to just get her sister out of her life, to forget her. But as this was a time in her life when she particularly felt the need to talk to someone, she couldn't help wishing she and Evelyn were close. She was the only family she had left.

She remembered the horrible accident in Dallas two years ago. Her parents hadn't known what hit them when a tractor trailer crossed the center line and collided with their car head-on.

Two years, and still the pain was fresh, raw. Never could Samona think of the accident without getting emotional. Her parents had been cheated. She had been cheated. And what made it worse for her to deal with was the fact that she hadn't seen her parents in more than a year because she'd stayed away from Dallas. She'd stayed away from Evelyn.

How could she get over all this, at least enough to forgive her sister? It wasn't Evelyn's fault, but Samona did partially blame her. If Evelyn hadn't stolen then married her boyfriend, Samona would never have left Dallas for Chicago. She would have spent more time with her parents before they died.

Samona sighed. Her parents were gone, and nothing would bring them back. But she still had a sister. Maybe it was time to make an effort at salvaging their relationship.

Tempting. Samona was too tempting.

Derrick closed his eyes as he lay on the well-worn living-room sofa. He tightened his fingers around the black beanbag in his hand, then relaxed them, continuing that routine for several minutes as thoughts whirled in his mind. Thoughts of Samona.

What he couldn't understand was why he had kissed her. Of all the stupid things to do, that had to be the worst.

Derrick squeezed the beanbag as hard as he could, but it didn't relieve the tension in his gut. He'd blown it, gotten too close to a suspect. How on earth had he lost his objectivity?

Opening his eyes, Derrick stared at the ceiling. The crazy part was, he didn't really regret doing it, even though he should. His brain told him that he was a fool but he couldn't forget the feeling of Samona's soft lips beneath his, slowly opening, accepting his tongue. Even now, he felt a rush remembering.

What was happening to him? He was a cop, and except for that one time, he always thought with his head, not his emotions. How had he let himself get so attracted to Samona?

He didn't have an answer. He only knew that in some way he was attracted to her. As much as he wanted to, he couldn't deny that.

It was hard to accept—whatever this attraction was. He'd only felt such a strong attraction for one woman before: Whitney Jordan.

Though he was over Whitney, he hadn't expected to feel something for anyone else in a long time. Maybe never. Now, his feelings toward Samona were unwanted and frustrated him. Frustrated him because he shouldn't feel anything for her. She was a criminal.

Good God, what was wrong with him?

Derrick got up and moved around the apartment, trying to get the kiss he and Samona had shared off his mind. But he couldn't. The taste of her sweet lips, the velvety soft feel of them, were constantly on his mind.

Finally he found himself at the phone in his bedroom. Picking up the receiver, he dialed Whitney's number. He didn't know why, other than the attraction he felt for Samona seemed in some strange way like a betrayal to Whitney, after all he'd felt for her.

When the butler answered, Derrick identified himself and asked for Whitney. Several seconds later, she came to the phone.

"Derrick!" she squealed. "How are you?"

Hearing Whitney's voice brought a smile to his face. A smile like the kind his own sister brought out in him. "I'm cool. How's my favorite girl?"

"Exhausted. Reanna and Marcus have me running around like a chicken with my head cut off. You know how it is—when one cries, the other cries. Now they're teething at the same time…."

"No, I don't know how it is, but I'll take your word for it."

Whitney laughed. "Sometimes I don't know if I'm coming or going. Having twins isn't easy."

"But it sounds like you're loving every minute of it."

"You know it."

"So where are they now?"

"Sleeping. Thank God."

Derrick said, "How is Javar?"

"He's great. Tired, but great."

Derrick could hear the smile in her voice and that gave him a deep sense of satisfaction. He wondered if he would ever have made her as happy as Javar made her. He doubted it.

"We've got to hook up sometime," he said. "I haven't seen those kids in so long." A year and a half ago, he would not have been able to picture himself as a welcome guest at Javar's house. Now, he was exactly that. It was amazing how things could change given time.

"And they've grown so much. I swear, it seems like only yesterday they were these tiny babies in my arms. Seven months later, my mother keeps asking me what I'm feeding them!"

Derrick chuckled. "Motherhood certainly suits you. I don't think I've ever known you to be happier than you are now."

"I don't think I have been. Javar and I finally have our lives back on track and everything is working out the way it was meant to be." She sighed, happily. "Well, enough about me. What's up with you?"

"Oh, the same old same old. Work and more work."

"When are you going to find some time to play?" Whitney asked. "You're too nice to let life pass you by without having any fun."

"I'm having…fun. Work is entertaining."

"Yeah right."

Derrick twirled the phone's cord around his hand. "One of these days, Whitney, I'll be as happy as you."

"Okay. What's wrong?"

"What makes you think something is wrong?"

"Because I've only known you since I was a kid. Something's up, Derrick. What is it?"

Derrick dragged his bottom lip into his mouth, wondering how much he should tell Whitney. He blew out a ragged breath. "It's a case I'm working on."

"What kind of case?"

"Undercover."

"Hmm… Let me guess—it involves a woman."

Derrick's mouth fell open. How on earth had she figured that out? "Why do you say that?"

"Because the only time I have to drag information out of you is when a woman is involved. Is she a partner in crime?"

"Not exactly."

Whitney paused. "Okay. Is she someone special, or is she like all the other women you've dated in the past—a passing fancy?"

"Hey," Derrick said. "What are you trying to say? That I'm some type of player?"

"No," Whitney replied. "But you certainly are a hard man to please."

"That's because all the good women are taken." He shouldn't have said that, but couldn't take back the words.

"Hmm," was all Whitney said. He was certain she knew the meaning behind his words, yet she said nothing. He was glad. He didn't want to make her uncomfortable. He was happy for her. Despite the feelings he'd had for her in the past, he knew that Javar was the right man for her. Javar was the man who could give her what she needed, wanted. Not him.

"I'm sure there are a few good women out there," she continued. "And if I'm right, you didn't really call to say hi, but to talk because you're confused. Maybe you're feeling something for someone you didn't expect to feel. Am I right?"

"W-well, kind of…" Derrick sputtered, shocked at how perceptive Whitney was.

"Then it seems to me like you've finally found someone you're interested in."

Whitney was too smart, Derrick thought as he shook his head, a crooked grin playing on his lips. He wanted to deny her allegation, but the words wouldn't come. He finally said. "It's a difficult situation."

"Work it out."

"Easier said than done, Whitney." Especially in this case.

The direction of his thoughts startled him. Without thinking, he had basically admitted that he did want things to work out with Samona.

"But you're thinking about it. Oh, I'm so happy for you. This is serious."

"Don't start planning my wedding yet."

"I'd just better be the first one you invite."

Derrick laughed. Javar was a lucky man. "If and when that time comes, you'll be the first to know."

When Samona heard the soft knocking on the door, her heart leaped to her throat. An image of Derrick smiling at her, his cute dimples winking at her, flashed in her mind. Why she couldn't get him off her mind she didn't know.

She sprang from the couch. A rose-colored silk nightie and matching robe reached her mid-thigh. It had been ages since she'd had the desire to put something sexy like this on, and now she knew she'd wanted to look sexy for Derrick in case he came by.

She was losing her mind.

At the door, she reached for the knob. Her fingers froze on the handle as she remembered two days ago. Remembered the note.

"Who is it?" she called instead.

"It's Derrick."

Just the sexy way he said his name made her pulse race. Slowly, she opened the door.

For a moment, Derrick merely stared at her, his eyes roaming her body from head to toe. His eyes seared her skin, making her hot. She loved the way he looked at her.

"I'm sorry, Samona," he finally said. "I didn't mean to disturb you."

"You're not disturbing me." *I'm glad you're here,* she thought.

"You look ready for bed." Maybe she was imagining it, but his voice sounded raspy. Because of her?

"No." She angled her head to the right, letting wisps of hair fall over her face. "Not yet."

Derrick's eyes caught the movement and she saw interest flash in their depths. He cleared his throat, folded his arms over his chest, then spoke. "I don't have your phone number, so I couldn't call."

"That's okay. So, what's on your mind?"

Holding her gaze, he said, "If I tell you that, I think I might be arrested."

Every inch of her responded to his words, knowing they were meant for her. Her nipples tightened, her pulse throbbed, her body thrummed with desire. He was attracted to her, like she was to him.

"Okay, time to get serious." He flashed one of his charming smiles and Samona wished he would take her in his arms and kiss her again. "I just thought I'd drop by to say that I really enjoyed today. And I was hoping you'd like to spend the day with me tomorrow."

Samona felt a niggling disappointment, but knew that Derrick was right not to take her up on the silent offer she was making. It was too soon to go too far in their relationship. They needed to take things slowly.

She took a moment to consider his proposal, not wanting to seem too anxious. "Sure. Why not?"

"Great. I can't wait."

"Great. I can't wait."

Good grief, what had he been thinking? Lying in bed, his hands behind his head, Derrick wondered what on earth had gotten into him.

When he had gone to Samona's apartment, he had planned to extend an invitation to spend more time with her. After all, that was what he was being paid to do. He hadn't planned to sound so excited about it.

But then, he hadn't expected to see her in that sexy silky number. She had been silently seducing him with every movement of her eyes, every gesture she made, every soft-spoken word. Somehow, he had respectfully declined.

For now. With his foolish "I can't wait" statement, Samona would surely be expecting something more in this relationship.

Maybe he should call the captain and tell him that he could no longer continue with this assignment. That he had lost his objectivity. That for some reason, around Samona he seemed to lose all reason.

"Yeah right, Lawson," Derrick said aloud. He could imagine Captain Boyle's "delight" at that news.

No, Derrick would continue with the assignment. He would push all thoughts of the tempting Samona aside and try to remember his reason for being here in this old house in Oak Park in the first place.

But deep in his heart, Derrick wondered if that was possible any longer.

Chapter 12

Samona sat cross-legged on the quilt, starting at the spectacular flower gardens in the distance. They were a dazzling array of colors—reds, whites, oranges, violets, pinks, blues. She should paint them, and capture the beautiful, sparkling blue water in the distance behind them. She would, one day, but not today.

She adjusted the rim of her floppy cotton hat to protect her eyes from the glare of the sun, and as always, to keep her identity adequately hidden. She was surprised at the number of people here. Despite it being a Monday, several people strolled the fabulous gardens and lawn, enjoying Grant Park. People must have called in sick to work, Samona thought.

She frowned. Not even she felt like working. The sketch pad in her lap was blank. Today, she didn't feel like sketching. Maybe finger painting, sponge painting or something fun like that. It felt like one of those "Crazy Days" as she would tell her students on those occasions when she felt like doing something different with her class. On Crazy Days, the students got to be creative in their own way, doing their own thing however they wanted. Later, if they wanted to, they could share their work with the class.

Her students… Crazy Days… Sighing, Samona closed her eyes.

"All right," Derrick announced. "What do you say we take a break from work and have some fun."

"Work?" Samona chuckled sarcastically. "What work? I've gotten nothing done today."

Derrick grinned sheepishly. "Neither have I."

"It must be the weather," Samona said. Or the fact that she couldn't forget his kiss and couldn't stop wishing he'd kiss her again. His kiss was ever present on her mind and had made her lose all interest in her art.

"Must be," Derrick agreed.

Samona turned, looking out at the lake, anything to try to gain control of her wayward thoughts. It was another beautiful June day. Though still officially spring, it felt like summer. But at least the heat was offset by the cool breeze coming off the water.

"You said something about fun?" Samona faced Derrick. She wondered what kind of fun he had in mind.

"Mmm hmm."

"Well…?" He certainly knew how to keep a woman in suspense.

"How about we go to the marina and see if we can rent a boat. Or pay someone to take us out on theirs. I'd love to go for a sail."

A boat… Roger. For a moment, Samona forgot to breathe. She tried to smile, to disguise her reaction, but couldn't.

Derrick flashed her a worried look. "You don't like that idea?"

"It's just that… I—I know someone who died on a boat recently…"

"Taking foot out of mouth." Jokingly, Derrick pretended to wrestle with his foot.

Samona's shoulders sagged with relief. With one silly smile,

Derrick had succeeded in easing the tension. He knew just what to do to make her feel better.

She stared at him for a moment. He was hard to figure out. One minute, he seemed depressed because of his own problems. The next, he seemed like he didn't have a care in the world.

Derrick caught her staring. "What? Something on my face?"

"No."

"Then what?"

"You're just…so interesting."

His eyes narrowed. "Interesting good, or interesting bad?"

"Good. You," she paused, cast her eyes downward, "make me laugh."

"A pretty woman like you should laugh more."

Pretty… As Samona stared at Derrick, she felt a tingling sensation spread through her stomach. She wanted to kiss him again. God help her.

Derrick clapped his hands together, breaking the moment. "Any other ideas?"

"We could get a hot dog."

Derrick made a face. "I don't eat that stuff."

Samona nodded, realizing how silly that suggestion was. Derrick was a health-conscious man. "Of course."

"How about an ice-cream cone?"

Samona jumped to her feet. "You're on."

Marie retreated down the steps and hustled to the car. She opened the passenger side door and slipped inside. She said to Alex in a whisper, "She's not home. Nobody is."

Framing her face, Alex kissed Marie long and hard. He was such a good kisser. That was one of the things she loved about him.

Breaking the kiss, he looked into her eyes. For the first time in weeks, he looked interested in her again, like he truly loved her. He winked, then said, "Let's do this."

Samona couldn't remember laughing so much in recent months. For two hours, she had forgotten she'd had a care in the world. She and Derrick had toured Grant Park extensively, walking along the paths to the Petrillo Music Shell where free summer concerts were held, to the Adler Planetarium and then the Field Museum of Natural History. They had strolled around Buckingham Fountain, a massive, circular fountain with many spouts. Derrick had even held her waist as she dipped a foot into the water, making sure she didn't fall. Later, they played an impromptu game of soccer with a crumpled paper ball on the grass. She was like a carefree child, frolicking and laughing.

Now, they were both outside her door, laughing once again. Laughing at something silly—she couldn't even remember what.

When the laughing died, their eyes met and held. It was the awkward moment after a date when neither knew what to say. It was a moment of anticipation. Would he kiss her? Would he not?

When he reached out and stroked her face, Samona knew then that he would. He made her feel so wonderful. So wanted. So distanced from her troubles.

As he lowered his head toward hers, the energy sizzled between them and it seemed like it took forever for their lips to meet. Finally, Derrick's delicious mouth covered hers. Having waited for this moment all day, Samona closed her eyes and surrendered to the kiss. She whimpered faintly, slipped her hands around Derrick's back. Trailed her fingers over his muscles. Squeezed, probed. Pressed her body closer to his.

Derrick moaned when she pressed her breasts against his chest. It was a deep moan, and seemed to rumble from his chest to hers. Never had she felt such need, the need to be close to another human being. To a man. To Derrick.

Derrick broke the kiss and looked at her. His hazel eyes had darkened with desire. His lips were wet and so seductive. His hand was still on her face, gently stroking her skin, exciting her. Samona covered his hand with hers, brought her lips to his fingers and kissed his rough skin.

"Samona…" His voice was a velvety rasp.

"Yes?" She looked at him with longing. What she was feeling now was so strong and she wanted to know that he felt it too.

"I… I've… I…" He lowered his head and kissed her again.

It was a kiss that ignited a fire in her belly. She had been hesitating at the door because she wasn't sure, but now she knew what to do. She knew what she wanted. Breaking the kiss, she said, "Derrick…let's go inside."

Derrick merely nodded. Turning, Samona found her key and unlocked her door as quickly as she could. She opened it and stepped inside.

In an instant, the excitement, the longing she had felt only a moment ago, died. She gasped. Threw a hand to her chest as she looked around her apartment in horror.

"Oh my God!"

Chapter 13

Derrick brushed past Samona, moving into the apartment slowly as she stood behind him paralyzed with fear. "What the hell?" he asked.

Someone had broken into her apartment. As she stepped cautiously into the living room, Samona's eyes registered the mess, saw the overturned chairs, the trashed artwork, papers all over the floor. Yet her heart didn't want to believe it was true. Who would've done this to her?

"Samona, do you have any idea who would have done this?"

Derrick was gripping her shoulders, looking into her face, but Samona hardly noticed. Her body was shaking.

"Samona?"

Her head moved slightly. It seemed that was all she could do. Derrick wasn't sure if her reply was a yes or a no. He only knew that she needed him. Wrapping her in his arms, he held her tight, offering comfort. She was so afraid, she trembled. He was afraid for her.

Somebody wanted to hurt her. He wished he could do more for her, protect her from the danger. Because he sensed she needed protection. According to her, she had nobody else.

He said, "Think, Samona. Think hard. Is there anyone—"

"No." She pulled out of his embrace and faced him. She

looked both confused and terrified at the same time. Derrick had seen that expression in his role as police officer many times. When he told someone that a loved one had been badly injured or killed in an accident. When he informed someone of a family member's arrest. Or murder. Or any number of other things.

"Just stay here a moment," Derrick said. "I'm going to check out the rest of your apartment. I'll be right back." When she didn't reply, Derrick shook her gently. "Samona…?"

Her head bobbed up and down in jerky movements. Her mouth was open but the only sound that escaped was wheezing as she struggled to breathe. Her eyes bulging, she clawed at her throat.

"Breathe, Samona." She was having a panic attack. He'd recognize one anywhere.

"I'm o-k-kay."

"No, you're not." He held her shoulders firmly. "Breathe, Samona. Concentrate. In. Out. C'mon, you can do it." As she followed his instructions, the wheezing slowed and died but it still seemed like it was an effort for her to breathe. "That's it. You're doing real good. Just keep breathing. I'm going to get you some water." Derrick ran to the kitchen and in seconds returned with a glass of water. "Drink this."

He placed the glass at her mouth, but Samona jerked her head away. "It's okay, Samona. I'm here with you and it's going to be okay."

She seemed to grow calmer at his words, and finally accepted the glass. She took a large gulp and choked.

"Not so much," Derrick told her. He rubbed her back until the coughing stopped.

"No…no water."

"You're sure?"

She nodded.

Her breathing was now regular, but she still seemed terrified. Derrick didn't know what to do to help her. He wondered if she always got panic attacks. "Will you be okay for a few minutes? I want to look around."

"O-kay."

For a moment, Derrick felt guilty. Guilty for leaving her there in the living room so distraught. But he was a cop. He knew what to look for and right now, had a job to do. Still, he couldn't forget the look in her eyes. That desolate, frightened look.

How had he gotten to the point where he cared so much? Cared for a woman who was accused of a heinous crime?

Ignoring that thought, Derrick headed to her bedroom. It was the same as the living room. The mattresses were thrown from the bed, drawers and clothes littered the floor. Amidst the mess, his eyes caught a pile of lacy lingerie, and for an instant, he tried to imagine Samona wearing something sexy for him. Something white and lacy and skimpy. The image disturbed him, and Derrick swallowed.

When he returned to the living room, he righted the sofa and returned the cushions to their rightful place. "Samona, come here. Take a seat."

"The kitchen. Everything."

Derrick took her by the shoulders, noting her skin felt clammy and cold. She jerked when he touched her. All he wanted to do was make her pain go away, but he couldn't.

She didn't protest when he led her to the sofa. When she was seated, he went to the kitchen. The stove had been moved from the wall, the paper-towel roll was scattered on the floor, the drawers and cupboards were open and their contents dumped. Even the toaster lay on the floor.

Why? Derrick wondered.

Moments later, he returned to the living room and sat beside Samona. He didn't know why her place had been torn apart like this, but he knew she needed to call the police. If she did, he would be a witness and his cover would no doubt be blown. He didn't care. He wanted Samona safe. "You have to call the police."

"No." Samona looked at her folded hands.

"Do you want me to call them for you?"

"No." Her reply was sharp.

"Why not? This is a crime scene. You need to—"

Samona threw her gaze to him and he saw then that her eyes were filled with tears. "I can't... You don't understand...."

But he did. She was afraid of the police. He wondered how she would react when she learned the truth about him. Would she hate him? It didn't matter. Her safety came first.

"This is serious," he said. "Somebody obviously wants to hurt you. The police can protect you."

She laughed sarcastically and he thought she would cry. Finally she said, "I'm not going to call the police. Please don't call them for me. I don't want them involved."

"But—"

"I'm not going to change my mind."

Frustrated, Derrick sighed. "Well if you won't let me help you that way, will you at least accept my invitation to stay with me tonight? You can't stay here."

He saw the first sign of relief in her eyes since he had offered her comfort. "Yes. Get me out of here, Derrick."

She hadn't said much since he'd brought her to his apartment, and now she lay sleeping on his sofa. He watched her from the neighboring arm chair. She lay on her side, her head resting on her arm, her small body curled in the fetal position. Her lips were slightly parted and strands of her onyx hair fell across her face. She was beautiful. She was forbidden. But there was something about her he couldn't resist. Something too tempting.

If they hadn't found her apartment ransacked, he wondered what would have happened when she invited him inside. He certainly wanted to make love to her. Wanted to more strongly than he had wanted anything. But would he have? Would he have broken his vow to the department? As much as he hated discovering Samona's apartment in such a state of turmoil, it had prevented him from making a terrible mistake.

Someone had ransacked her apartment, literally torn her place apart. This certainly added a new element to his investigation. Who had done it and why? He had no doubt it was connected to the robbery. Was it somebody who knew or thought she had the jewelry? And did this have anything to do with the private investigator someone had hired? The questions swirled around in his mind, but he had no answers.

The only thing he knew for sure was that he was glad he was with her when she'd returned home. There to protect her, comfort her the best way he could. The frightened look in her eyes still haunted him. She was so vulnerable, fragile. If she had walked in on her intruder, he shuddered to think what could have happened. She was only five foot four, hardly a match for a strong man with a deadly agenda.

Samona stirred, moaned. Instantly, Derrick moved to her side. Softly he brushed her hair off her face and looked down at her with wonder. How could a woman who seemed so soft, sweet, fragile, be behind such horrible crimes? But that question fled his mind as he lifted her into his arms. She snuggled her face into his neck and Derrick could only wonder why his body was betraying his mind. It was like he had totally forgotten why he was here, what job he had to do. Instead, his body grew warm in reaction to her need for him.

He was crazy.

He took her to the bedroom and placed her on his bed. She could get a good night's sleep here as opposed to on the sofa.

As he looked down at her sprawled on the blue comforter, his hands were sweating. Suddenly he was nervous. Not only did he need to slip her under the covers, but he needed to disrobe her. Just the thought felt like a violation. A violation because she trusted him when she shouldn't.

His mouth went dry and he closed his eyes. God, how could he do this? What if she awoke while he was slipping off her shorts? As a cop, he knew the possible ramifications. She could charge him with sexual assault, claim he had taken advantage of her. But as a man… No. He couldn't touch her. Instead, he took a blanket from the closet and covered her.

He was almost out the bedroom door when she called him. Her voice sounded soft and sultry, like she was calling to her lover. His skin prickled with excitement and heat pooled in his groin. If things were different…

"Yes?" He was surprised at the huskiness of his voice.

"I know you don't understand all this, Derrick, and you must think I'm crazy."

The urge to go to her, to take her in his arms was so strong, it was tangible. She looked so incredibly sexy with her slightly messy hair, her sleepy eyes. "No," he managed to say. "I don't think you're crazy."

Her lips curled into a grin. "Well, I just want to thank you. For understanding. And for being there."

"No problem."

"Good night."

"Night."

And then she laid her head back on the pillow and closed her eyes. Looking like she belonged there.

Derrick blew out a long, slow, steadying breath as he closed the bedroom door. He rested his forehead on the cool wood. The attraction he felt to Samona was indefinable, and it shook him to the core. Samona was intriguing, tempting—everything she shouldn't be, given the reason he was in this apartment. But that didn't seem to matter to his body.

Somehow, some way, he had to control his wayward feelings. He had to think like Derrick Lawson, the cop. Not Derrick Cunningham, the writer who found his neighbor a little too interesting.

"Stop pacing, will you? You're making me dizzy."

Alex's eyes narrowed as he looked at Marie. Sometimes, he didn't understand her. She knew how important it was to get his share of the jewelry. *Their* share. Yet all she wanted to do nowadays was nag him. "I'm thinking, all right?"

"For goodness' sake, you'd think we didn't find anything at Samona's place."

"What's your problem?" Marie was getting on his last nerve. Maybe life would be simpler if he just got rid of her. He had taken care of that Milano woman. He could do it again if he had to. "Forget Samona."

"Why should I? You can't."

"Not that again. I already told you she means nothing to me other than being my ticket to freedom."

Marie rose from the kitchen table and approached him. "Really? You don't find her attractive?"

Alex sneered. "Why are you doing this? Why are you acting so crazy?"

Marie exhaled harshly and placed a hand on his arm. "I just want all this over with. I want you back. Us. It seems to me you only care about Roger and Samona."

Alex drew her into his arms, rolling his eyes when she couldn't see. She was becoming a weak link and he was tired of pampering her. "Don't you get it? The way I see it, when we're through with her, she's gonna be going to jail for robbery and murder. Roger left us the perfect scapegoat. You told me that yourself. So, I'm damn well gonna use it. All I care about is getting what's owed to me, and then getting out of town. With you."

Marie sighed. "I know."

"Tell me you're ready to do this, Marie. This thing is almost over. I can feel it. But I need you. You can't go soft on me now."

"I know. I won't."

"Good. Because we have to do this tomorrow. The sooner we get what we want, the sooner we can start our life somewhere warm."

Marie looked at him, a weak smile playing on her lips. "You really think that her contact will be in that hotel room tomorrow?"

Alex nodded. He was certain of that fact. The one good thing that had come of today was what he and Marie had found on the notepad at Samona's apartment: a hotel name, a time, and the name "Evelyn Cooper." Tomorrow, he would pay a visit to this Evelyn character. He couldn't explain the feeling in his gut, but he was sure Evelyn was connected to Roger. Maybe Roger would be at the hotel, too. His jaw flinched at the thought of seeing him again. The louse would regret ripping him off.

"I'm sure of that," Alex said. "Tomorrow, we're gonna get what's ours."

Chapter 14

Desperate. Whoever had ransacked Samona's apartment was desperate, Derrick thought as he rummaged through her place, trying to get it into a manageable state. Her things had been thrown aside in a panic, not carefully searched. That told him the person or persons who had been here hadn't known what they were looking for. Rather, they had been searching for some type of clue to further whatever their purpose was.

It was early and Samona was still sleeping. Sometime during the night he had decided to wake before dawn and begin the task of putting her apartment back together. He thought that would be a nice surprise for her. After how frightened she'd been yesterday, he couldn't see her trying to put this place back together on her own.

He had also decided not to tell Mrs. Jefferson about the incident because he didn't want to alarm her. She may just insist on calling the police, and Derrick respected Samona's desire not to involve them. At least not yet.

Not involving the police meant his cover would not be blown. Not now, anyway. Deep down, he admitted to himself that he wasn't ready to end his relationship with Samona, whatever that relationship was.

He had been working on the place for more than two hours,

and still it looked like a tornado hit it. Every time he stopped and thought about what had happened, his stomach tightened into a painful knot. Samona wasn't safe. He didn't know what the person responsible for this wanted, but it was clear Samona wasn't safe while this person knew where she lived.

Why he cared was something he didn't want to think about. People like Samona—criminals—deserved what they got. Yet Derrick's heart wouldn't reconcile that belief with his brain.

He took a break and stretched. He'd never been in a situation like this before; he'd never felt so confused. He was a cop and knew what he was supposed to do. But he had never in his life felt so ambiguous. Part of him wanted to arrest Samona as soon as possible. Part of him couldn't imagine putting her away for the rest of her life.

And then there was that darn attraction he felt for her. He couldn't understand it. Didn't want to. He wanted to forget it. But even as he thought of Samona, he pictured her in his bed, sleeping, leaving her honeyed scent on his pillows. He pictured her smiling at him. He remembered the way her lips felt under his, soft, yielding to his mouth. Kissing Samona had stirred powerful feelings within him.

Sexual feelings. That's all it was. Derrick felt a modicum of relief as that thought hit him. Samona was a beautiful woman and it was natural to feel some sort of attraction to her. After all, he hadn't been with a woman for a very long time. His work was demanding and he had no time to date. The only serious dating he had done had been during his college years, after which he'd joined the police force and dedicated himself to his job. In recent years there'd been the odd date here and there, but nothing serious. Most of those women he hadn't seen again. So why, especially considering the fact that

Samona was under police investigation, could he not wait to see her again?

He was going to go crazy here, alone in Samona's apartment. Walking to the phone, he picked up the receiver and dialed the station. He asked for Nick Burns.

It took Nick more than a minute to answer, and he contemplated hanging up. Just as he was about to, he heard Nick's voice. "Burns," he said.

"It's Lawson."

"Hey, Lawson. How's it going?"

"Not good, man. Not good."

"Uh oh. Ms. Gray?"

"Yeah. I have to tell you, Burns, the more time I spend with her the harder it is to believe that she was involved in this crime at all."

"Why not?"

"Because." Derrick searched for the right words to say. "Because she just doesn't seem the type. I don't know how she ever got involved with that Roger character, but being with her, talking with her…she really doesn't seem capable of anything so heinous."

"Lawson, you've got to remain objective. I know this woman is a looker, but you have to see past that. Think of Milano. Brutally murdered. She didn't deserve that."

"I have thought of Mrs. Milano. Every day. But I'm telling you, I really have my doubts."

"Oh God. You're falling for her."

"I didn't say that."

"You didn't have to. It's pretty obvious."

Derrick groaned. "Yes, I think she's attractive. Who wouldn't? But that's all. You know me better than that. I'm a trained cop. I know how to do my job."

"And you're also human. If for whatever reason you think you can't be objective, you better let Captain Boyle know. I'm telling you, man. You don't want to get burned."

"I won't." The thought of walking away from this case now wasn't one Derrick wanted to consider. "She's starting to trust me."

Nick chuckled. "You don't want to leave her. You've got it bad, man."

"You're wrong. Trust me." The words sounded false even to Derrick's own ears.

"All right. I'll give you the benefit of the doubt. But I'll also give you a warning. Watch yourself. This is a big case and a lot is riding on you. You don't want to blow it."

"I hear you. Thanks for your concern."

"Who are you talking to?"

Spinning around, Derrick replaced the receiver. Samona stood about five feet behind him, her clothes wrinkled from sleeping in them. His heart raced. How much had she heard?

"Derrick? You didn't call the police, did you?"

"No." Not for the reason she had thought. "That was…a friend." Samona nodded. "I see."

He wasn't sure if she believed him. "You don't mind that I used your phone, do you?"

"No." Placing her hands on her hips, Samona looked around the living room. "Why didn't you wake me?"

Derrick's heart rate returned to normal. Thank God, Samona had not overheard more of his conversation. He approached her. "I figured you needed your sleep. I'm sure this has been very stressful for you, so I just wanted to help out."

"You didn't have to do this."

"I know."

Samona opened her mouth to speak, closed it, then opened it again. "Why?"

"Why did I do this?"

"Why are you being so nice to me?"

Why indeed? It was a question on his mind as well. In two strides, he closed the distance between them and placed his hands on her shoulders. The skin beneath her tank top was soft and smooth beneath his fingers. He wanted to kiss her again, to feel her surrender to him once more. But the conversation with Nick was still on his mind. "I just want to help. Is that a good enough reason?"

There was a flash of disappointment in her eyes. His throat tightened. Maybe she was hoping for a different answer. Why did it matter to him if she was?

Samona said, "I guess so." She shrugged away from his touch. "Well, let's get to work. There's a lot more to do here."

A few hours later, Samona's apartment was looking a lot better. Except for helping to put her bed back together, Derrick had avoided her bedroom. She wondered why.

Derrick was so confusing. One minute, it seemed as though he liked her. The next minute, she wasn't sure if he was being anything other than a friendly neighbor.

But he kissed you, a voice in her head told her. *Twice.* She paused over her dresser, closing her eyes for a moment as she remembered his kisses. The first had been the kind that said you were interested; the second had been the kind that could cause two people to lose control. Derrick had stirred an overwhelming passion within her. Yesterday, she had wanted him so badly. Despite her better judgment, she very well may have made love to him if she hadn't found her apartment ransacked.

Samona wrapped her arms around her body. What was it about Derrick? Even when Mark had kissed her, she hadn't felt the all-consuming emotions she had felt when Derrick pulled her into his arms.

She wasn't supposed to feel anything for anyone. Not now. Not with the cloud of suspicion hanging over her head. She didn't have anything to offer a man like Derrick. And it certainly wouldn't be fair to him to get involved with him when she knew any day she could be arrested.

The thought of getting arrested, the thought of losing Derrick, made her stomach swirl. For a moment in time she had let herself believe that maybe…maybe she would be able to love. Be loved. Have a normal life. Now, she realized what a fool she was.

She should go out to the living room and tell Derrick that she couldn't see him anymore. There was no point beginning something when she could see no future between them. That wasn't fair to either of them. But despite her thoughts, Samona stood rooted to the floor in her bedroom. How could she tell Derrick to leave when he was the best thing that had happened to her?

That thought scared her. Scared her because there was a very real chance that she could lose him. Lose him before she had a chance to love him.

Maybe that was for the best. But even though her brain said that, her heart couldn't accept it. When had her feelings for Derrick grown so strong?

When Samona heard the light rapping on her door, she jumped, throwing a hand to her chest.

"Sorry," Derrick said. "I didn't mean to startle you."

Facing him, she ran a hand over her hair. "That's okay."

He stayed at the door. "Is everything all right?"

"Yes. I was just thinking." *About you. Us.*

Derrick's gaze fell to the floor. Samona wondered what he was thinking. After several seconds, he finally looked at her. "The living room looks much better. And the kitchen. Your papers and artwork are in a pile on the coffee table, since I didn't know where you wanted them."

"Thanks."

"You're welcome. I was going to take off now, if you're okay."

"I'm fine. Go ahead."

"I can come back later."

"That's okay. I can handle the rest from here." *If you were talking about something else, please tell me now, Derrick.*

Derrick nodded. "All right. I'll see you later."

Samona saw him to the door. He didn't kiss her. He didn't even look at her with any special interest. She tried not to show her disappointment. She had no ties to Derrick Cunningham.

The instant he was gone, she hugged her elbows and leaned forward, hanging her head to her knees. That didn't relieve her stress much, but it helped her regain focus. She could not let Derrick have such a powerful effect on her.

Easier said than done. Groaning, she realized she needed to talk to someone. She rushed to the phone and called Jennifer. School was barely over and Jennifer might not be home yet, but Samona hoped she was. She could use her friend's advice.

When Jennifer answered the phone, Samona was relieved. "Jen, I'm so glad I reached you."

"Hey, Sammi. Everything okay?"

"I am so confused."

"Go ahead," Jennifer said. "I'm listening."

Samona walked across the room with the phone, then sank into the sofa, sighing. "Remember Derrick, my new neighbor?"

"How could I forget?"

"Well… Gosh, I can't believe I'm gonna say this." Samona paused briefly, then continued. "Despite everything, how messed up my life is right now, I think I'm falling for him."

"Falling for him as in you think he's cute? Or falling for him as in you're *falling* for him?"

"Falling for him as in…I can't stop thinking about him. Not at night. Not during the day. He's so attractive. But it's not only that. He's such a nice guy."

"Mmm hmm."

"Is that all you have to say?"

"Do you want me to say I'm surprised?"

Samona ran a hand through her hair. "I don't know. Yes. Yes, you should be surprised. I am."

"As you said, he's very attractive. And you are still a woman—one who's very much alive. You'd have to be blind to not notice that he's hot. Though I didn't get a chance to talk to him, just by looking at him I could tell he's one of the nice guys. So, no. I'm not surprised."

"This is scary. What I feel for Derrick I never felt for Mark."

"Ouch. So this is serious."

"I don't know. Maybe."

Jennifer asked, "How does he feel about you?"

"He's kissed me. Twice."

"Hmm. Lucky you."

"Stop it. You're happily involved."

"But I'm not dead." Samona could hear a smile in her friend's voice.

Samona frowned. "What do I do?"

"I say go with the flow."

"I want to. But how can I? My life is so screwed up. Any minute, the cops might find more evidence and arrest me. I couldn't take that—seeing the disappointment in Derrick's eyes if that happened."

"If the police had anything on you, they would have arrested you by now. You know it, and I know it."

Samona thought the same thing, but didn't truly feel free yet. Wouldn't until she was officially cleared. "I don't want to count my eggs before they're hatched. I can't help thinking that this is too good to be true. That it's all going to blow up in my face."

"Then why don't you tell him?"

"Are you crazy? I can't."

"Why not? You know what I say about honesty. Everything's possible if there's honesty in a relationship. And you're not guilty, so you have nothing to fear."

"It's not that simple."

"I know it's hard. But I've always believed in taking chances. Go for it. Don't let Roger ruin your life any more than he already has."

"You're right. I know you are. But I'm afraid."

"Afraid of what? Afraid that you might find the happiness you want? Or afraid that Derrick doesn't really feel for you the way you feel for him?"

Samona paused. After a long moment she said quietly, "Afraid of making another mistake. Of being a fool. Again."

"What does your gut say?"

"I don't know. I only know that I really like him. But after what happened with Roger…"

"With Roger, you were never sure. Remember? You told me

you were seeing him but you felt something wasn't right? Is that how you feel about Derrick?"

Samona didn't hesitate. "Not at all."

"Then, my dear friend, I think you have your answer."

Evelyn sat on the edge of the hotel's bed, her hands folded in her lap, thinking. If she could turn back the clock, she would not have hurt her sister. She had been wrong to go after her boyfriend, and knew Samona had been devastated when Evelyn married Mark. She had thought that seeing pain in Samona's eyes would make her happy, take away the bitterness she felt toward her, but it didn't. It only hurt her.

It wasn't that Evelyn didn't love Mark. She did, truly. But she should have made sure he ended his relationship with her sister before she ever dated him. So much pain could have been avoided.

Evelyn leaned forward. She wondered if God was punishing her for hurting her sister. Now, the one thing she wanted more than anything in the world she couldn't have: She and Mark couldn't have children.

There was a knock at the door. Her heart fluttering, she closed her eyes. She had been anxiously awaiting this moment since Samona had called from the hotel lobby. Finally, she would see her sister again after two long years. After Samona had left their parents' funeral without so much as a goodbye.

What would she look like? Thinner? Plumper? Visibly older? Maybe she had lost weight because of everything she was going through with the criminal investigation. While Evelyn ate when nervous or stressed, Samona didn't.

Would Samona smile when she saw her, or scowl? Or would

she simply be indifferent? Evelyn's stomach lurched. She could handle intense emotions—anything but indifference.

Rising from the bed, Evelyn smoothed her elegant slacks and walked slowly to the door. Her nerves were tattered and even her hands shook. God, she was nervous. This was an important visit—a turning point in their relationship. She hoped that Samona would want to work things out, that she wasn't here to tell her she never wanted to see her again.

There was another knock. Evelyn took a brief moment to check out her appearance in the bathroom mirror. She looked fine. *Just answer the door. Nothing is worse than not knowing.* She and her sister had a lot of issues to deal with, but they were the only blood family they had. It was time they made amends.

Evelyn steadied her hand and turned the knob, her heart racing. Before she could fully open the door, it was shoved open violently, throwing her backward. As she scrambled to regain her balance, a man and a woman marched into her room. A man and a woman she did not know.

Something was terribly wrong. She glanced at the intruders for only a moment longer before bolting for the door. She didn't make it. The man grabbed her forcefully, whirling her around. He punched her in the face, then threw her to the floor.

The room started to spin.

"Don't even think of doing that again, and don't even think of screaming. I have a gun, and I'm not afraid to use it."

Stunned, Evelyn merely stared at him. Who was this jerk? Who was this woman searching her hotel room? She was more angry than afraid, but she was no fool.

"Where's the jewelry?"

Blood from her nose trickled into her mouth. Her chest heaved. She didn't respond.

The man stooped beside her and grabbed her face. He squeezed it harshly, digging his dirty nails into her skin. "I said, where's the jewelry?"

"I don't know what you're talking about." Blood spilled from her mouth as she spoke. Oh God, there was so much blood.

"Wrong answer." He backhanded her across the face.

Angry tears filled Evelyn's eyes.

The woman spoke then. "We know you know where it is. And if you value your life, you'll tell us."

Evelyn's mind raced to find an answer that would satisfy them. Suddenly, she knew her life depended on it. She could think of none. "I don't know."

"Where's Roger?"

"R-Roger? Roger who?"

The woman poked her head under the bed, then rose. "He's not here."

"Too chicken to face me, huh?" the man said to Evelyn.

"I don't know any Roger." But she did. The one Samona had been dating.

"Give Roger a message for me. Or his girlfriend Samona— whoever you're here to meet." Pure evil flashed in the man's eyes as he raised his hand, this time with his gun.

Evelyn's heart went berserk with fear. "God no!"

He struck her with the butt of the gun. Once, twice. Many more times. She tried to use her arms to block the blows, but he was still able to make contact with her head and her face. Her blood spattered everywhere.

At some point, her body became numb and she stopped feeling. Slowly stopped acknowledging what was happening. Then finally, a welcoming, painless darkness overcame her.

Chapter 15

Samona sat on her bed with her arms wrapped around her knees, wishing she could pinpoint the moment Derrick had crawled under her skin and made his way to her heart. She couldn't. It didn't matter. He was there now.

In her heart. She blew out a shaky breath. So much was wrong in her life and she was so afraid. Afraid to love. Afraid she'd never love again. Afraid she'd lose the one good thing in her life before she ever really had it.

Derrick... She didn't know what it was about him, but it was something. Maybe his charming smile. Maybe his compelling eyes. Maybe his cute dimples. Maybe...

The phone rang, jarring her from her musings. Glancing at the wall clock, she saw that it was after six in the evening. Where had the time gone, she wondered as she grabbed the receiver. "Hello?"

"Hello, Samona. I'm glad I caught you home."

Immediately, Samona's throat tightened and she couldn't draw breath. Blood pounded in her ears. Her hands shook and she barely held on to the receiver.

"Samona, it's Mark."

Somehow she was able to swallow, wet her throat. "Y-yes," she croaked, "I—I know."

Mark. The one man she had loved. The man who hadn't had the courtesy to officially dump her before he'd started seeing her sister. Mark, the man she'd hoped to marry, but who had married her sister. Mark, whom she hadn't seen nor spoken to since her parents' funeral. Why now was he calling her?

"Samona, I'm calling about Evelyn."

Of course. Evelyn. The sister he had married. He probably wanted to reach her in Chicago. Maybe she wasn't in her hotel room and Mark thought she was with her.

She didn't care. She didn't know why her body was acting like she did. She was over Mark. But, God help her, the betrayal still hurt.

"Samona, are you there?"

"Hmm…yes. Yes, I'm here."

"Did you hear what I said?"

The urgency in his voice caused a shiver of dread to wash over her. "What is it? What's wrong?"

"Your sister's in the hospital."

"What!"

"I got a call from the police about an hour ago. Evelyn's been beaten up pretty bad."

"Oh my God." She felt dizzy, winded. "Beat up? Where? Why?"

"I don't know the details. I only know she's at Cook County Hospital."

"Oh God. Okay. Let me grab a pen." She put down the phone and searched for a pen and paper. With everything in disarray, she couldn't find one. Her hands were shaking so badly.

She stopped. Inhaled. Exhaled. Concentrated. In the living room on her coffee table, she found a pen and paper. She hurried back to the phone in her bedroom.

Mark gave her Evelyn's room number. He also told her that he was at the airport and his flight would be arriving in a few hours. "I'll meet you at the hospital," he said.

"I'm on my way now."

Samona hung up and searched for her purse. It wasn't in her bedroom. Frustrated, she squeezed her forehead and looked around. Where was it?

The living room. She hurried there and found her purse on the sofa. Exactly where she'd left it.

She felt lost, terrified. Almost as disoriented as she'd felt the day Roger had put a gun to her head. Her sister was seriously injured. It was hard to believe.

What if she had died in the attack?

Samona shook her head, dismissing the thought. Her sister wasn't dead. She was at the hospital and she had to get to her. Now. Her hands still shaking, Samona dug her car keys out of her purse.

Somehow she managed to lock her door. She turned to run down the stairs and stopped. Instead, she headed up the stairs to Derrick's door.

Her fingers were so jittery they were almost numb. She could barely feel them when they knocked.

It seemed like hours before Derrick opened the door. His eyes bulged when he saw her. "Samona. What is it?"

"My sister." Her voice sounded hollow to her ears. "She's hurt. Bad."

"Where is she?"

"The hospital."

"Which one?"

"C-Cook County."

Saying the words again didn't make it real. It seemed like she was caught in a bizarre dream that wouldn't end.

"Gimme a second. I'll drive you." Derrick disappeared into the apartment and returned moments later, his keys in hand. Placing a hand on her back, he gently guided her down the stairs.

Samona was barely aware of anything during the drive to the hospital. She was numb, afraid to feel. But when they entered the hospital room and she saw her sister on the bed, her face cut and badly bruised, sadness overwhelmed her. And guilt. A painful lump lodged in her throat.

After all this time, she hadn't known what she'd feel when she saw her sister again. She certainly hadn't expected to feel as much as she did. For years she had told herself she didn't care about Evelyn. That she didn't need her in her life. But seeing her sister horribly beaten proved two things to her. She loved her and missed her. She was the only family she had left. Today she had almost lost her without ever making things right.

She felt Derrick's hands on her shoulders. Felt him squeeze gently in a silent show of support. She leaned into him for strength, then moved to the side of the bed where her sister lay.

An oxygen mask covered Evelyn's nose and mouth. Her closed eyes were severely bruised and swollen. So were her lips, from what Samona could see beneath the mask.

Good God, who had done this to her sister? Though she had wanted to remain strong, tears spilled onto her cheeks. Tears for Evelyn and for herself.

Samona held a hand over Evelyn's body, afraid to touch her. Finally, she brought her hand to her sister's forehead, brushing her hair off her face. Evelyn didn't respond. She was still. Seemingly lifeless.

Samona thought of her parents. Wondered how bad they had looked after the accident. She hadn't been allowed to see them and the caskets had been closed. All she could do was hug their coffins and say her final goodbyes. She had felt so helpless. She felt helpless now.

Derrick ran a hand down Samona's arm, but she didn't turn. In slow, rhythmic movements, she stroked her sister's forehead.

"Samona, I'm going to find your sister's doctor."

She nodded absently.

As Derrick left the room, his own stomach coiled. Samona was in pain. Nobody should have to suffer the way she was. She had lost her parents, and now her sister was critically injured.

He remembered all too well the day his own father had died. At first, all he could feel was disbelief. Then, he had comforted his mother because she'd been devastated. It was only after his father had been buried that the reality of the situation had finally hit him. Alone in his room, he had cried. His father had died of a heart attack at the age of forty-seven. He'd had symptoms but ignored them, dismissing them as insignificant, and ultimately paid with his life.

That was twelve years ago, when Derrick was a teenager. After his father's sudden death, he had vowed to live a healthier life. Eat well and exercise. Get regular checkups.

"Hello, Detective Lawson."

Derrick spun around and faced the petite Chinese nurse he had seen on several occasions when he'd come to this hospital's emergency room. Immediately, he looked around, worried that Samona might be in earshot. She wasn't.

He looked at her name tag. "Pearl. Hello."

"Are you here on an investigation today?"

"Actually," Derrick began. "I'm here with a friend. Her sister was badly beaten, I was just about to look for her doctor."

"Who's the patient?"

"All I know is that her name is Evelyn."

"That must be Evelyn Cooper. She was attacked in her hotel room. Somehow she managed to make it to the phone before she lost consciousness."

Derrick's brow furrowed. Her hotel room. That struck him as an odd place to get attacked. Either she was at some sleazy motel, or she knew her attacker. "Do you know which hotel?"

Pearl shook her head. "I can't remember the name. But it's one of the posh ones downtown." She shook her head ruefully, then said, "Let me see if I can find her doctor for you."

Evelyn's doctor was a black man in his fifties. He shook Derrick's hand and said, "I'm Dr. Walker. Are you a family member of Ms. Cooper's?"

"I'm Detective Lawson with the Chicago Police Department." Derrick produced his badge for verification.

"A police officer was here earlier regarding Mrs. Cooper and I spoke with her."

"I'm not here in an official capacity. I'm here with the victim's sister, Samona Gray."

"I see."

"Naturally, Samona is very distraught and is by her sister's side. I was hoping you could tell me the extent of Evelyn's injuries."

"Certainly, Detective. Let me first say that Mrs. Cooper is a very lucky woman. The beating she received was a vicious one and could have had much more serious consequences. She's in critical but stable condition. She has a concussion and hasn't yet regained consciousness but I expect she will soon. Unfortunately, she also suffered extensive injuries to her left cornea. I don't want to alarm you, but it is possible that she may lose an eye. I won't know that for sure until we run a few more tests."

Derrick planted his hands on his hips as he contemplated the doctor's words. "That's pretty bad."

"Yes, it is. But as I said, I won't know the extent of the injury until the results of further tests. I'm hopeful. Evelyn is a fighter. Quite miraculously, she was able to call the hotel's front desk before she passed out. They then called the ambulance."

Judging by Samona's reaction, Derrick knew this new development would be especially hard for her to deal with. Wondering what to do, he bit his bottom lip. He didn't want to give her bad news, but he wouldn't lie to her. Not about this. Maybe he would wait until absolutely necessary before letting her know the extent of her sister's injuries.

"Any suspects?" he asked.

"None that I know of."

"Thanks, Dr. Walker." Derrick left the man and went to a pay phone. He called the district that would have dealt with this incident and spoke with Amanda Healy, the investigating officer. She told him that so far there were no suspects, but the crime unit was at the hotel testing for prints and looking for evidence.

Derrick hung up and folded his arms over his chest. He had goose bumps on the back of his neck. He didn't like this. Evelyn Cooper was in town on a business trip and had been assaulted? What were the chances of that?

Derrick's gut was telling him this was more than a random assault. His gut told him that somehow this had something to do with Samona. Something to do with the Milano case.

In the almost three hours that Samona had been by her sister's side, Evelyn had not regained consciousness. Samona had tried talking to her like she saw people do in the movies, but Evelyn had not responded.

Samona threw a quick glance at Derrick, who stood beside her. More than once she had told him that she would be okay, that he could leave, but he had refused. A smile touched her lips as she remembered. Truth be told, she didn't know how she would have gotten through the day if it weren't for Derrick. Thanks to him, she didn't feel as scared as she had initially. He had been gentle when he'd told her that her sister might lose an eye and had convinced her not to worry about that fact until necessary. Thought she'd been in pain, Derrick had made her realize that the most important thing was that Evelyn would be okay. Still, Samona wouldn't feel truly relieved until her sister woke up.

The sound of voices drew her attention to the door. Seconds later, the curtained partition opened and a nurse entered with Mark. Immediately, Samona ran to him, throwing her arms around his neck. "Mark...."

He kissed her cheek and squeezed her tightly for a long moment. "How is she? Really?"

She hadn't seen him in two years, hadn't wanted to because of his betrayal, but surprisingly Samona felt no bitterness. Once, his kiss and his embrace would have ignited some feeling within her. Now, she felt nothing. Nothing but a sense of happiness that the man who loved her sister was here for Evelyn. Pulling back, she attempted a smile. "Evelyn's going to be okay, Mark."

Derrick approached Mark and said, "I'm Derrick. Samona's friend."

"Mark." He shook Derrick's hand. "Mark Cooper. Thanks for being here. I appreciate it. Samona, the doctor wasn't available when I arrived. Did he tell you anything about Evelyn's condition?"

She told him everything, watched as pain contorted his

features as he learned the extent of Evelyn's injuries. Samona wished she could do more for him, but she couldn't.

When she finished her story, Mark nodded tightly, his eyes glazed as though he couldn't believe what he'd heard. He ran a hand over his short hair and blew out a ragged breath, then started for his wife's bed. Leaning forward, he kissed Evelyn's forehead, whispering something Samona couldn't hear. Then he lifted his wife's hand into his.

Samona jumped when Derrick ran his hands down her arms. The next moment she leaned into him for support. This was a weird moment when past and present merged. She felt a strange sense of bittersweet happiness watching Mark with Evelyn. Surprisingly, her heart felt light, free of the burden that had weighed her down for years. It was like she had gone through an instant metamorphosis. The bitterness and anger she had once felt toward Mark and Evelyn seemed to float from her body and dissolve in the air.

Mark was her past. He was her sister's husband. He loved Evelyn, and Samona could accept that now.

Derrick was her present. As she brought a hand on to his where it rested on her arm, Samona couldn't help thinking that the reason for this metamorphosis involved Derrick. Involved her feelings for him.

She couldn't deny now that she was falling in love with him. Silently, she wondered, *Will Derrick be my future?*

It was almost an hour since two orderlies and a nurse came to take Evelyn for testing. Mark walked back and forth, pacing the floor. Samona sat on a chair watching him. Derrick stood, watching her.

Samona didn't have to tell him that she had once been in love with Mark. It was obvious. Had been from the moment she had run into his arms and thrown her arms around him.

Derrick knew it didn't make sense, but he'd felt a twinge of jealousy when the two had embraced. It wasn't that he really felt threatened; Mark was married to Evelyn. But he wondered how close Samona and Mark had been. Had he been her one true love?

Derrick rubbed his tired eyes. He sensed Mark and Samona had been very close. If Mark had dumped her and married her sister, that was probably the reason why Samona and Evelyn were not close. And for Samona to be angry with her sister years afterward meant that she'd had strong feelings for Mark. No doubt, she had loved him. He didn't know for sure, and at this point he could only guess, but Derrick figured Mark had probably been Samona's one true love. Derrick had heard stories about how hard it was to get over one's true love—he knew it firsthand. But he had gotten over Whitney. Had Samona gotten over Mark?

His thoughts were interrupted when Evelyn was wheeled back into the room. She looked the same as when she had left: not unconscious.

Derrick, Samona and Mark all faced the nurse. She explained that the results of the tests would not be known for a couple of hours.

Mark sighed, exasperated, then immediately went to his wife's side. Samona walked to Derrick and he took her in his arms.

Facing them, Mark said, "You two don't have to stay here. Go on home. I'll call you if there's any change."

"No." Samona shook her head. "I want to be here."

Mark held Samona's gaze for a long moment, flashed her a weak smile, then turned back to Evelyn.

Derrick wondered about the look. Wondered why he cared.

* * *

Samona didn't know how much longer she would last. She was fading, despite her desire to stay awake until there was a change in her sister's condition. It would be so easy to fall asleep now, with Derrick's arms around her as she sat on his lap.

The intimacy between them wasn't forced. In fact, Mark must think they were an old couple. If Mark was thinking about anything other than Evelyn.

Derrick yawned and Samona knew he, too, was still awake. She snuggled against him, wondering when she had become so comfortable with him. Wondering why just being near him made her feel better.

Mark stood and stretched. Then he walked toward her and Derrick. His eyes were red; he was tired too. This was a long night and it wasn't over yet.

"Why don't you go home?" Mark suggested. "There's nothing you can do now. Get some sleep and come back tomorrow."

Derrick shifted beneath her, then placed his hands on her shoulders. "What do you say, Samona? Mark is right. You need to get some sleep."

Samona closed her eyes and thought long and hard. There was always tomorrow, but what if Evelyn took a turn for the worse during the night? She didn't know what to do.

All at once, a picture of her parents entered her mind and a feeling of peace washed over her. Somehow she knew then that Evelyn would be okay. She could feel her parents' spirits in the room with her as though they were actually there. They were watching over Evelyn, protecting her.

"Okay," she said. "Let's go."

She hugged Mark, then went to her sister and kissed her cheek. After promising to return as soon as she could tomorrow, she and Derrick left.

At some point during the drive home, Derrick reached out and took her hand. Samona looked at him, thinking he might say something, but he only smiled softly. The rest of the way home he held her hand, silently offering her comfort as he had for the past several hours.

Samona's heart felt full. Derrick hadn't spoken the words, but she felt loved. More loved than she had ever felt with Mark. Derrick had been there for her during the entire day without any complaints. Not only had he offered her support, he'd offered her hope. With him, her world didn't seem as dark as it once had been.

As they climbed the steps in their Oak Park home, Derrick said, "My bed is yours tonight—if you want it."

Samona's body thrummed with longing at his words. For an instant, she let herself fantasize. She let herself believe that Derrick was inviting her to share his bed—with him. God, how she wanted to wrap her arms around him and lose herself in this man.

"I don't mind taking the couch," he added.

The fantasy died. Samona sighed. She couldn't stay in Derrick's apartment and not be with him. After the trying day with her sister, she would want his comforting arms around her. "Thanks, but I'll stay at my place tonight. I'll be okay."

"You're sure?"

Samona nodded.

"Okay. I'll see you tomorrow."

He kissed her forehead, a chaste kiss, but one that set off sparks in her body. "Yes, tomorrow."

She watched him walk off until she couldn't see him anymore. But she didn't enter her apartment then. She stayed in the hallway, her back propped against the wall, listening. She heard him open his door above her.

When his door clicked shut and she heard the lock turn, Samona released the breath she didn't know she was holding, and closed her eyes. As she stood in the hallway, her eyes closed, her heart beating a musical waltz in her heart, Samona knew at that moment that she was in love.

Chapter 16

Someone was in her room, watching her. Someone with hard, cold eyes. Oh God…

Anxiety seizing her, Samona's eyes flew open but she didn't dare move. She could see nothing in the dark room, hear nothing but the windows rattling in protest as the night wind howled. Yet something had awakened her. An eerie feeling overcame her and her heart raced. Was her sister okay?

She sat up and was about to reach for the phone but stopped. Were those footsteps she heard? Fear skittered down her spine and she held her breath.

When in the dark night she heard nothing else, Samona let out a relieved breath. She was being ridiculous. Who would be in her apartment?

The person who had turned her place upside down.

She shook her head. No, she couldn't believe that. She was safe. She had to be. She was worried about her sister. That was all.

As she sat in the dark room trying to detect any foreign sound, a horrible thought invaded her mind. It caused goose bumps to pop out all over her skin. Her sister had been attacked *after* her apartment had been ransacked. She'd had a note by the phone with the information about where Evelyn was staying.

Samona's chest heaved as a shiver of nervous dread passed over her. God no. It was too horrible to be true.

But she hadn't seen the note. Not that she could have found it in the mess, but still she worried. Was it possible that the person who had broken into her apartment had attacked her sister?

It makes sense.

Right now, she wished she had stayed with Derrick tonight. She was afraid—too afraid to even leave her bed. She would be afraid until she awoke in the morning and found she was still alive.

Maybe she was overreacting. Maybe the events of recent days had her more frightened than she cared to admit. Nobody had been in her room. Her sister's attack had nothing to do with her.

Samona clung to that thought, but that didn't make her feel any better. Her gut told her something was wrong.

She was cold. There must be a draft from the window. Lying back, Samona pulled the blanket up to her neck, wrapping it around her shoulders to shield off the chill. But as she did, she couldn't be sure if the cold was really from the wind, or from somewhere deep within her.

"Where are you going?" the man asked.

"I'm leaving!" the woman shouted as she grabbed her clothes from the floor. Her neck hurt from where he had grabbed her. She wasn't going to stick around to let him treat her like he owned her. "You're crazy. I didn't know how much—"

"You're not going anywhere."

She screamed as he seized her arm harshly. "Let me go. I don't want to see you anymore. Okay? That's all. I just want out...."

He wrapped a thick hand around her thin neck. "Why are you doing this? You know I love you."

"You only love you. Not me, not anybody else. And I'm tired of it. I'm tired of your need to control."

"Really?"

He squeezed her neck and she almost gagged. She didn't like what she saw in his eyes. Hatred. Evil. She was talking to a dangerous man, she realized. She needed to take a different approach. "Look, I just need some time."

"You said you were leaving me."

"I… I didn't mean that. I just meant…"

He squeezed harder. "You wouldn't be just saying that now?"

"No," she wailed. She grabbed at his hands. "St-stop. Y-you're hurt-ing me."

He slapped her then. Her hand flew to her cheek and she looked at him, the man she had loved. Who was he? She didn't know him anymore.

Slowly, she began to back away from him. He walked toward her with confidence. Menacingly. Fear gripping her, she turned and ran.

He caught her in a few seconds. She screamed and scratched and kicked as he slapped and choked her. A kick landed in his groin and he yelled in pain.

She scrambled for the phone. Dialed 911.

"Derrick! Derrick, open up!"

When Derrick heard the pounding at the door, he threw off the covers and ran to open it. Samona rushed into his apartment, her eyes wide with fear. "Samona, what happened? Is it Evelyn?"

"No." Her chest rose and fell quickly with each rapid breath she inhaled.

"All right. Take a deep breath, then tell me what's going on."

"My apartment…someone was there last night. Someone…"

"Wait a minute. What do you mean? Someone was there while you were there? Or before you got there?"

Samona sobbed softly. "Last night, something awoke me. I thought...maybe someone had been there. But then I thought I was just overreacting. Then, when I woke up this morning, I found a note...."

"Where?"

"On my kitchen counter."

Derrick placed his hands on Samona's trembling shoulders. "Samona, where is the note now?"

"Downstairs. With the dead rose."

"Dead rose?"

She sniffled and nodded.

"Can you show me?"

She drew in a deep breath. "Okay."

He took her hand and they walked down the stairs to her apartment door. It was open. Samona hadn't even stopped to close it on her way out.

The note and rose were on the kitchen counter as she said. Not only was the rose black and dried, its petals lay scattered. Leaning over the counter, but careful not to touch the surface, Derrick read the note.

What happened today was just a warning.
Next time won't be so nice.
Give us what we want and everything will be okay. If you don't, you'll be sorry. We are very serious. We'll be in touch.

Smart, Derrick thought. Whoever had written the note had not implicated himself in any crime. Everything had been vague, with only enough information for the recipient to understand. But Derrick understood.

He said, "Did you touch anything?"

"No… I was too scared."

"Good. That was very good, Samona. You haven't tampered with the scene and now the police can dust for prints."

Samona's eyes flew to his. Confusion flashed in their depths. For a moment, Derrick's heart stopped. She knew. Knew he was a cop and that he had been lying to her.

But she said, "I…I can't."

Derrick's heart began beating, but he didn't know why he was relieved. Samona needed to contact the police. Needed to report this. With the attack on her sister, and now this rose and note, Derrick was certain that Samona's life was in danger. That she would find out he was a cop was a consequence he had to deal with. Right now, he only cared about her safety.

"Come here." He took her hand and led her to the living room. "We need to talk."

Samona looked at him, shaking her head. "Not here."

"Fine. Then we'll go to my apartment."

Samona agreed and they went upstairs. She sat on his sofa and he sat next to her. She linked her fingers together then rested her chin atop her hands. Derrick wondered how much more stress she could take before she completely broke down.

"Samona," he said. "Remember when I told you that I was here for you, that I would listen to you? I don't want to pressure you, but I think you should start talking. If not to me, then to the police. Whatever is going on here is very serious. I can't help but feel that you're in danger."

"I think so too."

"What does that note mean? What do you have that someone wants?"

Samona buried her face in her hands and moaned. Her head pounded and it felt like her last nerve was going to break. Why was all of this happening to her? She was a good person and she didn't deserve this. Finally, she said, "There's a lot you don't know about me, Derrick." She paused, afraid to go on. She couldn't take it if he turned her away now, even though she wouldn't blame him if he did. "You might not like this."

His body felt like a live wire, with energy flowing through him at rapid speed. This was the moment he had waited for. The moment she told him what he had been given the responsibility of finding out. Part of him wanted to stop her—he didn't want to know the truth now. Not if it could jeopardize what he was feeling for her. But he was a cop with a job to do. That came first. He would see this through to the end. He said softly, "Go on."

"The reason I can't call the police is because they won't believe me."

"Why would you say that?" Derrick asked, although he knew the answer.

"Because…" Samona sighed. "Because they believe I'm responsible for a crime that took place just over two months ago. If I call them now, they won't help me. They'll probably throw me in jail."

Derrick tried to act as though this information came as a surprise. "What did you do?"

"Nothing!"

Samona brushed her hair back with both hands and for the first time Derrick saw the scar. It must have been from the robbery, where she had been injured. He said, "I'm sorry. I didn't mean to say that. I mean to ask what the police think you've done."

"Please, Derrick. Please tell me that you'll listen to what I'm about to say with an open mind."

"I will." Derrick meant it. Part of his heart hoped now that Samona would offer him the explanation he needed, a reason to believe in her innocence.

"Okay." She looked down at her fingers, then back at him. "The police think I was involved in a robbery and murder."

"Murder?" Derrick hoped he sounded shocked enough.

Samona's face contorted with grief. "Yes. Murder." Her voice cracked and she took a moment before she continued. "It's not true. I didn't do it. I could never..."

"What happened?"

She couldn't tell by looking in his eyes if he believed her. God, she hoped he did. She couldn't take it if he didn't. Not after he made her fall in love with him.

"I was dating this guy. It wasn't serious—I didn't want it to be. On April Fool's Day, he took me to a jewelry store." She laughed mirthlessly. "At first I actually thought he was thinking of buying me an engagement ring. I was worried that he was going to do that because I wasn't interested in him in that way. Little did I know he had other plans in mind."

"He wanted to rob the place."

"Yes. And because I was with him, the police think I was involved."

"Surely the police must understand you had nothing to do with it—that you were just a victim, right?"

"I tried to tell them that, but they didn't believe me. You see, a woman was murdered. The store's clerk. Roger—my ex-boy-friend—fled the scene and got away. The people in this city want to see someone pay for the crime. Because Roger is no longer here, that someone is me."

"I can't believe that."

"That's because you're from Toronto. You don't know what it was like here two months ago. Every paper had a picture of me on the front page. And when the police couldn't come up with any concrete evidence to arrest me, people were angry. I lost my job, my life…"

"You still have your life, Samona. And from what you tell me, it doesn't sound like the police have anything on you." Man, did he ever feel like the biggest heel. Here he was offering her comforting words when he was her enemy. Why did she have to trust him? It would be so much easier if she had been snarky with him, rude, unapproachable. Not sweet, loving, vulnerable.

"They were watching me for several weeks. I think that they're trying to find out where the jewelry is. If they can positively link me to the jewelry, then they can arrest me with enough proof to make everybody happy."

"What about the murder?"

"Well, the police can't find a murder weapon, so they can't prove I fired the gun that killed the store owner. What I didn't tell you is that my loving ex-boyfriend knocked me unconscious at the scene. I guess I'm lucky. If I hadn't been out cold, he probably would have killed me too."

"Are you saying you didn't see the murder?"

"I don't know who killed that woman. When that happened I was dead to the world. Thankfully. I don't think I could live with that memory. It was bad enough waking up and seeing the body when the police had arrived."

Samona realized then that Derrick wasn't looking at her with contempt. Her heart leaped with joy. He didn't hate her. That meant he must believe her.

"Wow," Derrick said. "And you know nothing about where this Roger character is now?"

"He's dead. Apparently he got killed while trying to escape the country on a boat. He's the one I was talking about the other day...."

"What I don't get—and what the police probably don't get—is why this guy would have brought you along for a robbery if you weren't involved. I'm no criminal, but that doesn't make sense to me."

"I don't know. God, if I had known I never would have been there that day. But now that I think about it, I'm sure I was part of his sick plan all along. He probably planned to bring me along, knock me out and leave me there to take the blame."

"Sounds like a sick guy. How'd you get involved with him?"

"I had no clue that Roger was a criminal. Or anything other than a decent guy. He was just the uncle of one of the kids at my school—"

"School?" To a stranger, it would seem Derrick really did know nothing about Samona Gray. He was even surprising himself with how convincing he sounded.

Samona's eyes closed pensively then slowly reopened. "I'm a teacher. A teacher without a job because of all this. If I'm not officially cleared of this crime, I may never teach again."

She had answered all his questions without hesitation. Derrick wondered why the investigating officers hadn't believed her. She sounded convincing, seemed sincere.

"Do you believe me?"

Derrick paused. Thought hard. Tried to find a balance between what his cop head said and what his mind said now. He told her what she wanted to hear. "Yes. I believe you."

Samona sighed, relieved. "Thank you. You don't know how much that means to me."

"I think I do."

Her hand touched his face. Stroked softly. Derrick sucked in a breath as the soft scent of her skin drifted into his nose. Samona excited him. Overwhelmed him. One touch and he was lost.

"I don't know what it is about you." Her lips trembled and her eyes filled with tears. "I…"

He froze. "What?"

"I… I'm so glad I met you."

He should be happy. She was saving him from making the biggest mistake in his career. Instead he felt a mixture of emotions—anticipation, confusion, arousal, sadness.

He planted a soft kiss on her lips, a kiss that easily could have lasted longer but he didn't allow himself that pleasure. "How about we go see your sister?"

Nodding, Samona smiled. "Yes. Give me a minute to get into something decent and I'll be right back."

As she hurried off, Derrick lay his head back on the sofa and grimaced. He wished he had the guts to be as honest with her as she seemed to be with him. Wished he could follow his heart and tell her the truth about who he was. Maybe she wouldn't hate him if he told her now.

He thought of Captain Boyle, of the commander, of the mayor. These people expected a lot from him. Maybe too much.

He couldn't tell Samona. At least not yet.

Chapter 17

Samona sat by her sister's side while Mark slept in the armchair. When she and Derrick had arrived at the hospital, they had learned the good news. Not only had Evelyn regained consciousness, she wasn't going to lose her eye.

Mark had hugged her and said, "You were right. You said everything was going to be all right, and it is."

Samona had turned to Derrick and looked into his eyes. "Derrick was the one who convinced me not to worry," she'd told Mark. "He gave me strength."

Mark had smiled at Derrick. "Sounds like you're a special person."

Derrick had shrugged, and Samona had watched both him and Mark carefully. Though she didn't need his blessing, it was like Mark was telling her he approved of Derrick. If Mark had said those words even a month ago, she would have been tempted to give him a piece of her mind. Now, the irony of the situation made her smirk.

Mark…Evelyn. Samona looked down at her sister. Evelyn lay sleeping peacefully, and she didn't look much different from last night. But she had awoken. And, according to Mark, when she woke up around four in the morning, she hadn't stopped talking. Now, Samona hoped she would awake with her at her side. She had a lot she wanted to say.

If Evelyn would let her. Her lips twisted in a wry grin, Samona acknowledged that that was one thing that was going to change. From now on, Samona wasn't going to be afraid to tell her sister how she felt. If her true feelings about any given situation were out in the open, then they could try to work out their problems. She'd always been a bit intimidated by Evelyn, her older sister who seemed to do no wrong. Samona had found it hard to talk to Evelyn growing up. Then, after Evelyn had betrayed her with Mark, Samona had shut down her emotions where her sister was concerned. They had hardly spoken because Samona hadn't been able to see past the betrayal and hadn't wanted to find the true source of their problems. She hadn't been the only one—Evelyn had let their relationship deteriorate. Until now.

So, they had a lot of things to talk about. A lot of catching up to do as sisters. And Samona wanted to ask Evelyn about the attack. But most importantly, she wanted to tell her that she was going to be there for her from now on. Their problems were not too monumental to overcome.

Samona looked at her sister for a long moment. It wasn't going to be easy, she acknowledged. She couldn't expect to have a wonderful friendship with her sister overnight. But she had taken the first step in salvaging the relationship with her sister—forgiveness. The past was the past and it couldn't be changed but the future could and would be different.

Samona felt Derrick approach her even though she couldn't hear him. He said, "I'm going to the cafeteria to get some drinks. What would you like?"

"An orange juice, please."

He kissed the top of her head and heat flooded her. The way he would kiss her without notice, gently stroke her face, rub her arms—it was like he was her lover. He knew just what to do to make her feel better and when, as though he had been making her feel better for years.

"I'll be back as soon as I can."

Samona watched Derrick leave the room, hoping. Hoping she could have a future with him.

Evelyn stirred, and Samona's gaze immediately fell on her. Her heart beat rapidly with anticipation. After two years, she would finally speak to her sister face-to-face.

Evelyn shifted in the bed, made a face as though she was in pain, then settled. Samona wondered if she were actually going to wake up.

The next moment, Evelyn's eyelids snapped open. Looking around for a moment, it seemed she was trying to figure out where she was. Then her eyes rested on Samona.

She said softly, "Samona?"

"Yes, Evelyn. It's me."

Evelyn shut her eyes tightly, then reopened them. She moaned faintly. "Hi."

Samona's eyes misted. "What a way to get my attention."

A chuckle came from Evelyn's throat; her mouth hardly moved. "I told you I wanted to see you."

"Next time, kidnap me or something, will you? But don't scare me like this again."

"Okay."

"How do you feel?"

"Not good. But I'm alive."

"Yeah," Samona said softly. "Thank God." She squeezed Evelyn's hand.

"Where's Mark?"

"He's behind me on the chair. Sleeping. Do you want me to wake him?"

"No. Let him sleep."

They fell into silence, and after a long while, Evelyn spoke. "I'm glad you're here."

"I wouldn't be anywhere else."

A soft sob escaped Evelyn's mouth and a tear fell down her cheek. "This isn't what I had in mind, but if it got you here…"

"Don't say that."

"You know what I mean. I'm sorry, Samona. Sorry for everything. Sorry about falling for Mark."

"He's the perfect man for you. I know that now."

"But I hurt you."

"We don't have to talk about this now."

Evelyn nodded with difficulty. "Yes. I want to." She swallowed. "If I hadn't been jealous of you, I probably wouldn't have gone after Mark."

"Jealous?"

"Mmm hmm. You know—you were the pretty one. The apple of Daddy's eye."

"Yeah right. You were the apple of Daddy's eye. As far as he was concerned, you could do no wrong."

"Yeah, I got good marks, but so what? I had my head so far in the books I didn't know if I was coming or going. You, on the other hand, enjoyed life. Took chances. Lived on the edge."

"I did not. I was never extreme."

Evelyn huffed. "Remember the time you fell for Sean Garvey?" When Samona groaned and covered her face with a hand, Evelyn continued. "When Mom and Dad didn't want you to see him—they thought you were too young—"

"I was thirteen," Samona interjected, grinning. "I was old enough to have a boyfriend."

"Thirteen and didn't want to listen to anybody. Like you knew everything." Evelyn chuckled. "Remember how angry you got with me when I told Mom and Dad that you were planning to run away?"

Samona sighed wistfully. "Oh yeah. You were Miss Goody Two-Shoes, running off as quickly as you could to get me in trouble."

"That wasn't it. I told myself that was why, but the truth is I was jealous of you. I didn't want to see you having fun when I wasn't. All the guys loved you, but they didn't even notice me."

And that was why Evelyn had pursued Mark. She didn't have to say it; the flash of guilt in her good eye said more than words. Samona swallowed, determined to forget and forgive. None of that mattered now.

"Evelyn, what happened yesterday? Who did this to you?"

"I'd like to know that too." That was Derrick who had spoken. Samona hadn't even heard him return to the room. Now, she faced him. What had happened to her sister was really none of his concern, but she wanted him with her here.

"She tricked me. I thought it was Samona who called my room, so I gave that woman the room number...."

"A woman did this to you?" Derrick asked.

"There were two of them. A man and a woman. Black. They kept asking me about the stolen jewelry."

"Oh God," Samona said. "I'm so sorry, Evelyn. This is all my fault."

"No, it's not," Evelyn said. "I know you had nothing to do with that robbery. But whoever attacked me thinks you did."

"How did they know where you would be?" Derrick asked.

"That's what I don't understand. You're in town for one day and they find you?"

Samona's face contorted with guilt. "I think the same people who ransacked my apartment attacked my sister. I had a note by the phone with her name and the hotel where she was going to be staying…. God, how could I have been so stupid?"

Derrick touched the back of her neck. "Don't say that. There is no way you could have known—"

"But I should have. I should never have gotten involved with Roger. That's the reason for all of this. If I had just—"

Evelyn reached for Samona's hand and squeezed it. "I don't blame you. Don't blame yourself."

Derrick said, "Listen, you'll have to tell the cops this. I guarantee you, someone will be coming here to ask you questions."

"Maybe not," Samona said. "There are a lot of assaults in Chicago daily. The police don't have time to keep up with everything."

"Trust me, they will," Derrick replied.

"How can you be so sure?"

There he went again, venturing into territory he shouldn't. He lied. "I have a cousin who's a cop. So I know a bit of this stuff."

Samona stood and groaned, folding her arms over her chest. Evelyn said, "What's wrong?"

"She doesn't like cops," Derrick replied.

"It's not a matter of me not liking cops. It's a matter of them not liking me." She moved to her sister's side again. "Evelyn, I'm not telling you not to talk to them, but maybe you shouldn't tell them what you just told me. About the jewelry bit."

"Because you think that's enough to arrest you?"

Samona shrugged. "I don't know. I only know that the cops

have been trying to find a way to connect me to the stolen jewelry for two months...."

"That's—"

"Ridiculous?" Samona supplied. A tiny knot of tension began to tighten in her head. Just moments ago she and her sister were making gains. Now...

"I was going to say," Evelyn began slowly, "that I agree with you. That's something to be concerned about. So, if you don't want me to mention the jewelry, I won't."

Samona drew in a deep breath and let it out in an agitated rush. "I'm sorry, Evelyn. It's just that I'm so stressed."

"There's no need to apologize."

"Thank you," Samona said. "For understanding."

"I don't know." When Samona looked at Derrick, he was shaking his head. "I think it's important to be honest with the police. You want to catch these perps, don't you?"

"Of course," Samona answered.

"Evelyn, you saw them. You have a real lead for the police to follow. If you can identify the people who attacked you, then you can help get them off the street. And from what Samona has told me, I'd bet those people were the accomplices in the robbery and murder—the police need to know this." Derrick cupped Samona's chin. "This may just help you clear your name, Samona."

And he suddenly realized that that's what he was hoping for. For a way to clear Samona's name. Because he cared about her. More than he cared to admit.

"I think he's right, Samona," Evelyn added.

Samona's brain felt like it would explode, thoughts were whirling around in there so fast. She hadn't considered the fact that the ransacking of her apartment, the note and her sister's attack might actually provide proof in her favor. Now, thanks to Derrick, she had another reason to hope. How would she ever repay him for everything he'd done?

"Well?" Derrick asked.

"I think you should write police novels," Samona said.

Caught off guard, Derrick forced a laugh. "Why would you say that?"

"You seem to have a good head for that kind of thing."

Derrick shrugged. "You think so?"

"Yeah. You're a knowledgeable guy."

Evelyn said, "Huh? You've lost me."

"Derrick is a science-fiction writer."

"Not yet published," Derrick interjected.

"Wow. I'm impressed," Evelyn said.

Cocking an eyebrow, Derrick said, "Since you think I sound so 'knowledgeable,' does that mean you'll take my advice?"

Samona half shrugged, half nodded. "Evelyn, if and when the police get here, you tell them what you think is best. I don't know if I'm ready to face them yet, but I am tired of running. I just need some time."

"Fair enough," Evelyn agreed.

Derrick rubbed her back. "You've made the right decision."

Samona faced Derrick and smiled weakly. He was like a ray of sunshine on a cloudy day. An anchor in a stormy sea. Clichés flooded her mind and she wanted to tell him how she felt, but she didn't dare. Here in this hospital room, it was not the time nor the place to tell him what she was really thinking.

Instead, Samona said softly, "I hope so."

Derrick couldn't remember when he'd ever been on the hot seat to the extent he was when Samona had mentioned that he should write police novels. For a moment, he wondered if she knew. Knew and was baiting him. But if she did, surely she wouldn't want to talk to him. She probably wouldn't want to see his face again.

A hand on his chin, Derrick paced the floor by the pay telephones. At least twice he'd reached for a quarter to call Nick. On Wednesday, Nick didn't start work until the afternoon. Knowing his friend, he was probably sleeping now.

What point was there in waking Nick when he couldn't truly offer him any solutions, Derrick wondered. What Derrick really wanted was to come clean with Samona. In his heart, he knew he should. Felt he should before it was too late. Maybe if he told Samona the truth now, he could make her understand.

Before he drove himself crazy, Derrick grabbed a quarter and dropped it into the pay phone's slot. Sherry Burns, Nick's wife of three years, answered the phone almost immediately. "Hey, Sherry. It's Derrick. Is Nick around?"

"I think he's sleeping. Let me—"

"No," Derrick interjected. "It's okay. I'll call back."

"He should be getting up anyway. Just give me a second."

About a minute later, Nick came to the phone. "Lawson. You heard."

"Heard what?"

"About Milano. Isn't that why you're calling?"

"No." He paused, waited. "Well don't keep me in the dark. What happened?"

"His current girlfriend, Misty something-or-other, called 911 last night. From his place."

"Really?"

"Mmm hmm. It seems Angelo Milano got a little rough with Misty last night. When the beat cops arrived, she was terrified."

"Are you telling me Milano was arrested for assault?" Derrick asked.

"Actually, no. When the cops got there, Misty wasn't talking. Nada. Milano said something about an intruder breaking in—that he was in the shower at the time."

"And the 911 call?"

"Again, nada. Misty only said she was being assaulted, but not by whom."

"And Milano was in the shower at the time of the assault." Derrick shook his head and chortled.

"So he says. Apparently, when he heard Misty scream, he ran out of the shower, but the intruder got away. He didn't even get a description. Surprisingly, neither did Misty."

Time and again, Derrick had seen women change their stories in domestic-abuse situations. They would call 911, but by the time the cops got there, they didn't want their husbands or boyfriends arrested. Some actually pursued charges, but many of those women refused to testify against the men in court. As a cop, it was very frustrating. "Does anybody believe that story?"

"If so, I'll be looking for Santa Claus this Christmas. The problem is, we have nothing on him."

Derrick's palms sweat, his skin felt hot, and adrenaline flowed through his veins like hot lava. It was the way he felt every time he had a strong gut feeling about something. Now, a theory was taking shape in his mind. That theory fit this case like the last few pieces of a puzzle. But he had no proof.

"How's your case going?" Nick asked.

"A lot of interesting twists here too." Derrick told Nick about the attack on Samona's sister. "Somebody wants Samona and is going to great lengths to get her. In the last few days, her apartment has been broken into twice."

"Really?"

"Yep. The first time, her place was trashed. Someone was looking for something. Then, after her sister's attack, she got a note with a dead rose—basically a warning."

"To give up the goods," Nick offered. "So she *is* in this up to her ears."

Derrick paused, considered his words. "She says she isn't."

"You talked to her about this?"

"Yep. She opened up to me, told me the whole thing was her boyfriend's doing. That he left her alive to take the fall."

"And you believe her?"

Not only was Nick a fellow cop, he was one of Derrick's best friends. He could talk to him. He certainly needed to talk to somebody. "My gut tells me she's telling the truth. Not that I haven't been wrong before. But if you could just hear her talk, you'd hear how genuine she sounds."

"A lot of con artists are very convincing."

"True, but as far as she knows, she has nothing to prove to me."

"Maybe she has a thing for you."

"You're fishing."

"You're a handsome man—not as handsome as me, of course. Maybe she wants to impress you. She can't very well do that by admitting that she's a thief and a murderer."

"Maybe," was all Derrick said.

"You know how much I respect you," Nick said after several seconds. "So, if you have doubts about her guilt, then so do I."

A smile touched Derrick's lips. "Thanks, man."

"Whatever you do, Derrick, do it fast. My gut tells me this whole case is going to blow sky-high real soon."

Chapter 18

Derrick's conversation with Nick weighed heavily on his mind, even hours later when he and Samona had returned from the hospital. He had a feeling of foreboding, that something was going to happen, but he wasn't sure what.

It was Samona, he realized. He was worried about her. Had been since the break-in. Would be until this whole situation was resolved.

He had asked Samona if she was going to call the police, but she'd said she needed more time. He hadn't pressured her.

Samona hadn't wanted to go inside the house when they'd returned home. Instead, she'd said she wanted to go for a long, quiet walk. Derrick had offered to accompany her, but she had declined. She said she had a lot of things to think about—alone.

With her gone, Derrick was restless. What if something happened to her on the street? What if the people responsible for her sister's assault attacked *her?* Several times, he had started for the door, determined to find her and bring her home, but something had stopped him. His respect for her privacy. And the thought that he should distance himself from her before he became too attached.

Derrick chuckled sarcastically at that thought. It was way too late for that.

There was a knock on his door. *Samona.* Springing from the armchair, Derrick hurried and opened it.

"Oh hello, Mr. Writer." Mrs. Jefferson stood smiling, her arms crossed over her chest. "Sorry to bother you. But I was hoping you could help me with something. A danged thingy has blown. I have no power in my bedroom, bathroom and kitchen, and I'm no good at looking at that box in the basement. You know the one…" She snapped her fingers as she tried to find the word.

"The fuse box," Derrick supplied.

"Yes, that's it. Can you help me?"

"Of course, Mrs. Jefferson. Do you have a flashlight?"

"Right here." She pulled one from the waistband of her polyester pants.

"Great." Derrick's smile was forced.

As Derrick and Mrs. Jefferson made their way to the basement, a strange feeling crept over him. He wondered if the fuse had blown naturally, or if someone had tampered with it.

Samona hugged her elbows as a shiver passed over her. Though it was now dusk, the late spring evening was still warm. She wondered why she was cold.

It was a premonition, she realized. A premonition that something was going to happen.

She quickened her pace. How long had she been out? Glancing at her watch, she saw that she had been walking for more than an hour. Turning down a tree-lined street, she headed for home.

The feeling—what was it? It seemed to grow stronger. Samona stopped and jogged in one spot, trying to shake it off. It wouldn't go away.

She thought of her sister, but felt no anxiety where she was concerned. She thought of Derrick. He certainly couldn't be the cause of her worries. He made her feel things other than anxiety. Sweet sensations she hadn't experienced in a long, long time.

As she turned yet another corner onto another peaceful street, she realized what was bothering her. It was the thought of going home.

Home. She wanted to go home. Not to the house in Oak Park that had become her temporary refuge for these last few weeks. She wanted to go to her house in River Forest. She wanted her life back—her job, her home, her freedom.

She was tired of running. Tired of having to run. Tired of being afraid. Tired of wondering what would happen from one day to the next. She wanted the cloud that had hung over her head for the past two months to be replaced by a ray of sunshine.

She wanted to fight to regain what was hers, but she didn't know where to start. Maybe Derrick was right. Maybe she should go to the police with the information she had. Maybe they would believe her.

But what if they didn't? The prospect of spending the rest of her life in jail was not a pretty one. She'd never survive. Not if she didn't have a hope of ever being set free.

Why did Roger have to go and get himself killed? He was the one person who could prove her innocence. *I need you, Roger.*

A car slowed near her, and Samona's heart leaped to her throat as fear seized her. But the car drove past her. Its occupant seemed to be looking for an address.

Her nerves were frayed. The slightest sound made her jump. She was always on edge because her whole life was a mess.

Why was she thinking like this, she wondered. Her sister was going to recover nicely; she should be happy. But for some reason, she wasn't.

Derrick. It was like someone whispered his name into her ear. She sighed. Yes, she was worried about Derrick. Worried about where their relationship would go. If it could go anywhere.

She hadn't wanted to ask him when he was leaving town, but she knew he wouldn't be sticking around forever. He had a life to return to. So did she. His life was in Toronto. Hers was here. They hadn't known each other long, but if he asked her to move to Toronto with him, the way she felt now, she would say yes. If… That was a pretty big if, considering she didn't really know how he felt about her. She only knew she was in love with him.

She thought he was attracted to her. But she'd also thought that Mark would love her forever. She wasn't crying over what was; rather, she was concerned that she didn't really know anything when it came to love. Look how badly she'd screwed up where Roger was concerned.

She couldn't afford to make another mistake. As it was, she'd made two doozies. If she made another one…

The sun was setting fast and Samona realized that she had stayed away too long. She'd been so caught up in her thoughts. Now, she wanted to get home to Derrick. What did she have to lose by telling him how she felt?

"There you go, Mrs. Jefferson," Derrick said. Standing, he brushed the dust off his jeans. What he thought would be a ten-minute job had turned into a forty-five-minute marathon of chores. He could now add another title to his list of professions: handyman.

He had replaced the burned-out fuse in the basement, filled in a few large cracks in the wall, boarded up a window that for some reason wouldn't lock and now he had just finished screwing in the hinge on a cupboard door. One thing about old houses—it was important to maintain them. Otherwise they would crumble around you.

"I've gotten to everything you've asked me."

"Bless your heart, Derrick. I know I let some of this stuff stay way too long, but I don't know too much about these things."

Derrick nodded. He doubted Mrs. Jefferson knew anything about repairing a home. She seemed more interested in talk shows and tabloids. A man had probably taken care of the handyman responsibilities in the past. She wore a ring so he knew she was married. He wondered what had happened to her husband, but didn't dare ask. He wanted to escape while the night was young.

"Remember to call a carpenter as soon as possible. You really should have that deck's railing fixed."

"I will. Thank you so much." She yawned. "It sure is handy having a man around the house. At times like these, I really miss Arthur."

For a fleeting moment, Derrick thought he would miss this place when he left. Mrs. Jefferson would probably miss him and Samona. She may be a little eccentric, but she was a nice woman who was no doubt lonely.

"You're welcome," Derrick said. "I'll see you."

"Happy writing." Mrs. Jefferson smiled, then yawned again.

"Night."

Mrs. Jefferson watched him retreat, then closed the door. Derrick slowly climbed the stairs, thinking that he'd gotten in a good workout today without having gone to the gym. Bringing his nose to an underarm, he sniffed then grimaced.

A shower was the first order of business when he got to his apartment.

Samona frowned at Derrick's door when he didn't answer. Where was he? Straining to listen for sound, she thought she heard the shower.

For a moment, she was tempted to go inside and drape herself on his bed, then watch his reaction as he came from the shower and saw her. That would tell her whether or not Derrick was really interested in her.

Giggling at the thought, Samona decided she didn't want to give the man heart failure. She headed for the stairs and the back porch, not yet ready to face her own apartment.

Derrick opened the door to the back porch and watched as Samona whirled around, startled. Her eyes were wide, her lips were slightly parted, and tendrils of her dark, silky hair partly obscured an eye. His throat tightened. Man, she was beautiful.

He stopped in the doorway. "Samona, I didn't realize you were down here." That was a lie. He'd seen her from his window. "I'll leave you to your thoughts."

"No," she said quickly. There was a curious spark in the eye he could see as it met and held his. She let her gaze fall, then turned and faced the railing. Clinging to it with both hands, she looked at him over a shoulder. "I'd like you to stay with me."

"Okay," Derrick said, approaching her. There was something about her tonight. Something electric. He wondered if she was trying to seduce him. Cocking a hip against the railing, he asked, "Have you made a decision yet?"

"About calling the police? No. But I will soon." She paused, pinned him with a level stare. "Why are you so nice to me?"

"Why?" Derrick repeated, buying time to think of an answer. "Because I…like you."

She narrowed her eyes speculatively. "Hmm."

"Hmm? What does that mean?"

"Nothing." She leaned back on her heels, supporting her body weight with the railing.

"Whoa," Derrick said, placing a hand on her back. "Be careful. The railing is loose."

She stood tall. "Oh. Thanks. So, Mr. Cunningham, what brings you down here? Writer's block?"

"Actually, yeah."

"Because of me?"

"No…why would you say that?"

"Because you've spent so much time taking care of me recently. Being there for me. That must have thrown a wrench in your writing routine."

"A little," Derrick said softly. "But I'm not complaining. There are times when the real world is much more alluring than the fictional ones I create."

Was he saying she was alluring?

Derrick placed both hands on the railing and looked up at the sky. "Like tonight. It's much too beautiful a night to spend it inside."

"I know what you mean." Samona gazed up at the dark sky, sprinkled with golden stars. She would have to do a watercolor of the image soon. The stars were like rays of hope in a dark world. She wished she could reach out and snatch one, capture some of the magic she imagined they held.

"They're beautiful, aren't they?"

Derrick's words startled her out of the enchantment. "Yes. When I look at the sky, I see a large canvas." She gestured with her hands. "I would love to capture the beauty on paper. But I guess when you look at the stars, you see fictional worlds."

Derrick nodded. "Yes. Sometimes. But sometimes I just see it for what it is. A wonder of nature."

Samona nodded absently.

He was behind her now, so close she could feel the heat of his breath in her hair. A wave of longing passed over her and she shuddered.

"No matter how dark your world may seem now, a new day will dawn. You will have brighter days."

His soft words offered her more comfort than she realized she needed at the moment. And he seemed so sincere, the words meant so much.

Derrick's arms slipped through hers and landed on the railing next to her hands. Her skin prickled with excitement. She should turn and face him, slip her arms around his neck, press her lips to his throat. But she didn't dare move.

"Pick a star."

"Hmm?"

"Pick a star. Any star. Then make a wish."

Samona exhaled a shaky breath. A wish. Did she dare?

"Go on," Derrick urged. "Did you pick one?"

"Yes."

"Now close your eyes."

She felt safe with him, and closer to him right now than she'd felt to anyone ever before. Following his instructions, Samona closed her eyes. "Okay. My eyes are closed."

"Go ahead. Make a wish."

Samona paused, held her breath. Then made a wish. She

wished for freedom. The freedom to live her life as a whole person. The freedom to love and be loved.

Derrick pressed his lips to the back of her head. The warmest sensation washed over Samona. And the feeling that her wish had come true.

Slowly, she turned around and faced him. Looked up at him from lowered lids. She looked at his firm, squared jaw, then his lips. They were full and tempting and sexy. Her gaze passed his slim nose and met his eyes. Such intense eyes. The look she saw there was unmistakable. He wanted her.

They were drawn together like a magnet. His lips captured hers in a mind-numbing kiss. Everything—all thoughts of her problems, of her sister, of her foolish choices with men—fled her mind. She could only think of here, of now, of Derrick.

His musky scent consumed her, more powerful than any drug. She was lost in his kiss. His wide palm splayed across her back, his fingertips gently probing. Slowly, Samona's hands found his body. One found his hard, brawny chest; the other found the back of his neck and played with the short hairs on his nape.

Derrick groaned. She moaned. Her fingers explored the width of his chest, the firm muscular pecks, the groove between them, his rapid heartbeat. Finding a flat nipple, Samona gently stroked then tweaked it.

This had to be heaven on earth, Derrick thought as his body reveled in the thousands of exquisite sensations Samona's touch made him feel. He trailed his fingers down her back, over her shoulder blades, her bra straps, down to her waist. Never had he wanted a woman the way he wanted Samona. Deep down, he knew this was wrong, that he was breaching his trust as a police officer. But not even the image of an angry Captain Boyle could stop him now.

He slipped a hand around to the front of her body. He felt her sharp intake of breath when he cupped one full breast. Brushing his thumb over her breast, he could feel the outline of lace, wanted to free her body from it. He deepened the kiss, his tongue delving into her mouth desperately. He tweaked her nipple until it became a hardened peak through the fabric of her bra and shirt.

He wanted her. Right here. Wanted her with a passion that rocked him to the core of his being. His groin felt like it was on fire.

Breaking the kiss he said, "Stay with me tonight, Samona."

Her eyes were dark pools of passion when she looked at him. "With you as in you on the sofa, me on the bed—"

"As in *with* me. With both of us on the bed, or the couch or the kitchen counter for that matter." Her nervous giggle eased the tension. Derrick kissed her nose. "I don't care where. I just want to be with you. I've never wanted anything more in my entire life."

And that was true. He may regret this in the morning, but right now he didn't care.

"Yes, Derrick. Yes."

He kissed her once more, a long, hard, insistent kiss. Then scooped her into his arms. As he carried her through the door and up the stairs, Samona framed his face, kissed his forehead, nestled her nose against his ear. Giggled when she learned he was ticklish behind the ear. She knew that Derrick would fill her days with laughter. Maybe even her nights.

That night, Samona gave and received more love than she had ever known. Derrick took her to a place where time was suspended, where only they existed. He took her to a place of magic, laughter and love.

* * *

Hours after making love, Derrick couldn't sleep. Thoughts of the woman in his arms, of the profound experience they had shared, kept him awake. Making love to Samona had, quite simply, been the best experience of his life. Better than the day he'd met his new niece. Better even than the moment he'd learned Whitney was safe from danger. Better than anything he could have imagined.

Derrick snuggled against Samona's naked body, planting a soft kiss on her hair. Her hair smelled of apples. Her body felt like velvet against his. Her soft curves molded perfectly against him. They were a perfect fit.

She lay sleeping, the steady rhythm of her breathing like music to his ears. What sound was more beautiful?

Maybe only the sound of his name on her lips in the throes of passion.

Derrick slipped a hand around her small waist, pulling her close. She murmured and placed a hand on his, shifting against him like they had fallen into this position a million times.

This was perfect. Derrick had found a piece of paradise.

As he closed his eyes and savored the sweet feeling, he prayed the morning would never come.

Chapter 19

Alive. That's how Samona felt this morning. So incredibly alive, her heart incredibly full. Derrick had an arm possessively draped around her body, but his shallow, even breathing told her he was sleeping.

She wanted to stay like this forever, but couldn't. There were things she had to do today, like go to the police and hope they believed her story. It was time. Roger was dead and it was up to her to clear her own name. Derrick had given her the strength to pursue this.

Carefully, she slipped from beneath his arm and crawled off the bed. It squeaked in protest, but Derrick didn't move. He was out cold. Samona smiled to herself. She had tired him out.

For a long while, Samona watched him sleep. The edges of his mouth were curled in a grin. He seemed happy. She was happy too. Her eyes roamed the outline of his strong legs beneath the white cotton sheets. The blanket came to his waist. His chest—his beautiful, muscular chest—was bare and exposed. He had no chest hair, but sprinkles of dark curls began near his belly button and went intriguingly lower.

Samona should sketch him. Just as he was now. Maybe, once they were totally comfortable with each other, he would let her do a nude of him. He had a perfect body for clay sculpting.

She whirled around and faced the window. She shouldn't be thinking of tomorrow. Not until she had today figured out. If only she could suspend time, she'd climb back into bed with Derrick and wake him up with a slow, sensual kiss.

The possibilities were endless, once she had today figured out. Picking up Derrick's discarded T-shirt, she slipped it on. It hung to her mid-thigh. He continued sleeping peacefully even as she walked out of the room.

In the kitchen, she searched for tea. He had only packets of instant cappuccino. She wasn't much of an instant coffee drinker, but right now she didn't care. She'd drink instant coffee for the rest of her life—as long as that life included Derrick.

She hoped, prayed, she hadn't made a mistake. Hoped Derrick wasn't the type of guy who only wanted to get in her pants. She doubted that. There was something magnetic between them, something strong. Something real. Samona was sure of that.

She fixed herself a cup of cappuccino, then settled onto the sofa in Derrick's living room. Stretching her feet out, she looked at her toes. Plain. Boring. She would have to add some color. Maybe red.

This change in her was because of Derrick. And it felt good. She could see the silver lining on the cloud that hung over her.

Love. Love had changed her.

She sipped her cappuccino and sighed. Maybe she was getting too excited too soon. Derrick may feel something for her, but she certainly didn't know if he was in love with her. He made her feel special, he made her laugh, he'd given her hope. Yet in some ways he was still an enigma to her.

She didn't really know him.

Samona downed the remaining warm liquid and rose. She

pulled the edge of Derrick's shirt to her nose and took a good whiff, inhaling the musky scent that was his alone. Like a giddy schoolgirl, she twirled. Then giggled. She was being totally ridiculous. But being in love had never felt so good.

She wanted to get to know him better. She strolled the living room, but that didn't give her a good idea of who he was. Not even his laptop was here any longer.

She could wake him and ask him everything she wanted to know. Like how old he was. Like what he did to pay the bills while pursuing his writing career. She knew from his body and eating habits that he liked to exercise. Did he work out at a gym or run or mountain climb? Did he have any other passions? Anything crazy like parachuting or hang gliding?

No, she'd let him sleep. After last night, he was tired. But that didn't mean she couldn't look around.

Like her apartment, Derrick had two bedrooms. Maybe he was using the second one as his office. She arched a brow, intrigued. Maybe his manuscript was in there. She shouldn't snoop, but what would it hurt? It would certainly give her insight into an aspect of Derrick she hardly knew about.

Her hand clasped the brass doorknob. Casting a quick glance at Derrick's bedroom door, she confirmed that he was still sleeping. She would be in and out in just a minute. She'd only peek at his work.

The room was cool, but at least the floor was carpeted. It was a small room with three bookshelves filled with old volumes. Samona scanned the titles on the shelves. They were old classics. Shakespeare, Dickens, Bronte and many others. None of which were Derrick's, she suspected.

Tiptoeing, Samona made her way across the floor to the desk where his computer lay. The laptop was open, but the power was off. Several file folders surrounded the computer, and Samona's hand fell to one. These were probably his notes on his story, or maybe even some of his writing in long hand. He always took a notebook to the beach.

"Last chance to save your integrity and respect his privacy." In defiance of her words, her hand opened the folder.

Instantly, the smile on her lips died and her nerves danced like termites on speed. There was a black-and-white picture of her, one she didn't remember taking. In fact, she hadn't posed for that picture. It was when her hair was still braided. How would Derrick have gotten a picture of her then, when at the time she hadn't known him?

She flipped through the file, fear spreading through her veins like liquid ice. *No, please,* she thought, wondering for a moment if Derrick could be the person who wanted to hurt her. The one who was after the stupid jewelry she didn't have.

There were more pictures. Some color. Some black-and-white. All, of her when she'd had braids.

She dropped that file and picked up another. On the first page was written SAMONA GRAY FILE. A file? What kind of file? As she scanned the pages, the walls felt like they were closing in on her. She saw words like *suspect, investigation, made contact.* Everything else was a blur as she tried to make sense of it all.

"Samona."

She jumped about a foot when Derrick called her name. When she looked at him, his eyes were dark and intense as they bored into her. His face was contorted, but she couldn't read his expression. She didn't know if she should stay or flee. She knew only one thing: Derrick had lied to her.

Somehow, despite the fact that she was trembling, she managed to find a voice to ask, "Who are you?"

If the floor could open and swallow him right now, Derrick would have willed that to happen. Nothing had ever hurt him more than the look of pain and betrayal in Samona's eyes right now. God, he'd never meant to hurt her.

"Who are you?" she repeated, her voice a terrified whisper.

Derrick threw his head back. Closed his eyes. Then faced her and said softly, "I'm a cop."

Her eyes bulged. "A..." Her face twitched. "A cop?"

"Yes."

"Oh God."

He wished she would yell at him, charge at him and slap him. Anything but stand there looking absolutely crushed.

Derrick tried to swallow, but his throat was too dry and tight. He felt like a total, complete, certified idiot.

All his life he'd prided himself on honesty. He believed in telling the truth; he didn't believe in deceiving people. Yet he had deceived Samona. Deceived her because of the oath he'd taken to his job.

"Samona, I—"

"No. No. Don't say anything." She seemed to be both thinking and fighting off tears at the same time. She wouldn't look at him. Then suddenly, with a cry of despair, she stormed past him and into the hallway. He followed her but she ran into his bedroom and closed the door. Less than a minute later she appeared, dressed in her T-shirt and shorts. He stood, helpless, speechless. He didn't know what to say or do to undo the damage.

She scurried past him as though he was not even in the hallway. Watching her, it felt like somebody was literally squeezing the life out of his heart. Seconds later, she was at the door. Then she was gone.

Derrick ran to the door and flung it open. "Samona," he called. *Let me explain,* he added silently. The only response was the sound of pounding footsteps as Samona ran down the stairs. Away from him. Out of his life.

Chapter 20

Air. Samona needed air. She gulped to suck in as much oxygen as possible, but her lungs would only allow precious little bits at a time.

"I'm a cop." Derrick's words echoed in her brain over and over, taunting her.

Everything had been a lie. He was a cop. How he must be laughing at her now. He'd certainly gotten her to trust him. She'd even slept with him. She'd talked to him about the robbery. About how the police were trying to find enough evidence to arrest her. And all the while, he'd been the police. He'd been the enemy.

She was more than a fool. She was gullible, stupid. Why had she gone against her better judgment and started a relationship with Derrick? First Mark, then Roger, now Derrick—she was through with men. For some reason, she was cursed where they were concerned.

Samona hustled on the pavement, part jogging, part speed-walking as she put as much distance between herself and Derrick as humanly possible. He had called her name as she charged down the stairs, but she hadn't stopped.

"I'm a cop."

She should have known. By the little things he said and did.

Good grief, she'd suggested he write cop novels. Deep down a part of her must have known. So why had she so easily been seduced?

God, how could she have been such a fool—again? She was doomed when it came to men. She always chose the wrong ones—men who betrayed her.

Derrick had probably called the station already and the police would track her down on the street like an animal. A nasty lump formed in her throat as she realized the depth of his betrayal. How he'd met her, how he'd smiled at her, all those sweet, encouraging things he said—all lies.

All so that he could lock her in jail and throw away the key.

She'd never meant a thing to him. Not even when they'd made love. A tear trickled down her face. Even the lovemaking had been a lie.

If the police found her, she wouldn't resist arrest. Running would only delay the inevitable. If she was going to spend the rest of her life in jail, what difference would it make if that day came now?

Derrick slammed an open palm against the wall. Cursed. Cursed again. Samona had run out of here so fast she forgot her purse. He should be happy; she was in no condition to drive. But he wasn't. Wasn't because Samona was in danger alone on the street.

After she had taken off, Derrick had run downstairs to her apartment, hoping to find her there, but she wasn't. By the time he made it to the street, she was nowhere in sight though her car was parked in the driveway.

He would have to call the station before he went after her. Let Captain Boyle know that he had blown the assignment. He wasn't looking forward to this, but he may as well get it over with. All he really cared about now was Samona.

He picked up the receiver and called Captain Boyle. "Captain," he said when the man answered the phone. "It's Lawson. I've got a problem. A big one."

"What kind of problem?" Already, the captain sounded none too pleased.

"My cover's been blown," Derrick said into the receiver, deceptively calmer than he actually felt.

"What?"

Grimacing, Derrick put the receiver to his other ear.

"How the hell did that happen?"

"I can't explain now. What's important now, sir, is that Samona has taken off, and I have reason to fear for her safety. Sir, I believe she's innocent."

"You find her and bring her in!"

"Yes, sir."

Derrick hung up and grabbed his car keys from the kitchen table. His conversation with Captain Boyle had been brief, and he wondered how angry the captain really was, especially with his statement that he believed Samona was innocent. Hurrying through the door, Derrick acknowledged that right now, it didn't really matter. It only mattered that Samona was out on the street, alone. It mattered that he had a nagging feeling, telling him he was too late.

It mattered that he cared for her.

Samona angrily brushed away the tears that wet her cheeks. She didn't want to cry, certainly not over a man who wasn't worth her tears. Derrick had betrayed her and she had to remember that.

But every time she thought about the betrayal, her eyes filled with tears once again. What hurt was that she had started to care about him. Crossing the street, she quickened her pace. Who was she kidding? She was in love with him. Had been probably since their first dinner date—the pizza in his apartment.

A sucker—that's what she was. Her heart ached even more because Derrick had hurt her the most. Certainly more than Mark ever had, and he'd dumped her for her sister. At the time, she'd thought that was bad. But Derrick's betrayal topped that. Because she'd cared more about him than any other man. And now to discover that his feelings had all been a lie...

Maybe there was something about her that made men want to hurt her, betray her. How else could she explain three bad relationships in her life? She hadn't really cared for Roger, and until Derrick, she hadn't known what love was. Not really. Mark had been special in some ways, but now she knew that she'd only been infatuated with him—not in love with him.

She loved Derrick.

She bit down hard on her lip and squeezed her eyes shut, willing herself to forget that Derrick even existed. Somehow, she had to forget him.

Samona didn't notice that the car next to her was slowing. She didn't have time to scream as a hand came down around her mouth. Without much effort, she was dragged into the dark-colored sedan. Then, with only a dog barking in protest, the car drove down the tranquil street, unnoticed.

Chapter 21

Samona squirmed. Tugged. Tried to pull her hands and feet free of the ropes that bound her.

"Relax," the woman said. "We're almost there."

It was hard to breathe with the gag. She tried not to panic, but bile rose in her throat and she choked. *Breathe,* she told herself. If she had a panic attack now, she'd suffocate. She tried as hard as she could to breathe evenly through her nose.

"Shut her up," the man said.

"She ain't hurting nobody."

"I can't concentrate with her freakin' out like that. Shut her the hell up."

Samona's eyes darted to the woman in terror. She tried to beg for her life, but couldn't do anything but moan and groan because of the gag.

A false smile on her lips, the woman who sat beside her slipped an arm around her neck. "Don't worry, honey. This won't hurt a bit."

"Please let her be home," Derrick said as he descended the steps to the second floor. Though he knew it was unlikely, he hoped she had returned. Now more than ever, he knew her safety depended on it.

When Derrick's feet landed on the second level, he saw someone at Samona's door. A man dressed in dark, baggy clothes. He was about his height and his complexion, but a baseball cap hid his features. As soon as the man saw him, he tore off, sprinting down the steps.

"Hey!" Derrick yelled. That side profile... The man looked strangely familiar.

Roger!

Derrick sped after him like the devil himself chased him. His long legs carried him quickly. On the street, Roger was almost in a car. Derrick charged after him and caught the door before it closed. Roger rammed the key in the ignition and tried to start the car, but Derrick grabbed him and forced him out of the car before he could.

"Police officer! Don't move!" Derrick pinned him to the asphalt.

Roger groaned, then swore.

"Hands behind your back!"

Roger didn't put up a fight. Clearly, he'd been through the routine before. Behind his back, he crossed his arms at the wrists.

Derrick's heart raced with excitement. Roger was the key to finding Samona. Securing Roger's wrists, he heaved him off the ground. "You're under arrest, pal."

"Start talking." Derrick stood above Roger, who sat in the armchair in his living room.

"Not until I get to speak to a lawyer."

"There's no time for a lawyer. Samona—you remember her—the one you left to take the fall for a crime you committed." As Derrick said the words, he knew it was true. Had known it all along. What he didn't know was what Samona ever saw in Roger. He pushed that thought aside.

"I have nothing to say."

Derrick placed a hand on each armrest, facing Roger head-on. "Roger, we can do this the easy way, or the hard way. You can either start talking, or I can call for a car to take you to the station and you can talk there. But I guarantee you, the other cops, they won't be near as nice as I am. Everybody's sick of this case—and they've been itching to get someone real bad." He cocked an eyebrow. "If I hand you to them on a silver platter, you'll be like fresh meat to men who haven't eaten in months."

Roger squirmed. His tough facade was fading. "I'll take my chances."

"Will you? And are you willing to gamble with Samona's life, you spineless shell of a man?" Disgusted, Derrick stood and scowled.

Roger blew out an anxious breath. Derrick waited. Nothing. Finally Derrick said, "Tell me this—what brought you here? Back to Chicago? To Samona's place?"

"I got a call. I was told that Samona was here. I was also told a few other things that I won't repeat right now. I came here to check out if what I heard was true."

"Stop the riddles."

"Can I ask you a question?" When Derrick nodded, Roger asked, "Where is she?"

"Samona…left…a while ago. When I went to look for her, she wasn't anywhere in the neighborhood."

"Damn."

"What? Do you know something?"

"Someone told me that he'd take her—"

"Who?"

"Someone. Someone I owe. I was hoping that I would get to her first."

"To finish her off?"

"No, I—I cared about her. I wanted to warn her."

Derrick paced the floor in front of Roger. "You know," he began, facing the thug, "I don't know what points you think you'll gain by keeping tight-lipped. Maybe—maybe—if you come clean and help save Samona, that will earn you some points. But if you don't, and something happens to her..."

"All right." Roger buried his face in his hands. "Jeez." He mumbled something Derrick couldn't hear. "Okay."

"Who has Samona?"

"A guy named Alex Reilly."

Derrick nodded. He knew the name. Alex was one of Chicago's known criminals. "AKA Red."

"He and I...we both did that hit on Milano's store. Red's pissed 'cause I cheated him. We were supposed to split the jewels but I took off with everything."

"And faked your death."

"Yeah."

"So why come back? Everyone thought you were dead—you were home free."

"I shouldn't say anything else without my lawyer."

Precious time was wasting and Derrick's nerves were raw. "All right. That's it." He grabbed Roger by the collar. "We're going to the station. Not even your lawyer can get you off Murder One charges."

Roger threw his hands in the air. "Look, I didn't kill that woman, okay?"

"Don't you dare pin this on Samona."

"I'm not! Red took her out. That's why he's so pissed—he took her out and he didn't even get the payoff."

Derrick eyed Roger carefully. His nape prickled. What he'd just said implied something more than just a random robbery. "What do you mean the 'payoff'? Payoff as in the jewelry?"

"I mean the payoff for taking her out."

"Someone hired you to kill Sophia Milano." The words came out as a statement even though it was a question. God Almighty, it was all making sense.

"Jeez. We did this and we're not even going to get the money..."

Derrick looked Roger squarely in the eye. "Who hired you?"

"The woman's old man. Mr. Milano."

Her head hurt like the devil and she was groggy. Groaning softly, Samona tried to open her eyes. Tried to and couldn't. It took her only a second to realize that she was blindfolded.

Immediately, Samona remembered being abducted, bound and gagged. Her heart raced. She already knew what her abductors looked like, so why had they blindfolded her? There was only one thing she could think of: they didn't want her to see when they were going to kill her.

As terror seized her, her breathing turned ragged. Her nostrils burned as she inhaled and exhaled hastily. *Stop it,* she told herself. Desperately, she tried to control her panic. She wouldn't die like this—couldn't. From somewhere she got strength— strength to control her fear if even for a few minutes. How much more of this she could take, she didn't know.

She could hear angry voices. The man and woman from the car. Since she couldn't see, all Samona's other senses were heightened. She could feel the dust in her air cling to the perspiration on her skin. She could feel the tension in the room, and that made her worry. Something wasn't going as planned. She could hear the fear in her captors' voices. She could smell death in the air.

Never had she ever been so scared. Not even when Roger had put a gun to her head. Then, she couldn't bring herself to believe that he would actually shoot her. But she didn't know these two. They'd brutally beaten her sister just to send a message. God only knew what they would do to her.

Every sound, every footstep on the floor made her jump. Because each moment could be her last. *Please God,* she silently prayed, *protect me. Don't let me panic. Don't let me give up hope.*

Hope. Derrick had been the one to make her hope again. The thought of him and his betrayal brought fresh tears to her eyes, but she fought them. Fought them because they had nowhere to go, and beneath the blindfold, the tears only made her eyes sting.

The angry voices grew louder and clearer. "He'll come. He's got a soft spot for her..."

"It's been three hours," the female said. "Where is he? I told you this wasn't a good idea—"

"Give him time."

As footsteps neared her, Samona froze. This could be it, the end. Cold, rough fingers stroked her cheek and her heart felt like it would burst in her chest.

The man said coolly, "If he knows what's good for him, he'll be here."

Then he walked away chuckling, leaving Samona shaken and terrified.

Derrick had just spoken to Captain Boyle and relayed the news Roger had told him. Given Roger's evidence, some officers were on their way to arrest Angelo Milano on probable cause. Some were en route to join Derrick with both cruisers and plain cars. With Roger as their guide, they would search Alex Reilly's hideouts in an attempt to find Samona.

If anything happened to her, Derrick would never forgive himself. Closing his eyes, he prayed it was not too late.

When Mr. Milano opened the door and saw three uniformed police officers on his porch, his lips thinned with concern. "Officers, what's going on? Have you arrested my wife's murderer?"

"Angelo Milano," one officer said, "you are being placed under arrest for the murder of your wife."

"What?" His eyes widened in angry indignation.

"You have the right to remain silent—"

"This is crazy," Angelo yelled as he was placed in handcuffs. "You don't know what you're talking about."

The officers continued anyway, ignoring his protests. By the time he was brought to a cruiser at the curb, a small crowd of onlookers had gathered. His neighbors. The people who knew and respected him. They were all there to witness his demise.

Suddenly, this all became real. As Angelo was being placed in the cruiser's backseat, he burst into tears.

Samona drifted in and out of consciousness. It was easier to sleep, to forget the pain, although something told her she should fight to stay awake.

She didn't want to stay awake. Awake, her mind drifted to Derrick, his betrayal and the insufferable pain in her heart. Would she ever get over this?

She should have known better, but she was through kicking

herself. What mattered was that she had given her heart, totally and completely, to a man she didn't even know. If she ever made it out of here, she would never make that same mistake again.

Oh, Derrick, why? New tears filled her eyes.

Think of his betrayal, she told herself, willing herself not to cry. *Find your anger and get over him.*

She wished it were so easy. This time, she didn't know if she would ever find all the pieces of her smashed heart. If she could even find them, she didn't know if she'd be able to put her heart back together. Though she prayed she'd get out of here alive, she sensed after this she'd never truly be alive again. How, after this last heartbreak, could she be anything but emotionally numb?

All because she'd dared to believe in love one last time.

Never again, Samona vowed. If she made it out of here alive, she'd never love again.

Chapter 22

As each second came and went, more beads of perspiration popped out on Derrick's body. Constantly, he wiped his forehead and adjusted the air conditioning, but his glands were working overtime. After more than four hours of searching, Samona had not been found. He and his team of officers had checked out Alex's residence, an ex-girlfriend's home he apparently frequented and the home of a Chicago gangster whom he was reportedly good friends with. He was at neither place.

"He's gotta be here," Roger said as the plain car Derrick was driving approached a run-down, boarded-up building in Chicago's south side.

"Five-o!" he heard someone yell as the police cars advanced to the curb. Several young men darted down the street in both directions as if their lives depended on it. More young criminals, Derrick thought, shaking his head. Luckily for them, Alex was his concern today.

"What's this place?" Derrick asked. He suspected it was a buy-and-sell shop for illegal narcotics.

"It's a drug spot. You know." Now that Roger knew he might be able to cut a deal with the prosecutor, he was talking nonstop.

"Why didn't you tell us about this in the first place?" Derrick asked, frustrated.

"Because I didn't think of it 'til now."

Derrick rammed the car into park and he, the officer seated next to him and Roger jumped out. He signaled to the other officers and they cautiously approached the building with their guns drawn. Someone ran from the side of the building then, startling Derrick. Adrenaline flowing through his veins, Derrick turned, ready.

It was a young, harried-looking woman carrying a baby. "Don't shoot!" she yelled. "Please…"

Turning down the street, she ran off. Derrick blew out a ragged breath. Young kids on drugs, especially mothers, was a sad sight, but one Derrick was familiar with. Drugs needed to be removed from the streets, permanently. They were a poison, slowly killing people in the projects and even in some nicer neighborhoods. That's why he had devoted his time to the drug unit.

After a moment, he said, "Let's go."

He, his officers and Roger walked down the side of the building and approached a door. Looking around in the darkened building, it soon became obvious that it was empty. Remnants of crack pipes littered the ground, along with other debris, indicating that the place had been occupied recently. But the arrival of police cars had scared everybody away.

"The place is empty," an officer called from the dark room.

Derrick growled long and hard, both angry and frustrated. It was already dusk, and the chances of finding Samona alive after all these hours grew less likely.

He turned to Roger. "Think, darn it. Think hard. Where is Alex? You said he left a message for you on the street. If he wanted you to find him, then you have to know where he is."

"I don't know! We've been to all the places I can think of."

"That's not good enough."

"Okay. Wait. I think I know where he could be."

Derrick faced him with anticipation. "Where?"

"His mom's place."

"With Samona?" Derrick couldn't mask his disappointment.

"It's possible." Roger shrugged.

"All right." It was another lead and Derrick couldn't ignore it. He took a moment to tell his men the next place they would check out, although he wasn't putting much hope in that. Then, climbing into the unmarked cruiser, he said to Roger, "Lead the way."

"Here. Drink this."

The woman had ungagged her and now held a bottle of water to her mouth. As Samona gulped the liquid, she thought it was more precious than gold. Nothing had ever tasted as sweet. Her throat had been so raw and dry she'd thought it would crack.

Samona moaned faintly when the woman pulled the bottle away. She wished she could see. She said, "Please…take off this blindfold. I—I can't stand it."

"Really?" That was the man's hard, cold voice. "That's too bad. Baby, gag her."

"No…please. I swear I'll be quiet."

She felt a face near hers, could smell foul breath. A finger stroked her face and she jerked away. The man said, "Sorry. You might scream."

"No. I promise, I wouldn't. I won't…."

He said, "I can't take that chance." To his accomplice he said, "Gag her. Now."

"No—" Samona's protest died as her head was jerked back and her mouth forced open. As the gag was replaced, her throat tightened with fear.

"Don't worry," the woman said. "It shouldn't be too long now."

Too long for what? Samona's mind screamed. Deep in her heart, she didn't think she wanted to know.

The trip to Alex's mother's home had only accomplished two things. One, they learned that Samona was not there. Two, they scared Alex's mother. She had let Derrick and his team search her house, but cried the entire time. As Derrick and the other officers left the premises, Ms. Reilly begged them not to shoot her son.

If more children thought of the grief they caused their parents with their criminal activities, Derrick suspected less would get involved in crime. The trouble was, no matter what the crime, no one ever thought they would get caught.

Ms. Reilly would be doing a lot more crying.

This time when Derrick slipped into the cruiser, he dropped his head to the steering wheel. He couldn't give up. Not until he'd found Samona. But his men were getting tired. After several hours, they had no results.

Roger seemed exasperated. From what Derrick could tell, he was being straight with them. He would be going to jail the moment the search ended, so he had nothing to gain by sending them on a wild-goose chase.

An officer approached the driver's side of Derrick's car. Derrick rolled down the window. The officer said, "What now?"

"I don't know," Derrick admitted. "I know you guys are tired, and if you want to take off, I'll understand. But I can't give up. Not yet."

"Don't worry about us, Lawson. We want to get this perp as much as you do. Just name the place and we're there."

Detective Abdo opened the car door and took a seat beside Derrick. "I say we keep going."

Derrick appreciated his colleagues' loyalty. Now, they needed another place to search. Looking at Roger through the rearview mirror he thought that he had pushed him as far as he could, but maybe one last try. One last try before he relieved the other officers and brought Roger to the station. On his own, he would search for Samona until he found her.

"Roger, if there is any other place you know of—*any* place at all—you have to tell me."

Roger frowned. Thought hard. Then, after a long, tension-filled moment, his eyes lit up. "Wait a minute," he said slowly, excitement filling his voice. "I think I know."

Derrick turned and faced him, his heart once again filling with hope. "Where, Roger?"

Roger chortled. "It's gonna sound crazy, but Red is crazy enough—"

"Where?" Derrick asked again. *Let this be the one.*

"Milano Jewelers."

"That place is boarded up," Detective Abdo said.

"Yeah," Roger agreed. "And that's why it's perfect. It's where it all started, and it's where it all will end."

The back of Derrick's neck prickled. It made sense. Good God, it made a lot of sense. To the officer outside his window he said, "Milano Jewelers. That's where she is."

The officer ran off, shouting the next location to be searched to the rest of the team. Quickly everyone scrambled into their cars.

Starting the car, Derrick sped toward River Forest. He knew Samona was there, felt it.

He could only hope he got there in time.

Chapter 23

She didn't want to give up.

But doubts were starting to creep into her mind.

Where the ropes bound her, her skin was raw and stung each time she moved. Her breathing was shallow but at least even. Her energy was spent. She was exhausted. Shifting in the seat, Samona wondered if this was the way she would die. Here, attached to a chair, would she just fall asleep and never wake up?

Derrick. The thought of him always made her want to cry, but she couldn't cry. She swallowed. Choked on her saliva. Tried desperately not to give up the fight now. A coughing fit could cause her to suffocate. Slowly and deliberately, she regained control of herself. If she got emotional every time she thought of Derrick, he would be the death of her even though he wasn't physically here.

She had to forget him.

He took too much of her energy. Already, she was fading. Again. It was an effort to stay awake and she didn't even know if she wanted to be awake. Awake, she would face her death with fear. Drawing in deep, even breaths, Samona decided not to fight it. With sleep, there was no pain. Only peace.

As her world started to fade, she wondered if she would ever wake up again.

* * *

A block away from Milano Jewelers, Derrick stopped his car and killed the lights. The two cruisers behind him did the same. If Alex had Samona at this store—and Derrick prayed Alex did—Derrick wanted to approach unawares. Any sign of cop cars could scare Alex into doing something stupid.

Like kill Samona. If she wasn't already dead.

She wasn't. If she was, he would know it. Feel it. Just as he knew Alex was here.

Derrick and his fellow officers crept down the street to an alley. At the opening of the alley, Derrick instructed some of his men to go to the front of the building while he, Roger and a few other officers went to the back. Alex would not escape.

When they reached the back door of Milano Jewelers, Derrick paused. His heart was pumping so fast he thought it would explode in his chest. Samona was just beyond that door and he was afraid. Afraid that he might be too late. Afraid that something might go wrong. Afraid that if she were alive, she wouldn't want to see him.

He swallowed his fears. It was time to act.

Roger grabbed his arm, and Derrick turned and faced him. "I know Red is in there," he said. "He wants me. Let me go in there alone, talk to him. I'll try to free Samona."

"No way," Derrick said.

"You don't understand. Red always packs a piece. If you go in there, he'll panic. If he hasn't killed Samona already, he probably will. You don't want to risk that."

"He's right," Detective Abdo said.

Derrick gritted his teeth. "Yeah. He has a point."

"So you'll let me go ahead?"

Derrick placed a firm hand on Roger's shoulder. "If this is some kind of setup, so help you God."

"This place is surrounded. I'd be a fool to set you up now. I just want this over with."

"All right," Derrick said. "Be careful."

Derrick and the three officers with him exchanged concerned glances as Roger slipped into the store. His gun was drawn, and he was ready. Derrick prayed he didn't have to use it.

Moments later, a shot rang out in the night. Derrick's heart leaped to his throat. Fear propelled his feet through the back door and he charged inside, followed by the other cops.

The store was dark, softly illuminated by a light from a back room. Immediately, Derrick saw Samona in one corner of the store, gagged. As officers swarmed the store, turning on flashlights and calling out, Derrick ran to her.

Her head lolled forward. Derrick's throat constricted. Good God, was he too late?

"Lawson!" someone shouted. "We've got 'em. Two of them. But Roger has been shot."

Right now, Derrick didn't care about anything but Samona. Frantically, he fumbled with the gag and blindfold, then the ropes that bound her hands and feet. She didn't move, not even when he pulled her into his arms. "No! No, God!"

Officer Smith came to his side. "Lawson, is she okay?"

"I don't know." Derrick pressed his ear to her face, checking for breath. Relief flooded him. "She's breathing."

"An ambulance is on its way," Smith said. "Though it might be too late for Benson."

Derrick barely registered what Officer Smith said. Lightly, he tapped Samona's face. "Wake up. Come on, Samona."

Her head moved. First she moaned, then coughed. Then bolted upright, flailing her arms in the air. "No!"

Derrick pulled her to him, cuddling her head. "You're okay. Samona, it's me. Derrick."

She stiffened. Then pulled her head back and looked at him. She seemed dazed and afraid.

"It's okay," Derrick said. "It's over."

Samona whimpered. She tried to speak, but her voice came out as a croak.

Derrick didn't know if she understood him so he said, "You're free."

Samona sagged against him. Cried. Derrick held her, his own eyes misting with tears. What if he had been too late? He would never have had the chance to apologize to her. He would never have felt her soft body in his arms again. He would never have been able to tell her he loved her.

Love. The word surprised him. But he knew it was true. He loved her. Somehow, he had to make her understand that he hadn't meant to hurt her. He was only doing his job.

"Samona," Derrick began.

"Shh," she said. "Not now. Please."

"But—"

"Later," she said softly. "Not now."

"Okay."

The store was chaotic, filled with much noise and movement as the three people responsible for Mrs. Milano's death were taken into custody. But Derrick didn't notice. All his thoughts were on Samona. The woman in his arms. The woman he knew he loved without a doubt.

Samona was exhausted, but alive. Alive. Safe.

The night had been harrowing. After being checked out and okayed by the ambulance staff, she had been taken to the police station. After hours, she answered questions for both the police and the media. She had called her sister and Mark and given them the news. Then she had called Jennifer. Jennifer was with her now.

Derrick had saved her. And now, thanks to him, she supposed, she was free. Alex and his accomplice Marie were in custody. Roger, though critically injured from a gunshot wound, was in the hospital and expected to survive.

Alex and Marie had been Roger's accomplices. Roger had robbed the jewelry store and after he had knocked her out, Alex had killed Sophia Milano. It was all part of Mr. Milano's plan. Capitalizing on the previous jewelry store robberies, he had hired Roger to kill his wife and make it look like a robbery gone bad.

It was all so overwhelming. And to think she had been a part of it all—even though an unwilling part—was amazing. She was glad it was over.

Though tired, she had happily posed for pictures. This time when her face made the headlines, it would be as a free woman, not a wanted one.

She was happy.

Jennifer approached her in the small interrogation room, smiling. "You're free to go."

"Great." Never had she been so relieved in her life. Finally, the sun had burst through her gray cloud.

Rising from the chair, she turned to her friend. "Let's go."

Jennifer placed a hand on her arm. "Wait a minute. Aren't you going to say goodbye to Derrick?"

Samona shook her head. She hadn't seen Derrick in hours, not since he had brought Jennifer in to see her.

"I don't think so."

"Why not?"

"Because…"

"Because what?"

"Not now," Samona said.

Jennifer folded her arms across her chest. "Because he's a cop. Right?"

"I'm tired. I want to go home."

"You're going to run."

Samona slumped into the chair. "Jen, I'm not running."

"Yes you are."

Samona ran a hand over her hair. "Okay, fine. Maybe I am. But why shouldn't I? He lied to me—"

"He saved your life."

"That's beside the point."

Jennifer raised a skeptical eyebrow. "Is it? I thought that was pretty significant."

"More significant than the fact that he was hoping to arrest me for a crime I didn't commit?"

"He was doing his job."

"He lied to me. I can't trust him."

Jennifer dropped into the seat beside Samona. "My God, woman, you are one stubborn person. If you can't see that Derrick is in love with you—"

"Love…? Don't be crazy."

"You're the one who's crazy. That man loves you. It's as plain as day."

Samona made a face. "Yeah right."

"Fine. You should at least give him the chance to explain. Wouldn't you want the same if you were in his shoes?"

"I would never be in his shoes."

"And three months ago, you never would have dreamed that you'd be arrested."

Samona let out a ragged breath. "What's your point?"

"My point is that sometimes things happen beyond our control. Sometimes bad things happen to good people. Sometimes you get an assignment you hate. But you have to do it."

Samona stood. "Okay, Jen. I hear you. I'll talk to him. But not now. Later."

"Stubborn," Jennifer muttered.

"What was that?" Samona asked.

Jennifer flashed her a syrupy smile. "Nothing. Let's go."

Derrick stared at the phone as if it offered the answers to all his questions. He was confused and wanted someone to talk to. Right now, Whitney was that person. A woman might help him figure out what to do.

Afraid to see Samona, he had locked himself in his office while he worked on his notes. He could have gone home hours ago to his bed where he belonged, but he was too wired to sleep.

Derrick reached for the receiver. Lifting it, he stared at it for several moments. He replaced it. Picked it up again. Finally he slammed it down and groaned.

It was too early to call Whitney. Besides, she couldn't help him. He needed to help himself. He needed to talk to Samona. Hiding behind his desk and his paperwork would not negate that fact.

He stood and stretched. It felt like he had a thousand worms crawling in his stomach, he was so nervous. But he had to talk to Samona. Because he cared and he wanted her to understand.

When he left his office, he searched the entire station. Samona wasn't there. After speaking to another officer, he learned that Samona had been released.

Maybe that was for the best. If she hadn't sought him out to say goodbye, maybe she didn't want to see him. Maybe he should leave well enough alone.

If she hadn't had her things to pack, Samona would have gone crazy. Jennifer had helped her for a few hours but then had to leave. Of course, Jennifer had given her parting words of advice: talk to Derrick.

Samona couldn't. Not that she didn't want to, but what would that accomplish? Derrick didn't love her. He'd sweet-talked her, made her laugh, and made love to her because it was his job. Because he wanted to get her to confess to a crime she didn't commit.

Their relationship was a lie. What point was there in talking to him? He would go his way and she would go hers—separately.

If it was so simple, then why did it hurt so much? Dropping onto the sofa, Samona acknowledged that she didn't have an answer. Other than the fact that she cared. Cared too much. Even now, she wondered about him.

He hadn't come to see her. Part of her wished he would. The part that was a traitor. The part that had gotten her into trouble in the first place. Still, she couldn't help regretting the fact that she hadn't given Derrick a chance to explain back at the jewelry store.

It was hard to believe that just a couple of nights ago, she and Derrick had made love. Sweet love. For her, it had been a life-changing experience. For the first time in a long time her heart had felt full. Now, it felt empty. Her whole body felt empty, drained.

Stop thinking about Derrick, she told herself. *Forget him. Get up and go on with your life.*

She didn't move. Again, she willed herself to get up, to bring her things to the car. To leave and get on with her life. But she couldn't.

Finally, alone on the sofa, she fell asleep.

Derrick lifted his hand to knock on Samona's door, but paused. He was sure she didn't want to see him. So why was he here?

Because he had to make her understand. He'd had the entire day to think it over and he knew what he had to do. He faced many difficult situations as a cop, so why this particular situation scared him so much he didn't know.

That was a lie. He did know. He didn't know when or why it had happened, but he had given his heart to Samona. Now, all his hopes and dreams were in her hands. She had the power to hurt him the way no woman ever had.

He couldn't blame her if she did. He would deserve it for what he'd done to her. Still, he couldn't help hoping that she would hear him out and give him a chance.

His hands shook. His nerves were frayed. Closing his eyes, Derrick counted to ten slowly. When he reopened them, he knocked on the door, not giving himself the chance to back away.

When Samona heard the knock, she froze, sat upright and stared at the door. For a moment, she couldn't draw breath.

There was another knock. Her stomach coiled. She should get up, answer the door. But she was afraid. Afraid it wasn't Derrick.

That kind of thinking would get her nowhere. She couldn't stay here on this old sofa for the rest of her life. If it wasn't

Derrick at the door, then so be it. She would move on somehow. But she had to stop running.

Slowly, her stomach coiling, Samona rose from the sofa and went to the door. Her hand on the doorknob, she paused briefly. Then, she swung it open.

Derrick had been walking away, but when he heard the door open he turned around and faced her. Her stomach flip-flopped and her heart raced. She wanted to smile. Wanted to run to him. Instead, she stood with her hand on the doorknob, her back stiff, her face blank.

She said, "Derrick."

Slowly, he approached her, wondering what she was thinking. Was her pulse racing the way his was? Did she want to see him? He couldn't tell. Her face was devoid of any emotion. There seemed to be a spark in her eyes, but her lips were pulled into a thin line.

"Uh, Samona. I…uh, we didn't get to talk last night."

"I…know."

"I was…hoping we could…now."

"Uh, I see." She shifted on her feet. "Please…uh, come in."

Derrick approached her, the heat of his body enveloping hers. She didn't dare move as he passed her and walked into the apartment. Despite her resolve to get on with her life without him, she couldn't stop her heart from hoping.

He had come to her.

She closed the door and stepped into the room. Derrick's gaze was fixated on the Oriental rug. He had a newspaper rolled under his arm.

When she approached him, he spoke, "Uh, this is for you."

Extending both hands, Samona took the newspaper from him. It was the *Chicago Tribune.* On the front page, there was a picture of her, her lips curled in a grin. The caption read: SCHOOLTEACHER CLEARED IN MURDER CASE.

A laugh escaped her throat. Then she ran a hand over her face as she felt the onslaught of tears. It was official. She was free. She had her life back.

Her eyes flew to Derrick's face. He was smiling, though tentatively. "Congratulations," he said.

Samona said softly, "Thank you."

"Now everyone will know you're innocent."

"Yes. Finally." Her voice broke, but she didn't cry. Silence fell between them. Samona crossed her arms, then spoke. "Uh, is that why you came by?"

"Yeah." Derrick nodded. "I didn't know if you had seen the paper."

"I caught a bit of the news."

"So did I. You're quite the celebrity."

"This time in a good way." She stopped her lips from curling, even though she wanted to shout the good news to the world. Wringing her fingers, she averted her eyes.

"How are your hands?"

"Fine," she said quickly. She looked at him. "Just some bad scrapes but I'll get over that."

"So...you're okay?"

Samona nodded tightly. "I will be now."

"Good." Derrick pursed his lips and looked at her. She looked away. She didn't want to see him. He should go. "All right." He took a step toward the door.

"Are you leaving?" Samona asked.

Derrick's hand went to the back of his neck. "I...I don't want to bother you."

"Oh." She should tell him he wasn't bothering her. She

should tell him to stay. Once he walked out that door, he was walking out of her life forever. She knew that.

Derrick took a few more steps, this time passing her. Her lips trembling, Samona didn't turn around. He was leaving her. It was over. She was letting the best thing in her life walk away.

She didn't hear the door. Instead, she heard his footsteps as he approached her again. Derrick said, "Samona, I want to tell you something."

She turned to face him, her pulse pounding in her ears. "Go ahead."

"I want you to know that I knew you weren't guilty. Yes, I was supposed to investigate you, but I never could bring myself to believe you were involved in the robbery and murder."

"Why not?" She needed to know.

Because the moment I looked at you, I knew. "I don't know. I just did."

"Then why didn't you end the investigation?"

"Because..." His voice trailed off. Softly, he added, "Maybe because I couldn't face the thought of walking away from you."

Samona's stomach lurched. "Hmm."

"I'm sorry. Samona, I know it may not mean much now, but I do hope one day you can bring yourself to forgive me."

"I...I don't know. Derrick, you made me..."

"What?" He moved toward her, hoping. "What did I make you do?"

"Care," Samona blurted out. "God, I shouldn't have said that. I don't want to make you feel guilty. I know you were doing your job...."

"Is that what you think? That you were only work?"

"Wasn't I?"

"No." Derrick shook his head vehemently. "Samona, I wouldn't have made love to you because of my job."

"What are you saying?"

Derrick blew out a frazzled breath. How hard could it be to tell a woman that he cared about her, truly and deeply? He closed the distance between them and decided to go for it. He had nothing to lose. Right now, he didn't have Samona and wouldn't unless he took a chance.

"I know this is going to sound strange, but hear me out. I'm not sorry about my undercover job." At her puzzled expression, he held up a hand. "If I hadn't had that assignment, I would never have met you. I would never have fallen for you."

Fallen for you... Samona wanted to cry. Instead, she stared at him. If she was a fool for caring, then so be it. "Are you saying—"

"Yes." Derrick nodded. But he didn't actually say the words.

There was a sad expression in his eyes, and Samona's heart ached. But she couldn't go to him. Not until she had a few answers. "I know nothing about you. Not really."

"You know I'm not a writer. I'm a detective with the Chicago PD."

"But I know nothing else."

His gaze caressed her face. Somehow the energy between them had changed. It was no longer tentative. It was filled with sexual tension.

"Go ahead," Derrick said. "Ask me whatever you want to know. I'll tell you no lies."

"How long have you been a cop?"

Derrick reached out and cupped her chin. "Seven years."

It was hard to concentrate with him touching her. "I...I don't know how old you are."

"Twenty-nine. I'll be thirty in October."

"So I'm older than you."

"By eleven months and some days. You'll be thirty-one in November."

His gaze held her mesmerized. His touch made her body thrum. "That's not fair. You...you know everything about me."

Derrick shook his head. "No. I don't." He tangled his fingers in her hair. "Not everything."

"Like what?" she asked breathlessly. But she knew. She could see the question in his eyes.

"I don't know how you feel about me."

"I—" When his other hand touched her face, her breath snagged.

"I know you want me."

"I..." The pad of his thumb brushed her lip and for a moment, Samona's eyes fluttered shut. She couldn't deny it. "I know I shouldn't, but I do."

"Do you forgive me?"

"I shouldn't. I should be mad at you forever."

He inched closer to her face. "But that wouldn't be any fun, now would it?"

"You don't play fair." Her arms must have had a mind of their own for they circled Derrick's waist.

Derrick moaned. "Neither do you." His lips brushed hers and Samona's parted in expectation. "Samona, I know we haven't known each other long. But what I feel for you...it's more than just sex. This is the real thing. You did something to me, Samona. Somehow, you took my heart. Believe me, that's not an easy thing to do."

She wanted him to stop this torturous foreplay and kiss her. That was the last thing she should be thinking, but at this moment she knew she was crazy. Crazy for him. And despite what he had done she didn't want to live without him. How could she live without this?

Gently, he kissed her lips, then pressed his forehead against hers. He pulled her close and Samona could feel the evidence of his desire for her. She shuddered.

"I love you, Samona." He looked at her, his eyes honest, sincere. "And I'm hoping you love me too."

"I…yes." Her eyes misted. "Derrick, I do."

"Then kiss me. Hold me. Never let me go."

Molding her body to his, Samona did as he'd told her. She wrapped her arms tightly around him, ran her fingers up and down his back. Then slowly, she edged her lips close to his.

It was a sweet, slow kiss. A grateful kiss. A kiss filled with longing. A kiss that spoke of endings and new beginnings.

A kiss that promised many tomorrows.

Epilogue

It was the perfect day for a wedding.

It was warm, warmer than usual for the end of September, with just enough of a cool breeze to make the heat bearable. The sun smiled down at them from a cloudless sky, approving of his new union. Even the birds chirped and sang from the trees in Grant Park, as though happy for them.

Derrick nibbled on her ear. "What do you say we take off, go to our new house and christen every room...."

"And leave before our reception?"

Derrick flashed her a charming smile. "Nobody will notice."

Samona chortled. "Oh yeah. They won't notice the woman in white dashing to the limo."

"All right. You have a point. But you just look so good that I can't wait to get you out of that dress." His hand went to her lower back.

"Not so fast." She put a hand on his chest to hold him at bay. "This dress happened to cost a fortune, and I'm getting my money's worth."

"You already got that and more. Today you officially earned the title of most beautiful woman in the world."

"Oh, Derrick." Cupping his cheek, Samona planted a soft kiss on his lips. It was amazing how her life had changed. In just three months, she was a different person. The disastrous time in her life with Roger was now a distant memory. Roger had survived his gunshot wound but was in prison. He would be there for many years to come, along with his accomplices. Angelo Milano, knowing he faced the rest of his life in jail for the hit on his wife, had, while on bail, put a gun to his head and pulled the trigger. It was a tragic ending to a tragic story.

Samona stared at her new husband. Now, she had better days to look forward to. She had her job back at her old school. She and her sister were getting along well. She wouldn't have thought it a few months ago, but she had a new, wonderful life and was incredibly happy.

"Okay, everybody!" Evelyn yelled. She had taken charge today, and Samona was thankful for that. She couldn't have made all the arrangements on her own. "Before the bride and groom get carried away on the grass, I say we take a group picture!"

There were several chuckles among the guests, and blushing, Samona pulled away from Derrick. They, the wedding party and the guests hustled on the grass, grouping together near the spectacular flower garden. The photographer set up his camera.

Evelyn, her matron of honor, was to her immediate right. Then came Jennifer, a bridesmaid, beside whom was Derrick's longtime friend and also one of her bridesmaids, Whitney Jordan. To Derrick's left was Nick Burns, his best man. Next to Nick was her brother-in-law, Mark and Derrick's brother-in-law, Russell, both groomsmen. Everyone else crowded around them—Derrick's mother and sister; Whitney's husband, Javar; Mrs. Jefferson and their many other friends who consisted of police officers and teachers.

Derrick placed a possessive hand around her waist and pulled her close just as the photographer said, "Everybody ready?"

"Yes," they all replied in unison, followed by laughter.

The camera flashed.

"I think I blinked," Evelyn said. "Take another one."

The photographer did. He said, "Got it."

The crowd dispersed. Husbands found their wives. Girl-friends found their boyfriends. Children found their parents.

Samona watched it all in wonder.

Derrick cupped her chin and turned her face to him. He looked into her eyes. "In case you didn't know, you have made me the happiest man on earth."

"And you've made me the happiest woman. This is like a dream...."

"It is a dream. One we made a reality."

Samona framed his face. He was right. This day was a dream come true.

Derrick drew her close and captured her lips in a lingering kiss. Around them, the guests applauded and whistled.

Breaking the kiss, Samona looked out at all the smiling faces. Smiling for her. For Derrick. Snuggling against her husband, she smiled back, happiness overwhelming her.

It was the perfect day, she thought. The perfect day for a cele-bration of love.

FLIRTING WITH DANGER

Prologue

Monique's eyes flew open, greeting the darkness. For a moment she lay very still, wondering what had lured her from peaceful slumber to total consciousness. She wondered why her arms and legs were covered with goose bumps when the room was hot and muggy because the air conditioner had died. She wondered why she was afraid to even breathe.

Something had awakened her. But what? A noise? A bad dream? She didn't remember any dream, but it wouldn't be the first time she'd awoken feeling afraid because of something she couldn't remember. Her cousin Doreen would say that she woke up suddenly because she was about to die in her dream. And since dying in your dreams meant dying in real life, if you woke up terrified but alive, you should be grateful.

Yet Monique wasn't grateful for this feeling. For she *knew* something was wrong. She felt it with each *thumpety-thump* of her furiously pounding heart.

Drawing in a slow, quiet breath, she finally dared to move, darting her eyes from left to right, staring into the dark bedroom but seeing nothing. But that didn't mean that nothing was out there, lurking in the shadows. Perhaps outside her bedroom window, a stranger was scoping out the house, trying to get in. Against an unknown attacker, she was defenseless.

The sound of hyper barking sounded in the night, and feeling somewhat foolish, Monique instantly cracked a smile. Mr. Potter's dog. Of course. The neighbor's dog had awakened her on more than one occasion in the middle of the night. He must have spotted a cat, the way he was barking hysterically. Either that or he wanted back inside and was trying to wake his owners.

How silly she was, thinking the worst immediately. All her friends said she had an overactive imagination, and they were right.

Content, Monique rolled onto her side, snuggling against her pillow, determined to let sleep woo her once again. She let out a satisfied sigh. An instant later, she bolted upright.

What was *that?*

Now, she knew she wasn't crazy. She'd definitely heard something, something that made the hairs on her nape stand on end. Glancing toward her bedroom door, she cocked an ear. Listening for what had awakened her.

Monique's heart jumped into her throat. Oh, God. Were those footsteps she heard racing down the hallway? The front door closing? Or was her mind playing tricks on her? She couldn't tell, not with Mr. Potter's dog barking so loudly, but the cold feeling was suddenly back, and she gripped the blanket to her chest.

God, she never should have watched that horror movie last week! Her mother had told her not to, so she'd gone next door to her aunt's cottage and watched it with Doreen and Daniel. She'd regretted watching the movie as soon as it was over, and days later, she was still paranoid that some psycho would jump out of the closet and hack her to pieces.

Was that what had her so tense? Or was it something more?

Monique lay back down, pulling the blanket over her head. Her heart still raced, but maybe if she counted sheep she could calm herself enough to fall asleep again.

"Help..."

Monique stilled. Was that...?

"Help...me..."

The blood froze in her veins. Oh, God, that was her mother! Throwing off the sheets, she sprang from the bed. The cool wood floor was like a splash of cold water in her face, letting her know in no uncertain terms that she was not dreaming.

As she charged out her bedroom door, she heard a car engine roar to life outside, and for a moment she wondered who was out in this fairly deserted country area so late. But she soon forgot about the car as she ran across the hall to her parents' bedroom. God, she wished her father hadn't left angry, that he was still at their vacation home with them right now, not on his way back to New York. Right now, she needed him. Her mother did. He should be there.

Her mother's bedroom door was ajar. With an elbow, Monique shoved it open and raced into the room.

And found her mother sprawled on the floor.

"Mama?" Her voice was a horrified whisper.

"Help..."

The pale moonlight spilling in from the window was enough to illuminate a dark spot in the carpet where her mother lay, a spot that could only be one thing.

Her mother's life, seeping out of her body as she lay in a fetal position, her hands clutched to her stomach.

"Mama!" In a state of horror and disbelief, Monique dropped

to her mother's side. No, this couldn't be happening. This had to be a bad dream.

She reached for her mother's hand and felt a warm, sticky substance.

No doubt about it, it was blood. Too much blood. And it was everywhere.

"Oh, my God!" Monique cried. This was real. Oh, God, too real. As she listened to her mother moan softly, she was so numb and afraid that she didn't know what to do. Then her brain began working again and she remembered the phone. She scrambled to it and dialed 911.

"Mon…ique…"

"Please," Monique said, her tone anxious when the operator answered. "My mother's hurt. She's bleeding. Send help right away!"

"All right. Can you tell me…"

As her mother groaned again, the receiver fell from Monique's jittery hands. She hurried back to her mother's side, knowing the operator could trace the call. Right now, her mother needed her more.

Hot tears streamed down Monique's face, blurring her vision. Monique took her mother's head onto her lap, softly stroking her face and hair. Even though she was hurt, and blood stained her long white nightie, her mother still looked like an angel. She was that beautiful.

Monique couldn't lose her.

"Hang on, Mama. Hang on. Everything's gonna be okay. You hear me? I love you, Mama." Monique leaned down and pressed the side of her face to her mother's. "Oh, Mama. Please don't leave me. Not yet."

And then Monique stretched out beside her mother, pressing

her face against hers, wrapping her arms tightly around her body and gently rocking her, hoping and praying that she would be okay.

Hoping that she wouldn't die on her.

Chapter 1

Sixteen years later

"Oh, my lord," Vicky said, placing a hand over her heart as she watched the next model strut his stuff on stage. "I think I've died and gone to heaven."

Doreen whistled softly. "Mmm-mmm-mmm. He is the hottest thing I've seen since... Since forever."

Monique Savard shot a glance first at Vicky, a fellow model, then at her cousin, Doreen. Both women were clearly engrossed with the view of the half-naked model, enjoying every moment of this lustful pleasure. "Remember Hendrix, Doreen," Monique said, mentioning the name of Doreen's husband of four years, who happened to be a very attractive man, even if he wasn't quite as sexy as the model on stage.

Doreen snorted. "Hendrix who?"

Monique chuckled as she turned her attention back to the stage. She was volunteering her time this Saturday night at a charity fashion show and auction to raise money for the Brothas and Sistahs Community Center in the Bronx. Her cousin, Daniel, Doreen's brother, worked at the center as a counselor for troubled teens. Daniel had approached Monique about getting her and some of her model colleagues and friends to participate in a fund-raiser for the center. Initially, he had wanted to have the female models perform in the show, but given work obligations, Monique wasn't sure that idea would pan out. After discussions with her colleagues, Monique had come up with the idea to feature male models; most of her female friends were always hoping to find the right man, so she was certain more women would come to such an event. She and a few of the other models had agreed to volunteer their time for this Spring Fling event, dubbed the ultimate ladies' night; Vicky had come up with the brilliant idea of adding a charity auction as well.

And thus far, with the standing-room-only crowd, the event had been a huge success.

"I didn't know they made lawyers like that," Vicky commented, her voice dreamy. Half Hispanic and half African-American, Vicky had thick curly hair, honey-brown skin, and an exotic look that got her a lot of work as a model. "What I wouldn't give to see that man on my bed wearing nothing but those bulging muscles and a smile."

"Vicky!" Monique exclaimed.

"Like you wouldn't," Vicky retorted.

"He's not wearing much more than that right now," Doreen added, then sighed.

"Shh!" Emily, another model from the Cox agency where Monique and Vicky were represented, shushed her. "I can't enjoy the view with all of you making so much noise."

All heads turned to Emily, who, with her hands on her hips and her head tilted to the side, looked as if she were examining a precious piece of art. Which, no doubt, is what most of the women present thought of him, if their wild reactions were any indication.

His name was Khamil Jordan. Monique had made note of his

name after he first appeared on stage; he received such positive response that he'd be a good person to contact if the community center wanted to do this fund-raiser again. Right now, he was strutting his stuff at the end of the catwalk as though he was a natural. Monique suspected his confidence came from the roar of female voices that appreciated every one of his smooth moves.

He was definitely attractive. Approximately six foot one or two from what she could tell, broad chest, slim waist, smooth dark skin, and eyes that said, "I know you want me."

Yes, he was attractive, and he was sporting the bald look that she liked. It suited him very well. Would she give anything to have a man like that naked in her bed, as Vicky had suggested? It had certainly been a long time since she'd had any kind of action.

Naw, she quickly decided. While he was attractive, the cockiness in his attitude told her he definitely wasn't her type.

She wasn't hard to please, as Doreen often said. Her criterion was simple—fidelity. Unfortunately, not a lot of men believed in that. At least not the ones she'd met or gotten involved with.

Certainly not Raymond.

Monique released a bitter sigh, then put the thought of her ex-boyfriend out of her mind. After his betrayal, she'd decided to concentrate solely on her career, and she didn't regret the decision. Without the hassles of worrying about why a man who was supposed to love you wasn't calling or couldn't be found, she was happy. She didn't have time for love and didn't miss it in her life. Unfortunately, Raymond was still pestering her to give him a second chance. It didn't help that she often saw him on shoots, where he worked as a photographer.

Doreen didn't understand. She was happily married to a man

she'd met on a blind date, and she believed wholeheartedly in romantic love. Merely three months after meeting Hendrix, Doreen married him. Four years later, they were still lovey-dovey. Doreen affectionately called Hendrix her teddy bear, because he was tall and muscular, while she was short and petite.

Monique was happy for her cousin, but her own experience was quite different. She had seen her parents, whom she knew had no doubt loved each other, argue so often that she'd debated if it was ever worth it to fall in love. But life had a way of surprising you, and when she'd fallen for Raymond, she'd thought he was "the one." Mere months later, she'd learned how wrong she was.

High-pitched squeals filled the air, and Monique looked up in to time to see Khamil shrug back into a silk housecoat. Clearly, he'd let it fall off his shoulders to thrill the women. Well, they were definitely thrilled because as he coolly sauntered off the stage, women screamed and whistled and shouted for his return.

The bedroom wear was the last segment of the night before the auction was to start. After modeling several sets of clothes, it was clear that Khamil Jordan was the star of the male models. Monique had no doubt that he would fetch a great price at the auction when women would bid to spend a night with one of the men.

"Ladies," the emcee onstage began in a boisterous voice. "Is it just me, or are these some of the *hottest* men you have ever laid eyes on?"

Exuberant replies, agreeing with the emcee, filled the air.

"Mmm-mmm-mmm," the emcee continued. "Now, I know you all enjoyed the show, but now comes the real fun part. Some lucky ladies will have the chance to spend a night with the fine men we've seen up here tonight. As long as the price is right. Don't you all start fighting yet." The emcee and crowd chuckled when two women at a table near the front jumped to their feet and headed toward the stage. "Seriously, though, this is all for a good cause: support of the Brothas and Sistahs Community Center, which does a lot of work with our youth. So, keep that in mind when you make your bids." The emcee smiled. "Now, the first model is Robert Hawkins. Come on out here, Robert!"

The women cheered as Robert strolled onto the stage, dressed in formal wear. His smile could melt butter.

"Minimum bid, twenty dollars."

"Fifty," a woman from the back of the room yelled before the emcee had barely finished making her statement.

"All right. We've got fifty. How about sixty?"

"Sixty," another woman called out.

Monique stood at the back of the room and watched the women place bid after bid for a chance to go out with Robert. In the end, he was sold to the highest bidder, a woman who offered two hundred and sixty dollars to spend the night with him.

Monique watched in silence as the next four men were auctioned off, the most expensive bid being three hundred and ten dollars. But as Khamil Jordan strolled onto the stage to the frenzied roar of the women in the crowd, she knew he'd fetch a much higher price.

"Wow," the emcee said. "Did it just get a little hotter in here, or what?" She fanned herself with a hand. "All right, ladies. This is your last chance. Khamil is single, and says that he hasn't had any luck finding the right woman. Now that's a shame. But I know—no, I'm sure—that the right woman for Khamil is out there in the crowd. Am I right, ladies?"

The women replied with enthusiastic screams.

"Okay. Someone start the bidding."

"One hundred dollars!"

"One hundred. Ooh, I can tell the competition will be fierce for this one. Can I get one—"

"One-fifty!" another woman cried.

"Two-fifty," exclaimed the first woman who'd made a bid.

"Wow." The emcee gave out a low whistle. "Two fifty." She paused, then said, "Two-fifty going once, twice…"

"Three hundred."

"Four hundred."

Ecstatic cries filled the air at the high bid.

"Five hundred."

The crowd was momentarily stunned silent. But a low rumble escaped when the first woman said, "Six hundred dollars!"

"Six hundred going once, twice…sold! Khamil Jordan sold for six hundred dollars!"

The women in the crowd began clapping as the woman who'd won the bid did a little victory dance at her table.

Monique smiled to herself, then turned and headed toward the community center's kitchen where refreshments would now be served, and she'd be helping out in that regard.

The few times Monique had seen Daniel, he'd been running around like a chicken with his head cut off, worried that something would go wrong. But now that it was over and thousands of dollars had been raised for the community center, he would be happy. Tonight had been a definite success.

Monique saw him approach.

And when she realized he was headed straight for her, for some strange reason, her heart did an excited pitter-patter in her chest.

"I'm sorry," Monique said when he reached the table. "We're out of punch."

Khamil gave her a slow and easy smile. "Then it's a good thing I didn't come here for punch."

Monique gestured to the other tables. "We're all out of everything."

Khamil's eyes did a slow and deliberate perusal of her body. "I see the one thing I want."

Instantly, Monique's body stiffened, though she felt a strange tingle all over. Her instincts had been dead-on about Khamil. From the moment she'd seen him on the stage, she had figured him for a pompous playboy, and he was no doubt that.

"Oh."

Khamil chucked softly as he extended a hand. "Hi," he said. "I'm Khamil. One of the models."

Monique crossed her arms over her chest. "I know."

"Yes, of course." When Khamil realized she wasn't going to shake his hand, he pulled his back. "I guess you do, as you were here for the show."

Well, he must have been admiring his reflection somewhere when the celebrity models volunteering at the event were introduced. "Yes, I was here for the show. You were…good."

A hundred-watt grin exploded on his face. "Thank you. I didn't know what to expect, as this was my first time doing anything like this. But it seems I actually have some fans."

It was a simple enough statement, and clearly true since he had fetched the highest bid, yet Monique found herself curbing the urge to roll her eyes. The man had done one show, and now he had a following?

"So." His eyes did that flicker thing over her body again, making her feel as if he'd just seen her naked. "Did you…enjoy the show?"

It was the tone of his words that made Monique realize he wasn't referring to the show at all. He wanted to know what she thought of him.

She shrugged nonchalantly. "Sure. It was a good show."

"About time, right?"

"Pardon me?"

"Men have appreciated beautiful women for ages. It's about time women had the chance to enjoy the same. I was happy to oblige."

Monique wondered if Khamil was so dense that he actually believed this was the first time men had ever performed as models. She was tempted to tell him that it definitely wasn't the first and it certainly wouldn't be the last. But she didn't. Instead, wondering just how full of himself this man was, Monique cocked her head to the side and asked, "Is that right?"

"I believe in equal rights." His smile said he thought he was a god among men.

"I'm sure you do."

"And if you've got it, flaunt it, as they say." He flashed a boyish smile to make his words seem playful instead of cocky, but Monique wasn't fooled for one second.

"So they say."

As Khamil's chuckle died, he emitted a low whistle. "Man, you are one beautiful lady, you know that?"

"Who, me?" Monique pointed to herself and played coy. "Oh, you're too kind." She wanted to see just how far the fool would go. Did he think she was born yesterday?

"I'm just pointing out a fact. I'm a lawyer... I deal with facts. And you are undoubtedly the most attractive woman in this room."

"Thank you." She hoped her blush looked genuine.

"I'd really like to get to know you. How about we get together sometime? Maybe for a drink, dinner."

"Oh, I don't know…"

He fished in his jacket pocket and produced a business card and a pen. Before he handed her the card, he wrote something on the back. "Here you go."

Monique looked at the white car with the words *Burke, Lagger & Weiss* embossed in gold letters.

"My home number is on the back. But you can always reach me at the office. You can call me anytime you like."

"Can I?"

"Yes, ma'am. Now, how about that drink?"

"Shouldn't you be spending time with the woman who bought you?"

Khamil looked over his shoulder, as if expecting to find her there. "Actually, no. Our date is next weekend." Khamil raised an eyebrow. "So until then, I'm all yours."

"Really?" Monique feigned excitement.

"Did you come with anyone tonight?"

"Friends."

"Not a man?"

"No."

"Good." He took a step closer, and Monique couldn't help noticing his distinctly male scent. "Then how about we leave and I take you to a great place I know not too far from here?"

"I'm sorry, Khamil." She deliberately pronounced it "Camel."

"Kha-meel," he corrected, pronouncing his name clearly.

"Khamil." Monique took a step backward. He was too close, and she was uncomfortable. "I would…but I can't. I really can't leave my friends. In fact, I should get back to them. We're volunteering for the event tonight."

"Oh." For a moment, he seemed disappointed; then the charming smile was back. "That's great. I appreciate a woman who gives something back. I like to give back myself. That's why I agreed to do this tonight."

"Mmm-hmm. Well, I really need to get going." She moved to step past him. "As you can see, this place is a mess. I've got to start to help with the clean-up."

He blocked her path and flashed her what he must have thought was a drop-dead-gorgeous smile. It was, in fact, a little charming. But Monique ignored that, just as she tried to ignore how handsome he was up close and personal. "Before you go, give me your phone number."

She stared at him, not responding.

"Come on." He winked. "I promise I won't bite."

Good grief. When was the last time a man had actually winked at her? Mr. Jordan was the consummate player, she was sure.

"Hmm?" he prompted.

"Oh, why not?" Monique agreed, with a wave of her hand. "You don't seem like a stalker."

A deep laugh rumbled in his chest. "No. Just a man who finds you fascinating."

"You certainly know how to boost a woman's ego."

"I speak the truth." He handed her his pen and another business card.

Monique took the items and wrote a number on the back, then handed the pen and card back to him.

"Mary," he said, reading the information she'd written.

"Yes. Now, I really do have to get going."

"Okay." Khamil drew his bottom lip between his teeth. "I'll call you soon."

"All right." She smiled shyly, then stepped past him wondering if Khamil Jordan was the world's biggest fool.

When Monique entered her midtown Manhattan condominium, the phone was ringing. She dropped her purse off her shoulder and dashed into her penthouse suite. In the nearby living room, she grabbed the receiver. "Hello?"

The dial tone blared in her ear.

Hmm, she thought, mildly concerned. She'd reacted first, thought later, not even checking her caller ID. She hoped it hadn't been Raymond calling. She'd been avoiding his calls for three weeks now, and she hoped he finally got the point that she wasn't interested in speaking with him.

Monique replaced the receiver and dropped herself onto the sofa adjacent to the end table where the phone rested, letting out a satisfied sigh when she did. It had been a long night, but a successful one.

She allowed herself a small chuckle when she thought of Khamil, and what his reaction would be when he learned she'd given him a wrong number. The consummate player getting played. It served him right.

Once again, Monique lifted the receiver. She may as well check her messages. She dialed the access code for her call answering service.

After she entered her password, an automated voice told her that she had two new messages. She hit the key to access them.

"Hey, girl. It's just me, Doreen. I wanted to chat with you

before you headed out to the event tonight. Oh well. I'll see you there."

As Monique had already seen and chatted with her cousin, she deleted that message.

The next message began to play. "Hello. I'm trying to reach Monique Savard. Ms. Savard, this is Detective Darren McKinney of the Ontario Provincial Police. I'm calling about your mother's murder case. Please give me a call as soon as you can. We need to talk."

A familiar wave of pain and nausea washed over her after hearing the second message. Every time she thought about her mother's murder, she couldn't help feeling physically ill, even though the crime had happened sixteen years ago. For two years after the murder, her father had been the prime suspect. Ultimately, he'd been cleared—rather, the police couldn't put together a solid case against him—and in the end, the police hadn't found another suspect. The case had never been solved.

Monique quickly grabbed a pen and pad off the end table, replayed the message, then jotted down the number the man had given.

Replacing the receiver, Monique laid her head back against the sofa, and closed her eyes. The strange tingling that always accompanied the anxiety about her mother's death spread through her chest and arms, down to her hands. Her heart was now beating faster, and no matter how she inhaled and exhaled slowly, nothing made her feel less anxious.

Though her family had lived in Manhattan, her mother had been murdered in Barrie, a small city north of Toronto, where they'd had a cottage. They still had it, though neither she nor her father had gone there again after what had happened. Monique remembered so many happy summers at that cottage with her parents, especially the time she'd spent with her mother, and to go there without her mother would be too painful.

Like her mother, Monique had become a model. At the age of thirteen, she'd landed a contract with Elite Skin Care, and she'd done several print ads with her mother. The contract had been for five years, but her mother had died a year into the agreement, ending the job for Monique as well.

Once the police had officially dropped the case against her father, he had packed up and moved from New York to Florida. Perhaps the pain was too raw, the reality that he'd been the prime suspect too much to deal with, for him to stay in that city. But he'd received criticism from the media and his in-laws for seemingly not doing more to find Julia's murderer. Monique had wondered the same thing, but had witnessed firsthand her father's agony, and understood that his unwillingness to even mention his wife's name was his way of dealing with the pain.

Monique had reacted quite differently. She had vowed to follow in her mother's footsteps, becoming a successful model as Julia Savard had been. She didn't care about the possible danger and had gone to New York, always hoping to find some clue about her mother's murder. For months, her mother had been harassed by an unknown stalker, and she felt that stalker had followed her from New York to Barrie. Monique and her mother had been in Canada for a couple of weeks, taking some time off from their modeling contract with Elite Skin Care, and it seemed highly unlikely that someone who didn't know her or who she was would have found her at the cottage.

Monique's cousins, Doreen and Daniel, had also accompanied them on that trip. Only Monique had awakened when hearing her mother's cries for help.

Already, the painful memories of the past were giving Monique a headache. Her father hadn't been so much cleared as dismissed as a suspect because of a lack of evidence. Even though he hadn't caught his scheduled plane back to New York the evening of her mother's murder, and had later said he'd spent time in a hotel after a fight with his wife and had planned to see her in the morning to patch things up, his story sounded fishy, even to Monique. But when her father had looked her in the eye and plainly told her he hadn't murdered his wife, Monique had believed him.

Monique's family had always been close-knit. But after the murder, her father had moved to Florida to completely escape the spotlight. Monique had gone with him, but for years all she could think of was finding her mother's true killer, so as soon as she turned eighteen, she headed back to New York to pursue a modeling career.

Her father didn't want her to move back there. Knowing there had been a psychotic stalker after her mother made him hate the spotlight, and he didn't want his daughter to suffer a fate similar to her mother's. And with the killer never being caught, he could easily obsess over Monique once she made it big. Indeed, now that Monique was a woman, she eerily resembled her mother.

But Monique didn't care what the risk was; solving her mother's murder meant the world to her.

It was late Friday evening, but Monique took a chance at calling the detective. She frowned when she got his voice mail.

"Hi, this is Monique Savard calling for Detective McKinney. I got your message about my mother's murder, and I'm anxious to talk to you. I'll be here all weekend, and early next week. If you don't reach me, let me know the best time to reach you."

Monique disconnected the line, wondering why the detective had called. Was there news about her mother's murder? Was there another suspect?

Monique was about to call her father when she thought better of it. Unlike her, he seemed desperate to put the pain of her mother's murder behind him once and for all. It was for that reason that he'd moved to Jacksonville and had gotten an unlisted number. Monique doubted the police had been able to reach him. But she was back in New York, where they'd once lived as a family, always hoping that there would be some break in the case.

Raymond had often told her that she was too involved in the case; in fact, everyone had told her that. They didn't understand. How could she ever have a peaceful night's sleep, knowing her mother's killer was still out there?

"Forget it," she told herself, knowing she wouldn't. But for now, until she heard from the detective, she could allow herself to hope.

Hope that the detective had good news.

Hope that there was finally a suspect in her mother's murder case. Because if there was, and if that suspect was subsequently convicted, Monique could finally move on.

Chapter 2

Her long, slim legs were wrapped around him as he thrust long and deep into her. The sound of her passionate cries, the feel of her nails digging into his back, made Khamil's whole body burn with the need for release.

She was beautiful. Flawless dark skin, full, pouty lips. Looking down at her beneath him, watching her expression of pure carnal delight as he made love to her, was more than he could handle. Khamil had been trying to hold on, but he couldn't any longer…

Instantly, Khamil's eyes flew open. Though he knew immediately what the real deal was, he cast a quick glance to his left and right, confirming that he was alone.

He'd been dreaming.

About Mary.

One minute he'd been awake, thinking about all he had to do that day, the next he'd drifted off. And once again, Mary had invaded his thoughts.

He looked down at his erection and groaned.

"Mary." He said her name aloud, a smile forming on his lips. She was beautiful, no doubt about it. What he wouldn't give to have her beside him in his bed right now, naked. She had a somewhat shy demeanor, but he'd be willing to bet she'd be wild in bed. He had a sixth sense about these things and was rarely wrong.

Unable to sleep any longer, Khamil sat up. Though he'd worked almost eighty hours that week, and had participated in that charity event, he knew he wouldn't sleep anymore this morning. He was beyond fatigue to the point where he was wired and couldn't keep his eyes shut if his life depended on it.

There was a lot on his mind. He had work to do. It was always the nagging feeling that he wasn't completing the millions of tasks he had to do that kept him awake.

And Mary. She also kept him awake.

Khamil swung his legs over the side of his bed and dug his toes into the soft gray carpet. He sat silently, a curious smile playing on his lips. He definitely wanted to get to know Mary much better. And he wanted to find out if his sixth sense about her was right.

It wasn't as if he hadn't lusted over a woman before, but there was something especially intriguing about Mary. Maybe it was her beautiful dark skin or her arresting brown eyes. Maybe it was her dainty oval face, her high cheekbones, and those full, sensual lips definitely made for kissing. Or maybe it was her long, shapely legs. Or maybe it was the entire package. No doubt about it, she was definitely luscious.

Rising from his bed, Khamil gave his muscular body a good stretch. Mary hadn't called him, but it was still early. He shot a glance at the clock radio on his night table. Yep, it was very early. Nine-twelve.

Knowing he had a lot of work to do, Khamil headed to the kitchen, where he put on a pot of coffee. He waited while it brewed, turning on the small black-and-white television in his kitchen to catch the news on CNN. Nothing much caught his interest, so when the coffee was ready, he poured a cup and took it to the dining room table, which served as a desk for much of the work he did at home.

His briefcase already lay open on the table, the contract he needed to go over in a manila folder on top of other contracts. He took a sip of the coffee, then lowered himself onto the chair before the briefcase. Burke, Lagger & Weiss was a large law firm in downtown Manhattan that dealt with everything from civil lawsuits to criminal defense. Khamil had been with the firm for seven years, and dealt exclusively with entertainment law. He'd always had an interest in the entertainment field, because for as long as he remembered, he'd dreamed of being a musician. That was a dream he hadn't shared with his family. While his parents and siblings had known of his love for music, they'd always seen it as a hobby rather than a viable career choice. He'd never seen it as a career either, despite the fact that he'd always composed and played music on his guitar whenever he had some spare time.

Khamil downed the remaining black coffee, then placed the cup beside the briefcase. He withdrew the manila folder marked *Graves* and opened it. The firm preferred to deal with high-profile talent, but often it did contract reviews for up-and-coming actors or artists. Khamil believed that these very same artists had to start somewhere, and if in the future they made something big of their careers, they'd remain loyal to the firm.

Adam Graves was one such person. A talented actor, he still hadn't had a big break yet, and was willing to do almost anything to make that happen. Including work for low-budget productions that didn't pay a fraction of what he was worth.

Khamil lifted the contract, then briefly skimmed the first

page before setting it down. Emitting a frustrated sigh, he pinched the bridge of his nose. Despite the conversations he'd had with the producer on his client's behalf, this version of the contract didn't look much better than the last. If his client signed it, he'd be basically giving away his rights to future income. Yet when he'd talked to Adam the day before, Adam had been prepared to do just that, caring only about the exposure the film would bring. This was a vehicle to future stardom, Adam had assured him. Khamil hadn't bothered to point out that the last four similar contracts had gotten him nowhere. He knew that Adam wouldn't listen to reason.

Khamil had seen one too many contracts like this, one too many broken dreams. Independent producers, unless extremely lucky, just didn't have the resources to get their films the exposure needed that would result in an actor's being "discovered."

He went over the contract again, circling in pencil the clauses he wanted amended. He'd contact the producer once more on Adam's behalf, and see what he was willing to offer. He knew that whether or not the producer paid Adam a decent wage and gave him acceptable contract terms, his client was willing and ready to sign on the dotted line.

Khamil was en route to the kitchen for another cup of coffee when the phone rang. The first thought that entered his mind was that Mary was calling him. He hurried to the kitchen phone and snatched the receiver.

"Khamil Jordan."

"Khamil, you have been a very bad boy."

Khamil couldn't help rolling his eyes. Yet he sounded cheerful as he said, "Annette."

"You don't return calls anymore. And you're so hard to reach."

"I've been busy."

"All work and no play isn't good for the soul."

"So they say, but it can't be helped sometimes. This is one of those times."

"I miss you."

"Uh-huh." Khamil didn't tell her that he missed her as well, because he didn't. In the beginning he had, but she'd called too much, had seemed too desperate, and that had turned him off.

That and the fact that she'd mentioned on their third date how much she wanted to settle down and have a family.

"When do you think you'll have time for a break? You can come over and I can cook you dinner, give you a massage…"

"I'm not sure."

"Oh." She sounded disappointed.

"But if I get some time, I'll let you know."

"All right, sweetie. You know where to reach me."

She hung up, and Khamil held the receiver to his ear, listening to the dial tone for several seconds.

Finally replacing the receiver, he blew out a long breath. Annette was beautiful and willing to simply spend time with him, which he appreciated. She'd been great for nights out on the town and the occasional rolls in the hay. But lately, he had grown tired of her, the same way he had grown tired of others in the past.

Though his family and friends wouldn't believe him, he'd always had hopes of settling down one day, of starting a family the way his brother, Javar, had, of helping to keep the Jordan family name alive. In his twenties, he'd always figured he'd settle down one day—after he'd had enough fun to last a lifetime. In his early thirties, he'd pretty much had the same attitude. Though knowing he'd sown enough wild oats, he had been willing to entertain the thought of actually searching for the right woman. For whatever reason, the women he met and dated were good for the short term, but he couldn't imagine spending happily ever after with them. And in the back of his mind, he kept thinking that if he chose just one of the several women he dated to pursue for marriage, he'd feel as if he were in an ice cream parlor having just one flavor—forever. He couldn't do it. So, since he hadn't truly found anyone he'd cared to spend the rest of his days with, he'd stopped worrying about finding the right woman, certain that when he was finally ready to settle down, she would walk into his life.

But at thirty-eight, that hadn't happened yet.

He didn't know why the perfect woman eluded him. Maybe he was too picky. He knew that any woman he settled down with would have to have a career of her own, for two reasons. He spent so much time at the firm, a wife might get bored if she didn't do something fulfilling for herself. Also, many of the women he dated could only be classified as flaky, hoping to snag a wealthy husband, and he wasn't about to play that game. He'd be willing to give his wife everything, but she'd have to love him for him first and foremost.

Khamil filled his cup with more coffee, then strolled back to his dining room. Once again, his thoughts went to Mary. She was beautiful, classy, a woman he wanted to get to know. Yes, he was sexually attracted to her, there'd been definite sparks between them the night before. But would she ignite something else within him?

Maybe. There was something different about her that piqued his interest. Whether or not she would sustain that interest, only time would tell.

A quick look at the wall clock told him it was now just

minutes after ten. He wanted to talk to her, and sensed that she was the old-fashioned type who wouldn't call him first. He liked that. Unfortunately, a lot of women he met in New York were too pushy.

He hoped it wasn't too early to call her, but as he couldn't stop thinking about her, he figured he may as well.

He fished her number out of his card holder, went to the kitchen phone, and dialed it.

The phone rang three times, then a machine picked up. Khamil was about to hang up, then decided to leave a message.

"Thank you for calling Tony's Pizzeria," a male voice with a slight Italian accent began. "Unfortunately, we're closed right now. Our hours of operation are from twelve noon to one a.m., seven days a week. Please call back during that time."

Khamil looked at the receiver with confusion, then hung up the phone. He frowned. Maybe he'd dialed the wrong number. He dialed again.

Again, he got the same message.

Hanging up the phone, he leaned a hip against the kitchen counter. Something didn't feel right about this. Had Mary accidentally given him the wrong number? Or had she chosen to give him her work number?

A pizzeria? Did Mary work at a pizzeria? For some reason, Khamil couldn't picture that.

Oh well. He'd call back in a couple of hours and hopefully speak to her then.

Monique didn't exactly feel like being at this fitting so early on a Sunday morning. One, she was still tired from last night, and two, she wanted to be home in case the detective called.

She'd tried his line again, again getting a message. She

wouldn't have expected a call until Monday, but he had called her on the weekend, so she figured that perhaps he was working weekend hours.

Oh well.

"Huh, Monique?"

At the sound of her name, Monique turned and faced Vicky, who was sitting in the small room waiting with her and a couple of other models from their agency.

"Pardon me?"

Vicky held up a magazine and said, "Okay. I'll read this again. If you were walking along Broadway and found a wad of one-hundred-dollar bills, would, you, A, go immediately to the police and turn the money in, B, donate it to the charity of your choice, or, C, call your travel agent and make plans for the vacation of a lifetime?"

"Is there anything to identify who the money belongs to?" Heidi, another model, asked.

"Nope," Vicky replied.

"Then I'd donate it to the charity of my choice," Heidi answered. "Me."

Monique smirked as she shook her head. "You are too much, girl."

"It's true. If anyone can use the money, I can."

"For another pair of Armani blue jeans?"

"Hey, I don't work as much as you two, remember?"

"You're hardly starving," Monique countered.

"Still, if someone's dumb enough to drop a wad of hundreds, they obviously don't need the money."

Monique chuckled along with her friends, starting to feel better. Maybe it wasn't such a bad thing being out this morning. All last night, her mind had replayed the horror of the night she had found her mother dying, and it was nice having a reprieve from that memory, even if only for a short time.

"Hey," Heidi said, looking at Monique. "Guess who I saw yesterday."

Monique shrugged. "I don't know."

"Raymond. He asked me if I know what's up with you. Says he hasn't seen you around for a while."

Raymond. He'd been calling her, but thankfully, her caller ID enabled her to screen his calls. She had no interest in talking to him, not after what he'd done.

"Our paths haven't crossed, that's all."

"Well, when I told him you'd be working with me on this spread, he told me to tell you to call him."

"Thanks," Monique replied softly. She didn't discuss her personal life with her colleagues. Only Vicky and a couple of the other models she considered friends knew she'd been involved with Raymond. Vicky had shared Monique's concern that the man had started acting a little too clingy, obsessed even. Even though he knew Monique was a busy fashion model, he wanted an account of where she was at all times and who she'd spent her time with. He always said this was out of concern for her, that he wanted to know if any men got out of line with her, but Monique knew it was more. Though she and Raymond had only been seeing each other a few months at the time, he seemed to feel he owned her.

Monique looked at Vicky and she and Vicky shared a knowing look; then Vicky changed the subject. "Well, if I found a wad of hundreds, I have to admit, I'd be calling my travel agent to book the vacation of a lifetime."

"How many times have you been around the world?" Monique asked her friend, giving her a disapproving look.

"True. Okay, I'd turn it in. Isn't it true that after a certain amount of time, if the money remains unclaimed, you can keep it?"

"As far as I know," Heidi said.

"Then I'd turn it in and hope that no one came to collect," Vicky said, then smiled.

All the women shared a laugh.

Yeah, this was better than being at home, thinking about her mother's unsolved murder.

Fifteen minutes after noon, Khamil dialed the number Mary had given him once more.

"Tony's Pizzeria."

Khamil nestled the receiver between his chin and shoulder. "Hi. Uh, I'm looking for someone." He was convinced now that Mary had given him her work number. "I believe she works at your business."

"What's her name?"

"Mary."

"Mary? No one works here by the name of Mary."

"Are you sure?" Khamil asked. "Beautiful black woman. Tall and slim."

"Uh, no. She definitely doesn't work here. Maybe you took the number down wrong."

"No. She wrote it down."

The woman chuckled, and that said it all.

"Sorry to bother you," Khamil quickly said.

"I can't give you Mary, but I can give you a pizza."

"No. Thanks. Have a good day." Khamil hung up, but not before he heard the woman begin to relay the story of how some woman had duped him.

So, it was like that. Mary had given him a fake number. He'd bet double or nothing that her name wasn't Mary either.

He'd been played.

Chapter 3

Bright and early Monday morning, Monique got the call she was waiting for. Before the phone could ring a second time, she grabbed the receiver.

"Hello?"

"Ms. Savard?"

Monique sat up. "Yes, this is she."

"Hello. This is Detective McKinney of the Ontario Provincial Police."

"Hello."

"The reason I'm calling is about your mother's unsolved murder case. The O.P.P. has put together a task force to deal with what we call cold cases, cases of a serious nature that have remained unsolved for many years. Your mother's case is one of them."

Monique's heart fluttered. "Years ago, you never found any suspects, other than my father. What are the chances that, so many years after the fact, you'll actually be able to solve the crime?"

"One of the best things we have going for us now is DNA technology, which allows us to rule out previous suspects, or in fact confirm that they could have committed the crime."

"I see."

"Forensic scientists will be evaluating the samples we have on file to see if in fact they can still be used with any degree of accuracy. In the meantime, I'll be going over all the evidence that was collected regarding this case, including statements of witnesses. I understand you were the one who found your mother."

"Yes." Monique's voice was barely more than a croak.

"I may need to question you again in respect to what happened that night. And of course, if anything comes to mind that you realize you may have forgotten then, feel free to call me."

"It was so long ago."

"I realize that, but one never knows. Also, we'll be publicizing the cases we're reopening, so there's always the chance that witnesses who didn't come forward before may feel compelled to come forward now."

"I never thought of that."

"In fact, *America's Most Wanted* would like to profile this case on an upcoming episode they're doing featuring crimes in Canada. Because it was such a high profile case—"

"Yes, I understand. And I think it's a great idea."

"Good. Now, is everyone who was in some way involved in the investigation back then, in terms of your family members, still alive?"

"My father's still alive. My aunt. My uncle. Yes, all of them."

"I may need to talk with them as well, depending on how the DNA testing goes."

"I'll let them know."

"Great." The detective paused. "All right. That's all for now. I basically wanted to get in touch with you and let you know what was going on, before you heard about it in the media, of course."

"Thank you." Monique began to hope. "And I appreciate this."

"Hopefully we'll be able to get closure for your family once and for all."

"Yes, hopefully," Monique agreed, then hung up, allowing herself to experience real hope for the first time in several years.

The moment Monique walked into the women's clothing section of the department store where Doreen worked, Doreen saw her. A huge smile spread on her cousin's face.

Monique forced a smile as she sauntered toward Doreen. "Hey, you."

Doreen's smile instantly fell into a frown. "Uh-oh. What's wrong?"

"Nothing," Monique replied, giving Doreen a brief hug.

Doreen stepped back from Monique and gave her a skeptical look. "Come on. I know you better than anyone. There's definitely something bothering you."

Monique glanced away, strolling around a rack of cashmere sweaters to her right.

Doreen followed her. "Monique, I don't think you came here to shop for new clothes."

Stopping abruptly, Monique faced her cousin. "You're right. I didn't."

"All right. Then tell me what's up."

Not only was Doreen her cousin, she was Monique's best friend. They could discuss anything, even if they didn't always agree. "I got a call today from a police officer in Toronto. He said they're reopening my mother's murder case."

Doreen's eyes first narrowed, then widened, in surprise. "What?"

Monique blew out a weary breath. Even since learning the

news, she felt both a sense of fear and optimism. "I don't know why, but the detective said he thinks the new DNA technology may help solve this case."

"Wow." Doreen shook her head in amazement. Then she looked Monique squarely in the eye. "So, this is a good thing, right?"

"I think so."

"Then why don't you seem happy?"

"No reason in particular." Monique shrugged. "It's just not a pleasant subject."

"If you're worried about the DNA evidence—"

"The DNA evidence will exonerate my father," Monique interjected.

A hint of doubt passed over Doreen's face, which immediately put Monique on edge. "My father did not kill my mother, Doreen."

"I…" Doreen's voice trailed as she glanced away. After a moment, she faced Monique again. "I know you believe that."

"I *know* that, Doreen. No one knew my father better than my mother and I. Yes, they had their problems, but no, he never would have killed her." Part of her parents' problems was the fact that her mother had worked so much, and not spent enough time with her father, as far as he was concerned. Still, Monique was certain he'd loved her. In fact, he'd never remarried since her death. "He worshipped the ground she walked on," Monique concluded.

"Oh, Monique," Doreen began. "I'm not saying he *did* do it, but you have to acknowledge the possibility—"

"There is no possibility," Monique quickly responded.

Doreen was quiet, and Monique looked at her, but couldn't read what she was thinking. Doreen had pointed out to her time and again that most women were hurt or killed by men they knew, mostly lovers or husbands, as opposed to strangers. And while Monique knew that to be true, she also knew it wasn't in this case. She only wished her cousin had her back in this situation. Instead, Doreen probably thought she was crazy; a daughter who stubbornly refused to believe her father could commit such a horrible crime.

"What did the police say?" Doreen asked after a while.

"The detective said that recently, they've reopened a bunch of old homicide cases. Cold cases, they're called. Cases that were never solved years ago. There's a squad specifically dedicated to investigating these old crimes—the cold squad."

"I hear that's popular these days."

Monique nodded. "With my mother's case, they'll be reviewing everything, all the witness statements, evidence, et cetera. Hopefully fresh eyes can come up with something the original detectives missed." Monique hesitated, wondering if she should tell Doreen about the segment on *America's Most Wanted*. Decided against it, at least for now. She seemed to be the only one in the family hell-bent on finding her mother's murderer, while everyone else wanted to forget the whole ugly matter. It didn't make it an easy subject to talk about. "The police may need to speak to you."

"Of course. I'll help out any way I can. I'm not sure what good it will do, though. I didn't know anything then."

An image of her mother, bleeding on the floor, hit Monique with full force. She cringed as she suddenly fought back tears.

Instantly, Doreen wrapped an arm around her shoulder. "Monique." A little sigh escaped her. "I know I've told you this before. Somehow, you have to find a way to move on. What if they never find your mother's killer? What are you going to do? You can't let it eat away at you like this forever."

"I wish that was an option," Monique replied. "But it isn't. Every time I think I may be over it, something happens to remind me that I'm not. Sometimes it's a certain look a photographer will give me when he's photographing me, and I wonder if it was some sick pig who killed my mother because he fantasized about her in ways he shouldn't have. Or sometimes I'll be watching the news and I'll hear about a woman who's been murdered, and I'll see my mother's face."

Doreen hugged Monique harder. "You've never sought counseling in all this."

"Counseling isn't going to help."

"You should try it."

"Doreen, don't push this issue."

"Okay."

Monique stepped out of her cousin's embrace and walked toward another rack of clothing. She fingered one of the floral skirts. It was similar to a skirt she remembered her mother wearing one summer before she died. Which made Monique think of the fact that today was a gorgeous summer day. Fleetingly Monique wondered when the last time was that she'd taken time to enjoy such a day.

Not in sixteen years.

The summer reminded her of the cottage in Barrie.

And the cottage in Barrie reminded her of her mother's murder.

"The police will want to talk to Daniel, too. And probably your mother."

"We'll all do what we can."

"How often do you talk to your father?" Monique's uncle Richard had divorced Aunt Sophie around the time her father had moved to Florida, and he now lived in Ohio.

"We talk at least once a month."

"Well, if he can make himself available, that'd be great." Monique paused. "Maybe there's a clue right under our noses that we've been missing all this time."

"Maybe," Doreen said, but the word sounded placating.

"There's something else," Monique began, deciding to share everything with her cousin. "Because Mom was a high-profile model, they're going to run the story on *America's Most Wanted*."

"Well, that's good."

Monique was surprised that Doreen didn't voice any dissent, but then, Doreen knew how pointless that would be. Anyone who knew Monique knew that she wouldn't rest until her mother's killer was found. "Hopefully, if anyone saw or heard something strange back then, it will click if they see a show about the murder." Softly, she added, "And my mother can finally have some justice."

Doreen gave a grim nod. Monique knew she didn't understand her obsession with finding her mother's killer sixteen years after the fact, and she couldn't blame her. It hadn't been Doreen who'd walked into a bedroom to find her mother lying in a pool of blood. It hadn't been Doreen who'd felt so utterly helpless as she'd watched her mother's life slip away. It wasn't she who was haunted by those images even now.

Perhaps if Monique hadn't walked in and found her mother dying, this wouldn't be as bad for her. But her mother had begged Monique for her help and she hadn't been able to help her. It was something that haunted her to this day.

As if Doreen read her thoughts, she said, "There was nothing you could do, Monique."

"Maybe not then," Monique quickly replied. "But now. There's something I can do now. I can find my mother's murderer and let him face justice."

Khamil was in the checkout line at the grocery store when a magazine caught his eye. He did a double take, thinking the woman on the cover looked an awful lot like Mary.

Good Lord, it *was* Mary! Stopping, he grabbed the magazine.

"Sir?" the woman behind him asked. "Are you in the line?"

"Yes," Khamil mumbled in reply, slightly irritated with this woman's impatience. He stepped back into the line, taking the magazine with him.

No doubt about it, it was Mary all right. He'd recognize those sexy lips and beautiful brown eyes anywhere. Her eyes were staring at him, seeming to say, "Sucker!"

So she was a model. Khamil thought back to the night of the Spring Fling and grimaced. He remembered hearing that some professional models had helped organize the event, but he hadn't figured she'd been one of them. He'd met a couple of them, so why not her?

It made sense, thinking back. She was stunning. Of course, she could be a model. Yet Khamil had come on to her from the position of a celebrity speaking to someone who might have admired him that night.

Man, he was a fool!

"Is that everything, sir?" the cashier asked.

"Oh. Yes," Khamil answered.

"And the magazine?"

Khamil dropped the magazine onto the conveyer belt. "Yes. I'm taking this, too."

And hopefully he'd learn more about Mary, or whatever her true name was.

So much for that idea. The magazine didn't give Khamil any clue as to who Mary really was. She'd simply graced its cover.

He knew who would have an answer. Jeremy Leeming, another lawyer at his firm, who'd also been one of the models that night, knew one of the professional female models. In fact, it had been that model who'd solicited the men of their firm to perform that night. Jeremy was sure to have some answers.

Minutes later, Khamil had Jeremy on the line. He briefly explained all that had happened, how he now realized Mary was in fact a model.

Jeremy chuckled after hearing Khamil's story.

"All right, I know," Khamil said. "But how was I to know she was one of the models?"

"You're supposed to be smart, man," Jeremy jeered playfully.

"Even I have my moments. The point is, I want to find her."

"I can call Vicky. She'll know who she is."

"Let me know the moment you find anything out."

"Will do."

Monique almost choked on her glass of wine when she saw Khamil Jordan enter the restaurant. "Oh, no," she mumbled.

"What?" Vicky asked.

Monique frowned, then tried to shield her face with a hand. "That lawyer. One of the models from the Spring Fling charity event. He just came in."

"Oooh, the hot one," Vicky chimed.

"You can say that again," Janine, one of the other models in their group of four, commented, then whistled softly.

Monique splayed her fingers over her eye, allowing herself an avenue to see Khamil. "Oh, my God, What's he doing? Is he coming this way?"

"Sorry, Monique," Vicky said. "I forgot to tell you, Jeremy called me a couple days ago and said one of his colleagues was trying to get a hold of you."

"*You* sent him here?"

"I didn't think you wouldn't want to talk to him!" Vicky protested. "Besides, what could it hurt to meet him in a public place? Then you can figure out if you're interested in him or not."

"I already met him in a public place a couple weeks ago and I *wasn't* interested."

"Girl," began Renee, the fourth model in their group tonight, "don't tell me you're still hung up on Raymond. And if you are, this man can certainly help you forget that louse. Mmm. If he isn't the hottest brother I've seen in a long time..."

There was no use hiding. Khamil had seen her. Monique let her hand drop from her face and tried as casually as possible to reach for her wineglass. Though she kept her eyes straight ahead, she couldn't help checking out Khamil in her peripheral vision.

He did look fine. Dressed in a slick black suit, he looked as if he had stepped off the cover of *GQ* magazine. Indeed, many wealthy and high-profile people frequented this restaurant, so Khamil wasn't overdressed, but he certainly stood out among the crowd.

"Monique Savard." Khamil's voice was cool, yet his smile didn't quite reach his eyes.

"Hello."

His eyes did a slow perusal of her body, leaving her feeling hot—and exposed. "So," he began after what seemed like hours, "do you have a moment?"

"Not really."

"Let me rephrase the question. I'd like to speak with you. Alone. Now." He smiled to soften his demand.

There was something commanding about him, something mesmerizing, something that made it hard to tell him no. Monique drew her eyes away from him and faced her friends. "If you'll excuse me for a moment."

Vicky raised one perfectly sculpted eyebrow.

Monique gave her a cool look, a look that said she shouldn't make anything of this meeting. Then she pushed her chair back and stood.

Before she knew it, Khamil had her by the elbow and was leading her to the front of the restaurant.

"I agreed to talk to you, not to leave with you!"

"Relax," Khamil said, his voice as smooth as warm chocolate. "I just want a bit of privacy, *Mary*."

Monique's face grew warm with embarrassment. Okay, so she'd been childish giving him a false name and number, but he'd been so arrogant and full of himself, he'd been asking for it.

When Khamil had her in the entranceway of the restaurant, he spoke. "If you didn't want me to call you, why didn't you just say?"

Monique shrugged nonchalantly, not willing to admit she'd been childish. "You didn't seem like you'd believe it if I told you I wasn't interested."

"Hmm." Khamil studied her, trying to figure her out. And he wondered why he had actually come here. Yeah, she was attractive, but if she had lied to him about her number, then she clearly wasn't interested.

But there was something intriguing about her, he realized. Something that made him want to see her again. Coming to see her today had been like the second stage in a game, and he couldn't stop himself if he tried.

Monique stiffened her spine and crossed her arms over her chest. "Hmm what?"

Khamil gave a slight shrug. "I find you fascinating, that's all."

"Well," Monique said, as though his words didn't affect her

in the least. "That's nice, but I'm sure that's not the reason you came here tonight…" Her voice trailed off as she almost said, "Looking so good." She gave a tight smile. "Don't keep her waiting on my account."

"What?" Khamil asked, caught off guard.

But before Monique could give him an answer, she hurried back into the restaurant. A grin played on his lips as he watched her go. She didn't return to the table where she'd been sitting, as he'd anticipated, instead heading to the back of the establishment and the rest rooms.

Khamil's grin widened.

It was time for round two.

Chapter 4

Monique gasped and threw a hand to her chest when she stepped out of the bathroom door and saw Khamil standing directly in her path.

He merely smiled at her startled outburst.

Quickly recovering, Monique glared at him. "*Excuse* me," she said, moving to step past him.

Khamil stepped to the left, blocking her path with his muscular body. "Oh, I'm sorry," he mocked. "I didn't realize you were going to walk that way."

Monique flashed him a sarcastic smile. "Really?"

"Honest mistake."

"Fine." Monique stepped to the right, and once again, Khamil stepped with her, blocking her path.

"Ooops," he said, giving Monique a boyish look.

Monique was unimpressed. "There are laws against stalking in this state."

Khamil threw his head back and laughed. "Stalking?"

"What would you call it?" Monique challenged.

"I'm merely trying to get to know you," Khamil answered frankly. "And I'll do whatever it takes."

Something stirred within Monique, but she ignored the

feeling. "Didn't you get the hint when I gave you a fake name and number?"

Khamil raised an eyebrow. "Maybe you're just playing hard to get."

"You're too much," Monique said, shaking her head with chagrin. "Now please, let me pass." Once again, Monique tried to step past Khamil.

Again, he blocked her path. As Monique's dark brown eyes shot fire at him, Khamil quickly said, "All right. Maybe that was out of line."

"Yes, it was."

He stared at her a moment longer, wondering if he'd ever be able to crack the layer of ice around her. "I don't know how," he said softly, "but we've gotten off on the wrong foot."

"We haven't gotten off on *any* foot, Mr. Jordan."

"Ouch." But Khamil gave her another of his charming smiles, one that had always worked to ease tension with the opposite sex in the past.

Monique, however, seemed unaffected.

"And please," Khamil continued, wanting to keep the conversation going despite the chilly reception, "call me Khamil."

"Khamil, I have friends waiting for me."

Khamil's gaze followed a woman who brushed by him en route to the bathroom.

Monique guffawed. "Have a nice day."

"Wait." Khamil grabbed Monique's arm. "That's it? You're not going to allow me the chance to get to know you?"

"I've got an idea for you. Why not wait right here. When that woman you were just ogling comes out of the bathroom, you can see how far you get with her."

"Ogling?" Khamil looked at Monique as if she were crazy.

"She nearly bumped into me. I merely looked at her to make sure she had room to pass."

"Whatever."

This wasn't working. Monique was being so cold, Khamil was getting a serious case of frostbite. "I'm simply asking for a chance to get to know you. To let you see for yourself what kind of man I am."

"That's all?"

"Yes."

"Hmm."

"What?" Khamil sensed a sudden change in Monique's attitude, and when she slowly closed the distance between them, her eyes locked with his, he held his breath.

"All right." Boldly, Monique draped her arms around Khamil's shoulders, drawing his strong body to hers.

"Wh-what are you doing?" Khamil managed. One second he was cold, the next his body was on fire.

"This is what you want, isn't it?"

"I—I…I have no clue what you're talking about."

"Oh, come on. You see a woman you like, you pursue her in hopes of…well, in hopes of, you know. Sex." Monique raised a suggestive eyebrow, then slowly and deliberately, she placed a leg around Khamil. Khamil was powerless to do anything except stand there, powerless as she dragged her leg upward along his, stopping only when she reached his thigh.

Monique held Khamil's gaze, her dark eyes narrowed seductively. Khamil couldn't help it; his body reacted, instantly giving him a hard-on.

"Hmm?" Monique prompted. "Isn't sex what you want?"

"No. Yes. I mean no."

Monique cocked her head to the side and gave him a smug

look. "Isn't it? I know men like you, playboys, who live for having women fawn all over them." She paused. "So, what's the matter?"

What indeed? Normally, if a woman was offering Khamil what Monique was, he'd jump at the opportunity to bed her and walk away. Yet he felt flustered now. And while Monique had her arms around his neck, his arms still rested at his sides—definitely not like him!

And it wasn't simply where they were. It was not knowing how to accurately read Monique.

A slow smile formed on Monique's lips.

Khamil blew out a frustrated breath, then untangled himself from Monique's body. "No, that's not what I want."

"Really?" Monique sounded shocked.

Khamil looked away as he spoke. "Yes, really."

"Good." Monique straightened her clothes. "Because you're not going to get it. At least not from me. I'm not like other women, in case you haven't figured it out."

Khamil was too stunned to say a word.

Suddenly, Monique felt bad. She had no clue what possessed her to so brazenly come on to Khamil, only to let him down. Maybe because she'd met one too many guys like him over the years, especially since establishing herself as one of New York's hottest fashion models. But the bewildered look on Khamil's face, as well as the hint of embarrassment in his eyes, had her regretting what she'd done.

For the first time, Monique sensed a nice side to Khamil Jordan. Her shoulders drooped, the fight going out of her. "Khamil, I don't want to offend you, but I'm just not interested. You're not my type."

Khamil was still trying to make sense of whatever game

Monique was playing, and at Monique's last statement, he felt a painful little jolt in his chest. He didn't move or say a word, merely stared down at Monique, waiting for her to crack a smile—anything to let him know she was joking. But he received merely an unwavering, albeit somewhat contrite, look.

"I see," Khamil said tightly. He still didn't understand her, but now at least he'd gotten the point. She wasn't interested.

"Now, I really do have to get back to my friends."

Khamil gave a grim nod, then watched Monique turn around. He watched her stop midpivot, watched her body freeze. Instantly she spun back around. She hesitated only a second before marching toward him.

"Kiss me."

"What?"

Monique threw her arms around Khamil's shoulders. "Just—" Monique stopped herself short as she tipped on her toes and locked lips with his.

"Wait a…" Khamil mumbled against her velvety soft lips, but when Monique softly moaned and pressed her body closer to his, Khamil couldn't help reacting. He wrapped his arms around her, enjoying the feel of her curvaceous body in his arms. And when Monique parted her lips, he eagerly delved his tongue into her hot, sweet mouth.

While a moment ago he'd wondered what her game was, right now he didn't care. All he cared about was this beautiful woman, how sweet her lips tasted, how the delicate scent of her perfume was driving him wild. He wanted her, and he had the erection to prove it.

And as suddenly as it began, it ended.

Monique stepped away from Khamil and asked, "Is he still there?"

Khamil stared down at her as if she'd grown horns. "What on earth—"

"There was a guy behind me a moment ago." Monique spoke somewhat breathlessly, and knew she'd be lying to herself if she said it was because she'd seen Raymond unexpectedly. She hadn't expected Khamil to react to the kiss the way he had; she hadn't expected her own body to thrum with excitement.

She pushed the disturbing thought from her mind as she assessed Khamil's perplexed look. She may as well have been speaking Russian, considering how she wasn't getting through to him.

"There was a man," she repeated, her tone low. "African-American, around six feet tall, slim build. He was standing behind me a moment ago. Is he still there?"

A small scowl marred Khamil's handsome features as he looked past Monique. "I don't see anyone there now."

Monique's shoulders sagged with relief. "Good." She glanced over her shoulder to verify that Khamil was correct. There was no sign of Raymond. When she faced Khamil once more, she found dark, intense eyes boring into hers. He didn't speak, which unnerved her even more.

"I'll...uh...I'm going back now," she completed, gesturing a thumb over her shoulder to indicate she planned to head back into the restaurant's dining room.

Before she could move, Khamil darted a hand out, wrapping his strong fingers around her slim wrist. "You kiss me, then you plan to walk away without another word?"

"Well, I... Look, there was a guy behind me, someone I didn't want to see." She gave him a sheepish look. "I'm sorry I kissed you, but it was the only thing I could think of to do at the time, so he'd get the picture that I've moved on."

Khamil urged Monique closer, and she stumbled, falling against his thick chest. Her heart rate doubled, and she slowly raised her eyes until she met his look dead-on.

"Are you saying you kissed me to prove a point to someone else?" Khamil's tone sounded almost lethal.

"Yes," Monique said feebly, instantly hating how unsure of herself she sounded. "Yes," she repeated, firmly this time, even though she did glance away as she said the word.

But she couldn't look away for long. There was something about Khamil that was strangely compelling, even though she knew men like him and hated the type.

He raised an eyebrow as she met his gaze, a challenge sparking in his eyes. "So the kiss then…you didn't feel a thing."

Every nerve in Monique's body was on fire, yet she replied, "That's right. I didn't feel a thing."

"And when you wrapped your body around mine, that was just to show me how much you *didn't* want me?"

"Right again."

"Liar."

The word startled Monique, not so much because of what he said, but because of the intensity with which he'd said it. Because of how he'd neared his lips to a fraction of an inch from hers when he'd spoken. Because of how badly, at that moment, Monique had wanted to kiss him again.

This was wrong, all wrong. Why was she even thinking of the possibility of kissing him again? He wasn't her type, and she most certainly didn't want to get to know him.

Monique wrestled her arm from Khamil's grasp and took a step backward. "I'm leaving."

"Can't deal with your feelings?"

"Khamil, you're not my type."

"But you're still attracted to me."

"God, you have an ego the size of Mount Everest."

"I call 'em like I see 'em."

"Well, in this case you'd better get some glasses."

"Is that right?"

"That's right," Monique agreed, then spun around on her heel. She hurried away from Khamil, away from her confusing emotions, and back to the table where she'd left her friends.

"Hey," she said, taking her seat again.

"Hey?" Vicky gave her a disapproving look. "You disappeared forever with Mr. Hottie, and all you're gonna say is *hey?*"

"There's nothing to tell, Vicky," Monique quickly replied. "Except that I saw Raymond. Oh, no," she said as she looked around and saw him at the nearby bar. "I don't think I'm up for this tonight."

"Don't let him bother you."

Monique guffawed. "Yeah, right. Someone should tell him that." Monique had no doubt that he was there because he knew he could always find her there on Thursday nights. For someone who'd seemed so nice in the beginning, he certainly was acting like an obsessed idiot.

Monique pulled her purse strap over her shoulder and stood. "I'm gonna go."

"Oh, come on," Renee pleaded. "We'll make sure he doesn't bother you."

"I'm not in the mood to hang out anymore," Monique replied succinctly, then leaned over and kissed both Vicky and Renee on the cheek, then squeezed Janine's hand as she couldn't reach her for a peck. "Talk to you later."

She heard her friends mumbling about her as she turned to

leave, but couldn't make out what they were saying. Monique threw a surreptitious gaze in the direction of the bar. A wave of relief passed over her when she saw that Raymond was no longer there. In fact, she didn't see him anywhere. Still, she hastily made her way through the populated restaurant, heading to the front door.

"Monique."

She halted at the sound of Khamil's voice, as though his voice alone had the power to make her do anything he wanted.

"Monique," he repeated.

Slowly, she turned. Seeing him again was like seeing him for the first time; he literally took her breath away. Yes, he was fine. Too bad he was the type of brother who thought his good looks meant he was some type of god.

"Yes."

"You're leaving."

"Yes."

"So am I. I'll walk you out."

Monique didn't argue. And she didn't move away from Khamil's touch as he placed a hand on her back and guided her through the restaurant. As much as she told herself she didn't like him, there was something strangely comforting about his presence and his touch, especially right now when she was worried about where Raymond was.

Outside Khamil said, "Where do you live?"

Monique's eyes widened with alarm.

"I just meant, will you be okay getting home?"

"Oh. Yeah, I'll be fine. I live near Central Park. I'll catch a cab."

Khamil nodded, then looked at her, as though he wanted to say something else. Monique waited. When he didn't say anything, she spoke. "All right, then. Get home safe."

Monique turned before Khamil had the chance to say anything else. She hailed an oncoming cab, and within seconds she was inside, staring back at Khamil as the cab merged into traffic.

Chapter 5

Monique screamed when she stepped into her penthouse and turned on the light switch in the foyer.

"Raymond!" she exclaimed, clutching a hand to her heart. He was standing a few feet away from her, at the entrance to the living room. Until she'd turned on the light, he'd been standing there in the dark. Clearly, he'd planned to surprise her. "What in God's name—"

"I needed to see you," he said, walking toward her.

Monique stiffened her spine. "You gave me back the key. How did you get in here?"

"I made a copy," he admitted.

Monique wondered why he hadn't used it before now. Probably because he was giving her time to come to her senses and realize that she loved him, but considering she hadn't, he was now putting on the pressure. She'd have to tell the concierge that Raymond was no longer welcome in her home.

"Baby—"

"Don't call me that."

Raymond leaned against the wall and blew out a ragged breath. "You're right, I shouldn't have come here like this, and I'm sorry. I just needed to see you, and when you wouldn't return my calls…"

"There's nothing left for us to say, Raymond. I'm willing to be your friend, if for no other reason than I'll probably have to work with you again, but to be quite honest, you're making that very difficult right now."

"Who's the guy?"

"What guy?"

"The guy who had his tongue down your throat," Raymond snapped.

Monique kicked off her shoes and stepped past Raymond into the living room. "I want you to leave."

Instead of heading to the door, he was right on her heel, startling Monique. "You told me you were going to take some time and see what you wanted from our relationship."

"No, *you* told me that's what I should do. I told you it was over."

"Why?"

"Raymond, you cheated on me."

"And I'm sorry. It won't happen again."

"That's right, it won't. At least not with me." Monique paused. "Look, I think what happened shows that I just don't have time in my life right now for a relationship. Neither do you."

"This is about your mother."

Monique felt a stab of pain in her chest. She regretted ever telling Raymond about her mother's murder. Every time she felt down, he blamed it on that. When she couldn't forgive his affair, he blamed it on that. When she said she needed time away from him, he blamed it on that. He seemed to think that if he could make everything better in that regard, she would be his.

"This is about us," Monique responded slowly. "We're not right for each other."

"What if I could help you solve your mother's murder, would you give me another chance?"

Monique was momentarily startled by the question. She wondered what would possess Raymond to say such a thing. She asked him exactly that.

"What if I knew something, or knew someone who did?"

"Raymond, I don't have time for games."

"I want to help you, Monique, but if I'm going to give you something, you should be willing to give me something in return—another chance with you."

"Raymond, do you know something or not?"

He didn't answer, and his eyes said he expected her to agree to his terms before he'd tell her a thing.

Monique sneered at him. "Leave, Raymond. Now."

"Fine," he said, with a nonchalant shrug of his shoulders, one that said she'd made her choice and would have to live with the consequences.

Raymond had started toward the door when Monique said, "Give me the key."

He stopped, angrily fished the key out of his picket, then tossed it to her. It sailed past her, landing on the carpeted floor.

Monique didn't make a move for it, instead giving Raymond a lethal look that didn't match her inner trembling. She wasn't about to let him intimidate her.

Without another word, he turned.

Her body trembling from both anger and anxiety, Monique watched Raymond's slim form walk toward the door, then out of the condo. The moment he was gone, she ran to the door and bolted it shut.

Then she pressed her forehead and both palms against the door and rested there for several seconds.

What if he does know something? she asked herself.

He couldn't, she decided, heaving herself off the door. He would use anything to try and get her back, even the pain of her mother's murder. How low the man would stoop was beyond her.

If he cared so much about her before, then why had he cheated on her? Whatever the answer, Monique knew that this situation was too messed up for her to ever be dumb enough to give Raymond another chance.

How could she, when she didn't quite trust him?

A week after sharing that kiss with Monique, Khamil couldn't stop thinking about her.

He wasn't sure if it was because she had embarrassed him royally, but Khamil Jordan wasn't used to women playing him the way Monique had.

Maybe it was pride telling him he had to see her again and get one up on her. Play her and leave her feeling hot and bothered as she had done to him. But if he were to be honest with himself, he'd have to admit that his wanting to see her again had nothing to do with wanting to prove any such thing.

He wanted simply to see her again, and to know that this time he could have an effect on her.

Though he knew that he'd had *some* type of effect on her. She was either hot or cold with him, which meant she felt something. And he had watched her watching him as the cab had driven off. If he wasn't mistaken, he'd sensed a struggle within her as she'd looked at him. If not, why hadn't she simply looked away? She was attracted to him, despite that nonsense she'd said about him not being her type.

You didn't kiss someone the way she had kissed him and then say you felt nothing unless you were lying to yourself.

The phone rang, interrupting Khamil's thoughts. He hurried to answer it. "Hello?"

"Khamil."

"Hey, Javar!" Khamil exclaimed, elated to hear the voice of his elder brother by a year. "What's up, my man?"

"Just calling to see how things are going in your part of the world."

"Oh, same-old, same-old. Busy as usual."

"Take it from me, you need to slow down. I never listened to Whitney for years when she said I needed to take on a partner or two, but now that I have, I couldn't be happier."

Whitney was Javar's wife of seven years. The first two years they'd been blissfully happy, until a tragedy had torn them apart. Whitney had been driving her car with Javar's son, J.J.— her stepson—and had gotten into an accident. Unfortunately, the accident had killed five-year-old J.J.

At first, Javar had seemed incapable of forgiving Whitney for the accident, but he'd really been so consumed with grief that he hadn't known how to deal with it. Whitney had been torn up over the whole incident herself, living with a great deal of guilt. Although the roads were wet at the time, she still blamed herself for the accident. She'd needed Javar's love and support, and he hadn't been able to give it. Ultimately, she'd left him and gone to live with an aunt in Louisiana.

Two years later, she had returned to Chicago, where Khamil and his family had grown up, to seek a divorce. And when she'd ended up in another car accident that landed her in the hospital with life-threatening injuries, Javar had realized how much he still loved her and didn't want to lose her. Khamil had always liked Whitney, from the night he and his brother had met her in a Chicago club and his brother had fallen head over heels for her. Unlike his mother and sister, who wanted Whitney out of Javar's life, he had hoped they would work out their problems.

To this day, Khamil still had trouble dealing with the reality of just how badly his mother hadn't wanted Whitney in Javar's life. His own mother had tried to kill her, but luckily Javar had gotten to Whitney in time. But the worst part was learning that his mother had sabotaged Whitney's car, which had resulted in her not being able to control it on the rain-slicked roads as she'd driven with little J.J. It was his mother's fault that his nephew had been tragically killed.

Now, she was spending the next several years in prison.

But at least Javar and Whitney had worked out their problems and were once again happy.

"Khamil?"

"Huh?" he asked, realizing his mind had drifted.

"I asked, are you too busy to see your brother? I'm coming to town next week."

A smile spread on Khamil's face. "Of course I'm not too busy for you!" He didn't see his brother, nor the rest of his family, as often as he liked these days.

"Whitney was going to come, as we have a surprise for you, but she won't be able to make it now."

"A surprise? What, are you trying to set me up with one of her friends?"

"Hey, she knows better than to sic you on any of her friends."

"I resent that."

Javar chuckled. "Whatever."

"Then what kind of surprise?"

"She's pregnant again."

"All right!" Khamil couldn't help shouting. Then, he felt an odd moment of emptiness. These days, it felt as if he was living vicariously through his brother's life. Hearing this good news reminded him that he had yet to find the perfect woman, the one he would settle down and start a family with.

Once again, Monique popped into his mind, but Khamil did his best to block her out. She was definitely not wife material. Not that she wasn't beautiful enough, but any woman he would marry would have to like him first.

"Yeah, Whitney's almost six months along, but recently started cramping. We were worried she was going into premature labor, but she wasn't."

"Oh, no."

"No, everything's fine. The doctor just said she ought to take it easy, so she's gonna skip this trip."

"Wait a minute…did you say six months?"

"Uh-huh."

"And you're just telling me *now?*"

"Like I said, Whitney wanted to surprise you, but now that she can't…" Javar's voice trailed off.

"How are Reanna and Marcus?"

"Great." Javar paused. "Nothing will ever take the place of J.J., but I feel like I've been give a second chance to do things right. With J.J., I didn't make time to do things with him the way a father should, because I was always too concerned about providing for my family. Then, I lost him and couldn't make up for the years of misspent energy. Now, I'm definitely not making that mistake and I'm having a blast being a husband and father."

A smile touched Khamil's lips. "I'm glad to hear it, bro. You deserve it."

"My next wish is to see you settle down," Javar said, a smile in his voice.

"When—"

"—the right woman comes along. I'll be more than happy to settle down," Javar finished for Khamil, indicating just how many times he'd heard him say that.

Khamil chuckled. "Mock me all you want, it's the truth."

"I'll believe it when I see it."

Having spoken to his brother, Khamil couldn't concentrate on work. He was excited for Javar and Whitney, but once again, that empty feeling was back.

He wasn't exactly sure why that empty feeling had him thinking of Monique, but he did know that he needed to see her. According to his colleague, Monique and her model friends always went to Angel's on Thursday nights, and since it was Thursday...

He hadn't eaten yet, and the food was good there. He liked the ambience.

And hey, it was a free country.

Within the hour, Khamil was showered, dressed, and walking through the door of Angel's.

The host immediately greeted him. "Table for one?"

"I'm meeting someone," Khamil replied, looking past the young man into the restaurant. He glanced in the direction of the table where he'd found Monique the first time. Seeing Vicky, he smiled.

But the smile slowly disappeared as he headed toward the table and didn't see Monique. He felt a sense of disappointment, something he wasn't used to feeling. An instant later, he realized she was most likely in the bathroom, and joy lifted his heart once again.

Vicky gave him a bright smile as she looked up and saw him. "Khamil!"

She jumped out of her seat and wrapped him in a hug. The way she greeted him, you'd think she'd known him for years.

Khamil politely moved back, placing a chaste kiss on Vicky's cheek. He recognized her actions for what they were—an advance. She was letting him know in no uncertain terms that she wanted him. He was flattered, but also a little annoyed. Vicky was Monique's friend, and had to know that he was interested in her. Did Vicky's advances mean that Monique had told Vicky she had no interest in Khamil whatsoever, and that he was up for grabs?

"Where's Monique?" he asked.

Vicky's smile flattened. "Oh, Monique couldn't make it tonight."

"Really?" The disappointment was back, like a kick in the gut.

"Yeah, she had something to do. Personal business," she added with a little shrug.

"Hmm." Khamil was tempted to ask exactly how personal her businesses was, but didn't. He didn't have a right. Just as he didn't have a right to feel a pang of jealousy, yet he did. The way Vicky spoke made it sound as if Monique was out with a man. Was it the guy she'd tried to avoid when she had kissed him here in this restaurant, just last week?

"Feel free to join us, if you like."

Vicky's voice interrupted Khamil's thoughts. He looked down at the two other women at the table, knowing that it would be any man's fantasy to spend the evening with three gorgeous models, yet he said, "No thanks, I just came by to see Monique. I...I had to give her something."

"I can give it to her, if you like," Vicky offered.

Khamil shook his head. "Naw, that's okay. I'd rather give it to her when I see her." Of course, he was lying and wouldn't be able to produce anything worthy of passing along to Monique if his life depended on it. But Vicky didn't need to know that. "Just tell her I was looking for her, if she happens to come in."

"Sure," Vicky said.

Khamil gave a smile and nod to the other women at the table, who looked up at him sly grins. A faint voice in his head asked if he was nuts to walk away from these women.

No, he wasn't nuts. Monique was the one he was interested in, and he didn't want to confuse any of them, especially Vicky, by spending time with them if Monique wasn't around.

Still, as Khamil headed for the front door of the restaurant, he wondered when he had changed so drastically.

Chapter 6

When Monique finally arrived home, she went straight to her bedroom and collapsed on her king-size bed, letting out a loud moan as she did. The day's events had drained her. She'd done a catalogue shoot for lingerie and swimwear, which made for a long day as it was, but the day had been even longer as she'd been accompanied by a camera crew from *America's Most Wanted* on the shoot. The camera crew had captured film of her in her work environment for the show, and after that she'd done an interview about her mother's murder.

She was pleased with how it all went, even though the subject of her mother's murder had naturally brought her down. Hopefully, the airing of this story on national television would reach someone who knew something about the case, enabling the killer to be caught once and for all.

Monique rolled onto her back, resting her forearm across her forehead. She contemplated calling her father. She hadn't talked to him about the fact that the police were reopening her mother's murder investigation.

Part of her was afraid. She knew, based on past experience when dealing with her father about this subject, that he wouldn't be happy about it. That was the one thing that gave her pause on those very few occasions that she allowed herself to wonder if her father could possibly have had anything to do with her mother's death. But as quickly as that disturbing thought came into her mind, it fled. She suspected that her father's seeming indifference to whether or not her mother's killer was ever brought to justice had to do with the fact that he didn't trust the police to be able to do so.

After all, they had wasted two years trying to pin the crime on him. With only circumstantial evidence, they'd ultimately been unable to prove her father guilty of anything other than being perhaps a little intimidated by his wife's success.

She had deliberately avoided calling her father about this issue, but she would have to tell him what was happening before the show aired.

Sitting up, Monique stretched, then reached for the phone on her night table. She was caught off guard when she realized there was no dial tone.

"Hello…" a voice on the other line said.

"Vicky?" Monique asked.

"Yep."

"Oh. The phone didn't ring." She sat up. "What's up?"

"Nothing much. I was calling to see how things went today."

"Very well, I think," Monique responded. "I got to meet John Walsh," she added, her tone upbeat.

"Ah, so you did."

"Yep. He's really a sweetheart, made me feel very comfortable right from the beginning. It's obvious he really cares about the victims of crime and their families."

"I never watch the show."

"I do." Monique paused. "You never know, psychos may be walking among us, living next door, working with us." Her tone was lighthearted, but she was completely serious. And she was hoping that other people like her, people interested in justice, would watch the show and remember that muggy summer night sixteen years ago in Barrie.

"So what did you talk about?" Vicky asked. "For the interview, that is."

"He asked me how my mother's murder had affected my life—that sort of thing. Then we spoke about the fact that my mother had been harassed by a stalker before her death, and given that fact, why had I decided to follow in her career path." It was the very same question her father had asked her. "I told him I'd do anything to find my mother's killer."

"Hmm," was all Vicky said.

"They'll be heading to Canada next to interview the detectives working on this case. In fact, the entire episode is going to focus on Canadian crimes."

"And when will it air?"

"Next week." Monique paused, then asked, "How was it tonight?"

"The usual," Vicky replied casually. Then, "Oh, guess who dropped by?"

Monique's stomach instantly fluttered, though she didn't know why. "Who?" she asked, though she had a sneaking suspicion who Vicky was talking about.

"Khamil," her friend practically sang.

"Khamil?" Monique's voice was barely above a whisper as the butterflies went wild in her stomach.

"Mmm-hmm. He came by tonight."

Vicky had a flair for the dramatic, often making Monique pull information out of her. As much as Monique wanted to pretend that Khamil's showing up was of no interest to her, that was a lie. "So," she began after a moment. "What did he want?"

"He came by to hang out."

"Oh." Monique was disappointed. "So he stayed a while."

"A little while."

Well, there went any fantasy that he may have shown up to see her. Which, to Monique's chagrin, she realized mattered. The fact irked her, because she didn't want to give Khamil even a second thought.

"Tell me something," Vicky began. "Do you…well, are you interested in Khamil?"

"Why?" Monique asked quickly. Too late, she realized she may have sounded a tad defensive. But she couldn't help wondering why it should matter to Vicky if she was or wasn't interested in Khamil.

"I'm just wondering," Vicky replied casually. "He is fine. And…" Vicky's voice trailed off. "Well, he said he had something for you, so I was wondering if you're holding out on me or something."

"He had something for me?" Monique couldn't hide her shock. "What?"

"He didn't say. He just said he'd give it to you another time."

"Really?" Monique's mind worked overtime, trying to figure out exactly what Khamil could have had for her. And she also tried to figure out if Vicky was interested in making a play for Khamil. She wasn't sure.

"Really."

"I have no idea what it could be," Monique admitted. "But I'll call him. Thanks."

"So you have his number."

"Yeah, I do." Monique didn't offer any more explanation than that. "Anyway, hon, I'm exhausted, and I have to call my father."

"And Khamil." Vicky giggled. "Listen girl, I want all the details, you hear?"

Monique gave a little chuckle. "Sure. Talk to you later."

"Bye."

When Monique hung up, she stared at the phone, thinking she should call her father. But her curiosity over Khamil's visit got the better of her, and she decided to call him.

The card he'd given her with his number on it was in her wallet, so Monique reached for her purse on the floor beside her bed, withdrew the wallet, then searched for Khamil's card. Once she found it, her heart did an erratic pitter-patter in her chest.

Why was she so nervous? She was an adult. She could call him and be professional. Who knew what he had to give her?

Before she lost her courage, she punched in the digits to his home number.

He answered after the first ring. "Hello?"

Monique paused, then sucked in a nervous breath. She didn't realize she'd paused too long until Khamil spoke one more time.

"Uh, hi. Khamil?"

"Yes?"

"Hi." Monique forced a smile into her voice. "This is Monique Savard."

"Monique. To what do I owe this honor?"

"I heard you were at Angel's today."

"Yes, I was."

Monique waited, but Khamil didn't offer any further explanation. Maybe he hadn't stopped by to see her. Maybe he'd stopped by to see Vicky, and that's why Vicky had called to ask her about the nature of her relationship with Khamil.

"I was hoping to see you," Khamil said after a moment.

Monique felt a strange tingling in her arms, chest, and stomach. Excitement, she realized. Lord help her, she couldn't believe she was actually excited to hear that Khamil *had* gone to the restaurant to see her.

How long could she lie to herself and say she wasn't the least bit interested in Khamil? It was obvious. The mere sound of his deep, seductive voice made her head spin. And she had to admit she'd been insecure that he wasn't interested, and perhaps interested in Vicky, until he'd said the words she'd wanted to hear.

Her old insecurities from her relationship with Raymond had reared. Just because Raymond had played her didn't mean Khamil would.

"Monique?"

"Sorry," she quickly said, realizing she'd been lost in her own thoughts.

"It's probably none of my business, but Vicky said you had personal business to attend to..." Khamil's voice trailed.

"Yeah."

There was a pause; then Khamil asked, "Anything you want to talk about?"

"Not really."

"Oh." Disappointment stabbed him, like a knife in the heart. Which surprised him. It was a feeling he hadn't experienced in ages, since Dawn. Almost as if he were...jealous.

Yeah, he was jealous. Why else would Monique not want to say anything about what she'd done, unless that *personal* business had to do with a man?

Maybe Khamil was blowing the situation out of proportion, because in reality, she didn't owe him any explanation about what she did and didn't do in her life. Still, he couldn't shake the uneasy feeling in his gut.

"Vicky said you had something for me," Monique said after what seemed like ages.

"Uh…" Khamil didn't know what to say. Of course, he hadn't had a thing for Monique. That had simply been an excuse to drop by. Why couldn't he simply tell her that he wanted to take her out to dinner sometime?

Because he'd already told her he was interested, and she'd rebuffed him in a grand way.

But that kiss…

Meant to prove a point to some other guy. The last thing he had time for was a woman who was hung up on someone else.

"I was in the area and I had tickets for the theater tonight," Khamil lied. "So I figured I'd ask you. No big deal."

"I see," Monique said, but she didn't. Once again, she was feeling insecure. Khamil's tone now was aloof, and she wasn't sure if he was actually interested or not. "You could have asked Vicky."

"I would have, but I decided not to bother going. It was a spur-of-the-moment decision to even go, since I'm so busy with work and rarely take any time for myself. So, since you weren't there… Like I said, no big deal."

A lump of emotion formed in Monique's throat. Why she'd even bothered to allow herself the small fantasy that Khamil was interested in her beyond a physical attraction, she didn't know.

She remembered this feeling of disappointment well. It was further proof that she didn't have time in her life for a man and all the ups and downs that came with having one.

"Well," she announced, "I just figured I'd call to see what you wanted. Now I know." Pause. "I'll let you go."

Khamil didn't say anything right away, making Monique wonder if he wanted to say something else. *Silly,* she chided herself. Khamil was the kind of man who said what was on his mind. As she'd suspected, he'd been interested initially, but a player like him had already moved on to a new flavor.

"Okay, then," Khamil said. "Good night."

"Good night," Monique replied in a clipped tone. Then she quickly hung up, telling herself over and over that Khamil's lack of interest in her didn't matter.

Chapter 7

"*America's Most Wanted?* What the hell were you thinking?"

"Calm down, Daniel," Monique said. She looked from him to his sister, then to her aunt. She was at their Bronx home this evening for dinner.

"I don't see how this is going to help at all," Daniel continued. "You're a high-profile model. The only response you'll get is from nutcases who want attention, and they'll give the police all sorts of bogus leads."

Monique loved her cousin, but for as long as she'd known him, he'd always been a brooding man, one to see the negative before ever seeing the positive.

"He could be right," Doreen said.

"I don't think so," Monique countered. "The police are well trained in sifting through legitimate leads and bogus ones." She looked at Daniel, Doreen, and her aunt Sophie in turn. "Besides, this is great exposure. Yes, I'm a successful model, but that's the reason they want to feature this story. Because my mother was a successful model, murdered in her prime, and now I'm continuing her legacy. That's the kind of thing that interests people."

Aunt Sophie said, "A couple of years ago when that magazine featured your story, nothing came of that."

"Who knows who read that magazine? This show will reach a much broader audience—across the border as well where the crime actually happened. I have to hope someone who knows something will be watching the show when it airs."

"Your mother has been dead for sixteen years," Daniel suddenly said. "Yes, I'm sorry it happened, I'm sorry her killer was never brought to justice. But what good is it going to do to reopen the investigation now?"

Monique looked at her cousin point-blank, disappointed. "For one thing, it wasn't my decision to reopen the case. The police chose to do that. But I'm damn glad they're doing it, because my mother's killer has gone without justice for way too long." Again, she glanced at each of her relatives. "I thought you'd all understand that."

"I think," Aunt Sophie began, "Daniel is simply trying to say that this will all bring so much pain with it…and there's been enough pain. Sometimes, we just don't get the closure we want and need. But life has to go on."

"And if the opportunity arises for another chance to catch my mother's killer, why shouldn't I be glad?"

Aunt Sophie merely glanced at her food, then shrugged. No one was eating much of their dinner. "What does your father say?" she asked after a moment.

"I haven't told him yet," Monique confessed.

"Don't you think he should have a say in all this?" Daniel challenged.

"I'm not exactly sure why you're so against this, Daniel." Monique's tone was brusque, but she was most definitely annoyed now. "I'm the one who's going to be in the spotlight, if anything. The most the police will ask of you is to give them your account of what happened that night. How's that going to hurt you?"

"God," Daniel snapped, then pushed his chair back. "Why can't you just leave well enough alone?" He glared at her for a brief second before storming from the dining room.

Monique stared after him, both baffled and hurt.

Doreen gave a little shrug. "Don't mind him, Monique. He's got other things on his mind. He's really stressed at work. And he and Charlene are having problems—again."

"Mmm-hmm," Monique said, though Doreen's explanation for her brother's rude behavior didn't make her feel any better. She looked down at her plate, her piece of lasagna hardly eaten. No longer hungry, she pushed the plate away.

"Well, like I told you before, the show's gonna air tonight," Monique said. "I'm sorry I didn't tell you before now, but please understand this is something I had to do." She'd left a message for her father about the show, but he hadn't gotten back to her. She hoped he understood, too. Sometimes, it seemed she was the only one in her family who cared about getting justice in this case.

"And let's pray that this time," Monique added, "there are some results."

"Not tonight," Khamil told Macy.

"Oh." He could hear a frown in Macy's voice. "Maybe tomorrow, then?"

"Maybe," Khamil replied. He already had the remote in his hands and was flipping through the television stations until he got to the one he wanted.

"Listen, Macy, you know I'm gonna have to call you back. It's almost nine o'clock."

"Ah, that's right." Macy *tsk*ed. "You and that show."

"Yeah, me and that show. It's the one show I must see every week, as you know. So, I'll talk to you later, okay?"

Macy replied by making a frustrated sound and hanging up. *Oh well,* Khamil thought as he replaced the receiver. He didn't care. She must have thought he wouldn't reject her for a TV show, but such was life. Besides, he wasn't interested in hanging out tonight, plain and simple, and definitely not with Macy. Like the other women who'd come into his life, she had been fun for a while, but there was nothing special about her, and he didn't want to lead her on by spending more time with her if he wasn't truly interested.

He had friends who would continue to see women for companionship and sex, all the while knowing they had no plans for a future with them. Those same friends would come to Khamil for advice when the particular woman they were seeing gave them stress about wanting to settle down. In the end, there was unnecessary heartache, all of which could have been prevented if the men had just been open and honest about their feelings, and stopped seeing whatever woman when he realized there wasn't a future in the relationship.

Khamil found the station he was looking for, then settled into his sofa to prepare for the beginning of the show. *America's Most Wanted* was must-see TV for him, and he didn't like to miss it unless there was some type of emergency.

It wasn't morbid fascination with crime; in fact, Khamil always hoped he'd be able to recognize someone wanted for a heinous crime. He was a firm believer in right and wrong, at least where the law was concerned. If you do the crime, you do the time, was his favorite motto, and no one could accuse him of playing favorites. Three years ago, his mother had been convicted of attempted murder and involuntary manslaughter, and while he loved her, he knew she had to face justice the same way anyone else should. He also believed in forgiveness, and knew that people could change—only if they wanted to. Unfortunately, his mother continued to justify her actions—attempted murder as a way to protect her son from a woman she believed was a gold digger. His sister-in-law, Whitney, was so far from the calculating manipulative user his mother had made her out to be, and Khamil hoped one day his mother would finally see that.

Khamil watched the show, both horrified by the scope of the crimes and intrigued by just what made some people choose that path. Perhaps he was still trying to find answers for his mother's own bizarre behavior. While he knew his mother had been worried about Javar being taken advantage of, it was one thing to be a concerned parent, and quite another to take the step she had.

"Up next," the host said, *"a young girl finds her dying mother. It was too late for her to help her mother then, but maybe we can help her daughter get justice now."*

And then, to Khamil's utter shock, he saw Monique's face on the screen.

"It's a nightmare that haunts me every day," Monique said.

Then the show went to a commercial.

Khamil had been about to get up and get a soft drink, but now he remained rooted to the spot on his leather sofa, waiting for the commercials to end. Had he been imagining things, or had that actually been Monique Savard on the television?

It seemed like ages before the show returned, and as John Walsh began to speak about a young girl whose mother had been murdered sixteen years ago, Khamil's heart beat double time. The still pictures that flashed across the screen were of a woman who had to be Monique's mother. She looked so much like her, the two could pass for twins.

"But Julia Savard's career ended in the early morning hours of July 17, 1985, when someone brutally stabbed this successful model, mother and wife, leaving her to die." The pictures changed from beautiful shots of Julia Savard to quick pictures of a body lying on a bedroom floor, accompanied by sinister-sounding music. *"Hearing her mother's faint cries, Monique Savard rushed into her mother's bedroom and found her bleeding from multiple stab wounds."*

The scene went to a shot of Monique sitting on a chair, behind which were pictures of her mother and of her, in casual as well as professional poses. *"I still remember thinking that I must have been dreaming,"* Monique said. *"I remember walking into my mother's room and thinking I must have been having a nightmare. Well, it was a nightmare. It's a nightmare that haunts me every day."* Monique dabbed at her eyes, wiping a stray tear that had fallen. *"I keep wondering what would have happened if I'd gotten to my mother a moment sooner. Would she still be alive?"* Monique lowered her head as her voice cracked.

"Monique was young at the time of the murder, only fourteen years old," John Walsh said. *"She remembers hearing a car squealing off in the night, but as she hurried to call 911, she never managed to look outside.*

"Now, Monique has followed in the footsteps of her mother, and is a successful model in New York." The background music was now upbeat, as Monique was portrayed during some type of photo shoot.

"She knows her mother was stalked by an obsessed fan, but that doesn't scare her."

"I want to keep my mother's legacy alive," Monique said, the camera once again showing her sitting on a chair. *"I can't let the person who snuffed out her life snuff out her spirit. By doing*

what I'm doing, I'm honoring my mother. And if there's an element of danger, that doesn't scare me. All I care about is finding my mother's killer."

The screen went back to John Walsh, who was standing on a dark street somewhere in the city of Toronto. *"Monique and her family have had no answers in sixteen years, and they need them. Julia's husband, Lucas Savard, was initially considered a suspect in this heinous crime, but no charges were officially filed against him. It's been sixteen years too long that a killer has been able to walk the streets, unpunished. The Savard family will only have closure when Julia's killer is brought to justice.*

"There aren't a lot of clues in this case, but we've solved tougher cases than this one, and I know someone out there knows something. Don't be afraid to make that call. Now, on to our next case…"

Khamil let out a long swoosh of air once the segment featuring Monique was over, unaware that he'd even been holding his breath. Whoa, whoa, whoa! Monique Savard's mother had been murdered?

A million thoughts were going through Khamil's mind. How had he not known? That wasn't a rational thought, of course, because how *could* he have known? He and Monique weren't friends; in fact, they had barely spoken. It certainly didn't make sense that the first thing she'd say to him was, "Hi, my name's Monique. My mother was murdered sixteen years ago."

Besides shock and compassion, the other emotion Khamil felt was a sudden and intense burst of fear. Was she okay? If a stalker had harassed her mother, one could surely harass her. And if she lived alone in New York City… Khamil didn't want to entertain the possibility of how at risk she may be, given her high-profile career.

Wow. Monique's mother had been murdered. One would never tell to look at her, but then no one would know from looking at him that his mother was serving time in prison. While some people thought him shallow, namely because he was still single at thirty-eight and had had his share of women, he was far deeper than most people realized. He had the capacity to give love, the capacity to care. And he'd always empathized with victims of crime, understanding their pain and frustration in a way that even he didn't comprehend.

Now, knowing the truth about Monique's past, he felt a strange pang in his heart. Having watched Monique on the show, having seen her moved to tears as she recounted the night of her mother's murder, he couldn't help but feel pain on her behalf.

And, Lord help him, he felt like an inconsiderate fool.

She'd accused him of being a stalker, something he had laughed off at the time because he'd assumed she was simply playing hard to get, or at worst, giving him the cold shoulder. Now he knew her words had a deeper meaning. Maybe he *had* scared her by coming on too strong. And even if he hadn't actually scared her, he'd no doubt reminded her of what had happened to her mother.

Khamil slapped a palm against his forehead. What should he do? Apologize to her? He hadn't meant any harm by his actions, and he wanted her to know that.

But more than an apology, Khamil wanted to be there for her. If there was anything he could do to help her, he would.

Chapter 8

Days after the airing of her mother's story on *America's Most Wanted,* several tips had come in, but none were promising. Still, police investigators in New York and Toronto were looking into the various leads.

"It's going to take time," the detective from the Ontario Provincial Police had told Monique earlier today.

She understood that, but still, she was impatient. The longer it took, the less chance there was of the crime being solved. And she'd already been waiting for sixteen years.

"Afternoon, Harry," Monique said to the doorman as he entered her building, but she wasn't her cheerful self. Maybe she'd put too much hope in this television show being able to reach someone who'd miraculously know something about her mother's death.

"Good afternoon, Ms. Savard," Harry responded, smiling brightly as usual. "Away in some exotic locale again?"

"I guess so, if you call Los Angeles exotic." She'd left bright and early Sunday morning, right after the airing of *America's Most Wanted* the previous Saturday night.

"Palm trees…" Harry smiled, making his middle-aged face light up with the excitement of a young boy's. "I'd call that exotic."

"Don't forget the smog," Monique joked.

"That's why I'm moving to Florida when I retire. Plus, it's a lot less expensive."

"True," Monique agreed.

As she stepped past Harry, he turned and said, "There's a package for you in the office."

"Thank you, Harry."

"My pleasure. Glad to have you back."

Couriered packages often arrived for her, and because she was busy, they were left in the office when she wasn't at home to personally receive them. Stepping into the lobby, Monique first went to her mailbox, where she retrieved a handful of mail. There were a couple of flyers, which she discarded in the nearby trashcan. And a couple of bills.

Next, she went to the apartment's office, where she picked up the package that had been sent for her. One look at it and she knew it was from her agency. No doubt, this package held the new contract for the runway show she would do in France next month.

Walking back to the lobby, Monique slipped a finger beneath the envelope's tab, opening the flap as she headed to the elevator. Absently, she pressed the elevator's up button.

She glanced inside the envelope. Yep, it looked like a contract. But there was something else that caught her eye.

Inside the package was also a mauve envelope. Puzzled, Monique reached for it and pulled it out. It immediately struck her as odd, because it looked as though it held a card, and her agent wasn't prone to sending cards with contracts.

It was a card, she realized, just at the elevator door opened. A young couple stepped off, and Monique entered, then hit the button for the penthouse floor.

A Post-It note was stuck to the envelope, on which Elaine Cox had written *This came for you. No return address.*

It wasn't unusual for Monique to receive fan mail from her agency, but usually there were several pieces instead of one.

As the elevator ascended, Monique opened the envelope and withdrew the card. It had a floral picture on the front and the words *I'm thinking of you.*

Monique opened the card.

Instantly, her heart went into overdrive. Panic seized every nerve in her body.

Inside was written *Just the way I thought of your mother.*

Frantically, Monique searched the envelope again, knowing it would yield no clue as to where it had come from. But what did it mean? Clearly, someone was trying to taunt her—but why? And who?

The person who had stalked her mother?

Monique didn't realize the elevator door had opened until it started to close. Quickly, she jumped out and onto her floor. Then she looked both right and left down the hallway, a chill sweeping over her.

Her mother had received numerous cards and letters from some deranged psycho before her death, those letters also going to her agent.

But there was nothing overtly sinister about this card, nor its contents. Still, she couldn't help feeling creepy.

Monique hurried down the hallway to her door, then opened it as fast as she could and rushed inside. Was Daniel right—was she asking for more trouble in her life than she could handle, all because she was obsessed with finding her mother's killer?

Or was this letter from someone who had seen *America's Most Wanted,* and simply wanted to let her know she was in this person's thoughts? Not everyone was articulate and expressed exactly what they meant.

Still, as Monique locked and bolted her door, she almost heard the bubble bursting around the illusion of her safety.

Her mother hadn't been safe from the person who had wanted to hurt her. Why had she ever believed she would be?

The sound of the ringing telephone instantly woke Monique, making her wonder when she'd drifted off to sleep. Straightening herself on her plush sofa, she reached for the phone on the adjacent end table. "Hello?"

"Monique."

"Dad!" Monique exclaimed, elated to finally hear her father's voice. "Where have you been? I've left several messages for you."

"I could ask you the same thing."

"I've been out of town for a few days," Monique replied. She'd tried calling her father while away on business, but realized she hadn't called home to check her messages. "I was in Los Angeles shooting a commercial. I tried calling you while I was away."

"You know I don't like answering my phone unless I know who's calling. If the ID box doesn't say, I don't pick up."

"Yeah, I know." Not answering the phone was a habit her father had begun in the months after his wife's death, as all the calls were either from reporters or police telling him not to leave town. Now, even though that had all happened years ago, he hadn't gotten out of the habit. Which saddened Monique. He'd closed himself off from most of the world, as surely as if a big piece of him had died the night his wife had.

"So," Monique said, "how are you?"

"I'm still hanging in," he replied. "But what I'm really curious about is that message you left me. The police are re-opening your mother's murder case?"

"Yes." Unable to reach her father now, Monique had left him minimal details. Now, she filled him in on everything.

"I saw the show," he told her.

"You did?" Monique asked. "I thought maybe you were away, since you didn't answer your phone, and you didn't get back to me that night."

"No. I got your message all right."

"But you were upset with me," Monique said.

"A little, I guess."

"Dad, I know I should have told you about all this before any of it happened, but… Well, I was afraid of what you'd say. I know how much you want to put all this behind you, but the truth is, I can't. I have to do everything I can to see Mom's killer brought to justice."

Her father let out a long, sad sigh. "Oh, sweetie. You're so young, so full of hope. I wish I could believe that after all this time there could finally be an answer, but I don't trust the police. You know that, and you know why."

She did know why; her father had gone through hell as the prime suspect. Even now, his name hadn't officially been cleared. Still, there were many ways a crime could be solved, including wit-nesses coming forward after several years. She told her father that.

"We'll see, sweetie."

"Dad, this isn't only for Mom. This is for you, too. To clear your name."

"Which is why I can't be mad with you about not telling me sooner. I know you always have the best intentions. But I'm just so tired of it all."

And he'd stopped living because of it. He'd stopped fighting for justice, because clearing his own name had required so much of him, and still he hadn't been able to successfully do that.

"Well, the police may want to question you again, depending on how the investigation goes."

"I told them all I had to tell them for two years," her father said defensively. "I ain't gonna tell them no more."

"Dad..."

"I'm serious, Monique. Look, you do what you have to do, and I'm gonna do what I have to do. I've had enough stress to last ten lifetimes."

"I know it hasn't been easy—"

"There's nothing I can tell the police that they don't already know. And I don't want them to consider me a suspect again, whenever they get good and ready." He paused. "You didn't tell them where I am, did you?"

"No, but—"

"Good. Then please, promise me you won't."

Monique hesitated. "Dad, they never charged you with Mom's murder before. I doubt they will now."

"They think because we used to argue a lot, that means I killed her," Lucas Savard said, almost as if he was speaking to himself. "No, I won't allow myself to be the victim of another witch-hunt."

"Dad, what if they *need* to talk to you?"

"Promise me, Monique. Promise me you won't tell them how to reach me."

For a moment, Monique remembered what Doreen had said, that she was naive to not even consider the possibility that her father had killed her mother. Was she naive? Did her father have something to hide?

"You know the police can find you if they need to."

"If that's the case, then so be it. But you don't tell them where I am. You hear?"

Monique didn't answer.

"Promise me, Monique. I can't go through this again, all for another disappointment."

Monique exhaled a weary breath. "All right, Dad. I promise you."

As Monique hung up, she had an uneasy feeling in her gut. Did her father simply want to be left alone because he'd endured so much, or did he in fact have something to hide?

The question of her father's guilt or innocence bothered Monique long after she hung up the phone. Until now, she'd always been convinced of her father's innocence. Not that she wasn't anymore…she just wasn't sure.

The thought of her father, a man she loved and admired, killing her mother was too much to bear. And she had to ask herself if her resistance to even considering him a suspect was due to an inability to believe that someone she loved so much could do something so horrible.

Monique paced the floor in her penthouse suite, moving to peer through the blinds. Below, she saw people strolling, walking their dogs, and jogging through Central Park. She'd always felt safe here, but it seemed everything she once believed about her life was shattering like glass around her.

Groaning, she pivoted on her heel, marching back into the living room. She wouldn't do this anymore. If her father had killed her mother, she would *know* it. She'd have to.

Her mind drifted to the card she'd received, and her shoulders drooped with relief. Of course her father hadn't killed her mother. Her theory had always been that her mother's stalker had committed the crime.

Her moment of relief dissipated as the reality of her thoughts hit her full force. If it was a stalker, then that stalker could still be out there. He could be the one who'd sent her the card. And if he'd sent her the card...

Monique dropped herself onto the sofa, then buried her face in her hands. She'd been planning to head out tonight, to meet her friends at Angel's, but what if someone truly wanted to hurt her? What if someone knew her routine?

What she needed was a distraction, something else to think about, before paranoia got the better of her. Picking up the telephone's receiver, she decided to check for messages.

"Monique." Her heart instantly fluttered at the sound of Khamil's deep, sexy voice. "This is Khamil. I just saw *America's Most Wanted,* and figured I'd give you a call. I...I had no clue. Call me when you can."

There were a total of three messages from Khamil, all in which he called to see how she was doing and asked her to call him. The fact that he cared enough to call after seeing the show touched her heart. Perhaps because her own family members didn't seem to support or understand her quest for justice, it was refreshing to hear from someone who cared enough for her to talk about it.

Monique found Khamil's number, then lifted the receiver and dialed the phone. She was about to hang up when she heard Khamil answer the phone.

"Hello?"

Monique swallowed, then said, "Hi."

"Monique?"

"Yeah," she answered softly.

"I saw the show," Khamil said before she had a chance to say anything else. "I'm sorry."

"Thanks," Monique replied.

Khamil wanted to ask why she hadn't told him, though he knew why. They were barely getting to know each other. So he said, "If there's anything I can do to help, let me know."

"I appreciate that."

"You want to talk about it?"

Monique blew out a weary sigh. "There's not much more to tell other than what you saw. My mother was murdered sixteen years ago and the killer has never been apprehended."

"But the police are reopening the case?"

"Yes. I'm not sure why, but I can only pray that this time, the killer is caught."

There was a pause; then Khamil said, "I must say, I'm surprised that you became a model, like your mother. If indeed it was a stalker who killed her…"

"I know," Monique said softly. "None of my family understands that. I'm not even sure I understand it myself. But I don't want my mother's legacy to die, and if there's a chance I can catch her killer—"

"Wait a second," Khamil interjected. "What do you mean by that?" When Monique didn't answer, he continued. "Are you trying to say that you're *hoping* your mother's killer will come after you?"

Khamil felt a jolt of fear in his gut when Monique didn't answer. "Monique, that's crazy."

"I don't know what I'm trying to do," Monique finally said. "All I know is that I want my mother's killer caught."

"I can understand that. But not at the risk of putting yourself in danger."

"Khamil—"

"Monique," Khamil responded firmly. Then he paused. It wasn't up to him to tell her what to do, but he certainly didn't want to see her put herself at risk.

After a long moment, Khamil said, "Let the police do their job."

Monique didn't respond at first, and Khamil wondered if he'd offended her. But then she said, "I appreciate you caring. Honestly. Sometimes it seems like I'm the only one in my family who wants justice."

"I have to apologize for something."

"What?" Monique sounded surprised.

"You made a comment about me seeming like a stalker to you that night when I saw you at Angel's. Now I see… I realize that I probably really scared you. Given what happened to your mother."

"Oh. Well…" Truthfully, she hadn't thought of Khamil as a stalker. If she had, she never would have kissed him. The sudden thought of the kiss they'd shared made her feel hot. Lord help her, here they were discussing her mother's murder, and she was suddenly feeling hot remembering a kiss that didn't mean anything. What was wrong with her?

"It's no big deal," Monique finished. "I'm sure I overreacted."

"Still, I shouldn't have come on so strong, so please, know that it won't happen again."

Khamil's words should have reassured her, but instead Monique's stomach lurched, a queasy feeling washing over her as she held the phone. Why was she disappointed? She'd flat out told Khamil that she didn't appreciate his advances, yet part of her didn't want to hear that he'd never come on to her again. Surely there was something wrong with her.

"Uh-huh."

"All right," Khamil said. He wanted to invite Monique to a café where they could talk some more, but that was hardly appropriate right now. Besides, she'd made it clear she wasn't interested, so why couldn't he simply let go?

He'd always been too analytical, searching for a reason for everything. And right now, his brain told him that maybe, just maybe, Monique would give him a chance to really get to know her if it weren't for her mother's unsolved murder. She was stunning, and he sensed a fiery passion within her, but he also sensed that she was a no-nonsense type of woman who wouldn't spend her days and nights indulging in romance when something as serious as her mother's murder hung over her head.

"I've got some work to do, so I'm gonna let you go," Khamil said. "But please, if you ever need to talk about anything, do give me a call."

"Sure," Monique agreed.

Then Khamil hung up, and Monique felt a measure of sadness. Why was she suddenly feeling drawn to him?

No doubt because he was offering to be there for her, and she often felt as though she had no one.

Maybe she had judged him too harshly, thinking him only a playboy out to add more notches to his bedpost.

Well, she knew one thing for sure. She did appreciate his offer, and if and when she needed to talk, she wouldn't hesitate to call him.

Chapter 9

"Hey, if there's somewhere else you've gotta be, just tell me."

Whipping his head around, Khamil stared at his brother, Javar, who sat across the table from him at Angel's. "What? Why would you say that?"

Javar shrugged. "You keep looking at your watch, like there's somewhere else you've got to be."

"Naw," Khamil said, reaching for his mug of beer. "I don't have anything else to do."

"Then you must not miss your big brother."

"Older, not bigger." Khamil flashed a wry grin, then flexed an arm, displaying a huge muscle even beneath his long-sleeved white shirt. He'd played football in high school and college, while Javar's sport of choice had been basketball. As a result, Javar had a slimmer build than Khamil. "And why would you say I don't miss you?"

"Because if you have nowhere else to go, then you must be pretty bored with my company."

"What?" Khamil's eyebrows shot together, confused.

"You seem more interested in everyone else in this place."

"Huh?" But as Khamil asked the question, he instinctively glanced over his shoulder, then back at his brother.

"That's what I'm talking about," Javar said. "You looking all over the place like you're bored with the company."

Khamil straightened himself in the seat, resting his elbows on the table. "No, man. Of course not. I'm not bored. Just checking out the place."

Javar settled back in his chair and stared at Khamil. "Ah, I get it. You're expecting someone."

"Now you're tripping." Khamil's lips curled in a slight smile. "How could I be expecting someone when I'm here with you?"

"Okay, then." Javar took a swig of his beer.

"You were saying?"

Javar placed a mug back on the table. "Probably nothing that would interest you. At least not yet, little brother. Since you still refuse to settle down."

Khamil flashed his brother a mock-scowl. "Try me."

"Remember Derrick, Whitney's old school friend?"

"The cop who kept sweating you because he thought you were the one threatening Whitney's life?"

"Yeah."

"He's not still in love with Whitney, is he?"

"Naw," Javar replied. "He and Whitney are just friends."

"You sure about that?"

"Yep," Javar replied confidently. "He got married a couple years ago to a woman he was investigating for murder. But that's a whole other story."

"Wow."

"She wasn't guilty, of course. Anyway, Derrick fell in love with her—Samona's her name—they got married, and now he and Samona are expecting. In fact, she's due about two weeks before Whitney."

"Really?"

"Mmm-hmm. Samona and Whitney have become really close. In fact, I never thought it was possible, but Derrick and I have become good friends, too. Anyway, it's been quite an experience with the two of them being pregnant together—you can imagine the kinds of plans they're making for the new babies. They're driving me and Derrick crazy!"

A smile touched Khamil's lips as he watched his brother's eyes light up. Man, had it really been years since they'd both been single, hanging out in Chicago's hottest nightclubs? Back then, they'd talked about all the honeys, Khamil jokingly lamenting over the fact that there weren't enough hours in a day for him to date all the women he wanted. Now, here Javar was talking about pregnancies and family stuff.

"Sounds like you're loving every minute of it, J."

Javar's lips spread in a wide grin. Yeah, I am. Now, I'm just waiting for you to make me an uncle."

"Michelle's already made you an uncle."

"I'm not talking about our sister. I'm talking about you." Javar lifted his beer glass, tipping it slightly in Khamil's direction as if to punctuate his point. "You can't be a playboy forever."

"Just because I'm single at thirty-eight doesn't make me a playboy."

"Ha." Javar chuckled. "I know you."

The sound of female laughter caught Khamil's attention, and once again he turned toward the door. Instantly, he felt a nervous tickle in his stomach as he saw Vicky and a couple of the other models enter the restaurant. After a beat, he realized Monique wasn't with them. She always hung out with this group at Angel's on Thursday nights, so where was she?

If not for learning that someone had murdered her mother,

Khamil might not be concerned. But he found he was worried about Monique. He hoped she was okay.

Khamil was pushing his chair back when Javar said, "Hey, where are you going?"

"Excuse me a minute," Khamil said absently. He stood, then headed toward the models' table, determined to find out where Monique was.

Monique jumped out of the cab and ran toward the front door of Angel's, taking a quick glance around at the crowded Times Square sidewalk before entering the restaurant. Her heart raced frantically, and she was in no mood for a casual get-together, but she had no clue where else to go.

All she knew was that right now, she was too afraid to be alone.

"Hello, Monique," Aaron the host said. "The gang's already here at your usual table."

Monique managed a faint smile and nod before rushing past the host. But suddenly, she stopped mid-stride as she rounded the corner and saw Vicky and Khamil in an embrace.

Her stomach churned at the sight, and for a moment, she was so stunned, she didn't move.

Khamil and Vicky pulled apart. As if he sensed her presence, Khamil spun around, his eyes meeting hers.

Monique stared at him for only a brief second before turning and heading back toward the front door.

"Monique," Khamil called.

Monique didn't stop, instead picking up her pace. But a waitress carrying a tray of food was in her path, and she was forced to slow down as she tried to dodge past the woman.

"Monique, hold up."

Monique ignored Khamil as she stepped to the side, allowing the waitress to pass. However, before she could continue walking, she felt a hand on her shoulder.

Though she knew it was Khamil, she turned anyway. Frowning at him, she shrugged away from his touch, then started off.

"Monique, wait." Khamil's fingers curled around her wrist.

Monique blew out a frustrated breath, then faced Khamil. "What?"

He looked down at her with concern. "You tell me."

"Nothing."

Khamil linked fingers with hers, as if he'd held her hand like this a million times. And damn if she didn't feel a flush of warmth through her body at his touch. Still, she glared at him. "What do you think you're doing?"

Khamil moved in front of her, leading her toward the front door. "We're going to talk."

Monique wanted to yank her hand from Khamil's, but several of the restaurant patrons around them were staring at them, and she didn't want to make a spectacle of herself. So she allowed Khamil to lead her outside. Several people of all ages swarmed the sidewalks in Times Square, some casually strolling, while others walked briskly. Khamil dodged the mass of people and led Monique to the sidewalk's edge. Once there, she pulled her hand free.

"Monique, what's wrong?"

"Nothing," she lied.

"No, something's obviously bothering you. Are you okay?"

As she stared up at him, a lump formed in her throat. No, she wasn't okay. The last time she'd spoken to Khamil, she'd decided that she'd judged him too harshly, that perhaps he wasn't a shallow playboy. But seeing him all over Vicky…

This was stupid. Here she was, getting upset about a man she wasn't even dating, when her main concern should be the letter she'd received today. Another letter had arrived today, making the fear that someone was stalking her a reality. The letter might not have bothered her so much if it hadn't arrived at her apartment.

Khamil placed both hands on Monique's shoulders. "Monique?" Her eyes were slightly bulged, and Khamil's stomach knotted with concern. Something had happened. "God, tell me…"

"I got a letter," she answered after a few moments.

"A letter? What kind of a letter?"

Monique reached into her small purse and withdrew an envelope. Wondering what was going on, Khamil took the envelope from her hands. He lifted the flap and withdrew a folded sheet of paper.

Every day, I think about you.
Every night, I dream about you.
You don't know it, but I watch you.
I see you everywhere and you enthrall me,
Just like your mother did…

The moment Khamil finished reading the letter, he asked, "Where did you get this?"

Monique wrapped her arms around her torso, as if cold, even though the late spring evening was warm. "It came in the mail."

"To your *place?*" As Khamil asked the question, he checked out the envelope. It was addressed to Monique, and had been mailed via the U.S. Postal Service.

"Yeah."

"This is bad." Khamil pressed a palm against his bald head as he contemplated the seriousness of the situation.

"It's the second one."

"Second?"

Monique nodded brusquely.

"Have you gone to the police yet?"

"No. I just...I came straight here when I got that."

"Monique, you have to go to the police. Especially if this is the second letter."

"The first one went to my agent, so I didn't worry much about it. Besides, it wasn't threatening, at least not overtly."

"But this one went to your place."

"Yes."

"So this person obviously knows where you live."

Monique's bottom lip trembled, and she bit down on it. Then she said, "Okay, I'll go to the police. Then I'll let the doorman at my building know about this."

"You're not going back there."

Monique's eyes flew to Khamil's. "What?"

There was no way Khamil was going to let Monique go back home if there was even a hint of danger to her. "You'll come to my place."

While just a moment ago Monique's lip trembled with fear, defiance now flashed in her eyes. "Really? You *tell* me I'm going back to your place, and that's just it."

"I'm not going to let you go home."

"Khamil, you can't tell me what to do."

"This is serious, Monique. And I don't want to see you hurt."

An image of Khamil and Vicky in an embrace flashed in Monique's mind. "Fine. I appreciate that. But I can go somewhere else besides your place."

Khamil shook his head, dismissing that thought.

"Why are you shaking your head?" Monique asked. "You have no right to tell me what to do."

"Look, Monique, I'd just feel a lot better if you stayed with me. We can go back to your place and pick up some stuff you'll need, then head to my place."

Monique planted both hands on her hips. "In case you haven't realized, this is the year 2001—not the Stone Age."

Khamil held up both hands, as if in surrender. "Look, I know you have a right to make your own decisions. I'm not trying to tell you what to do. But…" Khamil's voice trailed off, as he brought a hand to Monique's face and gently stroked it. "Do you have a better idea?"

Monique's face tingled where Khamil's fingers had just been. "I…I could go to one of my girlfriends' places."

"Monique, if someone is after you, watching you as they say, then another woman won't be a deterrent. I'm not trying to be sexist, but I'm a big guy. I don't think anyone would mess with you if I was around."

At his words, Monique's gaze fell to his muscular chest and arms. Yes, Khamil was a big guy. In fact, he could easily be mistaken for a football player. He was right. No one would bother her if he was with her.

Still, she said, "I don't want to be an inconvenience."

"Monique, I won't be able to sleep for worrying about you."

"I see." Monique wanted to ask why he cared so much, but she didn't. Some liked to be heroes, to protect those who needed protection. She didn't want to read more into his concern than that. "Will you have to explain my being there to anyone?"

"Like a girlfriend?"

Glancing away, Monique nodded.

"If that's your way of asking if I'm involved with anyone, the answer is no. But you should know that by now."

Of course he didn't have a serious girlfriend. He was too busy playing with several.

"So," Khamil began after a moment, "you'll come to my place?"

"Sure."

Khamil's mouth curled in a smile. "Great. I've got to go back inside and tell my brother I'm leaving."

"Your brother?"

"Yeah. We were about to have dinner."

"Khamil, I don't want to keep you from your dinner."

"It's okay."

"Why don't we do this—you have dinner with your brother, I'll eat something with my friends, and then we can hook up to head to your place."

Khamil paused, "Sure. That makes sense. Besides, my brother's only in town for a couple of days."

"Khamil, like I told you, I can go to someone else's place."

"Don't worry about it. My brother's got work to do anyway, so it's not a big deal."

"All right. If you're sure."

"I am."

Monique gave Khamil a tentative smile, and warmth spread in Khamil's stomach. Funny that a smile could touch him in such a way, but perhaps hers made him feel good because she hadn't really given him one before.

Khamil placed a hand on the small of her back, and was about to guide her toward the door when he noticed a black car speeding toward them. Something made his heart race at the sight, instantly fearing the worst, while hoping it wouldn't be.

But when the car mounted the curb and headed straight toward them, every nerve in Khamil's body screamed.

Then so did Monique.

Chapter 10

A scream tore from Monique's throat when she realized the out-of-control black car was headed straight for them.

"Get down!" Khamil yelled a mere instant before he tackled her to the ground. Tires squealed as the car burned rubber off the sidewalk and back onto the road, speeding away.

It took Monique a full few seconds to realize what had happened; then she cried, "Oh, my God! Oh, my God!" Glancing at the road, she saw the tail end of the late-model sedan just before it darted in front of another car and disappeared.

"Are you okay?" There was a note of anxiety in Khamil's voice.

Her breathing ragged, Monique looked up into Khamil's dark eyes, eyes that were filled with both fear and concern. She managed a small nod, then, "Ow."

"What?" Khamil asked.

"My arm."

"Sorry," Khamil said, realizing that his full weight was on her slender body. Easing up, he saw that Monique was positioned partly on her side and partly on her back, one arm pressed against the sidewalk.

A crowd started to form around Khamil and Monique as

Khamil rose to his feet. Monique sat up slowly, as though with difficulty. He watched her chest heave as she inhaled and exhaled, watched the dazed expression on her face, and something in his gut ached. What if he hadn't been able to get her out of the way in time?

Khamil reached for her and pulled her to her feet. She collapsed against his chest, and he wrapped a comforting arm around her.

"You two all right?" a man in the crowd asked.

Khamil glanced down at Monique. She nodded. "I'm...fine."

"I can't believe this," Khamil muttered. Then, to the people surrounding them, he asked, "Did anyone get a look at the plate?"

People shook their heads.

"Damn," Khamil said. He pulled Monique closer, as though he'd held her like this a thousand times. She felt good in his arms, and he felt good knowing that she trusted him to give her support. He didn't know why, but her trust in him mattered more than it had ever mattered where a woman was concerned before.

"Khamil, what happened?" Monique asked. Her voice was shaky, and as he held her, he realized that her body was slightly trembling.

What *had* happened? Khamil suddenly wondered. Had the driver been on a cell phone and not paying attention? Or had he deliberately tried to run them over? The letter Monique had received had Khamil wondering if the near accident was actually an accident after all.

Before Khamil could answer her question, he saw Javar hustling toward him. "What the hell happened?" his brother asked.

"Some jerk mounted the curb and nearly hit us," Khamil

replied. Thinking of just how close the car had come to hitting them, Khamil gritted his teeth.

"New York drivers," Javar lamented, then shook his head.

Monique's gaze went from Khamil to this other man. Though he had a slimmer build, he had a narrow face, like Khamil's, as well as deep-set eyes. There was a definite resemblance between the two men. This had to be Khamil's brother.

The man's eyes met hers, and he smiled, then threw a suspicious glance toward Khamil. "So, Khamil," he began in a sing-song voice, "who's this?"

"Oh. Javar, this is a friend, Monique. Monique, this is my brother, Javar."

"Nice to meet you," Monique said, extending a hand.

Javar shook it. "Nice to meet you as well. So, you're the reason my brother deserted me at our table."

"We were just heading back inside," Khamil commented.

Javar's lips curled in a sly grin. "Mmm-hmm."

Khamil gave his brother a don't-go-there look. He could tell by his brother's lopsided grin that his brain was working overtime, trying to assess the nature of his relationship with Monique.

Javar leaned in close and whispered in Khamil's ear. "She's beautiful, man."

Khamil just nodded. "All right, you ready for some dinner?"

"Actually, I'm cool. I can pick up a burger, or order room service from the hotel."

"Oh, no," Monique interjected. "I don't want to ruin your dinner plans."

Javar waved off her concern. "Don't worry about me." To Khamil, he added, "Go ahead and hang out with your lady friend."

The inflection in Javar's tone said he thought she and Khamil had a relationship. She was about to correct him, but didn't bother. Instead, she said, "Will you both excuse me?"

Khamil's eyes met hers with concern. "Where are you going?"

"Inside. I'm gonna tell the girls I won't be hanging out tonight." At the thought of her friends, Monique's stomach felt queasy. What was the nature of Khamil's and Vicky's relationship? She wasn't jealous, but...concerned. She didn't want Khamil to lead her on, making her think he was interested in her, if in fact he was simply interested in playing the field. "Give me a minute."

"Sure," Khamil agreed.

When Monique disappeared inside the restaurant, Javar slapped him hard on the back. "So, little brother, something you've been keeping from me?"

Shaking his head, Khamil smirked. "She's a friend, Javar."

"Uh-oh."

"What?"

"Either you're getting mellow in your old age, or you've finally been hit by cupid's arrow."

"What?" Khamil made a face.

"When it comes to beautiful women, you never talk about them in terms of being *friends.* In fact, you're the first to comment about their various...attributes. And Monique is definitely *fine.*"

"Whatever."

"Mmm-hmm."

"Look, Javar, it's not like that."

Javar merely shrugged. "Well, she seems nice. Make sure you treat her good."

"Didn't you say you had something to do?" Khamil asked.

Javar chuckled. "Now you want to get rid of me."

"You're a trip, Javar. Give me a call later. We'll try to hook up before you leave town."

Javar wrapped his arms around Khamil in a spontaneous hug. "All right, little brother."

"Younger."

"Whatever."

Maybe she was being paranoid, but the first thing Monique noticed when she joined her friends was the plastic smile Vicky gave her before she took a sip from her water glass.

Monique pulled out the chair beside Renee and slumped onto it.

"What happened?" Renee asked. "You ran out of here like a bat out of hell."

"I…" Monique's voice trailed off. How could she admit that she'd run out of the restaurant because she'd seen Vicky and Khamil in an embrace? "I'm a little bit worried."

Janine's eyebrows bunched together. "Why?"

"I've gotten a couple of letters recently," Monique told them. "They're not particularly threatening, but they mention my mother. I wouldn't be so worried if the second letter didn't come to my home address."

"Oh, my God," Vicky uttered.

Monique nodded. "I don't know what to make of it, but it gives me the chills." And suddenly the thought hit her that the near accident outside might not have been an accident at all. Good Lord, had someone deliberately tried to run her down?

"Look, sweetie," Renee began. "You've got to go to the police."

"I will." Goose bumps popped out on her skin at the thought

that she'd come close to death, and that it may have been a deliberate attempt on her life. Who had tried to run her down, and why?

"Sweetie?" Renee gently rubbed Monique's forearm.

Renee's voice brought Monique back from her thoughts. "I don't feel much like hanging tonight."

"What's Khamil saying?"

At Vicky's question, Monique's eyes flew to hers. Yes, there was something strange about Vicky tonight. Her eyes were bright, yet they didn't hold the warmth they normally did. "Khamil says I should go to the police."

"Hmm." Vicky gave a brief nod, though she didn't seem satisfied with Monique's answer.

"In fact, we're gonna do that now." Monique pushed her chair back and stood.

"Khamil's gonna go with you?" Vicky asked.

"Mmm-hmm."

There was that plastic smile again. "Yeah, Khamil's a real gentleman."

Until now, Monique had never had a problem with Vicky, though she'd heard from some other girls at the agency that Vicky could be a backstabber. She had a reputation for going after what she wanted and not caring who she hurt. Monique had taken those rumors with a grain of salt. But now she had to wonder if Vicky, a woman she'd had as a friend for the past five years, would actually let something like a man come between them.

Because this *was* about Khamil. Monique knew that, even if Vicky wouldn't admit it.

"Tell Khamil we said goodbye," Vicky said, her upbeat tone contrary to the negative vibes she was sending Monique's way.

"Sure." Monique forced a grin. "I'll see you all later."

"Bye," Renee and Janine replied in unison.

"See ya." Vicky wriggled her fingers at Monique, then turned to Renee and Janine.

Monique turned and walked away.

"What's the matter?" Khamil asked.

"Nothing," Monique replied, but her tone was clipped. She and Khamil were in the elevator in her building, heading back downstairs. At her apartment, she'd collected some clothes and essential items.

Khamil placed a hand on her shoulder, and Monique jumped. "Monique." Khamil's voice was gentle. "It's going to be okay."

Monique didn't respond, instead staring straight ahead. Her mind was filled with so many doubts. Doubts about her mother's murder, and about who was possibly sending the letters. And as she tried to avoid eye contact with Khamil, she knew she also had doubts about him. Some moments, like right now, he could seem so gentle and compassionate, but then other moments, she didn't know if he was a thoughtless playboy.

It doesn't matter, she told her self. She couldn't allow herself to care about Khamil, anyway. Raymond had told her that she'd been too obsessed with finding her mother's killer to commit to someone, and maybe he was right.

Raymond. Monique's heart fluttered as she thought of him. He hadn't called her in more than a week, hadn't dropped by Angel's. Had he finally gotten the point—or had he resorted to another tactic? He'd already tried to entice her back into a relationship with him by implying that he had information about her mother. How far would he go to get her back in his life?

"Monique."

Drifting back from her thoughts to the present, she looked at

Khamil. He was pressing a hand against the open elevator door. Monique stepped past him off the elevator.

Harry gave her a bright smile. "Hello, Monique."

"Hello." Monique sauntered toward him. "Harry, has anyone come here looking for me—anyone you haven't seen before?"

Harry shook his head. "No."

"What about Raymond? Has he come around?"

Again, Harry shook his head. "I haven't seen him." He paused. "Is there a problem?"

"No, no." If Raymond hadn't been around, nor anyone else, there was no point in mentioning anything. At least not yet. "Just curious."

"Well, you let me know if I can be of any help to you."

"Sure," Monique told him.

When she felt a hand on her shoulder, Monique whipped around, slightly startled. She knew Khamil was with her, so why was she so on edge around him?

Maybe because he was too touchy-feely. And she suddenly couldn't help wondering if he was like this with every woman, or if he was being like this with just her.

"You want to get a bite to eat before we head to my place?"

A tingling sensation spread over Monique's skin. Such a simple question, but it conjured up all sorts of illicit thoughts in her mind.

And then she couldn't help wondering how casually Khamil invited other women over, women he ended up making love to…

Good Lord, what was wrong with her? There was no decent reason for her to be thinking of Khamil's private life, because it was none of her business. Besides, she wasn't heading to his place for sex.

"Maybe this isn't a good idea."

Monique didn't realize she'd spoken aloud until Khamil asked, "Why not?"

"The truth is, Khamil, I hardly know you." Monique spoke as she opened the lobby doors and stepped outside, partly because she didn't want to face him. There was something about his eyes when he looked at her that unnerved her.

"I think you know enough."

"Enough?" Still, Monique didn't turn, instead starting down the street.

Khamil kept pace with her. "Are we talking, or are we walking? Monique, if you'll slow down…"

She quickened her pace, knowing she must seem foolish, but she couldn't stop herself. Spending the night at Khamil's place suddenly seemed very dangerous.

Khamil placed a firm hand on her arm, and Monique stopped, the fight gone out of her. Slowly, Khamil turned her around, drew her body to his.

And then he covered her mouth with his, urgently kissing her. Monique kissed him back with just as much fervor, her hands slipping around his neck, his slipping around her waist. Their tongues mingled, their hands explored, the passion between them as strong and undeniable as if it had caught them in a web.

Panting, Monique finally pulled away. This was exactly what she didn't want.

"Monique…" Khamil's voice was husky, filled with desire.

"What was that?" she asked, looking around as if she'd heard something that had startled her.

"What?"

When Khamil glanced around to see what she was talking about, Monique slipped out of his arms. Trying to ignore the reality that she now missed his embrace, she hustled to the edge of the sidewalk. Thankfully, a cab was approaching, and she flung her hand in the air to hail it.

"Yo, Monique." Again, Khamil placed a hand on her arm, but she shrugged away from his touch. As the cab came to a stop, she opened the back door and jumped inside. Without another word, Khamil followed her.

"Where to?" the driver asked as they settled in their seats.

Khamil looked at Monique, but she didn't meet his eyes. So much for getting her input. "There's a little jazz bar on Fifty-seventh. A new establishment."

"I know the place," the driver said, his upbeat tone indicating he'd been there.

Facing Khamil, Monique guffawed. "Khamil, I'm not exactly up for dinner and jazz tonight."

There was something about her resistance that challenged him, challenged the side of him that had always been a joker. As a child, he'd irked more than one teacher with his class clown antics, and when he'd started liking girls, he'd shown his interest in them by teasing them.

He raised an eyebrow at Monique and said, "In a hurry to get to my place, darling?"

Muttering something unintelligible, Monique fell back against the seat and stared out the taxi's window.

Khamil turned and glanced out the other window, hiding his smirk. What had gotten into him? He felt as if he were in sixth grade again, teasing Cecelia Mathers. But he also felt a measure of satisfaction, because, like Cecelia, Monique's hot and cold routine around him told him exactly what he wanted to know.

She wanted him. Just as much as he wanted her.

Feeling her eyes upon him, Khamil faced Monique. Quick

as lightning, her head spun in the other direction. No doubt, she was hoping he hadn't noticed her staring at him. However, she hadn't turned away fast enough.

A soft chuckle fell from Khamil's lips. It was going to be an interesting night.

Chapter 11

Monique pulled at the neck of her shirt, holding it from her body to allow her skin to breathe. Lord, it was hot in here! It wasn't even summer yet and here she was, sweating.

She stole a glance at Khamil, his smug smirk making her angry. Why was she allowing him to get to her like this? She didn't have time for his games.

She blew out a hot breath. God, there was no fresh air in this car. She hit the window's power button, opening the window to let fresh air in as the taxi drove.

Khamil leaned in close and whispered, "I know. It's getting hot in here."

The low timbre of his voice caused a tremor to pass through Monique's body. She didn't dare say a word to Khamil, didn't dare look his way. There was no way she was going to give him the satisfaction of knowing that he'd gotten under her skin. She could only hope her cool exterior masked the desire burning within her.

Because that's exactly what was happening, she realized with chagrin. The more time she spent with Khamil, the less she could deny that there was something about him that made her blood stir. At first, she'd told herself that he made her blood stir in a bad way, because he irritated her. So what if she'd felt a tingle in places she hadn't in ages after their first kiss? She'd simply ignored that. But after the last kiss, she could no longer deny that Khamil made every cell in her body come alive in a way she hadn't ever experienced before.

Even if she didn't like it.

Not that she didn't like the feeling; she just didn't like the man.

When the taxi pulled up in front of the jazz bar, Monique flinched when she felt Khamil's breath hot on her ear. He asked, "Have you been here before?"

"I don't have much time for socializing."

Khamil raised a suggestive eyebrow. "So I'm the first to take you here."

His darkened gaze made Monique think of other firsts, and once again, she found herself getting hot. But she hoped she maintained her cool front when she asked, "Are you going to pay the driver?"

Khamil held her gaze, slowly drawing his full bottom lip between his teeth. Monique was unable to stop herself from staring, unable to stop her own lips from parting, almost as if she wanted to kiss him again.

She *did* want to kiss him again.

Monique quickly grabbed the door's handle and jumped out of the car.

Khamil watched Monique scramble from the car. Something had changed between them, no doubt about it, and if they didn't have an audience, Khamil would have taken her in his arms and ravished those soft lips of hers until she begged him to make love to her.

He knew just what he would do to her. Starting at her neck, he'd nibble a path to her navel, then lower...

"Sir?"

"Huh?" The cab driver's voice was like a splash of cold water—which was exactly what Khamil needed. Damn. Here he was getting hot and hard in the back of a taxi.

"Seven fifty-five."

Khamil dug the wallet out of the back pocket of his pants and handed some bills to the driver. "Keep the change," Khamil told the man.

Monique was already at the restaurant's doors when Khamil got out of the taxi. Her arms crossed over her chest, a frown marred her beautiful features. He felt a stab of disappointment in his gut. What was she afraid of? Was getting to know him such a horrible idea?

Yet he saw a vulnerability in her eyes as he strolled toward her, despite her cold expression.

She's afraid of caring, a voice in his head told him. And he knew it was true. Hadn't he acted the same way after his relationship with Jessica had ended his senior year in college? His family and friends acted as though he'd been incapable of giving his heart, but that wasn't the case. He'd given his heart to Jessica, and she'd broken it. A star college football player at Michigan State with a promising career ahead of him, Khamil's dreams of playing pro ball had ended when a severe hit had dislocated his shoulder. The shoulder hadn't been the same since. Neither had his relationship with Jessica, whom he'd subsequently found in bed with one of his best friends, the quarterback of the team. After finally giving someone his heart and getting burned, Khamil had vowed to never let a woman hurt him again.

And thus far, he'd kept that vow. He'd never given his heart to another woman the way he had to Jessica, and his life had been better for it. Not that he didn't miss the feeling of being in love on occasion, but for the most part, relationships without all the serious emotions had been much less complicated.

So he understood Monique's fear, if she was indeed afraid of getting involved. He had no idea what her past relationships had been like, but he understood that the fact that her mother had been murdered when she was still a child was enough to make her fear getting close to anyone.

"Busy night," Khamil said as he reached Monique, glancing around at the populated street.

"Yeah."

"You ready to go inside?"

In response, Monique turned to the door. She felt so...on edge. What was wrong with her? She was an adult; she could handle a dinner with Khamil, couldn't she?

But could she handle spending the night at his place?

Monique's thoughts were interrupted by the sound of laughter. Two women were exiting the restaurant. Both smiled, though their gazes went beyond her, and Monique knew they had to be looking at Khamil. Something inside her stomach tightened painfully, and she couldn't help turning to see how Khamil would react to them.

Khamil returned the women's smiles with a charming one of his own. Monique rolled her eyes, suddenly more irritated than she had the right to be.

"Are you coming?" she quipped.

Khamil's eyes met hers. "What's with the attitude?"

"I'm not the one with the attitude," Monique retorted.

Khamil's gaze narrowed. "If you've got something to say to me, why don't you just say it?"

Monique looked over her shoulder, and satisfied that no one was within earshot, spoke. "Fine, you're an attractive guy. You obviously know that. But you're taking *me* out to dinner. Is it really that hard for you to put aside your flirtatious ways for such a short time—"

"Flirtatious ways?"

"Do not even try to deny that you were flirting with those women."

Khamil pinned her with his dark eyes. "And that bothers you, does it?"

For a moment, Monique couldn't say anything, almost as if Khamil's eyes had the power to leave her speechless. Trying desperately to concentrate on something other than Khamil's heated gaze, Monique twirled a loose tendril of her ebony hair. She shouldn't have said anything. All she'd done was flatter Khamil's incredibly large ego.

His eyes looked like sparking black jewels in the dim illumination of the streetlights. "Well?" he prompted.

Monique swallowed. "All I'm trying to say is that it's disrespectful for you to ogle other women when you've got a woman by your side. If you can't understand that—"

"But you're not my woman." Khamil paused. "Or is that the problem—that you want to be?"

Monique was quickly losing control of this situation, but laughed sarcastically to give Khamil the impression that he couldn't be more wrong. "You always have to twist everything to flatter yourself, don't you?"

"Why don't you answer the question?"

"Because that's not the issue—"

"I think it is." Gently, Khamil ran a finger along Monique's jawbone. "I think you want me to look at only you. Only notice your beauty." His finger trailed a path to the soft spot on her neck. "Is that it, Monique? Are you jealous?"

Lord help her, Monique knew she should step away from his touch, but she was unable to move. Why did he have this power over her?

"You couldn't be more wrong," she finally managed to say.

"I'm not so sure about that," Khamil said, but his tone said he was totally sure that she wanted him. "Or are you so used to men looking at you that you don't expect them to look at anyone else?"

Khamil's comment broke the spell he had her under. Anger swept over Monique, and she stepped away from him, meeting his eyes with cold ones. "I didn't get into this business for the attention, if that's what you're trying to imply."

"But I'm sure you've become accustomed to it. No doubt men all over the world admire your beauty."

Maybe that was part of her problem, she silently conceded. Working in this business, she'd seen how so many men went crazy for a beautiful woman. Yes, she'd rather be beautiful, but she wanted to be appreciated for more than that.

And if an obsessed stalker had killed her mother, then Julia had died because someone had idolized her beauty above all else.

Monique enjoyed modeling, mostly because she was helping to keep her mother's legacy alive. And of course, the money was great. But she had other plans for her life. She couldn't model forever, nor did she want to. Her dream after this career ended was to become an interior designer.

Monique placed her hands firmly on her hips. "I'm not as shallow as you obviously think. And believe me, I know that beauty is more than skin deep."

Monique spoke the last words sharply, her comment no doubt meant for him. Khamil opened his mouth to reply, but the sound of footsteps stopped him. A group of people walked by him and Monique, obviously staring at them, clearly curious as to what was going on. Glancing inside the restaurant, Khamil noticed that the two hostesses in the front were watching them as well.

"What?" Monique asked. She followed Khamil's gaze, but didn't see what had caught his interest.

Facing her, he felt a smile tugging at the corners of his mouth. "Monique, everyone thinks we're having a lovers' quarrel."

Horrified, Monique looked inside the restaurant once more, noting the curious stares of the two hostesses and a couple in the foyer. And when she saw three women approach from across the street, their eyes fixed on them as well, Monique grunted and turned on her heel, ready to walk anywhere but this embarrassing situation.

Khamil's strong fingers wrapped around her slender arm, forcing her to stop. "Honey, will you ever forgive me?" he asked, loud enough for the nosy spectators to hear. A man scurrying by slowed to watch them. Then Khamil pulled Monique into an embrace, squeezing her tightly.

For one fleeting moment, Monique forgot that she was standing in the middle of one of New York's busiest streets, surrounded by curious onlookers. She could only think of how good it felt to be pressed against Khamil's hard body, how right.

But only for a moment.

"Let me go." Monique's voice was soft but her tone was lethal.

"Promise me you'll be nice," Khamil whispered, "and I'll let you go."

Monique closed her eyes, willing the unexpected tantalizing sensation spreading over her body to dissipate. "Just let me go," she said after a moment.

"Not until you promise me that you'll be nice." Khamil's breath was warm against her ear. "Can we both go inside and try to have a nice evening?"

"Forget dinner. Let me go; then you can go home, and I'll go back to my place."

"I'm waiting," was Khamil's reply.

He was really enjoying this! Monique was both furious that she was letting him get to her and embarrassed that people were witnessing this show. This had to end. Now.

"All right," Monique conceded.

"All right, what?"

"I'll be nice," Monique quipped. She hoped he was happy. The man was absolutely incorrigible!

Slowly, Khamil released his hold on Monique, but still kept one hand firmly planted around her small waist. With the other hand, he opened the door to the restaurant and led her inside. He smiled at the two hostesses and proudly announced, "It's okay. She forgives me."

"She'd be a fool not to," one hostess muttered to another; then both young women giggled.

Monique forced a smile, though what she really wanted to do was strangle Khamil.

"Table for two?" one of the hostesses asked.

"Yeah," Khamil answered. "Nonsmoking. Something private."

The hostess grabbed two menus. "Right this way."

As Monique and Khamil followed the young woman, Monique whispered, "You are an absolute jerk. And you can let go of me now."

"Not yet."

The hostess led them to a quaint table in the back corner of the restaurant. "Here you go," she chimed. "I hope this is okay."

"It's fine," Khamil replied.

The hostess placed the two menus on the table, then gave Monique a knowing smile and walked away.

Monique finally jerked her body free of Khamil's strong grasp. She shot an angry look at him, then plopped into her seat.

The smile Monique had once thought charming she now found annoying as Khamil flashed it at her again. "Okay," he said, sitting down. "No more scenes like the one outside."

"I didn't cause that scene," Monique hissed. *"You're* the one—" Monique stopped midsentence and inhaled a frustrated breath. She was going where she didn't want to go. Getting more upset than she already was in the small confines of a restaurant certainly wouldn't do her any good. She needed to relax.

"Maybe I did cause that scene," Khamil admitted. Then he shrugged. "Now we're even." Khamil lifted his menu.

"Even?"

He lowered his menu and pinned her with his eyes. "At Angel's. When you kissed me outside the bathroom. You want to talk about a scene. You gave everyone there something to talk about for weeks."

"Nobody saw us," Monique said softly, suddenly wondering if anyone other than Raymond had seen them. She'd never done anything so…shameless.

"Except that guy."

"Right." Monique's tone was sheepish. How could she have been so silly as to kiss Khamil for Raymond's benefit? If she hadn't, she probably wouldn't be here now, dealing with a man she knew she'd be better off staying away from.

"And that's why you kissed me. So he wouldn't bother you."

"We already discussed this."

Khamil rested his elbows on the table and leaned forward.

"You know what, Monique? You can deny it all you want, but I know you enjoyed that kiss. You enjoyed me—"

That did it. Monique was *not* going to go there. She shot to her feet faster than Khamil could blink, grabbing her purse and overnight bag as she did. But before she could get away, Khamil grabbed her by the waist and pulled her down onto his lap.

Her breath snagging in her throat, Monique's eyes met Khamil's. Neither said a word, but the moment between them was so intense that it seemed they were the only two people in the world.

"Hey, none of that hanky-panky until *after* dinner."

Horrified, Monique looked up to see a pretty Asian woman with long black hair standing over the table with a pen and pad in her hand. "We want to make sure you at least pay the bill," she added, grinning. "Hi, I'm Alice, your server tonight. What can I get you to drink?"

"I'll take a beer," Khamil said. "Whatever you have on tap."

"I'll have a water," Monique told the server. *To throw all over you*, she added silently, glaring at Khamil.

"Bring her a strawberry margarita," Khamil instructed Alice. "She'll like that."

Alice made some notes on her pad, then slipped it in a pocket of her apron. "I'll be right back."

When the waitress was out of earshot, Monique heaved herself off Khamil. "I hope you enjoy the strawberry margarita, because I certainly won't be here to drink it."

"Where are you going to go?" Khamil challenged, his dark eyes daring Monique to answer him. "You know that if you walk out that door, I'll be right on your tail. I'm not letting you go back to your place, Monique. So you may as well stay put, and enjoy your evening."

Knowing he meant every word he said, Monique glared at Khamil for several moments, then slowly sank back into the seat across from him, resigning herself to a night of hell. "Just remember why I'm going to your place tonight."

The waitress returned with their drinks, and Khamil ordered a cheeseburger with fries. Monique decided on an appetizer of chicken fingers.

Monique wasn't big on fruity drinks, preferring a glass of wine to any other type of alcohol. And tonight, she certainly wasn't in the mood to drink at all—certainly not with Khamil. So she fiddled with her straw before finally putting it to her mouthy and taking a sip of the strawberry margarita. To her delight, the drink was sweet and refreshing. She took another sip.

"So," Khamil began, "when do you want to go to the police about the letters?"

"I don't know," Monique replied. She'd been considering what she should actually do. "I'm kind of thinking that maybe I'm being premature. I mean, what are the police going to say? The letters aren't truly threatening—"

"The threat is clear, Monique."

"Yes," Monique answered, getting serious. "I guess…going to the police will make this all more real."

"You can't ignore this."

"I'm afraid," Monique said softly. Visions of the night she'd found her mother dying on the bedroom floor flashed in her mind. A chill swept over her. Were these two letters possibly from the same person who'd killed her mother?

"I understand that. That's why I'm going to be here for you, Monique. I won't let anything happen to you."

Khamil spoke with confidence, and Monique believed every

word he said. She didn't know why, but she did know that he would do whatever he could to keep her safe.

She felt a moment of sadness. Her father hadn't been able to protect her mother. She hadn't been able to save her, either.

"I'll go to the police in the morning," Monique said, fighting the sudden urge to cry.

"Hey." Reaching across the table, Khamil covered one of her hands with his. "It's going to be all right, Monique. I know how important it is for you to get closure, and I'm going to help you do that."

A smile touched Monique's lips. Khamil's words gave her comfort, comfort she desperately needed. Why did he seem to care where her own family did not?

Monique stared into Khamil's eyes, looking for an answer to her question. His dark eyes held compassion. She was confused. One minute she wanted to get away from Khamil, the next she felt like throwing herself in his arms and letting him wash away all her fears. How could he bring out both desires in her?

The waitress arrived with their food then, and both Monique and Khamil ate in silence. When they were finished, Khamil settled the bill; then both he and Monique headed outside, where Khamil hailed a taxi. As a taxi pulled up to the curb, Khamil said, "Last chance. My place, or the police station?"

"Your place," Monique told him, then hoped she had made the right choice. Because whether it was about protection or not, she knew that spending the night with Khamil would be far from uncomplicated.

Chapter 12

The moment Monique and Khamil stepped into the lobby of Khamil's upper west side condo, Monique's heart went berserk. All she could think of was how many other women had been to his place, how many had spent the night.

What was she doing here?

Khamil placed a hand on the small of her back and led her to the elevators. When the elevator door opened, she swallowed.

A beautiful young black woman exited the elevator with a fluffy white poodle. "Hello, Khamil," she said, greeting him.

"Hello, Diane."

Monique threw a glance at Khamil, wanting to ask who the woman was, but bit her tongue. Instead she asked herself, since when had she become so…jealous. Yes, she realized with chagrin, she *was* jealous. Maybe Khamil had been right when he'd said that she wanted him to give only her his attention.

But why? She didn't want a relationship with him.

She'd never been like this with anyone else. Even when Raymond had cheated on her, she'd simply told him it was over without a second thought. So why did who Khamil slept with matter to her one bit?

Khamil led Monique onto the elevator. He hit the button for

the fifth floor. Moments later, the elevator came to a stop, and the doors opened.

Khamil started off the elevator, but Monique didn't move. Realizing she wasn't going anywhere, he paused, then faced her. "What's the matter?"

"I can't do this," Monique whispered.

"Can't do what?"

"What's up with you and Vicky?" Monique asked before she could stop herself.

"Me and Vicky?"

Monique angled her head to the side as she leveled her gaze at his face. "Yes, you and Vicky." Having seen them together in an embrace had been bothering her all evening, and she finally had the courage to ask him about the nature of their relationship. "Has she been here? To your place?"

"What are you talking about?"

To her own ears, she sounded ridiculous. Yet she continued. "You and Vicky seemed very *chummy* earlier. In fact, Vicky gave me some attitude when she questioned me about you, so…" Monique paused. "So, if there's something going on between the two of you, tell me now. Because I have to work with Vicky, and I don't want any unnecessary animosity between us."

Khamil let the elevator door close, then hit the stop button.

Monique's eyes bulged as she looked at him. "W-why are you—"

Khamil closed the distance between them and swept Monique into his arms. Without hesitation, he brought his lips down on hers—hard—swallowing Monique's moan of protest. Damn, she felt good. She was like an intoxicating drug, one he needed more and more of. Yet only kissing her wasn't enough.

He wanted all of her.

And he was tempted to take her, right here and now, and probably would have, if Monique hadn't slipped her hands between their bodies and pushed him away. As she stared up at him from lowered lashes, her chest rose and fell quickly with each breath she took.

"Does that answer your question?" Khamil asked.

Monique looked away. "Th-this is exactly what I—I don't want…"

"I think it's what you *do* want." When Monique's eyes flew to his, Khamil raised one eyebrow in challenge. "Otherwise, you wouldn't care less what was up with me and Vicky."

Monique's heart thumped hard in her chest. "So there *is* something between you and Vicky?"

"No, there isn't."

"Then why did she act like I was encroaching on her territory?"

"You'll have to ask her that."

It was suddenly hot in the elevator. Too hot. She believed Khamil, which surprised her, because a part of her had wanted to cling to the possibility that he was involved with someone else—anyone else—if for no other reason than to give herself an excuse to stay away from him. But there was something about Khamil that had her forgetting why getting involved with him would be wrong, and instead had her wishing that he'd take her in his arms and kiss her silly again.

Monique had to stop thinking like that. She hit the button to start the elevator. Then she pressed the button for the main level.

As the elevator started to move, Khamil hit the stop button again. Once again, Monique's heart beat anxiously in her chest.

She was both excited and alarmed at being trapped in an elevator with Khamil.

"You're not going back home, Monique."

She swallowed as her body shivered from the intensity of his words. "Fine," she told him. "I'll find my way to the nearest hotel."

"You are not staying at a hotel."

"Oh, yeah?" Monique said. "Try and stop me."

"I will, if that's what it takes."

Her eyes were wide with indignation, but Khamil held her gaze, letting her know he was not going to back down. He was crazy, but he wanted her. Wanted to take her in his arms and tear the form-fitting black pants and black tank top off her body. Wanted to take her wildly, right here on the elevator floor.

"Fine," Monique huffed, but Khamil got the feeling it was all for show. Then she started up the elevator again. "But first thing in the morning, I'm gone."

We'll see about that, Khamil thought, the edges of his lips curling in the slightest of smiles.

God help her, Monique was losing it! What was it about Khamil that made her angry one minute, then hot and bothered the next?

"Monique, do I need to invite you in?"

She was standing in the doorway of his apartment, but hadn't even realized it. Holding her head high, she strolled over the threshold.

"It's beautiful," Monique said, meaning it. She surveyed the small but quaint, modernly decorated condominium. Bright white walls contrasted with the black lacquer coffee table, the black and brass lamps, and the black leather sofa. Instantly, her mind started conjuring up ideas of how to add to the living room's appeal. Perhaps an area rug that added a splash of color, some classic paintings on the walls that mixed an old flavor with the modern.

Monique walked farther into the apartment. At the far end of the living room was a glass solarium. In the solarium, there was a beautiful glass dining table with black and brass trimmings. Two white candles rested on ether end of the table in brass candleholders, complemented by a floral centerpiece.

The candles made Monique think of romance, and she couldn't help wondering how many romantic evenings Khamil had spent here...

Monique inhaled a steady breath, deliberately ignoring the direction of her thoughts. Retracing her steps through the living room, she went to the hallway. As she further explored the apartment, she discovered there was only one bedroom.

"Can I get you anything to drink?"

Startled at his voice, Monique spun around to find Khamil standing behind her. Maybe it was because she was at his bedroom door, but illicit thoughts crept into her mind, and she couldn't help throwing a glance over his entire body. Her gaze lingered on his thighs, which looked large and powerful beneath his black pants.

Oh, how she'd love to reach out and touch someone...

"Monique?"

Her eyes flew to his face, embarrassed that he'd caught her staring. "Uh...sorry. What did you say?"

"I asked if you wanted a drink."

"A drink," Monique repeated, as though she didn't know the meaning of the word. Drinking and Khamil would not mix, not here at his place, when she couldn't stop noticing just how devastatingly sexy he was. "Uh, no." She forced a yawn. "I'm starting to drift. You know, get all blurry-eyed. I'd just like to go to bed."

His eyes held hers a moment too long, but she wouldn't look away. Couldn't. "I understand," he finally said. "The bed's all yours."

"Oh, no," Monique replied. There was no way she'd sleep in Khamil's bed. "I'll be fine on the couch." To prove her point, she walked back into the living room and sank into the softness of the black leather sofa.

Khamil followed her. "Monique." His voice was deep and oh-so sexy. Just the way he said her name made her skin tingle. "You get the bed. No arguments."

"No." Khamil's bed was too…personal. Sleeping in it would be crossing some sort of line. She brought her feet up to the couch and stretched out. "Just bring me a blanket and I'm good to go."

"The bed sheets are clean. I changed them this morning."

"Khamil—"

"You're taking the bed, Monique."

A small frown played on Monique's lips. "Do you always have to have your own way?"

"I'm trying to be a gentleman."

She flashed him a plastic smile. "Offer appreciated. Declined."

"Suit yourself." His hands went to the front of his shirt, and started undoing the buttons—slowly.

"*What* are you doing?"

"I'm sleeping on the couch, Monique. You're my guest. You get the bed."

"But you're too tall. You'll get a kink in your neck sleeping on the couch."

"I'll be all right." He pulled the shirt off his body.

Monique had forgotten just how sexy Khamil had looked without a shirt on the night of the charity fashion show, and now her breath snagged in her throat at the sight of his beautifully sculpted arms and smooth, dark chest. Damn, but this man was *fine*.

What was wrong with her? Only teenage women gawked at men the way she was gawking, didn't they?

Her mind returned to the dilemma at hand when she heard Khamil unzip his pants. "Hold up, Khamil," she said, throwing out a hand to stop him. She didn't want to see the rest of his magnificent body. She'd never maintain control of her raging hormones if he dropped his pants.

"Did I get the couch?" he asked, a sexy smile playing on his lips.

"Yes." She leaped off the couch. She'd agree to anything just to get away from him.

"Do you need a shirt to sleep in?"

She shook her head. "I've got nightwear in my overnight bag, thank you."

That shouldn't have excited him, but it did. Hell, it did. She'd look sexy in anything, but he wondered what she preferred to wear to bed. Sexy teddies, or a simple T-shirt? He wouldn't mind seeing her in one of his plaid shirts, unbuttoned to her cleavage.

"I'll just go to…bed now."

"Okay," Khamil replied. "See you in the morning."

"Good night." Monique made a hasty retreat, grabbing her overnight bag along the way. When she closed the bedroom door behind her, she laid her forehead against it for several seconds.

Goodness, Khamil was hot! And so was she, just thinking about his hard, muscular chest, his smooth dark brown skin, his firm butt, and those sexy thighs… She sucked in a sharp breath and let it out slowly. The scent of him filled her senses. She couldn't sleep in his room. In his *bed*. She would call a cab and go to a hotel.

She reached for the doorknob, then stopped. This was crazy. *She* was crazy. If she left, he'd chase her. Her heart thumped at the thought. Gosh, she really was crazy. She actually liked the idea of Khamil chasing her, that he didn't want her to leave…

There was a knock at the door. "Monique."

She froze.

"Monique," he repeated softly.

"Y-yes?"

"I'm going to use the bathroom. Give me five minutes; then it's all yours."

"Okay." She waited, wondering if Khamil was going to open the door. *Wanting* him to. But all she heard was the soft sound of his footsteps as he walked away.

Frustrated, she sighed. This was going to be one *long* night.

Chapter 13

Khamil couldn't sleep. There was no point even trying. The knowledge that Monique lay in his bed, just down the hallway, consumed his thoughts.

What would she be like in bed? Would she be wild, digging her nails into his back and calling out his name? Or was she the quiet but intense type?

The irony of the situation wasn't lost on him. He rarely had a woman in his apartment if she wasn't sharing his bed. And despite the fact that Monique wasn't here to be his lover, he wanted her. Wanted to press himself against her curves, sink his body into her soft, hot spot.

"Cool it, Khamil," he told himself. He closed his eyes and started counting sheep, hoping that would take his mind off the woman in his bed.

Monique couldn't sleep. Groaning, she rolled over onto her side and buried her face in the pillow. Then she rolled over again.

This was pointless. At most, she'd had a few precious minutes of sleep here and there throughout the night. And now, sunlight spilled through the blinds, overpowering the darkness.

Fresh sheets may have been on the bed, but Khamil's scent was everywhere. Surrounding her, invading her senses.

Khamil… It was hard not to imagine him in the bed with her. Hard not to imagine how his gaze alone had made her shudder with longing. Hard not to remember the rush of excitement she'd felt when he'd pulled her to him in the elevator, crushing her breasts against his solid chest.

Her eyes flew open. Was that a sound she heard outside her room? Heart pounding, she swallowed and waited.

Nothing.

Chiding herself for feeling disappointed, she rolled onto her side. Something caught her eye.

She screamed.

He'd just drifted to sleep when the bloodcurdling cry bolted him awake. *Monique.* Scrambling from the sofa, Khamil darted to the bedroom. Threw open the door.

Stopped dead in his tracks.

"Khamil!" Monique cried, relief evident in her bulging eyes. "Oh, God, it's there. Right *there.*"

He could hardly concentrate on what she was saying. Standing by the window, she wore only some scrap of ivory on her skin. Ivory lace. God, he was lost.

"Khamil! You have to do *something!*"

"W-what is it?"

"I don't know. Just kill it!"

Khamil ventured farther into the room, his eyes darting to the spot where Monique was pointing. When he saw the object of her fear, he shook his head. "This is why you screamed bloody murder?"

"Kill it. Khamil, please kill it." With each word, she backed farther away.

"It's only a bug."

"It's god-awful ugly, that's what it is! Ew! Look at all those legs. It's disgusting. And I've never seen anything that big in my life. Good grief, you should charge it rent!"

Khamil looked at the offending bug, which was on the wall beside the bed. Monique was right. It was ugly. He wasn't sure if it was a centipede or what, but it had about a gazillion legs and was probably two inches long.

He took a step forward. Monique jumped. He looked at her closely. She was shivering. God, she was really afraid. He suddenly wanted to comfort her, make the fear go away. "Don't worry. I'll get rid of it."

Khamil grabbed a Kleenex from the box on the night table, then rounded the side of the bed to get near the bug. Moving slowly, he covered the creature with the Kleenex, skillfully capturing it without killing it.

"I'll be right back."

Monique let out a sigh of relief as Khamil left the room, then immediately felt like a fool. If she could take this all back, she would. Screaming at the sight of a bug! It was absolutely absurd.

She could handle spiders, lizards, snakes even, but not that horribly disgusting bug that looked about a foot long.

Moments later, Khamil returned. "It's gone."

"Where?"

"I opened a window and let it outside."

She'd been too absorbed in the bug drama to notice what Khamil was wearing—or rather, *not* wearing. White cotton boxers covered the bare essentials—barely. Through his pants, it was clear Khamil's legs were muscular, but naked—he was perfect. Every part of his body was taut with beautiful muscles.

He was walking toward her. Monique's body stiffened, but she was helpless to move. Her eyes caught his, held his gaze.

It seemed like an eternity before he reached her.

"Khamil—"

"Monique—"

They spoke at the same time.

"Go ahead," she said, surprised to find her voice was barely a whisper.

He opened his mouth to speak. Closed it. Stared at her.

Her lips suddenly felt very dry and she flicked her tongue out to wet them. Immediately, she saw the response in Khamil's eyes. They darkened. Narrowed. She licked her lips again.

"Don't…do that."

Deliberately, she ran her tongue over her bottom lip. "This?" she asked innocently. She was teasing him, tempting him, and she didn't know why.

"Yes, that."

Something passed between them, something electrifying, exciting. He was so close now his breath fanned her forehead. In the silence of the room, she was sure she could hear her blood flowing through her veins.

He reached out and captured her wrist, stroking the inside with his thumb. The simple action made her heart pound furiously.

"Unresolved," he muttered.

"Hmm?" All she had to do was stand on her toes and her lips would brush against his.

"Ever since the first night I met you, I've wanted you. I think you feel the same way." Khamil gently stroked the smooth skin of Monique's face. She quivered at his touch. "God, Monique, I love the way you respond to my touch. It makes me hot."

Monique's throat constricted, preventing any words from escaping. She was completely distracted by Khamil's touch, by his words, by his heated gaze.

"We've been skirting around the issue," Khamil said, his voice husky. "But it's clear we want each other. There's so much tension between us…"

Before she knew what was happening, Khamil tilted her chin upward and lowered his lips to meet hers, surprising her with a delicate kiss. His mouth was as soft as velvet and lingered on hers, gently parting her lips with his tongue. He reached for her face with both hands, cupping it tenderly. His tongue was warm as it danced with her own, teasing her, exciting her beyond anything she could ever have imagined.

The kiss sent a tingling sensation all through Monique's body, electrifying and awakening every cell. When Khamil finally pulled his head away from hers to catch his breath, Monique felt as though someone had doused her with a glass of cold water. She hungered for more of what she had just experienced.

"You are the most beautiful woman I have ever laid my eyes on." Cupping Monique's chin, Khamil smiled down at her, a genuine, dazzling smile. Monique stared back at him in stunned silence.

"I want to make love to you."

"Khamil…" His name escaped on a breathless sigh.

"That's it, Monique. Let me know how much you want me." He trailed a finger from her neck to one soft mound of her breast.

"I want you," she said softly, surprised at her words.

Khamil covered her lips with his and wrapped his arms around her. Knowing that there was no turning back now, Monique wrapped her arms tightly around his neck.

And she didn't want to turn back.

"I want you so much," Khamil whispered against her ear as he urged her back onto the bed.

And then he was kissing her again, slowly at first, teasing her. But then his warm, wet tongue delved into her mouth with urgency, and the kiss became an explosion of desire.

Monique surrendered to the kiss, to the blinding desire that consumed her. Her tongue danced with Khamil's in a desperate song of passion. His mouth was warm and sweet and intoxicating. She moaned against his kiss, enjoying the here and now, not thinking about tomorrow.

Breaking the kiss, Khamil looked deeply into Monique's eyes. "Are you sure?"

Bereft of speech, Monique nodded.

Khamil's eyes crinkled as he looked down at her, heated longing evident in their depths. He brought his hand to her lips and softly traced the outline of her mouth with one finger. One finger, yet the light touch was so stimulating, Monique's entire body tingled with sexual fervor.

With his skilled hands, Khamil trailed a sensuous path down her smooth neck, then pulled the string that held the front of her lacy camisole together. The camisole loosened, and Khamil spread the material apart, exposing her breasts. He groaned softly, then brought his tongue to her searing skin and kissed the smooth, soft flesh between her breasts. Monique shuddered with delight as Khamil ran his tongue along her skin, up the hollow of her neck, and back down again.

"You're so beautiful," he said softly. Bringing both hands to her breasts, he stroked and kneaded the supple flesh. Then, he lowered his head and circled his tongue around a hard peak. Thrilled with the glorious feel of his tongue, Monique arched her back seductively, wanting more. She moaned Khamil's name when he took her nipple completely into his mouth.

Fire soared through Monique's veins right to her feminine

core. Wantonly, she clasped Khamil's head, holding it to her breast as he suckled, as ripples of pleasure coursed through her body.

She was mad with sweet longing, unlike anything she had ever experienced. Both hot and wet, her center of pleasure was throbbing incessantly. And just when she thought she would die of the ecstasy, Khamil slid a hand beneath her camisole and began daintily caressing her most private part. A rapturous moan escaped Monique's lips, and between ragged breaths, she said, "Oh, Khamil, I need you."

Monique pulled herself up onto her side and reached for Khamil's boxers. Her fingers were shaking as she tugged at them. Khamil eased himself up, allowing her to slip the boxers over his hips. Hastily, Monique dragged them down the length of his muscular legs.

Khamil pulled her to him. A sliver of desire skittered down Monique's spine as her hardened nipples grazed the solid muscles of Khamil's chest. She brought her mouth to his neck and ran her tongue along it, wanting to excite Khamil the way he was exciting her. Khamil gripped her arms, a raw sexual groan emanating from his throat. Feeling a sudden surge of power, Monique skimmed her tongue down to his chest, across the heated, brawny flesh, then over to one of his small nipples, taking the peak between her teeth.

Khamil shuddered, then pushed Monique onto her back with a force that thrilled her. She stared up at him from lowered lids, and watched as he brought his hand to her breast, gliding his fingers along the full, soft flesh. He reached for the camisole and Monique moved her body, allowing him to take it off.

Khamil's breath caught in his throat as he took in Monique's exquisite beauty. Her firm, flat stomach, her slim waist, her full, soft breasts and their dark erect tips. "You're perfect, Monique," he uttered softly. "Absolutely beautiful." He lay beside her and kissed her lightly, then with his fingers trailed a fiery path from her neck to her stomach, stopping just above her lace panties.

"Don't stop," Monique said, stroking his face. "Make love to me."

With delicate hands, Khamil skimmed the white lace panties over Monique's round hips, then over her long, smooth legs. An inferno of passion was burning in his loins as his eyes roamed her body, her silky, dark skin and tempting curves.

His gaze holding hers, Khamil lowered himself onto Monique's body, gently parting her legs with his own. Slipping a hand between their bodies, he found her throbbing center, then moaned softly when he discovered she was wet and ready for him. He immersed a finger deep inside her, enjoying the way she arched her back at his touch, the way an excited moan escaped her lips. He played with her until she was whimpering and groaning and tossing her head from side to side, until he could no longer stand not being inside her.

"Just a second." Easing himself off the bed, Khamil reached for the top drawer on the night table. He pulled out a condom, tore open the package, then put the condom on.

Monique still lay ready for him, and he settled himself between her legs. Then, capturing her mouth with his, he entered her.

A half moan, half cry fell from Monique's lips. She dug her nails into Khamil's back, squeezing hard as he thrust deep inside her. Nothing had ever felt as glorious as this. Her body was alive with sensations, wonderful sensations that threatened to take control of her very being. "Oh, yes!" she cried. "Oh, Khamil…"

Monique was driving him crazy. She knew just how to touch him, how to meet his wild thrusts. It was as if they were familiar with each other's bodies, with what thrilled and turned each other on. Yet they were lovers for the first time.

"Khamil!" Monique squealed, gripping his firm buttocks as the most delightful dizzying sensation swept over her. She let out a loud, ravished moan as her hips bucked savagely, as contractions rippled through her core, one after the other until every ounce of strength drained from her body. As the contractions subsided, she clung to Khamil's slick body, luxuriating in the aftermath of her splendid climax, knowing that what she had experienced was heaven on earth. She wished she could stay in his arms forever.

Khamil seized Monique's lips in a short, fierce kiss, just before his head grew light and his body grew taut. He plunged into Monique's sweet warmth one last time, collapsing on top of her as he succumbed to his glorious release. As sweet sensations rocked his body, he held her to him tightly, knowing that he had never experienced anything quite as wonderful as this with any other woman.

They stayed there like that, holding each other, their bodies wet, their breathing frantic. And finally, when their breathing returned to normal, Khamil slid off Monique and lay beside her.

"My God, Monique." Khamil kissed her temple as he wrapped an arm over her waist. "What have you done to me?"

Monique turned in Khamil's arms, surprisingly content. Their lovemaking had been explosive, and there was no point in denying that. "The same thing you've done to me."

Silence fell between them as they snuggled up together.

"Maybe now I can finally get some sleep," Khamil whispered.

Monique chuckled softly. "Me, too."

Khamil pulled her closer, and Monique closed her eyes. Yeah, she'd sleep well. At least for a while.

Chapter 14

The sound of Monique's beeper going off jarred her from sleep. For a moment she was stunned to find herself in a strange bed. But the strong arms around her instantly reminded her of where she was.

In Khamil's bed.

Khamil stirred. "What was that?"

"My beeper," Monique answered. She glanced at the digital clock on Khamil's night table. It was thirteen minutes after nine. "That's probably my agent."

Monique moved to the side of the bed and reached for her purse on the floor. She dug out her beeper and checked the number. Her family also had her beeper number, but were instructed to use it only if there was a dire emergency. Thus far, that hadn't happened.

"Yeah, it's my agent," Monique said.

"You need to use the phone?" Khamil asked.

"Yeah. I'll go to the living room."

"No, go ahead and use this phone. I need to get up anyway."

Khamil threw the covers off his body and climbed from the bed, naked as the day he was born. Monique couldn't help checking out his firm butt as he walked to the closet. Seconds later, he slipped into a terrycloth robe.

The sight of his naked body was an all too real reminder of what had happened last night. As Khamil exited the bedroom, Monique wondered what today would bring. Was last night simply a one-time deal? And did she want any more than that? Between her modeling career and her quest to find her mother's killer, she wasn't sure she had much to offer a man in a relationship.

Putting those thoughts out of her mind, she reached for the phone and dialed her agent. Kelly, the receptionist, answered.

"Morning, Kelly. It's Monique Savard. Is Elaine in?"

"Yep. One second."

A moment later, Elaine said, "Elaine Cox."

"Hello, Elaine. It's Monique."

"Hi, Monique." She paused. "Listen. There was a message for you on the office voice mail this morning."

"Really?" Who would leave a message for her at her agency, rather than at her home number?

"Yeah. And it's kind of cryptic, but sounded important, so I figured I'd call you right away with it."

Monique sat up. "Okay."

"The person's voice sounded muffled, so I couldn't make out if it was a man or a woman. But the message said that you should check the house in Canada, that she probably kept the letters. They will give you the answers you're looking for."

"What?" Monique asked, more out of confusion than because she hadn't heard what Elaine had said.

Elaine repeated the message, then said, "Hopefully, you know what the heck that means."

"I think so," Monique answered, though she really had no clue. But more baffling than the cryptic message was the issue as to who had called her agent. "And this person didn't leave a name, or a number where I could reach them?"

"Nope. Sorry." Elaine paused, the asked, "Is this about your mother?"

"I'm sure it is." That had to be the "she" the mysterious caller had referred to. Confused, Monique blew out a frazzled breath. What letters? And what kind of clue did they hold as to the identity of her mother's murderer?

There was only one thing she was sure of. If there was some type of lead at her family's cottage in Canada, then she had to go check it out. Immediately. "Look, Elaine. I'm gonna head out of town for a few days, but I'll be back in time for the Cover Girl shoot next week."

"Monique." Elaine's tone was wary. "I'm worried about you."

"I'll be fine," she told her. "But this is something I have to do."

"Please be careful."

"I will."

"And call me with a number where I can reach you."

"All right. I will. Thanks for giving me the message."

"Of course."

"I'll talk to you later," Monique said, then replaced the receiver. She pulled her legs to her chest, her mind trying to make sense of the information she'd just received.

What was going on? Who had called? Someone who'd seen *America's Most Wanted* and was calling with a tip? And if so, why hadn't they called the police?

The knock at the door interrupted her thoughts. Monique adjusted the blankets over her breasts, then said, "Come in."

As if he sensed something was bothering her, Khamil looked at her with concern. "Everything okay?"

"I don't know."

"What do you mean you don't know?"

"I got a weird call from my agent," Monique explained. "Someone called and left a message for me to check the house in Canada because there'll be answers there. They mentioned some letters."

"You still have the house?"

Monique met Khamil's eyes. "Yeah."

"Then whoever called is someone you know."

A chill slithered down Monique's spine.

"Otherwise, why would they tell you to check the house? If it was someone you didn't know, they wouldn't know if you still had the house. Hell, they wouldn't know about any letters."

"You're right." At first, Monique had wondered if the call had possibly been a prank. But Khamil was right. If someone knew her family still had the house, then there was no way the message could be a prank.

Still covering herself with the bedsheet, Monique reached for one of Khamil's shirts, which hung on a bedpost. She slipped it on. Then she stood and reached for her overnight bag.

Khamil walked farther into the room. "What are you doing?"

"I have to go." Monique reached into the bag and pulled out her bra and a clean pair of underwear.

"Where?" Khamil asked, his tone wary.

"I have to go to Canada."

"Wait a second," Khamil stopped before her. "You get a weird call about some clue and you're just gonna get up and take off to Canada?"

"I have to, Khamil." Monique slipped the underwear on. "If there are answers there, I need to find them."

"Fine. I hear you. But you can't just get up and go."

"Why not?"

Khamil shook his head in dismay as he stared at Monique. She didn't look at him as she slipped her bra around her waist, fastened it, then pulled it over her breasts. Last night, they'd spent an incredible night making love, and now, she was ready to run off as if nothing had happened between them.

"Don't you want to have a shower?"

"I can have one at home."

Khamil couldn't help feeling a sense of disappointment as he watched Monique slip into her pants. "And last night…"

"I don't have time to talk about that right now."

"I see." Turning, Khamil walked toward the bedroom door. He didn't know what to make of Monique. Last night, she'd been concerned that he was involved with someone else, making it seem as though she may have wanted more from him. Now, she was acting as if she didn't give a damn about him in any way, not even the fact that they'd made love.

Khamil faced Monique again. She was now fully dressed. "Are you going to the police?"

"Yeah, I'll go. After I head home and make my travel arrangements."

Monique returned Khamil's shirt to the bedpost, then took one last look around. Satisfied that she had everything, she headed for the bedroom door.

"All right," she said, stopping before Khamil. "I'll call you later."

She stepped past him, but Khamil took hold of her arm, stopping her. "That's it? You spend the night with me, and you leave?"

"I'm sorry, Khamil." Monique ran her free hand over her hair. "I've got a lot on my mind."

"Fine," Khamil conceded. "Will you call me when you get there?"

Monique nodded. "Sure."

Khamil didn't like this. He didn't like Monique's indifferent attitude toward him, and he sure didn't like the idea of her chasing some lead about a murder by herself. "Be careful," he told her.

"I will."

Lowering his head, Khamil surprised Monique with a soft kiss on the lips. Even though the contact was brief, she savored the feel and taste of him. Glancing into his eyes, she saw sincerity in their dark brown depths, and butterflies danced in her stomach.

Last night with Khamil had been nothing short of wonderful. He was a skilled lover, but she'd known he would be. He seemed sincere enough, and had been good to her, yet she wasn't sure she was ready to consider anything more than last night. For one, Khamil hadn't said he wanted anything more. And until her own life's messes were straightened out, she didn't know if she'd truly be able to give her heart to anybody.

Yet she couldn't deny they'd shared something special. Reaching for his face, she palmed one of his cheeks. "I have to go."

Khamil turned his face in her hand so that his lips met her palm. He gave her hand a brief kiss. "Please call me later."

"I will," Monique promised.

Khamil had already called the office the night before to let them know he'd be working from home today. But he was completely unable to concentrate on the contracts that lay before him on his dining room table.

All he could think about was Monique, and what kind of trouble she might be getting herself into.

He was worried about her.

He'd called her apartment once already, but she hadn't answered her phone. No doubt, she was at the police station. That thought should have given him comfort, but it didn't. There were way too many cases in which the police didn't and couldn't do anything about an anonymous threat until it was too late.

Standing, Khamil gathered the loose files from the table and dropped them into his briefcase. If he stayed at home and worked and anything happened to Monique, he'd never forgive himself.

Javar had had a premonition the night their mother had tried to murder Whitney, and that premonition had brought him to his wife's side in the nick of time. And one night long ago, during college, Khamil had had a premonition that had saved his life. He'd refused to go out after a football game with two other players from the team who were heading across the border to Windsor, Canada, for a night of clubbing. Eric and Trey had been hit by an out-of-control truck that had crossed the median en route to the Canadian border, and both were killed instantly. Their car had been a mass of crushed fiberglass and metal; Eric and Trey hadn't stood a chance.

If Khamil had gone with them, there was no doubt he would have been killed as well.

He believed in instincts, believed in trusting them. As a lawyer, he had to—and they never steered him wrong.

Right now, Khamil's instincts told him that Monique needed him. And they were too strong to ignore.

His briefcase closed, Khamil quickly headed to the bedroom to dress, hoping he wasn't too late to reach Monique before she left for Canada.

* * *

Having called her travel agent on the way home and learning that there weren't any flights for Toronto until the afternoon, Monique had decided to do as Khamil had suggested and went to the police station to report the threatening letters she'd received. As she'd guessed, there wasn't much the police could do about the letters, except open a file for her case.

"If you get anything else, let us know," the officer she'd dealt with had told her.

Now, Monique sat in the back of a taxi, heading home where she would pack. She still had four hours before her flight from JFK, but already she was anxious. What kind of clue could be in the house? And who would know about it? Surely if her father knew about the clue he would have brought this to the police's attention years ago.

Unless it was something that would further implicate him in the crime.

For the second time, she allowed herself to consider what Doreen always tried to impress upon her. There *was* a possibility that her father could have killed her mother.

That was nonsense, Monique concluded almost as quickly as the thought had formed. Deep in her heart, she knew that her father didn't have anything to do with her mother's death. Still, it was obvious that someone knew something, and the fact that someone knew her family still owned the house in Canada deeply disturbed her.

It had to be someone close to her.

But who?

Or, she suddenly realized, it could be someone who still lived in the neighborhood where they'd had their summer home. Yes, she thought, a wave of relief washing over her, that made sense. A neighbor might know that the house had never been sold, and may even know something that had happened that horrible night. For whatever reason, this person may have been scared to come forward—until now.

That thought comforted her, even though she was no closer to having any answers. Bottom line, she didn't want to think that anyone close to the family might have known and withheld vital information about her mother's murder from the police.

The taxi pulled to a stop in front of her building. She paid the driver as Harry opened the door. She smiled at Harry, but her smile quickly faded as she looked past his shoulder and saw Khamil standing near the building's front door.

"You have a guest," Harry told her.

"Yes," Monique said absently. "I see."

Monique headed toward Khamil, noting the briefcase and small piece of luggage at his feet. "Khamil, what are you doing?"

"I'm going with you," he replied simply.

Monique narrowed her eyes as she looked at him. "Going with me where?"

"To Toronto."

"Toronto?" She gaped at him. "What on earth for?"

Khamil replied, "I have business up there."

"Really?" Monique sounded skeptical.

"Toronto has a booming entertainment industry. Many talent from there work on both sides of the border, and vice versa. In fact, a New York producer is up there filming a feature right now, and he needs me to look over a contract for one of the secondary characters who wants to do some negotiating. So I have plenty to do."

Monique's expression said she didn't believe him.

"And," Khamil continued, "I don't want you to go alone."

"Khamil..."

"Don't bother telling me to go home. The man who killed your mother is still on the loose. There's no way I'm going to let you put yourself at risk."

Monique felt a little jolt in her heart at his words, and her entire body got warm. God help her, his stubbornness turned her on. "Why not?"

"We're friends. I'm always there for my friends."

Disappointment bubbled in Monique's stomach at Khamil's description of their relationship. Yet that's all they were— friends who had shared a passionate night of lovemaking.

"I'm sure you have better things to do than baby-sit me," Monique told him.

Khamil lifted the briefcase. "I've got work in here. I've got my cell phone. I'm good to go."

Monique blew out a sigh. The idea of having company on this trip made her feel much better. "All right. If you're sure."

"I am."

"Well, I still have to pack," Monique explained, stepping into the building as Harry held the door open for her. She passed him a few bills. "I went to the police station, but like I thought, there's not much they can do."

"You filed a report, right?"

"Uh-huh. So, we'll see." Monique hit the elevator button. "But I'm not about to wait around for the police to do anything. Do you know how many times my mother reported the threats she'd been receiving? In the end, it didn't do her any good."

The elevator doors opened. A couple exited, and then Monique and Khamil entered.

"I called about flights," Monique began when the door

closed. "There's one that leaves JFK for Toronto at three fifty-five this afternoon."

"Cool. That'll give us time to stop to get something to eat before we head to the airport."

The elevator made a soft pinging sound as it landed on the penthouse floor. The doors opened and Monique made her way off the elevator, followed by Khamil.

They walked in silence down the hallway, Monique reaching into her purse for her keys. At her apartment door, Monique tried inserting the key, but it wouldn't go in.

Holding up the key chain, Monique sorted through the keys until she found another similar one. She often confused the two keys. She placed the second key into the slot and pushed, but like the first one, it wouldn't go in, either.

"Having trouble?" Khamil asked, his breath warm on Monique's neck.

Monique's eyes fluttered shut as Khamil's breath tickled her neck. "No," she replied as calmly as she could.

"It looks like you're having trouble to me," Khamil said, putting his hand on hers. "Let me help."

With his slightly callused hand resting delicately on hers, Khamil helped her insert the key in the lock. You'd think he was slowly disrobing her, the way Monique's body got excited at Khamil's touch.

And that was the problem, she realized. With Khamil around, she didn't focus on what was important because she couldn't seem to keep her raging hormones under control around him. Right now, she should be concerned with whatever clue might be at the cottage in Canada, not with how wonderful it had felt to be in Khamil's arms last night.

"This is the key?" Khamil asked.

"I think so," Monique replied.

Khamil's fingers wrapped around hers. He tried to turn the key, but it wouldn't move. "Wait a second," he said. He wiggled the key in the lock. "That's strange. It won't go all the way in."

Monique's gaze fell to the key. Khamil was right. Maybe she'd messed up with the first key. "Try the other silver key."

Khamil tried the second silver key, but again, it didn't insert completely into the lock. He withdrew the key and bent his head to inspect the lock closer. Then his eyes flew to Monique's, panic written on his face.

"What?" Monique asked. She hugged her torso, suddenly feeling cold.

"It looks like someone tampered with the lock."

"What?"

"The edges of the slot are bent slightly. Damaged. See?"

Monique looked where Khamil indicated. Then she nodded, acknowledging that he was right.

"Almost as if someone took a screwdriver to it or something."

Something made Monique reach for the door handle and turn it. And when it opened, she threw a worried glance at Khamil. She never left her apartment door unlocked.

Khamil saw the concern in Monique's eyes and matched it with a look of his own. After a moment, he put a finger to his mouth, indicting for Monique to be quiet.

Then he silently edged open the door and stepped into the apartment.

Chapter 15

Monique's heart pounded as she watched Khamil creep into her apartment. She was so frightened, she couldn't move.

"Oh, God," Khamil said.

"What?" Monique's stomach lurched with fear.

"Damn." Khamil turned to face her. "Someone's definitely been in here, Monique."

Hearing Khamil's words, she felt a shiver pass over her body. Yet she'd known that had to be the case the moment she discovered the apartment was open. As much as she'd wanted to believe she could have accidentally left the door unlocked, she knew that wasn't likely.

As Khamil continued to stare at her, Monique slowly entered her penthouse unit. A startled cry fell from her mouth at what she saw.

On the wall, written in red, was the word *Whore*.

And all over the floor, there were red rose petals. The petals had not only been ripped from their buds, many had been crushed into her carpet with someone's shoe heel.

Monique closed her eyes tightly as panic swept over her. "Oh, my God."

Khamil placed both hands on Monique's shoulders, and she opened her eyes to find him staring at her intensely. "Monique."

Khamil pressed his fingers into her shoulders softly, but firmly. "Do you have *any* idea who could have done this?"

She thought a moment, then said, "Raymond."

"Raymond?"

"The guy who was at Angel's that night," Monique explained. "When I kissed you. He's the only one who had a key."

Khamil stood straight, his hands falling to his sides. "He had a key to your place?"

Monique nodded.

"So the relationship was serious."

"I guess," Monique said. "I trusted him. But then he started acting crazy. He cheated on me, so I broke up with him. But then he wanted me back."

Khamil's eyebrows shot together. "How crazy? Crazy enough to be the person behind the threats?"

Monique blew out a hurried breath as she contemplated the thought. "Maybe. And he *does* know where I live. He knows my agency. He works a lot of the models' shoots."

One of Khamil's eyebrows shot up. "He does?"

"Yes." Oh, goodness. Could Raymond really be the one behind all of this? "He did make some weird comment about knowing something about my mother's death. At the time, I brushed that off as another lame attempt on his part to get me back, because he said he'd tell me what he knew if I got back together with him."

"And this guy still has a key to your place?" Khamil asked, his tone incredulous.

"Not because I want him to. He made a copy," Monique explained. "But when he showed up here the last time, I asked him for it. He gave it to me." Glancing at the floor, Monique frowned. "I suppose it's possible he had a few copies made."

Her eyes wandered back up to Khamil's face. "But if he had a key, why break into the apartment?"

Khamil pursed his lips, contemplating the question. "Maybe he didn't break in," he said after a long moment. "Maybe he opened the door, came in and did all this, then tampered with the lock afterward to make it *look* like a break-in." Khamil paused, his forehead furrowing. "And you said 'the last time.' When did he show up here?"

"A few weeks ago."

Alarm flashed in his eyes. "Did you call the police?"

"No. I asked for the key back, he gave it to me, and I thought that would be the end of it."

"Monique…"

"Fine, I made a mistake. I had no clue he'd be so…insane." Monique's bottom lip quivered as she glanced at the wall, then back at Khamil. "But what if it *wasn't* Raymond? What if it was someone else?" Hugging her torso, she turned away at the disturbing thought. "Oh, God."

"I'm calling the police," Khamil announced. "In the meantime, pack a suitcase. A large one. I don't want you coming back here."

When the police finished taking their statements, they promised they'd send a detective to talk to Raymond. In the meantime, they had retrieved the building's security tape to see who had gone in and out of the apartment in the last twenty-four hours.

Still shaken, Monique sat on her sofa, her elbows resting on her knees, her chin resting in her palms.

"You still want to go?" Khamil asked.

Monique looked up at him, knowing he meant whether or not she still wanted to go to Canada. She nodded. "Yes. I have to."

Khamil lowered himself onto the sofa beside her. "This could simply be a coincidence. The person who sent you the letters referring to your mother might not be the person who did this. In fact, it makes perfect sense that it was Raymond who trashed your apartment, angry at you because he saw you with me."

Monique lowered her gaze to the cream-colored carpet. Her eyes caught a spot where the red roses had stained. It looked like a spot of blood....

"Help...me..."

Monique squeezed her eyes tightly, trying to block out the haunting memory. But she couldn't. Her mother's blood had stained the carpet in the bedroom just as these red roses had stained hers.

Was this a coincidence? Or was the person who'd stalked and killed her mother toying with her?

Monique shot to her feet. "I need to get out of here."

"Monique."

Not wanting to fall apart in front of Khamil, Monique turned toward the window. A second later, she flinched when he wrapped his arms around her.

"It's okay, Monique," he said softly. "You don't have to be strong all the time. I know how hard this is for you."

"How do you know?" Monique asked. "How could you possibly know?"

"Because I've been through my own share of tragedies, Monique. My uncle was killed in the line of duty at a routine traffic stop in Chicago. Yes, his killer was caught, but the grief never quite goes away. And..." Khamil's voice trailed off. It was still hard for him to admit this to anyone, and very few people knew the truth. "My mother is behind bars for attempted murder."

Monique turned in his arms, staring at Khamil with curious eyes.

"It's a long story, and I'll tell it to you someday, but the gist of it is that my mother hated my brother's wife, and tried to kill her a couple times. The first time, she succeeded in killing my nephew—her own grandchild."

Monique threw a hand to her mouth. "Oh, Khamil. I'm so sorry."

"He was only five," Khamil went on. "Of course, my mother never expected him to be in the car she'd sabotaged in an effort to get rid of my sister-in-law, Whitney. My mother's actions tore our family apart, and ruined my brother's marriage for a couple years. Javar blamed Whitney for the accident, because Javar Junior hadn't been buckled in. And of course, you can imagine what kind of guilt my sister-in-law lived with. It wasn't until a couple years after my nephew's death that we learned the truth about the accident, that it wasn't Whitney's fault."

"How?" Monique asked.

"My mother tried to kill Whitney again. My mother's a doctor and she'd drugged Whitney, with plans of drowning her in the lake."

Monique gasped.

"Yeah, I know. Anyway, to make a long story short, Javar got to her before it was too late, and my mother confessed to everything."

"Khamil, that's so horrible." She placed a hand on his forearm and gently stroked it. "Did your brother and his wife work things out?"

Khamil nodded. "Thankfully. And everything's fine now

between them. They have three-year-old twins and I just found out they're expecting another baby."

A smile touched Monique's face. She loved happy endings. It was what she still hoped for in her mother's case. "Oh, that's wonderful."

"Yeah," Khamil said proudly. "But my mother…she's in prison, and she'll be there for a very long time."

"I'm sorry," Monique said. In a small way, it gave her comfort to know that she wasn't the only one who'd gone through something devastating, even though the kind of pain she'd suffered wasn't something she would wish on her worst enemy. But for the first time, she felt that someone not only cared, but understood.

"She did the crime, now she'd doing the time," Khamil said, as though it was no big deal. But Monique could see the pain in his eyes.

"Do you talk to her?"

"My mother?"

Monique nodded.

"Not really. She still blames Whitney for everything that's happened, and to tell the truth, I can't deal with her."

"I see." Turning, Monique strolled to the window and peered down at the view of Central Park. It was a picturesque day, with a cloudless blue sky. What she'd give to be carefree and able to stroll through the park without any worries about anything.

Except, perhaps, falling in love.

Butterflies danced in Monique's stomach at the direction of her thoughts. *In love?* Why on earth had that come into her mind?

But she knew. Spinning around, she saw Khamil. He was staring at her, and his eyes met hers.

He was an enigma. Playful yet serious, cocky yet not full of himself… She was falling for the caring side she saw in him, despite the fact that his playful, cocky side made her wonder if he was a seasoned playboy.

What if he is? she asked herself. *Can't people change?*

Once again, she faced the window, the hope she'd felt a moment earlier fizzing. She was too old and had been in one too many relationships to delude herself with the wish that someone could change their ways. Once a player, always a player, as the saying went. While she had no doubt that Khamil was attracted to her, she seriously doubted if the attraction would last. There were no pictures of women in his apartment, indicating to her that none stayed in his life for any length of time.

Why should she be any different?

She wouldn't allow herself to get her hopes up, because that would only lead to disappointment. She would accept his friendship—because she needed a friend, and he seemed to understand her pain.

But she'd certainly make sure to guard her heart.

It seemed like days later that Khamil and Monique arrived at Pearson International Airport in Toronto, when in fact it had only been hours. Because of the break-in at her place and having to give reports to the police, they'd had to catch a later flight than planned. Now, it was evening in Toronto, and Monique had no desire to head an hour and a half north of the city to her family's cottage.

As if reading her thoughts, Khamil said, "It's late. Maybe we should get a hotel and get some rest, then get to work in the morning."

"I was thinking the same thing," Monique told him. "In fact,

I'd meant to call my cousins and my father to let them know I'm here. I can do that from the hotel."

Their luggage in hand, Khamil and Monique headed outside the terminal. The first shuttle they saw was for the Holiday Inn, and they got on board.

Khamil placed his arm around Monique's shoulder as the bus started to move, and she rested her head against his shoulder. Glancing down at her, Khamil stroked her jet-black tresses.

He felt comfortable with Monique, more comfortable than he'd felt with any other woman he'd ever been with. Perhaps it was because she wasn't like the others. She was strong, independent, and she sure didn't act as if she needed him. Which, Khamil had discovered, was a quality that attracted him. It was exactly what he wanted. A woman who was self-sufficient, who didn't need a man for anything but wanted one for a satisfying relationship.

He frowned at the direction of his thoughts. Why was he thinking of a relationship? What they'd shared was sex, pure and simple. Besides, not only had Monique not made any mention of wanting anything more, she'd practically run from his bed and his apartment the morning after, seeming not to care about even the possibility of more with him.

Maybe that's what intrigued him. The chase. So many women these days did the chasing, taking away that traditional role from men. Not that he was the most traditional guy, but there was a part of him that enjoyed the pursuit of a woman— the hunt, as some would say. The more Khamil thought about it, the more he realized that it was the women who were the boldest who turned him off the most.

But he didn't want to get ahead of himself. He had chased Jessica, and in the end, she had broken his heart. He'd had female friends over the years who told him he was hung up on that fact, that because Jessica had bruised his ego, he didn't want to give his heart to another. And maybe, he finally conceded, they were right.

Khamil twirled a tendril of Monique's silky hair between his fingers. Was that his problem? Had he been a coward all these years, guarding his heart because he didn't want another woman to break it?

He didn't know. All he knew was that for the first time in years, when he thought of Jessica, he didn't feel the bitterness that he used to. Whether or not that was because of the woman who now laid her head on his shoulder, he wasn't sure.

Whatever the case, it could only be a good thing.

"I'm gonna take a shower," Khamil announced the moment after he stepped into the hotel room and placed the luggage on the floor. At the front desk, he'd almost asked Monique if she wanted separate rooms, but decided against it. The memory of last night had been with him all day, and now that they were actually settling down for the evening, he knew without a doubt that he wanted her by his side, sharing his bed. He wanted to spend the night with her again, making love to her as he had less than twenty-four hours ago, and unless she voiced any opposition to spending the night with him, he'd decided there was no reason for him to suggest otherwise.

"All right," Monique said. She lowered herself onto the edge of the king-size bed. "I'm going to make some calls."

Khamil winked at her. "Feel free to join me when you're done."

Monique flashed him a small smile. "Sure."

Leaving Monique sitting on the bed, Khamil sauntered into

the bathroom, where he placed his hands on the counter and leaned forward. He stared into the mirror long and hard. He looked like Khamil Jordan. Yet he felt like a different man. Something had changed about him in these last few days, and he wasn't quite sure what it was.

He missed Monique, which didn't make a lick of sense, considering she was just outside the bathroom door. He glanced at the door, hoping it would open, and when it didn't, he felt a modicum of disappointment. When had he ever gone to a hotel room with a woman he wasn't going to make love to? Never.

He wanted her, no doubt about it, and he had to admit that his ego was taking a small beating at the reality that she clearly didn't share his desires. If she wanted him even half as much as he wanted her, she'd be in here with him, ready to get wet...

Khamil blew out a ragged breath. Yeah, he had it for her bad. He wanted her in the shower with him, wanted to lather her body up with soap, touch her in all the places that would make her moan...

Maybe that was his problem. He was *horny.* A chuckle fell from his lips. How could he not be? The night he'd spent with Monique had been one of the best sexual experiences of his life. She knew just how to move with him, how to touch him. There hadn't been the awkwardness that he usually experienced with a new lover.

Now, he had an erection.

Khamil walked to the bath and turned on the water, adjusting it until it was the right temperature. Maybe he should blast the cold water, he thought with chagrin. What good would it do for him to have an erection when Monique was preoccupied with whatever clue may be at her family's cottage.

And it would certainly be insensitive of him to try and tempt her away from that to satisfy his carnal urges.

Trying to forget about Monique, Khamil stripped out of his clothes, then got into the bath where he pulled the lever to start the shower. The warm water felt wonderful, sluicing over his body. Closing his eyes, he let the water massage his body and face.

He jumped when he felt a hand brush against him, then whirled around. Opening his eyes, he saw Monique smiling up at him.

A slow grin spread across his face.

"You said I could join you, didn't you?" Monique asked.

"Hell, yeah," Khamil answered. His eyes ventured lower, taking the view of her exquisite body. No doubt about it, she was perfect. Slim waist, legs for days, full beautiful breasts, smooth, dark skin. He reached for a nipple, tweaking it with his fingers.

Monique closed her eyes and moaned softly. The nipple puckered at his touch. "You like that?" Khamil asked.

"Mmm."

"How about this?" Lowering his head, he captured the nipple in his mouth.

Monique arched her back and mewed.

"Spread your legs," Khamil told her.

Monique obeyed, and Khamil cupped her, then gently caressed her with his thumb. White-hot heat exploded at the center of her womanhood.

"You like that?"

"Yes," she whimpered.

Khamil dropped to his knees before her, startling Monique. She couldn't tell which was hotter—the water or his breath gently fanning her.

"I want to see you," Khamil said. He ran his thumb over her nub. "I want to taste you." He flicked his tongue where his thumb had just been.

"Oh, God…" Monique clutched his head and held him to her, luxuriating in the glorious feel of his tongue on her most private spot.

"Damn, Monique. You're driving me crazy."

She couldn't speak, only toss her head from side to side as she moaned. She hardly recognized the passionate cries escaping her, but she'd never felt this good. Khamil flicked his tongue over her, then suckled softly, driving her absolutely mad with desire. With each skillful flick of his tongue, her body coiled tighter and tighter, like a spring.

And then the spring popped, and she dug her nails into his head and cried out as she was catapulted into an abyss of dizzying sensations. Her body rocked with spasms, and still he didn't relent, until Monique was so overcome with the glorious feeling coursing through her body that she collapsed against Khamil. She slithered down and wrapped her arms around his neck.

Khamil kissed her fiercely as the warm water cascaded over their bodies. He wanted to spread her legs and ease himself inside her right then, but the slippery bathtub was hardly ideal. "Let's go to the bed," he whispered.

He stood, helping Monique to her feet as he did. He kissed her once more, then turned off the water. The air in the bathroom instantly chilled them as they got out of the shower, and Khamil quickly reached for a towel. He wrapped it around Monique, rubbing it over her body to help dry her.

Monique stood on her toes and slipped her arms around

Khamil's neck. She didn't feel cold when the towel fell from her shoulders into a heap at her feet.

All she could feel was heat as Khamil scooped her into his arms.

And all she could think as he carried her out of the bathroom and set her down on the king-size bed was how much she wanted him, right here and right now, even if it was only for a moment in time.

Chapter 16

The next morning, Monique awoke to a feeling of sadness. She wasn't sure why. Her head rested against Khamil's strong chest, and his arms were wrapped snugly around her. She lay listening to the sounds of his steady breathing, as though she'd done this a million times before. There was no denying the comfort level between them, yet something still bothered her.

Monique lifted her head and looked over Khamil's chest to the clock radio. It was only minutes after seven, meaning she hadn't had more than four hours of sleep. She was still tired, but she knew she wouldn't be able to sleep another wink.

Not in Khamil's arms.

Very carefully, Monique slipped out of Khamil's embrace, then sat on the edge of the bed. She threw a glance over her shoulder. Khamil hadn't moved.

What was wrong with her? Both nights she'd spent with Khamil had been wonderful, and during their lovemaking she hadn't been shy about sharing her body with him. But both mornings after had brought a measure of anxiety and distress.

Monique frowned, not quite sure what it was that bothered her. Deciding her energies would be better spent on planning her day, she got up. In her suitcase, she found a T-shirt and slipped it on. Then she walked the few steps to where her purse lay on the sofa. It was early, but her father normally rose with the sun. Before she went to the house, she wanted to let him know about the message she'd received and that she was in Canada to do some investigating.

As Khamil was sleeping, she didn't want to use the room's phone. She dug her cell phone out of her purse and started for the bathroom.

"Monique."

Monique froze, hearing the way Khamil's voice sounded when he called her name. The sweet deepness of his voice, the softness it portrayed as he called her... Her stomach suddenly felt like a home for frenzied butterflies.

She turned.

Khamil glanced at the clock, then back at her. "What are you doing?"

"I'm going to make some calls."

"It's eleven minutes after seven," Khamil said matter-of-factly.

"I know that. My father's already up, and I want to—"

"Come back here."

Khamil's statement took Monique by surprise—and made a shiver of desire pass over her.

"Come back here," Khamil repeated.

Khamil's tone left no room for negotiation, and after a moment's hesitation, Monique headed back to the bed.

"Sit down," Khamil told her.

Monique sat. Khamil's eyes roamed over her, from her face to her thighs, then back to her face. He slipped a hand beneath the edge of her T-shirt, resting his fingers on her leg.

"Khamil—" Monique protested.

"Why did you put this on?" Khamil asked, his fingers tugging on the T-shirt.

"Why does anyone put clothes on?" Monique retorted.

"I've already seen all of you," Khamil told her.

"What's your point?"

"Yesterday morning, you got up and left after we made love. Today, you're doing the same thing."

"I've got a lot on my mind."

Khamil edged himself up on an elbow. "It's more than that."

Monique met Khamil's eyes, first wide with indignation, but after a moment, she looked away.

"What are you afraid of, Monique?"

Monique opened her mouth to reply, but nothing came out.

"We've spent two incredible nights together, and you gave me all of you. Yet you can't stay in bed with me the morning after. You don't feel comfortable being naked with me." Khamil slipped a hand beneath the T-shirt and softly stroked one of Monique's breasts.

The delicious feeling that flooded her was too much. She couldn't deal with this, not now. So she stood.

"Monique, don't run away."

Monique swallowed, then met Khamil's eyes. "What's happening between us?"

"We're attracted to each other," Khamil replied simply.

"Yes, but—" Stopping abruptly, Monique turned away.

"But what?"

Monique whirled around. "Is that all it is? Sexual attraction?"

Khamil's shoulders moved in a slight shrug. "Would that be so bad?"

Disappointment swirled in Monique's stomach, making her feel queasy. "I… This is the last thing I need."

Khamil sat up fully and reached for her. His hand on her leg, he gently guided her to the bed. "Look, I don't know what's happening between us, either. But I do know… Maybe we should go with the flow, see where it takes us."

"I don't need any distractions, Khamil."

Khamil placed a finger on Monique's chin. "Is that all you see me as? A distraction?"

A shaky breath escaped her. "No."

"Good. Because I don't want to be a distraction."

"What do you want with me?" she asked.

"I could think of a number of things," Khamil replied, a devilish grin prancing on his lips as he trailed his fingers from her chin to her ear.

For a moment, Monique was stunned, her throat too constricted for speech. Khamil's sexy smile and suggestive words suddenly had her tingling with longing. For a moment, she felt totally sexy and utterly desirable.

But she said, "I'm serious, Khamil."

Khamil dropped his hand. "I don't know."

His response upset Monique more than she'd expected. She had no clue what she wanted, yet hearing Khamil say that left her feeling…empty. She wanted him to care more. She wanted to know she meant more to him than anyone else did.

Her heart thumped quick and hard. God, what was happening to her? But the question was rhetorical, for she knew. Somewhere along the line, she'd started caring for Khamil more than she'd ever planned to.

"I don't want this to mean nothing," Monique whispered, surprised to find she'd voiced her thoughts aloud.

Khamil merely nodded, leaving Monique feeling more insecure than she'd imagined possible. When had she started caring?

Maybe it was because Khamil seemed to understand her, understand her need to resolve the one thing that haunted her most in life. She hadn't found that level of care or understanding from any other man she'd dated. Every other man thought she was obsessed and needed to "let go." Even her family felt the same way.

Yet Khamil hadn't said those words to her. Instead, here he was with her in Toronto to help her get answers.

"Have you ever been in love?" Monique suddenly asked.

A muscle in Khamil's jaw flinched, and his dark eyes grew even darker. But that was the only evidence he had heard her question, because he stared straight ahead, silent.

"Khamil?"

"Yeah." His voice was quiet, and Monique was sure she heard a hint of resentment in his tone.

"What happened?" Monique couldn't help asking. Why this was important to her, she wasn't sure.

"It didn't work out," Khamil replied nonchalantly.

Something flickered in his eyes as he looked at her. Pain. Anger. Khamil had a way with women, a confidence and ease that made Monique believe he'd left a string of broken hearts across the U.S. Yet there was no doubt that Khamil's expression was one of hurt.

Was it possible that someone had broken his playboy heart?

Yes. The pain she saw in his eyes was real.

"She hurt you," Monique said simply.

"Uh-huh. She cheated on me once she realized I no longer had a shot at playing pro ball."

"I'm sorry," Monique said.

"No big deal. That was a long time ago."

It may have been a long time ago, but he was still hurt.

Monique could see that as plainly as she could see the sun shining outside the hotel window.

Khamil stretched, and Monique couldn't help but admire his wide shoulders, finely cut arms, and slim torso. Every part of him was so well toned, so taut with muscles. He was a big man, one who Monique knew would never let anything bad happen to her.

Was that part of his appeal?

"We've got to see about getting a car," Khamil announced.

"Oh." Monique sounded disappointed.

"You said your cottage is about an hour away, didn't you?"

"Yes."

"So unless we take a cab, we're going to have to rent a car."

"Mmm-hmm," Monique agreed.

Khamil gave her an odd look. He saw confusion written on her face, which matched the way he felt. Instinctively, he knew that she was disappointed that he had changed the subject from his love life to the reason they were here. But his bad experience with Jessica was something Khamil didn't want to discuss, and as far as he was concerned, it was better left in the past.

Khamil swung his legs off the bed. "So what do you want to do? Call your father?"

"Yeah. I want to tell him what I'm doing."

"You want some privacy?"

"No, I'm cool."

Khamil stood. Catching Monique off guard, he swept her into his arms, pressing her soft body against his hard one. But the kiss he gave her was surprisingly gentle. "Give me a few minutes to get dressed; then I'll head downstairs."

"You don't have to do that, Khamil."

He brushed his lips across her forehead. "It's okay. I brought some work with me."

Khamil released her. Her heart filling with warmth, Monique watched as he dressed. She'd been so wrong with her first impression of him. He had a sensitive, caring side, one she'd never imagined.

And it endeared him to her.

"I'll see you in a bit," Khamil said, then left the hotel room.

When he was gone, Monique sat on the edge of the bed. A sigh oozed out of her. She was afraid of what she was feeling, because her attraction to Khamil had taken her by surprise. No other man had ever made her feel quite the way Khamil was making her feel. But she'd witnessed so many relationships that went bad, including her own parents'.

Her father and mother had fought often, more in the years just before her mother's death. Julia traveled a lot, and from the arguments Monique had overheard, Lucas hadn't approved of all the time she spent away from home. The night her mother had died, her parents had argued. Monique had only overheard loud voices, and wasn't sure what they'd argued about. And she hadn't come out of her room when her father had stormed off. Later, he'd told her and the police that he'd headed back to New York because he and her mother had had a nasty argument, which is why he hadn't been around when she'd been murdered.

The last few times Monique had spoken to her father about that night's events, she'd sensed the guilt he carried. If he hadn't argued with her mother and left, she would probably still be alive.

Unfortunately, it was exactly his account of what had happened that night that had led the police to consider him as the prime suspect.

Despite their problems, her father had loved her mother, of that Monique was sure. He couldn't have killed her, much less left her to die in the same house where his daughter slept.

Monique grabbed the receiver and dialed her father's number. After two rings, he answered.

"Hi, Daddy," Monique said, a smile spreading on her face.

"Monique. Hello."

"How are you?"

"I'm okay, sweetheart."

"You sound out of breath."

"I was just heading outside to do some gardening when the phone range, so I ran to get it." He inhaled a deep breath. "I'm surprised. You're calling early."

"Yeah. I wanted to let you know that I'm in Canada."

"*Canada?*" Lucas asked, clearly surprised.

Instantly, Monique's back stiffened, bracing for the disapproval she had come to expect from her father where the subject of her mother's murder was concerned. "Dad, I got an anonymous message via my agent. Someone said that I should check the house, that there's some clue to Mom's murder there."

"And you up and ran to Canada as soon as you got this message? What's wrong with you, girl?"

Lucas's words stung Monique, much like a slap in the face. "You know why I came. One of us had to, and it sure as hell wouldn't be you!"

"Don't you take that tone with me."

Years of frustration finally found a voice. "You know what I don't understand, Daddy? Why you haven't done more to find Mom's killer. Fine, you went through hell with the police investigation and being suspected of the crime. But for God's sake, she was your wife. If you loved her, how can you not spend every waking hour trying to find the truth?"

"Sometimes the truth is better left alone."

Monique paused, then asked, "What on earth does that mean?"

"When you search for the truth, you have to be prepared for what you may find. It might not be what you expect, maybe even something you can't live with. Are you prepared for that?"

Monique felt a strange tingling on her nape. "Why are you talking like this? Is there something you know that you're not telling me?"

"Leave it alone, Monique."

"Leave what alone?" she asked, pressing the issue. If her father knew something, why hadn't he told the police?

"Did it occur to you that this could be some kind of trap? That the person who killed your mother wants to get you to the house so they can do you harm?"

Monique's body trembled at her father's words. After a moment, she said, "Yes, Daddy, it did occur to me. But I don't believe that's the case. If someone wanted to hurt me, they'd be taking a big chance in hoping I'd head to the cottage just because they called and left some cryptic message."

"Unless they know how determined you are to solve this case, and therefore know that you'd be on the first plane out of town."

Her father's statement gave Monique pause. Was that the case? Was someone trying to set her up?

Monique's eyes wandered to the hotel room door. For the first time since she'd arrived in Toronto, she felt genuine fear. And she was glad that Khamil had insisted on coming with her.

Yesterday, she'd thought she knew what she was doing. Now, she was confused. "But, Daddy, if someone is trying to set me up as you suggest, and it's someone who knows we still have the cottage in Barrie, then that means someone close to us killed Mom..."

"I want you to head home, Monique. Right now. If the police

are reinvestigating the case, fine, let them do their job. I want you to be no part of this."

An eerie feeling passed over Monique, the feeling that her father knew more than he was telling her. Good Lord, what was going on?

"I don't understand, Daddy."

"You heard me." He paused, and when he spoke again, his voice cracked. "I already lost your mother, I don't want to lose you, too."

Monique's throat clogged with emotion. "You won't lose me."

"Please, Monique. Let the police deal with this."

Monique's body was so filled with fear, her hands shook as she held the phone. Part of her conceded that her father was right, that perhaps she was in over her head. But the other part knew she couldn't give up now, not if she indeed was close to learning the truth.

"Promise me, Monique."

Help...me...

Her father was asking too much, more than she could give. She wanted to forget the helplessness she'd felt that night as her mother lay dying in her arms. She wanted to forget the image of all that blood that was permanently etched in her brain. She wanted to forget how her mother had begged for help, and that she hadn't been able to help her.

Monique wanted, needed, for the nightmare of what had happened that night to finally end. It wouldn't end until her mother's killer was apprehended—and until then, she had to do all she could to make sure that happened.

"Daddy, I have to go."

"Monique—"

"Bye," Monique said, then quickly hung up. Her hand lingered on the receiver, a million questions spinning in her mind, leaving her dizzy.

For the first time, she wondered if there was something she was missing, something she *should* know about what had happened that night.

Something that would, like a puzzle, fit together—if she could find all the pieces.

Chapter 17

"You haven't touched your food."

Khamil's voice actually startled Monique; she was so absorbed in her thoughts.

She looked up at him, then down at her plate. The scrambled eggs and pancakes were no doubt cold by now, making the thought of eating even less appealing than when she had entered this restaurant.

Monique pushed the plate away. "I'm not hungry."

"You have to eat something."

Monique replied with a quick shake of the head.

Watching her, Khamil took a bite of his waffle, then washed it down with coffee. Something was bothering her. He'd known that the moment he'd returned to the room. She'd been tense, preoccupied. He'd asked her what was wrong, but she hadn't answered.

Feeling his gaze, Monique met his eyes. "Are you almost finished?"

Khamil gestured to his side order of bacon in response. "Not yet."

Monique blew out a harried breath. "I'd kinda like to get going."

"We will," Khamil told her.

A frown played on Monique's lips. She balled a fist, then placed it against her mouth. A second later, she closed her eyes.

Khamil placed his fork and knife against his plate. "Monique, will you please tell me what's wrong?"

Opening her eyes, she looked at him. "I just want to get to the house. That's all."

"You're not going to be any good to yourself if you head up there on an empty stomach. You need energy, Monique. You don't know what you're looking for. We could be there for hours."

"Don't you think I know that?" she quipped. Then her face crumbled. "God, I can't deal with this…"

"Damn it, Monique." Khamil stared at her with concern. "What's going on with you?"

"I need answers. That's what's going on."

"And we're going to get them. Today."

Monique gave a brief nod, but her expression lacked confidence. She said, "I'm starting to wonder if there's more going on that I ever realized."

Khamil's eyebrows shot up. "What do you mean?"

"I mean…" Monique fiddled with the stem of her water goblet. "I spoke with my father, and he doesn't want me going to the house. Khamil, he almost sounded as if he knew who killed my mother."

"What?"

Monique shook her head. "I don't know. He didn't say that, so I could be jumping to conclusions. But he said some weird things to me for the first time that have me wondering how much he knows."

"I don't understand, Monique."

"Neither do I."

Khamil watched her, watched her rest her cheek in her palm and glance away. He could almost see the burden on her shoulders.

"I know this is hard, Monique," he began gently. "But trust me, you have to take care of yourself. Not eating won't help the situation."

Monique wanted to eat, but her stomach was a ball of nerves, and she knew she wouldn't be able to keep anything down if she tried.

"I…" She glanced down at her plate and instantly felt queasy. "I can't."

Khamil swallowed a piece of bacon, then spoke. "What about the Canadian police? Are you going to contact them before you head to the house?"

"I thought about calling that detective who's in charge of my mother's cold case, but…"

"But what?"

Monique shrugged. "I'll call after I check the house and see if there's any type of clue there." And she suddenly wasn't sure of anything anymore, least of all if she should call the police. "I don't know."

"What?"

"It's just…" Monique's voice trailed off. "My father was the prime suspect for a long time, but ultimately, the police didn't have enough evidence to charge him. He always maintained that he had nothing to do with the murder, and all these years, I believed him. But—" Monique stared into Khamil's eyes. "But, Khamil, what if I'm wrong?"

Nearly two hours later, Khamil pulled their rented Jeep Cherokee up in front of a quaint-looking cabin on a small street in Barrie. The cabin was surrounded by brush, and the grass clearly hadn't been cut in years. Wildflowers and weeds grew all around, making the cabin seem as if it were part of a wilderness landscape.

The nearest house was approximately twenty feet away on either side.

Khamil turned and found Monique staring ahead blankly.

"Hey," he said.

"It's been so long," Monique whispered. Her father had never sold the house, partly because she'd insisted that he not do so. But she hadn't been back here since her mother's death.

Once, this place had held so many happy memories for Monique and her family. She and her mother had come here to spend many summers, her father joining them when he had his two weeks of summer vacation. The times they'd been here, her parents had rarely argued. Except for that fateful night…

"You sure you want to do this?" Khamil asked.

Monique looked at him and nodded. "Yes. I have to."

"All right." Khamil opened his car door, got out, then went to the passenger side and opened the door for Monique. When she didn't make a move, he extended his hand.

Monique took his hand, thankful to have him with her, thankful for the strength he was offering. She climbed out of the Jeep.

"You have the key?" Khamil asked.

A small smile touched Monique's lips. "Yes," she replied. "Wouldn't that be something for me to get all the way here, only to have forgotten the key?"

"We would have gotten in somehow."

Monique met Khamil's eyes. "I'm sure we would have."

"It's nice to see you smile," Khamil told her. "You have such a beautiful smile."

"Thank you." The smile wavered, and Monique bit down hard on her bottom lip. "God, Khamil. I'm so afraid."

"Hey." Draping an arm around Monique's shoulder, Khamil drew her to him. He could only empathize with what she was going through, but he knew this had to be incredibly hard. He still had trouble going into his little nephew's room when he visited Javar and Whitney in Chicago.

Monique blew out a loud breath. "Okay. Let's do this."

Taking her hand, Khamil walked with Monique to the porch. There, she dug the key out of her purse and slipped it into the lock. A second later, she pushed the door open.

The smell of dust and mold was the first thing that hit Monique; then sadness hit her in the gut. The last time she'd been here, she and her mother had giggled happily as they'd stepped over the threshold.

Help...me...

Monique shook her head, trying to lose the memory.

"It's not too late to change your mind," Khamil said.

"No." Monique swallowed and squared her shoulders. "I have to do this."

She stepped away from Khamil, walking farther into the house. "She's been gone for years, but I feel her." Monique did a three-hundred-and-sixty-degree turn. "I feel her everywhere."

"Where did it happen?"

Monique faced Khamil, then pointed to the door beside her. "In this room."

The next second, she reached for the door's handle. The door creaked in protest as she slowly opened it.

Help...me...

Monique's knees buckled. But before she fell, Khamil's strong arms were around her.

As Khamil held Monique, her breathing came in quick, ragged gasps. He glanced into the room. It was completely empty, as though it had never been lived in, but he felt a presence there.

"My father got rid of everything in this room, but I can still see it. I don't even have to close my eyes."

Khamil placed a hand on Monique's, taking it off the door's handle. Then he closed the door. "If there's nothing in this room, then there's nothing here that can help us."

Monique's gaze flitted to Khamil's. "Yes, you're right. You're right."

With the door closed, Monique stood tall once again. Khamil ran both hands down the length of her arms. "All right. The caller said something about letters."

"Yes."

"Where might they be?"

Monique's eyes went to the staircase. "There's a loft up there, where we kept a lot of things. From what I remember, my mother had a chest of personal items up there. Memorabilia from her career and whatnot."

"Then that's where we go."

Khamil led the way. The stairs squeaked as they made their way up.

In the loft, dust motes flew in the air. The area was large and housed several items, all of which were covered by large, white sheets.

Monique sauntered to the large bay window, which let in lots of sunshine. "My cousins and I used to love to hang out up here. We used to spy on the neighbors. See?" Monique gestured to the house across the street. "You can see right into the backyard from this angle. There were a girl and her brother who used to live there. Talk about spoiled."

"Your cousins used to come here with you?"

Monique faced Khamil. "Uh-huh. See the house on our left? They owned that one."

"Really?"

"Yeah. My mother bought it for them. She liked the idea that we could take family vacations with our extended family. She was very close to my uncle Richard and aunt Sophie."

"Sophie was her sister?"

"No. Uncle Richard is my father's brother. He and Aunt Sophie are divorced now." Monique walked away from the window and to the middle of the room. She grabbed a white blanket and pulled then waved her hand around as dust flew into the air.

"If my mother had any letters, they should be in her chest," Monique explained. She pulled another blanket off more hidden objects. "Ah. There it is."

She lowered herself to the floor, sitting cross-legged. Khamil sat beside her.

As Monique lifted the lid on the chest, Khamil said, "Tell me about your father."

She looked at him. "My father?"

"Yeah. What does he do?"

"Well, he's retired now, but he used to work as a customs officer at LaGuardia. In fact—" Monique smiled. "That's how he met my mother."

"You're kidding."

"Nope. She was heading back to New York from France, I believe, and she went through the line my father was manning. He fell for her instantly, asked for her number, and the rest is history."

"Wow. It's like they were destined to meet."

"Yeah." Monique's voice became wistful. "This was the one place I remember them being happy."

"They had a rough marriage?"

Monique shrugged nonchalantly. "No worse than anyone else's, I don't think. Uncle Richard and Aunt Sophie always argued. My dad once told me that the Savard men were very passionate in every way. They didn't hide their emotions. My mother traveled a lot, and my dad missed her. I think that was their biggest problem. I think that was my aunt and uncle's biggest problem, too. Uncle Richard is a pilot, and he was always away from home. And I'm not sure if this is true, but Aunt Sophie always thought Uncle Richard was having affairs."

"That's rough."

"From what my cousin, Doreen, used to tell me, Aunt Sophie was pretty paranoid about the whole issue."

"Distrust like that is enough to drive two people apart."

"I know."

"And your parents?"

"Infidelity was not an issue," Monique quickly said. "My dad was thirteen years older than my mother. He didn't get married until he was forty. He told me he'd waited all his life to meet the right woman, and when he met my mother, he knew she was the one. He was devoted to her. Which is why he missed her so much when she was away for work. Then, when she started getting weird letters from fans…" Monique's eyes lit up. "Maybe that's what that caller was referring to. A letter from the guy who was obsessed with my mother."

Monique quickly began going through the items in the box. She pulled out two large scrapbooks, then placed them on the floor.

"May I take a look at this?" Khamil asked.

"Sure."

Monique continued rummaging through the contents of the chest while Khamil opened one of the scrapbooks. Aside from the scrapbooks, there were family photo albums, some framed photos, and a large quilt.

"Wow. Your mother was beautiful," Khamil commented.

Pausing, Monique looked at him. "Yeah, she was. She was still modeling at forty-two, when she died."

"Really?"

"Yep. Her skin was flawless and smooth, even at that age. She didn't look a day over twenty-five."

"I see why she was a successful model." Khamil flipped a page. "Elite Skin Care?"

"Uh-huh. That was her biggest contract."

Khamil turned the page. A grin spread on his face. "Hey, is that you?"

Monique leaned forward, and Khamil held the scrapbook toward her. She giggled as she looked at the picture of her and her mother, both wearing white sundresses, Monique sitting beside her mother, resting her head against her shoulder. "Yeah, that's me."

"You two modeled together?"

"Yeah. My mother negotiated a contract for me with Elite Skin Care as well, so we could work together. Because she was spending more and more time away from home, she wanted to be with me as much as she could. That was my first experience modeling. They loved the idea of having mother and daughter model together. I guess they were trying to say that if you used their products, you could look as young as my mother did. Of course, my mother naturally looked like that, with no help from Elite."

Khamil chuckled. "She didn't use their products?"

Flashing him a wry grin, Monique shook her head.

Khamil turned to another page, and Monique went back to the chest. She lifted the heavy quilt and placed it on the floor.

Then her breath caught in her throat.

There were envelopes—several of them—lining the bottom of the chest.

"Khamil," she said. When he looked at her, she announced, "I found the letters."

Chapter 18

"How many are there?" Khamil asked.

Monique reached for a stack of letters secured with an elastic band, pulling it out of the chest. "A lot."

Khamil extended a hand. "Here. Give me some."

Monique passed him a stack.

"What am I looking for?" Khamil asked.

"I don't know," Monique replied, pulling out another stack of letters. "*Anything.*"

She slipped the elastic band off the letters she held, then lifted the first letter in the pile. "This is my father's handwriting," she said. She flipped through the envelopes. "These all are from him."

"He wrote her a lot of letters?"

"I guess so. She was away a lot."

Monique reached inside the chest and took out more letters. She didn't want to read the letters her father had written to her mother. Not only did it seem like an invasion of their privacy, there was no point in reading her father's letters, as she was sure they didn't hold the clue the caller had been talking about.

Monique sifted through the news envelopes. The penmanship on all were different, leading her to believe these were from her mother's fans. "There might be something here," she said. "I think this is fan mail."

"This letter is from your father to your mother," Khamil announced. "I don't know if you want me reading it."

Monique smiled, appreciating his concern. "Go ahead." She paused. "I think you're the better person to read those, anyway—just in case I've been blinded by love and family loyalty all these years."

Khamil gave her an understanding nod, then began reading the letter.

For the next several minutes, Monique and Khamil read letter after letter. Finally, Monique said, "I don't think there's anything in these. They're all nice fan letters, telling my mother that they admire her, that they like the skin care products—stuff like that." Monique groaned. "I'm not even sure the mail from her stalker would be in here. The police probably have it."

"So far, these are all love letters from your father to your mother. You're right. He adored her."

"Yeah," Monique agreed absently. She withdrew another bunch of envelopes. This was like searching for a needle in a haystack, only she didn't know what the needle looked like!

She opened another envelope and scanned the letter. She was about to toss it aside until she saw the words *I'll always love you.*

Her interest piqued, Monique's eyes went back to the first line. She began reading.

Dear Julia,

I miss you, more than you could ever imagine. It's lonely here without you. I hate when we have to say goodbye, and miss you the first second we're apart. I hate having to keep my feelings for you secret. I know this is a tough situation, but there must be a way we can work it out. I can't imagine not being able to be with you forever, freely. We've both tried to protect everyone else, putting our own feelings aside. I can't do that any longer. I need to be with you, Julia. Now and forever.

I'll always love you.

Your Pooh-Bear

"Monique."

At the sound of Khamil's voice, Monique looked at him.

"My God, Monique. What's wrong?"

A sick feeling was swirling inside her body. God, what did this letter mean? It wasn't from her father.

Khamil reached for the letter, taking it from her fingers. After he read it, he asked, "Who's Pooh-Bear?"

"I have no clue."

"It's not your father." It was a statement, not a question.

"Obviously not."

Khamil held Monique's gaze. He saw the pain in her eyes, and didn't know what to say to make this easier for her. "Monique," he began cautiously. "Did you know that your mother was having an affair?"

"No!" She buried her face in her hands, then looked at Khamil once more. "Oh, my God."

Khamil didn't say anything, merely stared at her.

"I know what you're thinking," she suddenly said.

"You do?"

"My father didn't kill my mother. This doesn't prove anything."

"It's motive, Monique."

Monique shot to her feet. "I don't care what you think it is. My father didn't do this."

Khamil stood to meet Monique. "How do you know?"

Monique's lips trembled before answering. "He couldn't have."

Khamil reached for Monique's face, but she stepped away from his touch. After a moment, he said, "Why don't you take a break? I'll go through the rest of the letters."

"No." Monique shook her head. She was missing something, she was sure. There was a memory in her reach, but she couldn't quite grasp it. "I'll keep reading."

Monique dropped to the floor once again and continued going through the letters. Khamil sat beside her, looking over her shoulder as she read. After the fourth letter, Monique knocked the stack across the floor. "Gawd!"

"Monique."

Her eyes flew to Khamil's. "Do *not* tell me this is okay, because it's *not*. God, I've just found out that my mother was having an affair. I can't believe this."

Khamil took both Monique's hands in his. "You know what? I think you should call the police." When Monique whimpered, he continued. "They should know this, Monique." Khamil placed a hand beneath Monique's chin, forcing her to look at him. Her eyes glistened with tears.

"Look, I understand your fear," he said. "The last thing I wanted to believe was that my mother could possibly be responsible for taking my nephew's life, or trying to kill my sister-in-law. But you know what? When we all learned the truth, as painful as it was, it was a relief. The truth won't always make you happy, but it will bring a measure of closure."

"My father asked me if I was prepared to learn the truth. He said sometimes it's best left alone. Do you think he knew about my mother's affair?"

Khamil palmed her face. "I think he did. Something he said in one of his letters now makes sense."

Monique looked at Khamil expectantly. "What?"

"He said something about forgiving her for what had happened, that he still loved her more than life. That's all."

Monique glanced at the floor, deep in thought. Nothing in life was easy, Khamil realized, knowing how much pain she was going through. Everyone had some issue or other that they were dealing with. But he was a firm believer in the adage that what didn't kill you made you stronger.

And Monique was strong. A survivor. She'd dealt with more than any young child should ever have to deal with, yet she still had a zest for life, a passion she wanted to share. He'd felt that both times they'd made love.

"I think you're right," Monique announced minutes later. "I should call the police." Getting onto her knees, she crawled the few feet to where her purse was. She took out her cell phone and her wallet. She'd placed the number for Detective McKinney in there.

Monique dialed the number for the detective, then waited. When his voice mail came on, she frowned.

"What?" Khamil asked.

"I got his voice mail," she explained. "It's the weekend." Looking down at her paper, she began punching in another number.

"Who are you calling now?"

"He left me his home number as well."

As Monique listened to the phone ring, Khamil watched her. She chewed on her bottom lip and thrummed her fingers against her thigh.

Her eyes lit up. "Hello. I'm looking for Detective McKinney."

She threw a relieved glance Khamil's way, and anxiety danced in his stomach. "Hello, Detective McKinney. This is Monique Savard. I'm sorry to call you at home…"

Khamil rose to his feet and sauntered to the window, affording Monique some privacy as she spoke to the detective. He glanced outside. The branches of the large maple tree outside the window swayed in the gentle breeze. As his eyes roamed through the tree, he spotted a nest filled with eggs.

Just then, a sparrow flew by the window, landing on the branch with the nest. The bird was so close that if the glass weren't in the way, Khamil could reach out and touch it.

It was a sight he didn't see in New York City, and it filled his heart with warmth.

Yeah, this place was idyllic. Here, surrounded by nature, one had to sit back, relax, and enjoy.

He glanced over his shoulder at Monique. A lump formed in his throat as he looked at her hunched form. He wished they could be here under different circumstances—on a romantic getaway, rather than a search for her mother's killer.

Maybe. One day.

Khamil turned back to the window. The sparrow was now nestled on her eggs. Children needed their mothers, no matter how old they got. Monique's mother's life had been cut short. His mother had been taken from him due to her own crazy actions.

They had something in common. Maybe that's why he felt such a strong pull toward her. That and the fact that he sensed her vulnerability, and Khamil wasn't one to walk away from someone who needed him.

"Khamil."

Khamil turned when he heard his name. "You told him?"

Monique got to her feet. "I told him, but he already knew."

Khamil frowned. "He did?"

Monique strolled toward him, then passed him and went to the window. She leaned a hip against the frame. After a moment of staring outside, she faced Khamil. "I'm not sure what's real anymore."

Khamil walked over to her. "What do you mean?"

"There's so much my father didn't tell me. I'm not sure if he thought I was too young to know, or…" Monique whimpered.

"You don't want to tell me?" Khamil asked gently.

Monique met his eyes. "Of course I'll tell you. You're the only one who seems to care." Monique paused, then continued. "Detective McKinney knew that my mother had had an affair. Apparently, another man's sperm was found in her body when they did the autopsy. When they questioned my father about it, he told the cops that he knew my mother was seeing someone else."

"Wait a second. Are you saying that on the night of your mother's murder, she'd been with someone else?"

Monique squeezed her head with both hands. "I remember my parents fighting. I remember my father leaving. But I had no clue anyone came over after he left. Other than the person who killed her."

"Maybe…" Khamil paused. "Do you think your mother may have been raped?"

"I asked the detective that. But he said that there was no sign of force at all. And…" Monique blew out a quick breath. "My mother was also pregnant."

"What?"

Monique shook her head, still unable to believe all she'd learned. "If it was my father's child, wouldn't my parents have told me about the baby?" She hugged her torso, suddenly cold. "God, maybe that's why my parents were arguing that night."

"Hey." Khamil's eyes lit up. "If someone else had been with your mother after your father left, then doesn't that exonerate your father?"

Warmth flooded Monique's body as she stared at Khamil. Ever since her mother's murder, she had wanted her family members to say something as simple as this, but they never had. She knew they were secretly convinced of her father's guilt. That Khamil offered her a reason to once again believe in her father, given the new evidence, meant the world to her.

Lord help her, she was falling for him.

Hard.

"I was so wrong about you."

"Excuse me?"

Khamil's question made Monique realize that she'd spoken aloud. A smile played on her lips as she met Khamil's eyes. "I said, I was wrong about you."

"Oh?"

"You don't want to know what I thought about you in the beginning." She chuckled softly.

"If the way you rebuffed me is any indication, I can only imagine." But he smiled, letting her know whatever she may have felt before didn't bother him now.

"I thought you were—" She grinned sheepishly. "Well, I thought you figured the world revolved around you."

Khamil flashed her a surprised look. "It doesn't?"

Monique laughed. "You're so silly."

"I'm just glad I can make you smile." Khamil softly stroked her cheek.

Monique's laugh faded. "Yeah. So am I." Once again, her expression grew serious. "I want to believe my father had nothing to do with my mother's death, but the detective raised a good point. What if my father came back to the house, saw my mother's lover leaving, and became enraged? My father was never able to verify his whereabouts after he left this house that night. He said he drove to Toronto and went to the airport, but wasn't able to catch a flight back to New York until the morning. I never wanted to consider this, but that would have given him enough time to head back up here..." Monique stopped abruptly, unable to go on.

Instantly, Khamil swept her into his arms. Monique sagged against his strong chest, feeling as though his strength was helping her to carry this heavy burden.

"Until we know otherwise," Khamil said, "don't think the worst. I know you, Monique. I can understand your loyalty to your father, but I don't think it's unfounded. You're smart. I know you'd rather know the truth, no matter how horrible, than stick your head in the sand."

A soft moan escaped her, and Monique was surprised to feel a tear run down her cheek. How did Khamil know her so well in such a short time? He was absolutely right. She hadn't pursued the truth for this long without knowing that she had to be prepared for the worst, no matter how inconceivable it might be.

I love you, she thought.

Monique pulled her head back and looked up at Khamil. He looked down at her. She felt a little jolt in her chest.

God, it was true. She'd gone and fallen in love with him.

As Khamil stared down at her, the edges of his mouth curled in the slightest of smiles. His eyes were full of compassion, and something else she couldn't quite read.

Did he feel about her the same way she felt about him?

The thought caused her stomach to churn with anxiety.

He was here for her, being a wonderful friend to her, giving her the support that she so desperately needed. But maybe this was simply about friendship—nothing more.

Before she knew what was happening, Khamil covered her mouth with his. A surprised squeal bubbled out of her throat, but Khamil caught it with his tongue.

Monique instantly melted in his arms, her head growing light with desire. Never before had a man's kiss made her dizzy the way Khamil's did.

She could get used to this.

Monique's cell phone rang. Startled, both Khamil and Monique jumped apart. Then they laughed.

Khamil rested his forehead against hers. "You better get that."

"Yeah."

The phone continued to ring. Groaning, Khamil stepped away from her. Monique ran to retrieve her phone.

"Hello?"

"Monique, it's Doreen."

"Hey. What's up?"

"You tell me."

Monique glanced at Khamil. He mouthed, "Who is it?"

She mouthed back, "My cousin." Into the phone, she said, "I guess you heard."

"You're in *Canada?*"

"Yes. My father called you?"

"He got off the phone with my mother a couple hours ago. I've been trying to reach you, but kept getting your message service."

"I didn't turn my phone on until recently," Monique explained.

"Your father's really worried about you, and frankly, so am I. He said you got a call about some clue at the house."

"Yes." Briefly, Monique filled her cousin in on the call that had come to her agent, then what she'd learned about her mother's infidelity.

"Holy," Doreen said.

"I think my father was trying to protect me," Monique explained.

"Or keep the truth from you for other reasons."

Monique hesitated, then said, "Yeah. Maybe."

"Hon, I know you've always thought I don't understand, but I do. You've gone through so much pain already. What if you learn something you'd be better off not knowing?"

"Like the fact that my father may have killed my mother?"

"Yeah."

"Nothing can be worse than the fact that I held my mother in my arms as she died. I want to know the truth, Doreen, no matter what."

"I hope so." Doreen spoke as if it were already common knowledge that Lucas Savard was guilty of the crime. "I'm talking to Monique. Wait a sec—"

Monique heard some rumbling, then, "Monique."

That was Daniel's voice, stern.

"Daniel, hi."

"So, you're up at the cottage."

"Yeah." She didn't want to hear her cousin's disapproval. "I already told Doreen everything. She can fill you in."

"So, someone called you?"

"Someone called my agent, yes."

"Who?"

"I don't know."

"What did they say?"

Monique sighed. "Like I already told Doreen, the person said something about there being letters at the cottage, that these letters would give me answers."

"And?" Daniel prompted.

"I did find some letters. Letters that made it clear my mother was having an affair."

"That doesn't surprise me."

"*Excuse* me?"

"Look, Monique," Daniel went on, ignoring her. "Everyone's worried about you. Why don't you give up this wild-goose chase and just come home? How do you know that whoever called you isn't setting you up?"

"I'm fine," Monique told him.

"You're just so stubborn, Monique. First, *America's Most Wanted,* now this. You may as well put a target on your head and stand in the middle of Times Square."

Monique rolled her eyes. "I'm fine," she reiterated. She looked to Khamil. "I'm here with someone."

"You are?" Daniel was clearly shocked.

"I'm smarter than you all give me credit for. Now, why did you say that it didn't surprise you that my mother had an affair?"

"Who's with you?" Daniel asked.

"A friend," Monique replied testily. "Look, Daniel, if there's something you know that I don't—"

"Seems to me you have all the answers you were looking for."

"I only know that my mother was having an affair." She was getting annoyed. "I don't know who killed her."

There was pause, then Daniel said, "Did it ever occur to

you that someone was trying to protect you—spare you from the truth?"

Was there a conspiracy going on in her family? Did everyone else know something except she? And if so, what? "I'm a big girl now," she said.

"Come home, Monique."

"Tell me what you know."

"Get on the first plane and get out of there. Leave the past in the past, Monique."

"Do you know who killed my mother?" she asked.

"You heard me," Daniel snapped.

There was dead air. "Daniel? Daniel." Monique grunted as her eyes went to Khamil. "He hung up on me."

"That didn't go well, I take it."

Monique shook her head.

"Who's Daniel?"

"He's my other cousin. He and Doreen are my uncle Richard and aunt Sophie's children. They used to spend as much time here during the summers as my family did."

"From your end of the conversation, it sounded like Daniel was upset."

Monique folded her arms over her chest. "Daniel's always a little…testy. He's manic-depressive, and he has awful mood swings. When he's happy, he's wonderful. But when he's upset, you're best off staying clear from him." Monique ran a hand through her hair. "Plus, Daniel's always been overprotective. You should have seen what he was like when people picked on Doreen or me. I think his overprotective nature developed when he learned, at a young age, that his parents wouldn't live forever. About a year before my mother died, Aunt Sophie got pretty ill. For quite some time, she was bedridden with some mysterious illness the doctors could never quite pinpoint. Because Uncle Richard was away a lot—he needed to work to support the family—Daniel became the one who took care of his mother. He was the oldest of the children, but even for a seventeen-year-old, that was a serious burden. Anyway, I know for a while he was really scared that he would lose his mother. So was Doreen. We all were." Monique paused. "I know he's only upset now because he's worried about me."

Khamil nodded in understanding. "You think he knows something and isn't saying?"

"I don't know. He wasn't at all surprised about my mother's affair. But then, he was four years older than me. Maybe he was privy to some things that my parents kept from me, simply because I was younger."

Several moments passed, then Khamil asked, "What do you want to do?"

"I think I've learned all I'm going to learn here," Monique replied, looking around the large loft. As well, she wasn't sure she could spend much more time here and not completely break down with the memory of what had happened sixteen years ago. The happy memories of the time she'd spent here were overshadowed by that awful night.

"Besides, it certainly seems like my family knows more than I do. So—" she met Khamil's eyes "—I want to go back to New York. I want to find out exactly what it is that my family has been keeping from me all these years."

Chapter 19

"I'll call you later," Monique told Khamil as she got out of the taxi and stepped onto the sidewalk in front of her building.

"Are you sure you'll be okay?"

"Yes, I'll be fine." Khamil had offered to come up with her, but she had declined. It had been a long day, and Monique's brain was still churning with all she'd learned. Tonight, she simply wanted to take a long, hot bath, then get some much-needed sleep before talking to her family tomorrow.

She continued, "If Raymond was the one who trashed my apartment, he won't be stupid enough to come back here. He'll have to know I called the police."

Khamil didn't respond. Instead, he turned to the driver and passed him some money. A moment later, he stepped out of the taxi.

Monique gawked at him.

"I'm going upstairs with you."

"Khamil." Monique spoke his name in protest. "That's not necessary."

"Humor me," Khamil said. "I want to make sure you're safe. Then I'll leave."

Monique's heart beat faster. The thought of Khamil coming up to her apartment made her think of the two incredible nights they'd shared. And it made her wonder what the future held.

"Okay," she agreed. By now, she knew Khamil well enough to know that he wouldn't take no for an answer.

Minutes later, they were at her apartment door. The locksmith had installed a new lock before she'd left for Toronto, and finding the new key, Monique inserted it.

She paused, throwing a glance over her shoulder at Khamil. He nodded, and Monique opened the door.

Khamil stepped past her into the apartment, and wary, Monique watched him. But after a moment, his shoulders drooped with relief. He faced her. "Seems like the coast is clear."

Monique crossed the threshold into her apartment. "Thanks."

"All right," Khamil said. "I'll go now. Make sure you bolt your door."

"I will."

Khamil slowly strolled out of the apartment, then faced Monique. "Look, if you need anything, anything at all, call me."

Monique offered him a soft smile. "Will do."

Khamil didn't move, instead lingering outside her door, staring at her. Monique's flesh tingled beneath his gaze.

Oh, yes. There was definitely a sexual chemistry between them, and they were wonderful in bed together. But she wanted more than that. Yet what she'd learned about her parents' marriage today made her wonder if a happy relationship was only an illusion.

She asked, "Why are you so good to me?"

"We're friends, right?"

A lump of disappointment soared to Monique's throat from her heart. Forcing a smile, she nodded, unable to say anything.

Khamil raised an eyebrow. "And of course, I love your body."

"Of course." Her voice was clipped, but she couldn't help it. She was disappointed.

The playful expression on Khamil's face disappeared. "What's wrong?"

"Nothing. I'll see you later...*friend.*"

Khamil's eyebrows shot together. "What..."

"Nothing. Don't mind me. I'm tired."

"Hey," Khamil said softly. "Don't jump to any conclusions. You're a..." He paused. "Special friend."

"Sure." Again, she smiled. "Look, thanks for going to Toronto with me. I'll call you tomorrow."

"Okay." Khamil gave her an odd look.

"Good night." Before Khamil could say anything else, Monique closed the door and turned the lock. Disappointment washing over her, she rested her head against the door.

What was wrong with her? Hadn't she known that it was dangerous to care? Her parents hadn't had a good relationship no matter how much she'd lied and told herself otherwise. Her uncle and aunt hadn't had a good relationship. Daniel's relationship with his girlfriend was constantly up and down.

Why, oh why, did Monique expect a proclamation of undying love from Khamil, a man she'd known was a player the moment she'd seen him?

Still hoping, Monique pressed an ear to the door, listening for sound. Seconds later, she heard the *ping* of the elevator door as it opened.

She closed her eyes tightly, willing the unexpected hurt to pass.

It didn't.

"We're friends," she heard Khamil say.

No doubt, he'd bedded lots of his *friends*.

"Don't do this." Monique told herself. When she'd slept with Khamil, there had been no promises. Indeed, she hadn't wanted any. They'd both been mature adults, sharing the act of sex. It was her fault if she'd read any more into it.

She'd done a helluva lot more than that. She'd gone and fallen in love with him.

Monique wasn't exactly sure when it had happened. But she did know that she loved him. He was in her heart.

Vicky often said that men came and went in your life, that relationships didn't last forever, but that you should take the positive from them, no matter how short they were. Was that what Monique was supposed to do—take the positive out of her experience with Khamil?

Exhaling a sigh, Monique walked down the hallway to the bathroom. She needed to take that hot bath. Trying to forget Khamil and her feelings for him, she sat on the edge of her Jacuzzi tub and started the bathwater, then added a liberal amount of lavender scented bubble bath. As it ran, she headed to the bedroom, where she checked her messages.

"Hey, girl," came Vicky's voice. "Give me a call. I think we need to straighten some things out."

Monique couldn't help it; she felt a spurt of anger. She wasn't sure she wanted to call Vicky back. For years, they'd been friends, and she never would have let a man come between them. Clearly, Vicky didn't share the same sentiment.

Beep. "Monique." Pause. "It's Raymond. Look, I need to talk to you. Call me. Please."

Beep. "Hey, Monique. It's me again. You need to call me. I got a weird message, and I think it pertains to you and the search for your mother's killer."

Beep. "Monique, it's Raymond. I hope you're not avoiding me. We need to talk. I'm sorry if I acted like a jerk, but there are some things I need to tell you, things you need to know."

"Whatever," Monique said. The last thing she'd do was call Raymond back. After what the man had done to her apartment, she wanted nothing to do with the psycho.

Having heard all the messages, Monique went back to the bathroom. The tub was almost full and she turned off the faucets. Next, she stripped out of her jeans and T-shirt, then slowly eased herself into the warm water.

"Mmm," she said aloud. The water felt good.

She laid her head back and closed her eyes, staying like that for several minutes. When was the last time she'd relaxed like this? Too long ago for her to even remember. It was something she needed to do more often. Already, the warm water was working out the kinks in her neck.

Monique reached for her sponge and dipped it in the water, then held it above her body and squeezed, releasing a waterfall of bubbles and steam. Her mind drifted back to Khamil. She knew she needed to forget him, but how could she? Already, she regretted sending him home instead of asking him to spend the night with her.

She missed him, missed his warm embrace. She missed what they'd shared just last night in the shower at the hotel.

A quivering sensation ran throughout her body as she remembered the feel of Khamil's lips on her body. Never had a man's tongue felt so good before, so much so that she craved it now, craved it as a nicotine addict craved a cigarette.

She closed her eyes and let herself imagine…

Khamil was resting against the doorjamb of the bathroom, his lips curved in the slightest of grins. His eyes were dark with desire as they probed every inch of Monique's wet body. Slowly, he entered the bathroom, pulled his T-shirt over his head, and slipped out of his perfectly snug jeans. His body was magnificent, corded with muscles in all the right places.

And he was ready for her. His erection was testament to that.

How she wanted him! She needed him in this tub with her, his slick body pressed against hers.

"Khamil."

A seductive smile spread on his face as he approached her. Stepping into the steaming bathtub, Khamil gradually lowered himself on top of Monique's moistened body. She closed her eyes and unleashed a soft, passionate moan.

With exquisite tenderness, Khamil explored every part of her body with his hands. Caressing. Tweaking. Fondling. Teasing. Mercilessly, he ran his tongue along her wet, hot skin, tormenting her with passion as he glided his tongue in circles around one of her taut, throbbing peaks. And just when Monique thought she was going to go crazy with desire, Khamil took her nipple in his mouth and sucked, sending ripples of pleasure coursing through her. Monique arched her back in heated longing.

"Oh, Khamil." Her own voice startled her, and the cold realization hit her.

Khamil was nowhere near the bathroom.

Lord, she had it for the man bad!

Never, ever, had Monique gotten so absorbed in a sexual fantasy the way she had just now. Her body was thrumming with sexual longing, for which there was no cure.

Except Khamil.

But while his body would satisfy her physical needs, she needed more than that. She wanted all of him—body and soul.

* * *

Groaning, Khamil turned from his back onto his side. He adjusted his head against the pillow, then promptly rolled onto his stomach.

He closed his eyes, but a moment later, they popped open. Oh, what was the use? He'd been tossing and turning since he'd gotten into bed more than an hour and a half ago. He could no more sleep than he could stop thinking about Monique.

"Monique." Her name escaped his lips on a sigh.

He felt a niggling of disappointment. He didn't like how things had ended between them earlier. He had known what she wanted from him, yet he hadn't been able to give it to her.

He'd recognized that spark in her eyes, the same spark that he'd seen in the eyes of so many of the other women he'd dated. No matter how much she had fussed and rebuffed him in the beginning, she'd fallen for him.

And that scared the crap out of Khamil.

Monique was beautiful, caring. Strong, yet vulnerable. The sexual chemistry between them was undeniable. He hadn't felt such a strong attraction for a woman since…

Since Jessica.

And that was the problem, he realized. He'd fallen hard for Jessica, given her his heart completely. And she'd hurt him.

The reality that after all these years, he was finally feeling another strong attraction for a woman had him in a quandary. Over the years, he'd learned to turn off his emotions, to guard his heart. Yet there was something about Monique that had made him let that guard down.

But he didn't want the guard down. He wanted it back up around his heart.

Rolling onto his back, Khamil blew out a frustrated breath.

Man, he really *was* afraid of getting hurt. He had never quite acknowledged his feelings over the years since Jessica had broken his heart, no matter what his friends had told him. Instead, he'd concentrated on having fun. And he'd turned into the heartbreaker, all so he wouldn't get too close to anyone.

Wow. The realization shocked him.

He was thirty-eight years old. Certainly he couldn't go on like this forever. Yet the thought of taking a chance on a relationship with Monique scared him more than he cared to admit.

Khamil turned onto his side, lay there for a moment, then promptly sat up. He flicked on the light on his end table. With the room illuminated, he stood and walked across the bedroom to his closet. Reaching inside, he found his guitar and took it out.

Khamil went back to the bed, where he sat, positioning his guitar in his arms, ready to play. It had been ages since he'd touched it.

He strummed a few chords, getting used to the feel and sound of it. And then he was playing the tune to DeBarge's "A Dream," thinking of Monique.

Thinking of her and how she fit the lyrics.

He wanted to turn the fantasy he dreamed of—that he had finally found the woman to spend his life with—into reality.

For years, the dream had eluded him. What he'd experienced with Monique in the last few days had made the dream come alive again. Unlike DeBarge, he didn't want to wake up knowing that the dream would never come true.

But dreams didn't come true without any effort.

He'd put forth that effort in his career for years and had achieved success. He'd never let fear of failure stop him. Why let fear of rejection get the best of him now?

It was just that he'd seen so many up-and-down relationships that he'd come to believe he may never find true love. But, he realized, his fingers stopping on the guitar strings, he'd also seen the power of love heal.

The power of Javar and Whitney's love had brought them through the dark hours of their marriage. Khamil didn't doubt they'd remain happy forever.

Yes, Jessica had betrayed him, and as a result, he'd hardened his heart to love. But when he compared Monique to Jessica, there was no comparison. Thinking back, he recognized a self-centered side to Jessica, one he hadn't noticed until after their breakup. While with her, Khamil had been so enamored with her beauty that he'd hardly notice her flaws.

And while Monique was a model and most definitely beautiful, she hardly seemed to know it. There was nothing about her that was conceited. There was nothing about her that was self-centered. Except for the fact that he'd been attracted to both women, Monique was nothing like Jessica.

He and Monique connected in a way that he and Jessica never had.

Annoyed with himself, Khamil stood. He returned the guitar to the closet. Now that he thought about it, really thought about it, he'd been wasting his pain and insecurity on someone who didn't deserve it. Jessica hadn't been the person he'd thought she was, and instead of conceding that he'd simply made an error in judgment, he'd let that negative relationship prevent him from being open to meeting someone else he could love.

But maybe he hadn't been open to letting that happen because the right person hadn't come along.

Until now.

Khamil climbed back into bed, propping his hands beneath

his head. Was that it? Had it simply taken him all this time since high school to find the one person who was perfect for him?

And if Monique was the woman for him, how could he let fear and confusion get in the way of something that could potentially be wonderful?

He couldn't.

And he wouldn't.

It was high time he put the issues of distrust and fear as they pertained to Jessica where they belonged—in the past.

No one ever achieved anything worthwhile without taking a chance.

Chapter 20

As Monique got out of the tub, she heard the loud rapping on the door. Instantly, her stomach lurched with anticipation. It was late, after one in the morning, and she could think of only one person who'd be coming over this time of night.

Khamil.

Smiling, Monique grabbed a thick white towel, wrapped it around her body, then hustled to the door. Victor, the doorman who'd been on duty when she and Khamil had arrived here, had obviously recognized Khamil and let him back into the building.

At the door, Monique glimpsed through the peephole.

He stomach sank to her knees.

Raymond!

"Open, up, Monique," Raymond said. "I know you're in there."

Stepping back from the door, Monique looked around frantically. What should she do?

"C'mon, Monique."

God help her. "Raymond, I'm going to call the police."

"I don't think you want to do that."

"I don't want you here, Raymond."

"We need to talk."

"Go away."

"You want the truth about your mother, don't you? I have some answers for you."

Monique's hands were shaking. "I don't believe you, Raymond. Please, don't make me call the police. They already know you broke into my apartment and trashed my place."

"Actually, if you call them, they'll tell you they interviewed me. I have an alibi for the time your place was broken into."

Monique swallowed.

"They checked the tape, Monique. They didn't see me coming into your building."

Monique remained silent, and after a moment, Raymond said, "Come on. Do you really think I wouldn't be in custody if they had any evidence at all against me?"

"Why are you here?"

"There are some things you should know about your mother. Monique, I used to work with her."

A chill ran down Monique's arms and back. Raymond had worked with her mother? Why had he never said so before?

"I…"

"She was with the Snoe Agency on Sixth Avenue. It's since gone out of business."

"How do you know that?"

"Monique, for God's sake. Just open the door."

Monique whimpered, then bit her lip. The fact that Raymond knew even those details gave her hope that he was indeed telling the truth. But she didn't trust him, and she didn't want him in here.

Yet if he knew anything, she needed to hear what he had to say.

"Give me a second," Monique told him. She scurried to the

bedroom, where she slipped into a robe. Then, she headed to the kitchen and took a butcher knife from a drawer.

She wasn't about to take any chances.

Monique opened the door, and Raymond quickly stepped into the apartment. He stopped short when he saw the knife Monique held.

"Holy, Monique."

She held the knife firmly ahead of him. "Look, I don't trust you. But I'm willing to hear you out. So tell me this news you came to tell me, then leave."

Raymond ground out a frustrated grunt. "Can I at least sit down?"

With the knife, Monique gestured to the living room.

"How did you get up here, by the way?" she asked once Raymond sat on her sofa.

"Victor let me up."

Victor. Damn. Monique hadn't spoken to him about her problems with Raymond, only Harry.

Raymond ran the back of his hand across his forehead, wiping away sweat that had popped out on his brow. "Do you have to...hold that knife?"

"Yes," Monique replied succinctly. "You have ten seconds to start talking before I start cutting."

Raymond held up both hands in surrender. "All right. I worked with your mother years ago. I photographed her on many occasions. I was fairly new to the business then, but I had a lot of contacts, and I was lucky enough to be able to work with her."

"What do you know about her murder?"

"I'm not sure."

"Get out."

"Will you wait a second?" Raymond's eyes implored Monique

to listen. "What I'm saying is I can't be sure of who killed her, even if I have my suspicions."

"Keep talking."

"I never mentioned anything to you before, Monique, partly because I didn't want to tell you anything..." His eyes went skyward, as if searching for the right word. "Negative."

"What's that supposed to mean?"

"I know how much you adored your mother. I didn't want to burst that bubble."

Monique glared at Raymond. "Listen, if there's something you want to tell me, tell me. If not—"

"Your mother, for lack of a better word, was a flirt, Monique." Monique shot Raymond a startled gaze, and he continued. "She cheated on your father. More than once."

A ragged breath escaped her as she sat down on the sofa opposite Raymond. "God, please don't tell me what I think you're saying..."

"No, I never slept with your mother. But not because she didn't try."

"God, no..."

"Yeah. She tried to seduce me, Monique. More than once."

"And you never slept with her?"

"I was attracted to her, yes, but no. I didn't sleep with her."

Monique shot to her feet, paced a few steps. She stared at Raymond long and hard. "So, you dating me...what was that about? Your sick infatuation with my dead mother?"

"No," Raymond said, appalled. "Of course not."

"I don't know what to think," Monique said, her voice barely above a whisper.

"I fell for you because of you, Monique. Not because of your mother. I still care for you."

"You care so much that you cheated on me."

Raymond sighed. "I already told you, I'm sorry."

Monique waved a hand in front of her, dismissing the issue. "That's a moot point. Our relationship is over."

A frown played on Raymond's lips, but Monique held his gaze with a firm one. She wasn't about to back down on this issue.

"Anyway," Raymond said after a moment. "I'm not gonna lie. Your mother was an attractive woman, and I might have slept with her—if she hadn't been involved with one of my best friends."

Monique lowered herself back onto the sofa, a lump the size of a baseball forming in her chest. Who was her mother? She didn't know anymore.

"Like I said, that's the reason I never told you anything before. Because I knew it would hurt you. But your mother was involved with one of my colleagues and best friends. They'd been having an affair for several months."

Monique shut her eyes tight. How could this be true?

"He'd even been to your family's cottage in Canada."

Monique's eyes flew to Raymond's. "How do you know about the cabin?"

"I told you, Monique. My friend was having an affair with your mother. And…and he became obsessed with her."

"So he was Pooh-Bear?"

Raymond nodded slowly. "Yes. That's what she used to call him."

"Oh, God."

"Your mother tried to break things off when she realized he was getting too serious. That's when he started writing her letters, calling nonstop."

"If my mother knew it was him, how come the police don't know the identity of her stalker?"

"She didn't know it was him," Raymond explained. "He waited a while after she dumped him before starting to stalk her. He was trying to scare her. He just couldn't let go."

Monique stood and walked toward the living room window. Her mind was racing with so many questions, she was as breathless as if she'd just run a marathon. She remembered her father's question about whether or not she was prepared to learn the truth about her mother, no matter what.

Nausea churned in her stomach. All she'd wanted was to learn the identity of her mother's killer. She hadn't been prepared to learn this.

She turned.

And screamed.

Raymond stood mere inches from her.

Quick as lightning, he grabbed the wrist that held the knife.

Adrenaline took over. Monique fought for dear life to hold onto the knife while Raymond twisted her hand, trying to make her drop it. She screamed as she struggled. Raymond was stronger than she, and her wrist was throbbing with pain from how hard he was twisting it.

But she wouldn't let go.

Couldn't.

"You're even more beautiful than your mother," Raymond whispered in a voice so cool, you'd never know he was actually struggling with her. "Oh, God. You don't know how badly I want you."

Grunting, Monique shoved a shoulder into Raymond's

chest. The effort paid off, and she stumbled as her body went free of his grip.

But Raymond recovered quickly, then walked slowly toward her.

"It doesn't have to be like this, Monique. If you'll love me, the way it's supposed to be, we can have everything."

"You're deranged." Monique took a few steps backward, rounding herself around the coffee table. All the while, she kept the knife aimed at him. If he made a move for her, she wouldn't hesitate to stab him.

Help...me...

The memory of her mother dying in her arms hit Monique with such velocity that she actually shook. But she didn't stop moving. The phone was close, just a few feet away. If she could reach it...

Raymond's eyes flitted from her face to beyond her shoulder. She knew he'd read her thoughts.

He lunged for her. Without thinking, Monique threw the knife at him, then dove for the phone. She couldn't risk him overpowering her and using the knife against her.

She knocked the receiver off the hook and hit the first programmed button her fingers could meet.

"Help!" she cried. "Please come quickly. Raymond Stuart, he's a photographer—"

Raymond's eyes grew wide with alarm. He stood over her for a moment, then quickly retreated and darted out of the apartment.

The moment he was gone, Monique sprung to her feet. She charged for the door, quickly locking and bolting it.

Then she slumped down the length of the door. She couldn't stop the tears.

"Oh, God. Thank you. Thank you." Not even knowing whom she'd dialed or if she'd reached anyone, Monique had acted as though her call had gone to the police. It had been enough to scare Raymond off.

The phone. She had to call the police. Monique got to her feet and hurried back into the living room. She grabbed the receiver and held it to her ear.

"Hello?" she heard.

A sob escaped her. "Aunt Sophie?"

"Monique. My God, what's wrong?"

"Oh, Aunt Sophie." Monique broke down. Then she told her aunt what had happened.

"I'm on my way. Make some chamomile tea. When I get there, we'll call the police."

"I'll call them now."

Aunt Sophie hesitated, then said, "I'd like to be there with you when you make the call, sweetheart. I know you've been confused about a lot of things for a long time, and it's time you got some answers."

"Aunt Sophie?" Monique asked, perplexed. But she'd already hung up.

Monique stared at the receiver for several seconds. In twenty-four hours, her life had turned completely upside down. Never in a million years would she have expected to learn what she had about her mother.

Why had her mother cheated on her father? Despite her parents' arguments, Monique had known that her father adored her mother.

So many questions. She wanted answers.

Monique stood and went to the door. She glanced through

the peephole. Satisfied that Raymond was gone, she went to the kitchen to make some tea, as her aunt had suggested.

But in the kitchen, she leaned a hip against the counter and closed her eyes. Her stomach was too queasy even for tea. Besides, tea wouldn't do anything for her. Only answers would.

"Raymond," she said sadly as she headed back to the living room. "How could you do this?"

Monique sat down on the sofa, burying her face in her hands. After a second, her head whipped up. Her heart suddenly beat so fast, she thought it might explode.

Had Raymond killed her mother?

He had to have killed her, the same way he'd planned to kill her tonight. The pieces fit together...so why didn't it feel right?

Monique went to the phone and picked up the receiver. She dialed the number to her father's home in Florida. It rang and rang until the machine came on. She hung up and dialed again.

This time, her father answered after the second ring. His voice was groggy as he said, "Hello?"

"Daddy."

"Monique." Pause. "It's nearly two in the morning. Why are you calling so late?"

"Dad, someone tried to kill me tonight."

After her father's startled gasp, Monique filled him in on the night's events.

"My God," her father said. "This man worked with your mother years ago? He's the one who killed her?"

"I thought that," Monique said slowly. "But I'm not so sure anymore."

"Why?"

"Daddy, I need for you to tell me the truth. No matter how

awful it might be. No matter what may have happened that night, I'll always love you. I want you to know that."

There was a pause, then Lucas said, "Are you asking me if I killed your mother?"

"Did you?"

Lucas didn't respond right away, and Monique's heart dropped to her knees. God, no. All this time, she'd so desperately wanted to believe in her father's innocence.

"No," her father finally said.

A sigh of relief oozed out of Monique. Her father's tone was soft, but it didn't waver, and Monique knew without a doubt that he was telling the truth.

"But you knew she was having an affair?"

"Yes."

"Why didn't you tell me?"

"I didn't want anything…" His voice cracked. "I didn't want to ruin the image you had of your mother."

It was love Monique heard in her father's voice, love she heard among his tears. And her heart spilled over with love for him then, appreciating the fact that he'd done all he could to protect her from a truth that would have hurt her.

But Monique knew there was more to the situation than that. So she said, "Even after what Mom did, you still loved her?"

"Yes," Lucas said sadly. "I love her still. She was my life."

The tears she heard in her father's voice brought tears to her own eyes. Her mother had had a wonderful man in Lucas Savard. Why hadn't she appreciated that?

Sadly, Monique realized that she would never know the answer to that question. Her mother had taken those answers to her grave.

"I love you, sweetheart," Lucas said. "You're all I have left of Julia, and I don't want to lose you. Please, please, take care of yourself."

"I will, Daddy." A mixture of happiness and sadness swirled within Monique. While she'd always known in her heart that her father couldn't have killed her mother, she hadn't quite understood the depth of his love for her. She understood now.

"Listen, Daddy. Go back to sleep. We'll talk in the morning."

"Okay," he said.

He sounded so frail, and Monique was reminded of life's cruelest lesson. She wouldn't have her father forever. "I'll visit you soon. Maybe even next week."

"I'd like that," Lucas said. "I miss you."

"I miss you, too. And I love you."

"I love you, too."

Hearing a smile in her father's voice brought happiness to Monique. Yeah, she'd go see him as soon as she could.

She ended the call, but held the receiver to her heart for several minutes. She couldn't feel any more love for her father than she felt at that moment. He was such a special man.

Her mind wandered to Khamil. He was a special man, too. He'd been by her side during this whole ordeal, never casting judgment against her mother or her father, instead lending her a shoulder to cry on.

She wanted to call him, but she was afraid. She was in love with him, and wanted to share things with him for that reason. But could she deal with the fact that he might only want to be her friend?

Now wasn't the time to think about that. All her life, she'd carried the heavy burden of what had happened that horrible night on her own, and it had felt good to have Khamil carry some of that load with her. He'd not only shown her that she didn't have to be strong all the time, he'd offered to be strong for her.

Yes, she'd call him. She needed him now.

The phone rang twice and Monique was about to hang up, figuring Khamil was sleeping. But he answered.

"Hello?"

"Hey. Khamil. You sound wide awake."

"I couldn't sleep." Pause. "Are you okay?"

Thinking of the night's events, Monique was suddenly overwhelmed. "No. I'm not."

"I'm on my way."

Before she could say goodbye, Monique heard the dial tone.

Yeah, Khamil was a very special man. A special man, just like her father.

Chapter 21

"Sure," Monique told Victor, the doorman. "Send him up."

"Will do."

"Oh, and Victor," Monique quickly said before he could hang up. "I'm expecting someone else. Khamil Jordan. When he arrives, please send him up."

Monique stood and strolled to the kitchen. Her nerves finally settling, she was now ready for some tea. She was glad to know that her cousin was on his way up and that Khamil was on his way over. She didn't feel alone.

Monique filled the kettle with water, then plugged it in the wall.

There was a knock on the door, and she hurried to answer it. Opening it, a smile spread on her face. "Daniel."

"Hey, cuz." He gave her a brief hug, then stepped into the apartment. His expression grew serious, "What the hell happened?"

"God." Monique wrapped her arms around her torso. "Raymond. He's a nutcase. He came here with some cock-and-bull story and I...I let him in." She explained to her cousin how she'd gotten a knife before doing so, how that knife had given her a false sense of security.

"I told you what you were doing was dangerous."

"I know. Everyone did. The thing is, I got involved with Raymond before the police reopened my mother's murder case. This would have happened one way or another."

Daniel nodded grimly. "Well, at least you're okay."

"Yeah." Thinking of the reality of how differently the night's events could have played out, Monique shuddered. "I've got the kettle on. I'm making some tea. Would you like a cup?"

"Sure."

"I'm having mint tea. Is that okay with you?"

"Mint tea sounds great."

Monique started for the kitchen. "Take a seat and make yourself comfortable. When I come back out, we'll talk."

In the kitchen, Monique busied herself with putting tea bags in mugs, then filling the mugs with water.

"You want sugar?" she asked.

"Two spoons, please."

Monique did as instructed, then brought both mugs into the living room. She handed Daniel his, then sat on the love seat across from where he sat on the sofa.

"So," Daniel said. "This Raymond guy, he killed your mother."

Monique brought the mug to her lips and cautiously took a sip. It was still too hot. "Actually, I'm not sure he did."

Daniel's eyes shot up. "You're not?"

"I don't know," Monique said, shaking her head. "It doesn't feel right."

"The guy tried to kill you. He was obsessed with your mother, and now with you."

"I know, but…" What was it that was bothering her? She couldn't place her finger on it. All she knew was that her intuition said Raymond hadn't killed her mother.

"So he was Pooh-Bear?"

Pooh-Bear.

"Don't tell you're still going to continue this crazy quest of yours, Monique."

"Until I'm sure Raymond killed my mother, you can't honestly expect me to give up now."

"Monique, what's wrong with you?"

As her cousin voiced his disapproval, Monique's mind wandered. Pooh-Bear. Why did that ring a bell?

"Where's your mother?" Monique suddenly asked Daniel. "She said she was coming." She brought the mug to her lips.

"She's dead."

The mug fell to the carpet, hot liquid splashing everywhere.

His eyes turning black, Daniel leveled his gaze on her. He placed his mug on the coffee table, then stood. Horrified, Monique stared at him.

"What did you say?" she asked.

"My mother is dead."

"Dead?" A moan fell from Monique's lips. "My God, why didn't you say something?"

Daniel started toward her, the coldest expression she'd ever seen on his face.

"You should have stopped this when I told you, Monique."

"Why do they call you Pooh-Bear, Uncle Richard?"

She heard the question in her mind so clearly, she wondered how she had ever forgotten it.

"You?" she managed between ragged breaths.

"Your mother was a whore, Monique. She was a whore who slept with as many men as she could. But when she tried to take my father from us, I had to stop her."

"Oh, my God." Monique shot to her feet.

"My mother never let me forget it. Every day, she told me how your mother had ruined her life, how she thought she was literally dying of a broken heart because of what she'd done. I thought…" Daniel paused as pain flashed across his face. "I thought I was losing my mother. Do you know that I found her unconscious in the bathroom? She'd overdosed on pills, Monique. She tried to kill herself, because of what your mother did to her."

Monique was so light-headed, she thought she might pass out. "What are you saying, Daniel?"

"Do you believe that after all these years, after my mother practically made me kill your mother, she wanted to come clean?" His lips pulled in a taut line. "I'm not going to jail, Monique. Not for a whore."

Oh, my God, oh, my God. Think, Monique. Think! "Daniel, no one's sending you to jail. You were young when you committed the crime."

"I was eighteen, Monique. Legally an adult."

Slowly, Monique took a step backward. She didn't recognize the Daniel who stood before her, and she had no clue what he was capable of. "You need help, Daniel. We can get you help."

"That's what my mother said. Right before I killed her."

Monique threw a hand to her mouth as she gasped.

"She was going to come over here and tell you everything. I couldn't let her do that."

He was crazy. If he'd killed her mother and his own, surely he would kill her.

Monique swirled around, darting into the kitchen.

Daniel gave chase.

Monique screamed when his fingers dug into her shoulders. He spun her around and slammed her against the wall, ramming his forearm against her windpipe.

"Please, Daniel." Monique gasped for air. "Please don't do this."

Daniel's body pressed her against the wall with a quick shove and again, Monique screamed. A moment later, when she saw him fall to the floor, she looked up, stunned.

And saw Khamil.

It took her only a second to realize that Khamil was actually there and not a figment of her imagination. A relieved cry escaping her, she jumped into his arms.

"Oh, Khamil." She wrapped her arms tightly around his neck.

"Monique." He squeezed her hard, as if he wanted to meld their bodies together.

"Oh, thank God you came."

Khamil pulled back to look at her. "Are you okay?"

Monique managed a jerky nod. "Yeah. I'm okay now."

Khamil held her to his body again, and Monique closed her eyes, savoring the wonderful feel of him. After a moment, she told him how Raymond had showed up first.

Monique looked down at her cousin's motionless body. "Is he…"

"He's out cold, and will be for a while. A move I learned in martial arts." A sly grin spread on Khamil's face.

"You're a man of many talents, aren't you?"

"So I'm told."

Monique pressed her head to Khamil's chest. She was safe. The nightmare was finally over.

"Damn, girl," Khamil said after a long moment. "You were going to get yourself killed before I had the chance to tell you that I love you?"

"It's been a night of close calls, but—" Stopping abruptly,

Monique tilted her head and met Khamil's eyes. "What did you just say?"

Khamil met her gaze, steady and strong. Then a small smile spread on his face. "I think I just said that I love you."

Monique's heart thumped erratically. Did Khamil mean what he'd just said, or had his words merely been a reaction to this situation?

"And...do you?" Monique asked. "Love me?"

His smile grew until it was a wide grin. "Yeah," he replied, nodding. "I do."

A squeal erupted in Monique's throat.

"I've never met anyone quite like you, Monique. And until I did, I figured I just might spend the rest of my days as a bachelor." His hand found her face, and he trailed his fingers along her cheek. "But I know now that I don't want that. I want you."

"Oh."

"When I heard your scream, then saw you pressed up against the wall... God, I was so afraid I was going to lose you before I ever had the chance to love you."

Happy, Monique squealed again. "This isn't a dream? You're not just saying this?"

Khamil shook his head. "You know how well we connected, Monique. We found something rare, and I don't want to lose that." He paused, then narrowed his eyes as he looked down at her. "Wait a second. I'm telling you all this, yet I don't know how you feel about me."

Monique angled her head to the side and framed Khamil's face. "Yes, you do. A connection this strong couldn't be one-sided." She paused, happy tears filling her eyes. "I love you, Khamil Jordan."

He smiled again, then lowered his lips to hers. He kissed her until they were both breathless.

"Will you marry me?"

Monique's eyes registered shock.

"Why wait?" Khamil asked. "When you find something that's real, why let it slip away?"

Why indeed? And Monique knew that Khamil was special, rare. He was a good man, a passionate man, just like her father.

So she said, "Yes. Oh, Khamil. Yes!"

Khamil held her to him, lifting her feet off the ground. And as he spun her around, Monique couldn't stop giggling, knowing that her dream of finding that one man who would love her forever had finally come true.

Epilogue

"Wow," Javar said.

"I know." Khamil had just finished telling his brother about all that had transpired a few days ago. Even now, it seemed too incredible to be true.

"After what happened with Mom and Whitney, I figured I was the only one in the family who was going to see this much drama," Javar commented.

Khamil looked to Monique's naked, sleeping form on the bed beside him, bathed in the morning sunlight. The sight did his heart good. At last she was getting some decent rest, once and for all putting the whole nightmare of her past behind her.

"Yeah, who would have thought?" Khamil said after a moment, answering Javar. "Hopefully there'll be no more drama like this."

"From now on, just diaper drama and feedings in the middle of the night, right?" Javar laughed. "Like what I have to look forward to?"

"Hey, sounds good to me," Khamil replied.

There was a pause, then Javar said, "Man, I can't believe I'm hearing you talk like this, little brother."

"Hmm." Once, Khamil wouldn't have pictured it, either. Now, the idea was actually appealing. And compared to stalkers

and other psychos, diapers and feedings would be welcome—
when the time came.

In the days since the attack on Monique's life, a lot had
happened. Both Daniel and Raymond had been arrested, Daniel
for two counts of murder and Raymond for stalking and attempted murder. Daniel indeed had murdered his own mother
to keep her from telling the horrible truth about the past; she'd
played on young Daniel's emotions, making Julia Savard out
to be a threat to the family because she was sleeping with
Richard. Daniel, who'd been chronically depressed for years,
was afraid he'd lose his mother because of Julia, so he'd killed
Julia. In his mind, he'd been doing the right thing, hoping to
save his own mother, who'd been withdrawn and suicidal
because of her husband's affair. Now, Daniel would no doubt
spend the better part of his life behind bars. It was a sad situation all around.

Raymond had admitted to police that he'd broken into
Monique's apartment and trashed it, leaving the rose petals and
vandalizing the wall. But as disturbing as all that was, Monique
actually received some peace of mind from Raymond when he
admitted that he'd lied about her mother's character. Yes,
Raymond had worked with her years ago. He'd been infatuated
with her then, but they'd never had an affair, and she hadn't had
an affair with any other photographer. However, she'd considered
Raymond a friend and had confessed to him that she'd made a
mistake and gotten involved with her husband's younger brother.
Raymond had always held out hope that by being there for her,
she'd come to realize that she loved him. To that measure he'd
begun stalking her, hoping in his sick, twisted way to once again
show her that he was there for her, that she could count on him
to protect her, and that as a result she would come to love him.

Years later, that infatuation had carried over to Julia's daughter. Once again, he'd resorted to head games and manipulation in an attempt to control the new object of his desire. He'd succeeded in dating Monique, but was always afraid he'd lose her. And when he'd cheated on her, he had actually hoped to make her insecure enough that she would cling to him—all in a bizarre effort to keep her. When that failed, he'd begun stalking her with letters, the way he had stalked her mother, hoping that she'd realize she needed a man—him—in her life, to feel safe.

"So," Javar said, a smile in his voice. "You're really going to take the plunge?"

"Yep." Khamil trailed his fingers along Monique's spine, bringing them to rest in the groove of her back. Stirring, she moaned softly. "In less than a week, my bachelor days will be over."

"It's about time," Javar quipped playfully.

"It's kind of amazing," Khamil said. "You search all your life for the right person, not knowing if you'll ever find her. Then bam, just like that, she walks into your life."

"That's the way it was with me and Whitney. I knew the moment I saw her." Javar paused. "And I thank God every day that we worked our problems out."

"I hear you."

"Well, I can't wait to see Monique again, the one woman who's done what we all thought impossible—stolen your heart."

Khamil chuckled. "You will. We'll head to Chicago after the honeymoon. And you know we'll be there when Whitney has the baby."

"You better," Javar told his brother. "Hey, we found out she's having a little girl. And Samona is having a boy. Man, this is gonna be fun."

"I'll bet." Khamil glanced at Monique. He wondered if she wanted to start a family soon. Well, he knew they'd at least have fun trying.

"How's Jamaica?" Javar asked.

"Beautiful," Khamil crooned. "Wish you were here."

"I'm sure you do."

Khamil chuckled.

Monique stirred, turning onto her back. Opening her eyes, she smiled at him. "Who is that?" she asked softly.

"My brother," Khamil replied. He brought a hand to her breast, tweaking a nipple. Monique giggled.

"Okay, little brother," Javar said. "Sounds like you're busy. Call me after you've jumped the broom."

"Don't think I'll do it?"

"Hey, with you, I have to see it to believe it."

"Believe it," Khamil said. "'Cause my bachelor days are over." He winked at Monique. "And speaking of that, my future wife beckons."

"All right. Later."

Khamil hung up the phone, then slid across the bed to Monique. He took her naked body in his arms, then nuzzled his nose against her neck.

She giggled. "Stop!" She fought to get away from him, but Khamil didn't relent. "Come on. You know I'm ticklish, Khamil!"

Chortling, Khamil finally let up. He brought his mouth to her lips, kissing her briefly but passionately. Then he pulled back and gazed down at her. "So, Mrs. Jordan-to-be. What shall we do? You feel up to some snorkeling today? Or sailing maybe?"

"Actually." Monique brought her hands to Khamil's chest. "The future Mrs. Jordan isn't feeling very well." She flashed a playful pout. "She thinks she's going to have to spend the entire day in bed, being taken care of by the very handsome Mr. Jordan—whom, by the way, she can't wait to marry."

Khamil arched an eyebrow. "Is that so?"

Monique raised her head, stopping her lips a fraction of an inch from his. "Uh-huh. Think you're up to the task?"

Khamil gave her a sexy smile. "I think so."

"'Cause if you don't do a good job of taking care of me, I may not be able to marry you."

"In that case…" Khamil draped an arm across her waist, then flicked his tongue over her ear. "I'd better start taking care of you right now."

"Ooh, I love a man who listens to me."

Khamil skimmed his lips across her cheek. "Hey, I'll do my part to make sure you're…*well*."

"Mmm." Monique ran a hand over Khamil's bald head. "I'm liking this already."

Khamil brushed his nose over hers. "No doubt you are."

Monique wrapped her arms tightly around his neck. "Come here."

"Oh, baby…" Khamil did as told, settling on top of her.

He was liking married life already.

He wasn't going to miss his bachelor days. Not one bit.

Author's Note

Kayla Perrin lives in Toronto, Canada with her husband of four years. She attended the University of Toronto and York University, where she obtained a Bachelor of Arts in English and Sociology and a Bachelor of Education, respectively. As well as being a certified teacher, Kayla works in the Toronto film industry as an actress, appearing in many television shows, commercials, and movies.

Kayla is most happy when writing. As well as novels, she had had romantic short stories published by the Sterling/Mac-Fadden Group.

She would love to hear from her readers. Mail letters to:

Kayla Perrin
c/o Toronto Romance Writers
Box 69035
12 St. Clair Avenue East
Toronto, ON, Canada
M4T 3A1
Please enclose a SASE if you would like a reply.

Pleasure SEEKERS

Part of the Hideaway Legacy

A sizzling, sensuous story about Ilene, Faye and Alana—
three young African-American women whose lives are
forever changed when they are invited to join the
exclusive world of the Pleasure Seekers.

Rochelle Alers

NATIONAL BESTSELLING AUTHOR

"Fans of the romantic suspense of Iris Johansen,
Linda Howard and Catherine Coulter
will enjoy [*Pleasure Seekers*]."
—Library Journal

Available the first week of January wherever books are sold.

sepia™

www.kimanipress.com   KPRA0360107TR